The Good House

Also by Tananarive Due

THE BLACK ROSE

MY SOUL TO KEEP

THE BETWEEN

THE LIVING BLOOD

FREEDOM IN THE FAMILY

The Good House

a novel

TANANARIVE DUE

WSP

WASHINGTON SQUARE PRESS
NEW YORK • LONDON • TORONTO • SYDNEY

Washington Square Press
1230 Avenue of the Americas
New York, NY 10020

ISBN: 978-0-7434-4901-4

First Washington Square Press trade paperback edition July 2004

10 9 8 7 6 5 4 3 2 1

For information regarding special discounts for bulk purchases, please contact
Simon & Schuster Special Sales at 1-800-456-6798 or business@simonandschuster.com

Manufactured in the United States of America

For my grandmother
Lottie Sears Houston

May 3, 1920–December 25, 2000

We miss you, Mother

—

For my grandmother
Lorna Stark Houston

May 1, 1926–December 21, 2000

We miss you, Mom-Mom

In Eden, who sleeps happiest?

The serpent.

— DEREK WALCOTT

A mudslide on Walnut Lane last Saturday, brought about by heavy rains, has left eight families without homes as a "river of mud" swept whole houses from their foundations and smashed them to bits at midnight. Miraculously, there were no human lives lost, but there were great losses in property and livestock. Only the house built by Elijah Goode still stands on the entirety of Walnut Lane. This is Sacajawea's first such mudslide in recent memory.

Our neighbors need our prayers and clothing donations for their recovery. Bring any donations to Sacajawea First Church of God.

— *THE SACAJAWEA EAGLE*
June 21, 1929
(From the archives of the Sacajawea
Historical Society)

The Good House

⚞ prologue ⚟

SACAJAWEA, WASHINGTON
JULY 4, 1929

THE KNOCKING at her door early Thursday afternoon might have sounded angry to an ear unschooled in the difference between panic and a bad mood, but Marie Toussaint knew better.

The knocking hammered like a hailstorm against the sturdy door Marie Toussaint's husband had built with wood he'd salvaged from a black walnut tree knocked over in the mudslide. The mud's recent wrath had left their two-story house untouched, but sprays of buckshot fired at the house during cowardly moments, usually at night, had pocked and splintered the old door. The mere sight of the damaged door had always made her angry, and Marie Toussaint no longer trusted herself when she was angry.

From the ruckus at the door, there might be two or three people knocking at once. Before Marie could look up from the piano keys that had absorbed her while she tried to command her fingers through Beethoven's *Sonate Pathétique*, John swept past her, his thick hand wrapped around the butt of his shotgun. He kept his gun leaning up against the wall in the kitchen like a whisk broom, ready for finding.

"Get in the wine cellar. Latch the door," he said.

"Maybe it's Dominique, John."

"Hell it is."

She knew he was right. They had driven Dominique to the church an hour ago in the wagon. Her daughter would never walk back home by herself—and not just because of the mile's distance between their house and the church that had accepted Dominique for summer Bible classes in an unprecedented gesture of goodwill since the slide. Today, Dominique was at a special Independence Day class, where she was no doubt learning about how much God had blessed America. Marie had lectured Dominique on the dangers, though. She was a smart, obedient girl. If she walked home alone, she might become a target to those who disapproved of the church's decision to treat her like any other young citizen despite her brown skin.

These visitors had nothing to do with Dominique.

John crept like a cat near the door, as if he expected it to fly open despite its locks. Very few townspeople in Sacajawea locked their doors during daylight hours, or even at night, for the most part, but peace of mind was a luxury Marie and her husband could ill afford.

Watching her husband's caution, Marie felt knowledge bubble up inside of her. She sensed the ever-knowing voice of her guiding *esprit*, a voice she had first heard when she was six. That voice had guided Marie well in the twenty-five years since. Her *esprit* had led her from New Orleans to Daytona to San Francisco to Sacajawea, this riverfront town hidden in the Washington woodlands. As a girl, Marie had named her *esprit* Fleurette because that was *Grandmère*'s name and therefore must contain some of her wisdom, she'd decided. And Fleurette was a wise one, indeed.

Fleurette did not want Marie to open the door. Her burning ears told her so.

"Who's there?" John called out in a big, barking voice that stopped the ruckus cold.

"That you, Red John?" a reedy man's voice came back through the door. Marie recognized Sheriff Kerr's voice, though he sounded unusually nervous and winded. The sheriff was neither friend nor protector to them, despite his tin star. Sheriff Kerr's rifle had fired most of the buckshot that had ruined their door, she was certain.

"Red John, you open this door. On my word, there's no shenanigans. We've got a sick child out here, and folks tell me your colored gal has some nurse training. They're sayin' she saved livestock hurt within an inch of their lives after the slide. God knows we need her now."

John glanced back at Marie, who had risen to her feet without realizing it. Her ears still burned, but Fleurette's voice was lost beneath the sudden, concerned beating of her heart.

"Who's sick?" she said, but John waved to shush her.

"The woman you call my 'colored gal,' she has a name. Speak of her proper," John said to the closed door, unmoved.

"Goddammit, Red John," the sheriff said, sounding more like his old self. "We've come for Mrs. T'saint. Is that what she wants to be called, you ornery injun? She can call herself King George of England, for all I care. I don't like this any more'n you do, but Hal's girl needs doctoring in a hurry, and we've got to put the past aside. I can't fathom any God-fearing woman who'd nurse pigs and goats at this house and not people. Would you have this girl die here on your stoop? Open this door before we break it down. I mean it, Red John."

"*Please*, Red John." Another voice came through, Hal Booth's. A sick child's father.

"Do it, John," Marie said, and only then did her husband unbolt the two locks. He did it on her word, not on the sheriff's or Hal Booth's. John made his position clear by the look he gave Marie with a stab of his deeply set brown eyes.

Five people tumbled into the house with the stench of fear and summer perspiration, tracking red brick dust from the front porch into the foyer, onto the front rug already muddied beyond repair by the refugees who had crowded here the night of the slide. All of the arrivals were men except for Maddie Booth, who was sixteen, twice as old as Dominique. Maddie was limp in her father's arms. Maddie was a small-boned girl, but she weighed more than a hundred pounds, surely, so they must have suffered quite a climb up the twenty-one stone steps that led to Marie's house from the road below. The steps were steeply set apart.

Marie wouldn't have recognized Maddie except that they had named her, because her appearance was so changed. Her waxen blond hair was usually neatly braided, but today it was a hive of straw atop her head, matted and untamed. And her eyes! Marie could see only the rims of Maddie's gray irises, which were rolled up unnaturally high; the rest was just pink and bleary, sightless. Saliva streamed from the girl's mouth, dampening her rumpled dress in a large V across her breast. At the instant her dangling feet touched the red dust on the floor, the girl suddenly shuddered like someone who'd felt the lash of a horsewhip. It looked exactly like an epileptic's convulsive seizure, Marie thought. She had studied epilepsy at the Mary McLeod Hospital and Training School for Nurses in Florida, so she knew a few things about the brain disorder that would be a great help if Maddie's ailment were what it appeared to be.

But that was not so. Whatever was troubling this girl might *look li* epilepsy, but surely it was not. Fleurette's warning rose to a screec' Marie's head, as if trying to split her skull in two. Never, *neve*

Fleurette carried on so. That was how Marie came to the terrible realization, although she'd suspected the truth from the mere sight of Maddie, especially after the girl's resistance to the red brick dust Marie had ground and freshened every morning to protect the house since the mudslide. To see how the girl's legs had jerked away! Marie had heard of such cases from *Grandmère*, but she had never seen one this pronounced with her own eyes.

And then there was the smell. Maddie Booth stank.

"Papa," Marie said, mute except for that word. She stopped in her tracks. What name was there for this? A *baka* had been brought to her house, in a flesh disguise.

"She's had a fit," Maddie's father said, his blue eyes imploring. "She's never before been sickly, not like this. But it started yesterday morning. Said her stomach was ailing her. Then this morning, she was out of her mind, talking senseless. Her skin's burning up one minute, cold as a block of ice the next. And her breathing . . ."

Yes, Marie could hear Maddie's breathing. The girl's chest heaved with her labored breaths, and the sound was like choked gurgling from a deep well. Unnatural. The intervals between her breaths were horrible in their length, nearly interminable. This girl was dying.

John's lean, rigid form stood tall over the other men, and Marie saw his eyes. He knew the truth, too. The lines of his jaw grew sharper as he locked his teeth.

"Help her, Mrs. T'saint," Hal Booth said, thrusting Maddie toward her like a sack of flour. "Please do something. She's our only girl, our baby. If something happens to her . . ."

Marie wiped her hands on the dustcloth she always carried in her apron pocket, not because her hands were dirty, but because her hands needed something to do. She must *think*. "Lay her down on the sofa in the parlor. Keep her head propped up so she's not choking. Watch her close," Marie said. "Wait for me."

Those sure-spoken words might as well have been someone else's, because Marie was not at all sure. Her hands felt like frail corn-shucks, drained of blood. Until now, today had been an ordinary day, she realized. She'd been about to soak her green beans and begin drying her herbs, like any other weekday. She'd had no telling dreams, no whispers from Fleurette to shake her from her sleep. The only odd thing about today had been John coming home from his logging camp twenty miles down the road because his back was hurting him—but even that wasn't so odd, because his back hurt from time to time when he forgot to drink his tea. She'd never taken John's backaches to signify anything special, and she'd been glad for his unexpected company.

Yet here she was, facing this thing. And in her own home. Where had her warning been?

Then, she remembered one of the first lessons *Grandmère* had taught her: There is a cost for all things, one mirroring the size of the other. Marie could hardly say she hadn't known to expect it. She had brought it here herself, as surely as if she'd called it.

Fleurette was in a frenzy in Marie's head. Marie's ears burned so badly now, she wished she could pull them clean off and be done with the pain. If she could heed Fleurette's soundless voice, she would run all of these intruders back out where they'd come from, even if it was at gunpoint. Then, she'd be wise to begin lighting candles right away, if it wasn't too late already.

As she turned toward the stairs, Marie began whispering prayers she had never uttered.

"Marie?" John said, taking long strides to follow her.

"A girl so young . . . ," Marie muttered, and her hands trembled. She could still smell Maddie even here, at the staircase, and the stench nearly turned her stomach. If any of the rest of them had the ability to smell it as she did, they would not be able to bring themselves to touch that child, she thought. She wondered how she could touch Maddie herself, when the time came. "*C'est tragique*, John. *C'est sinistre.*"

"This is not your fight." John had never been a whisperer, and Marie was sure everyone in the house heard him when he spoke, his low-pitched voice bouncing across the walls. He followed her as she took the wooden stairs two at a time.

"Help me find the blankets. We'll need an armload. What if that were Dominique?"

"What if it was?" John said, and for the first time she heard something in his voice that was not borne of their bitter time in Sacajawea. He took her shoulders and roughly turned her around, forcing her to look at his face, which was nearly hidden in the long, loose strands of his jet-black hair. But his eyes were not hidden. John's eyes spoke his heart, and his heart was not filled with the anger that had consumed him for the past three years— his eyes told her that his heart was sad and scared. She was not accustomed to seeing fear in John's eyes.

"Don't do it, Marie. Send them away. We'll say prayers for them. Or if you must be stubborn, take them to the woods, to the grounds. Not here. This is where we *live*."

"She would be dead before we get out there. You see how far gone she is."

"Then let it have her. It's not our place. Don't let pride—"

Marie had never once wanted to hit John in the three years since she had allowed him to move into her house as her devoted student with the privileges of a husband. A ritual by his grandmother, one of his Chinook tribe's last remaining elders, bound them together—not any white man's certificate or covenant, as their neighbors had never failed to notice. The unconventional nature of their union had only fueled their neighbors' resentment toward the colored woman and red man who shared such a grand house in their town. John was now both husband and student to her, respectful most times and utterly insolent others. His unfinished accusation stung her heart. *Pride!* Did he really think that little of her?

"Yes, that's right," John said. "Pride, I said. And guilt besides, I think. But you weren't wrong for what you did. They had that coming and worse."

"You *hush*," Marie said, hating to hear him even speak of it. They had agreed to forget the events of that night, and it was dangerous to give the memory language. Speaking of past events kept them alive, and he knew that as well as anyone. By now, the trembling of Marie's hands was nearly violent. She couldn't say if it was because she suddenly understood the truth of John's warning or because of the child waiting for her downstairs. She had rescued a Chinaman in San Francisco in '21, but that had been different. That *visiteur* had been weaker, not nearly so dangerous. And she'd had no role in rousing it, not like this time.

John was right. And so was Fleurette, clanging in her head like a hundred fire-bells. But the child was dying, and Marie had no more choice in this than she did the rhythms of her heart.

"Get the blankets, John. Light candles. I'm going to fill the tub and fetch *Grandmère*'s ring," Marie said. That was how she told him it was decided.

"You have great skills, Marie . . . but luck is a creek that often runs dry. Don't expect to draw your water there day after day," John said, his face so pained that he seemed to blurt the words against his will. "Don't take this on, Marie. I'm begging, woman. Do you hear? You know I beg for nothing." To make his point, he repeated his plea in his Chinook language, holding her face between his large palms. "*Yaka humm. Wake okoke skookum deaub. Wake alta.*" She could feel his meaning more keenly when she didn't recognize his words, watching his emotions light his face while the foreign speech washed over her. She had to look away.

"I have to do it, John. I am responsible."

John sighed, leaning closer to her until their foreheads touched. She enjoyed the current of his warm breath, just as she relished the wisps of his feather-light hair brushing her brow. Tears smarted in her eyes. She shook her head gently, nudging him away. "I must, John. This is the cost that has been decided for me. Can you understand? Marie Toussaint cannot turn away a child to die on her front stoop. Not at my own house. Anything but that, you see?"

"My wife, I know you well. Your enemy, I see, also knows you well. This is a well-laid trap for you," John said, and she heard in his voice a grudging admiration for the *visiteur*, the *baka* with no name. He kissed her forehead lightly. John's next words, although they broke Marie's heart, came from a place more gentle than the place of whispers.

"I will do as you ask," her husband said. "But we both know it has already won."

THE PARTY

... A real live nephew of my Uncle Sam's,

Born on the Fourth of July ...

— "YANKEE DOODLE BOY," GEORGE M. COHAN, 1904

⚔ *One* ⚔

ANGELA TOUSSAINT'S Fourth of July party began well enough, but no one would remember that because of the way it would end. That's what everyone would talk about later. The way it ended.

Angela didn't want to have a party that day. Maybe it was the lawyer in her, but she was too much of a stickler to enjoy hosting parties, brooding over details. *Is there enough food? What if there's an accident with the fireworks? Will somebody have too much beer and break his neck on those steep steps outside?* Angela didn't have the hostess gene, and she couldn't remember why she ever wanted to throw a Fourth of July party at Gramma Marie's house. Like most of the well-intentioned plans in her life, the party had grown into something to dread.

"*Shit on me.*"

Angela's digital clock said it was just after six. The first guests would be here in less than a half hour, and she wasn't fully dressed. Still damp from the shower, Angela tore through her jumbled pile of shirts in the top drawer of her grandmother's old mahogany dresser, searching for a T-shirt that wasn't political enough to raise eyebrows and draw her into an argument from the start. TREATMENT, NOT PRISON. IT'S A WOMAN'S CHOICE. STRAIGHT BUT NOT NARROW. She opted for a peach-colored Juneteenth T-shirt a promoter in L.A. had given her last year, and she wiggled into it. Frankly, she'd rather be hosting a Juneteenth party anyway, commemorating the end of slavery. What had the War for Independence done for her ancestors?

Two clamplike hands encircled Angela's bare waist from behind. She froze, alarmed, unable to see because she was trapped inside the cotton shirt, her arms snared above her head. "Tariq?"

"It's Crispus Attucks, back from the dead to give you a brother's perspective on the Boston Massacre," a low-pitched voice rasped.

Angela's heart bucked. Jesus. She poked her head through the shirt's collar and found Tariq's smiling face behind her. She gazed at the deeply graven lines that carved her husband's features, at the unruliness of his bushy moustache splaying toward his cheeks as if it intended to become a beard, and it occurred to her that Tariq wasn't handsome so much as sturdy. At U.C.L.A., watching him dart through and around bigger, stronger men with a football cradled under his arm like a bundled infant, she had felt her juices flowing on a much deeper level than her juices had flowed for any of the men she'd met at law school. Much to her surprise, Tariq Hill had scorned hoochies and loved his books, planning to get an M.B.A. one day— and her juices swept her away. Then, as her punishment for letting her juices do her thinking, time had taught her the downside: Tariq's demeanor often mimicked his rugged look; unyielding, impatient, even unkind. He made her nervous. Not always, by any stretch, but far, far too often.

So, Angela couldn't help it. She let out a tiny gasp, even after she saw Tariq's face.

She hoped he hadn't heard her gasp. He had.

"What the hell's wrong with you? It's just me," Tariq said, no longer sounding playful. That was *the tone*, understated, nearly robotic. She hadn't heard this tone from Tariq since he'd been here, but there was no mistaking it. The tone was Tariq's mask, flung clumsily over his anger. Hiding everything he didn't want her to see.

Damn. She'd pissed him off, and right before the party.

Angela forced a bright smile. "Sorry. You scared me," she said.

Tariq's lips curled ruefully, and Angela saw his annoyance shift from her back to himself. His eyes were suddenly soft. Angela was only five-foot-three, and this was one of the rare times the twelve inches separating her face from her husband's did not feel like an impossible distance. She had to dial her head back more than fifteen years to remember seeing Tariq's eyes this soft.

"My fault, babe. I should've knocked. That's on me." He kissed the top of her head, massaging her damp, short-cropped hair with one hand.

Apology accepted, she thought. But were they going to spend all of their time apologizing to each other from now on, tiptoeing around each other's weaknesses?

Angela wasn't used to having Tariq here. Summers belonged to Corey. She'd come to Sacajawea expecting nothing more than summer visitation with her son, when she took a two-and-a-half-month leave from her law firm to become a full-time parent, rediscovering the person her son was turning into since he'd moved to Oakland with his dad. This trip was their third year running, a tradition. More like a reunion.

But two weeks ago, Tariq had shown up in his faded old VW van, the one he had driven when they eloped to Vegas when she was pregnant, and his presence created a reunion of an entirely different kind. The three of them were spending the warm months here at Gramma Marie's house, in the folds of this quiet logging and fishing town on the banks of the Columbia River in southwestern Washington state, with ninety minutes isolating them from Portland, the nearest major city. Peace and seclusion, no distractions, no excuses. And if they could live together, just for a summer, Angela believed there was still hope they could dig up something warm and living from the ice that had settled over their marriage long ago. Their last chance.

The shredded, soulful moan in Otis Redding's "I've Been Loving You Too Long to Stop Now" playing on Angela's bedroom CD player was barely audible beneath the Will Smith bassline shaking the walls from Corey's room across the hall, but Redding's vocal caresses filled the room in their silence. Tariq's eyes turned glazed and wolfish. "I love this song," he said.

Angela's thighs squirmed. Last night, once again, Tariq had tapped on her bedroom door and asked for an invitation into her room wearing nothing but his boxers. She and Tariq had made love five times since his arrival, and she felt their sexual play creeping back toward the much-anticipated ritual it had been in the old days, dueling appetites. Last night, she'd dismounted him after her sweet, sudden orgasm and enveloped him within the hot moisture of her mouth and tongue.

"What are *you* thinking about, Mr. Hill?" Angela said, knowing full well. She hadn't given him oral sex since a year before he moved to Oakland. Today, she guessed, Tariq was one happy man.

"I'm thinking about what's in those Levi's," Tariq said, his eyes boldly assessing the modest spread of her hips. "And a certain debt I can't wait to repay."

She wanted to say, *I can't wait either,* but she only smiled. There was still an artifice to this, occasional puppet strings flitting into her vision that kept her from sinking into the fantasy. For one thing, they had separate rooms and were still hiding from Corey like two boarding-school students ducking from their dormitory monitor. And neither of them had dared utter the terrifying words "I love you," for fear of the silence that might follow. But God, this felt good. Not quite right, but maybe it was getting there.

"Baby, please hold that thought, okay? It's after six. I need to go downstairs. . . ."

"Yeah, I think I need to go on down, too." He teased her with his fingertip, drawing his index finger across her breast until her nipple sprang to attention. His voice was a breath in her ear. "I'd like to go down right now."

Somehow, despite her fluttering chest and a persistent smoldering where her thighs met, Angela pulled herself away, leading Tariq out of the room by the hand, toward the stairs. Tariq walked behind her, rubbing just close enough that she could feel the solidness of his erection beneath his grilling apron. It was a tempting invitation. More than tempting. Until a week and a half ago, Angela hadn't had sex in exactly five hundred days. With Tariq behind her on the stairs, Angela's body went to war with her reason, and almost won. She squirmed against him, then found her resolve. "You better quit following me around with that thing and go put the ribs on."

"Yes, ma'am," Tariq said. And he stepped back.

No argument. No sarcasm. That was good. There hadn't been much sarcasm from him all summer. Mostly smiles, and easy cooperation. Tariq had cut down to one or two cigarettes a day, smoking on the deck outside without being asked, a ritual more than an addiction. This was not the same Tariq who left four years ago. She'd hardly met this Tariq. She had a lot to learn about him.

He kissed the top of her head again. "I'm gonna check on those ribs."

Maybe Gramma Marie's house would cast some sort of cleansing spell on their family, Angela thought. Gramma Marie would have loved the idea of her coming back to the house she'd called "that ugly old house" when she'd been too young to see it for what it was, before she knew about the magic it could work. She tried to work the same magic every summer with Corey, and up until exactly two weeks ago, she'd begun to think the magic wouldn't happen. She'd begun to think that maybe Gramma Marie wasn't preserved in this house after all, that maybe she should take Corey away to New York instead, or somewhere mind-blowing like Egypt. She'd been mourning the loss of the magic until the moment Tariq's van had driven up and Corey had looked out of the living room's picture window and said, *Dad's here*, his tone dazed, his face emblazoned with an expression of pure joy Angela would never forget.

At last, it was happening, after all this time. Gramma Marie's magic was back.

In the living room, Angela surveyed her grandmother's 1920s-era quartered white oak furniture, relics from another time. She rested a warm gaze on the old Starr upright player piano against the wall, remembering how she'd hated that scarred piano—once, not merely because of Gramma Marie's mandatory one-hour daily practice sessions—Angela could play decent blues and gospel piano to this day for no other reason than her grandmother's stubbornness—but because of the way the keys moved by themselves when Gramma Marie put on her music rolls, as if an invisible man, a ghost of some kind, were sitting at the bench. Now, she treasured the piano. It held Gramma Marie's spirit intact. So did the tall, oak grandfather clock that had kept Angela awake all through high school until age finally silenced it. And the matching rocker where Gramma Marie had spent her days rocking against the cushioned leather seat, gnawing peanuts. And, of course, Gramma Marie's collection of porcelain figurines were all preserving pieces of Gramma Marie's spirit, too; strawberries, dogs, ballerinas, flower vases, miniature teapots, juicy watermelon slices, and little dark-skinned children sporting short pants or unruly plaits. Even the ugly-as-sin, featureless, little dark clay dolls scattered among the figurines, which Angela had never much cared for because they seemed unfinished and vaguely misshapen, were helping bring Gramma Marie back to her. Gramma Marie's house, she decided, would bring them all good luck.

Tariq's head emerged from the French doors leading to the dining room, his face framed between the whitewashed wood panels. "Hey, Snook?" he said softly, using his long-ago pet name. "All playing aside, I'm glad I'm here this summer, babe. I should have said that before now. This is long overdue."

"Not as glad as I am," she said. "*Glad* isn't even the word."

"We have some talking to do. Tonight, after this party. All right? Real talking."

Unexpectedly, Angela's entire body felt rigid. "I swear, Tariq, I don't know if I have it in me to sit through another one of our bad talks. I really don't."

"I know," Tariq said, blinking. "Let's do better this time then, Snook. I've . . ."

But his voice trailed off. Angela heard quick-paced footsteps descending the wooden staircase, and Corey appeared from the foyer. At fifteen, Corey was bony and only five-foot-six, although he'd hoped to inherit his father's genes for height and musculature. So far, Angela's tiny stature had offset any memorable growth spurts, something else she figured her son blamed her for.

"What's going on?" Corey said, suspicious. If she and Tariq were talking too long, their son assumed they were fighting. She couldn't blame him. Fighting was the one thing she and Tariq had always been good at together—over money, over parenting styles, and their worst, over that raggedy damned handgun a friend of Tariq's had given him years ago. She'd finally convinced him to sell it, but had they ever recovered from that one night? That fight with Tariq was the closest Angela had felt to having a nervous breakdown, and even as she had listened to herself screaming in rage, she'd wondered why Tariq wasn't trying to comfort her. Instead, she'd seen something change in Tariq's eyes, tightening. His forearm had knotted, and his closed hand had risen suddenly, ready to strike her.

That was when Corey had come out of his room. Nine years old, crying because Mommy and Daddy were yelling. The sound of their son's cries had snapped both of them back to themselves. Ever since, it seemed, Corey had been their wary referee. His face still wore the same expression, prepared for chaos.

"Nothing's going on," Angela said, swatting Corey's backside in his too-baggy denim shorts. "Go upstairs and turn that music off. I don't want that blasting when people get here. I'm about to put on some jazz."

"Oh, you afraid we're gonna sound too ghetto? It's just Will. It ain't like I've got on nothin' hard-core." Corey was purposely butchering his grammar, an affectation he'd adopted since he'd moved to Oakland, trying to pretend away all his years of private school so he wouldn't stand out. The sound of it grated on Angela's ear.

"Go on back up and do what your mama says," Tariq said. "Don't get smart."

Corey leveled a gaze at his father, as if he had turned traitor. Then he seemed to lose focus, as if he were exhausted. He cut his eyes away before turning to amble back toward the stairs. "I thought maybe Sean was here," Corey mumbled. "I gotta go to Sean's later."

"What about the fireworks?" Tariq said.

"I dunno, Dad." Corey's voice was muted as his feet shuffled up the stairs. "I don't feel like it. My stomach's not right today, man."

"What'd he say? His *stomach?*" Tariq said, angry. He sprang into the living room with one of those sudden motions that had always made Angela wonder if a man that big could hurt someone just by moving so fast. His size had always scared her, even if the presence of the gun had scared her more. "Does that boy know we spent two hundred dollars on fireworks? Lemme go talk to him."

Watching Tariq follow Corey, Angela knew that the frail opportunity that had just bloomed between her and her husband, whatever it was, had been lost for now. His mood had changed, an aspect of the old Tariq she remembered very well.

Let's do better this time then, Snook. I've—

He's what? Angela wondered, frustrated. She felt a certainty, every bit as irrational as it was gloomy, that their conversation couldn't wait, not this time. A part of her was convinced that if she didn't find out *right now* what feelings she had stirred in Tariq, she would never know. All of Angela's worst nightmares tended to come to merry realization one after the other, as if they were on a hellish train schedule, so it was no wonder she struggled against her grim imagination. There was always something worse waiting. One more bad thing.

Tariq called out to her from upstairs. "Snook, did you remember the ice?"

Shit. She'd forgotten. Their freezer's ice machine was too slow for a party.

"You want me to go?" Tariq called again, guessing at her silence, and Angela felt herself relax. His mood must not have changed that much after all.

"No, you put the ribs on," she said. "It'll just take me a few minutes to run into town, baby."

Angela found her pocketbook on the red upholstered seat of Gramma Marie's glossy mahogany chair sitting near the foot of the stairs, the empty throne. It was an eye-catching chair, almost more artwork than furniture, standing on lovely legs carved to look as if they were braided, mirroring the seat-back's twisting, lacelike designs. Beside the chair, an old-fashioned telephone table displayed a yellowed photograph of Gramma Marie and Red John taken during the 1920s, when they had both been young. Angela gazed at the picture, amazed to realize that her grandmother must have been in her early thirties when this photograph was taken, younger than Angela was now. Gramma Marie's midnight skin was model-smooth, her broad, prominent nose was as intriguing as an African maiden's, and she wore her thick hair in well-kept French braids that wound around her head, the same style she had favored until the end of her life. Angela had never met her grandmother's husband because he had died in a logging accident long before Angela was born, but to Angela, her strong-featured grandmother and Native American mate, with his long hair and dark, meditative face, were still the Lord and Lady of this manor.

" 'Bye, Gramma Marie," Angela said softly to the photograph, as habit compelled her. And the photograph spoke back to her, or at least it always seemed to because Angela could best remember her grandmother's husky voice when she gazed at her preserved face: *Adieu, cher.*

Outside, Angela could smell her past buried among the ferns and salal in the earthy scent of the cool forest floor. She stood atop the high ridge where the house was perched, accessible from the private clay road below only by climbing the twenty-one stone steps—a climb Gramma Marie had been perfectly capable of achieving, thank you very much, until her sudden death from pneumonia at the age of ninety-two. Above the steps, the house appeared like a doll's house set against the wilderness, prominently displaying the large picture window Angela and Tariq had built after they claimed the house as their own. Gramma Marie's house had been built in 1907, and except for the picture window, internal refurbishing, roof work, painting, and electrical and plumbing updates, the roomy house remained as it had always been: a cheery blue post-Victorian with five bedrooms, twin pairs of narrow white columns on either side of the porch to greet visitors, and a round window positioned like a watchful eye from the attic. The boxy second story sat atop the smaller first level like a fat, nesting bird. The house bordered nearly virgin woods and a creek that had been in Angela's family for three generations now. Gramma Marie had left plenty of money, too, but the property meant more to Angela. *I never got my mule,* Gramma Marie used to say, *but I damn sure got my forty acres.* The true number was closer to sixty acres, Angela had since learned. Those acres were hers now, and Corey's.

The clay road below, which locals called Toussaint Lane, petered out about thirty yards beyond Gramma Marie's house, vanishing as a thin dirt trail into the woods. Local kids, herself included, used to hike a half-mile into those woods on Gramma Marie's property to The Spot, a large clearing with a fire-pit and ring of logs where they drank beer, smoked, and necked. And that wasn't all they could do there, she had discovered in high school. Myles Fisher, her high school sweetheart and first true friend, had become her first true lover one day at The Spot. Two blankets, a layer of fir needles, and mutual eagerness had cushioned their bodies from the hard ground.

No lovemaking experience had felt quite like it, although Myles's tentative touches, unlearned but earnest, didn't rival Tariq's hungry assuredness. Tariq was the best lover Angela had ever known. But there had been something about that time at The Spot, something it had taken years to work out of her memory that revisited her each time she thought about the ground where their naked bodies had lain.

Myles, like her, had left Sacajawea as soon as he had his high school diploma, and she hadn't seen him since. They had both been in such a hurry to get away, and sometimes she wondered why. This was a place of healing. Gramma Marie had always said so, and the people of Sacajawea still seemed to believe it, as if they considered this house their town's temple, a place to whisper their wishes. A place to make things right after they'd gone wrong.

"I want a family again," Angela whispered to the house and the forest that embraced it.

In the woods, a hidden bird shrieked. Exactly as if it were laughing at her.

Marlene Odell's age-spotted fingers tapped in the price code for bagged ice at her cash register at Downtown Foods, a dimly lighted grocery store with shelves crammed tight. Year by year, Angela noticed rarer items springing up around the store: Brie, couscous, Thai seasonings, black-eyed peas, instant grits. There was even a small section of sushi on ice in the back. More like civilization. This store was small, but Marlene and her husband cared about what people wanted.

"I hear you've got a surprise coming later," Marlene said.

"What kind of surprise?"

Marlene shrugged, gazing at Angela through loose puffs of silver hair. "The kind you have to wait to see for yourself. Someone I expect you'll be happy to see."

"I'm not sure I like surprises," Angela said, but she left it alone. She and Tariq had planned for thirty guests exactly, but the world wouldn't come to an end if one more showed up. Angela dug for loose dollar bills crumpled in her back pocket. "Thanks for working on the holiday while the rest of us are having a good time, Marlene. This street is like a ghost town today. I was afraid I'd have to go over to the bait shop on the river for ice."

"Don't thank me, thank the cheap SOB who thinks he's my boss. Rolf sent me out here bright and early. I was happy as a clam drinking my coffee and watching the colored man, Bryant Gumbel, on the morning news."

Angela took a deep, calming breath. Marlene Odell must be seventy-five by now, and a lifetime ago she'd caught Angela stealing a handful of Tootsie Rolls from this store. She'd also driven over to personally report the theft to Gramma Marie, thereby becoming responsible for the worst whipping of Angela's life. So, Angela couldn't think of a tactful way to tell a woman who'd known her since she was a thieving child that the term *colored* was woefully

outmoded. Young or old, Sacajawea residents freely referred to Gramma
Marie as their *colored pioneer,* oblivious to how insulting it sounded. *Colored*
outdated *Negro,* even! But, hell, after Angela and Myles moved away for college and then Gramma Marie passed on, no other black person had lived in
Sacajawea. Maybe a lily-white town couldn't know any better.

It was the crowning irony: Angela loved her grandmother's house, but
she hated living in such a speck of a town. She always had, starting with the
summers she spent at Gramma Marie's house when she was very young.
As a child, downtown Sacajawea had reminded her of the set of *Little House
on the Prairie,* and she'd wandered through the streets feeling jarred by the
foreignness of everything around her. Where was the convenience store
where she could buy pickled pigs' feet and a hot sausage? Where was the
record store? The game room? As a transplanted *Los Angelina,* the concept
of camping meant nothing to her, and she had decided after one outing
that fishing was a whole lot of hype about nothing. All these years later, she
was still searching for something interesting in Sacajawea to catch her eye.

If not for Gramma Marie's pioneering days, Angela would never have
heard of this out-of-the-way logging town, which was accessible from Portland only by a two-lane riverfront road from Sacajawea's larger neighbor,
Longview, or a ferry from Westport, Oregon, beyond Puget Island. Sacajawea's main street was home to the grocery store, the courthouse, the fire
hall, a pharmacy, a saloon, the old hotel, three antique stores, Ming's Chinese, a used-book store, the U Save gas station, a drive-thru espresso stand
called Joltz, the diner, and Subway Heaven, which sold sandwiches and
hand-churned ice cream. There was no movie theater, no health club, no
McDonald's. Main Street really *was* the main street. Aside from the River
Rat Lounge off the pier, some warehouses, and a few offices converted from
homes on the surrounding streets, Main Street was nearly all there was.

But if Angela wanted to spend summers in her grandmother's house,
Sacajawea came with it as a package deal. And each year Angela returned, she
could practically hear Gramma Marie whispering in her ear: *When do you plan
to invite folks over proper, Li'l Angel?* Because despite Sacajawea's clear summer
skies, a placid river perfect for sailing, and the genteel backdrop of Mount
Hood amid the Cascade range, this was not a resort town where people
camped for the summer and kept to themselves. Tourists drove farther west
for that, to the sands of Long Beach on the Pacific coast. Aside from the
handful of vacationers who frequented the town's two popular B&Bs, most
people in Sacajawea had lived here for generations, earning hourly wages
in the mills in Longview or taking down trees in the woods. And even if

Sacajawea had been a more sometimey place, the rules would have been different for Angela, or anyone else who was kin to Marie Toussaint.

Marlene and the other townspeople would be deeply offended if they knew how she, Corey, and Tariq cackled about Sacajaweans' quaint habits. Like how the proprietors of the small cluster of businesses that called itself "downtown" always had their radios tuned to the same oldies station that played The Four Seasons, Bobby Darin, and Elvis Presley, creating an overall effect Corey called "Time Warp, U.S.A." And how even the beefiest-looking bill-capped rednecks with gun racks mounted in their pickups' rear windows drove past them in town and greeted them with wide grins and neighborly waves like characters straight out of a Frank Capra movie. Angela tried to imagine her neighbors in L.A. waving at her with big smiles as they drove through Hollywood Hills on their way to work, and it was a good laugh. Oh yes, and that *colored* thing. That could be funny, too, in the right mood. Sure enough, Angela noticed "Teen Angel" playing on the store's tinny speakers. Time Warp, U.S.A., all right.

"How's Corey doing?" Marlene asked, her gaze suddenly probing. "I keep seeing him with that new boy, Sean. They're always running here and there, those two."

Marlene's tone put Angela on alert. Teenagers became secretive as part of their code of behavior, and Corey gave vague answers when she asked how he and his friend Sean spent their time. He'd come home with an ugly scrape on his arm the other day, claiming he'd been thrown by Sean's horse, but the skittishness in his eyes had made her wonder what more there was to the story. "They're not getting into trouble, are they?"

"Oh, no, nothing like that," Marlene said, but Angela was sure Marlene's inquiry had left something unsaid, a judgment. Sean Leahy's family lived in a trailer on the land adjacent to Gramma Marie's property, and as newcomers, the Leahys were subject to disapproving scrutiny from the residents. Either new people were considered city-folk trying to spoil their town, or they were vagabonds who couldn't be trusted. Sean seemed to be a good kid, though. His father was a single parent, and although Mr. Leahy was eccentric in his dress—he strung beads and feathers through his shaggy blond hair—Angela hadn't noticed anything worrisome about him. The guy had three foster kids, which made him a good citizen in her book.

"I'm just glad Corey's finally found a real friend here," Angela said. "I need all the help I can get dragging him here every summer. But I'm afraid *not* to, with all the nonsense waiting for him in the city. Gangs, drugs, guns, all that. It's unbelievable."

"Oh, I believe it," Marlene said with a knowing look. "Your poor grandmother had such a time with you. But you were a breeze compared to Dominique. Now, *she* was a handful at Corey's age, believe me."

Angela had not expected to hear her mother's name today. This was one of those rare days she had not thought once about her mother. Now, she remembered why she kept her interactions with Sacajawea residents to a minimum: They knew too much. They knew the things she rarely mentioned to even her closest friends in L.A. Here, casual conversation was painful.

Everybody here knew what had happened to Dominique Toussaint, that she had swallowed a bottle of Sominex with her morning glass of orange juice. At the start of Angela's freshman year in high school in L.A., she had found her mother slumped dead across the kitchen table. Angela had come home from school, walked through the back door, and seen her mother with one long arm reaching across the Formica, holding on to the table like a raft in the middle of the sea. But they didn't know everything. They didn't know the first words in Angela's mind as she stared at the top of her mother's braided scalp in its death-pose on that tabletop: *Thank you, God.*

"Gramma Marie was the best thing that ever happened to me, Marlene," Angela said quietly, nudging those memories away. "I'm just hoping this town has been good for Corey, too. Even if Gramma Marie isn't here."

"Oh, sure. Harder to go wrong here. We all know where you live."

Angela suddenly noticed the display case beneath the cash register, where she saw a collection of gleaming pellet guns for sale, beneath a handwritten sign promising TWENTY PERCENT OFF. Guns always caught her eye. The guns looked real to her, like the kind that used bullets. People in Sacajawea gave their children pellet guns and BB guns the way her friends gave their children Game Boys. God, she hated guns! Two years as a public defender right out of law school had taught her that—along with a harrowing incident at twelve, when she'd walked into her mother's bedroom to find Dominique Toussaint standing in front of her bureau mirror with a handgun in her mouth. *It's not loaded, sugar,* she'd offered Angela quickly, as if that made it all right.

Angela's party mood, as much as she'd mustered one at all, was suddenly gone.

If she could have been honest, she would have told Marlene she wished she'd never planned a party, because she wasn't the kind of person who could enjoy several hours with people she had known a long time but had never known well. And she wanted to be alone with her family, because she had no way of knowing if this was the last time they would live together.

And, to put it plainly, if she *was* going to throw a party, she'd rather do it in L.A., where she could also invite her more rhythmically inclined black, Latino, and gay friends and spend the night dancing to salsa and old-school funk. But none of those reasons were quite right, Angela realized. She just didn't want this party to happen—she never had, not from the start—and she wasn't sure why.

Suddenly, the bag of ice she'd been cradling on the counter above the gun display felt so cold at her fingertips that it seemed to nip her. As she drew her hands away, a too-cold sensation seized her hands, racing up her arms. She shuddered, and it was gone. Angela stared down at her reddened fingertips, surprised. How could she have gotten a cold-burn that quickly?

"Have a good time, Angie," Marlene said as Angela jangled through the automatic door with her ice. "That party at the Good House will be the talk of the town. Folks'll be glad to see you."

"If I hadn't done it, Gramma Marie's ghost would have whipped my hide," Angela said.

By the time Angela loaded the ice onto the scrap-covered passenger-side floor of Tariq's van, she was bothered by Main Street's quiet. The street was festooned with red, white, and blue streamers and bows that had been up for weeks now, but it was too still. Angela didn't like the absence of cars and pickups beside the curb, the empty parking lot at the courthouse, the dead neon signs hanging in the windows of Main Video and Joltz, drained of light. And there wasn't a single person on the street. She saw a few sailboats listing lazily on the river, in need of stronger breezes, but everyone else in town seemed to be hidden away. Angela locked her door as soon as she climbed into the van, an L.A. habit she usually forgot after her first few days back in Sacajawea. She sat a moment before turning the key in the ignition, watching Marlene through the wall-size window as she shelved cans in the deserted store. The image struck Angela as lonely. No, more than lonely. Like something to grieve, something inevitable.

Angela wished she could stay here and put off the rest of the day. Just for a while.

But the ice was melting, and it was time for the party to start.

—

The first guests arrived at 6:30 sharp, on Angela's heels. They would have less than an hour to sample Angela's 7-Up punch, and they would never taste Tariq's marinated beef ribs. That wasn't the way it was planned, but that's the way it turned out.

Everyone she'd invited came, and most of them brought stories.

"I haven't set foot inside the Good House since I-don't-know-when," Art Brunell said, clasping Angela's hand warmly as his squat figure filled the doorway. His brow was dotted with sweat from his climb up the steps. "It's going on twenty-five years now. My mother used to send me out here for your grandma's root teas. Boy, did I love coming over to Mrs. T'saint's house. I memorized the order of all the presidents once just so she'd let me have a piece of pie, and believe me, it was worth the trouble. How you doin', Angie? Hope life's as good for you as it is for me."

His green eyes shone through his wire-rimmed eyeglasses with the same zeal and ardent kindness Angela remembered from high school. It was hard not to like Art, even though, like most locals, he pronounced Angela's surname phonetically instead of saying *Too-SAUNT*, the French pronunciation she preferred.

"That's a tall order for mere mortals, Art, but I'm doing all right. Where's Liza?"

"Huffing and puffing right behind him," Liza Brunell called, breathless. "And I have those jars of elderberry preserves I've been promising you. My friends get samples whether they want them or not." Liza's careworn face had been much more luminous in her senior picture as Liza Kerr, the school's star actress with an eye toward Broadway. She'd been damn good, too. In those days, Liza had considered Art a cornball like they all did, and she'd never imagined birthing Art's freckled six-year-old son, who was at her side. The boy's hair was an orange nest, reminiscent of Liza's, and he fidgeted as if his skin made him itch. All three Brunells wore campaign T-shirts proclaiming YOUR TOWN'S FUTURE—ART BRUNELL FOR MAYOR. Angela had never asked Liza if she'd made her peace living in a place she'd sworn to escape, but she envied the way Liza and Art fit each other. Maybe Broadway had never been real to Liza, but this was.

"Is this your baby *Glenn?*" Angela said. "He's growing fast, just like Corey. Children are definitely not forever, are they?"

"No, they're not, thank goodness," Liza said. She nudged Angela as she walked into the foyer, her eyes dancing. "Oh, I've got a surprise for you."

"Liza, this town can't keep a secret. You're the second person who's brought it up in twenty minutes. Just tell me what's going on."

"If I told you, it wouldn't be a surprise, would it?"

Before Angela could press Liza, Glenn began screaming as he gazed at the foyer ceiling. "Lookit, Mom! This house is *way big!*" Angela could only imagine how he must act at home.

"Well, keep it down. You don't have to throw a fit. It's not like you've never seen a nice house," Liza said, as if her son's outburst cast doubt on Art's much-whispered Big Bucks from his law practice in Longview. Angela heard rivalry in her friend's voice. All through high school, she and Liza had raced to see who could get more, faster. Liza had never left Sacajawea, but she'd still done just fine: Rumor had it that Liza only worked part-time at the grocery store with Marlene because she chose to, since Art quietly owned a million dollars in real estate throughout western Washington. Art and Liza never talked about how much they had. They lived in a three-bedroom house on five acres near State Route Four, like anybody else.

"No, Glenn's right. The Good House is special," Art said, as somberly as if he were speaking of a church. He gazed up at the foyer's chandelier, which sparkled from its recent cleaning. Illuminated by the stained-glass window built in a half-moon shape in the door, the chandelier cast rainbow-colored teardrops onto the staircase and throughout the foyer. Art rested his hand on his son's head, and Angela noticed their identical sunburns, probably from a day's fishing. "Wow, this is a hell of a house. Hasn't changed a bit, Angie."

"Don't say *hell*, Dad," Glenn said, teasing.

"Stop that, Glenn," Liza snapped. "I've told you, repeating it's not funny."

Angela recognized the quick look that passed between father and son, because she had seen that look countless times between Tariq and Corey: *Lighten up, Mom.*

In the living room, Rob Graybold, another former classmate who was now the county sheriff, was holding court near the French doors, entrancing a huddle of guests with stories about transients running crystal meth laboratories in the woods. Crowding attentively near him were a new physician, Rhonda Something from Portland; the Everlys, an older couple who served as caretakers for Angela's house and yard during the months she was away; and June McEwan, the Sacajawea County High principal. Laney Keane, president of the county historical society, was admiring the player piano in a corner by herself. And Angela could hear laughter from a bigger knot of guests who had gathered in the kitchen, the room that somehow became the nucleus of any party. The murmur of combined conversations was a roar to Angela, burying the melodic squeal of Coltrane's saxophone on the stereo. If a bomb dropped here today, she mused, Sacajawea would be history.

"Dad, how come it's called the Good House?" Glenn Brunell asked.

Laney Keane gave the boy a smile that softened her pinched face. "In the first place, Glenn, this house was built in 1907 by the town pharmacist, Elijah Goode. He chose this place because he said the land felt 'blessed beyond all description,' or in any case that's what he wrote to his brother in Boston. Marie Toussaint worked for him for a time, and he left her this house in his will."

"Are you kidding me?" Art said, hoisting his son onto his back with a grunt. "I never heard that. I always figured it was something to do with Mrs. T'saint and her teas."

"Oh, no, it's much more than that," Laney said, as if their ignorance distressed her. "In 1929, three years after Marie Toussaint took ownership of this house, a mudslide destroyed the other homes on this side of town. Mrs. Toussaint and her husband brought their neighbors in, pulling some of them out of the muck with their bare hands. Have you heard that story, Angela?"

"Only every other Sunday," Angela said, remembering Gramma Marie's fondness for elaborate storytelling. In another era, her grandmother might have been a *griot*. "She told me she even had her neighbors' goats in this living room. Chickens, pigs, you name it. She had to throw out her foyer rug." Gramma Marie also told her she'd been treated badly by her neighbors until that mudslide. Angela repressed a sour chuckle, wondering how her guests would react to *that* portion of their heritage. *And did you hear about the time Sheriff Kerr shot up Gramma Marie's door and shattered the round attic window with buckshot? Have another Bud and I'll tell you. . . .*

"Did people die?" Glenn asked Laney eagerly.

"No, thank goodness," Laney said. "And as far as I know, this house has been called the Good House ever since."

"Well, it's those teas I remember," Art Brunell said. "Those weren't just your normal teas. My papa used to swear up and down that Mrs. T'saint's teas could cure anything from a head cold to a cold bed. He said it was voodoo for sure."

Angela felt her ears burning with embarrassment in the ensuing laughter, and she slowly eased her way out of the living room, toward the now-empty foyer. She knew where this was going: Sooner or later, someone would ask her what Gramma Marie used to put in those teas, treating Angela like the progeny of a legendary medicine woman. Gramma Marie had earned a nursing degree, that was all, and her Chinook husband, whom most people condescendingly called Red John, had likely taught her a thing or two about the medicinal qualities of regional herbs. Gramma Marie, despite her roots in Louisiana and her Creole surname, had not been some kind of witch doctor. Would anyone assume she had been a witch if she and her husband had been white?

But the townspeople weren't the only ones to blame, Angela reminded herself. Gramma Marie had played the stereotype for all it was worth, giving her customers mystical-sounding instructions—*Now don't you ever drink this in a bad mood, or it'll have the opposite effect*, and other nonsense Angela overheard from time to time, remnants of old bayou superstitions. That kind of talk had crept up in Angela's mother, too. During her bad spells, Dominique Toussaint had claimed she was hearing the voices of demons laughing in her ears—before she'd silenced them with a bottle of downers, that is. Maybe Gramma Marie had sown the seeds for her mother's delusions, Angela thought. She was glad her grandmother had never tried to pass any of it on to her. As a child, she'd been afraid whatever was wrong with her mother might be catching somehow.

Angela went to the kitchen, where Melanie Graybold and Faith Henriksen, both of whom owned shops in town, were red-faced with laughter over a joke she had missed. Angela snuck behind them and glanced out of the breakfast nook's bay window toward the patch of grass cleared away for their backyard and deck. Half a dozen men congregated around the grill with Tariq. With the back door propped open, she could smell beef cooking and hear the men debating starters for a fantasy football league.

Earlier, she'd overheard the men talking about some new law against mole-trapping while Tariq nodded sagely, pretending an escapee from the Chicago projects knew anything about outdoor life. Tariq wouldn't know a mole from a raccoon. She was glad he had steered the conversation back to comfortable ground. Tariq *knew* football—that, and a few volumes' worth of finance, economic theory, and post-Reconstruction history and sociology, if he could find anyone who cared. The more he enjoyed himself at the party, the better his mood later. The better for both of them.

A glass of Pellegrino on ice might help her nerves, she decided. She'd brought a supply of the sparkling mineral water from L.A., and she drank it constantly, a substitute for the Chardonnay she no longer allowed herself to enjoy because she enjoyed it too much. Pellegrino was safer, since the last thing Corey needed was a mother as incapable of coping with daily life as hers had been.

After finding a glass, Angela clawed into the half-empty bag of ice sagging in the kitchen sink. That cold-burn sensation seized her arm again, exactly as it had at the store, except, if anything, it was more pronounced this time. Like her arm had been injected with ice.

Angela yelped, drawing her hand away with a spasm that nearly knocked the glass from the counter. *"Dammit,"* she hissed, shaking her arm out. It tingled, then the strange sensation vanished. Great. Now she was probably having an anxiety attack, just in time for the party.

"Mom?"

Corey walked from behind her, gazing at her with those almond-shaped eyes that mirrored her own. Although he was slightly bent over, Corey stood above her, a new development this summer that was hard for Angela to get used to. Corey was less a child each day.

"Can I talk to you? I have to give you something." Corey sounded distressed.

Angela forgot about her arm. "Baby, how's your stomach?"

"Whatever, it's a'ight," Corey said. He took the crook of her arm, steering her toward the privacy of the foyer that ended behind the stairs, near the closed door leading to the wine cellar. He took a breath. "Mom, I did something, and I have to make it right. It's been heavy on my mind."

Shit, Angela thought. Something in Oakland. Or something with Sean. Suddenly, Angela remembered Marlene's inquiry about Sean at the market: *They're always running here and there. . . .*

Angela felt inexplicably panicked. Her belly was as tight as it got some nights in L.A., when she lay awake wondering where Corey was at that precise moment, if his father had met any of the parents of the kids their son was spending his time with. Wondering if Corey was already sexually active, in danger of becoming a parent or catching a disease. Or if Corey might be in the wrong car at the wrong time when an Oakland cop might show up with an attitude. The worries came in a flood, deepening and multiplying. That was the thing about summers—during the summers, she didn't worry as much. But she was worried now.

Corey slowly raised his closed palm, then unfolded it painstakingly, like a flower-bud. There, nestled among the dark crisscrossing lines that foretold her son's future, sat a small gold band with tiny figures sculpted all around it. When Angela saw the ring, her mouth fell open with a long, stunned gasp. Her eyes beheld it, unblinking.

"At first, I was gonna play like I'd seen it at a yard sale or something, and say, 'Hey, Mom, look what I found, it's just like Gramma Marie's.' But it's the same one."

Angela's heart bounded, although she was afraid to trust her eyes. The solid gold ring was carved with African symbols that looked both geometric and oddly singular, unknowable. Gramma Marie had been wearing that ring the day she died. She'd motioned for Angela to come closer, then she'd slipped the slick, warm gold across Angela's finger, making her promise to keep it always. This ring had been Gramma Marie's good-bye to her, and Angela hadn't seen it in four years.

It had been stolen. Whatever bastard had broken in through her bedroom window and stolen this ring had also somehow broken her life, the parts that mattered.

Now, the ring was back. This was impossible. Angela stared at the ring, not touching it.

Corey's voice wavered as he met her confused eyes. His explanation tumbled out. "I threw the brick and broke your window, Mom. It sounds dumb now, but there was this girl I liked, right? Her name was Sherita, and I knew the ring was special to you, and I thought maybe it would be special to her." Corey swallowed, glancing away. His voice became a monotone, signaling that he had spent time rehearsing this speech. "It was just dumb kid stuff. I said I'd let her wear it for a week. But she said she saw me talking to some girl before the week was over, and she wouldn't give it back. I was afraid to tell you I took it. So I threw the brick and broke the window and knocked your jewelry all over the floor, and you thought somebody stole it. I said to myself, 'If she asks me if I did it, I won't lie.' But you never did ask, Mom."

He looked relieved to be finished, blinking fast.

Angela took the ring and stared at its beautiful symbols, which looked like shiny golden light-etchings against the sunken surface. A triangle with a cross in the center, a double wave, a pear shape. Slowly, she slid the ring onto the bare finger where she had once worn her wedding ring. It was snug, but not too tight. Perfect fit, like the day it had been given to her. Thinking of her grandmother, Angela could nearly smell the rose-scented talcum powder Gramma Marie had dusted herself with. She felt a shift in time, as if she were standing before this cellar door with her grandmother again as she had when she was Corey's age. Angela had hauled box after box of preserves down those steps, stacking the jars in the compartments that had been built for wine. *Now, Li'l Angel, you be careful on those steps.* The jars were dusty now, and the preserves inside were surely dried or rotten, but some of them were still down there exactly where she'd put them.

Angela felt a single icy fingernail brush the back of her neck, hearkening to the strange cold-burn she'd felt at the store and in the kitchen. Something felt wrong.

"How did you get this ring back?" she whispered.

Corey didn't look her in the eye. "I wrote letters to see if Sherita was still staying down there, and she was. I paid her for it with extra money I made from Sean's dad, grooming his horses. I was thinking about how stealing your ring was one thing I wish I could take back. So I did."

No wonder Corey had been behaving so strangely! He must have lain awake half the night, wondering how he was going to finally tell her the truth. And yet, it wasn't all truth, either. Not yet. Corey spoke quickly when he was lying, like now.

"And she still had it?" Without meaning to, Angela had shifted into her courtroom voice.

Corey shrugged. This time, he looked at her and smiled, trying to imitate his father's playfulness, the Hill men's charm. "Well, it's a damn nice ring. Like they say on TV, I cared enough to give the very best. You know what I'm sayin'?"

Corey knew better than to cuss in front of her, no matter how grown he thought he was, and she'd told him she would skin him alive the next time he dropped *youknowwhatimsayin* into a conversation with her, which sounded as ignorant to her as Jimmie Walker's *Dy-no-mite* had sounded to Gramma Marie. She wanted to slap her son's face. How many times had she told the story of her stolen ring as a woeful loss? How many times had she felt genuine hurt over it, sometimes at the mere sight of Gramma Marie's photograph, as if allowing someone to take her ring had been a shameful act on her part? How *dare* Corey let all these years go by without saying anything!

Then, Angela's anger melted, swallowed by relief. Bliss. She breathed in deeply, feeling lightheaded. Could this be real? Maybe her secretly spoken wish was coming true after all. She squeezed her own fingers, enjoying the solidness and texture of the ring.

"I know you're mad at me, huh? Well, I've been thinkin' about a punishment—"

"Corey . . ." Eyes smarting, Angela cut him off. She cupped his chin in her palm. "I don't know if you remember, but not long after you took this ring, everything fell apart for us. Your daddy and I lived in separate houses, in separate cities, and we forced you to choose between us. I think maybe that's punishment enough. What do you think?"

Now, it was Corey's turn to be silent. His lips were mashed tightly together, thinned out. He was fighting tears, she knew.

"Come here, baby," she said, reaching up to him, and he leaned against her in a hug, as he hadn't in far too long. Angela felt her heart pounding from the simple pleasure of embracing a child who rarely gave her the opportunity anymore. "When you stole this ring, you were being a selfish, thoughtless little boy. But getting it back to me—saving your money, writing a letter to that girl, using your head—that was the work of a young *man*. That makes me proud of you, Corey. That lets me know you're doing all right despite everything we've put you through. I'm glad, and I thank you with all my heart."

"It ain't all that, Mom," Corey said. She heard moisture in his nose.

"Yes, it is. I love this ring. And I love you."

Corey exhaled, and his breath warmed her neck. He gave her a tight squeeze before releasing her. Then, his gaze was dead-on. "Mom, did Gramma Marie tell you stuff about the ring? Like, those symbols. Did she tell you what they mean?"

"It's West African, she told me. She got it from her grandmother, and I forget how far it goes back before that. At least another generation. I guess she thought it was a good-luck charm."

He lowered his voice. "But what about the symbols? She never told you anything about them? Like . . . if they're supposed to have powers or something like that?"

"Powers?"

"You know," Corey said sheepishly. "If they could . . . make things happen?"

Angela didn't have the heart to ridicule him. The guests' speculations about Gramma Marie must have fired up his imagination, and how would he know any better? Corey had only been five when Gramma Marie died, and he barely remembered her. This was the first time he'd asked about his great-grandmother with real interest, as if he wanted something from her memory.

"What kind of things, Corey?" she said. "I don't understand."

Corey's gaze shifted away, then back again. His sigh seemed to harbor real sadness. "Nothin'. Forget it."

"Well, hold on. Gramma Marie held on to a lot of old folks' superstitions, so she might have mentioned something about the ring," Angela said quickly. One of Corey's major complaints about her was that she didn't take his concerns as seriously as Tariq did. "I'll have to sleep on it, okay? Ask me tomorrow. When it's not so crazy."

"Yeah, a'ight," Corey said, although his face didn't brighten. "Things are good with you and Dad this summer, right? I hear ya'll sneakin' around at night, those floors creaking. Ya'll ain't fooling nobody. Thought you should know."

Angela laughed, rubbing his short, wiry hair. "Don't get your hopes up, but we're trying."

"Cool. Guess we all make mistakes, huh? Some small and some big." Corey's eyes were unusually solemn and wistful now. He pressed his hand to his abdomen, like a pregnant woman feeling her baby kick. "And you just gotta' try to fix them, right?"

"Corey, you look awful. Are you sure you're all right? You don't have to help with the fireworks if you want to go lie down. I'll explain it to your dad."

Angela saw uncertainty on her son's face—or, more precisely, what she saw looked more like he could not choose one facial expression. First he looked nearly stricken, then sharply annoyed, then resigned. Corey rarely allowed his emotions to surface so baldly in front of her, and watching his face reminded her of studying her mother's warring emotions as a child, trying to guess which version of Dominique Toussaint would emerge next.

"I'm *fine*, dag," Corey said impatiently.

"Then do me a favor and go to the cellar and bring some sodas up, okay? They're stacked in the corner. Bring up a couple of cases. And you might as well bring the fireworks up, too."

His eyes flickered to the cellar door and back. She thought she heard the *thckk* as Corey sucked his teeth. Gramma Marie would have knocked her across the room for making a sound like that, but she and Corey had just had a rare nice talk, an actual conversation, so she ignored it.

"I have to go to Sean's," Corey said.

"Take that up with Tariq, but we both know what he'll say. I tried to talk you guys out of a big light show, but your dad's looking forward to it," Angela said. "Now go get the sodas, please."

Corey didn't answer. What was wrong with him today? Angela watched him prop open the cellar door and stare down a moment before he descended the stairs in silence.

She heard Gramma Marie's voice in her head: *Now, Li'l Angel, you be careful.*

Angela was about to tell him to tug on the string and turn on the light when he suddenly leaned back to gaze at her from beyond the narrow doorway. All at once, his tentative expression shed itself of everything except the unrestrained love he'd shown her when he was four and five. So loving he almost looked feverish. Little Corey. God, she missed that sweet, happy young kid. And he was here again, smiling at her like a photograph from easier days.

"I'm gonna take care of you good, Mom," he said with an exaggerated wink. "You wait."

Angela never forgot that smile from Corey.

If she had glanced at her watch, she would have noticed that it was 7:15 P.M. Exactly five minutes before the party would be over.

—

At 7:16, the doorbell rang.

Tariq was standing over the backyard barbecue grill cooking ribs, talking draft picks with Logan Prescott, Gunnar Michaelsen, and Tom Brock, who were all long timers with the Sacajawea Logging Company. A few yards from them, the seven young children at the party, including Glenn Brunell, were playing kickball in the clearing. Only the bigger kids were allowed to go after the ball if it got kicked too far into the woods, because there was a very steep dropoff that could be dangerous.

So far, so good.

In the living room, the player piano was limping through an atonal version of "Getting to Know You," and it irked Angela that Laney Keane or someone had put on a piano roll without her permission. The piano wasn't a toy, as Gramma Marie always used to say. Sheriff Rob Graybold had wrested the conversation away from Laney Keane's historical reflections, and the group was listening intently to his theories on why people became child molesters. Because he hadn't expected to be on duty today, Rob was halfway through his second Bud Light.

All talk of Elijah Goode or Marie Toussaint and her cure-all teas had been forgotten.

Angela answered the door, and it was then that she received the second of her three big surprises of the day: A dark-skinned black man stood on her front porch with a half-dozen huge sunflowers. The man on the porch had shaved his head clean, sported a thin moustache, and had no sign of the round-frame glasses he'd worn in high school, but she knew his *mouth*. His teeth. His eyes. Myles Fisher was waiting on the porch just as he had when he'd come to fetch her on prom night. "Well, I will be *damned*," Angela said.

Liza Brunell squeezed Angela's shoulder from behind. "Aren't you surprised?"

In Myles's hand, the sunflowers truly did look like sunshine on stems. Angela squealed, laughing. "Myles, look at you!"

Myles stepped toward her and hugged her with unself-conscious firmness. She tried not to notice the pleasant, refined scent of his cologne or how broad his shoulders had grown since high school. She gave his lips only a polite peck before she pulled away, but she felt giddy in a way that scared her. Myles's eyes shone like burnished copper pennies, and his shaved head suited him well, making him look self-assured, controlled. She couldn't pull her eyes away from his face.

"Angela Marie Toussaint," he said, pronouncing each syllable of her name slowly, with affection. "For once, I don't know what to say."

"I thought you were in D.C.!"

"He's interviewing to be the new boss at the *Lower Columbia News* over in Longview," Liza broke in, excited. "He came to the market Tuesday and I couldn't believe my eyes. I said he should come to the party and surprise you."

"That's the only reason I didn't call sooner," Myles said, his gaze deepening. "I wanted to see this look on your face. Liza nabbed me my first day back in town."

Myles had been working as an editor at *The Washington Post* for years, she'd heard. Why would he leave the *Post* for such a tiny paper? Myles patted her hand, seeing her bewilderment. "Ma's sick," he said quietly, and Angela suddenly understood. His adoptive parents had been older, and Ma Fisher's husband had died when Myles was only a junior in college. She must be close to ninety by now, and she was probably the only family he had left.

"I'm so sorry about Ma Fisher, but I'm thrilled to see you, Myles. When some people leave town, they *leave town*. I haven't seen your sorry ass in more than twenty years."

"You've obviously mistaken me for a much older man." Myles's eyes drank in the details of the house with the same appreciation he'd shown for her, and she understood that, too. He'd had many good times here. "Look at this place! Angie, you've done good. Gramma Marie is beaming down from Heaven, darlin'. She says, '*Fantastique, cher.*'"

She squeezed his hand. "I hope so."

Angela was glad Tariq was out back grilling and couldn't see her face, because she didn't want to learn whether or not her husband's jealous streak was still intact. After a couple of beers, Tariq could act foolish over nothing. And frankly, this might be the one time it wasn't exactly nothing, because Myles looked good. His face had rounded out in an attractive way, and his build had grown stocky, shedding his adolescent lean-muscled wiriness. The defining lines of his chest were visible through his tight, bone-colored Lycra shirt. He worked out, apparently. Not in the rigorous way Tariq lifted weights to feel like he was still an athlete, but enough.

Liza caught Angela's gaze and wagged a finger at her, and Angela smiled. For an instant, she felt as if she were back in the hallway of Sacajawea County High, an odd, gratifying feeling. She wondered why she hadn't had a party like this long ago.

"I need to meet the man who stole my girl," Myles said. "Where's this Mustafa guy you married? The big, bad football player? Is it true he can read, too?"

"Fool, you better hush. His name is *Tariq,*" Angela said, slapping at his shoulder. "Nobody told you to go to Columbia. Maybe if you'd gone to U.C.L.A. like we both planned . . ."

"Is that Myles Fisher I hear?" Art Brunell's voice thundered from the living room. "Mark my words, folks: The first thing I'm gonna do when I'm elected mayor is set up restrictions so we don't have any more of these deadbeat yokels moving back into town!"

Everyone laughed then, a sound that resounded throughout the house. Angela couldn't remember the last time she laughed that hard, like someone dizzy on champagne.

Then, it was 7:20.

For the rest of her life, this was all Angela would remember: loud, braying laughter. Off-key piano strains. Children outside shrieking, *Get the ball!* Then, smothering everything else beneath it, the powerful sound of something exploding in a *POP.*

Whatever it was, it was right near them, in the house. In the foyer.

Angela looked at Myles at first, as if his arrival had brought the sound somehow, but he only looked deeply startled, shoulders hunching. Then, she realized the sound had come from *beneath* them. The cellar.

"What the hell—" Rob Graybold said. "Who's setting off firecrackers?"

The explosion brought a hush to the room. Even the children outside were quiet. So was the piano, the birds, and any other sounds that had been present, near or distant, before then. Or, at least they *seemed* to be silent. In the silence, the memory of the sound loomed larger. The sunflowers were on the floor, at her feet.

Corey, Angela thought, her mind splintering. Then, she shouted his name.

Sheriff Rob Graybold went down the cellar stairs first, and she leaned on him, pushing. He'd told her to stay back, to let him take a look, but she didn't hear him, and she wouldn't have listened if she had. The cellar light was on, a naked bulb shining overhead. Her eyes followed the neat brick patterns on the cellar wall, blurring lines. She couldn't see past Rob. She couldn't see Corey.

"What happened? *An-geee?*" she heard Tariq call in alarm, from miles away.

She smelled gunpowder. Goddamn fireworks. They were illegal in California, with good reason. Children lost limbs and eyes. Why the hell had she let Tariq go out with Corey and buy rockets that were meant to light the sky?

It won't be too bad. There's a doctor here. Whatever it is, it won't be too bad.

Rob Graybold went frozen where he stood on the steps, and Angela couldn't move past him. She heard the air seep out of his lungs in a *whooshing* sound because she was so close to him, pressed tight. She felt his heart pounding, and she could smell pungent perspiration from his underarms, beneath the stink of burnt powder.

"Dear Mary and Joseph," Rob Graybold said. He turned around and tried to take Angela's arm, tugging so hard it hurt. "We need to get that doctor in here, Angie," he said, pale as milk. "Don't go down there."

But by now, Angela was screaming. She writhed against Rob Graybold until she squeezed herself past him, and her struggle brought both of them stumbling down the cellar stairs, off-balance.

Corey was lying on his stomach in the exact center of the cellar floor. His head was turned away from her, one arm raised nearly to his face, the other limp at his side, palm upward. He looked like he was taking a nap. And he must have dropped some of the drinks, some of the red ones, maybe some bottles of cherry syrup, because his head lay in the midst of a red puddle that reached almost as far as the wine shelves against the far wall. And the puddle was growing.

Another smell threaded its way through the scent of smoke and perspiration, a thick odor she couldn't allow herself to recognize yet, though she knew perfectly well what it was.

She didn't see any bags of fireworks or cartons of soda near Corey. The only thing she *did* see was a very realistic black toy gun in the middle of the red puddle, inches from Corey's hand. The gun bore a remarkable resemblance to the gun Tariq had, a black Glock with a taped butt, the one he'd kept in his nightstand drawer until she finally won the fight and he took it to a gun shop and got rid of it. Yes, he got rid of it. He said he did. He marched into the house and said, *I hope you're happy now, bitch,* and showed her the receipt. It was the first and last time he had ever called her that word, and he'd later said he was sorry. But he'd gotten rid of it because she'd screamed at him, telling him how she'd walked into her mother's bedroom to find Mama standing there with a gun in her mouth when she was twelve, and it just wasn't safe to have a gun, not with a child in the house. Angela always tried to be careful, just like Gramma Marie said.

"He got rid of it," Angela rasped, even though she was seeing that gun again, with that same tape wrapped around the butt, a mirage from a life she had left behind. *"He got rid of it."*

Angela repeated those five words and nothing else for the next half hour. All the while, Gramma Marie's gold ring gleamed on her finger as absolute proof that some things can come back after they're gone.

As far as most of the guests at Angela Toussaint's Fourth of July party knew, it was the first bad thing that had ever happened at the Good House.

HOMECOMING

Your home stands behind you, patient.

It knows, *cher*, you will return.

— MARIE TOUSSAINT

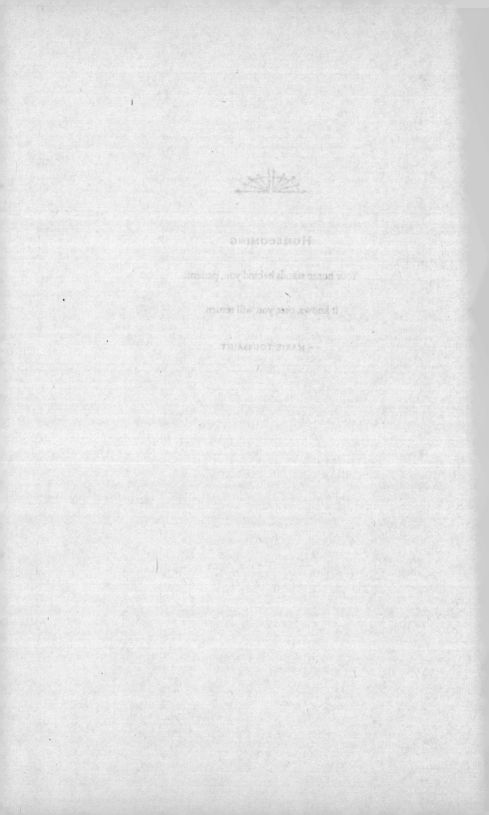

☆ Two ☆

By THE BEGINNING of her third mile, Angela Toussaint was flying. Her lean, corded legs reached a rhythm of their own accord, piston machinery propelling her white running shoes as they hit the ground. Angela no longer perceived gravity's work on her feet, or the tiny shocks of impact on her legs and hips. She no longer felt the searing sensation that had been dogging her lungs as she struggled to take in enough oxygen. She only felt the dawn air in her face and the blood rushing hot through her taut body's arteries. Flying. Finally, flying.

This was Angela's favorite time and place to be. She was nowhere and nothing. She had no beginning, no end, no present, no future. When she was flying, she disappeared from herself. Let it last forever this time, she prayed. Let it last.

But it never did. Angela could run ten miles or more without much trouble if she slowed her pace, but she had never learned how to run slowly. When Angela ran, she liked to *run*, to push her body to the end of what it had to offer. She'd vowed to start slowly today and train the way the experts instructed, but the next thing she knew, she'd been flying again. But she couldn't fly long. Angela could sustain her faster pace for only a mile—maybe a mile and a half, on very good days—but then her body began to complain. A monstrous stitch in her side. Burning lungs. Rock-hard shoulders. Tightening muscles in her legs threatening to knot themselves.

With a squeal of frustration, Angela began to slow down, her strides landing harder and more clumsily, and the world that had been passing in a blur while she was high on endorphins took its mundane shape again. She trotted to a stop on the path at four-thousand-acre Griffith Park, nearing the Los Angeles Zoo. This was her favorite morning jogging route despite the number of other runners here even by 6 A.M., when the park off of the Golden State Freeway officially opened. It was a hazy morning, so the daylight was muted and weak, and a pale shroud hid the top of the Santa Monica mountain range at the park's horizon.

Gasping for air, Angela made her way to a bench, where she propped up one leg and doused her head with water from the bottle she carried in a leather pouch slung across her back. When she'd emptied nearly half the bottle on herself, she took it to her lips and began to gulp. The lukewarm water was gone fast. She tossed the empty bottle into the L.A. County Parks recycling bin and doubled over to try to slow her breathing, locking her arms against her knees.

Nearly three miles at full speed and no puking today. That was a good sign. She hadn't done too much damage to herself this time.

"You must wake up every morning feeling like you've been hit by a truck," a stranger's voice said, and Angela looked up to see a man stretching in the grass ten yards behind her, his legs splayed wide open as he faced her. He was shirtless with a concave abdomen, a typical specimen of Los Angeles perfection—if she'd been into the Richard Gere type. Or if she'd been into anyone. This would be the part in a movie where she and the stranger would strike up a chat, share breakfast together, and then live happily ever after. Except that this was real life. In real life, there was always an *ever after*, she knew, but happy had nothing to do with it.

"Good guess," Angela said through her labored breaths.

"You're out here almost every day. Are you training?"

"Death Valley Marathon. December," she said. She did not recognize him, but why should she? Faces passed her without definition when she was running. That was what she liked best.

He pursed his lips at the mention of Death Valley, then smiled. Capped teeth, healthy tan. His handsomeness made her uneasy, strangely. "Braving the desert, huh?" he said. "I do the California International Marathon. That's in December, too. This your first?"

"I turned forty this year," she said. "It's now or never."

"I'm forty-four, and that's not true. I'm on my third." Despite his slightly thinning hair, Angela would have guessed he shaded closer to thirty-five than forty-four, but she took his word for it. The man stood up, brushing grass from the backs of his thighs. Maybe he'd felt self-conscious, thinking his goodies might spill out of his gray gym shorts, she thought.

"Listen," the man began. "I know from experience this is ten times easier with a training partner. My wife used to be mine, but the divorce killed that. At the risk of sounding like I'm pulling a cheap line, would you like to meet here and train? I run every day except Sundays and Mondays. My name's Ryan."

Hidden away in a dank, abandoned cave, Angela heard her female soul screaming, *Yes, yes, YES*. She preferred men with a chocolate hue, but she wasn't blind. Even if she never did anything with him except run, this guy would provide a damn scenic motivation never to miss a day. This was a storybook moment, she thought, the moment lucky women experience and rush to tell their girlfriends about. But she was not a lucky woman.

Angela stepped back as Ryan came forward, his hand outstretched for a shake she never returned. "You know what? That's a generous offer, but I prefer to train alone," Angela said.

He cocked his head, genuinely puzzled. People who looked like him were not accustomed to the word *no*. She saw him make a polite glance at her left hand, checking for a ring. There was none—Angela never wore jewelry when she ran. The one ring she still treasured was far too precious to risk losing again. The man shrugged. "All right, then. I'm sure I'll see you around. Let me know if you change your mind. Can I just . . . give you a little advice?"

"Go for it."

His face was as caring as any stranger's she had seen in a long while, despite the fact that she had just blown him off. She felt annoyed with herself, at the same time she was annoyed with him for breaking the peace of her refuge. "Try not to run so hard at the start and the finish. You'll hurt yourself. Once you're warmed up, run has hard as you want until the last mile, then . . . just relax."

Relax.

"Thanks. I appreciate that," Angela said, thinking how sad it was that he had just advised her to do the very thing she had long since forgotten. He might as well have just told her she should flap her arms and fly up to the summit of the mountains wreathed in morning fog.

"Don't bullshit me, Angela. Just tell me what those cheap jerks said."

Naomi Price spoke with such precision that she sounded elegant even while cursing. Every syllable was crisp and rich. Even on a speakerphone, Angela imagined she could see Naomi's perfectly lined crimson lips caressing her luminescent teeth as she spoke, the careful result of her degree in theater from CalArts. Hollywood's hottest rising black starlet had presence even when she wasn't in the room with you—and Angela could remember Naomi when she'd been a pudgy twenty-year-old on a daytime soap.

She stared out at Sunset Boulevard's cityscape from her tenth-floor office, rocking to and fro in her leather chair, twirling the stirrer in a cooled latte. The morning's haze had burned off, and the noonday sun lit up the glass office towers in her view like sparkling ice sculptures. Across from her window, twin billboards announced a new diamond necklace from Cartier and a new explosion-happy Bruckheimer flick, selling penitence on one side and heroism on the other.

Angela had dodged Naomi's calls as long as she could. She'd only picked up the ringing line because her secretary was at lunch and she'd thought it would be Stan Loweson from FilmQuest. Stan called when he didn't expect her to be in the office, preferring voice mail to true interaction.

"They're saying eight hundred is as high as they'll go," Angela told Naomi.

The speaker made a sound as if it had just been hit by a blast of air.

"This is a premature conversation," Angela said before Naomi could regain speech. "I don't know why you always do this. You pay me a percentage so I can hide the ugly underbelly from you. It's called a ne-go-ti-a-tion. This is foreplay. We say no, they come back higher. But I'm warning you— it won't be *much* higher. You'll peak at a million. You don't have the box office yet, Naomi."

"You better remind them that *People* magazine said—"

"They know all about it. Stan said congratulations."

"And on *Hollyview* last week, Tom Cruise mentioned me as someone he'd like to work with. You sent them that tape, right?"

Angela ignored that last comment. She'd dutifully put in a call to Cruise's representation, and until they called back, that was all talk. Cruise was too savvy to have said it publicly unless he meant it, but she'd still look like a fool bringing that up with Stan.

"A million, Naomi. And we'll be sweating for that."

"They expect me to show my stuff in bed with this overrated white boy for that kind of money? He's almost old enough to be my father, and you know what they're paying *him!* Angela, this is racist *bullshit.* If I was—"

"Girl, stop it," Angela sighed, cutting her off. "Stay focused on what *is*, not what isn't. A million is your biggest payday to date. You build a career a step at a time. I wouldn't care if you did this one for Guild minimum—it's that important. One day, God willing, you'll be doing love scenes with Denzel for ten million dollars a pop. But that day, my dear, has not arrived."

Naomi made another indistinguishable sound, a cross between a scream and a howl, forcing Angela to turn down the volume on her speakerphone.

"Naomi, am I good at what I do?" Angela said in the ensuing silence.

Naomi sighed, and a wind billowed through the speaker. "The best," she said at last.

"Then trust me. I'll fight to get you a million. Then we move on to the next step."

Thankfully, Angela's line beeped. Stan, of course. Twelve-fifteen on the dot.

"My line's beeping. Just leave this to the pros, Naomi. Go do some crunches or whatever it is you beautiful people do."

"Fuck you, Angela," Naomi said. Then, sweetly: "We still on for dinner?"

"Yeah, but not Roscoe's. I don't know how you eat fried chicken, but I can't eat that stuff when I'm training. I'll call you later and we'll pick a place."

The phone beeped again, trampling part of Naomi's response. "—eat there one day a month, and this is my day. You know you love those wings and waffles. Come on, Angela, I've been looking forward to it for weeks!"

OUT OF AREA, the phone display read. Not Stan's usual I.D., but he might be calling from a cell phone. "Let me go. It's probably Stan."

"Well, if it is, you need to tell him those Butterfly McQueen days are over, and he'd better wake up and realize black actors need to get paid some real money, too—"

Angela cut her friend off in mid-rant. She switched over to the other line, donning her best don't-mess-with-me voice. "Angela Toussaint."

Silence at first. She glanced to make certain the telephone display said Line 2. It did.

"Hello? Angela Toussaint," she said again.

An uncertain, frail-sounding woman finally spoke. "Angie?" she said. "Goodness, you sound so different at your office. You really threw me for a loop, sweetheart. I hope this isn't a bad time."

Angela couldn't answer at first. She couldn't open her mouth. She sat with her palms pressed flat on her desktop, frozen in place. Her insides seemed to draw up, squeezing her lungs so tightly that she decided not to breathe. At least for a while.

It was Laurel Everly, the caretaker of Gramma Marie's house in Saca-jawea.

"Angie?" Mrs. Everly said. "Are you there?"

"I'm here." Angela hadn't meant to sound so clipped, but those were the only two words she could manage. Mrs. Everly had sent her three let-ters in the past two months, and she hadn't opened them. She opened none of her mail except bills. Angela had changed her number and become a ghost. Clients had her cell phone number, and that was all that mattered.

Two weeks had passed since Mrs. Everly's last letter, forwarded from her old Hollywood Hills address. Angela hadn't thrown the letters away like she had most of the other letters that found her, but she'd managed to convince herself that she'd forgotten they were there. Mrs. Everly must have called Directory Assistance, and she'd found the sixteen-month-old Toussaint Talent Agency.

The things Angela had attached meaning to lost their relevance—her new office suite she shared with a secretary and assistant, the running shoes under her desk, the photograph she had taken with Sidney Poitier six months ago, the framed *Variety* article profiling her after she orchestrated a comic's $10 million payday, her biggest feat. That version of Angela Tous-saint was foreign, and she found herself confused to be sitting in her place. She was only Angie again.

"Well . . . you sound busy," Mrs. Everly said, unable to conceal her hurt feelings.

Angela picked up the handset, then she closed her eyes, rubbing her temple. She could feel her heartbeat there. "No, uh . . . actually, this is a good time, Mrs. Everly. It's lunchtime. I know you've been trying to reach me, but I've been . . ."

POP

The sound she heard in her memory—the sound she had never stopped hearing, really—was a mere echo, nothing like it had once been, but it was enough. Angela's mouth went dry. She tried to squeeze away the images that began battering her: The brick wall. The empty wine racks. A growing puddle of bright, ugly red on the floor, snaking toward the wall.

Then, gone. Angela had grown amazed at her power to sweep her mind clean.

"How are you? How's Mr. Everly's back?"

"Some days are good, some not," Mrs. Everly said. "But could be worse. Joseph turned seventy-six last month, and I'm not far behind him. We still do all the work ourselves, except we had to hire out some of the roof work after all the rain last winter. You remember . . ."

Angela didn't remember. When was the last time she and this woman had spoken? Angela's mind had shoved all of Sacajawea into a tamed, formless shadow, at least while she was fully awake.

"I hope you won't be angry with me, Angie, but I showed the house even though I never heard back from you. They're about to drive me batty, calling me every other day. They're a very nice couple—the man is colored, and his wife is from New York, probably Jewish, I think. They have another B&B in Seattle, he said, and when I told them about Marie, well, you should have seen his face light up. He said he could make the house part of some kind of heritage tour, put it in a directory. He talked about a bronze plaque with Marie's face on it, telling her history. They'll keep with tradition and call it the Good House, he said."

At first, Angela couldn't make sense of Mrs. Everly's words, or the pride she heard in her voice. Then the meaning washed over her. "You opened Gramma Marie's house to strangers?"

"I know it's an unusual liberty, but I wrote you about it—"

Angela's next question came suddenly, surprising even her. "How much are they offering?"

"The same I said in my last letter."

"I don't remember what you said in the letter, Mrs. Everly." Angela fought not to sound as irritated as she felt. Mrs. Everly had been Gramma Marie's friend, so she was a small piece of Gramma Marie left behind. Angela didn't dare disrespect Mrs. Everly.

Mrs. Everly lowered her voice, shy about discussing money. "Four hundred. I don't know if that's a good price, even if real estate's depressed. The house is so special, and the land to boot. But they don't care so much about the land and the timber—it's the house they love. We only hate to see it standing empty, you see."

We meaning her and her husband. *We* meaning the whole town. It was none of anyone's business if the house was empty. The line beeped in Angela's ear, someone else trying to get through. "Thank you so much for calling, Mrs. Everly. I'm sorry I've been so hard to reach. I hope you can understand, after everything." *Everything* was a small word for what it was, the sum of it.

"Oh, yes," Mrs. Everly said, suddenly more motherly than business-like. "Of course I understand, Angie. I was just afraid you'd be sore at me."

"Don't worry about that. I'll give you my answer soon. I have another call, so . . ."

Mrs. Everly clicked off without argument. Angela didn't pick up the other line right away, waiting for Caller I.D. to do its work so she wouldn't be caught off-guard again. FILMQUEST PICTURES, the display said. Stan Loweson, king of the lunchtime callback.

Naomi Price was about to get her million dollars, whether Stan liked it or not. Anyone who thought Angela Toussaint was a pushover had no idea who they were messing with.

POP

But as the phone rang three times, then four, Angela didn't move to pick up the receiver.

Her million-dollar call went to voice mail, and it was gone.

Roscoe's House of Chicken 'n Waffles in Hollywood, tucked inconspicuously at Sunset and Gower, could be hard to find if you didn't already know where it was, but it was a Los Angeles staple. It offered the usual soul food, depending on the day's specials—greens, grits, and biscuits—but its true lure was the fried chicken and waffles celebrated in its name, served together in a combination that seemed mismatched only to people who had never tasted it. Tourists who bought celebrity home maps and hung out at Planet Hollywood would be much better served grabbing a quick meal at the no-frills tables at Roscoe's, Angela thought. Over the years, she had seen everyone from Bobby De Niro to Sam Jackson getting their soul-food fix at the Hollywood or South Central locations, dressed down and ready to eat.

Tonight, the biggest name dining at Roscoe's was Naomi Price. Their table was in the back, but although most other diners had either failed to recognize Naomi or only nodded cordial recognition, two high school girls with microscopically braided weaves stood at their table gushing over Naomi while she signed autographs. "My mama is not going to *be-LIEVE* this . . . ," one of the girls was saying, so excited she was whipping her hands in the air as if they were on fire.

And Naomi was eating it up. She always had time for *her people,* as she called the well-wishers who flocked around her. In the past year, there hadn't been a single time they'd been out together when Naomi hadn't stopped to chat with a fan, whether it was at Starbucks, the movie theater, or the ladies' room. That degree of renown hadn't been true in the beginning, when Angela first opened her agency and Naomi had been one of the few name clients who'd trusted her enough to hire her. Luck had instigated it: They'd known each other in passing while Angela was still at the law firm, they had mutual friends, and Naomi had been ready for a change. The rest, pure magic. After a decade in the business, with Angela's guidance, Naomi had become an overnight success.

Angela had been an agent for only sixteen months, but even as a rookie she was living out an agent's dream, creating an ascendancy. She and Naomi were making a lot of money together, and they were about to make much more. Together, they watched it unfold, as humbled by the process as they were amused. *Magic* was the only word to describe it.

Naomi had a smooth, oval-shaped face that made her look like a Somali model. Her complexion was a shade lighter than Angela's and two shades darker than Halle's, and she had a natural bustline that put Angela's B-cup to shame. Being Naomi Price was a full-time job, Angela had observed, from Naomi's strict nutritional habits to the killer workout routine she lived by to combat her tendency toward chubbiness. Tonight, in a casual white designer jogging suit and a thick braid nestling her back, Naomi wore gold-tinted eye shadow and fiery cinnamon lipstick that looked as if it had been born on her mouth. Naomi was so lovely, sometimes the sight of her stopped Angela's thoughts cold, the way she might stop to stare at a striking sunset.

"Thank you, Miss Price," the girls said in chorus, and they vanished back to their table. Neither of them had afforded Angela a second glance. Naomi gave her instant invisibility.

"So damn cute. That tall one reminds me of my cousin Betty," Naomi said, before slipping a fork full of syrup-drowned waffles into her mouth. This was Naomi's designated "Cheat Meal," the one day a month she ate what she chose. Naomi's face melted with delight as she ate. She chewed her waffle as if she'd never tasted sugar before.

Angela had finished her food long ago, so her plate was a graveyard of stripped chicken bones. "I want to talk about Stan," Angela said. Their usual habit was to avoid discussing business until their after-dinner coffee, but Angela was making an exception.

Still hunched over her plate, Naomi looked up at her with one eyebrow raised. "You better not be about to give me any bad news while I'm eating my waffles, Angela."

"This deal is still fine. But I want to be honest. Stan tried to call me about five minutes after I hung up from you at lunchtime. I didn't pick up the phone. I couldn't talk to him," Angela said, and she felt her unspoken words being sucked back down her throat. She realized she had just swallowed a sob. Quickly, she wiped the corners of her eyes. Naomi wasn't the kind of friend Angela wanted to cry in front of. Maybe an old friend, if she'd hadn't been hiding from them, but not a new one, especially a client. Why had she brought it up?

She must be desperate to talk to someone, she realized. Life in the outside world wasn't as ordered as it had been at The Harbor, with daily friendship sessions scheduled at two. Paid friendship, after all, was better than having no one to tell.

"Honey!" Naomi said, blanketing Angela's hand with the warmth of her own. "What's wrong? Do you want to get out of here?"

Angela shook her head. "No, enjoy your food. I'm sorry."

"Sorry about what? I thought we were friends."

"We are friends." Angela had spent more time with Naomi in the past year than anyone else. Angela didn't see many old memories reflected in Naomi's face, and that alone made her precious.

"You have to listen to enough of my shit, don't you? Tell me what's wrong."

So, against her better judgment, Angela told Naomi about Mrs. Everly's call, the offer on Gramma Marie's house, the time she'd spent in Sacajawea as a child. There were things she didn't say, but she didn't have to. Black Hollywood was a small circle, and there were some things everyone knew. "I think I just want to be rid of that place," Angela finished.

Naomi's eyes, watching her, were wide and all-absorbing. "That's deep, girl."

"Ain't it, though?"

Naomi smiled, virtually blinding Angela with her teeth. "That's the first time I've ever heard you use that word. You never say *ain't.*"

Despite herself, Angela laughed. She dabbed her damp nostrils with her crumpled napkin. "Yeah, well, Gramma Marie drove that word out of my head. I tried to come to her every summer all grown, 'You don't tell me what to do and what to say' and all that mess. By the time she was through with me, I got scared when I even *thought* the word *ain't.* Gramma Marie didn't play."

"That sounds like Mama June, my grandmama in North Carolina, part of that Booker T. Washington generation. Putting your best foot forward. Representing for the race."

"Yes," Angela said, heartened and surprised by this unexpected strand of kinship. "Gramma Marie made me read all of Booker T.'s books—*Up from Slavery*, the books about Tuskegee. Oh, and I had to read *The Souls of Black Folk* by DuBois, too. Had me writing book reports on my summer vacations. Way back when, Mama wasn't allowed to go to school in that town because it was segregated, so Gramma Marie taught her at home. When I came along, she put all that schooling on me, too." And I tried to put it on Corey, she thought, keeping that part to herself. The thought hurt, but not nearly as much as it usually did.

"Just like me!" Naomi said. "Mama June was the first person to make me recite Langston Hughes poems. And she taught me how to walk with books on my head for my posture. I thought she was crazy, but just look at us now, Angela. God bless those strong black women, huh?"

"Yeah. God bless them," Angela said. A rare radiance flooded her heart. She hadn't permitted herself to think about how much she missed even her memories of Gramma Marie, given that so much of her grandmother was locked inside a house she could no longer stand the sight of. Tears came, but they didn't feel bitter. Nor drain her strength.

"I'm'a tell you what I think," Naomi said, leaning closer. "Your decision about selling your grandmama's house and that history, that's between you and Jesus. Maybe selling the house will be the best thing, in the end. But something else Mama June used to tell me: I have intuition. I've got a good feel for people and situations. And it sure comes in handy in this town, where people kiss your ass for an hour and forget you an hour later. So I have a feeling about you, Angela."

Angela believed in intuition, too, she realized. She hadn't always, but she did now. She had irrefutable proof of it: She'd *known* something was wrong that day of the party. All day long, she'd known it. That might be what had driven her crazy for a little while, just knowing that she'd known. And that knowing hadn't mattered. It hadn't helped her stop it. *POP*

"What's your feeling?" Angela said.

Naomi put her face was so close to Angela's that their noses nearly touched. "You can't make that decision until you go to the house again. Spend a few days with it. See if you're ready to say good-bye."

Angela pulled away. "I can't do that."

"You *think* you can't. But I think you have to, Angela. If you never go back and you decide to sell that house, you might wake up one day and realize you made a mistake you can't fix. And all because you didn't know you were ready. What you gonna tell the ancestors then?"

The ancestors. Now, Naomi sounded like Gramma Marie. It dawned on Angela that she'd never learned more about Naomi's life outside of the business because she hadn't shared more of herself either. So much of her job entailed trying to soothe Naomi's artist's ego, she'd tricked herself into believing that was all there was to this woman. Naomi knew her better than she'd thought, and she didn't know Naomi nearly well enough.

"You know what happened in that house, Naomi." This was the closest she'd come to talking about the Fourth of July with someone who wasn't a shrink.

"Yes, ma'am, I do."

"Then you know why I can't go back there right now."

"I also know that's your grandmama's house, and you can't run from it. If you go back there and the love has been buried by the pain, all right then. That's when you'll *know*. Go on and sell it, let someone else love it. But you can't walk around thinking you're the same person you were two years ago—because I saw you two years ago, girl, and it ain't true."

Had Naomi been at the funeral? Of course she had, because almost all of her old law firm's clients and other industry types had attended out of respect. They hadn't been doing her any favors, either. Ironically, Angela mused, her display at the funeral was probably the reason so many clients had hesitated to hire her. But not Naomi. She had seen the whole thing— the beginning of what had felt like Angela's irretrievable descent into a mental bog—and it hadn't mattered to her.

"I can't go through that again," Angela said.

"Angela, you *won't*. Look, I'm not saying it won't hurt—of course it will. But my intuition tells me you need to do this. Not a little bit, either. A *lot*. And you know what? If it'll make it easier, I'll go with you."

A young couple in African-style clothing was hovering a few yards from their table, pretending to read a newspaper article framed on the wood-paneled wall while they glanced at Naomi every few seconds with fevered recognition. They were both in their twenties, an age Angela could barely remember, a figment of her own imagination. Angela both pitied and envied the woman she'd been then, always railing at life because she thought it was so hard—when she still had no idea what hard really was. Hard had just been getting started.

The couple took steps toward them, and Angela knew she was going to lose Naomi's attention to fans—"spreading good juju," Naomi called it. But Naomi did something Angela had never seen her do before: She shifted away from the curious couple. Nothing overt, but enough that her body language spoke volumes, a big red neon DO NOT DISTURB sign. The couple got the message. With sad faces, they drifted back to their seats.

"Think about it, all right?" Naomi said, holding Angela's eyes. "Maybe after you get me my million from FilmQuest. My next shoot isn't until the end of the month. Why don't we celebrate in . . . what's your grandmother's town called again?"

Suddenly, Angela felt a bubble break.

How could she expect Naomi Price to drop everything to go up to Gramma Marie's house with her? Naomi wouldn't be caught dead in Sacajawea. People like Naomi Price went through life governing their satellites, and Angela was just another of her satellites. Angela had seen Naomi talk to fans and producers alike with this identical intense sincerity, and Naomi's ability to make people believe they were the center of her universe was her greatest star quality.

Down girl, Angela scolded herself, looking away from Naomi's eyes. She was obsessing, a feeling she recognized from a squeezing sensation in her chest. As the shrinks had pointed out, her tendency to obsess and second-guess had betrayed her many times before. What was so damned hard about allowing herself to have one true friend?

"It's called Sacajawea," Angela said, ignoring her misgivings. "And I'll think about it."

And maybe, God help her, she really would.

⋈ *Three* ⋈

THIS WAS GOING to be one of the hard nights.

A daily menu of tragedies on the ten o'clock news blared from Angela's television set while she untied the melted ice-pack from her sore left thigh. Early on, she used to coddle herself when she felt tweaks and twinges while she was running, but now she'd learned to endure the punishment and distinguish between normal and abnormal pains. She iced at night, and in the morning she'd wake up groaning and hissing as she swung her cadaver-stiff legs over the side of her bed. How had the gorgeous guy in the park put it? Feeling like she'd been hit by a truck. Right on, mister.

But she could live with that. Physical pain was the easiest part of her life.

As Angela stood at her kitchen counter unwrapping herself, she sipped from her cup of herbal tea and dreaded going to bed. She couldn't put it off much longer. If she didn't hit her pillow by ten-thirty, she'd have no chance of getting up by five-thirty, which was the only routine that gave her enough time in the mornings to jog, read the *Times* and the trades, and start making her East Coast telephone calls before the New Yorkers headed to lunch.

She hadn't turned on her lights. The dancing, flickering parade of colors glowing from the television set cast strobelike shadows across the stacks of boxes crowding what was supposed to be her living room. There was a sofa in there somewhere, but mostly the room looked unchanged from when she'd moved into the Sunset Villas apartment eight months before. The only difference now was that most of the boxes had been ripped open. She had never really unpacked, constantly searching through boxes. She could think of much more practical uses for the $2,500 a month she spent on this secure downtown apartment and its 1,500 square feet of glorified storage space. She'd moved in with the dream of an elegant place to entertain her clients: Her kitchen had Italian granite floors and counters, the balcony was large enough for a party, shaded by potted palm trees, and the obscenely large master bathroom was equipped with a black marble jetted soaking tub she and her aching muscles practically lived in.

So far, no one had seen any of it but her, and the longer she lived here, the more she doubted anyone ever would. She slept here and occasionally ate here, but the apartment felt more cold and austere all the time. She was a visiting drifter. Every morning, Angela awoke to the chaos of boxes and asked herself if she believed this was the way a healthy person would live. The answer, of course, was *hell no*. But as much as she hated not being unpacked, she had not claimed this space either.

The newscaster's voice made its way past her thoughts. ". . . Century City toddler is dead tonight after his six-year-old brother accidentally shot him with a handgun their father left within the boys' easy reach, police say. The tragedy happened—"

Instinctively, Angela picked up the remote and changed the channel. She found Lifetime, where *The Golden Girls* were wisecracking in the safety of their comfortable, pastel world. How could she have forgotten never to watch the news before bedtime? Maybe she'd been testing herself, hoping she was ready to reenter the detached society of people who didn't take the nightly news personally. If so, she'd just failed the test.

Angela finished her tea, hoping the valerian root, passionflower, and kava-kava would take her down fast, since it was late and she didn't have time for a hot soak tonight. Supermarket tea wasn't as good as Gramma Marie's, but it would have to do. She wouldn't go foraging in her medicine cabinet for her bottle of Xanax, either. Those days were over. She would learn how to do this on her own, all by herself.

"Welcome to Helltime," Angela sighed, and she limped toward her bedroom.

Helltime. Bedtime. One night at a time.

—

My mama is not going to be-LIEVE this
Mom? Can I talk to you? I want to give you something

Angela's eyes snapped open. Eleven o'clock, the bright red numbers on her clock said.

She thought she'd made it. She almost had. But as soon as she'd felt her limbs finally loosening with occasional tiny sleep-spasms, the lid on the Pandora's box in her mind had toppled out of place, releasing the voices. She'd heard that teenage girl from Roscoe's, the one who'd wanted Naomi's autograph. And then Corey next.

The voices almost always led to Corey.

Some people had bad dreams. Not Angela. She wasn't certain she dreamed at all; she couldn't remember a dream she'd had in years. But Helltime was the weakness in Angela's defense system—she couldn't control her thoughts when she was in that space between waking and sleeping, vulnerable. The closer she floated toward sleep, the more animated her mind's menagerie became, playing random images, voices, and whole conversations, as if an entire cast of characters sat in her head waiting for the curtain to rise.

Why, *here* you are, Angela. So nice of you to join us again, old girl!

Sometimes she bobbed to consciousness and realized she couldn't follow the nonsensical trains of thought, and she drifted to full sleep, relieved and unmolested as the harmless babble whispered in her imagination. But sometimes—oftentimes—her thoughts came back to familiar, painful refrains. Her thoughts took her hostage. When that happened, she felt herself fleeing to wakefulness like she had fallen into a well, flailing for light and air.

My mama is not going to be-LIEVE this

Corey and that girl from Roscoe's would be about the same age now, seventeen. If Corey had been at the restaurant having dinner with them tonight, he might have thought the girl was cute. He might have pretended to be looking elsewhere while he glanced up at her with quick, sly flicks of his eyes, the way she'd first noticed by the time he turned thirteen. My God, she'd thought to herself when she observed it, Corey is changing. Corey is growing up.

Except that he wasn't growing up, not anymore. Corey was dead. Dead.

A handgun his father left within easy reach

POP

You fucking sonofabitch. Look into this coffin and see what you did. Just like Emmett Till's mama said when they beat her son to death, I want you to SEE it. *You did this, Tariq. Look at his face. Look what you did to him with*

*that gun and your lies. It doesn't even LOOK like him anymore! YOU KILLED HIM
YOU FUCKING SONOFABITCH*

I'm gonna take care of you good, Mom

Angela jerked to full wakefulness again. Her heart had lobbed itself
into her throat, beating hard. She raised her hand to the spot, wondering if
her air passage was blocked. But, no. She could breathe, even if her breath
had hitched slightly. She felt a thin sheen of perspiration across her neck,
tracing it with her index finger to her collarbone. When Angela saw the
boxes stacked around her bed, she stared and blinked for a few seconds,
confused. Where had these boxes come from? Dr. Houston wouldn't like
these boxes in her room. She didn't have clearance for so many things. It
was against The Harbor's regulations.

But she wasn't at The Harbor, was she?

Angela recognized her venetian blinds slatting the moonlight, the red
numbers glowing from the digital clock. Eleven-twenty. This was the apartment. She wasn't still living at the private mental retreat where she'd
checked herself in for three months after Corey's death. She had left The
Harbor nearly eighteen months ago. Dr. Houston had written her a prescription for Xanax, referred her to an outside psychotherapist, assured her
of how much better she was doing, and told her she was free to go. Resume
your life, she'd said. Start your new business, your talent agency. Go home.

Home.

Dr. Houston's pleasant face and manner had disarmed Angela from the
start, even if the woman's good humor had seemed naive. *A ball of smiles*,
Angela had thought when she'd first sat in her office at The Harbor. No
white coat, no clipboard. She'd offered Angela hot tea and chocolate-chip
cookies fresh from the kitchen's oven. She had a sunny dress and gentle
questions.

Why have you decided you should be here, Angela?

Angela had not *decided* that she should be there, she thought. It all had
been decided for her.

I'm afraid I'm going to hurt myself or someone else, Angela told her.

Who are you afraid of hurting besides yourself?

My husband. My ex-husband. She liked the sound of *ex*, an erasure. An
undoing.

She told Dr. Houston how she had browsed through a *Soldier of Fortune*
magazine one day at a newsstand in the months after Corey's death, sobbing, wondering not-so-idly if it was true you could find a hit man in the
classifieds section. That was what the rumors said. She thought of a movie

she'd seen, one of those Japanese animés Corey had liked so much—she couldn't remember the name—where someone ordered a hit on himself and then changed his mind. Would she change her mind, too? Probably. She'd be much better off if she followed her mother's example and swallowed a bottle of pills, she thought. Then, standing there, she'd imagined what it would feel like to hire someone to kill Tariq instead, and she knew she wouldn't change her mind about that. She'd instruct the hit man on exactly what to say: "Tell the truth and I'll let you live." And Tariq would sputter and beg, and he'd finally tell the whole truth: *Yes, I lied about getting rid of the gun, and I brought it with me to Sacajawea. It was in my suitcase. Corey must have found it. I lied the whole time. Half the words that come out of my mouth are lies, and they always have been.* And the hit man would say to Tariq, "I lied, too. This is for Corey, from Angela. A life for a life," and after Tariq's eyes went wide with terror, his killer would pull the trigger. He'd shoot him in the head. Just like Corey.

That fantasy, she told Dr. Houston, was the only thing of late that brought her any happiness.

You have a very active imagination, Dr. Houston said. *When did you first start believing you would like to kill your husband?*

When I saw that my child had been shot with that gun.

Well, not right away, she recalled, amending her response. At first, since Tariq had promised her he'd gotten rid of the gun years ago, she had tried her best to argue God and the universe out of the impossible thing they had conspired to try to make her believe. Corey could not have Tariq's gun, and therefore Corey could not be dead. She could not be seeing what her eyes thought they were seeing. It could not be. He got rid of it. He said so.

How did your husband explain the gun's presence in the house?

Lies, Angela said. If he had told her the truth when it happened—if he had fallen to his knees with the sobs of a sinner and admitted that he'd brought the gun with him to Sacajawea—she might have been able to forgive him. She'd wanted so badly not to feel so horribly alone after Corey died. Because, you see, in the end, you are alone. In the beginning, it was everyone's concern—the people at the party, the sheriff's office, the forensics experts who did their tests to determine that the wound, indeed, had been self-inflicted to the head. From day to day, Angela had been able to busy herself with the details of trying to understand what had happened, how it had happened, the exact time it had happened, searching for a suicide note (there had been none, thank God, so the final ruling was *accidental death* although everyone conceded they would never really know), and planning the funeral. The details at the opulent funeral home had been endless and traumatic in their specificity—what to write on the headstone, what kind of pillow to have in the coffin—yet it had all been perversely comforting to her, a last project for Corey's sake. Her last chance to be his mother.

Every step of the way, she'd been surrounded by people for whom Corey's death was their most important priority. Sympathetic tones and earnest eyes. *We'll look into this. We'll take care of this.* But as time had passed, the number of people in that circle of concern had shrunk, and they all went on with their lives. The police took longer and longer to respond to her calls, and even when she talked to Sheriff Rob Graybold and asked him to repeat facts for her, she could hear the beginning of impatience after a time. *There's really nothing more to it, Angie,* he'd told her one day with nearly impolite finality, and she'd felt a flash of aching embarrassment. One by one, they were all gone, until she'd been the only one left.

If only Tariq had told her the truth, if he'd said he was sorry about the gun, she would not have been alone. The aloneness had been almost as bad as seeing Corey's bleeding head in the cellar.

But, no. Tariq had not told the truth. He'd stuck to his original lie, the one he'd first birthed the day he came home and said, *I hope you're happy now, bitch.* He got rid of the gun, he swore to the police. He didn't care if the gun Corey had shot himself with was identical to the one he'd had, with the same silver packing tape wrapped around the butt. He'd been like a hustler trying to con his way out of a petty charge, never telling the truth, not even to save his soul in the wake of his own son's death. He blubbered and sobbed and moaned, lying the entire time. And Sheriff Rob Graybold and the county police decided Corey must have found the mysterious gun on his own, that it did not belong to Tariq. A big coincidence, they said.

It wasn't enough that Angela had lost her son. She'd lost her son to a lie.

And people wondered why she'd made such a scene at the funeral, throwing a metal folding chair at Tariq that glanced off of his jaw and shoulder before clattering to the floor, destroying the mournful tranquility of the church like a bomb. Why it had taken three people to pull her off of him.

And now you're afraid you might hurt yourself? Dr. Houston said.

Yes, because life has fucked me by leaving me no one to love, Angela had told her. If you want the truth, doctor, every day feels like a ritual punishment I have to endure before I'm allowed to die. I can stay in bed for days, pretending I'm dead, and I like it. I finally understand my mother—she was such a regular visitor to the psych unit, she should have had her own wing. Now I know why she always ended up there every summer like clockwork. My mother heard the demons laughing, and she saw the truth. You want to know what the truth is? Happy people are just people who haven't learned better yet. Once you know that, it's hard to go back to the bullshit. But I want to unlearn what I know. I want to reclaim the fantasy. I want to go back to sleep like the happy people.

Going back to sleep, Angela learned each night, was easier said than done. Eighteen months after she'd left The Harbor, two years and two months since Corey's death, getting to sleep at night was still the most treacherous part of her day.

In the dark, Angela opened her nightstand drawer, which was empty except for what appeared to be a hardcover copy of Alex Haley's *Roots*. But it was not. Angela had fitted the book cover atop a small safe built in the shape of a book, a marvel she'd ordered from a spy shop when a client raved about how she was fooling her housekeeper by keeping her jewelry in what looked like a can of WD-40 oil spray. Corey's confession the day he died had done little to make Angela feel more at ease about the possibility of theft. She didn't own much she considered of value anymore, but Corey's death had made her more resolute that she would not take any chances.

The book safe was filled with padding. Beneath that, a small felt ring case. And inside the ring case, Gramma Marie's gold ring.

Even with only the moonlight, Angela could see the ring's tawny glow, dulled by darkness. She slipped the ring onto her left ring finger and squeezed her hand, exactly the way she had when Corey had brought it back to her. She closed her eyes as the precious metal bit gently into her skin.

Mom, I did something, and I have to make it right

This was progress, she thought. For the first year, she'd shunned the ring. She'd kept it safe, knowing that it had been Corey's last gift to her, but she'd found it too hard to look at the ring in the beginning. But she had worked her way back into wearing it again. On the days she didn't run, she wore it to work. When her assistant, Imani, complimented the ring a few weeks ago, Angela had said, *It was my grandmother's,* and it had felt good to mention Gramma Marie again, honoring her. When Angela wore the ring at night, she believed it helped her sleep. Not always, but sometimes. The spirits of both her grandmother and her son lived in this ring, and perhaps she felt so lost because she was not communing with them often enough, she thought.

Gramma Marie's good-luck talisman. Corey's good-bye token.

Hot tears washed Angela's face, but she was so accustomed to tears that she almost didn't notice them. At least she wasn't doubled over in sobs, her throat peeled raw. Those exhausting nights, thankfully, seemed long behind her. Tonight's tears, like those she had shed in front of Naomi, were not the bitter poison that had driven her to The Harbor. These tears were different.

Go home, Dr. Houston had said.

Barefoot, Angela padded across her bedroom's lush carpeting to her hallway and the living room's hardwood floors, making her way to the little-used kitchen telephone hanging on the wall above the counter. She dialed the number and waited while the phone rang only once.

"Hey, Naomi," Angela said after the voice mail's chipper message. "I'm calling on your cell because it's after midnight, too late to bother you at home. I've been thinking about what you said, and you know what? You're right. I need to visit the house. I think I'm ready, and I need to make this sojourn whether I'm ready or not. If you'd still like to come with me"—her voice faltered. Why was *this* the hard part?—"well, I'd really appreciate it. Maybe you could come up just for a weekend or something and I'll stay a few days after you go. We can work it out. But I wanted to tell you now, before I change my mind. Let's toss around some dates tomorrow, okay?"

By the time Angela went back to bed, she slid into the bosom of sleep as effortlessly as a toddler who had never known loss and had yet to learn fear. No muddy, dreamy voices plagued her.

With Gramma Marie's ring hugging her finger, Angela slept straight through until dawn.

⚔ Four ⚔

*W*HERE YOU GOING?"
The question caught Rick Leahy by surprise. His son's voice had nearly been washed out because it had come from the left side, Rick's bad ear. He'd just touched the doorknob of the double-wide trailer he shared with his three kids, expecting to slip out unnoticed, but Sean was slumped down on the sofa in the living room, nearly invisible between two piles of unsorted clean laundry. Rick hadn't seen him at first, but now Sean's white-blond hair was unmistakable, the cloned image of what Rick's hair had looked like until it had darkened to a honey shade in adulthood. Sean was staring at the television screen, a bowl of cereal balanced on his knees.

What was Sean doing up by ten on a Saturday? The other kids were still in bed.

"Quick ride," Rick said. It wasn't a lie, but it wasn't truthful, either. "Want to come?"

Sean shook his head. His cheeks and chin were overgrown with what looked like phosphorescent stubble, in need of shaving. He knew Rick was full of crap, but both seemed content to play it this way, not pushing too hard. Sean might not like where he was going, but there wasn't anything he could do about it, either.

"Be back in an hour," Rick said.

"Do the words *bad karma* mean anything to you?" Sean said.

Rick didn't have an answer for that right away, and he didn't want to argue.

"I wish I could bring your friend back, kid, but I can't," Rick said after a pause, in his most patient voice. "I really am trying to understand how you feel about this. We just disagree."

"Yeah, whatever," Sean said. In other words, *Yeah, screw you, Pops.* "It's your life."

Rick felt like he was antagonizing his son, a feeling he did not enjoy, especially after the nightmare Sean had been through these past couple years. But he wasn't going to conduct his life according to Sean's superstitions either. If Sean had his way, the property next door would have been walled off since his friend Corey's death.

"Be back in an hour," he said again, and he eased his way outside.

Chestnut was Rick's favorite riding horse, the six-year-old mare he'd bought soon before he found the cheap parcel of land in Sacajawea he now called home, five acres of mostly flat meadowland abutting the woods. He had five other horses now—three were his, and two were retired racehorses biding their time while their owner in Portland waited for buyers or takers for stud services. Named for her coloring, Chestnut was a sweet girl, an animal who understood Rick's whims without much prodding. Rick shouldered a woven basket and took a short running leap to climb the horse's back, with only a thick, patterned Navajo blanket serving as a saddle beneath his well-worn jeans. By now, after riding for years without a saddle, he figured he had *cojones* of iron. Rick clucked, spurring Chestnut with his heels. "Come on, girl," he said, and she began a spirited trot away from the barn.

His sister said he collected children and horses, and maybe Bonnie was right. He loved both. Sean was his biological son with a one-night stand who'd given the boy up shortly after his birth, but Tonya and Andres were adoptive children who had lived with them for nearly four years now. Miguelito, the four-year-old he'd had as a foster child, had been adopted out last year when an uncle came forward and the caseworker decided he'd be better off with family. That hole in their home still hurt like hell. The agency had warned Rick something like that could happen, but imagining it and experiencing it were very different, like trying to *imagine* what it would feel like to get his leg sheared off. Kids needed homes, sometimes only for a short time, and he'd willingly offered his—but he'd gotten too attached to Miguelito. After Miguelito left, he'd brought in the two racers instead of applying for another foster kid. He would soon, maybe, but not yet. The horses were not his to keep either, but he knew the sting wouldn't be nearly so bad when it was time for them to go.

Above him, the sky staged a skirmish between the blurry morning sun and soupy clouds. As usual in the fall, the clouds seemed destined to win in the end, but not yet. So far, it was so bright and warm that Rick took off his denim jacket and tied it around his waist. Indian summer, he thought. Good. With sunshine burning off the morning dew, conditions were perfect for his morning enterprise. The ground would be good and dry.

Rick's acreage was long and narrow, on a slight incline. The cross-fencing he had built prevented a direct path to the Toussaint woodland directly beside him, so Rick rode Chestnut all the way down to his front gate, which was open, and doubled back to find the trail to the woods he had beaten into the soil over the past two years. There were only a couple of spots that weren't too steep to give his horse access, if he wanted to avoid having to ride all the way down to the dead end of the road and then take the same trail the kids used on their way to The Spot. Rick wasn't interested in The Spot. He had his own path, closer to his property line. The woman who owned the house, Angela Toussaint, had given him permission to ride on her property anytime he chose, but he wasn't really after a morning ride today. That was what he'd lied about.

He wanted to stock up on herbs.

Sean called it stealing, but Rick saw it differently. Angela Toussaint had seemed like a cold character when she'd first come to his house and announced her policy of meeting the parents of any of her son's friends, but she'd invited him to help himself to any of the gifts her land had to offer; walnuts, blackberries, blueberries, apples, or a half-dozen other fruit varieties he could find if he searched long enough. *Otherwise, it all just goes to waste,* she said. She hadn't mentioned the unattended herb garden behind the house by name, but why should it be excluded?

Chestnut stumbled slightly and slid a half-foot where the soil was loose and damp at the most dramatic drop in the makeshift path. Then she got her footing, and they traveled safely beneath the canopy of evergreens that shaded the Toussaint land, the biggest remaining parcel of forest in town. The path was narrow, barely a path at all. Rick's face was *thwapped* by brittle, dead limbs he didn't duck in time to miss. Rick kept his elbow up, guarding against upcoming limbs that might be meaner. At Chestnut's pace, a good pop would knock him on his ass.

There were still enough clear views between the trunks and limbs for Rick to see the rear of the regal house on the ridge above him, every window darkened. Occasionally, Rick saw Joseph Everly tooling around in the backyard, tending the rosebushes or mowing back the brush always trying to reclaim the small back clearing. And sometimes Rick saw a light on in the house, or open windows, signaling that Laurel Everly was doing her work inside. But aside from the presence of the Everlys, the house was dead. A beautiful post-Victorian, lifeless.

Rick fantasized about buying the house if it was ever put up for sale, but he knew he could dream on. He'd won a workmen's comp settlement ten years ago, and lived very carefully as a full-time father ever since, but there was no way he could afford a house like this one. Must be five thousand square feet, maybe more, and Sean had told him it was like a museum inside. Besides, Sean would flip out if he tried to buy the Toussaint place. He wanted nothing to do with it.

Apparently, Angela Toussaint felt the same way, Rick mused. Sorry damn shame.

Rick loved beautiful, unappreciated things. Maybe that was the root of his love of foster kids, he thought. Rick couldn't stand to see kids unloved. He'd fought for sole custody of Sean after the boy's Deadhead mother confided that she was planning to sell their blond-haired, blue-eyed baby boy to the highest bidder. And all of his "found" kids had special needs: Tonya had been five when he'd met her, legally blind, her contemplative dark eyes hidden behind thick, owlish glasses. Andres was a mixed-race Puerto Rican with a killer talent for drawing, saddled with his share of learning problems and a touch of attention deficit hyperactivity disorder. Miguelito had been a dark-skinned Mexican, his ethnicity alone serving as a liability in a system where most adoptive parents were searching for infants who looked more like Sean. But aside from the factors that had trapped the children in foster care for most of their young lives, Rick knew his kids were beautiful.

Beautiful and unappreciated. Just like Angela Toussaint's stately shell of a house.

Overhead, a raven taunted Rick with a piercing squawk. The ravens on this property were goddamned possessive, chattering at him as if they expected him to pay a toll. Protecting their nests, no doubt. This one was right on schedule, like the ogre under the bridge in the children's fairy tale. "Fuck off, bird," Rick muttered, and he heard the bird's wings flutter in what sounded like a fury.

Once the house was no longer in sight, Chestnut slowed, unsure of where to proceed as the rough path forked before them. Rick urged her to go left, past the large cedar tree with a heart-shaped crater in its trunk that served as his landmark. They came to the creek-bed bordered by salmonberry and horsetails, where the rushing waters had begun to rejuvenate with the infusion of October rainwater. In summertime, this portion of the creek dried to nearly nothing, although it never vanished. Chestnut splashed through the shallow creek to the other side, and the evergreens gave way to red alders and bigleaf maples, and then to a small clearing.

There, Rick saw a crooked configuration of three waist-high wooden fence-posts, blackened with age. There was no fence, and the remaining fence-posts, wrapped in vines and crabgrass, had probably been standing here since the Depression. At one time, old lady Toussaint must have come out here regularly tending to her herbs, because the plants still grew wild in clusters that seemed most abundant where her fencing might have stood. Rick had come across the herb garden by accident during one of his first rides here, and he'd been thrilled with his find.

He had a smorgasbord out here. Already, he spotted the ring of sweet basil plants, with their hairy stalks and yellow-white flowers. He could smell basil from a mile away. Not too far from there, closer to the creek, he saw a cluster of flowering valerian plants. And sweet woodruff growing behind one of the fence-posts. And some thin, practically leafless stalks of dill. His eye also caught the pretty yellow blooms of large-flowered mullein plants basking in a patch of sunlight. About ten yards east, he saw a few large elder shrubs, recognizable by their tiny yellowish white flowers and clusters of violet globe-shaped fruit, nearly black. It all grew of its own accord, some of it out of season. The plants didn't care about the calendar. This was herb heaven.

"Good catch today," Rick said, dismounting.

He untied the leather string on his basket and opened it, pulling out his dirty work-gloves, a small paring knife, and the honed-edge sickle he used to gather herbs. Once he collected and dried these plants, he would make teas that would help him and his kids cope with headaches, indigestion, constipation, sleeplessness, overexcitement, and any symptom a cold or flu might throw at them. Not to mention that the basil plain tasted good, the secret ingredient to his kids' favorite spaghetti and herbed chicken recipes.

Somehow, the basil he grew in his home garden didn't have the same flavor, and he couldn't get valerian to grow from seeds at all. Besides, no other homegrown or store-bought herbs could offer anything close to the potency of the herbs he found on the Toussaint property. When he and his kids came down with the flu last summer, he'd knocked it out of their systems within a day. People in town said the old woman had been famous for her teas, and now he knew why.

Maybe it was something about the land, the nutrients in the soil. Whatever it was, Rick chuckled as he imagined the pretty penny he could earn if he ever found the nerve to plant a couple hundred marijuana seeds out here in the abandoned Toussaint herb garden. He'd have an empire in green. Better than Lotto, he thought.

But that was just idle thinking. Rick had given up grass at the same time he'd given up college, when he'd found himself responsible for raising a child. If he had an entrepreneurial bone in his body, he'd strike a deal with Angela Toussaint to grow more herbs out here, cultivate them, and market them, even if it was just to a local clientele. Hell, he could make money on the woman's name alone, the way people in town talked—*Madame Toussaint's Magic Teas!* Use the old lady's picture on the box. He could envision it, all right.

But Rick Leahy had more ideas than he had drive or discipline. If he hadn't lost the hearing in his left ear after a forklift broadsided him in the shipping yard at his old job in California, he'd probably still be working there today, fantasizing about his escape and hating every minute of it. But God looks out for children and fools, or so the old proverb said. His sister had hired him a good lawyer, and he'd walked away with five hundred thousand bucks, even after attorney's fees and taxes. Someone with a fire under him could have invested that money and made something of it, Bonnie always said, but Rick was happy with his little chunk of land, his kids, and his horses.

Beside him, Chestnut chuffed restlessly. Her hooves came too close to the dill, so Rick guided her to a safe distance from his cache, looping her reins around the Y intersection on a thick branch of a fallen alder trunk. Fall leaves crunched under his boots as he walked back toward the dill, where his basket was waiting. Good a place to start as any, he decided.

Another bird complained, and when Rick looked up, he noticed a raven perched on each fence-post, all three of them regarding him with a convincing imitation of intelligence. Their black eyes were unblinking, appearing to follow his movements. Weird. He couldn't think of a single time he'd come out here when the ravens didn't gather around the garden to watch him. Still, he couldn't spot the nests. "Ah, I see you brought friends," Rick said cheerfully. "Well, fuck your friends, too."

A mosquito whirred in Rick's right ear, and he absently slapped at it before beginning his search for the ribbed fruit on the dill plants ripe enough to be of use. Had to be brown, and most of it wasn't ready yet, but some was. Good enough. The flowering stems were good medicine, too.

The Doobie Brothers popped into his head, "Black Water," so he sang quietly to his horse, the trees, and the ravens. "I wanna hear your funk in

Dixieland . . . hey Mama, won't you take me . . ." He was sure he was butchering the lyrics, like always, a disability Sean razzed him about. But he knew the melody, and this song always took him back to his childhood in Santa Cruz. Watching *Happy Days* with his sister, who'd had a crush on Chachi. Eating Now N' Laters. He could almost taste the candy now, tangy and sweet on his tongue. "By the hand, hand . . . gonna take your hand, little Mama . . . gonna dance with your daddy . . ."

Rick had thought he was in a good mood, so the sadness caught him by surprise.

He'd had his share of bad news in life, and he'd learned how to shrug it off with a sense of routine. He fixed things. If he couldn't fix it, like losing Miguelito, he shed his tears and learned to live with it. That would be his key to longevity in life, he always said. But after fifteen minutes of collecting herbs, soon after he'd moved from the dill to the valerian root he gave Andres in small doses to help him quiet his mind at night, Rick noticed that he felt so sad that his muscles had turned leaden. He could have just been kicked in the gut, for all the sorrow he felt knotted in his middle. The shift had been so gradual, he hadn't even noticed until he was stewing in it, on the verge of tears.

Rick stopped singing. What the hell was going on with him? He looked up from the small mounds of soil where he'd uprooted the valerian plants and stared around him. One raven had flown off, but two still remained, staring. The ravens no longer amused him.

"Go on, get away," he said, chucking a stone at the nearest fence-post. He had a good arm, so he hit it dead center. With unpleasant cries, both birds flew off. But they didn't go far. He could hear them in the treetops, all three of them up there, probably. Or more.

Rick saw an image in his mind, then. But not exactly. It was more like reliving the moment when he'd first seen the image, crisp and clear: Miguelito's brown arms reaching toward him from the caseworker's embrace the day she and the boy's uncle came to pick him up. They'd done the transfer slowly, letting the uncle spend time with Miguelito in the weeks preceding the change, and Miguelito seemed to like the guy, which had been a relief to all of them. They'd acted out the pleasantries in the living room, him and the other kids pretending they were greeting Miguelito's thin, pock-faced uncle as a good friend because the caseworker thought it would be less traumatic that way. But when it had been time for Miguelito to *leave*, the kid had let out such wounded howls, his arms outstretched, brown eyes imploring as he called for Rick. Remembering the horror of that instant, Rick felt tears prick his eyes. His vision blurred.

"Mother*fuck*," Rick said, tasting his anguish anew. First Sean's friend had shot himself in the head, then they'd lost Miguelito a year later, when his uncle materialized out of nowhere. "Who the hell did we piss off? Can you tell me that one goddamned thing?"

Rick didn't know who he was talking to, but he felt certain someone could hear him. God, perhaps, the orchestrator of it all. That sense, rather than giving Rick satisfaction, made his grief and anger more keen. What was the point of trying to spread love and do the right thing if it came to nothing in the end? What was the point of any of it?

Whatever it was—whoever *He* was—was watching Rick right now. He knew it.

"You *bastard!*" he shouted suddenly, nearly pitching himself off-balance. He had never been more angry, and the shout tore at his throat. His phlegmy, altered voice echoed deep into the heart of the shady woods before him, toward The Spot and the reaches he rarely explored. "You heartless bitch-bastard! Go fuck up somebody else's life! *I've done my share!*"

Spittle sprayed from his mouth. Both hands were locked into fists, rock-hard. He wanted to hurt someone, maybe to kill something. Rick was breathing in furious gasps.

Then, the moment broke. Rick was left crouching beside his basket with a clear mind, the terrible mood lifted, hearing the whirs and whistles of insects around him. What the hell had *that* been about? He could hear his last shout even now, bouncing in the woods. A stranger's words in his own voice. He'd gone from singing the Doobie Brothers to screaming like a lunatic in the space of mere minutes. His underarms were damp, itching uncomfortably.

Do the words bad karma *mean anything to you?*

For the first time, the words *bad karma* meant a whole hell of a lot to Rick Leahy. Rick began to feel caught in a net, as if the tree branches surrounding him served as webbing. Almost as if—and this next thought made the hairline on his neck sizzle slightly—*he could not leave here today when he was ready.* Rick had never been claustrophobic, indoors or outdoors, but now he understood what the affliction meant. He felt trapped.

"This is nuts. I'm actually sitting here bugged out for absolutely no fucking reason," he said. He tried to use an old trick he'd learned as a kid when he had nightmares, using his voice as assurance, a window to reason. Buoyed by his wave of rationality, Rick laughed at himself. "You're letting Sean's head-games get to you. This is priceless, Leahy."

What happened next hadn't happened to him as a kid, or at any other time.

At first, the scraping sound he heard in the leaves behind him sounded like the noise a small animal's hurried passage might have made. A rabbit, a squirrel, maybe a creature as large as a fawn. The sound startled him because it was so close—ten yards, maybe fifteen—but he didn't see any movement. Chestnut, sensing the shift of his mood, stirred with a snort, taking tentative steps forward and then backward, as much as her tied reins would allow.

"Easy, girl," Rick told her, really talking to himself.

The sound came again, a little louder this time, though not as close, and from the opposite direction. Rick's head whirled around. Nothing but the forest ahead of him, where it grew more densely, away from any clearings, gardens, or beaten paths. Where very little sunlight bled through.

A man might have made that sound. Or something bigger.

"Mr. Everly?" he called.

The mosquito's whine in his ear was deafening this time, and Rick slapped at his earlobe so hard that it stung. Then, his hand froze where it was, like the flustered pose Jack Benny used to strike all the time, except that Rick didn't feel flustered. He felt numb. His left hand was raised, and he'd slapped his *left* ear. He hadn't heard a sound out of that ear in ten years, and yet he'd just heard a mosquito buzzing there, big and bad.

"What the fuck . . . ?" he whispered.

Rick snapped his fingers outside of his ear, straining to hear, but the sound was indistinct, his right ear fooling him by taking up the slack. The dead space on his left side was still there. The judge had ruled he had *permanent hearing loss*, with five hundred thousand bucks to back it up. But Rick had heard something there a moment ago. A mosquito, or some insect. Something.

Rick's heart cranked up, and he felt dizzy from the rush of blood to his head. He didn't know what was going on this morning, but he didn't like it. Not a puny little bit. He also wasn't going to stick around to see if he'd come to like it any better. He was remote from everyone out here. He could shout himself hoarse, and no one would hear him.

"Know what, Chestnut?" he said. "I think I'm about ready to . . . ."

He didn't finish the sentence, because the noise had started again, a motion of dry leaves scraping the forest floor. But this time, even with his bad ear, he made no mistake: It wasn't a rabbit, a deer, a man, or anything else living. This was much louder, bigger. The mass of leaves shifted with a sustained rustling hiss, there was a short pause, and then the massive shifting came again. The noise reminded him of what it might sound like if someone had an impossibly large broom and was slowly sweeping, sweeping, sweeping. An acre's worth of leaves seemed to move at once, as if the ground was methodically shaking them from its back. There was no breeze to speak of, so it couldn't be the wind. What, then? Rick stared, seeing no movement anywhere in his line of vision. But he heard it, and that was enough. The sweeping.

Coming straight at him, from somewhere in the woods.

Blood-flow seared Rick's face. He sprang to his feet, abandoning his basket and tools. He freed his sweating palms from his gloves, still breathing hard. Chestnut whinnied when he approached her, wild-eyed, and he shushed her as nervous perspiration dripped into his eyes. He stroked her nose and muzzle, clucking, telling her she was a good girl. Chestnut was pulling so much that he had a hard time untying her reins, and when he did, he was afraid she wouldn't stand still long enough to mount.

Horses were neurotic as hell, but this wasn't like Chestnut. She was scared, the way she'd be scared if they were surrounded by a hidden pack of wolves. Using the felled alder to gain height, Rick flung himself across his horse's back, landing hard and off-center. His testicles flared with hot pain. After making a confused half-circle, Chestnut turned toward the creek, back the way they had come. "Come on, girl," he said, and man and horse began their flight from Marie Toussaint's herb garden together. Some kind of bird, perhaps one of the ravens, wailed behind them.

Paw-paaaaaaaaaaaawwwww

For a horrible instant, the cry sounded precisely like Miguelito's, the day they sent him away. Pure instinct made Rick sit straight upright, looking back. He saw only his basket, the fence-posts in the clearing, and the shadows in the woods. Goose bumps blotched Rick's arms, and he spurred Chestnut faster, hunching down close to her mane. "Jesus . . . That was *not* Miguelito," he murmured once, then twice, and soon he believed it.

Halfway home, when he could no longer hear the eerie sounds of rearranging leaves or birds parroting human cries—and was discovering rapid solace in the notion that he had imagined most of what he had heard—Rick cursed himself for leaving his basket of herbs. He had one hell of a stomachache, and a cup of dill tea would take care of him good.

⚞ *Five* ⚟

OCEAN BEACH HIGHWAY in Longview took drivers through the city beneath hilltops dotted with expensive homes half-hidden behind evergreens. Because the streets were slick from earlier rainfall, the noon-time sun made the four-lane highway's asphalt gleam as if it were topped with glass.

The roadside scenery, though, was less impressive: Ocean Beach was flanked by fast-food chains, grocery outlets, and strip malls. Taco Bell. Starbucks. Chinatown Restaurant. McDonald's. Wal-Mart. Video King. The chains were more densely packed than Angela remembered, but the city of thirty-five thousand did not seem to have changed much, carrying on its existence without her just fine, thank you. She and Naomi would soon pass the more scenic portion—the historic affluence of the Old West Side and Lake Sacajawea—but Angela hadn't come to Washington to spend time sight-seeing in Longview. In the most literal sense, she was just passing through.

She and Naomi had arrived at Portland International Airport an hour ago, picking up their rented Ford Explorer for the road portion of their trip after the two-hour flight. Getting to Gramma Marie's town, as always, was nothing short of an expedition, and Angela always felt a little like the town's Native American namesake when she set out for Sacajawea, as if she, too, were guiding Lewis and Clark through the wilderness. Once they had crossed the bridge from Portland's airport to drive north, entering the state of Washington, most signs of settlement vanished, with a nuclear power plant and scattered highway signs interrupting the meadowlands, farmhouses, miles of greenery, and a town facing the highway called Kalama that evoked images of a 1950s movie set, with few other reminders that they were still in the twenty-first century. It was pretty, all right, especially on sunny days like today, with the fall leaves in full plumage, but Angela was a city girl at heart. Her eye was wary of open spaces, accustomed to man-made distractions. Longview was about an hour from Portland, and there were countless commutes in L.A. that took the same time—but for some reason, the drive here always felt longer.

Naomi was asleep on the passenger side, strapped safely into her seat, her black miniature poodle, Onyx, curled at her toes. Angela didn't like that dog—she might be able to respect a small terrier, but a *poodle?* She and her friend had come close to their first real argument when Naomi insisted on bringing him. Angela had given in, remembering that people who spent as much time away from home as Naomi often needed security blankets, and Onyx was Naomi's. No matter where she was, as long as she had her dog with her, Naomi could feel she was at home, and Angela envied that about her. Silly haircut or not, Angela understood the dog's value. His purple collar was on the gaudy side, but at least Onyx wasn't trussed with little pink bows.

For now, Angela was glad both pet and master were asleep. She didn't want a single aspect of Longview to catch her friend's eye—*Ooh, girl, can we stop for a latte?* or *Hey, is that a Thai food restaurant?* or *Where's that lake, Angela? Let's pull over and take Onyx for a walk.* In spite of how long as she'd been putting off her return visit, once Angela had made the decision to return to Sacajawea, she'd hardly been able to think about anything else. Nervousness still fluttered beneath it all, and she'd suffered through her usual hellish nights, but mostly she felt eager. She longed to see Gramma Marie's house, the round attic window, the walnut tree, all the touchstones of her childhood. Even the pain waiting there intrigued more than frightened her. In the past few weeks, she had learned to view her return to the place of Corey's death as any other challenge she had faced in her life—something she could vanquish. And even if she was wrong, if she could not salvage any of the joy she had once felt in Gramma Marie's house, at least she would know, and that knowledge would be hers to keep. Knowledge would give her its own strength, an end to her limbo.

Thirty minutes to go. Almost there. Angela's heart was already throbbing.

"I can't believe I'm back here," she whispered, amazed at her courage.

"Bless you, Naomi. I owe you a big one. I'm gonna work my ass off for you. That first million is just the beginning."

Naomi, still sleeping, offered a delicate snore in response.

City reverted to country in a blink of an eye. Ocean Beach Highway became State Route Four, shrinking to a narrow lane heading west out of Longview's city limits. Immediately, the convoys of logging trucks began, some in pairs, some in fours, each strapped with a dozen or more thick, freshly cut trees with their sap-orange cores exposed, stripped of limbs. The trees were long and somehow proud despite their fallen state. The strip malls were replaced by swampy canals on either side of the road, until the land grew steep on the northern side, transforming into rocky ridges where small waterfalls of frothy rainwater tumbled down. ROCKS, a yellow highway sign warned. Fencing was draped high across some of the stony ridges to keep the rocks in place, to prevent them from escaping and smashing into the windshields of passersby. On the south side, the water grew less swampy, widening until it converged with the green-brown waters of the Columbia River. If she kept driving, Angela would end up at the Pacific Ocean, but that was a couple hours' trek, and it wasn't her destination. Sacajawea was only thirty miles from Longview. It was close.

As always, Angela gripped the steering wheel more tightly on the Four, looking out for tumbling rocks, stray wildlife, and a dozen other hazards that plagued this road. A speed sign warned her to slow to thirty miles per hour because of an upcoming curve. From now on, Angela knew, this road would require her full concentration.

Following one of the sharp curves in the road, Angela was uplifted by a new angle of the wide water before her, reminiscent of the ocean she would never reach. Across the river on the Oregon side, the waters were skirted by mountains that nearly blended into the clouds hanging above them. The clouds' bellies were dark, bloated with unshed rainwater, but their edges still shone cottony and white, brightened by the sunshine prevailing in the noontime sky. Seagulls and other seabirds wheeled around each other, some of them so far away they were pinpricks. This was beautiful.

"Naomi," Angela said. "Wake up. You'll want to see this. We're almost there."

Blinking, Naomi stared at the panorama. "Oh, yeah, girl, this is so pretty. *This* is where your grandmama lived?"

"Pretty close."

"No wonder she didn't mind being isolated up here in the middle of nowhere."

"It has its moments," Angela said.

Naomi squirmed like an excited child. "This'll be like going to a spa, huh? Toussaint Lodge."

Why not? Angela loved the claw-foot bathtub in the upstairs bedroom, the living room's picture window was perfect for deer-watching in front of the fireplace, and she and Tariq had installed a hot tub on the backyard deck, one of their last home improvements. People paid good money to visit a place like that. "Yeah," Angela said, smiling. "I hope so."

Her mother used to say that hope was nothing but a heartache that hadn't happened yet. But Angela was still addicted to it. She had never learned how to give it up.

—

Tariq's VW van was parked on the roadside at Toussaint Lane, waiting.

"Jesus," Angela said, jamming the brakes. Her heartbeat fell mum.

"What?" Naomi said. Onyx had been gazing out of the window with a dog's euphoric devotion, and only Naomi's hug kept him from toppling to the floor after the sudden stop.

"Tariq is here. That's his van," Angela said. She stared hard, as if she thought the van would disappear if she gazed at it long enough. It didn't make sense. "What the *fuck* is he doing here?"

"Slow down, Angela. Look at the van," Naomi said with uncharacteristic calm. "Tariq isn't using that van unless he's been driving with two flat tires. See?"

Angela's eyes followed Naomi's pointing finger. The van favored one side: Both the front and rear tires were flat on the side facing the road. The ground near the doors was littered with aluminum cans and food wrappers. Local kids were treating the van as an abandoned vehicle, probably using it for a clubhouse, make-out den, and God knew what else.

When Angela exhaled, she felt as if the three-hundred-pound man who'd decided to sit on her chest had moved on. Now, her heart was racing again. She wished Mrs. Everly had warned her that the van would still be parked outside.

"You're right. He must have left it here. It's probably been here . . ." Ever since the Fourth of July, her mind calculated. She might have been the last person to drive this van, when she went to the grocery store to get more ice for the party. She hadn't even reached the house yet, and the memories were potent enough to startle her.

No, this was not going to be like staying at a spa.

Naomi suppressed a laugh. "I wish you had seen the look on your face just now when you thought he was here. I know it's not funny, but I would not have wanted to be that man if he'd really been sitting up in your house."

"No, you wouldn't," Angela said, remembering *Soldier of Fortune*. Her voice was venom.

Naomi's lips turned up playfully, but her eyes shone with concern. She gave Angela a quick hug, engulfing her in Giorgio. "You gonna be all right now?" she said.

Angela nodded. "I'm sorry. I wouldn't wish the way I feel about him on anyone. It eats you. There is nothing worse on this earth than a liar."

"I heard that."

The two of them struggled up the stone steps with their rolling flight bags, while Naomi kept Onyx from scurrying free by keeping a tight grip on his leash. Despite being in good shape, both women were breathing heavily by the time they reached the top. This was the hardest part about visiting Gramma Marie's house, just making it up the twenty-one steps, especially with luggage. Angela remembered looking up at the house from Toussaint Lane as a child and feeling as if it would be like climbing to the top of Jack's beanstalk.

"Those steps are *serious*," Naomi huffed, slumping onto the white wooden porch bench. Onyx, barking manically, tangled his leash as he ran around her leg.

"Sorry about that. I . . . *shit*—" Angela nearly dropped her pocketbook, where she'd been searching for Gramma Marie's key.

If Angela had just taken a courtroom oath at that moment, she would have sworn that she was seeing Tariq's hulking shoulders appear from the corner of the porch on the right side of the house, where a garden path led to the backyard. She would have sworn that she could see his face, intent on her as he approached. But instead, her eyes overpowered her imagination and she realized it was only white-haired, balding Joseph Everly, dressed in overalls, with a small stepladder balanced across his shoulder. Mr. Everly wasn't nearly Tariq's height, but maybe the ladder had thrown her off. A moustache of perspiration was perched above Mr. Everly's top lip. Freckles or age spots, she wasn't sure which, dappled his bald crown.

No wonder Onyx was barking, Angela realized. He'd heard him coming. Or smelled him.

"Sorry, Angie, didn't mean to sneak up on you," Mr. Everly said. He had bright new dentures, and they fit his mouth so well that they seemed to take years off his face, although his walk had a halting quality that bespoke his age. "Welcome home, little gal. We've missed you."

"Missed you all, too, Mr. Everly," Angela said.

"I see you brought a watchdog with you this time. How you do, miss?" Mr. Everly's half-bow in Naomi's direction was polite, but he clearly had no idea who she was. Freed by Naomi, Onyx raced to Mr. Everly's ankles, sniffing them furiously. Once introductions were over, Mr. Everly rested his ladder against the house and wiped perspiration from his face with a grimy towel from his front pocket that was so dirty, Angela expected it to leave stripes on his face. "I wanted to catch you as soon as you got in, Angie. I hate to greet anyone with bad news, but I don't think this can wait."

"What?" Angela said, her heart already sinking. Had something happened to his wife?

Mr. Everly beckoned her off of the porch. "Come on down with me a quick minute. This is something I have to show you."

He stood before the massive, ropy trunk of the black walnut tree, which still had most of its leaves although less hardy trees in the yard had already begun shedding theirs. With garden-dirty fingernails, he pointed to the center of the trunk. "You see this? Come get a good look. This tree's got to come down, Angie."

A rotting V-shape sliced the tree's trunk straight down the center, and there was nearly enough room for a grown person to fit inside the growing crevice. It was a miracle that the tree hadn't simply fallen apart already. Once the tree split fully, one huge side of it would fall against the house. The tree was still standing, but it was as good as dead.

Shit, shit, shit.

Gramma Marie's house would seem naked without this tree. Its leaves shaded the front of the house, littering the porch's roof with green fruitlike casings that, once opened, revealed soft walnuts inside. Angela's second-floor bedroom window had looked out on this tree when she was a child, and she'd thought many times about using the sturdy branches to stage a daring escape into the night. She'd never tried it, but she'd always felt reassured knowing that she *could*. And once, after an argument, Myles Fisher climbed that tree at one in the morning to beg her to go to the senior prom with him. She'd said yes, and they had made love on prom night. This tree was her running buddy from way back.

Besides that, Gramma Marie used to tell her that the spirit of her grandmother lived in this tree, and that she herself would come rest there among its branches after she died. It had sounded like a fanciful wish at the time, but somehow didn't anymore.

"I sure am sorry, little gal. I'm sure this tree means a lot to you."

"What happened?" Angela said, running her fingers across the dark, moist area of rot.

"Can't say it's any one thing. Mostly, I think it's age, Angie. Catches up to all of us. Trees live a long time, but they don't live forever. And now that the rain's started up again, this one can't handle its own weight."

"I want to have a few days with it. Can you wait until I leave to have it taken down?"

"Could be, but don't dawdle too much. She would knock an ugly hole in your house. We don't want the rain working on her too much longer. It's already worse from the last time I was here, and the wind's picking up to boot, especially at night."

Naomi didn't say anything about the exchange when Angela returned to the porch to unlock the front door, but Angela thought something in her friend's knitted brow said, *I can't believe ya'll were out there making that big a fuss over a sick tree.*

City folks, Angela thought.

"By the way, Angie," Mr. Everly called from the yard as she pushed the door open, "I don't suppose you've been back long enough to hear what happened to your neighbor."

Considering the bad news at the start of her visit, Angela's return to the house went better than she'd thought it could. Having Naomi with her was a big help, a distraction. Serving as Naomi's tour-guide, Angela was able to see the house through fresh eyes without dwelling on the memories of Corey preserved in each room. Naomi's exclamations gave Angela new feelings of delight at each turn: *Your grandmama looks like an Ashanti warrior princess in this picture, and just look at that fine hunk of man next to her. Angela, this piano is wonderful! Is this all original furniture in the living room? Does this water pump in the kitchen really work? I bet some of these books in the library are a hundred years old. I love the little sinks in the bedrooms—I've never seen that before. Angela, you never told me this house was so big. If you sell it, call me first.*

Naomi's enthusiasm was contagious. She loved the cushioned window seat on the second-floor landing positioned to stare out the quarter-mile distance to downtown Sacajawea and the river beyond it, she loved the old-fashioned daybed in one of the guest bedrooms, the ruffled curtains, the carved designs that decorated the wooden bannister, the black-and-white checkered kitchen tiles, the porcelain figurines collection, the smell of cedar and lavender that sat in the house. She loved details of the house Angela had stopped seeing before Naomi reminded her: the coved ceilings in strategic spots, the Greek key mosaics built into the borders of the flooring in the living room and library, the large butler's pantry beside the kitchen that evoked a different time, the sunny breakfast nook with so many large windows it seemed more like a patio, even the faded old wallpaper against the staircase, patterned with bouquets of pink flowers gilded with tiny golden bows. Naomi did not miss a single manifestation of grandness in Gramma Marie's house. Their tour took a solid hour.

Angela avoided the trouble spots, of course.

The wine cellar at the end of the foyer remained in shadow, its door firmly closed. Likewise, Angela was glad to discover that Mrs. Everly had closed the door to Corey's room, and Naomi had sense enough not to ask her to open it. Angela felt an ache when they walked past Corey's white door— the door to the room that had been hers in high school, but would be Corey's forever. Again, distraction got her through the moment gracefully. She would go in there, she knew, but not now. Not today. Angela did show Naomi the room Tariq had been using, and she was glad to see that although his van was still parked outside, all other traces of his presence had been removed, either by Mrs. Everly or by Tariq himself. Just a made-up bed and wicker furniture. Thank God for small blessings, she thought.

But Angela wasn't happy about everything she saw. The large bedroom upstairs that served as storage space—a repository for furniture, junk, and papers collected by Angela, her mother, Gramma Marie, and probably even Elijah Goode before her—apparently had not been aired out in some time, and the musty smell crept beneath the closed door before Angela opened it to show Naomi. The smell irritated her. Mrs. Everly knew she wanted those rooms aired out regularly. She did not like the smell of old, unused things. When Angela glanced inside, she felt a twinge as she realized that Corey had been in the midst of straightening this room as part of his assigned chores just before he died, and the memory of their arguments resurfaced before flickering away. The room was so dusty, she could see dust motes floating in the sunlight like swarms of tiny insects. The only attractive feature in the storage room was its closet door, painted a bright blue that matched the exterior of the house. The closet door was open, revealing more mess on the closet floor.

The bigger problem was the upstairs bathroom.

The bathroom's appearance was soured by a narrow ring of dark residue around the claw-foot bathtub's drain. There was a similar patch of black, grainy residue hugging the bottom of the toilet bowl. She also saw a soggy yellow-brown leaf Mrs. Everly must have carelessly dropped inside without flushing it away. Those kinds of sloppy touches weren't like Mrs. Everly, and they shouldn't be, as much as she was paid. All it took was a blast of water from the faucet to melt away the ring in the tub and a single flush to clear the toilet. Mrs. Everly was getting old too, she thought.

Still, the bathroom seemed most unchanged of all to her, with its old-fashioned sink with brass double-faucets, authentic claw-foot tub of cast iron rigged with a shower spout, a toilet with a pull-chain dangling down, a rusting washboard decorating the wall, and Gramma Marie's wooden shower stool still sitting in the corner from the days when it had been more difficult for her to bathe herself. The tall, rectangular mirror above the sink, with its regally designed ornamental brass frame, had reflected passing faces for a hundred years. Within this bathroom's intimate space, Angela felt closest to the house's past inhabitants, as if their voices were murmuring against the wallpapered walls.

Corey's voice was in here, too. Her ears couldn't hear him, but something inside her could.

Angela taught Naomi the tricks and nuances of operating the house's appliances and gadgets—always let the water mingle in the sink in the bathroom because the water heater is set so high you might get scalded otherwise, don't use the hand-pump in the kitchen because it leaks beneath the sink, don't leave any luggage in front of the wall's electric heaters.

It was after two before they knew it, and they hadn't eaten lunch yet. With the arrival of the food, the visit felt like a slumber party. They both sat in their slippers in the living room on the Oriental rug in front of the fireplace, eating slices of a large no-cheese, all-veggie pizza from Pizza Jack's, the only pizzeria in town that delivered. Angela found a bottle of Merlot in the kitchen cabinet, someone's offering to the Fourth of July party, so they busted their diets and emptied it together. Soon, they were both giggling over the renditions of the songs on Gramma Marie's piano rolls, so off-key they were unrecognizable. After they tired of the piano and Naomi turned on the CD player—where the same Coltrane CD from the party still sat—Angela didn't turn it off even when the first song, "A Love Supreme," brought a clear image of Corey's face to mind, from the party. Music could do that. The intensity of the flashback nearly made her stomach lurch, but the feeling passed quickly. Angela finished off her glass of Merlot, feeling a wave of sadness as she remembered the problem with the walnut tree. And the worse news, which had come out of the blue.

Happened a week ago Thursday, out on Main Street, in the middle of the day, Mr. Everly had said. *Terry Marlow was taking a logging rig around the corner, you know, on his way to the Four, and Rick Leahy walked right into it. Crossing the street, you see. Marlow was in the right, that's what Sheriff Rob Graybold says, and a half-dozen witnesses say so, too. Rick Leahy walked smack into the truck. It about near tore him in half. They say he had a bad ear on his left side, and that's the way the truck came. Maybe he didn't hear it. Shame about the kids, though. He left behind a whole trailer full.*

"So . . . did you know your neighbor very well?" Naomi said, following Angela's thoughts.

"No, not really, to be honest. I met him a few times. He used to ride his horses on my property once in a awhile. His son was Corey's only real friend here."

Naomi stared wistfully into the fireplace's flames. "I'm sorry, but it sounded so casual, the way that old dude put it. Both of ya'll looked like you were about to break down crying over that tree, and then he gives you this terrible news about your next-door neighbor like he's talking about the weather. Like, 'Hey, by the way, your neighbor walked into a logging truck, don't you know. Guess he should look both ways before he crosses the street.'"

Naomi was an excellent mimic, and her imitation of Mr. Everly's non-chalant speech made Angela laugh. She'd pinned him. "Yeah, that's Saca-jawea for you. They like to gossip, and folks here can be cold when you're new. Mr. Leahy hadn't lived here that long before Corey met his son that last summer." Angela realized that this was the most casual reference she'd made to the summer of 2001 in as long as she could remember, and also the most times she had mentioned her son's name without tears. "I don't think the town ever warmed up to him. He was probably just a stranger to them, so they consider it an interesting story to tell."

Angela wondered what had happened to Sean and his foster siblings now that their father was dead. Sean had lost his friend and then his father, a lot of loss for a kid. If the kids were still in town, she would have to see the boy and give him her condolences.

"How are you feeling?" Naomi said.

"Good. I hate to say it, but I don't think I have too much room for other people's tragedies today. I'm still working on my own."

"True."

"This visit is great for me, Naomi. I really owe you."

Naomi winked at her. She was about to say something else when she suddenly looked away, glancing around the room. "Where's Onyx?" she said. "I can't believe he's not in my face trying to steal my pizza."

Onyx wasn't in sight. It might be a half hour or longer since Angela had seen him. Naomi had sworn the little dog was house-trained, but Angela was convinced she'd find at least one soiled rug during this visit. Naomi whistled loudly. "Onyx?" she called.

They heard a bark from nearby, but Onyx didn't come. Naomi came to her feet, calling again. Angela felt slightly dizzy when she stood up to follow Naomi—too much wine, she chided herself. Naomi was in the foyer, where Onyx was before the front door, looking at them over his shoulder. He stood against the door on his hind paws, scratching in a flurry of black fur.

"Shit. Naomi, don't let him do that—"

"Onyx, *stop*," Naomi said, then she crouched next to Onyx. "He never goes to the door like that in a new place." Angela examined the door for scratch-marks, and was relieved to see none. Her grandfather had built this door, and she'd hate to have to kill her friend's dog the very first day. "Can I let him out front by himself? I don't have my shoes on."

"I wouldn't let him run free if I were you. There's no fence and sixty acres," Angela said.

"You sure, girl? Onyx knows not to go far."

"Trust me, you don't want a poodle out there running loose. The coyotes would love him."

Naomi fixed a devastating look on Angela at the word *coyotes*. Maybe it had never occurred to her that if there were deer and elk nearby, there would also be coyotes and other less cuddly creatures. Gramma Marie had always had cats for mousing, but she'd kept them indoors after losing her favorite tabby to a howling pack of coyotes. But Gramma Marie hadn't begrudged the coyotes; she'd told Angela a story from Red John's grandfather about how the Coyote spirit made the Columbia River and protected men from monsters, and how he and a host of other protective spirits dwelled in her backyard. She said her land was a crossroads where all the spirits met.

"Look, the coyotes aren't going to come break the door down, sweetie," Angela said, seeing Naomi's face. "But I live near the woods, and that's what woods *are*, a place where animals live. Raccoons, bobcats, deer, coyotes. Nothing's going to bother us, but Onyx needs a chaperone."

"What about bears?" Naomi's eyes were comically wide.

Angela laughed, shaking her head as she climbed the stairs to retrieve her shoes. "Oh, Naomi, stop. There might be a black bear or two around, but Gramma Marie told me they aren't prone to attack people. It's the grizzlies you need to worry about, and we don't have those," Angela said. "You forgot to ask about the lions and tigers, hon."

"This ain't funny," Naomi called after her. "And what *about* lions?"

"This is Sacajawea, sweetheart, not the Serengeti."

Despite all references to uncivilized forest creatures, after Angela and Naomi walked the dog and drove into town to rent the mom-and-pop video store's only copy of *How Stella Got Her Groove Back* ("I'm in shock that they even have this," Angela told her friend, clutching the video like a brick of gold), she and Naomi slept well that night. Angela would soon come to regard the memory of that Friday night with Naomi as her most pleasant time since Corey's death, in the most unlikely place imaginable. It was also her last lingering instance of tranquility in Sacajawea.

Neither Angela nor her friend would sleep well for long.

Six

SATURDAY

*B*Y MORNING, Onyx was missing.

Angela decided to postpone her early-morning run to whip up a home-style breakfast for her friend, using the recipe cards Gramma Marie had left in her strawberry-shaped cookie jar. Cooking had been like a religion to Gramma Marie. There were more than a hundred recipes in that jar, all of them unique to her: sweet potato biscuits she'd learned from a traveling teacher, oxtail soup and corn fritters she'd learned from her father, fried rabbit from a church elder, a salmon recipe from Red John, a recipe for a baked plantain loaf passed on from her *grandmère*'s African grandmother. Angela's attempts to recreate her grandmother's cooking were another way of keeping Gramma Marie's spirit alive. By 9:30 A.M., the lower floor was steeped in the smells of buttermilk biscuits, scrambled eggs, cheese grits, and salmon croquettes.

Angela heard Naomi calling for Onyx upstairs, her voice louder as she neared the kitchen. The dog would turn up, Angela knew. There were only so many places Onyx could go. She just hoped he wasn't leaving a trail of piss and dogshit behind him.

"If it's not the right day for your cheat meal, that's too bad!" Angela called out.

When Naomi poked her head into the kitchen, the sight of her was startling. As much time as Angela had spent with Naomi, even at the gym, she'd never seen her without makeup. Fresh from sleep, Naomi still retained her own brand of prettiness, but her mouth seemed slightly drawn, her skin was dull, and her eyes appeared much smaller without mascara. She looked like Naomi Price's plainer older sister. "I can't find Onyx," Naomi said.

"He's just exploring, I'm sure. There's nowhere for him to get lost."

Naomi shook her head. "No, Angela, this is weirding me out. He was in my room, and our door was closed all night. When I woke up, the door was still closed, but there's no Onyx. Did you let him out?" Her voice was thin and scared.

"No, sweetie," she said. Naomi's face fell, and Angela remembered how pet owners regarded their animals as children. The dog had probably gotten out through a cracked-open bedroom door. Angela dried her hands on Gramma Marie's strawberry-print dishtowel. "Don't worry, we'll find him. He can't have gotten far."

Calling and whistling in chorus, they started their search upstairs. By the second sweep of the house, Angela found herself opening closed room doors—even Corey's, where she caught a glance of her son's Janet Jackson poster on the wall before she hurriedly shut it again. Not a whimper from the dog.

After a time, the bad thoughts appeared. Had the dog gotten sick? Eaten something he shouldn't have, like a cleanser or poison? She glanced at the door of the wine cellar, but she would not go there, not for anything, and Naomi did not think to look there either. But they looked everywhere else—under the sofa, behind the piano, in cabinets. They abandoned reason as it began to feel more certain that something was wrong.

"Keep calling him inside. I'll go look outside," Angela said.

Naomi's head whipped around, her face worried. "Is there any way he could have gotten out by himself?"

Angela was already pulling on the black wool coat she kept in the closet beside the front door. The coat smelled like a stranger's, it had been so long since she'd worn it. "No way I can think of, but we haven't found him in the house. Don't panic, Naomi. We *will* find Onyx."

Angela heard a yappy bark outside as soon as she opened the front door. Naomi heard it, too. The women ran out onto the front porch, their eyes sweeping the front yard and its clumps of hedges. No Onyx. "Onyx? Here, boy! Come here, boy," Noami said, stooping to search the rhododendron shrub near the porch. But when the dog barked again, it was clear he was much farther than the front yard. The sound seemed to have come from the road.

Angela didn't see him until she'd nearly reached the top of the stone steps. From her perch, she could see Toussaint Lane below, and Onyx was in the tall grass beside Tariq's abandoned van, running back and forth in the frenzy dogs usually reserve for mail carriers outside their gate. The dog's tail wagged with recognition, but he didn't come toward her. He ran and barked, as if a fence restrained him on the other side of the road.

"You stupid dog! How did you get outside?" Naomi scolded Onyx after they had climbed down to retrieve him. He did a happy-dance around them as they stroked him, chasing himself in circles. Angela was happy to see him, and he was one happy little dog. Naomi wrapped her arms around Onyx's neck, and the dog washed her face with his tongue.

"Onyx, you scared the shit out of me," Naomi said.

The episode cast a pall over breakfast. Naomi didn't talk about it, but Angela knew she had been shaken up. She had awakened to the idea that her pet was gone, that he might be hurt or dead or lost, with no warning or explanation. Angela knew that feeling of suddenness well. Although Angela was disappointed not to hear raves over her cooking, she let Naomi sort the morning out in her head as they sat and ate a silent meal together in the breakfast nook. Angela saw Naomi slipping Onyx pieces of her carefully prepared croquettes under the table, barely eating herself, and she understood. How long had the dog been out there? What if he'd met a coyote after all?

Their true visit had begun, Angela thought. This was not a trip to a spa or a girls-only slumber party. Life's meanness had brought them to Gramma Marie's house—a death had brought them to this house—and that particular brand of meanness surfaced anytime it damn well chose.

This would be their last full day together, Angela realized. Tomorrow, Naomi would go back to Portland to catch a seven P.M. flight to L.A. By Tuesday, Naomi had to be in Vancouver, British Columbia, to prepare for her three-week shoot. Angela would be alone here for the next few days and nights, with her own trauma to sort out. She'd lost a hell of a lot more than her dog, and Corey wasn't going to be waiting for her outside in the grass by Tariq's van, no matter how much she wished for it. Corey's absence was going to fill up every crevice of this old house, not just the bedroom she would soon have to be brave enough to face.

Angela's eggs were cooked to perfection, and Gramma Marie's seasonings rang true, but that morning the food didn't have the slightest flavor.

Later, at mid-morning, with Onyx on a leash, Angela and Naomi made their way down Toussaint Lane, jogging west on River Drive, a road that sloped steeply downward for a quarter-mile, then they turned north onto Main Street. Angela planned to run past town to the boardwalk alongside the river, maybe as far as the bait-shop. She was impressed at how well Onyx kept up, his small legs skittering like a caterpillar's. "Onyx runs with Mommy four times a week. He's my personal trainer," Naomi said proudly.

Naomi Price might be the more recognized face in Hollywood, but Angela was royalty in Sacajawea. They drew stares as they ran, mostly because people were surprised to see Angela fly past them in a jogging suit. Liza Brunell was in the window hanging a poster at Downtown Foods—CHILEAN CHERRIES! $3.99/LB—and her face glowed when she saw Angela. She made the universal telephone gesture, cocking her hand beside her ear, thumb and pinky extended: *Call me.* Angela waved and returned the gesture, a promise, although she never slowed.

A passing pickup honked with two welcoming bleats, and Angela waved back at the driver's extended arm even though she hadn't turned around fast enough to see his face. And at the colonial-style Sacajawea County courthouse, Angela and Naomi jogged straight past Sheriff Rob Graybold sitting in his parked sheriff's unit. Angela had a wave for him, too, and he leaned out of his window so his arm could billow more enthusiastically. "Hey, Angie!" he called, gifting her with a rare smile. He couldn't have looked happier to see her if she'd been his own sister.

Poor Rob, she thought. She'd harassed that man to death after Corey died.

"These are some friendly-ass folks," Naomi observed, her strides chopping her words. "Even the cops, huh? I should've brought my camera to take a picture of that."

"They're friendly if they know you." A lot of them had been at the party. In many ways, they knew her better than anyone.

Back at the house, Angela showered, but Naomi preferred a bath, so she soaked in the claw-foot tub upstairs for nearly an hour. After lunch, they retreated to different rooms to work. Naomi had pages to study for her shoot, and Angela caught herself up on the messages she'd missed Friday: Her golden comic's negotiations for a series at Fox were at an impasse over the pilot script, an actress she'd just signed had been sentenced to court-ordered rehab, and Stan Loweson wanted to add two weeks to Naomi's January shoot in Prague. Like hell. Not for free, if that was what he was thinking.

She'd been away from her desk for one day, and all hell had broken loose. But no one had told her this would be easy, Angela reminded herself.

Anything that comes too easily is a lie, Gramma Marie used to tell her at every chance, until Angela practically heard the words in her sleep.

At five o'clock, someone knocked on the door.

Onyx barked in hysteria, as if the knocking were a personal insult. "Well, *damn,*" Angela muttered, leaving the library, where she'd set up her laptop and the portable phone. She didn't mind a visitor, but she couldn't stand the barking. No wonder she'd never owned a dog.

Onyx was posted at the front door, chastising the new arrival through the wood. "Hush all that racket. You're not going to scare anybody, sounding like a damn wind-up toy. And you let me find *one* puddle of piss in this house," Angela said, tugging at the soft, neatly groomed ball of fur atop his head. She called upstairs. "Naomi, Onyx is out loose!"

No answer except what sounded like a muffled conversation upstairs. Naomi was in the world of her character, memorizing lines behind her closed door. This dog would have to sleep on a leash tied to Naomi's bed tonight, Angela decided.

When Angela opened the door, she expected to find Liza Brunell. She didn't.

Instead, Myles Fisher stood on the porch in a red plaid shirt, holding a cane fishing pole like a walking stick. Angela couldn't speak at first, lost in the memory of when she'd last seen him: the scent of his cologne the day of the party. The sunflowers he'd brought. Her happiness when he'd arrived, interrupted by such horror. His patient helpfulness after Corey's death, when he'd been all but invisible to her through her veil of grief.

Myles and Liza Brunell had been the only two Sacajaweans to come to L.A. for the funeral, and Myles had organized Sacajawea's public memorial service for Corey. He'd mailed her the program afterward, which had been lovely, with someone's charcoal sketch of Corey's face. He'd attached a note informing her that two hundred people had attended. But Angela hadn't sent him a return note, nor had she answered his concerned calls or letters since, just like with Mrs. Everly.

Now, here he was. Angela felt sick with guilt. She hadn't even called him to let him know she would be in town.

Without a word, Myles rested his fishing pole against the doorframe and stepped into the house. He came within an inch of Angela, pulled her to him, and wrapped both arms around her, squeezing hard. She hugged him back, nearly falling into him. He smelled like he'd been outdoors baking in the sun, but underneath that sharpness was the Myles she remembered from high school, boyish and intimate, almost more her cousin than her boyfriend. Almost, but not quite. Silent tears melted across her face as she held on to him.

"I'm sorry," she said.

Myles didn't answer her at first, holding on. Then, close to her ear, he said, "You really know how to disappear, lady. More than two years. I've been worried to death."

"Forgive me?"

"I'll think about it, but I haven't decided yet." At that, Myles pulled back slightly and searched her eyes. He rubbed her tears into her right cheek until most of the moisture vanished, blending. "You sure you're all right?"

She nodded, smiling. "I wasn't always, but I am now. I'll tell you all about it."

"Okay, then," Myles said, and for a long time, they just stared. Both of his palms clasped her face gently, and for a moment Angela's heart flipped as she wondered if he might lean over to kiss her lips. The thought of it made her stiffen and nearly pull away, but she didn't. Myles did not kiss her, nor had he probably intended to. In high school, he had been so powerful in his affection, even his platonic affection, that he had often confused her. Angela had spent years misreading Myles's signals, and she'd just done it again. For all she knew, he was married by now.

"How long are you here?" he said at last.

"About a week."

He smiled, surprised. "Good. You planning to keep the house?"

Angela fought to swallow as her throat constricted. "I don't know."

Until they heard Naomi coming toward the stairs, neither of them had noticed the way Onyx was pitching himself against their legs in his excitement, trying to intrude on their reunion. With the approaching footsteps, they both instinctively took a step away from each other.

"You have big, furry rats," Myles said, noting the dog. "I could call someone about that."

"Shhhhh. My friend Naomi Price is here. He belongs to her."

Myles squinted. "Naomi Price the actress?"

"That's the one. She'll be thrilled you know who she is. You're the first so far."

"Angie, what happened to your walnut tree? There's a . . ."

Before he could finish his question, Naomi appeared on the staircase. She was wearing only a long T-shirt and lounging pants, but her face was highlighted with a stunning assortment of earth tones. Myles gave Naomi a toothy grin, leaning over to offer a handshake.

"Miss Price, it's a true honor," he said. "You were wonderful as Coretta King last year."

The magic words. Naomi's pet project had been a candid script she'd optioned about Martin Luther King, Jr.'s widow, Coretta Scott King, and Angela had finally been able to help her set up the project at TNT. The audience hadn't been overwhelming—five times as many people had seen Naomi play a stripper, Murder Victim Number Three, in the forgettable Keanu Reeves vehicle released the same year—but Naomi had been nominated for an Emmy and a Golden Globe for her performance in *Coretta*. It was her best work on film.

"You saw that?" Naomi said, a smile igniting her face. "How wonderful!"

"Naomi, this is Myles Fisher," Angela said. Then, a beat later: "My high school boyfriend."

Naomi gave her a quick, perceptive glance. Enough said. Angela could almost *see* Naomi pocket the blast of sensuality she'd been about to hurl at Myles. She meant nothing by it, but she was a hell of a tease, another aspect of her star power. Even at a low hum, Naomi could make men flush and forget that their wives and children were standing next to them.

"I didn't know this town had any brothers."

"I'm the one."

"Then you'll have to stay for dinner with us, Myles," Naomi said.

Myles looked at Angela for guidance. "Well, I don't want to be . . ."

Angela squeezed his hand. "No, of course you should. Are you free?"

A boyish grin broke through. "Too busy for dinner with Angela Toussaint and Naomi Price? Do I look like a fool? Of course I'm free. I'm just all funky from fishing. Let me go home, clean up, and come back."

God, he sounded enchanted. Angela couldn't help wondering if he was more amenable to dinner because Naomi was here, but she decided she might not want to know. "Come back at seven, Myles. How's that?" Angela said.

"Seven it is." His voice had pitched to a throaty rumble she had never heard before. Gallantly, Myles took Naomi's hand and kissed it. He did the same to Angela's, although his gaze was slightly winking when he looked at her face. "Ladies."

"Girl, he's *fine*," Naomi said once Myles had vanished into the yard. "Did you see that?"

"Oh, I saw it," Angela muttered. She'd never seen him kiss a woman's hand before. Myles should have been an actor, too, she thought.

"You need to pack him up with you when you come back to L.A. Or send him to me."

Angela didn't answer. She couldn't be fooled by her childish echoes of jealousy, or by Myles's sudden display of chivalry in the presence of an actress he admired. By now, she and Myles had been apart longer than they'd been together, and the last time they had shared a true friendship they'd been no more than children. Twenty-two years was a long separation.

Besides, Myles hadn't been kidding when he said he hadn't decided whether or not to forgive her for withdrawing after Corey's death. He might try to give her false reassurances out of politeness, but she knew him too well. He must have written her a dozen times, and she'd never acknowledged a single letter; she probably hadn't read more than one or two. He was hurt, and could she blame him? She'd pulled the same vanishing act in high school, finding herself suddenly busy for weeks at a time just when he'd thought they were growing closer, and he'd gotten fed up with it. Myles, unlike her, knew how to accept his losses.

She had run away from him. She had done it after what happened at The Spot when they were eighteen, and she had done it again after Corey died. She owed him an explanation, and she would finally give him one, she decided. Hell, he'd seen her behavior at Corey's funeral. How hard would it be for him to picture her in a loony bin? He'd probably have a harder time figuring out why someone would set her loose.

Like mother, like daughter.

Crazy was in her blood.

"Myles, how's Ma Fisher?"

"Ma is still hanging in there," Myles said, scooping steamed broccoli onto his plate. The table setting was more formal than Angela had intended, but she liked imitating the way Gramma Marie had served food on her good china on special occasions. Angela had made jerk chicken breasts, brown rice, and broccoli, the closest she'd come to a dinner party in ages, and she was enjoying herself. The antique oak table seated eight, and they were clustered at the far end, closest to the window. "She doesn't recognize me anymore, not as her son. She used to in spells, up until about Easter. She can still walk, but the Alzheimer's is doing a number on her brain."

Angela's heart sank. She wished she'd been able to go visit Ma Fisher at least once before her mind dimmed for good, but when Corey died, Angela had forgotten the significance of everything else for a time. She should have called her, even while she was at The Harbor. She'd heard Ma Fisher was sick, she knew how old she was. Between Gramma Marie and Ma Fisher, Angela had gained two mothers after Dominique Toussaint's suicide.

Gramma Marie had tutored Myles in black history and literature from the time he was ten. The Fishers thought the lessons would be good for their new adopted black boy, and Ma Fisher had sat in on the sessions too, inquisitive and eager. That was how Angela had first met Myles's mother, three weeks after discovering the meaning of the word *orphan* herself. Angela's mother had just died, and her father had been a one-night stand whose name Dominique Toussaint had never known. When Angela saw Myles and Ma Fisher sitting together at Gramma Marie's library table, she'd felt envy. Ma Fisher's skin was white, but Myles had a mother. Anyone could see it.

"That's awful about your mother," Naomi said. "I'm sorry."

Myles half-shrugged. "She's happier now that she's not fighting to hang on to her memories, thank God. She smiles a lot. So, I'm feeling a little relief for her sake. It's hard, though. I finally had to figure out this isn't about me."

"Is it all right to leave her alone like this?" Angela said.

"We have two nurses now. The weekend nurse is a good lady. Her name is Betsy, but Ma calls her Sandy."

"Sandy? Like your old dog?" Angela said. The sudden memory surprised her.

Myles smiled, looking at Angela with appreciative eyes. "Yes."

Myles and his golden retriever had been inseparable, until Sandy crossed a hunter's scope when Myles was sixteen. That had been the first time she had seen him cry. But not the last.

"Myles, I'm gonna keep your mama in my prayers," Naomi said. "Even the scientists are admitting prayer makes a difference when folks are sick."

Those words struck Angela as something she should have said, but her feelings rarely leaped out into words that way. She wished they did.

"That's good of you to say. Angela, this is a very nice lady."

"Yes, she is. I wouldn't be back here if Naomi hadn't offered to come with me."

"Is that so?" Now, Myles gazed at Naomi with an added spark of admiration. "Then we both owe you. You saved me the expense of hiring a private investigator to track her down."

"Don't forget, she's my agent. I'm gonna keep her healthy and happy, no matter what."

"I thought that was supposed to work the other way around," Myles said.

Naomi leaned closer to Myles across the table. "Honey, she just got me my first million-dollar deal," Naomi stage-whispered. "Believe me, I'm *happy*."

Myles raised his crystal water glass. "To a million dollars and the future of the lovely and *très* talented Naomi Price—you better wear sunglasses, sister, because it's gonna be bright."

"Damn right," Angela said, and they tinkled their glasses together.

"Wait," Naomi blurted. "Also, to Angela Toussaint—the strongest, smartest woman I know."

"Hear, hear," Myles said.

"You mean the bitchiest," Angela murmured.

"Girl, hush. Don't be talking about my friend like that," Naomi said.

Angela's eyes stung during the second toast, and she could feel blood rush to her face. After isolating herself from companionship for so long, her heart seemed to be drowning in their combined warmth. She was moved, and at the same time she felt unresolved.

"It's my turn," Angela said, her words nearly too big for her throat. "To Myles Fisher . . ." She faltered, wrestling with herself. "For the truest kind of friendship. A friendship that forgives."

"*Merci, chérie,*" Myles said, but Angela thought she saw a small wince in his eye.

"Don't tell me you speak French!" Naomi said.

"Only the little bit her Gramma Marie taught me. Nothing to brag about."

By the time they were eating the fruit salad dessert, the three of them had toasted Gramma Marie, Naomi's father and late grandmother, and Pa Fisher, which brought a tear to Myles's eye. Angela called for the final toast.

"To Corey. He's in good hands. He's with his grandmother," she said. Myles and Naomi said *amen* as they toasted. It was only then that Angela realized she'd made a breakthrough Dr. Houston would never believe. She'd toasted Corey and she hadn't crawled under the table to bawl. Gramma Marie's magic again, she thought. Simply being inside this house made her feel stronger.

And death was destined to be their dinner subject.

"Myles," Angela said, "what happened to Rick Leahy?"

Myles shook his head, pushing his chair away from the table. "Rick, Rick, Rick," he sighed. "I still can't believe it. What a waste. He got hit by a truck right on Main Street in the middle of the day. I wrote the obituary. I'll bring it next time I'm here."

"You write at that paper? I thought you were the boss."

"I'm the managing editor, so I do hire, fire, and grumble. But I made a special dispensation for Rick. We used to go fishing every once in a while, philosophizing. He was a good man."

Myles and Rick were both outsiders in some ways, Angela realized, and as an adopted child himself, it was only natural Myles would be drawn to a man who rescued children. Myles had come to Sacajawea at ten, after spending a couple of years in foster homes. Myles was only two months older than Angela—*You could be twins*, Gramma Marie used to say—although Angela had avoided him until she enrolled in Sacajawea High if only because Gramma Marie had tried so hard to push them together every summer. To Angela, Myles had always been a skinny, bookish boy, dark as tar, who tried too hard to please adults, keeping his hair cut too short, calling his white mother "ma'am" and his white father "sir." In high school, though, she couldn't ignore Myles anymore. He had been the only boy who seemed to see her, to notice she was a girl. That had meant so much to her, it scared her.

"What happened to his kids? Sean Leahy was Corey's best friend," Angela said.

"I know. Rick talked about that. I think an aunt is here staying with them. They're still next door, Sean and his brother and sister."

"There's no mama?" Naomi said.

"Rick was a single father," Angela told her.

"And the little girl has been orphaned *twice* now. Two of Rick's kids were adopted," Myles said, and Angela and Naomi shook their heads, murmuring their *umh-umh-umhs*. "Sean turned eighteen this year, and he may try to win custody to raise the kids here, so they won't have to leave their friends and be uprooted again."

Eighteen. Only a few months older than Corey would have been. Angela could hardly believe a child so close to her son's age was facing such a large responsibility. She remembered Sean's pale blond hair, his nasal laugh, the way he and Corey had often huddled together like mad scientists, being kids together. Corey would have been nearly a man now, and Sean was one already.

"His father just didn't hear the truck coming?" Angela said.

Myles clasped his fingers together, and he didn't answer at first. Angela wondered if maybe she'd probed too deeply, if Myles didn't want to discuss it any more. But Myles finally leaned far back in his chair and met her gaze. "Well . . . that's the bizarre thing," he began. "There were two witnesses who weren't as far from Rick Leahy as we are from that china cabinet, and one of them was the driver. You know—Terry Marlow. I feel terrible for the guy. They both say Rick saw the truck. They say he looked dead at Terry's face and then walked into his truck's path."

"Suicide?" Angela said. Suicides always took her back to her mother's breakfast table.

Myles shook his head, shrugging, as if he were shedding a hot, uncomfortable cape. "Terry says Rick was grinning from ear to ear when he did it," he said. "He tells me it's giving him nightmares, not just what happened, but the *way* it happened. The way Rick looked at him."

Grinning. A distinct shiver started at the top of Angela's head and wound its way to her neck, shoulders, and both arms, leaving a trail of cold skin. Suddenly, she'd heard more than she wanted to know. She slid her shaky hands beneath her thighs.

"I shouldn't have said anything," Myles said perceptively.

"No, it's all right, Myles. I asked." Angela tried to smile.

"I think it's time to play Scrabble," Naomi said. "I brought my game from home. You know who busted out with a-s-p-h-y-x-y for seventy-five points to beat me the last time I played? Will Smith. It's true. That man is so smart. I met him back . . ."

Naomi told stories like no one else. For the first time since the Fourth of July party, there was raucous laughter at the Toussaint house. This time, it went uninterrupted for hours.

✠ Seven ✠

ANGELA WAS WIDE AWAKE by 5:30 A.M., grateful for the fledgling sunlight that meant she'd made it through the night. Gramma Marie's bedroom seemed too beautiful a place to have offered her so little rest.

She lay in the center of Gramma Marie's canopied bed draped with sheer white curtains, a bed her grandmother was rumored to have once shared with Elijah Goode before she shared it with her common-law husband, John. With a shiny mahogany dresser, a tiny sink with a white skirt, and a private window seat, where she could sit and stare out at the woods if she chose, the room should have been a comfort. But if Angela had slept, she didn't remember it. All she remembered was her racing mind, Corey's words assaulting her.

I'm gonna take care of you good, Mom.

In her half-waking state, Angela recalled the words exactly as they'd been spoken to her—not *I'm gonna take GOOD CARE of you, Mom,* which was a devoted son's promise, but *I'm gonna take care of you GOOD,* which might be something else altogether. A threat. A presaging. He'd said those words minutes before he shot himself in the head, inflicting the most damage the best way he knew how. *I'm gonna take care of you good, Mom.* And Corey had said it with a smile. No, a grin. Just like Rick Leahy before he walked into the truck.

Angela felt a burning, hurting brand of angry. She'd never let herself feel mad at Corey for long, but she was mad now. She wanted to have her son back if only so she could slap him senseless.

What if, just supposing, Corey had shot himself out of spite? To spite her for forcing him to stay with her in Sacajawea? To spite her and Tariq for making a mess of his family? What did those words mean if it *wasn't* an accident, if it was another family suicide after all? Angela's greatest fear was that when she finally went into Corey's room, she would find a big fat suicide note taped to his mirror even though none had been there before. *I'm gonna take care of you good, Mom.*

And he had, hadn't he? He'd taken care of her good, all right.

Angela sat up in bed, hoping to shake the poison from her head. Her throat and stomach felt bloated, as if she might vomit. She would take a quick run before Naomi got up. Four or five miles of hard running along the Four would knock out the bad thoughts. Sore muscles were good for that. Traffic would be sparse this early on a Sunday.

Happy to have a plan, Angela slipped on her black jogging suit, the same one she'd worn yesterday. The crotch was still slightly damp because she'd left the sweatpants balled up on the floor, but she'd make do. She strapped on her running shoes, fixed her headband. One stop at the bathroom, and she'd be gone.

Stepping into the hallway, Angela noticed that Naomi's room door was half open. Damn. That probably meant the dog had gotten out again, and he might have figured out a way to reprise whatever escape route he'd found yesterday. Angela peeked into the doorway, hoping she'd find both Naomi and Onyx in the daybed.

Instead, she found neither. The covers were turned back, the bed empty. Naomi was not at her glass-top tea table either, where her script pages were spread out beside a coffee mug.

If Angela knew nothing else in life, it was that Naomi Price was not an early riser. On days she wasn't working, Naomi couldn't drag herself out of bed until 9:30 or 10 A.M., sometimes later. Naomi would not be up before six. Angela felt the first vibration at the base of her skull when she saw the empty room; a small vibration, but perceptible. She didn't like it.

The bathroom door was ajar in the hallway, too, and the light was off. Angela didn't think Naomi would keep the light off, but she looked in the bathroom anyway. Empty. Angela sat on the toilet and made herself relax, allowing her full bladder to squeeze itself empty. After flushing and drying her washed hands on her clothes, she went downstairs to look for her friend.

"Naomi?" she called.

No answer. None of the lights downstairs were on. Angela flipped on the foyer light when she reached the bottom of the stairs, bringing life to the chandelier, which cast a sunny, mottled glow throughout the foyer. Maybe Naomi was outside walking her dog, she thought. Or, maybe she and Myles made some kind of plan behind her back and were screwing each other blind back at his place. That last thought, a nasty jab, annoyed her to a surprising degree even while she told herself it was ridiculous. But the front door was still locked from the inside, even the dead bolt. Naomi might have locked the doorknob lock from outside without a key, but not the dead bolt. Unless she'd gone outside from the back.

When Angela turned to walk toward the kitchen, she saw that the door to the wine cellar was wide open for the first time since her arrival. Her flesh seemed to leap away from her.

Why the fuck would Naomi go down there?

"Naomi?" Angela called, not moving. Her heart was taking deep dives into the pit of her stomach, then slamming back up against her chest. "Naomi, if you're in the cellar, please come out."

She heard a thump against the roof of the porch, a walnut rolling like a midsized stone. But nothing else.

Open door or no open door, Angela decided she was not going near that wine cellar. The cellar door could have popped open by itself because of an air pocket in the foyer. There was no reason in the world for Naomi and her dog to be down there, and Angela wasn't going to poke her head in that cellar unless she had a list of good reasons herself. At least twenty, maybe more.

Instead, Angela unlocked the front door and stood on the porch in the cool morning air, calling Naomi's name. The early-morning sky was gray and unpromising. Angela went to the stone steps and surveyed Toussaint Lane, seeing Tariq's van parked on one side and the Explorer parked on the other. No Onyx, and no Naomi. She walked on the smooth bluestone garden path along the right side of the house until she was climbing the cedar steps to the backyard deck. No Naomi at the patio table, sitting beneath the umbrella in one of the chairs. No Naomi in the hot tub, which was covered with its foam seal, unused.

"Naomi!" she shouted into the woods beyond the drop-off behind her house, toward the herb garden she had not visited in years. She turned again, this time north, facing The Spot, and called her friend's name again. Her voice tripped into the foggy treetops, unanswered. Naomi was not outside. Her friend wouldn't venture into the woods, as scared as she was of coyotes. Naomi was either in the house or taking Onyx on a walk toward town. Simple deductive logic.

But as Angela let herself back in through the front door, embraced again by the warmth of the heated house, she came face-to-face with the open door of the wine cellar at the other end of the foyer. At that instant, Angela knew: Naomi was down there. It seemed as obvious as the fact of her own existence. And for some reason, Naomi was not answering her.

"Naomi!" she shouted, loud and cross. If this was a prank, it was a cruel one, and she couldn't imagine Naomi being that cruel. Naomi knew what had happened in there.

Without any understanding of what or whom she was arming herself against, Angela found one of Gramma Marie's old black umbrellas in the coat closet, the kind Angela had once fantasized about taking flight with like Mary Poppins. Keeping it closed, she brandished the umbrella and its pointed tip like a sword, clasping the polished wooden handle. She kept it close to her body as she took her first steps toward the cellar.

Angela's heartbeat was doing calisthenics she didn't know it could do. "Naomi, please come out if you're in there," Angela said, pleading. "I'm not playing with you. This isn't funny."

She was four feet in front of the door, not yet close enough to see down inside. She waited a long time, unable to go on. Then, she felt herself taking the last few steps to the cellar doorway, and she was standing fixed in the one place where she had never thought she would stand again. She stared down past the stairs. The narrow cellar's light wasn't on, and it was dark inside, but the light from the chandelier provided just enough illumination for Angela to see through the darkness.

Pale clothing against dark skin. A person was lying on the cellar floor.

"Oh, no," Angela said, staring hard into the pitch, praying the figure would dissipate into a hallucination. Instead, it just became more clear. Angela flung the umbrella away and tugged the string to turn on the cellar light. "Naomi?"

Naomi Price was lying in the center of the cellar floor, her head facing away from Angela. One arm was splayed out, the palm upward, and she looked—

Like Corey.

The room whirled momentarily, but Angela fought to keep from fainting or fleeing, whatever her body was trying to do. She flew down the stairs so quickly that she nearly tripped over her feet. Just like last time. "Naomi?" She knelt at her friend's side, shaking her.

"Mmmmpppphhh . . ." Naomi made a sound. Yes, praise Jesus, she had made a sound. And her back was rising and falling with her breaths, and now she was *moving*, rolling over onto her side.

"What the hell are you doing down here?" Angela said. Tears were flowing, mingled tears of utter panic and a kind of relief she could never describe.

Naomi blinked up at her without comprehension, her eyes and face bleary. Naomi's brow was so furrowed, her eyebrows almost met. "What?" Naomi said, irritable at being awakened.

"Why are you down here on the floor? You're in the cellar."

Naomi blinked twice more, and then she sat up as if she'd been doused with cold water. She stared around her with saucer eyes, first at the brick walls and the wine shelves, then at the floor. She peered especially hard at the floor, touching her pajamas, gazing at her own palms, and Angela suddenly understood what she was looking for: blood. Yes, she knew what had happened in the wine cellar.

There was no blood, not even dried blood. Now that Angela was down here, she saw that the floor had been scrubbed clean. The spot where Naomi sat had been *more* scrubbed than the rest of the floor, with smears of cleanness standing out against age-old grime at the borders, where the scrubbing stopped. She was sitting exactly where Corey had died, but there was no blood.

"What happened?" Naomi said, and tears came to her eyes too.

"You don't remember coming down here?"

Naomi looked at Angela, so lost and horrified that Angela pitied her. *"What is going on?"*

Angela spoke slowly and clearly, trying not to alarm her further. "Naomi, I saw you weren't in your room, so I came down looking for you. The cellar door was hanging open, and here you are, lying asleep on the floor."

Naomi waved at her, dismissing her explanation. "No, no, no, no," she repeated, running the scenario through her groggy mind. "That can't be right. That *cannot* be right. How did I get here?"

"I don't know. Maybe you . . . walked in your sleep?"

"I don't do that." Naomi's face wrenched with disbelief.

"Sweetie, you did it. Look at you. You got down here somehow."

When Naomi's face didn't change, paralyzed in place, Angela pulled her close and hugged her, smoothing back the matted hair at her hot forehead. She gave her methodical, soothing strokes. "It's all right, Naomi. You were just sleepwalking. You didn't get hurt."

She heard Naomi sob, and her heart sank. In her own fear, she'd scared Naomi needlessly. Now that she had her friend's fear to contend with, Angela magically forgot her own. She was here in the wine cellar crouched where her boy had died, and she was the one doing the consoling. God definitely has a sense of humor, she thought.

"This is weird shit, Angela," Naomi whimpered. "There is some weird shit going on."

"Sleepwalking is not that weird. I know it seems freaky if it's never happened to you before, but it happens more than you think." Something else occurred to Angela, and her voice brightened. "And you know what I just figured out? I think I know how Onyx got out yesterday. I think you let him out, just like when you came down here this morning. You just don't remember it."

Immediately, Angela realized she'd screwed up. She'd spoken without thinking.

Naomi pulled away, more shaken than before. "Angela, where's Onyx?"

Angela had no idea.

For more than an hour, Angela and Naomi combed the house and the outdoor areas bordering the house, and there was no sign of Onyx. This had turned into one of those mornings that felt like an entire day had passed before nine A.M. The sun had grown gleefully bright for a while, but now the sky had surrendered to the gray clouds, foretelling oncoming afternoon rain.

Angela called the Humane Society and Animal Control, leaving messages at both places. Then, she and Naomi drove toward town, moving slowly, watching every alleyway, every garbage can. They went to the boardwalk, to the bait-house, talked to the early-morning fishermen camped up and down the river, and then to the Four, driving a couple of miles up and down in each direction. A dead raccoon by the side of the road—its legs straight up in the air as if in four-paw salute—made Naomi shriek before she realized the dead animal wasn't Onyx.

On the way back home, they stopped at the front gate at the Leahy place. A pigtailed girl in eyeglasses was in the front yard playing on a tire swing. After telling her how sorry she was her family was having a sad time, Angela asked if anyone in her family had seen a dog. The girl ran inside the mobile home to check. The answer, she reported breathlessly on her return, was no.

"Fuck," she heard Naomi whisper, just below the child's hearing.

The hard truth sank in: It was after nine o'clock, and they hadn't been able to find a sign of the dog. This search could take all day, and Naomi had to leave by four-thirty to get to the airport on time. At best, they had been robbed of a good part of their day together. At worst, Naomi was going to have to miss her flight. That wasn't *really* the worst-case scenario, as Angela knew full well, but her imagination wouldn't allow her to consider what that might be.

They would find Onyx. Angela just didn't know when.

She had to start searching her acreage, and she would need help. She'd pretty well managed to spook Naomi out of the idea of going near the woods, so she found herself leaning over her kitchen counter at 9:15, spooning yogurt into her mouth as she dialed Myles Fisher's number.

The phone rang only once before someone picked up, but there was no greeting. A silent line.

"Hello?" Angela said. "Is Myles there? This is—"

"Oh, just make it stop!" Ma Fisher said crankily. Her voice bellowed, distorted because her mouth must be too close to the mouthpiece. She had aged, but Angela recognized the voice right away from the countless times she had called for Myles in high school.

"Excuse me?" Angela said.

"It hurts, Mrs. T'saint. Why won't you please make it stop? Go on, make it stop, you coward. You know how. Just like you did in 'Cisco. Don't be scared. Whatcha scared of?"

Angela's words died in her throat. In 'Cisco? What the hell did that mean? She didn't know what to say, nor exactly what she had just heard. It took Angela several seconds to remember that Ma Fisher's mind had been lost to Alzheimer's. Angela heard interference and a few muffled words, then Myles's voice came on. "Hello?"

"Myles, it's Angela."

"Sorry, Angie. Ma got hold of the phone again. She likes to answer it, even if she doesn't know who she's talking to."

"But Myles, she *did* know. She called me Mrs. T'saint."

"Yeah . . . She saw the Caller I.D. She still seems to be able to read, when she wants to. It's not real likely she recognized your voice. I never say never, but she's just . . . not here."

He was right, of course—the old Ma Fisher would have called her Angie, like everyone else in town, not Mrs. T'saint—but Angela was rattled by the exchange with Myles's mother. After a morning like she'd had so far, rattling her was not difficult.

"What's up? We're all sitting down to breakfast," Myles said. There was a distance in his voice that felt crushing. She didn't know who *we* was, if he was simply referring to his mother and the nurse or someone else who had a breakfast pass. Angela almost changed her mind about why she'd called. But then she glanced out at the backyard deck, where Naomi was sitting at the table with an untouched glass of orange juice, staring out accusingly toward the woods.

"I'm sorry to interrupt your meal. It's just . . . Myles, Onyx is missing."

"Who?"

"Naomi's dog." She forced herself not to come to tears while she told him the story, even the part about the cellar. She didn't want him to feel manipulated, as if she were having some kind of breakdown. But she hoped he would want to help.

Myles's voice dipped with concern. "Okay, let me finish up here," he said, "and I'll meet you at your place within an hour. Listen, I don't want to alarm you, and you probably shouldn't share this with Naomi, but a dog that size out back in your woods—"

"I know," Angela said. "I'm trying not to think about that."

"Sorry about your crappy day, doll-baby. I'll be there soon."

⸺

Once, Gramma Marie had said, Elijah Goode had a carriage house where Toussaint Lane dead-ended, where the clay road lost its will and conceded to the mouth of the dense woods. But the carriage house had been taken down decades ago, and the path seemed to have vanished, too. In Angela's memory, there had been a clear trail back here, the one she and the other kids in Sacajawea knew would take them to The Spot. Once, someone had hung up an old pair of gym shorts on a cedar limb as a landmark, and when Gramma Marie took them down, a bra had gone up instead.

All landmarks were long gone now. Corey had led her and Tariq on the path after Tariq's arrival that summer, and she'd realized then that she might never have found her way without her son's knowledge. The path wasn't clearly appointed like a nature hike; it was a narrow trail of red-brown needles carved by footfall over time, winding in a seemingly random snake through ferns and the trunks of narrow hemlocks and pillarlike red cedars that grew in crowded stands back here.

Together, tentatively, Angela and Myles sought out the path. Some-times they reached blockages, and Angela was sure the thin trail had van-ished—then she saw it reemerge at an odd angle, around a rotted tree stump, or beyond a fallen log carpeted with bright green moss. When she lost her balance and braced herself against a maple, she marveled at the springiness of the soft moss beneath her palm. The tree might be dead, without a single leaf, but it was so trussed in moss that it looked like it was wearing a majestic robe, dressed for company.

The growth was so dense, the sunlight had all but vanished except for patches of light tricking their way past the thinning fall leaves of the alders and maples. Angela wished she had worn a jacket over her sweatshirt, be-cause the temperature dropped without the sun's favor. The woods smelled damp, of composting leaves and a fir scent that was so vivid and fresh that it put air fresheners to shame. This was *beautiful*. Angela had her own per-sonal nature refuge back here, and it was a crime how rarely she visited. Even before Corey died, she'd rarely come out here. To her own land.

Angela and Myles followed the path in silence much of the walk, ex-cept to call for Onyx and point out each other's way when the path tried to lose them. Silence felt right. Angela had expected to hear a symphony of in-sects and noisy birds, but the forest might as well be a chapel. When she fi-nally heard a small animal stirring in a nest of vines beside the path, she thought Onyx would dash toward them with his pink tongue hanging from his mouth. But he didn't. Whatever it was camouflaged itself so well that Angela couldn't see a peek of it.

Squirrels. Raccoons. Moles. They had their own world out here, hid-den from her.

"Do you think he had sense enough to stay on the path?" Angela asked Myles.

"I don't see why not. The deer use it. See?" Myles said, nudging his foot against a pile of round, pale droppings. Leave it to Myles to recognize deer shit, she thought, smiling. He had always been more enamored of Saca-jawea, more rooted to the region. She'd forgotten most of what she'd known about outdoor life, and she didn't remember ever knowing much.

The walk to The Spot took longer than Angela had remembered, nearly twenty minutes. Thick, knotty tree roots helped her keep her foot-ing as the path steepened, then the sunlight's influence grew as they reached the clearing, which was stark in its lack of growth of any kind. The Spot was barely larger than a public swimming pool, a circular bed of fallen fir needles and leaves around a fire-pit. She could have sworn it was bigger than this, but she'd thought the same thing the last time she'd been here. In her imagination, The Spot was huge.

The makeshift grill Tariq had laid over the fire-pit to cook hot dogs with her and Corey was still here, only more rusted, and the logs and large stones ringing the pit were nestled in new trash. Dozens of beer cans. Newspapers. Cigarette butts. A crushed KFC bucket. When Angela saw a faded, discarded red box of Trojan condoms, her jaw tightened with anger.

"What's wrong with these nasty kids?" Angela said. "We never left this kind of mess here."

"No, it's a disgrace," Myles said. "We'll clean it another time."

Angela was so annoyed by the lack of respect the kids had shown for the land that she didn't notice Myles's use of *we* until seconds later, and the word warmed her. Maybe all was forgiven. But then again, Myles had his own memories anchored here, and he probably was just as offended as she was. They had been eighteen, seniors, when they had come here looking for privacy the night of their prom, her chiffon dress swishing in the underbrush on the trail. If there had been anyone else here, they'd planned to park Pa Fisher's truck somewhere secluded down the Four, on one of the old logging roads, but Angela had been relieved The Spot was theirs that night. The truck wouldn't have been the same.

Myles had been a virgin when he came with her to the heart of Gramma Marie's woods, and she'd decided she would give him her virginity, too, that she'd kept it for him despite the four times she'd had sex already. She'd been so young before, a thirteen-year-old kid in awe of a band instructor who had pretended to be her friend, feeling grown because he offered her his beer and his dick. Angela had never told Mama or Gramma Marie about her visits to Mr. Lowe, but she knew damn well Gramma Marie would have put that SOB in jail even if Mama hadn't been able to collect herself enough to care. With Myles, Angela had been ready to erase those times; the times that had made her feel sullied and used as soon as a minute passed and she knew better.

She'd wanted it to feel right. Here, nothing could feel wrong.

That night, Angela had seen Myles's dark, firm nakedness poke through the zippered mouth of his jeans, surprising her with how wide and man-sized he was when she thought of him as a skinny boy. Angela remembered the ground beneath the blanket, hard despite the cushion of needles, bothering her shoulder blades until the sweet moment when everything was suddenly perfect. Myles had pushed slowly, nudging inside her, and she'd felt locked tightly to him, possession and possessor.

That was the first time she'd understood how profound it was to have a man *fill her*. She'd lost her breath, digging her nails into Myles's shoulder blades. Only Tariq had made her feel anything close to it since, in days that felt so ancient by comparison that her experience with Myles at The Spot could have been last week. Or yesterday. Angela's stomach loosened, fluttering.

Angela glanced shyly at Myles, certain he must have the same memory in his eyes, but his attention was on his task. *"Onnnnnnn-yyyyyyyyx,"* Myles called, cupping his mouth as he shouted into the woods. He stuffed two fingers past his lips and produced a whistle that hurt Angela's ear.

A fully reborn echo repeated his call to him before fading. The whistle, too, seemed to weave its way through the woods before it fell silent. No Onyx.

The trail that had brought them here didn't reappear on the other side of The Spot, at least not that she could see. Angela helped Myles search the areas bordering The Spot, but they didn't wander far from the clearing. In the light, she noticed pockmarks on his cheeks, acne from high school that had not properly healed, or marks from razor bumps. The small marks gave his face a sterner, more finished quality, evidence that his journey from boyhood to manhood had not been without scars.

"I'd feel better with a compass," Myles said.

"Could we get lost?"

"For a couple hours? You bet. It's easy to get disoriented."

"Screw that, then," Angela said. She had heard about a *Village Voice* editor named Joe Wood who had never returned from an afternoon hike while he was in Seattle for a minority journalists' convention a few years back, something that happened to hikers too often for her liking. Angela had never met the man, but the news of his vanishing had chilled her. That could have been her. That could have been anyone. "Let's head back and check the other side, by Gramma Marie's garden."

"Before we go back, there's something I need to tell you," Myles said, grave.

This was it, then. They were alone for the first time, and he was going to speak his mind. She tried to find words to tell him her side of the story—how she'd felt so mortified after attacking Tariq at the funeral, how she'd gone to The Harbor for those months. How she'd been afraid that if she allowed Myles to befriend her again during that time, she might have been such a madwoman that she would have damaged their friendship for good. Or she might have melted into Myles's presence, losing herself entirely. Her son had died, for God's sake. What the hell did he expect? Angela's thoughts were so crowded, she couldn't choose one.

Myles's eyes blazed in the sunlight as they neared the shaded path. "When we first set out, I saw some remains by a shrub," he said. The word *remains* did not have immediate meaning to her. Myles went on: "Some blood and fur. I noticed a dark patch, so I took a peek. It's pretty well eaten, but it's definitely a small animal. Maybe it's been there a couple days already, and there wasn't enough for me to say for sure if it was the dog . . . but the fur was dark, and there's a chance. A good chance, I'm beginning to think."

"Lord Jesus," Angela said. "On the path right near the house?"

"Where the path begins. I didn't see a collar, but you can look for yourself on our way back. I don't know what you'll want to say to Naomi."

At the mention of Naomi's name, the woods seemed twice as cold. A newborn headache squeezed Angela's temples. It would be bad enough if Onyx had run away or been stolen, but how could she tell Naomi there was evidence that some animal might have eaten him? Naomi would be traumatized, and she had to report to her shoot in two days.

"*Shit* on me," Angela said. "Shit, shit, shit."

"Sorry."

"This is not happening. Why is this happening?"

"Things always happen, doll-baby," Myles said. He slipped his arm across her shoulders, where it rested broad and sure, but now she couldn't enjoy it.

Angela didn't want to examine the remains, but she had to. She'd spent more time with Onyx, so she would be more likely to recognize him.

As Toussaint Lane and Tariq's van came into distant view from the trail, Angela asked Myles to show her the carcass. Stooping down, Myles pointed behind the expansive trunk of a red cedar at the edge of the trail, and Angela laid her hand upon the tree's trunk as she peeked around. She saw four ravens pecking at what looked like a mound of leaves. A closer look told her the leaves were stuck to something underneath. Angela couldn't see more from where she was standing, so she walked beyond the tree, past Myles, until she was only five feet from the thing. Then, she squatted.

Three of the ravens flew away, but one remained, tugging at the mound. The last raven pulled out a string of red flesh, snapping it away from the mound with its beak. Angela felt her morning yogurt tease the back of her throat, flavored with stomach acid. The bird was eating the dead animal. She had almost forgotten ravens did that. "Get away!" she said, angry, and the bird flew off.

The raven had been feeding on something fleshy, covered in old blood. The flesh seemed much too small to be a dog at first, but when she looked more closely, she realized these were only *partial* remains. This portion had been separated, but it had been bigger, maybe twice the size of what was left. There was too much blood to tell what the consistency of the animal's fur might have been, but a pinhole of sunlight from a gap in the trees above gave her perfect light where she needed it: She saw a small patch of fur, bright and damp. Black fur.

"Shit on me," Angela whispered. It wasn't certain, but it was possible. Turning probable.

"See what I mean?" Myles said.

"God, I hope this isn't Onyx. Please don't let this be Onyx."

"What are you going to tell her?"

"We can't say anything. Not now. We have to be sure."

"Your call," he said, but she wondered if he was disappointed in her.

Silent again, she and Myles circled the house to go to the backyard. The path down to the herb garden from the backyard was steep and overgrown, so they had to cling to jutting branches to make it down the rocky, muddy soil without stumbling. Gramma Marie's words came back to her: *Before you grab hold of any branch, see that it's friendly,* she had said, warning her to test any branch's strength before relying on it, a phrasing that had made Angela think of mean trees plotting to hurt her. Exposed roots grew in descending rows that were perfect as makeshift steps, and Angela clearly remembered making this descent as a teenager.

But the underbrush had grown since she had been here last, and Angela couldn't remember her landmarks, or whether the herb garden was right or left of where they stood. This side of the property had a very different feel than the portion leading to The Spot, more a marshy thicket than a forest, although there were still stands of trees. Long ago, an acre or more back here had been cleared. Gramma Marie had kept chickens, goats, and pigs, growing her vegetables on one side and her herbs on the other. Now, left to its own will, the land had grown wild again. A nest of gnats circled Angela's ankles from a puddle of mud she nearly stepped into.

"There," Myles said, nodding to his left. "I think the creek is that way."

This path was much less traveled, no longer a path at all. A bed of chest-high ferns stood in their way, so they waded through. There were so many spiderwebs strung between the ferns, the sea of green branches seemed to be waving from a marionette's hand. Angela knocked down spiderwebs as she walked, pulling them from her hair and skin when she felt their sticky tendrils. In October, the black garden spiders reappeared in force, and Angela hoped she wouldn't run into one of the webs' caretakers, because they were too big for her comfort.

"*Onyx!*" Angela shouted, almost a scream of frustration.

Myles joined her calls for the dog until they reached the creek, following it until they saw the three fence-posts marking the flat land where Gramma Marie's herb garden had once stood. It was no more than a small clearing now, overrun with weeds. Gramma Marie would be sad if she could see it, Angela realized. She imagined Gramma Marie in her straw hat, stockings falling down her thick calves as she bent over her garden, hacking and pulling. She'd worn big rubber boots in her garden. My God, yes, Angela could almost *see* her. The memory of Gramma Marie was as strong here as her memory of lovemaking with Myles at The Spot had been. Close enough to touch, almost.

A raven landed on one of the fence-posts with a squawk, its shiny eyes watching her. Angela used to feed ravens and crows when she was younger, mesmerized by their shiny jet feathers, but she'd lost her fondness the first time she'd seen a raven eating a dead squirrel. The feeling was back now, in force. The bird's stare made her uneasy.

"Look at this," Myles said. She hadn't noticed that he was out of her sight until he came behind her carrying an open straw basket.

Angela didn't recognize the basket, nor the tools inside. "Not mine. Do you think Gramma Marie left it out here?"

"No, it's too new. I'd swear Rick Leahy had a basket just like this."

"He used to ride here," Angela said, inspecting the basket more closely. It was woven with what looked like a Native American or African pattern, not something to discard lightly. Work gloves, a knife, and some other kind of tool were inside, atop dried plants that had lost all but a shadow of their greenness. Dead plants and a dead man's things.

"Could you take it to his kids and see if it's his?" Angela said. Her earlier visit to the house had been awkward enough. She didn't want to go back.

"Yeah," Myles sighed, closing the basket. He tied the basket's thin leather string to clasp it.

"I almost gave up drinking, but now I'm glad I didn't," Angela said. "I want a glass of wine tonight. A nice cold one. Maybe five or six. Does this town sell liquor on Sundays?"

"No, but I have some hard cider I can bring you later."

"Bring enough for Naomi. If she's still here tonight, I'm sure she could use some, too."

Liza and Art Brunell were leaving the house as Angela and Myles returned. Just wanted a progress report, they said, but Angela knew they were there to make sure she was all right. Liza had let her run off Missing flyers without charge at the store and then volunteered to hang them around town for her. Angela knew she must have looked pretty distraught when Liza saw her.

"Our black lab Miko's the apple of our eye, so we understand," Art said, squeezing both of Angela's elbows hard in lieu of a hug. Art flirted up a storm when Liza wasn't with him, all in good fun, but in his wife's presence he was downright priestly. Liza Kerr was still the homecoming queen in her husband's eyes. Art had shed both a little hair and a few pounds since the last time she'd seen him. He still had his trademark double-chin, but he looked good. Liza, too, looked suntanned and healthy with her hair cut in a pageboy style that was cute on her, not as severe as such a blunt haircut looked sometimes. Life had not been good to Angela lately, but it had obviously been good to the Brunells, and she was glad.

"Did I hear a rumor that you won the election, Art?" Angela said.

"That's why I'm here," Art said, winking. "Missing dogs are part of the mayoral duties."

"Call us if you need us, sweet pea," Liza said, as they headed for the stone steps.

"How's Glenn?" Angela called after them, remembering her manners.

Art was the one who answered. "Doing great! Just turned eight. We're goin' fishing today."

Inside the house, Naomi was as much a wreck as Angela had expected her to be. She'd already called the airline to postpone her flight, and she asked Angela to do her best to reach her director, a kid on the rise from music videos named Vincent D'Angelo. Naomi wanted to put off her first day on set, maybe until Thursday. Angela knew what the answer would be. D'Angelo was on his studio's schedule and wouldn't have any room in his budget for delays. All delays cost money.

While Angela waited for a return call, she wrestled with her ethics. *You need to treat people as if you're staring into a mirror,* Gramma Marie had said, and Angela was a big believer in the Golden Rule, too. If she were in Naomi's place, she would want to know about Myles's discovery. She wouldn't want false hope. And if Angela were acting solely as a friend, no matter how painful, she would tell Naomi about the remains outside for the sake of honesty.

But as Naomi's agent, Angela wasn't so sure.

This is why you don't befriend your clients, Angela reminded herself through gritted teeth, consulting her Palm Pilot to try to find a number for anyone else on the production staff. Five years ago, Naomi had dropped out of a project because of mood swings and fatigue from a weight-loss drug. Angela's law firm had settled the producer's suit, but the damage was done—Naomi had been labeled a flake, and it hurt her career. Some producers still asked Angela about Naomi's stability, and she didn't blame them. She couldn't let Naomi jeopardize another job, not over a dog.

The world's longest day was getting longer.

From where she stood at the kitchen telephone, Angela could see Myles and Naomi sitting outside at the deck table, where they had quietly excused themselves. Naomi's hands were clasped in front of her with her elbows resting on the table, and Myles's hands were draped over hers. Their heads were very close. It was a hard sight for Angela. Myles has always been a rescuer, she thought sarcastically, and was mad at herself for the thought. How could she begrudge her best friend any comfort she could get? Yet, here she was, feeling petty.

She felt more petty than ever when they came back into the house, closing the door gently behind them, and she overheard Naomi say, "Thank you for the prayer, Myles. I needed that."

"My pleasure. Just trust in God, sister. You'll be all right."

Trust in God. That was something Angela hadn't been able to do since her mother died, when she'd decided religion was wishful thinking in a world filled with examples of how God was asleep on the job, or else a sadist outright. Corey's death hadn't changed her opinion, but she envied Myles and Naomi for their belief. Good for them, she thought.

It was a quiet night. Myles went home and called later, begging off on his promise to bring over the hard cider. Ma Fisher had had a difficult day, he said, and he wanted to stay with her.

Every half hour, Angela went outside to walk around the house, calling for Onyx. Naomi stopped going with her, having fallen silent the rest of the day. They both ended up on the living room sofa, hardly listening to the music on the stereo. Naomi's listless behavior reminded Angela of the way she had felt after Corey's death, nearly catatonic. Grief looks the same, she realized. The degrees might change, but grief was grief.

At eight o'clock, when both of them were so tired of mind and body that they were already talking seriously about going to bed, the telephone rang.

"Maybe someone found Onyx!" Naomi said.

"No, sorry. It's long distance," Angela said, noting from Caller I.D. that the call was from Vancouver, British Columbia. Someone from the production getting back to her, finally. She took the portable phone into the kitchen so she could answer out of Naomi's earshot.

It was Vincent D'Angelo, deeply wired, about to start shooting his first feature film with twenty million dollars of someone else's money. "A dog? You're kidding, right?" he said in a flat voice. He sounded relieved it was something so easy to say no to.

"He can't do it," Angela reported to Naomi, and she nodded, resigned. Angela had never seen Naomi's eyes so red. Jesus, she was going to look a mess if she didn't snap out of this, Angela thought. "He says he's expecting you at the hotel for a read-through tomorrow night. You're really going to have to leave as early as you can tomorrow."

Naomi nodded again, silent. She was hugging one of the sofa's decorative Oriental-style pillows to her chest, a mother craving her lost child.

Angela really didn't want to feel angry—she could think of no good reason to feel anything but empathy for her friend—yet she was growing angrier all the time. *You think this is bad? Losing a dog? Try losing your son, Naomi. Try having him shoot himself in his goddamned head in your own house, splattering pink and gray brain matter on the floor. Try knowing you were kneeling over the exact spot it happened just this morning. The blood is gone, but I can still smell it, Naomi.*

"So, how do you want to play this?" Angela said. "I think I should go with you to Vancouver. Either me or Suzanne." Suzanne Ross was Naomi's personal assistant, a part-timer with brains. She was good at handling Naomi, and she'd be glad for the work.

"Yeah, call Suzanne for me. I want you to stay here, Angela. He might come back." Naomi sounded as if her throat were stuffed with straw. "Do you think he will?"

At that instant, the part of Angela that was Naomi's friend won out over the part that was her agent. "I don't know, sweetie," she said. "I wish I could reassure you, but I can't do that. To be honest, I'm getting discouraged."

Naomi seemed to half-smile, as if she were glad to hear the truth. But it was far from a smile; her face looked like she had just witnessed a horror. "Can I sleep in your bed with you tonight? I don't want to be alone in my room," Naomi said.

"Sure. Of course you can. Whatever you want. My bed has plenty of room."

Naomi finally met Angela's eyes. Ringed by smudged mascara, Naomi's eyes looked Asiatic, haunted. Her nose was a dark cherry red. "Angela, you know how I told you I have intuition?"

"Yes."

Naomi lowered her voice. "Sell this house, Angela. Just stay here a few days, to see if Onyx will come back. Truth is, I feel bad asking you to stay that long. I think you should just leave."

The same thought had been gnawing to the surface of Angela's mind, especially after that morning's episode with the cellar. The discovery of Rick Leahy's abandoned basket by the herb garden bothered her, too. It was probably nothing, but she was beginning to feel like bad things were drawn to this house's doorstep.

"What does your intuition tell you about Onyx?" Angela said, hoping Naomi knew.

Naomi stood up wearily, dropping the pillow to the floor. "He's gone. Something's wrong. I don't sleepwalk, Angela. And even if I did, why would I go to sleep in the cellar where your son died? What would make me do that? You know that's not right. That's no damn coincidence. And then Onyx just happens to disappear? *Bullshit.*" Naomi lowered her eyebrows, her face suddenly fierce. "There's something about this house. That guy who came here before—the mayor and his wife—he said people here call this the Good House. Well, I don't know why. Girl, believe me . . . it's not a good house. I don't know what it is, but it isn't that."

Onyx was still missing by morning. After her last, sleepless night in Angela's bed, Naomi left without her dog to catch a 10 A.M. flight to Los Angeles so she could pack for Vancouver. She and Angela shared a hug at the airport's curbside, then Naomi vanished into the crowd of travelers who had their own schedules, their own sorrows. Watching her friend leave, Angela was ready to fly to L.A., too. Instead, she pulled her Explorer into the airport's traffic, then drove north.

Toward Sacajawea.

⚔ *Eight* ⚔

JUNE 10, 2001
Two years earlier

I'M A REBEL, don't misspell, an' I don't take *shit* . . . Got the rhymes, ain't done time, and my beats don't *quit* . . . Ya'll niggaz lemme *school* ya, or watch me while I *rule* ya . . ."

Corey Toussaint Hill's head bobbed as he recited his favorite rap under his breath, a rhyme called "Rebelution" he'd written before summer break. He didn't rap as well as his friend T.—T.'s gravelly voice was a dead ringer for DMX's, especially when you closed your eyes—but Corey liked the way the rhyme flowed, one line bridging smoothly to the next. *You got it, man*, T. had said when he heard it, whipping his arm around to catch Corey's palm in a slap and shake. *You got it, Corey.* This would be the title cut on the CD they were planning to make in the fall, with T. dropping the beats and laying the rap tracks while Corey wrote the rhymes. T.'s brother had a mixer, and they would do it themselves and sell it at school and at parties, just like the Sugar Hill Gang and Puff Daddy used to do when they first started out. That was how a lot of rappers started.

Standing outside of Downtown Foods with one Air Jordan propped against the brick wall, Corey stared out at the sunlight gleaming on the river and imagined he was back at home at his dad's place, kicking it in his room. Playing BET videos, eating barbecue potato chips with grape soda to chase them down, maybe sharing a roach from the ashtray of T.'s brother's car. Corey had tried smoking weed the first time T. brought him a roach, and he hadn't felt anything except his burned fingertip when he tried to light it, but T. said he had to learn how to hold the smoke in his lungs right.

T. had promised Corey he would steal one of his brother's big-ass blunts so they could smoke it all up themselves. If not, they'd just turn the music up real loud and get high on that, T. had said.

Corey knew what he meant. He was high on the music in his head now. He needed to be high on something around here.

Corey knew he could find prettiness around him if he wanted to look for it, but he wasn't in the mood to see pretty. The river, the boats, the trees, it was all right for seeing in movies, or maybe a long weekend. But after a week in Sacajawea, Corey was ready to hitchhike his way back to Oakland. Just when things had started getting good at home, he had to leave and come to this sorry town. Just when his phone had started ringing every night, when T. had introduced him to his friends, *This here's Corey Hill, his dad works for the Raiders, he's got brains, and he writes mad rhymes,* when all of a sudden he'd had the keys to the kingdom.

He almost thought he'd made a mistake after he moved to Oakland in the seventh grade, not knowing anybody, kids making fun of his clothes and the way he talked, saying he sounded like a white boy, calling him Urkel after that goofy boy on the TV sitcom. At Hollywood Academy, he'd always been different just because he was black, and the other black kids he knew from school, or his mom's friends' kids, didn't mess with him. But in Oak-Town, he was an alien in public school, at least until T. came along. If you were in with T., you were *in*. Girls who used to pass Corey in the hallway like he was somebody's old gum mashed on the wall had started noticing him, he started getting invited places, and everyone asked the same question: What you doing this summer?

Summer meant concerts, cookouts, the dopest movies, and sleeping late. No homework, no projects, no essays, no equations. T. had said Corey might get laid this summer, for real, because Vonetta thought he was cute, and she was sixteen and knew what she was doing. She'd date a younger boy if he was mature enough, T. said. Corey wasn't sure if he thought Vonetta was cute because her nails and hair were too fake, but he did like the idea of her lips kissing him, her fingers taking charge, undoing his clothes. She gave him looks in the hallway like she had plans in her eyes. She was a cheerleader and took honors English with him, so she had a body and a brain going for her, too, not just those lips. But some days, Corey thought her lips might be enough. They were big and full and soft, the kind of lips he thought about in the shower and when he couldn't sleep at night.

None of the girls in Sacajawea had lips like that. First of all, you could hardly *find* any girls in Sacajawea—there were only six hundred people in this whole town, a quarter of the people in his high school, maybe not even as many as his senior class. And even when he did see a couple of girls walking around town, these white girls looked at him like, *Wow, imagine that, a real Negro.* Sometimes they gave him shy smiles, but he didn't see that look in their eyes like he saw in Vonetta's. All they gave him was curiosity. Corey had never gotten any play in Sacajawea before, and he could already tell it wasn't about to start now just because he'd grown three inches since last summer and would get a car in the fall when he turned sixteen, a promise from Dad, their secret.

Corey looked at his watch and sighed. Only noon. Days dragged on in this town like they were getting paid by the minute. He'd still be chilling in bed if Mom hadn't made him come shopping with her to help her load grocery bags into the car. He'd hoped she was going to one of the big supermarkets in Longview, because at least they had bodybuilding and PlayStation 2 magazines, which were better than nothing. Instead, Mom had come down the street to this tiny little store with hardly any food, never mind the stuff you could find in a *real* grocery store, a store with some sense. A store in the twenty-first century.

After a few minutes, Corey had told Mom he had to wait outside. He couldn't stand the music in that store another minute. The music wasn't just antique shit, it was *bad* antique shit, the kind of music that made Corey wonder who would pay to record it. He could imagine the singers in front of those big, old-fashioned microphones with their suits and ties, crew cuts and silly-ass grins, singing about the Blue Moon or Venus or being a Teenager in Love and Walking in the Rain. Just corny. It wasn't like Corey thought all the music from the 1950s and 1960s was bad—he liked Chuck Berry and James Brown and even some Elvis Presley, because after all Elvis hadn't done anything except reheat some old blues songs, even if he didn't give any of the bluesmen their props. But the radio station playing in the shops in this town seemed to be on a mission to put people to sleep. Sometimes Corey thought the deejay was going out of his way to personally piss him off.

T. would never believe this place, Corey thought as he surveyed the street. He wouldn't believe a downtown with no streetlights, or even a stop sign. He wouldn't believe there was a bar downtown called the River Saloon, like something out of an old-school Clint Eastwood cowboy movie. He wouldn't believe how there was hardly any neon anywhere, or how lame the selection was at the video store, which used to be somebody's little house and had lace and doilies everywhere and still smelled like peppermint and coffee. And he damn sure wouldn't believe a town with nothing but white faces. Nothing. *Nada.* Welcome to Our Planet, Stranger. Anytime Corey saw brown skin on anyone, he'd already learned they must be Mexican. There were Mexicans here and there.

And now here was something else T. wouldn't believe, Corey noticed. Two boys stood outside the River Saloon across the street sharing a cigarette, and the bigger, dark-haired one was wearing a black T-shirt printed with a big Confederate flag. The boy was giving him a look Corey didn't like, like he was daring Corey to say something about it. The boy looked more fat than muscular, with his gut stretching out the tucked-in shirt beneath the flag, but he was a good size, not someone to be played with. He might be a senior, probably a football player who thought he was special because he didn't know how big the world was yet. Someone like that could be a problem, Corey thought. He met the boy's gaze, and after a while the kid and his buddy started talking, looking away. Corey would never show it in his face, but he was relieved.

Nobody Corey knew would have the nerve to wear that rebel T-shirt on the streets. Why the hell did people wear rebel flags way up here anyway? Washington hadn't been in the Confederacy, and that war was over. Just ignorant, Corey thought. He'd never understand why Mom always brought him to this town, except to punish him for being happy the rest of the year.

A gray horse and rider came clopping from around the corner into the middle of Main Street, like it belonged in the traffic of pickup trucks and other slow cars. The horse looked good, Corey had to admit that. He hadn't seen a horse that color before, that deep, ghostly gray with a tail and lush mane to match. A car would be all right, but a *horse* was where it was at.

Corey didn't notice the rider until he was right in front of him, passing by. The kid on the horse was his age, with long hair so blond it was almost white, like an albino's. He had on a faded Public Enemy concert T-shirt, which didn't fit the picture at all, unless it was a joke.

The horse slowed as the boy gave the reins a casual, expert tug, and Corey felt weird about the way those sky-clear eyes bored into him. He didn't want any hassles, so he looked away.

"Hey, man," the boy said. "It's good to finally get some variety around here."

The boy was staring at Corey in a way he didn't like. Too interested. Either he was a stone redneck or another wannabe. There were wannabe boys like this at his school, talking shit and trying so hard to be ghetto and then going home to their all-white neighborhoods in the sports cars their silicon daddies had bought them. No cops were pulling *them* over for nothing, so what the hell did they know about it? Just like Cowboy Joe here probably didn't know a damn thing about rap.

"Where'd you get that Public Enemy shirt?" Corey said. "A time machine?"

The boy's head snapped back in surprise. "That's harsh. What do you have against P.E.?"

The horse wanted to keep walking, but the boy held him in place, tugging the rein with one hand, hardly thinking about it. This kid had probably been riding horses his whole life, like it was nothing. Corey wasn't sure why that mattered to him, but suddenly it did.

"Nuttin'. You just look to me like another white boy tryin' to front like he black," Corey said.

The boy grinned. "To me, you sound like another black boy trying to front like he's a nigga."

"Bitch, *what* did you just say?" Corey could hardly trust what he'd heard, that a white boy had called him the N-word to his face. He took two steps, his hands braced to start punching.

The boy was smiling. "Dude, you know the way I meant it. Nig-*gah*. All I'm saying is, why can't you just relax instead of trying to come off all hardcore?"

"Man, you don't know me. Who the hell you think you're talking to? Why don't you get down off that horse and say that?" Corey said. He *wanted* a fight now, never mind if he might get a busted nose, get one of his eyes swollen, or hurt his knuckles. Corey knew it hurt to hit people because he'd done it before—it wasn't like in movies. But he was itching to fight in a way he hadn't since fifth grade, at Cesar Chávez Elementary School. One day a kid had kicked a basketball out of his arm, and Corey felt like he blacked out. The next thing he knew, the other kid was lying on the ground in front of him with a fucked-up nose, too scared to get back up, saying he was sorry. Corey had scraped the skin off his own knuckles, but that had felt good, he had to admit it. For once, *he'd* been in control. After that, Mom and Dad sent him to private school, probably mostly Mom's idea, like he'd never seen white kids with good grades and college funds kicking the shit out of each other, too. Corey had steered clear of any other fights, but he still remembered how much he'd liked kicking that kid's ass. He would like it now, too. More.

But Corey knew he would have to cool out. The guy in the rebel shirt and his friend would probably jump in, and he couldn't fight against three, even after tae kwon do classes. Worse than that, he was standing in front of the grocery store's picture window, and his mother could see every breath he took. She was always watching him, expecting him to fuck up. If he started whaling on somebody right now, this summer would go from bad to worse. Things would get ugly. Uglier than now.

The boy waved him off. He had no idea how close he was to getting hurt, Corey thought. "Whatever. You know what I meant," he said. "I'm not tryin' to mess with you like some people around here would." With a subtle motion of his head, the boy pointed out the two boys across the street, who were still talking, ignoring them. Or at least they seemed to be.

"All I know is, you can get your little white ass killed behind that where I live," Corey said.

The boy started laughing. *Laughing!* Corey had suspected this fool might be certifiably crazy, but now he knew for sure. "Okay, forget it, man," the boy said. "I didn't mean anything." He snapped the reins again and his horse sprang into a lively walk.

"Yeah, you *best* ride on. You better hope I don't find out where you live, Opie, 'cause we'll see how funny you think it is then." Corey barely recognized his voice. He sounded exactly like T. when he was in a bad mood. T. didn't fight, mostly because the sound of his voice scared people off.

Corey must have raised his voice, because the boy in the rebel shirt and his friend were staring now, too, paying close attention, not talking anymore. Without looking back, the rider waved at Corey over his shoulder. "*Adiós*, homey. You don't fool me. We're not all hicks around here, you know. I'm from Santa Cruz, and my grandmother sounds more street than you."

By now, Corey's face was burning. It was as if this boy in Sacajawea, a stranger, were wearing X-ray glasses and had seen all the way through him to Hollywood Academy. *Whassup, Oreo? How you doin', Urkel?* Corey wished he could launch after this fool and pull him off that horse. Smug motherfucker. Who did he think he was?

"You better learn some respect, or somebody's gonna teach you," Corey called after him, loudly. He didn't care who heard him say it.

"Public Enemy rules!" the boy shouted into the sky with a raised fist. "It Takes a Nation of Millions to Hold Us Back!"

A man in a billed cap leaving the River Saloon and an old woman in a flowered dress about to walk into Sacajawea Collectibles stopped to look over to see what the boy was talking about. The boy with the rebel flag and his friend were still looking, too. Looking hard.

"Crazy-ass white boy," Corey muttered as the boy on the horse rode off. *It Takes a Nation of Millions* definitely *was* his favorite P.E. album because it included "Don't Believe the Hype." But that boy was going to need some sense knocked into him.

"Corey, give me a hand, please. I brought you here to help," his mother called. She was pushing a rickety cart crammed with brown bags, a load of work for him. She used the voice he hated, the taskmaster voice, like his damn teacher. She was trying to whip his lazy butt into shape every summer, always taking it to extremes. He wouldn't have minded helping with dishes and stuff like that, but she had him outside pulling weeds and clipping trees in that hot sun. Or going up and down Toussaint Lane, or deep into the woods to The Spot, to clean up other people's trash. She never remembered to ask nicely. Half the time, he wouldn't mind if she would just ask another way. Instead, she treated him like a slave, and all because she was mad that Dad didn't give him any chores at his house. Dad had a housekeeper for that. So what?

Dad had promised he would talk to her and try to find a way to make things different this summer. Before Corey left Oakland, Dad had promised he would call Mom and try to work it out so she wouldn't take him to Sacajawea that summer, so she'd keep him in L.A. That could have been all right. He could have seen his old friends, gone to movies every other day. Even better, Dad had said he would offer to pay half of whatever it cost for Mom to take him to New York, or somewhere overseas. Shit, she could have taken him to London. It was cheap to go to London, especially if Dad paid half. He wanted to do something to remember, something *good*. But Corey was stuck in Sacajawea for the third summer in a row, and it was the same old shit. Dad had let him down. Corey wondered if he'd called Mom like he promised. Probably not.

Probably didn't want to deal with her. Corey couldn't blame him.

Corey hated to remember how hurt she'd looked when he worked up the nerve to tell her he wanted to live with his father instead of staying with her. He'd survived a year with her after she and Dad split up, but that was all he could stand, the way she got so tight. *If you don't like it, move out,* she'd said, and he'd said that was cool with him. She'd just about cried as soon as he told her, but it had to be done. With Dad, he always had someone he could be himself with, watch whatever movies he wanted to, not worrying a cussword would slip out of his mouth, because Dad just laughed at it. Mom was so tight, Corey felt like she was choking him.

It wasn't his damn fault they were so messed up they couldn't live in the same area code.

"Thought we'd have backyard burgers today," Mom said, trying to make him smile. She said he never smiled anymore, at least not around her.

"Sounds good," Corey said, helping her load the bags into her BMW without another word. He knew Mom hated it when he was so quiet, but what was he supposed to do? He had plenty to say, and she never wanted to hear it. Dad could groove to just about anything—sports, movies, music—but Mom was all about school and goals and chores, and that was about it. When he'd tried to tell her that T. liked his rhymes so much he was going to record them on a CD, all she'd said was *What kind of name is T.? Has your father met his parents yet?* And then she'd said, *That's fine for a hobby, but I hope you have higher aspirations than being a rapper.* Thanks a lot, bitch.

No wonder Dad sometimes wanted to slap her. He never had, at least not that Corey had seen, but his father's eyes gave it away: He *wanted* to, and Corey didn't blame him. That thought felt wrong, but its wrongness didn't make it less true.

As his mother drove back toward home, Corey searched for the boy on the gray horse. At the end of the street, just when he was sure he must be gone, Corey saw the horse's flanks. The boy was still mounted, beside a bright red pickup truck with a bed full of baled hay. The boy was having an animated conversation with a large man who looked Mexican. They were at the edge of the road, a few feet from Corey's car. Through his cracked window, Corey could hear the boy's voice, and it sounded like Spanish. *"¿Es verdad? ¿Estas seguro?"* he heard him say, and Corey understood him because he'd studied Spanish for two years and was making A's. *Is it true? Are you sure?*

"Hey, Mom, would you slow down?"

"What, Corey?" She sounded irritated, as usual, but the car was slowing.

"Just a sec," Corey said, and he thumped his window to get the boy's attention. The boy looked at him, smiling with recognition. He waved like they were buddies.

Corey pointed at him, then made a slow, deliberate slicing gesture across his throat. *You're dead,* he mouthed silently, so Mom wouldn't hear. In return, still smiling, the boy gave him the finger, pretending to scratch his chin. This boy was looking for an ass-kicking.

"Have you made a friend?" Mom asked, trying to glance back in her rearview mirror. She hadn't noticed the kid's middle finger because he was too sly.

"Yeah, something like that," Corey said.

He couldn't wait to run into that smart-ass kid again.

———

That same day, sweating in the late-afternoon sun, Corey fantasized about Vonetta's lips while he bagged weeds he and his mother had pulled the day before along Toussaint Lane. Shit work, but at least he was out of the house. As he got closer to the property line, where the trail of uprooted weeds stopped, Corey noticed a little boy who was almost the same color as T., the color of the lattes his mother liked to pick up at the Joltz drive-thru window. The boy was about eight, he had a sloppy reddish Afro, and he was standing next to the neighbor's wooden fence. He was wearing denim shorts and his legs were skinny, with big, knobby knees.

There were black folks living next door? Corey couldn't believe *that*.

Walking closer, Corey noticed that the young black boy was talking to that same kid who'd been riding the horse in town. He couldn't miss his bright hair and Public Enemy shirt. Opie was painting the wooden ranch-style gate with sloppy strokes of a white-dipped paintbrush while he talked to the younger kid, too wrapped up in conversation to notice Corey.

A man's call made both boys look back toward their house, and suddenly the little kid scampered off. The next thing Corey knew, Opie was looking right at him. Then he went back to his painting without saying anything.

Corey walked toward him, shielding his eyes from the sunlight with one hand as he left the shade of his mother's property. Opie's house sat far back on the incline, a big trailer with curtains in the windows. There was a barn or a stable back there, too, which Corey had never noticed. The little kid disappeared inside the trailer's front door.

If he wanted to thump this kid good, just one shot to the mouth, there was no one to see. But Corey had lost his fire for it now. "Where's your horse?" he said instead.

"Grazing out back."

"What kind of horse is that color?"

"She's an Andalusian. Her name's Sheba."

"Yeah, a'ight," Corey said. He dropped his plastic bag to the ground, watching Opie's paint strokes on the fence. He hoped his mother wouldn't see this kid painting and get any ideas.

"Want me to get you a brush?" the kid said.

"Hell, no, Tom Sawyer. Do I look like Huckleberry Finn to you?"

The boy laughed. "No, I guess you look more like Jim."

Corey suddenly remembered why he'd wanted to kick this kid's ass, because people called the character *Nigger Jim*, and anybody knew that. But he decided to let it go. "Who was that black kid out here a second ago?" Corey said.

"Andres? That's my little brother."

"You've got a black little brother?"

"He was born in Puerto Rico. Must be black people in Puerto Rico, too."

"There's black people all over the Americas. You know, the transatlantic slave trade? Learn your history," Corey said. "So he's adopted?"

"Yep," the boy said. He suddenly stopped painting and looked at Corey's face. "Why'd you have to be such a jerk in town?"

"Me? Lemme tell you something, because obviously no one bothered to school you on this before," Corey said. "Here on *this* planet, you can't just say the first thing that pops out of your head. 'Cause I'm serious—if it'd been somebody else you were saying that 'niggah' shit to, you would've been knocked off that horse."

The boy thought about it for a while. "Okay, maybe you're right. I'm always pissing people off. I say what I see. Maybe I'm too honest."

"No, you're too *stupid*."

"Anyway, sorry."

Corey shrugged. "Yeah, me too, I guess. I wasn't being cool."

Corey had run out of things to say. He was about to ask this kid where all the girls in Sacajawea hung out when the boy spoke again. "If you think I'm stupid, you're wrong," the boy said. "My I.Q. is 148. Sometimes it's higher. Depends on the test."

"You always go around telling people your I.Q.? That's tacky, man. My I.Q.'s 150, and I don't go around bragging about it. What, you want people to think you're better than they are?"

"You're lying. Yours isn't that high." For the first time, the boy looked irritated.

"What, you thought you were the smartest guy around?"

The boy frowned and went back to his painting. Corey could definitely tell this kid must be a magnet for bullies. He'd met other kids like him who could tear up any test you put in front of them, but who were retarded when it came to getting along with anybody. Corey used to feel that way, too.

"I bet you listen to a lot of gangsta rap," the boy said.

"Sometimes. I like Snoop, Dre, DMX, you know."

"Figures. That's sellout crap for the radio. That's not about anything."

"Ya'll white boys in the suburbs are the ones spending all that crazy money, trying to piss off your parents. Don't complain to me. What do you listen to?"

"Rappers who've got something to say. Political rap, consciousness rap. Public Enemy, Sistah Souljah, Mos Def, Arrested Development, Speech, the Roots, Wyclef Jean. Some of it's old, but my dad turned me on to it."

"That's all cool with me," Corey said. "I'm down with that stuff. Mos Def's a poet for real."

"You ever heard of a group called the Orishas?" the boy said.

"I know that word. What are they called again?"

"The Orishas. They're Cuban."

"Yeah, I've heard of that," Corey said. He had a Cuban friend in Oakland, Osvaldo, who practiced *santería*. Osvaldo's family went to ceremonies where *santeros* sacrificed goats and chickens for the Orishas in ceremonies that lasted all night sometimes, away from the eyes of the police. Osvaldo had a fire of belief in his eyes that made Corey want to know more about *santería*, and Osvaldo never ran out of stories. He told Corey how the ceremonies helped bring his family safely from Cuba, or saved his father's life in Vietnam, or helped bring his aunt back from her deathbed. Osvaldo said he'd seen a man on crutches leap nearly six feet into the air, ridden by an *orisha*, his face full of bliss. Osvaldo also claimed he'd put a hex on the guy his girlfriend was stepping out with by covering his hand with a special powder and offering the poor guy a handshake. *Fucked him up good*, Osvaldo had said, and he wasn't kidding, either. Corey had been careful about shaking Osvaldo's hand after that. You never knew.

Corey would give anything just to see real magic happen once. When he was little, he'd ordered a dozen card tricks and magic sets from the back pages of comic books, always hoping the magic would be real. Something disappears. Something comes out of thin air. Something moves across a table. But it never happened. All the magic sets he ordered were full of illusions, sleight of hand, decoys. None of it was real. But there might be real magic out there somewhere, he figured. People in Sacajawea said Gramma Marie had known voodoo—she fixed problems and gave people tea for good luck and helped bring the fish to the river when the fish were missing, people said. *That* was magic. That was Osvaldo's kind of magic.

"Is your CD about *santeria?*" Corey asked the boy, hopeful.

"No, man. It's rap music. Orishas is just the name they use. Some of the rhythms might be from ceremonies for gods or whatever, but these are young guys from Cuba who've got something to say. It's in Spanish, though. People who don't know Spanish are missing out."

"I'm taking Spanish," Corey said, although he was sorry there wasn't more about magic on the CD. "You're not the only one who knows some Spanish."

The boy's face lit up. "Oh, then you gotta hear the Orishas. I'll go get it." He dropped his brush into the paint can, about to run off. "What's your name anyway?"

"Corey."

"I'm Sean. Are you sure you're gonna listen to it?"

"I guess," Corey said. "If it's supposed to be good."

"You have to bring me one of yours, a trade. When you're done, we switch back."

"Most of my good shit's at my dad's house. But I've got *Doggy Style* by Snoop."

"Yeah, all right." This time, Sean started running back toward his trailer.

"Thought you didn't like gangsta!" Corey called after him.

"But that one's classic. I always make an exception for a classic."

"Cool," Corey said, smiling. He'd have to go in the house and sneak into his secret stash in his closet to find *Doggy Style*. Mom censored his music, and he wasn't supposed to have any CDs with explicit lyrics, which meant he was only allowed to play radio edits and Will Smith on his bedroom stereo. Mostly, he used his Discman and hoped he wouldn't get caught. It would be good to share his music with someone instead of hiding it all the time. T. would probably think Sean was a trip, Corey thought. T. liked old groups like Arrested Development, too.

The trade complete, Corey went home.

In the privacy of his room, he first heard the Orishas' blend of oldschool Cuban ballads and hip-hop, and he dug each cut more than the last. The music was different, but it was good. He recognized it a little, because Osvaldo played Cuban music during the sixth-period yearbook class—they were free to crank up the boom box in that class because they were in a portable classroom and the teacher was cool. Chango was always there in the words of the songs Osvaldo played. Corey recognized his name every time he heard it. Osvaldo said Chango was his personal god.

The Orishas sang about Chango, too. Their drums were probably playing to Chango, Corey thought. Osvaldo had shown him a dance for Chango, clowning in class one day. Flapping his arms like a chicken, hips quivering. The other kids had laughed, but Corey thought it looked cool as hell, dancing for a god. Osvaldo's skin was white, but Corey realized when he saw him doing that chicken dance that Osvaldo was more African than he was. Africa was still living in Osvaldo.

"This music's all right," Corey said, nodding to the Orishas' beat.

With twenty-four days to live, Corey Hill started to believe the summer might not be so bad.

—

That night, Corey dreamed of a door painted bright blue, an endless blue. It was the same dream he'd had every night since his arrival in Sacajawea, always returning as soon as he was asleep, the lone fixture in his dream space. Corey settled into the dream as if he were returning home, bathed in whispers without true voices as he walked toward the door he visited so often.

Behind the blue door, Corey heard someone calling his name.

⋈ Nine ⋈

Present-day
MONDAY

*I*T HAPPENED WITHOUT FORETHOUGHT. Instead of going left toward the master bedroom where she had planned to take a nap after driving Naomi to the airport, Angela went to the bedroom across the hall from hers, next to the window seat, the room with the closed door. She turned the brass doorknob, pushed the door open, walked in.

Since the curtains were open, the sun soldiering outside washed the smallish bedroom in light. Bare wooden floorboards reflected the sunlight, bouncing it back up against the white walls. The room looked like a dream-space, and for an instant it seemed to be a living thing because so many of the sights impacted her at once: Janet Jackson flirting in the poster on the wall with a sculpted midriff, Corey's jeans and bath towel thrown across the back of his chair, his desk covered in CD jewel cases, his wire notebook open beside them, an overflowing black duffel bag stuffed halfway into the open closet door, Corey's Air Jordans in the middle of the floor—one toppled on its side, the other standing upright, just tossed off. Corey must be standing behind the door, Angela thought, certain of it. She could almost hear him breathing.

There was a neatly folded note on the pillow mound on the made-up bed. Angela was so calm, she did not feel the maws of panic when she saw the note, even though a part of her nightmarish vision had leaped into reality. There had not been a note in here That Day. She and Tariq and Sheriff Rob Graybold had searched this room for a note—they had opened the desk drawers and flipped through Corey's notebook full of poems and rap lyrics—and there had been no note explaining why he was dead. This note was new. Angela unfolded the piece of stationery and read the familiar jittery script, an old woman's:

Angie—
I made the bed, but I didn't see fit to move anything without your say so.
If you would like this room cleaned, please let me know.
Rgds, Laurel Everly

Bless you, Mrs. Everly, Angela thought. It would be better if the bed hadn't been made, but this was good, too. An untouched room was the only way to commune with Corey now, where she could spend time in his personal space and take note of the evidences of him.

She needed to see him again.

Angela looked behind the door, and Corey's brown bomber-style leather jacket hung there. She'd given him that jacket for Christmas, and he liked it so much he'd brought it to Sacajawea despite the summer heat. The jacket's brown leather still smelled new. Gently, Angela took the jacket from its hook and searched for her son's scent. The leather smell was strongest because the jacket had not belonged to him long, but Corey was there at the neckline. A teenager's cheap cologne, glycerin and oils from a hair moisturizer he'd started using to make his tight, wiry black locks glisten. At the armpit, the jacket's black lining smelled of deodorant and a whisper of tart musk. *Yes.* Corey'd had a strong smell since puberty, with strong body salts, like his father. Smelling him was a shock. Angela's legs felt weak, but only in a twinge. She wished she could bottle Corey's smell and keep it.

What had kept her from coming to see her son? Corey had been here all along.

She went to his desk next, reading the poems left behind in his notebook. She had tried once before, desperate to find traces of him, but hadn't been able to finish. This time, she wasn't as bothered by the sexuality and profanity as she had been right after he died, when she'd wanted so much to find only his childlike affection preserved, not his burgeoning manhood. She'd felt so crushed by the disappointment of what *wasn't* in his words, in her memory Corey's poems had been pornographic, a source of shame. Now, she read Corey's writings with appreciative eyes.

Sweet honey cream,
wild woman of my dream,

will you swallow me h-o-l-e?
Can I be the burrowing mole
in your field of streams?
Can you hear my (eager) screams?
Hold my Lust with your fevered hand.
Let me taste the Promised Land.

"You were becoming a writer, weren't you?" Angela said.

For an hour, Angela sat at the edge of her son's bed and read, forgetting about Naomi and Onyx. The creations from Corey's pen awed her. Corey's love poems were full of surprisingly astute sexual metaphors, but not all of the poems were sexual. She was amused to see that he'd written a poem about Sean's horse, Sheba. And his rap rhymes, although they were littered with the requisite *fuck* and *shit* seasonings to make them palatable to young tastes, were more than the empty bravado she'd assumed they were. One longer rap, called "Rebelution," seemed to be a plea to young blacks to look beyond society's expectations of them. One of her favorite passages from "Rebelution" was: *Five-O? You best just go. / You ain't got shit on me. / This niggah don't subscribe to slave mentality. / Your prisons don't define me, / This rebel's got a mind, G.*

Inevitably, she came to a blank page, and then another. And another. She'd reached the end of Corey's work. Angela flipped forward into the notebook, finding nothing until she was nearly at the end, with only five or six pages remaining. There, she saw Corey's handwriting in block letters so large that five words nearly took up the entire page: WE HAVE FUCKED UP <u>BIG</u>.

The word *BIG* was underlined six times. The ink was dark, and the paper was deeply indented, so she knew Corey must have been bearing down hard on the page. The sight of the ominous phrase was such a stark contrast to the other writings that Angela felt her fingertips thrill when she touched the words. The next pages in the notebook were bleak white. She checked them one by one. Empty.

Secret sex poems. Secret fears. Her son's secret life.

Angela massaged a cramp in her neck. Corey might have written those last words close to the date of his death. He'd separated that page from the work he cared about, perhaps choosing it at random in a moment of anxiety. Had he met a girl and gotten her pregnant? Had he killed himself because he'd been afraid to tell her and Tariq about something he'd done?

"Was it really so hard to talk to me, Corey?" Angela said. "Was I that bad?"

It wasn't a suicide note, not exactly, but it was evidence that Corey had been upset about something. That wasn't a surprise. She knew he'd been upset that day. She'd asked him several times what was wrong, but this was the first clue she'd come across. Why hadn't this notebook been taken into evidence? How had this been overlooked?

Suicide. The word raked at her, but Angela had always known it was possible. No, it was probable. Would she rather believe that a boy as bright as Corey had found a gun, accidentally put it to his head, and pulled the trigger? A young child might do that, but a teenager? Yes, it happened, Sheriff Rob Graybold had said. Teenagers play Russian roulette all the time. Or, Corey might not have realized the gun was loaded. She'd accepted the accidental death theory only because it was more gentle than the alternative.

Corey's last note had nothing to do with her, and Angela felt relief roll across her soul. Who did the "we" in the note refer to, then? And was there a relationship between WE HAVE FUCKED UP BIG and his last words to her, *I'm gonna take care of you good?* Angela's heart raced, although the racing had nothing to do with the fear that had kept her away from Gramma Marie's house and Corey's room for so long. This was something else. Resolve. Excitement, even. She could solve this. She would find the answer because she was no longer afraid to look for it.

Angela went to Corey's closet, where a few of his clothes were hanging up neatly while most of them were piled on the floor, hidden from sight. This time, she didn't pause to search for his scent. Angela studied the clothes on the floor, which were mostly dirty, stained with grass, mud, and dried perspiration. She checked the pockets of his jeans. She found a movie stub for the R-rated *The Fast and the Furious,* which Tariq must have snuck Corey in to see in Longview, damn him. An Almond Joy wrapper. Loose change. She didn't know what she was looking for, but she figured she would know it when she saw it.

Angela moved on to the duffel bag, and she found a box of condoms in a zippered compartment. The box had been opened, so she counted the wrapped condoms inside, finding eleven. One was missing, then. That made sense, she remembered: There had been one condom hidden in Corey's wallet, which he'd had in his back pocket at the time of his death. She'd brought that wallet home with her, and it was probably in her box of Corey's things, somewhere in her bedroom. She wished she had brought it with her.

Angela found a dozen CDs in the duffel bag, all of them marked with Explicit Lyrics parental advisories. Little stinker, Angela chuckled. She'd run the same game on Gramma Marie in high school, keeping her Richard Pryor albums hidden from her grandmother's prying eyes, listening to them late at night, with the volume turned low. She couldn't help thinking that Richard Pryor was definitely the better end of the artistic deal, but every generation has its heroes, she reminded herself. She'd been looking forward to the day when Corey would no longer be a minor, when she wouldn't feel responsible for shepherding his values, and she might have said, *Okay, Corey, put on some Snoop Dogg and tell me what's so special about his dope-smoking and pussy-hunting.* The day Corey graduated from college, she had planned to share a glass of wine with him, and on that day they could have started becoming friends instead of just two strong-willed individuals with conflicting agendas, the role they had been mired in all his life.

Tariq had never pushed the parent space with Corey, behaving like a buddy from the day the kid could talk, and she'd always felt forced to take up the slack. Dominique Toussaint had never been stable enough to keep track of where Angela was, who she was with, or what she was doing, leaving her to make her own decisions, and as a consequence Angela had been drinking Schlitz and smoking pot at twelve, having sex a few months later, when she was thirteen. Gramma Marie had given her boundaries. Corey had never had the chance to grow up and understand why Angela had been so rigid about discipline, so fanatical about not exposing him to predators and seemingly innocuous traps. To Corey, she'd been the Bad Cop to his father's Good Cop, and it wasn't fair. She'd never had the chance to be his buddy, too.

Angela felt some of her newfound strength seep away as new tears fell. She needed to lie down. She went to Corey's bed and lay atop the bedspread, her knees pulled close to her chest in a fetal position. She waited for sobs, but they never came. A raw sense of regret burned in her chest, flaring hot, but it would cool soon. Grief in smaller, manageable doses.

She could do this.

Angela faced the window's sunshine where she lay, and her eyes rested on the window seat, which Corey had left piled with his good-sized boom box, a stack of clean socks, and copies of *Vibe* magazine. Staring, Angela felt memory tickling her, and something more nebulous than memory. Something she could not put a name to.

The window seat in this room, like the ones in the master bedroom and the hallway, opened up to reveal a cranny beneath the seat, she remembered. Angela wasn't sure if Corey had known the space was there, but she felt an overpowering desire to see if anything was inside. Something *was* inside. For the first time since her Fourth of July party, Angela felt genuine intuition.

Angela moved the items on the window seat carefully to the floor, clearing the cushion. That done, she gripped the whitewashed wood beneath the upholstered padding and lifted with both hands.

Angela gaped. And gaped more, her eyes traveling from one end of the space to the other.

A white towel lay there, spread out with one stone at each corner, as if to hold it in place. A white bowl from the kitchen sat in the center, with a discoloration that told her it had probably been full for some time, the water slowly evaporating. Beside that, she saw an oft-burned white candle, half-melted, with a charred wick. There was some kind of tarnished saint's medal with a faded blue ribbon. And a photograph.

Her fingers trembling, Angela reached down to bring the photograph closer to her face, so she could be sure what she was seeing: It was a picture of Corey at three years old, grinning in the arms of snow-haired Gramma Marie. Her face was already thinning out, the way it had much more in the little time she had left to live when this picture was taken.

Christmas 1988. Two years before Gramma Marie died.

It was an altar. Gramma Marie had kept altars in her bedroom, with candles galore, pictures of Jesus, and all kinds of trinkets, although she had never explained the meaning of the altars to Angela beyond saying it was the place where she prayed. Gramma Marie had often left bowls of water sitting around the house, too, both on her nightstand and on top of the refrigerator, meant to serve as some kind of blessing. Warding off evil. It had always seemed silly to Angela.

Angela put the photograph back, noticing three paper bags crammed in the corner of the cranny, beyond the towel's border. All of the bags were wrapped tightly at the mouth, although the one closest to her was the most loose. Angela took that one first, and it was heavier than it looked. She peeked inside. It was half-filled with dark soil.

The second bag was lighter, spotted with faded dots of grease at the bottom. This one was full of dried chicken bones. No gristle or meat. Just bones.

"Jesus help," Angela said, surprised. Her spine vibrated, singing from the massage of invisible cold fingers. Cautiously, she brought the bag to her nose, sniffing. Just dryness and the vaguest memory of flesh. Any maggots' work was long finished. These were old bones.

Confused, Angela unrolled the crumpled mouth of the third bag—and this time a black feather suddenly poked out at her. Angela dropped the bag with a gasp, falling onto her backside, her palms steadying her against the floor.

The bag lay on the floor before her, stock-still. Several black bird feathers had spilled onto the floorboards, but the movement had been her imagination, she decided. This bag was just filled with feathers. Raven feathers.

This must be one of Gramma Marie's old altars. This altar was crude, not nearly as lush as her old bedroom altar. Angela had regretted not leaving Gramma Marie's altar intact, and now she'd accidentally unearthed one she had never seen. She checked the space one more time, and she found a stack of index cards bound by a red rubber band. She'd almost missed the cards because they were upright, leaning against the side closest to her, nearly out of her vision. She unwound the rubber band. Each card had a single symbol drawn in black Magic Marker. A triangle. A double-squiggle. These symbols looked familiar to her. Where had she seen them?

The answer was on her left ring finger, she realized. Gramma Marie's ring.

Angela compared the markings on her ring to those on the index cards, a dozen in all, and each symbol had a match, even if some were rendered less convincingly than others. The cards were hand-numbered, and Angela suddenly recognized the looping numerals. When she did, she felt what seemed like a stab of electricity.

This was Corey's handwriting, not Gramma Marie's. Jesus, was this *Corey's* altar?

Sitting alone in the bright stillness of her son's bedroom, Angela held her breath. Corey had asked her about the symbols on her ring the day he died. She couldn't remember his exact words, but he had asked if the symbols had power. By God, he had. He had.

Angela didn't know what it meant, but she knew it was important. This mattered, and the fact that it mattered was slowly but surely scaring the hell out of her. Condoms and profane CDs were one thing, but Corey had been hiding a part of himself she hadn't known a trace of. How had he learned to make an altar? Gramma Marie had died before she'd had a chance to teach him, and Gramma Marie had never taught her or her mother anything significant about her *vodou* roots, so why would she teach Corey? And if not her, then who?

Raising herself onto her knees to gaze back into the heart of the window seat's cavity, Angela surveyed the assortment of objects inside with growing trepidation. Her eyes couldn't leave the photograph of Gramma Marie and Corey that he must have placed there himself, for a reason she couldn't fathom. Gramma Marie looked old and tired, almost too weary to smile, and pudgy-cheeked Corey was bursting with the joy of new life. The two of them were posed together, their cheeks pressed close, frozen in time.

WE HAVE FUCKED UP <u>BIG</u>, Corey's note said.

Angela had a firm inkling who the "we" was. And although it was terrible timing, she was going to find every scrap of information she could about her son's last few weeks of life. She'd asked questions once before, long ago, and gotten nowhere.

This time, she had gotten somewhere already.

☙ Ten ☙

THE DOUGH-FACED WOMAN who answered the door looked harried and distrustful, as if she were accustomed to unprovoked cruelties from strangers. She did not smile, and although she was probably no older than Angela, her forehead was already deeply grooved with lines.

"I'm your neighbor," Angela said. "I brought some things for Sean. He and my son were friends. I'm so sorry about what happened."

The woman's smallish eyes were dull, unresponsive. "Thank you," she said.

"Would it be possible for me to talk to Sean?"

The woman stepped aside. Her profile made her look heavier, with most of her weight carried behind her. "Come on in. He's in his room," she said.

Angela took a quick glance around the trailer before she followed the woman's pointing finger. She saw dishes piled precariously high in the sink in the kitchen near the entryway, and in the living room two young children who looked eight and ten were sitting in front of the television set. The little girl's thick glasses reflected the television screen, and the darker-skinned boy, who was older and taller, had an uneven Afro in dire need of either trimming or combing. His hair must be a mystery to whomever was grooming him, Angela thought. Neither of the children glanced in her direction, transfixed by after-school television.

Sean's room was the first bedroom to her right, recognizable by the posters plastering the door and the raucous squeal of a rock guitar from inside. Angela knocked.

"I turned it down already!" came an annoyed shout. He might as well have been Corey.

"Sean, it's me, Corey's mother. Angela Toussaint."

After an instant, the music vanished in mid-riff. The door flung open, and Sean stood there with hair hanging over his eyes. His hair was shaggier than Angela remembered it, closer to the way his father had worn it. Sean had also grown substantially. He was six feet and rangy, towering.

"Hi, sweetheart," she said, smiling sadly. "I'm so sorry about your dad."

Sean flipped his hair away from his eyes, resting his palm against his forehead. He gazed at her for a moment with an unreadable expression, more than simple surprise. "Yeah. Come in," he said, and he closed the door behind her.

Sean Leahy's room was a disaster. The floor had a few clear spots, but every other space was covered with clothes, concert posters, books, traffic signs, naked store mannequins with bizarre body paint, or charcoal sketches, all of it marked with the scent of tobacco. Sean dumped a pile of clothes from his folding metal desk chair and turned it around to offer her the seat. Then, he sagged down onto his bed.

Angela sat, too. "I was going through Corey's room, and I found a few CDs I thought you might want. I remember how much you both enjoy music. I wasn't sure what to bring you, so maybe you can come to his room sometime and find something else you'd like."

Angela had brought Sean ten of Corey's CDs, mostly the ones with the explicit lyrics, because she couldn't bring herself to part with anything else, even music she had never heard of. Now, in Sean's presence, she felt magnanimous. She wanted to do something more for him.

"That's nice of you. I bet that was hard to do," Sean said. He looked inside the bag only briefly after resting it on the floor between his legs.

"Corey would want this."

She'd hoped the gift would relax him, but after his initial probing gaze, the boy was not making eye contact with her. He wasn't obvious about it, but he only glanced at her at short intervals before his eyes went to the wall behind her or to the floor. Anywhere but back to her face.

"You're going through a horrible time," Angela said.

A short sigh, but no answer.

"I'm really so sor—"

"Shit happens, huh? Excuse my language."

This was not the same carefully mannered boy who had visited her home and spent so much time discussing the books in her library with her, Corey's cheerful companion. Sean was skittish and distant, and Angela got the feeling that if she didn't come to her point soon, he would ask her to leave. From experience, she knew grief left little room for hospitality.

"What happened to your dad is awful," she said, "but I wanted to talk to you about Corey."

Sean shifted his body weight, rubbing the back of his neck. His pale blue eyes skipped toward her, then away. "What about him?"

Angela reached into the back pocket of her jeans and pulled out the index cards marked with the symbols from her ring. This was a long shot, she knew, but it was the quickest way to answer the most troubling question that had arisen from her visit to Corey's room. She extended the cards to him. "Would you look at these and tell me . . ."

But Sean was on his feet. He held his palms up like he was being robbed, stumbling away from her. "I don't want those."

Angela paused, surprised by his reaction. "You know what these are?"

Sean didn't answer. His jaw had gone hard, resolute. This was the same way Sean had behaved when she and Sheriff Rob Graybold had questioned him right after Corey's death, volunteering nothing with a cornered look in his eyes.

"Put those away," Sean said, his voice at the barest edge of civility. It nearly scared her.

"All right, I'm putting them away," she said. She stuffed the cards back into her pocket, out of sight. "See? They're gone."

Sean eyed her warily, then sat again, clasping his hands between his knees. He was silent for a minute or longer. Angela sat in silence, waiting him out.

Sean rubbed his fingers together absently, probably craving a cigarette. "I didn't know you were back here until Mr. Fisher came over yesterday," Sean said. "He brought Dad's basket. There's a dog missing or something?"

"Yes. My friend Naomi's dog disappeared overnight. I'm still looking for him."

"That dog's history."

The certainty in his voice chilled her. If she were a police officer, she would have been sure Sean had something to do with Onyx's disappearance. But it wasn't that, not exactly. It was something else. "Why do you say that?"

Sean shook his head, but didn't speak.

"You have something you want to tell me, Sean."

"You're not safe over there. If I'd known you were thinking about coming back, I would have called you and told you no way. Everything about that land you have is fucked up. I told Dad, too, but he didn't listen."

"Well, I'm listening."

Sean leaned back on the mattress, propping himself on his elbows. He thought, then sighed. "Dad rode over there a couple of weeks ago, early on a Saturday morning. He came back all shaken up, and he didn't have his basket with him, but he wouldn't say why. He said he didn't feel good, a stomachache or something. I said, 'I told you so, didn't I?' He was out of it for a couple of days, then he seemed all right. A week later, he was dead."

"I know. It's horrible, Sean. But why do you think that has something to do with my land?"

His eyes swept up to hers again, searing. "Because I know."

"But *how* do you know, Sean?"

"Corey and I both knew it. We were gonna try to fix it, but we ran out of time."

"I don't understand. What were you going to try to fix?"

For the first time, Sean looked near tears. Years melted from his face. "What we did."

Angela felt a cold breeze bathe her as she remembered the words WE HAVE FUCKED UP BIG. Her brain suddenly flickered with a macabre image of Sean and her son burying a body in the woods, their shovels chomping into the soil.

"What did you do, Sean?"

He pursed his lips, not answering.

"I'm not going to get you in trouble. I just need to know," she said.

"We pissed it off."

"You pissed what off?"

He blinked, and dropped his head. "Your land." It was a whisper.

Angela struggled to make connections, and it was like trying to see in a blizzard. "You . . . think you did something to the land?" Sean didn't affirm what she'd said, but he didn't deny it either, so she went on. "And what you did had something to do with the symbols on the cards?"

"We were just playing around. Corey found some stuff about spells, and he figured out how to get you your ring back. Then it got way out of hand."

Spells. The image of a secret burial forgotten, Angela felt herself hiding Gramma Marie's ring from sight beneath her palm, feeling protective. "My grandmother's ring? The one he wrote the girl in California to get back?"

Sean glanced at her sidelong, grinning weakly. "Is that what he told you?"

"What really happened, then?"

"He lost your ring a long time ago, when he was a little kid. With the spells, we figured out how to bring back lost things. There's a way to do it, you know. You use this saint's medal, St. Anthony. Anyway, that was how it started. Like I said, we were just playing around, no big deal, but it got out of hand. Now it's all pretty well fucked, and we didn't have a chance to *un*-fuck it. So, yeah, that dog's gone. And Corey is gone. And my dad is gone. And you'll be gone, too, if you don't go back to California the first chance you get." He peered at her hard, almost *through* her. "Stay away from that house, Mrs. Toussaint. And especially The Spot. Leave and don't come back."

Jesus, this child was certifiably delusional, Angela thought, despite his echoes of Naomi's identical warning. Had Corey fallen into a similar delusion? She'd seen what looked like a saint's medal beneath the window seat, in the cavity, so Sean wasn't making this up. Not all of it, anyway. He sounded like someone who'd fallen victim to a cult. What had *happened* to these boys in the space of a few weeks, a single summer?

"Sean, did someone tell you something is wrong with my land?"

"Nobody had to tell us shit. We weren't blind. You're the one who's blind, Mrs. Toussaint." He was mumbling, not looking at her again.

The first chance she got, Angela decided, she was going to talk to Myles about convincing Sean Leahy to see a psychiatrist. The other two kids probably needed serious therapy, too. Something had been ruptured in this household, and whatever had happened here might have crept into her house, too. Into Corey. Why hadn't she seen it before?

Angela's heart slammed her chest. "Sean, did Corey ever talk about killing himself?"

Sean shook his head.

"Did he ever show you that gun or tell you where he got it?"

Again, the answer was no, assuming he was telling the truth, and Angela felt relieved at the small comfort. At least this boy hadn't had any part in helping Corey carry out his death. It was a horrid thought, but in the bizarre turn of their conversation, that scenario had occurred to her, too.

"But you both believed you carried out acts of magic using spells. Corey believed this?"

"*We did.*" Sean's teeth were gritted.

"And you both believed you had done something bad. And the land was tainted as a result."

Sean suddenly clapped his hands to his cheeks, shaking his head. Tears streaked his face. "Man, you're just like him!" he said, his voice stripped. "Just like my dad. You think this is bullshit."

Angela brought herself to her feet. The woman staying with the children, the aunt, would not like her upsetting her nephew. "Calm down, Sean. I think I'd better go."

"You'll get it soon, Mrs. Toussaint. It's all gonna be clear, in living color."

"I really hope so, Sean."

"That's what you think," Sean said grimly. Angela was eager for her exit, but as she neared the door, Sean called after her in a much softer voice: "Hey . . . one thing before you go?"

She faced him again, and his eyes were glazed. "What is it, sweetheart?"

"Before Corey died, did he seem normal to you?"

Angela felt a ripple of pain. "No," she said. "He didn't, especially right before. I knew something was wrong. He was anxious one second, happy and smiling the next. It was strange, and I was worried. He wasn't himself at all."

"Neither was my dad," Sean said. "Not unless it's normal to grin like a fool and then jump in front of a truck when you went to town to get some subs for your kids to eat for lunch. Your kids you fucking *adored*. So if you think I'm talking crazy, maybe you should ask yourself about that. Ask yourself what Corey and my dad had in common."

In some ways, it was the most reasonable thing Sean had said yet. This family was definitely connected to Corey's death, Angela decided, and she had more than a slight feeling that once she solved this puzzle, it would be worse than two dead people. Much worse, maybe.

"I will," Angela said. "I promise you, Sean, I'm already asking."

—

"Wow," Myles said over the telephone once he'd heard about her conversation with Sean.

"Wow is right."

"That's strange. I don't know what to make of that."

"I'm going to get more out of that kid, too, even if I have to bring the sheriff next time."

Myles sighed. "Wow," he said again. "I hate to make reckless statements, but . . ."

"You might as well go on and say what you're thinking, Myles."

The rain that had threatened for days was finally falling with a steady, persistent drumming across the rooftop, sounding like it wasn't going anywhere soon. Rain in southwestern Washington was stealthy, without thunder or lightning, but this was a full-fledged storm. Angela lay across her bed, stripped down to her T-shirt and panties. She'd planned to take a nap, but her mind had been racing, making sleep impossible. With the sky darkening through her window, she'd decided to call Myles, as if it were a long-standing habit. His voice on the phone calmed her.

"I'm thinking what you're thinking," Myles said. "The deaths of Corey and Rick Leahy may be connected somehow. Sean's always adamant about me never going near your property. I wrote it off as superstition because he'd lost his friend there, and his father and I talked about it once. But Sean never said anything about magic or spells, and neither did Rick. That's the part that has me stumped. I don't know what to think. I'm at a loss over it, just like we all felt last year after June McEwan."

June McEwan, the Sacajawea High School principal, had been Angela's home economics teacher long ago. She still had blazing red hair, and Angela remembered seeing her at the Fourth of July party, even though she hadn't had a chance to talk to her.

"What happened with June? Is she dead, too?"

"No, no. I forget, you've been completely out of touch, haven't you? Last summer, June invited her brother over for Sunday dinner, their tradition, then she got up from the table, walked behind his chair, and started choking the hell out of him. She almost killed him, Angie. His neck was black and blue. He literally had to fight her off with her steak knife."

Angela sat up, cradling the phone close to her ear. "June McEwan tried to kill *Randy?*" Randy McEwan, closer to Angela's age, was one of the gentlest men she had ever known. He and his sister were inseparable.

"But you already have enough on your mind," Myles said. "Let me drop it."

"Don't you dare. What the hell happened? Were they arguing?"

"Nope. He insists everything was fine between them. She'd been in a good mood right before it happened, he said. Then she started screaming about how she had to kill him. He was forced to commit her for a while, then she moved away. I thought about June after Rick died because of the suddenness of it, how uncharacteristic it was. There's just been a lot of it lately. Corey's death was the first thing, because everyone was devastated about that. They really were, Angie, the whole town. A year later, June bowled everyone over again. Now, this thing with Rick."

What little light had been left through the cloud cover was disappearing rapidly with nightfall, and Angela didn't like the new darkness enveloping her bedroom. Quickly, she switched on the lantern-style lamp at her bedside. In the light, she felt less jittery. But just a little. This would be her first night sleeping alone in Gramma Marie's house, and already she was dreading the darkness.

"Any new word on the dog?" Myles said.

"No, unfortunately," Angela sighed. "That was something else that bugged me about Sean. He was *so sure* the dog won't be found."

"Have you talked to Naomi?"

"Yeah, I caught her at home about an hour ago. She's still a wreck, but she told me to thank you for everything, by the way."

"My pleasure. She's a sweet lady. I'm glad to have met her."

Angela paused, feeling the uncomfortable stirrings that had visited her when she'd watched Naomi huddling in prayer with Myles. "I could put in a good word for you with Naomi, you know. She's single, and you're exactly her type."

Myles laughed, although the laugh sounded forced. "Don't bother. She lives in Hollywood and I live in Sacajawea. That wouldn't be much of a relationship, would it?"

Touché. That sounded like it might have been directed at her more than Naomi, and Angela was sorry she'd brought it up. "Myles, I want to talk to you about why I disappeared on you," she said. "Is there any chance you could come over?"

"You mean now?"

Angela almost lost her nerve, but didn't. "Yes. Tonight."

"No, sorry, Angie. It's dinnertime and it's pouring outside. And to tell you God's honest truth, I'm sure that wouldn't be a good idea."

Sitting alone in her bedroom in Gramma Marie's house, the twenty-two years since high school felt only imaginary. Here she was trying to ask Myles's forgiveness after an emotional pothole, probably trying to lure him into her bed for a man's touch after an eternity, and he was politely keeping his distance. Just like old times, when she messed up and fell from his grace.

"I'm not angry," Myles said, filling the silence. "Your son died, Angie. Besides that, we hardly knew each other anymore. You had no responsibilities to me. You have your own life."

Ouch, ouch, and ouch. Two left jabs and a right cross. At The Spot, making love, she and Myles had sworn to each other that they were soul mates. They might have been kids, but it had felt real as could be at the time. It damn near felt real now.

"That's not true," she said. "We've never stopped knowing each other."

He didn't answer right away, but when he did his voice was full of closure. "Well, I have a chicken on for Ma, so let's consider this a rain check. Thanks for the update on Sean. The magic angle is disturbing, I agree. You shouldn't ignore this."

He sounded eager to go, but Angela wasn't ready to hang up and surrender to the empty house. Not so soon. "Yeah, that kid *believes* in the magic, too," Angela said, fishing for a less prickly subject. "You should have seen the way he jumped when I pulled out the index cards with Gramma Marie's *vodou* symbols."

Myles took the bait. "Is that what those symbols on the ring signify?"

"That's what I'm assuming. Gramma Marie believed in *vodou*, like a lot of people. You remember."

"Sure do. The *loas* and all that. You showed me her bedroom shrine."

"It's a shame, but I don't know anything about her ring or those symbols."

"Then that's your first step," Myles said. "You need to learn whatever Corey knew. You need to find out what he and Sean were so afraid of. Why there would be a curse."

His matter-of-fact tone made Angela's scalp itch. "You think Sean's story might be true?"

"No. But if there's any possibility your son killed himself because of his beliefs, you should know what those beliefs were. That ring keeps coming up, so it's a good start, doll-baby. I really have to run, though. Are you all right?"

No, Angela realized. She was not all right.

"I'm fine. Have a good dinner," she said.

They said their good-byes, and the line clicked dead. Angela immediately became aware of all the sounds around her. Rain battering the house in torrents. Three hard thumps on the rooftop in quick succession, more walnuts. The rain collecting in the gutter outside her window, rattling as loudly as a rickety engine trying to come to life. She remembered Mr. Everly's warning about the tree, but she whisked her mind clean, her old, useful trick. She was not going to sit in a dark house pondering the loss of her tree or Naomi's missing dog. And she especially was not going to sit here worrying about Sean's belief in curses and spells. If all of those unpleasant thoughts were going to assail her at bedtime anyway, she might as well put them off as long as she could.

She needed a hot bath. In the commotion, she hadn't had a single soak since she'd been here.

After pulling off her T-shirt, Angela went to the bathroom and turned on the light, examining the sloping fullness of her bare breasts in the bathroom mirror. Not bad for forty, she decided. Her chest had tightened since she had started running, and her breasts were still alert; not an eighteen-year-old's, but not drooping toward Mama Earth as much as she'd feared. Myles's lips had sucked on these breasts at The Spot, so sweetly and gently that she'd barely felt him except in moist brushes. How much more assured would his mouth feel on her breasts now? She would probably never know, and that only made her curiosity more keen.

Jesus, was she falling for Myles again? Or was she just horny?

When Angela bent over the bathtub, she instantly forgot Myles and her breasts.

The floor of the white tub was coated with streaked, gritty brown dirt that had not been there two hours ago. Two wet brown leaves with dark, rotting spots lay beside the drain, like the leaf in the toilet she'd seen her first day back. The mess in the tub didn't smell like raw sewage, and it looked more like plain old mud, but Angela slapped her bare heel angrily into the tile floor when she saw it. On top of everything else, she was having plumbing problems, too? One more thing to look forward to, she thought.

"*Shit* on me," she said, turning the light off. This was tomorrow's problem, not tonight's.

The bathtub drain gurgled, ever so quietly, behind her. Angela heard the noise amplified against the bathroom's walls, just loudly enough to make her turn back around to peer into the dark. She saw her own long shadow in the light cast from the doorway, but she couldn't see beyond the bathtub's shiny white rim. She heard something splat into the tub, probably more mud, then that gurgling from the drain. The muted sound varied in pitch, lower and then higher, merry and playful. The bathtub seemed to be singing to itself.

Angela's fingertips tingled, ice-cold. So cold they seemed to burn.

Mom, can I talk to you? I have to give you something.

Angela expected something startling to happen, and it did.

Above her, outside of the house, there was a thunderous cracking, then the violent swishing of wet leaves. The sound surrounded her, descending with the promise of impact. With a cry, Angela crouched and thrust her arm upward as if to keep the ceiling from caving in on her. Angela was frozen, her veins prickling.

She couldn't worry about the bathtub now. The walnut tree was falling.

"Oh, God—"

She was practically standing right beneath it. By the time it occurred to

Angela that she'd be safer if she ran, the tree was landing. Its impact shook the ceiling and wall beside her in the hallway with an unsettling *thump*. Angela felt the floor vibrate beneath her feet, and she cried out again. The decorative mirror at the front of the hall swung precariously right and then left, but came to rest at a crooked slant without falling.

And that was all.

Angela caught her breath, standing stock-still as she gazed upward, expecting to see zigzagging lines race across the ceiling as the tree fought its way inside the house. But there were no cracks, and there was no more sound. Nothing but silence now except for the rain. The tree had fallen, and now it was down, and there was nothing else.

Angela breathed again, and rational thought began to shine through. She wasn't hurt. The damage to the house might not be worse than scraped paint, or maybe a few displaced shingles. She was damned lucky. But Angela didn't feel lucky. She stood in the same defensive stance in the hallway, unmoving. Listening. Waiting.

Because there *would* be something else. She knew that from a place that did not adhere to rationality, a wordless, unmapped place. She'd felt that tingling in her fingertips, the same sensation she'd experienced on the Fourth of July, and that tingling signaled big things, catastrophic things. She hadn't realized until now how much she'd been living in dread of the day that cold-burn would return, imagining what awful surprises it would drag in its wake.

And it had come. Tonight. Right before the tree fell. This time, she wouldn't ignore it.

Knowledge rustled inside her, trying to birth itself. Angela stood still, hardly breathing, because it seemed to her that if she stopped breathing for a short while, she would know why her fingers had tingled. The tree was only the smallest part of it. She knew that much.

Angela's heart ballooned and deflated in a manic rhythm in her chest. "Are you trying to talk to me, Gramma Marie?" Angela whispered. "I'm listening. I'm listening for you."

Her only answer came in the barrage of steadily beating rain on the rooftop, in a language she did not know.

VISITEUR

Fight the Power.

We've got to fight the powers that be.

— CHUCK D, PUBLIC ENEMY

⚔ Eleven ⚔

OAKLAND
TUESDAY MORNING
1 A.M.

IT HAD BEEN SO LONG since Tariq Hill had felt fine, he'd forgotten he was capable of it. But tonight he was fine and then some. He felt like himself again, better than himself, walking toward the entrance of Club Paradiso with his nephew DuShaun and three other rookies with an easy stride, the way a man walks when life is on good terms with him. As he and the players neared the warehouse-style club's velvet rope, the crowd outside stirred beneath the bright solar lamp. A tangible current sparked through the line as onlookers' eyes danced with daydreams of what it must feel like to make a stadium of sixty-three thousand football fans rise to their feet and scream.

Twenty-ten. That was a good win over the Rams, especially on Monday night. Something to make the Rams think twice when the team went to St. Louis later in the season.

"Way to go, DuShaun!" a woman shrieked, hoping to catch his nephew's eye. DuShaun glanced in the direction of the call with a boyish grin, waving. The woman who'd yelled was with a group of friends, college girls maybe, their bulging breasts fighting to pop out of their blouses, skirts riding up their asses. Almost like children playing dress-up, except for the way those bodies smoldered. DuShaun's eyes drifted away from the girls and he shared a glance with Tariq, as if checking to see if his uncle was still there. DuShaun was a strict Baptist boy dating a new girl he'd met at Bible study, and although he was only twenty-one, he was talking about wanting to get married before too long. He hadn't come to Paradiso looking for girls.

But temptation was temptation. Tariq knew that better than anyone. "They might as well go stake out a street corner," Tariq said, steering DuShaun past the girls.

"That's cold, Uncle Tariq," DuShaun said, chuckling.

"Are you football players?" A small voice behind them. Tariq turned around and saw two teenagers huddled against the wall, not far from the entrance. The taller one was a slouching boy with overeager eyes who looked about fourteen, but it was the girl who'd spoken. Her spiked hair was the color of orange juice. Despite her four-inch heels and enough makeup for three, her elfin body was unfinished. She was tall, but she wasn't even fourteen. Where were her mama and daddy?

Instinctively, Tariq grazed his palm against her hair, gently touching the dry, prickly tips. He'd always hoped he and Angela would have a girl, too, but things had never worked out that way. Things hadn't worked out any kind of way. "Sweetheart, you don't have a damn bit of business out here," he said. "Go on home 'fore I send somebody out here after you. You'll have a long time to be a grown woman."

"Are you football players?" the girl repeated. She flicked a thin black strap from her bony shoulder, baring it to him. "My friend's got coke."

Tariq didn't want to break his good mood, since he had no idea when he'd have another one. "Take your little asses on home," he said, more firmly. "See what happens if you're still here in a while, when I come back to check. See if I'm playing."

As the steroid-inflated bouncer at the door waved him in, Tariq gave the kids a last stern daddy's stare. Their faces, staring back, were blank. The players patted Tariq's shoulder, laughing as they followed him. "Out here in front of the club preaching," Reese said. "Man, you're worse than DuShaun. You ain't gonna save no souls here. They ain't hearin' you."

"For real," DuShaun said. He sounded as if the sight of those kids was enough to make him nearly lose his appetite for nightlife.

But this was a celebration. DuShaun had run a grueling seventy yards in tonight's game, and he'd stunned the Rams' defense when he'd taken a handoff from Gannon and thrown a perfect missile thirty yards down the field, setting up his team's last touchdown. The DuShaun Hill Special. Not only could the new kid run, but oh yeah—he could *throw*. Thought you knew.

Tariq wasn't a coach, but he'd decided to work on DuShaun's arm, remembering the precision of that kid's passes when he was a quarterback in high school. As a running back at FSU, DuShaun never tapped that potential, but Tariq had figured his touch was still there. Tariq had run patterns for him a couple hours each day when the Raiders' practice sessions had ended that summer, forcing DuShaun to find him with the ball. Thirty yards. Forty yards. Fifty, sixty. The boy could throw. The Raiders had drafted him in the sixth round without much expectation, but DuShaun Hill was becoming a star, and the season was just getting started.

Tariq wanted to share the good news with Angie. She hadn't taken his calls since the divorce, but she was still his phantom confidante, the person he thought about first when he had news about his family. To Tariq, there were two Angies: the woman he'd made love to that summer in Sacajawea, who had shown him with every breath and word that she still loved him like she had at U.C.L.A.; and the new Angie, the raving Angie who'd emerged from the wine cellar.

He would call Angie's office later and leave a message for her about DuShaun, he decided, even if she never called back. Before Corey died, she'd always wanted to know how his brother Harry and his kids were doing, their safe harbor during difficult conversations. DuShaun was nearly her nephew as much as his, and it would probably do her some good to hear how well the kid was doing. DuShaun wasn't Corey, not by a long shot, but in the months since his nephew had moved in with him, Tariq had felt better in a way he hadn't expected he could.

That one good thing helped make up for the rest, the aspects that weren't good at all. Tariq had a doctor's appointment tomorrow, and he wasn't expecting any news he wanted to hear. Tonight, he felt like a new man, praise Jesus almighty. At least for one night.

"I'm about worn out. I'm feeling it now, Uncle Tariq," DuShaun said, his voice nearly lost in the rallying beat of Montel Jordan's "This Is How We Do It." For an instant, Tariq was blinded by the club's swirling white and red strobe lights. The dance floor was full, even if the rest of the club was half-empty because the bouncers only allowed people to enter in a trickle, making space inside seem precious. All eyes in the cavernous room tracked them as they walked toward the bar; the effect was like flying, Tariq thought, as if he could float on those worshipful gazes.

"You're gonna feel it, a game like that. That was rock solid, DuShaun. I'm proud of you," Tariq said. "Let's hang out here awhile, then you can go crash. You've earned it."

The bartender was eager to take their drink order, anticipating his tip as if he thought every ballplayer was a millionaire. DuShaun and his friends were rookies, and only Reese had topped seven figures when he was signed. But not for long, though. Not for very long.

While Reese and the others got Amstel Light, DuShaun followed Tariq's lead and ordered a ginger ale. In Tallahassee a D.U.I. arrest had scared DuShaun off beer and pot in college, which was just as well, Tariq had told him, because addictive personalities ran in the family blood. He and DuShaun would keep each other out of trouble. Tariq wouldn't sneak off to the bathroom to do lines of coke the way he used to while Corey lived with him, until right before the end. Tariq had decided to get his act together and try to convince Angie to move to Oakland with him, and he hadn't looked at coke for six months before Corey died. Nor anytime since. He'd lost the taste for it. He'd even lost his taste for his Marlboros, and cigarettes were supposed to be the toughest bitch of all to kick. Corey's death had finally helped him do it. Sometimes staying clean felt so effortless that Tariq couldn't figure what had been wrong with him before. He'd rather have died a slave to coke than lose Corey getting sober, but if he couldn't have one, he'd settle for the other.

From where they stood at the bar, Tariq recognized a group of veteran defensive linemen shuffling to the music on the dance floor, three-hundred-pounders in tight black T-shirts and ill-fitting jackets surrounded by women with flowing weaves and transparent dresses. "DOOOOOOO-Shaun!" one of the tacklers called out, a warrior's whoop. The other players joined in, scattering applause.

"Good arm, dawg."

"Thrill Hill, baby!"

DuShaun raised his glass, smiling shyly. His broad, square-jawed face glowed.

Yep, Tariq thought, this was what he'd wanted. DuShaun rarely hung out with the players on his downtime, preferring videos and his sound system in his room. Tariq heard rumors that some of the players had mistaken DuShaun's choirboy mentality for an attitude problem, but here at Paradiso, DuShaun could show his teammates he was one of them. His coming-out party.

Tariq's mood soared. He'd had a whole day of feeling good, from sunup until now.

Until he looked across the club and saw a man in a white jacket.

A nondescript middle-aged man with a U-shaped hairline was sitting on one of the club's plush black sofas across the room, not looking in

Tariq's direction. Seeing him, Tariq somehow knew exactly how it would play out: The guy's drink was low, and he'd need a refresher. He was going to walk up to the bar and try to talk to DuShaun. And then he was going to get hurt.

The man was wearing a white jacket like he thought he was Don Johnson on *Miami Vice*—out of date for decades. Sometimes, Tariq felt kindred to that kind of man, the kind who had trouble figuring out which parts of his life were long done with, people who went through the motions for no other reason than habit. Tariq felt sorry for the man at first. But the man in the white jacket carried himself as if he had money—his watch glistened from across the room—and his sense of entitlement was going to get him in trouble. This was how Tariq saw it in his mind: The man was going to come up to the bar talking to DuShaun, saying things that were uncalled-for.

And Tariq was going to hurt him. That part, in his mind, was most vivid.

Tariq watched the man in the white jacket launch himself up from his seat, his empty glass in hand. He began weaving his way to the bar, past the bobbing bodies on the dance floor. Even his loping walk looked exactly the way Tariq had imagined it.

Tariq no longer cared how he knew when things were going to happen beforehand. He'd felt the sensation earlier at the game, watching from the skybox: Before DuShaun had even left the huddle, Tariq had seen his nephew cutting away after Gannon's handoff, twisting free of his first tackle and letting that ball soar. Tariq had seen it in his mind, and it had happened a beat later. His future sight was a startling development—frightening, really, like flashbacks in reverse—but with all the worries Tariq had been plagued with in the past two years, he'd come to see a drop of psychic ability as a small, useless thing. He hardly had the energy to notice.

Besides, he usually didn't like what he saw.

"You're DuShaun Hill!" the man in the white jacket said, arriving at last, and Tariq heard his voice slur. The man smelled like a couple hours' drinks, precisely as Tariq had known he would.

DuShaun, who had been sharing a private comment with Reese, looked at the man warily. Most people knew to keep their distance at the clubs, but there was always somebody who didn't. "Whassup, man," DuShaun said, always polite, the way Harry and his wife had raised him.

"What happened to your game, D-Hill?" the man said, using DuShaun's college nickname. "You were running a hundred-twenty, hundred-thirty yards a game at FSU. It ain't like college ball no more, huh? I thought you came to Oak-Town to *play*."

Tariq felt the young players near him stiffen, mumbling. DuShaun was smiling some, but Tariq could see his nephew's annoyance in the angles of his eyebrows. "I don't know what game *you* were watching tonight, man," DuShaun said. "But I'm sorry. I'll try to do better for you next time."

Reese laughed, deep and loud, covering his mouth with his huge palm.

"I hope so, D-Hill," the man said, missing DuShaun's sarcasm. "I thought you were gonna *bring* it. That showing off you were doing out there today ain't nothin' but—"

"Watch your mouth," Tariq said.

Tariq's voice had cleaved the conversation down the middle, ending it cold. The man snapped his head to look at Tariq, and he must have seen his immediate future in Tariq's eyes. He took a step backward, raising his empty glass as if to deflect a blow. "Chill, man. I'm just tryin' to tell—"

It wasn't *exactly* the way Tariq pictured it, he had to admit that: In his mind, he saw himself snatch the empty glass from the man's hand and hammer it against his temple. Then, when the man bent over trying to see if his skull was busted, Tariq saw himself hoist his knee into this man's nose, flattening it into a bloody piece of clay. And that would be just to get himself warmed up.

That wasn't what happened at all. Instead, Tariq felt something like a flashbulb pop in his head. After that, the man was on the floor, skidding backward on his ass. Tariq's palm had shot straight out, shoving the man down hard. The man would feel that handprint against his breastbone for at least a couple of days.

"What the *fuck* . . . ," the man said, cradling his chest. His glassy eyes had gone sharp and sober. He was more scared than hurt. He didn't know if that was Tariq's only blow, or if it was just the first. Tariq hadn't decided himself.

The club-goers in their radius moved away, eyeing Tariq to try to assess what he might do next. Tariq saw a woman give him a disapproving glare, and he felt a prick. She reminded him of Angie, disappointed yet again. DuShaun took hold of one of Tariq's arms, Reese the other.

"Get your ass on away from here," Tariq said to the rumpled man on the floor, keeping his voice measured. He didn't want to ruin this for DuShaun. "Next time, don't come acting ignorant."

The man crawled backward like a spider; then, when he'd decided his distance was safe, he wobbled to his feet and blended his way into the crowd fast. The tense moment left the club-goers' minds, and they resumed their conversations and drink orders. No blood. Nothing to look at.

"How's that dude gonna come up on us like that?" Reese muttered. "He was trippin'."

It hadn't ended soon enough, or maybe that flashbulb in his head had popped something vital, because Tariq's good mood had vanished. It was absurd to him that he'd been enjoying himself only a moment before. His stomach was hurting, and he could smell a familiar sourness rising from his pores. He remembered his doctor's appointment tomorrow, and the idea of it made him feel a tarry anger that settled over the entirety of his spirit. Again, he thought of Angie. He'd found himself thinking about her a lot lately, conducting one-sided conversations with her. Yes, he would have to get in touch with Angie soon, he vowed. He and Angie had a lot to say.

For one thing, Angie was in trouble she didn't even know about. Deep trouble. You-can't-walk-away-from-it-but-you-better-fucking-try kind of trouble. Sometimes, he could see that, too. In some ways, he could see that best.

"You cool, Uncle Tariq?" DuShaun said.

"Yeah," Tariq said. "You all stay put. I need some air."

Tariq Hill had a whole new vision in his head, and his future was waiting for him.

⚔ Twelve ⚔

SACAJAWEA
TUESDAY

A NGELA AWAKENED to the racket of chainsaws.

Last night's deluge had never stopped, it had only slowed, so there was a still a steady rainfall, a drizzle one moment and a clothes-soaking downpour the next. But the rain didn't silence the buzzing, popping, and loud idling of chainsaws in front of Angela's house, the sound of concentrated industry. More than that, it was the sound of community.

Angela had called Mr. Everly last night to tell him about the tree, asking if he could contact a removal company. "Nonsense," Mr. Everly had said. "If it's already down, I'll put the word out. We'll make sure no harm comes to the house."

Sure enough, when Angela looked through the upstairs window at the top of the stairs, she saw men from Sacajawea in the front yard below, most of them gray-haired retirees in hickory shirts, suspenders, and billed caps. She counted six men sawing the trunk or removing debris. Mr. Everly was there, of course, and Angela recognized the others: Logan Prescott, Gunnar Michaelsen, and Tom Brock, who had all been at her Fourth of July party; and a much older man named Rex, who occasionally gave talks at the historical society about the region's logging past. Even Art Brunell was out there, wearing a windbreaker and wool cap as he helped drag branches across the yard after the experienced loggers sheared them from the tree's trunk. Wood chips flew in mini-blizzards as the teeth of chainsaws chewed through wood. Faintly, Angela could hear their voices and laughter through the window—*You sure you got that? Whoa, watch out for that one, Rex*—both camaraderie and counsel. All of these men had seen logging accidents. Rex moved cautiously, unable to do much more than monitor the work and rake piles of twigs out of the way, but Angela couldn't remember the last time she'd seen so much pep in the old guy's step. He was happy to be a part of something again, however small.

They had come for a burial, she thought. A lost tree, a lost era. The logging industry was depressed, nothing like it had been, and these guys had memories of a different time. Angela felt a fresh sadness, seeing the tree's mighty trunk split in half, with one side bent toward the stone steps under the weight of its thick branches of leaves, the larger half resting on the house. But this was also a homecoming. She was back where she'd grown up during the best part of her childhood, and these people loved her. And if they didn't love *her*, they had loved Gramma Marie. It was a good feeling, nearly enough to make her forget last night's fears. Nearly.

Angela went to get dressed. It was time to see the damage to the house.

Outside, Joseph Everly was breathing hard, coated with perspiration and fresh wood shavings. He spoke authoritatively, as if he were the foreman of a large site. "Knocked off a few shingles up top," he told her, shouting to be heard over the saws. "You can't see it from here, not until the last of that tree comes down, but I took a look up on the roof. That upstairs attic window has a nasty crack in it. We'll have to get that replaced. But aside from that, she's lookin' good, Angie. The house is tip-top. You've got yourself a minor miracle on your hands."

His wife would have his hide if she knew he'd been climbing on the roof with his bad back, Angela thought. Two men now on the roof were leaping so nonchalantly as they maneuvered around the immense tree branches that Angela was certain they would fall. Neither man was as old as Rex or Mr. Everly, but they were at least in their sixties. Gunnar Michaelsen, one of the men on the rooftop, had white hair and a matching white beard. He looked like he should be playing a department store Santa Claus, not standing on her roof with a chainsaw in his gloved hands.

"That looks dangerous up there, Mr. Everly," Angela said.

"It's only dangerous if you don't know what you're doing. And these boys *do*." Mr. Everly's voice shook with pride. "I was with Weyerhauser thirty years. Gunnar, Tom, and Logan were with Sacajawea Logging twenty-five years apiece. Rex was with Morrell, I believe, going *way* back. Rex, how many outfits you work for?"

Angela hadn't noticed Rex inching behind them, lured by their conversation. The older man's clothes smelled of pipe tobacco. Either he didn't have dentures or hadn't bothered to put them in, so his words were gummy in his mouth. "Ma was a camp cook for Morrell, so I started with them when I was twelve, stayed on 'til they closed. Then I went to Crown Zellerbach, and that was the biggest one in the forties, through the war. I cut trees 'til I was sixty, then I worked on the loading machine 'til I retired in eighty-five."

Weyerhauser. Sacajawea Logging. Morrell. Crown.

Angela didn't know a thing about logging except that her grandfather John had lost his life to that tough work in the woods, but she heard the names of the companies often, even those that were gone. In Sacajawea, men identified themselves by their logging affiliations like combat troops identified themselves by their military divisions, especially the older loggers. The last *griots* of a bygone time.

Suddenly, Angela missed Gramma Marie—not in the fuzzy way she'd settled into missing her in the thirteen years that had passed since her grandmother's death, but really *missed* her, the way she missed Corey. The daily, empty kind of missing that made her life feel wrong, off-kilter. Stolen. What if the spirits of Gramma Marie and her grandmother before her *had* lived in this tree? Where had they gone now that the tree had died?

"Watch out below!" Gunnar shouted. His chainsaw screamed, and a large mass of wood from the rooftop fell with a ground-shaking thud. It landed with the sharp, pervasive smell of sap, the tree's lifeblood. The men on the ground gathered around the thick, mossy five-foot mass of newly shorn tree trunk, admiring it. These men loved trees in their own way, even if it was only the special way a hunter loves his hunted. They loved trees more than most, she thought.

Someone patted Angela on the back, and she turned to see Art's eyes, bright with concern. "How ya' doin', Angie?" he said. He wrapped one arm around her, squeezing her close. Art's kindness was another forgotten comfort of home. He'd given her a similar squeeze outside of their English class in the hallway of Sacajawea High School after he'd heard that she and Myles had broken up, a week after the senior prom. *I dunno, Angie, I guess of all people I thought you two were made for each other—not just a high school thing, but a forever thing,* he'd said, and she'd nearly burst into tears because she hadn't known other people could see it, too. That forever knowledge was what had scared her. That, and knowing she could never be what Myles deserved.

Back then, at eighteen, she'd had everything to look forward to, or so she'd thought. Now, Angela was growing accustomed to the certainty that the best of her life was behind her, the way these loggers knew their best days were behind them.

"I hate to lose anything, Art," she answered, watching her tree taken apart piece by piece.

"Yep. Me, too," he said in a voice that understood almost too well, a voice that might have sounded like a politician's empty empathy if she hadn't known him for so long. "Me too, Angie. I guess there isn't a person alive who doesn't."

"I about flipped when Art said he was coming over here to help," Liza Brunell confided while she, Angela, and Mrs. Everly fixed breakfast for the team of men outside. They made fried-egg-and-bagel sandwiches in an efficient assembly line in the kitchen, echoing the routine of the loggers. "I hope nobody gives him a chainsaw. Art would probably cut himself in half."

"That's a shame, Liza," Angela said, laughing.

"But you remember what a klutz he is. That hasn't changed. Mrs. Everly knows."

Mrs. Everly's face flushed red. Laurel Everly was a soft-spoken woman who wore her thinning gray hair in attractive French braids, exactly the way Gramma Marie had. Watching Mrs. Everly with Gramma Marie during their regular visits and card games, Angela had thought Mrs. Everly was unfriendly, but she'd come to learn that the woman was just painfully shy. Mrs. Everly rarely came to work when Angela was at the house, preferring to leave notes behind. Today, she'd made a special trip because of the tree.

"Well, I wouldn't use the word *klutz,*" Mrs. Everly said.

"Mrs. Everly's too nice—he's a klutz," Liza said. "That doesn't mean I don't love him. Art's a whiz at a million things, but I see him for who he is and who he *isn't.* He's just happy being mayor, so he can have an excuse to be into everything. He's like a pig in shit out there playing lumberjack."

Mrs. Everly winced at Liza's profanity, a game Liza liked to play with her. "He's been one of our best mayors," Mrs. Everly said diplomatically.

"Best goddamn mayor in a long time," Liza agreed, and Mrs. Everly winced again. Mrs. Everly touched the large silver cross she wore around her neck, as if to remind her Savior that she herself did not condone blasphemy even if it crept occasionally into the company she kept.

"Where's Myles?" Liza asked Angela suddenly.

"Why are you asking me? He's at work, I guess."

"You two looked cozy Sunday, is all."

Angela shook her head, smiling. "There you go again, in my business."

"Like I wasn't always. So?"

Mrs. Everly suddenly busied herself in the butler's pantry, not exactly out of earshot but far enough away that they could all pretend she was. Angela sighed and met Liza's hungry gaze. "I'm not picking up any vibes from him. I think he's seeing someone."

"Not here in town he isn't," Liza said. "I'd know. There's nothing going on with those nurses he has for his mom, in case you wondered. The younger one's got a boyfriend, and the other one's not into men, if you catch my meaning. She and her 'special friend' live in Skamokawa."

"You're so nosy, Liza. It's someone else, then, maybe in Longview. I just have a feeling. Either that, or he's still mad about getting his heart trashed in high school."

"That's ancient history, Angie."

Angela thought of Myles's dark nakedness from that day at The Spot, and her stomach shivered. "I don't know. I'm not so sure it is."

"I've got a plan," Liza said. "How long will you be here? Art renovated the little theater for me, the one in the old hotel? They used to stage burlesque shows there back in the thirties. It's really tiny—seats about forty. But we're opening Friday night with my first play. Why don't you invite Myles to come with you? For old times' sake."

"You're in a play?"

"Yep. It's a three-act. I wrote it, I directed it, and I'm starring in it. You won't believe the cast we put together; one guy from here, a wonderful woman from Skamokawa, and a couple of kids from Longview. It's my first produced play, Angie. Nothing to get excited about, but—"

Angela hugged Liza, cutting her off. Liza had found a way to accomplish her dream, and with Art's backing, no less. Hugging Liza, Angie felt waves of alternating joy and envy for her friend. Liza's choices all seemed to have worked for her, and not a single one of Angela's had. She'd lost her family the moment she decided to stay in L.A. rather than move to Oakland with Tariq. It hadn't been fair of him to accept a job without consulting her—and she'd always known his offer from the Raiders was just an excuse for a fast flight away from her—but she should have gone anyway, law partner or not. She and Tariq were equally stubborn, and Corey had been caught between them.

Tariq had made a series of wrong choices in his life, God knew, but Angela had to admit her own mammoth share. For the first time since Corey's death, Angela thought about her ex-husband with something other than rage. Tariq had made a point of driving to Sacajawea in his old van, the one from college. He had touched her like a lover, seemed eager to discuss a future. They had come *so* close to salvaging their family, that one irretrievable casualty of their separate dreams.

"That's so great, Liza," Angela said, meaning it. "I'm happy for you."

"Yep, we're lucky. We bought the theater space, and we're naming it the Little Theater in Sacajawea. I'm surprised Art didn't give you a flyer. He always has them in his pocket, passing them out like they're reelection buttons."

"I can't wait to see it."

"You'll invite Myles?"

Angela smiled ruefully. There was always the small chance Liza's happiness was infectious. "Sure. Why not? He can only say no."

"Stick to the good thoughts," Liza said with a scolding look. Liza had been heavily influenced by positive-thinking tapes even when she was in high school, the indoctrination of her parents. Angela wondered how different her own life might have been if Dominique Toussaint had been capable of thinking about anything except her laughing demons.

Something about the memory of her mother—she had no idea what—made Angela remember the bathtub upstairs. "Mrs. Everly, who's your plumber? I'm having problems with the tub."

Mrs. Everly's face appeared from beyond the pantry door, much more solemn than Angela would have expected. In fact, if her face had been red only a moment before, it looked nearly pale now. "The bathtub upstairs?"

"Yeah. Have you noticed a problem with mud in the drain? Something was coming up last night. I think it was mud."

The room went silent except for the growling of chainsaws outside. Liza had been slicing bagels a moment before, but she'd stopped in midchop, her knife hovering over the cutting board. Angela could no longer mistake Mrs. Everly's complexion: Her face had gone pallid. Her lips pursed so tightly they nearly vanished. Angela looked at Liza, and her friend's face looked strange, too. Thoughtful, slightly alarmed.

"What's going on?" Angela said.

Mrs. Everly and Liza looked at each other with confusion. Liza went back to her chopping, and neither of them spoke. There was a secret in the air. Maybe two, by the look of it. Angela leaned close to Liza, watching her friend's jaw tense. "Tell me," she said. "Go on."

Liza shook her head. "I don't know anything about a plumbing problem, Angie. When you mentioned the tub upstairs, you just brought something to mind. . . ."

Mrs. Everly drifted away from the pantry, intrigued. She wanted to hear more, too. "Something about mud?" the older woman prompted.

Liza covered her mouth with her hand as she smiled. "You're both going to think I'm nuts, and those guys are hungry. Let's take them their breakfast."

"Breakfast can wait," Angela said. "What do you know about the tub?"

Liza sighed. "Okay, well, here goes. I'm warning you beforehand, it's silly. There's a story my grandfather told me—actually, he told me this story a lot—and it has to do with the tub upstairs."

Angela felt her heart leap, and the tiniest cold sensation tickled her fingers. If not for last night's experience, she wouldn't have noticed it. But she did notice, and her mind was primed to absorb Liza's every word.

"Grandpa was the sheriff in Sacajawea in the 1920s and 1930s. Maybe you knew that. He had lots of stories, but nothing like this one he told me about this house and that bathtub upstairs. I'll start at the beginning: You already know about the mudslide on this side of town in 1929, right? All the other houses that had been built between here and River Drive, gone. Now, they weren't *strong* houses—some were shotgun houses put up by poor families with help from their neighbors, people who couldn't afford land. Grandpa said the houses weren't even legal, some of them, so the people were squatters. And this big, grand house was right at the end, the beacon at the top of the bluff. For a long time, this was the finest house in Sacajawea. Hell, maybe it still is. This entire street had been buried in mud, and all the homes were gone except this one. A couple weeks later, something happened. Grandpa used to tell me the exact date, but I don't remember anymore. It may have been July Fourth." At that, Liza stopped. She'd startled herself. "Yes, it was July Fourth . . . I remember that now. Independence Day. Grandpa got a call from a man named Halford Booth, who used to have a cannery here." Angela's ears had foamed over at the mention of the Fourth of July. Her hearing faded, then sharpened.

"I remember Hal Booth," Mrs. Everly said, smiling with a fond recollection.

"One of his children was sick—Grandpa never would tell me which one. Grandpa always called the kid the Child, keeping it a secret. He said the child was feverish, convulsing, and Mr. Booth needed Grandpa's help finding a doctor. I don't know why there was no doctor in Sacajawea, but some doctors used to travel back then, dividing their practices between towns. Anyway, Grandpa took one look at the child and decided there was no time to go to Longview or Skamokawa to find a doctor. The child was near death, he said. I can hear him now saying it: *near death*. He said he knew as soon as he laid eyes on the child. He got a couple of men together and they all brought the child here, to your grandmother's house. He said it was a hell of a struggle, finding a way past the mud, then having to carry the kid up all those steps, but he knew this would be the right place. He said he'd never felt more sure of anything in his life, like divine inspiration. You may not know it, Angie, but folks here didn't like your grandmother too much back then. The real fact is, Grandpa liked her less than most. He'd been raised in Alabama, and . . ."

Angie had heard Gramma Marie's stories about Sheriff Kerr. About the guns and the buckshot that had marred the front door, until her husband built her a new one.

"That was a different time," Angela said simply, so Liza would move on. This was a story Gramma Marie had never told her about the Fourth of July, and that was more important to her than a discussion about racial politics in Sacajawea—even if times might not have changed as much as Liza would like to think. Corey had complained about nasty looks from local kids, too.

"Yes, times were different," Liza said, relieved to be past the subject. "But that's just to let you know what a step it was for him to bring the child here. He always said, 'Something else made me do it, a higher power.' He swore that until he died. Mrs. T'saint had a reputation after the 'slide, when she helped those people and nursed all those animals, so this seemed to him like the right place to go. Mrs. T'saint and Red John didn't want to let Grandpa and the others in at first, but they finally did. And your grandmother knew right away, just like Grandpa, that something terrible was wrong with this child. He could see it in her eyes. Mrs. T'saint was scared. And the way he put it, she wasn't scared because she thought the child would die—it was like she was scared for *herself*. Grandpa told me he didn't realize that right away, but he realized it later, after what happened.

"She gave instructions, almost like she'd been expecting them. Take the child upstairs, she said. The kid was delirious, taunting her, calling her names. He was also burning up, so Mrs. T'saint and Red John wanted to put him—I'll just call the damned kid *him*, for God's sake—in the bathtub. Mrs. T'saint filled that tub with ice-cold water, and Red John brought ice, too. Another thing you need to remember is, most people didn't have indoor bathrooms like that in 1929, at least not around here. A lot of people, Grandpa included, were still using outhouses. So that bathroom stuck in his mind as something special—a sink, a bathtub, that mirror, a toilet with a pull-chain, and all of it *upstairs*, spanking new. He'd never seen anything like it. He felt like he'd brought the child to a real hospital, a modern place.

"But there were other things he noticed he didn't like. Candles burning. Unusual smells, probably incense. And a drum Red John had in there. That drum really made him nervous. Grandpa said the minute he heard Mrs. T'saint start talking in 'swamp-nigger mumbo jumbo'—pardon the expression—he thought he'd made a mistake Mr. Booth would never forgive him for. Mr. Booth had put a sick child in Grandpa's hands, and here was this lady practicing what sounded like hoodoo. Grandpa says he told Mr. Booth flat out they needed to go somewhere else, but your grandmother had a private word with Mr. Booth and Mr. Booth said they would stay here, and that was that. He really put his foot down. He said he believed in her, and nothing would change his mind."

"Hal Booth was a headstrong man," Mrs. Everly added quietly.

"Mrs. T'saint had a bowl filled with water, and she sprinkled some of the water on the floor in a pattern. Grandpa was paying close attention because he'd already made up his mind that if something happened to that child, your grandmother would have to bear the legal responsibility. Yessir, he'd made up his mind about *that*. Once the child was in the bathtub, Mrs. T'saint used her fingers to spread drops of the water on the child's forehead, on his neck. The way someone would with holy water—but Grandpa said the water smelled like it had rum in it to him. The whole bathroom smelled of rum, he remembered that. She said a few words in a strange language that sounded like French to him and yet *not* French."

"Creole," Angela said, her mouth dry.

"Exactly. She was probably saying some kind of prayers, that was what he thought. Praying to *whom*, he didn't know—and that was the part that worried him. But she'd started in on her praying, doing whatever she was doing with the water in the bowl. And then, while they all stood there, something began to happen. Grandpa told me at first he thought the child was passing gas under the water. There were just a few bubbles from between his legs. But the bubbles didn't go away. Instead, there were more and more. Grandpa swears the whole tub got to boiling like a stewpot on top of a stove. The water wasn't hot, but it was churning like mad, splashing everyone. That took them all by surprise, he said—even Mrs. T'saint. She got that look on her face again, like she was seeing her own death. The next thing they knew, the water in the tub wasn't only bubbling and churning, but it had turned brown. Then, it turned *black*. Grandpa always told me he was a monkey's uncle if that tub didn't fill up top to bottom with mud while they all watched it happen. Mud was flying all over the walls. He said he never forgot the sight of that child's face just above the mud in the bathtub, grinning like a Cheshire cat—but with his eyes rolled upward so you could only see the whites."

Angela's cold-burn was back, this time at full strength, locking her arm. Without realizing it, Angela was holding the edge of the kitchen counter for support. Mrs. Everly slowly sank down until she was sitting atop one of the bar-stools, her eyes rapt.

Angela didn't want to hear any more. But she couldn't open her mouth to say so.

"Somehow, through all that ruckus, Red John started drumming and Mrs. T'saint went to chanting. He said she became like a crazy woman, the way she acted. Like she wasn't herself at all. Her voice sounded different, louder and coarser than her voice was, or any woman's voice. Grandpa decided right then and there he'd lived to witness the Apocalypse. All he could think about then was ways to try to make himself right with God, apologizing for every sin he'd ever committed, going back to boyhood. But after a time, he said, the mud stopped flinging. The child in the tub stopped grinning and started crying. And your grandmother was on the bathroom floor on all fours, panting like a dog. Tears streaming from her eyes. And she said, 'The child is well.' It was done. But it *wasn't* done. I'm just not sure if I should say the next part or not, Angie." Liza's eyes were red. She'd told her story with a passion Angela had mistaken for enthusiasm, but she looked worn out.

"Go on, Liza," Angela said.

Liza blinked, and tears appeared. "Your mother, Dominique, wasn't in the house when Grandpa and the others came. She was about eight years old then, and she was at church, at a special program. It *was* Independence Day, because that was what the program was about. Red John had taken her there, and they hadn't picked her up yet. But before Grandpa and Mr. Booth could gather up the child they'd brought, someone came knocking on the door. Grandpa said his blood went watery as soon as he heard the knock, because it wasn't the way someone knocks when they're coming to call. It's the sort of knock when there's bad news.

"It was someone from the church, one of the Sunday school teachers. Grandpa said the man looked like he'd seen his own special version of Hell that day, too. It was Fenton Graybold, if I remember right, Rob Graybold's grandfather. He'd run all the way from town to tell Mrs. T'saint and Red John something was wrong with Dominique. She'd been sitting up in class singing with everyone one moment, and then she'd clapped her hands over her ears and started screaming like she was trying to raise the dead. Nobody could calm her down and she wouldn't let anybody touch her, so Fenton Graybold ran a mile to tell Mrs. T'saint and Red John to come fetch her. Grandpa said Mr. Booth never had a day's trouble from his child after that, but Dominique was never right in the head since. He said it was as if . . ." But Liza didn't finish, sighing. She looked at Angela apologetically, emerging from her spell. "It's an old story. I shouldn't have brought up that last part about your mom."

Angela's jaw trembled. "What did your grandfather say, Liza? He said it was as if . . . what?"

This time, Mrs. Everly spoke with the rasp of a longtime smoker, although she was not. "Whatever Marie cast out of Hal's child went to Dominique instead," she said.

Liza didn't have to acknowledge it; they all knew that was what her grandfather had meant, even if he hadn't worded it that way. The three women sat in a long, steeped silence. Eventually, the chainsaws quieted outside as the men neared the end of their task. This was an ordinary afternoon in the twenty-first century, the age of technology, yet the three of them were in the kitchen making breakfast while they talked about an honest-to-God demon, an *Exorcist* kind of demon. Worse yet, none of them had laughed.

Angela's brain had locked away her thoughts, and she fought to find them. "Why didn't you mention that before, about the Fourth of July?"

Liza clasped Angela's hand with a damp palm. "I swear, I didn't make the connection until now, talking to you. Sweets, come on—it's one of Grandpa's old stories. It doesn't mean—"

"It's not just a story," Mrs. Everly said. She looked nervous when they turned their attention to her, but she went on: "Marie never told me all the details, but she often called Dominique's condition 'her punishment.' I asked her about Dominique once, about her illness, and she said Dominique was born a normal child, was a sunny child for years, and that she'd only fallen ill later. Marie said Dominique had been taken away from her to punish her. She never told me what she meant, or why she thought she was being punished. But she spoke of it with such certainty, such sadness. I always felt sorry for Marie, with Dominique that way. When we played cards, I think I saw her pain the way few other people did, even though she didn't speak of it. Not even to you, Angie. She was insistent about keeping anything remotely painful far away from you."

Angela's head hurt. She'd had only two migraines in her life, with dizziness and nausea on top of the viselike pressure against her temples. A migraine was coming. Worse than a migraine. "Mrs. Everly, why did you react that way when I mentioned the bathtub upstairs? I saw your face. Did Gramma Marie tell you about this?"

Mrs. Everly lowered her eyes, embarrassed. She busied her hands arranging the plates of very cold fried-egg-and-bagel sandwiches. "There's nothing she said. Marie was a very private person. We played Hearts and I helped her clean the house, and that was the extent of it," she said. "But I've never liked that bathroom, the one upstairs."

"Why not?"

"It makes my ears play tricks on me. I've often thought I . . . heard things. Footsteps, usually. A door slamming. Once I was on the stairs and I thought I heard someone cry out from that bathroom. Not a little boy, though—it sounded more like a girl. When I went to look, there was no one there. Another time, I was walking past the bathroom and I thought I heard splashing in the tub. Water, I thought. But when I went to see . . . I found mud."

"In the tub?"

"Yes, in the tub, on the floor, in the toilet bowl, on the sink. There was quite a bit of mud. This was perhaps six months after Corey died, and I didn't want to trouble you with it. I called a plumber then, but he found nothing in the pipes to explain it. I haven't seen any mud since that day."

"Well, there's some there now," Angela said. "And my friend's dog vanished from a locked house into thin air. And that's not all of it. There's probably more."

Once again, that brought a deep silence to the kitchen. They all listened, expecting to hear a strange noise from upstairs that instant, but they didn't. The three women's minds brewed separate horrors around the question consuming them: *What was going on in this house?*

Their thoughts might have remained unbroken for a long time if Art and the other men hadn't come swaggering inside to demand their breakfast, soaked with sweat and rain, enjoying the shared memory of their feat over nature.

Angela had only seen newspaper newsrooms in movies, *All the President's Men* and *Absence of Malice*—where newsrooms felt important, the headquarters for vital work—so the Longview offices of the *Lower Columbia News* were a disappointment. The newspaper wasn't as small as she'd feared, but it was too tidy, and despite the large headlines from old editions posted on the walls, the room bore no sense of urgency. No one was hurrying to deliver a photograph or disk here or there, the telephones were nearly silent, and the few staff members in the room were languidly completing the tasks of their day. No deadlines. No pressure. No work that was changing the world.

It was nothing like a place someone as smart as Myles deserved to be.

But Myles's office was a different story. The waiting area was decorated with mauve patterns on the wall and a matching sofa beside the secretary's desk, and Angela could tell even with the door closed that the office must be large. One person was waiting to see Myles, a middle-aged man in a tie and dress shirt who looked anxious. At least Myles has power, she thought. The sign on the office door was brass and stylish: MYLES R. FISHER, MANAGING EDITOR. Not bad.

The fiftyish secretary, who wore too much eye shadow, arched her eyebrows and asked Angela how she could help her. Angela said she wanted to see *Mr. Fisher*, and no, she didn't have an appointment, but please buzz in and tell *Mr. Fisher* she was here. If he was busy, she would happy to be wait on the sofa until *Mr. Fisher* was ready to see her.

Myles came out right away, and a half-dozen men and women carrying notebooks trailed behind him. It seemed likely that Myles had cut their meeting short when he heard she was here. Angela admired Myles's deep violet dress shirt and silver-gray tie beneath his tailored gray suit. He might be dressing like a woodsman in Sacajawea, but when he came to work in Longview, he still looked like Washington, D.C.

"Where did you learn how to *dress?*" Angela said as he hugged her. She wished she'd kept her mouth shut when she noticed the secretary's curious eyes, but it was too late now. Myles gave her a mock frown, then patted her shoulder to guide her into his office. Myles told the waiting man he would need a few more minutes. The last thing Angela saw before Myles closed the door behind them was the waiting man's solicitous grin.

"Well, look who's the H.N.I.C.," Angela teased. "Mr. Head Negro In Charge."

"It's not as much fun as it looks. I might have to give out layoff notices early next year," Myles said, offering her a seat in one of two leather chairs before his desk. There was a conference table for six by the window, flanked by mahogany bookshelves. Somehow, even potted palms were getting enough light in here, growing like a jungle. The office was beautiful.

"I can see why the paper is having money problems," Angela said. "Was this office like this when you got here, or did you give them a list of demands?"

"I made a few suggestions about the work environment I prefer, and in return they have a better newspaper that sells more copies," Myles said, his eyes laughing. There was a touch of shark in him, just as there was in her; they'd always recognized that in each other. Myles sat at the edge of his desk, where the pressed gray leg of his pants was four inches from her knee. She couldn't remember the last time she'd noticed anyone's proximity like that, but she enjoyed noticing it.

"I'm thrilled you're here, Angie. I wish I'd known you were coming, but"—he shrugged—"can you stay in town another hour, until five? I'll take off early, and we'll have coffee. There's a Starbucks here now."

"Yeah, I'll just go to my room," Angela said. "You can pick me up when you're ready."

Myles's expression changed, dimming. "What do you mean? What room?"

Angela hated to let go of the playfulness she'd been holding on to since she walked into the newspaper building, but she must have wanted to talk about it, because there it was. "I'm not staying at the house tonight," she said. Her voice didn't crack, no small accomplishment.

Myles leaned closer, concerned. "Is it because your tree fell?"

"Jesus," Angela said, laughing despite the sting in her throat. "Are you running a story about it in tomorrow's paper? How did you hear about my tree?"

"Small town, doll-baby. Art came to see me about a news story earlier today. He told me."

"No, it's not the tree. It's a lot of other things. You don't have time to talk now, so can you come to the Red Lion later? I'm in Room 205. Or I can meet you at Starbucks. . . ."

"No, no," Myles said, standing. "Of course I'll come pick you up. Room 205. I'm just sorry you're having such a hard time up here, Angie. I wish I didn't have this last meeting. But I should be finished in an hour, and I'll zip right over. We can have an early dinner. There's a decent Red Lobster close to your hotel. Good biscuits."

"It's hard to say no to good biscuits."

"Then we're on," Myles said, smiling.

They had shared only a handful of words, and Angela felt brighter already, at least in some small space of her psyche. She was trusting her instincts—she felt determined to, since intuition had served her so well over the last couple of days—and her instincts had brought her to Myles. She hoped she wasn't only using her worries to flirt with him, but she couldn't help that. She needed him.

As Myles had promised, the Red Lobster near Three Rivers Mall in

Longview had excellent biscuits. Angela was grateful to be in a large, busy restaurant. In L.A., she'd always complained that she ate out too much, but after a few days of fixing meals at home, Angela was glad to eat out. Already, she felt more steady, back on familiar turf. The menu was endless. She ordered a frozen margarita just because it was so easy.

Myles heard her story from beginning to end, everything that had happened since their telephone conversation. The long series of events surprised even her, given that fewer than twenty-four hours had passed. But it was all there, in its amorphous awfulness.

"And now you think I'm a raving lunatic," she finished.

Myles had been gazing at the ceiling while she spoke, concentrating. He looked at her and squeezed her hand across the table. "No, I don't. I promise you."

"Then you believe my mother might have been possessed in 1929?" Her story told, Angela's mood lightened again. She found herself smiling. "It would damn sure explain a lot."

"It would explain a lot in *most* families," Myles said. "You're looking for the easy answer, Angie. There's a lot your demon theory doesn't explain. If your mother was possessed in 1929, what does that explain about Corey? That was more than seventy years later."

There, Angela was stumped. She'd been trying to think up the answer to that since Liza's story. "I don't know," she sighed. "It's an inherited curse? It jumps a generation? Or maybe it's something in the house itself, something he got too close to. The tub, for all I know."

"And Naomi Price's dog?"

Angela sighed. "Maybe coyotes. Or, maybe the dog has something to do with it, too. I don't know, Myles. But I can't spend another night there. I'm in the film business, remember—and if this were a movie, this is the part where the audience would be screaming for the woman to get out of the house. So that's exactly what I'm doing."

"That feels like good, sound judgment to me."

Angela stared, skeptical. "Really?"

"Absolutely."

"You think I have a good reason to be afraid of the house?"

"I think you need to sleep somewhere you won't be afraid."

She wanted more, but she could live with that. He wouldn't humor her; Myles had always had an honest soul. He told you what he thought, no bullshit. She'd learned long ago never to ask him any questions she didn't want the answers to. Angela sipped the last of her margarita, checking for the waitress so she could start on another. Her head already felt lighter, more detached. "Myles, I know you would sit here and talk to me all night if you thought you needed to. But you have to go, don't you? I get the feeling you have someone to answer to."

"Ma has a nurse."

"I'm not talking about Ma Fisher."

Impatience flitted across Myles's face, but quickly melted away. He stared at the tablecloth and sighed, resting his back against the booth's cushion. "You have too many other things going on to worry about that, Angie."

"I'm sorry, but I don't like not knowing. Every time I'm around you, I feel someone watching over your shoulder, and I'm trying to understand why," she said.

Myles waited to answer, but not long. "Her name is Luisah. She lives here in Longview. She's a yoga instructor. We've been seeing each other for six months." He delivered his news with little inflection, hands clasped on the tabletop.

The pain came, a small ripple over her. She waited for it to subside, but the wait took longer than she'd expected. *Damn.* Myles had a girlfriend. "My instincts are amazing me lately," she said, but for a moment, neither of them could think of what to say next. Angela heard clinking silverware, a drone of conversation, and Latin-themed Muzak. She missed her margarita, badly.

"You were right. This wasn't a good time," she said.

Myles laughed, but it wasn't a happy sound. "I didn't think it would be." He wasn't about to tell any more than he needed to, damn him. He was too merciful.

"Do you love her?"

At that, surprise sparked in Myles's eyes. "Why are you asking that?"

"It's something else I want to know. If you love her."

Instead of answering, Myles searched for their missing waitress, and he found her with a wave. He asked her to bring the check before Angela had time to order her second drink. "Okay, I withdraw the question," Angela said after the waitress hurried off.

"You don't have to withdraw the question. It's just not an easy question, and it's especially hard to talk about it with you. I hope you know why."

"Of course I know why," Angela said. "It's harder for me. I'm pretty sure my ex-husband had a girlfriend named Luisa. She's a recurring character, and I'm beginning not to like her."

Myles smiled sadly, a faraway look in his eyes. "You would like this one," he said. When he exhaled, her napkin fluttered in his breath. "I'm sorry, Angie. I should have told you right away. But I didn't know if . . ."

"If it would bother me."

He shrugged. "Yeah."

"I wish it didn't," she said. "But it does."

"So I can see." The check came back with lightning speed. Myles had left his American Express Platinum Card on the table, so the waitress took it and vanished again. "Do you think maybe we ought to talk about your grandmother's house instead?" he said.

"No, that's okay. I've said what I wanted to say. I'm just tired now. I want to get back to my room and fall asleep to HBO."

"Angie, listen," he began. "Luisah is . . ." He didn't finish.

Shit. He does love her then, Angela thought. "She's what?"

"She's a good person. She's mixed, black and Japanese. She's a vegetarian. We have fun together. We go to plays and art-house movies in Seattle. There's an A.M.E. church up there we like, so we go a couple times a month. We go hiking. Am I in love? I don't know. The last time I knew I was in love, I was eighteen years old."

Angela felt unsettled by the magnetism in Myles's eyes. She could not look away from him, and she didn't have a snappy response this time, except in her quickening heartbeat.

"Six months isn't a long time," she said, already sorry for saying it.

"It isn't a short time."

Their waitress returned right in time.

The drive back to the hotel was practically no more than crossing the rain-slick street, and Angela didn't have time to think of a way to extricate herself from her conversation with Myles painlessly. She'd wanted to know, but knowing was giving her gas. The true sign of love, she thought. As Angela concentrated on calming her bowels, her mind flashed her an image of a bathtub full of churning water, turning brown, then black, and she felt her throat constrict.

The Red Lion was at the edge of Kelso, Longview's sister city, near the freeway ramp. Myles's black Saturn came to a stop before she realized it, parked in front of the automatic double doors at the hotel lobby entrance. An empty luggage cart gleamed in brass outside. Most people who stopped here never ventured beyond room service, she figured. It was a business hotel for people passing through Longview on their way to other places, and in that sense it suited her perfectly.

Myles allowed the car to idle, but when she didn't move, he switched the engine off. With the windows rolled up, the scent of the cologne she recognized from the Fourth of July party filled the car, spicy and pleasant. Angela's arms and legs felt like hot oven coils, the way they had in high school when she and Myles sat beside each other on Gramma Marie's couch, trying to touch and yet not touching. This was a familiar place for them. Then, as now, Angela wanted to lean over to kiss him, or reach boldly for his thigh. A king-sized bed was waiting in her room, and Gramma Marie was no longer monitoring her chastity, or what had been left of it.

But Angela had started this, and she had to finish it.

"I'm happy for you, Myles," she said. "Guess I should have come back six months ago."

Myles gazed at the steering wheel, blinking. "There is that." His voice was solemn.

"Our matchmaker friend Liza's sure going to be disappointed. She thinks you're waiting for me."

"I was," he said, gazing at her askance, and her heart twitched. "That summer you came back. I'd heard you were in town with your son, your marriage was in trouble. I wanted you to be happy, that was the main thing. But with Ma getting sick when she did, it started to feel a little like . . . it was supposed to happen that way. I'd be back, you'd be back. Something might happen. We'd pick up where we'd gone wrong. Then, Tariq came. And Corey died. It's in my letters."

Angela closed her eyes. Her chest seemed to be splintering. "Shit. I couldn't read them." She could hardly remember why, except that she'd tried to blot out everything after July Fourth. "One more reason to wish my son had never died," she said finally.

Her comment felt ugly, but some things you just had to laugh at. You laugh or you cry.

He kissed her cheek, pressing his lips firmly. "The least reason," he whispered.

Angela held his face with her palm. His skin was rougher than it had been in high school, marred but still wonderfully his. Two inches separated their lips. "What's wrong with me? Is it normal to hang on to a high school thing?" she said.

Myles covered her hand, then brought it down from his face until her hand rested on her own knee. He patted her knuckles before taking his hand away, and she felt the absence of his body heat. "It's not normal, and it's not just you," he said. "What happened with us is the closest thing I've known to magic. And it hurts like a sonofabitch sometimes, speaking for myself. But here's the thing, doll-baby: We had something special at your Gramma Marie's house, just like we had something special at The Spot. I can't explain it. But you know."

"Yes," she said.

"Well, let's keep that memory, then. That's our mutual gift. As for the rest of it, I've spent years banging my head against the wall over why we're always pushed together and pulled apart. That almost drove me crazy after high school, lady, and it started to drive me crazy again after Corey died. But it dawned on me one day that I'm not *supposed* to understand—and as long as I remember that, I'm at peace." And he was. Myles sounded serene. Angela tried to remember ever seeing this kind of serenity up close, much less experiencing it.

Myles rubbed her chin. "I don't know what's going on at the house lately, why horrible things have happened there," he said, "but I do know it can't be that house itself. I kissed you in that house, on your grandmother's sofa. Any place that can give us what we felt can't be marked with some kind of evil, some curse. Not your Gramma Marie's place. I don't believe that, Angela. I won't."

"I don't understand it either, Myles. But I think it is. Somehow, it is."

They ran out of words. The silence in the car only heightened Angela's awareness of Myles's physical presence, his maleness, and their nearness felt insufferable. She wished she and Myles were different people, because truly selfish people always seemed to get what they wanted, no matter what the consequences. But she'd learned too much about consequences to ignore them.

"Tell Luisah I'm sorry I kept you," Angela said.

"I'll do that," Myles said. She heard the relief in his voice.

"Tell her if she gets tired of you, I don't mind secondhand goods."

"I'll leave that part out," he said, smiling. He paused. "I love you, doll-baby. Always have."

"Me, too." Her voice was a squeak. It took more strength than Angela would have thought imaginable to push open her car door and climb out to stand on her own feet, and more still to watch Myles's car round the driveway and leave.

The eighteen-year-old she had been when she had left Sacajawea shouldn't have had the power to make the decision to send Myles away, she thought. An eighteen-year-old had no way to understand how many acts in life, once done, could not be taken back.

⚛ *Thirteen* ⚛

SACAJAWEA
JUNE 20, 2001

"THIS IS SOME BULLSHIT. As usual, this lady is tripping," Corey muttered.

The upstairs junk room looked worse than he remembered, clusters of things tangled into each other in a mess; scarred old bureaus, vanities and bookshelves, faded draperies and linens, piles of books and newspapers, and boxes stacked until they were as tall as he was, making him feel like he was standing at the entrance of a maze. The room was on the sunny side of the house, hot as Mercury because there were no shades or curtains over the large double window. This room felt airless, and dust was already tickling his nose. He'd told Mom his hay fever had gotten worse in the past year, but she'd given him a look like she thought he was making it up to get out of doing some work. Why was she so quick to believe she was being lied to all the time?

"This lamp is awesome," Sean said, his voice muffled because he was hidden behind boxes, out of Corey's sight. "I bet it's, like, eighty years old. Think your mom'll let me have it?"

"The way you're so busy kissing her ass all the time, she'll let you have anything you want," Corey said, half to himself. Sean treated every visit to his house like a field trip, pulling his *oh, gosh* act. *What an awesome library, Mrs. Toussaint! Do you mind if I borrow this book? Oh, yes, we read Richard Wright and Zora Neale Hurston in my honors English class in Santa Cruz last year, Mrs. Toussaint. This is such a great photograph of your grandmother, Mrs. Toussaint. Have you thought about enlarging it and framing it on your wall? Your job is so cool, Mrs. Toussaint—I'd love to meet celebrities all the time.* Corey figured Sean was acting like that because he didn't have a mother, just his dad and his sister and brothers, but it still got on his nerves. Let Sean come here and try to live with her a few days if he thought his mom was so damn great. That would give him a quick reality check.

Straightening up the junk room was the latest project Mom had laid on him, as if she weren't already taking up all his time. She'd made him read two books and write reports on them last summer, but this year he had to read three—and they had to be books in Gramma Marie's library, so he could forget about Stephen King or Steven Barnes or Tom Clancy, the books he read for fun. He'd tried to find the shortest, thinnest books he could, but James Baldwin's *Go Tell It on the Mountain* was too full of problems to enjoy on a summer's day. Baldwin's language was deep, and Corey could relate to the teenage character wrapped up in his family's dramas, but he couldn't give himself over to the book. Maybe he was too pissed at Mom to let himself like it. Corey felt like he spent all his time working and reading, but he'd rather be reading than cleaning, that was for damn sure. He hadn't made this mess. Why should he have to clean it up?

"I don't know what the hell she expects me to do with all this shit," Corey said.

"She said to make it neat. Maybe you should put the furniture on one side and the boxes on the other," Sean said, straining his thin arms to open the window. When he heaved, the window gave way with a grating squeal, and fresh air flew into the room. "I'll help you. It won't take that long. Then we can go ride out back."

Corey almost smiled at that idea. Sean had first let him ride Sheba a few days after they met, and he'd liked sitting high atop the horse's broad back, feeling the jarring motion of Sheba's strides beneath him, snapping his neck back. He'd gone horseback riding at summer camps when he was younger, but it was different to be on your own, riding on a trail or downtown with Sean, talking while they let the horses walk. He had the hang of it pretty much, pulling the reins to get Sheba to go where he wanted. He'd love to be riding in the shaded woods behind the house, over to the creek the horses liked to drink from, instead of standing here in all this mess.

"She's got people she pays who could do this. That's the fucked-up part," Corey said.

"You cuss a lot. You ever notice that?"

"And if I bend over at the right angle, you can kiss my ass. You ever notice that?"

Sean laughed. "I'm just saying. Miguelito's going around the house saying *bullshit* all the time now, and my dad thinks it's my fault."

Corey laughed. "I keep forgetting to watch my mouth around little kids. Sorry. It's a habit."

"Everybody's got their bad habits," Sean said, and suddenly Corey smelled cigarette smoke. He whipped around and saw Sean leaning out of the open window, blowing smoke outside while his arm dangled over the windowsill. He was gazing out toward the woods.

"Put that out, man. For real."

"The window's open," Sean said, like he couldn't see that with his own eyes.

"Shit, I don't care. My mom's got a nose like you wouldn't believe. She's probably smelling that all the way downstairs, and she's gonna come up here fussing. Your dad might let you smoke at your house, but that's a hippie thing. My mom's not like that."

Sean shrugged, and smoke floated out of his nostrils in two streams, the way Warner Brothers cartoon characters looked when they were supposed to be mad. "He wants me to quit, he just doesn't hassle me about it. Know what, though? I think I'm hooked on these things."

"Yeah, like my dad. He can't go five minutes without lighting up. But that's not my problem. You can take your nicotine junkie ass outside and smoke, but you've got to put that shit out in here."

Sighing, Sean mashed the cigarette out against the sole of his shoe and flicked it out of the window. "Whatever."

"You better go find that cigarette later, too. If she finds it first, she'll be all over me."

"You're really scared of your mean ol' mom, huh?" Sean said, grinning at him.

"Fuck you. You don't have to live here."

"I bet you can't go ten minutes without cussing."

"That's a bet. Five bucks," Corey said.

"Make it twenty minutes for ten bucks, then. Starting now."

"You're on. Easy money," Corey said, and they shook on it. Then, Corey sneezed. After he sneezed, he had to stop himself from saying *goddamned dusty-ass room*. He almost lost the bet, just that fast. Corey picked up one of the old newspapers, a Portland *Oregonian*, and the headline was from the 1970s, something about Watergate. If he dug to the bottom of the newspaper stack, he'd probably find headlines about everything from the first space flight to the start of World War I. Maybe older stories than that. There must be a hundred years' worth of junk in the room alone.

Corey and Sean pushed an old wicker bureau and rickety wooden dining room chairs to one side to begin clearing a path. His mother had told him she wanted to be able to walk through and sort out what to keep, but if it were up to Corey, he'd just hire a crew to bag it all up and haul it to a dump. What was the point of letting it pile up? Dad said being a pack rat was a defense mechanism, a way people tried to hold off death. If that was true, it must have been genetic, because Gramma Marie had it, and Mom was the same way at home. She hardly threw anything away. She had every school paper and holiday card he'd ever written in boxes in her closet somewhere.

Sean started rattling about the Seahawks and why he thought they were going to have a better season this year, probably better than the Raiders, which was a joke. Corey kept his mouth shut because he knew Sean was only trying to goad him into cursing. He wouldn't fall for that.

But Corey lost the bet anyway.

After he and Sean moved a stack of boxes out of their path, Corey got his first good look at the closet door in back of the room, behind a coatrack draped in fabrics. He sneezed again, but he nearly swallowed it back in surprise. Goose bumps swelled on his arms. He stumbled toward the door, toppling the coatrack as he shoved it out of his way.

The closet door was painted bright blue.

"Holy *shit*," Corey said.

Sean let out a triumphant laugh. "Seventeen minutes! Aw, man, you had me going, but I knew you couldn't last. You're so pathetic. You owe me ten bucks."

Corey ignored Sean, standing before the door as he gazed up and down. The paint looked fresh and vivid, exactly as he'd known it would. His gaze rested on the glass doorknob, and his body felt charged with electricity. "I dream about this door," Corey said, very softly.

"If that's the best you're doing in your dreams, I feel sorry for you."

"No, I'm serious," Corey said. "Man, it's *this* door. It's a room with white walls and boxes, and this door is in the back. And there's a glass doorknob. And in my dream, the doorknob starts to shine like a light." In his mind, he faintly saw a flash of blue-white light, the light he'd seen in his sleep. Then, nothing. "But I always wake up before I can open it."

If Sean had asked him this morning if he'd ever had a dream about a blue door, he would have said no. He hadn't remembered the dream until now, seeing the door in front of him, and now that he'd seen it, Corey thought it was possible he'd had the dream several times this summer. Maybe every night since he'd been in Sacajawea.

Corey's limbs went cold.

"You look freaked out," Sean said.

"I dunno, it's just weird. Like déjà vu or something."

"Well, what are you waiting for? Dreams are messages, dude. Maybe there's a stash of money in there and you're supposed to find it. Or, wait—maybe there's a safe."

With those words, Corey felt his foreboding vanish. There *might* be something valuable hidden in there, and it was finder's keepers, as far as he was concerned. An afternoon of drudgery had just turned into an adventure. He felt his shoulder pop when he tugged hard on the doorknob. The door was locked. "Shit," he said.

"Second curse in twenty minutes. Did we make a rule for that? I forget."

"Fuck you. Hand me that little knife you carry."

"You better hope there's some money in here, *hombre*, because you're deep in debt."

While Sean stood behind him, watching, Corey manipulated the keyhole with the slender nail file in Sean's Swiss army knife, trying to trigger the release. His hands were slightly unsteady, residue from his shock at seeing the door and the memory of his recurring dream, but he kept at it, searching for the right pin. He just had to find the sweet spot.

"You're doing it wrong," Sean said.

"Like you know any better."

"Seriously, it's the other side—"

In mid-argument, Corey heard a click, and the door flew open.

Corey's feet flew backward, so he bumped into Sean, who took a step back too. The door opened so quickly, it was almost as if there had been a weight behind it, a spring. But nothing emerged from behind the door, which was open hardly more than a crack. Corey smelled stale air floating out; old clothes, mothballs, cedar. The smells were strong, triggering a sneezing fit. The air felt thick. His eyes watered as he sneezed.

"Bless you," Sean said.

"Thanks."

The closet was narrow and small, but the space was crammed. Clothes on hangers were packed against each other, dense and tight, and the closet overflowed with shoes, ribbons, papers, a walking cane, a dull steel shotgun with a narrow barrel, and too much else to see. In a room full of junk, Corey thought, here was the junk Mecca.

"I don't see a safe," Sean said, disappointed.

But Corey didn't want to give up that fast. Why would he have been dreaming about this door unless there was something to find here? "I'm gonna dig around a little. But first, we've got to move these clothes."

Corey carried out armfuls of wooden hangers weighted with heavy coats and suits, and Sean took each load from him, finding a place in the room to pile them. The itchy woolen fabrics felt rough against Corey's forearms, scratching him. He was sneezing so much that he would need to grab some tissue soon, or else he'd have snot all over his face.

"Hey, Corey, you know what? Check out these *clothes*," Sean said. "This suit looks like it's a hundred years old. There's places we could sell stuff like this."

Sean held up a suit on a hanger for Corey to see. The dark gray suit had a long coat that didn't look like any fashion Corey recognized, unless it was a tuxedo coat, but it didn't look quite like a tuxedo because the buttons and collar went up too high. It was just different. Old, like Sean said. He sniffed the fabric, but his nose tickled from the sharp scent of old mothballs. These clothes had belonged to someone who was dead now, Corey thought.

"Hey, man, you're right. We could sell stuff like that to antique stores, costume shops . . ."

"And places that sell props for movies and plays," Sean said.

"Hell, yeah. My mom could hook us up."

Corey's excitement flickered when he thought of his mother. She wouldn't let them sell things from the closet for themselves. She'd say *no* for no good reason, her favorite word.

The shotgun leaning inside the closet caught Corey's eye suddenly, and he ran his fingers along the cold barrel, which was longer than newer shotguns he'd seen. He lifted the gun up; it wasn't as heavy as it looked, only about ten pounds. Corey examined the gun, trying to recognize the age of the wooden stock, but he didn't know enough about guns. This one was definitely real, though. He'd had a real gun in his hands only once, the time Dad let him touch his black handgun when he was nine, a gun with tape wrapped around the butt. Mom said no when Dad asked to take him to a shooting range like he begged him, so he hadn't seen it since. Dad always offered to take him shooting now, but Corey didn't want it now the way he had then, when it would have mattered.

"This gun's been around awhile, too," Corey said.

"My dad would know better than me, but that looks like a breechloader, maybe," Sean said. "It could be eighty or a hundred years old. A collector might want it."

Corey lifted the gun, resting the solid stock against his chest, stretching his arms out to balance the barrel. He felt a swell of power, mimicking a sniper's stance. The gun had a tiny goalpost-shaped sight, and Corey closed one eye, squinting, lining up his targets as his finger massaged the steel trigger. He aimed toward a corner of the wall above the door frame. Then at a lightbulb sitting atop a lamp stripped of its shade. Then at Sean's ducking head.

"*Fuck.* Hey, don't play around. You don't point a gun at people," Sean said. All playfulness had leapt from his eyes. Corey almost didn't recognize him as the laid-back guy he'd been hanging with for the past week, the guy who hardly cursed and always had something funny to say.

"Sorry," Corey said, lowering the gun. Suddenly, he felt a snake of ice down his spine. He'd had his finger on the trigger of a gun that might be loaded, and he'd pointed it at Sean's head without thinking twice about it. He might as well be nine again, he thought. "I'm really sorry, man. That was me being a dumb-ass."

Sean didn't look reassured. "We don't know if that's loaded or what, right?"

"You're right. I messed up. I guess I thought the gun was so old, it probably wouldn't work." Sean was right to be pissed, but at the same time Corey wished he could let it go. He didn't have patience for people who made a big deal out of things. He hoped a joke would snap Sean out of his funk. "This gun looks so old, I thought some cowboys might have been using it to slaughter the local Indians way back when."

Sean's lip curled slightly. "Whatever, no big deal. But even if it was that old, that doesn't mean it wouldn't work."

"True."

"And anyway, just so you know how it really happened, cowboys didn't slaughter Indians in this area. Most of the tribes died off from disease back in the 1800s, like the Wahkiakum and Cathlamet tribes, and a lot of the Chinook tribe. It was more like a medical slaughter, because they didn't have immunity. I read that at the historical society," Sean said, and Corey knew things were cool between them again. Sean the know-it-all was back, leaning on his knowledge like a one-legged man leans on crutches, Corey thought. Still, he was glad Sean wasn't too pissed.

"You must have been bored if you were hanging out at the historical society," Corey said.

"Bored? When we first moved here, I wanted to kill myself."

"Glad it's not just me." Corey put the gun aside, embarrassed at how careless he'd been. Life in Sacajawea had been ten times better with Sean around, so he needed to be more appreciative of the guy. "Sorry again about that. Let's get some music going in here."

Corey turned on the boom box he'd set up on the floor, and the Cuban percussion and vocals of the Orishas filled the room. Cowbells, shakers, trumpets, acoustic guitars. The music made Corey think of palm trees and the beach, and suddenly he didn't feel so far from California. The more he heard the CD, the better it got. It blew him away. The song playing now, "Madre," was a tribute to a mother who sacrificed for her children, Corey's favorite. Singing in Spanish, Corey forgot about horseback riding. He and Sean worked in the sweltering room, sifting through the closet.

Corey got excited when he saw a large, rusting strongbox on the floor beneath a shoe rack. There was no lock, and when he pulled it out to open it, he found receipts and ledgers for an E. J. Goode Pharmacy on 150 Main Street in Sacajawea, dated from 1922.

"We should take that to the historical society," Sean said.

"Yeah, I guess," Corey said, emptying it out. He hoped he'd find money inside, but no luck. The papers were just the financial records of the same dead man whose clothes they had found. This had been their biggest thrill so far, and it was nothing. Maybe he'd never really dreamed about this door, Corey thought. Or, if he had, maybe it didn't mean anything. He wasn't sure anymore.

"I've got to go," Sean said when the CD had repeated three times and they were both covered in dust. "I need a smoke, like, *now*. And Dad's expecting me back by five."

"Yeah, man, all right," Corey said.

At the door downstairs, Corey gave Sean the quick, one-armed embrace he gave his friends in Oakland when they had to take off. Sean was cool, he thought. They would have been friends anywhere, probably, not just in Sacajawea. Standing in the foyer, Corey smelled spicy food cooking. Dinner would be the high point of his day, as usual. Mealtime was the only thing he and his mother could agree on.

Corey popped his head into the kitchen from the butler's pantry. His mother was standing over a pot while she held a recipe card up to her face, stirring a wooden spoon as she read.

"Can I have a Coke?"

She didn't look away from her card. "How many have you had today?"

Damn. She was really something else, managing every detail of his life. "Just one."

"Okay, but two's enough. Too much sugar. Your father's family is full of diabetes."

Anything that had to do with his father had something wrong with it. No surprise there. Sighing, Corey opened the refrigerator, and the blast of cool air felt good. He stood there fantasizing about what this house would feel like if it had air-conditioning. Mom kept saying it didn't need it, but she was tripping. This house might stay cool in the fall, but it was hot as hell in summer.

Corey grabbed his soda can, flicking open the tab. "What's cooking?" he said, peeking into the orange pot she was stirring. He saw chicken chunks, fat sausage pieces, tiny shrimp, and okra in a golden red sauce. Whatever it was, it was bound to be good.

His mother smiled at him, and he was amazed again at what a smile did to her face. "Gumbo," she said. "One of Gramma Marie's recipes."

"Well, that sh—" Corey stopped short. He'd been about to say, *That shit smells great*, like he would have said to his father. If Sean had been here, he would have busted a gut laughing. "That sure smells great, Mom. I can't wait for dinner."

"Really?"

Corey turned to look at her because of something in her voice, and her face made him fidget. His mother's eyes had gone gentle, an expression that reminded him of the way the fat girls at school stared at the quarterback, Rodrick Lovell, in the hallway. Wanting something they know they can't have. He felt bad for those girls when he saw them, and he almost felt bad for his mother now. "You've always been a great cook, " he said, looking away from her eyes and how they made him feel. "Anyway, I'm still working upstairs. Call me when it's ready, a'ight?"

"Sweetheart, you don't have to keep working. Just do a little at a time."

"No, it's cool. There's some good stuff up there." He didn't tell her about his dreams and the blue door. He would feel like an idiot, and she would look at him like he *was* one. But even after he'd decided not to say anything, Corey wished he could tell. Not telling left a hole in the air.

"What did you find?" Mom said. She always seemed to know his mind.

"Old clothes, papers, you know. Just stuff." He was already on his way back out to the foyer. Maybe he'd talk about it later. For now, he had to find what he was looking for. He was glad she didn't call after him.

When he went back upstairs to the junk room, Corey realized that except for the path that led from the door to the window, and another path from the window to the closet, the room looked worse than before. The closet had seemed small at first, but the crush of things had spilled into the rest of the room. Piles of clothes. Stacks of papers. Just looking at all of it gave him a headache, and for a moment, he was mad again. What did this have to do with him?

But when he got back to the closet, his eagerness returned.

The clothes were gone, leaving the core of the space empty. The warped, peeling white paint on the back wall was visible for the first time in decades, Corey figured. He noticed a few more strongboxes up on the top shelf, but they had lost their intrigue after the disappointment of the last one. He'd save those for last, his final shot for cash, gold, or stock certificates. For now, the floor was still densely packed with shoes, unrecognizable gadgets, and fallen clothing. What if there was a hidden floorboard?

Corey was ready to find something to change everything. Something that would matter.

As it turned out, Corey's search didn't take more than another ten minutes.

Nothing else caught his interest as he waded through the mess on the closet floor, and he couldn't find any loose wooden floorboards, so his eyes wandered back to the top shelf, to the strongboxes. He grabbed a chair and balanced himself, pulling them down one by one. Of the four strongboxes he found, two were locked, one was filled with unmarked prescription bottles and empty vials, and the last one had another pile of receipts, these from 1925. Corey laughed when he saw the product names listed in sales columns: Age Reversal Pills. Vision Restorer. Manhood Cure.

What a load of crap, he thought.

E. J. Goode had a great year in 1925, Corey noticed as he glanced through the paperwork. That year's income was $100,000, about five times what he had made in 1922. The mail-order business brought in most of the money, not the pharmacy at 150 Main Street, so Corey decided the pharmacy had been mostly a front. E. J. Goode might have been the friendly neighborhood pharmacist, but through the mail he'd been selling products he knew good and damn well were quack bullshit. There hadn't been penicillin in those days, much less Viagra. Age Reversal Pills? How did Goode get away with selling that junk? Didn't people know it was bullshit?

Unless it *wasn't* bullshit, Corey thought, and his imagination stirred.

Corey went back to the strongbox full of empty bottles and opened it, shaking the bottles and vials, holding them up to the light. A few had powdery residue stuck solid to the glass, but most were empty. E. J. Goode could have been putting anything in these bottles, Corey thought. But, then again, hadn't Mom told him Gramma Marie had taken up with Goode for a while before he died? What if she'd helped his business along with a little magic? A little conversation with the *orishas?*

Corey's ears seemed to ring, and he felt dizzy. He stood up to regain his balance, and when he did, he realized that he hadn't checked to see if there was anything else on the top shelf, behind the space where the strongboxes had been. Corey found yellow, crumbling newspaper pages, and he swept them aside to make sure nothing else was hidden beneath them.

Something was. Corey grabbed it, pulling it out.

It was a large black satchel, so dusty it was coated gray. But everything about it felt *right:* the weight, the size, the appearance. Instead of déjà vu, this time Corey felt as if he were walking through his future. He held the satchel, his heart thudding.

Corey couldn't make himself open it, and he couldn't put it aside. He was glad Sean was gone, because Sean wouldn't have understood what it was like to discover something he knew he was supposed to have, but at the same time he knew he *wasn't* supposed to have it. It was his, and it wasn't. Corey's thoughts swam, confused. If he didn't know better, he'd think he was scared of it.

"I'm losing my damn mind," he said, and there was no one in the room to argue.

He had turned off the boom box long ago, so the room was silent. Corey took a deep breath before he turned the satchel's tiny metal pin. Carefully, as if it might break, he pulled the leather tongue free and opened the mouth wide. It was filled with papers, not money. *Damn.*

Corey pulled out the thick stack, about a hundred pages. He only realized he was holding a manuscript when he saw the title page: *Le Livre des Mystères*, it said in the dead center, typed with typewriter keys that smudged the ink on the *e*'s.

It was French, so Corey wasn't sure of the words. He'd been taking Spanish, not French. Still, the language seemed similar enough that he could figure out every word except one. The *something* of the Mysteries, it said. *Livre. Libre.* Freedom? No, that didn't make sense.

Livre, livre . . . ?

The answer came to him in a flood of adrenaline: *Livre* meant *book*, of course, like *libro* in Spanish. This was called *The Book of the Mysteries*. Corey grinned, feeling triumphant. There was no author's name typed beneath the title, but Corey saw a signature scrawled on the bottom right side, dated by the year, 1929. *Marie F. Toussaint* was spelled in a stylish, womanly signature, so pretty it was almost calligraphy.

Corey felt blood charging through his veins. Gramma Marie had written a book, and Mom didn't know anything about it. Mom cooked Gramma Marie's recipes, sang her songs, and read the books in her library like the whole house was a tribute to Gramma Marie, but Corey was sure his mother had no idea this book existed. Mom was going to go crazy when she saw this.

Crouching to the floor, Corey flipped to the next page. It was full of type, single-spaced, written with hardly any paragraphs. And Corey didn't need a translation for the word typed at the top center of the page, under the Roman numeral I: *Magie*.

Magic.

"This whole thing better not be in French," Corey said, scanning the first page, and he was relieved when he recognized the words as English.

I am fearful to commit the words to paper, but I fear their loss more. I leave these words here so they will be documented, and I pray I can steer the appropriate spirit to these pages when I am gone, at the dawning of the new millennium. Perhaps I will steer you, Dominique, when you are well again, or your son or daughter who is yet to be born. Or, perhaps I will find a great-grandchild who is the very image of grandmère and steer her sleep to this piece of her destiny. And when she wakes, I will show her the story of her line.

As he read, Corey hardly remembered to breathe. Gramma Marie had said she would steer her great-granchild here in sleep. What else could she mean, except through *dreams?* He was the great-grandchild! And this year, 2001, was the new millennium, even though most people had made the mistake of getting excited last year, stocking up on food, water, and flashlights like it was the end of the world.

Gramma Marie had called him here, like she said she would.

How could someone who was dead steer his dreams?

"Ho-ly shit," Corey said, and his profanity shocked his ear, as if Gramma Marie were in the room with him. His skin went clammy, from the back of his neck to the backs of his thighs. Could it be something like the ghosts in *The Sixth Sense?*

Maybe he couldn't see dead people—but could dead people see him?

Corey's memories of Gramma Marie were almost dreamlike because he had been so young when she died, but he remembered how she used to give him a quarter every time he sat on her lap, pulling it from his ear, or at least that was what it looked like to him with her quick flick of her wrist. Gramma Marie had been dead since 1990, the year he was five and her death ruined Christmas day. She'd been dead for eleven years. Yet, Corey felt an aliveness in the room, something other than himself. He looked around, searching for signs of anything unusual; a flickering lightbulb, movement beneath the curtains draped over the furniture, rustling inside the boxes, unusual insects. He didn't see or hear anything to explain what he felt, but the stillness seemed deceptive. Deliberate.

"Is someone here?" he said, not sure he was really hoping for an answer. If something talked back to him, he thought, he would scream like a third-grade schoolgirl.

But nothing answered. His breathing was the sole sound, heavier now. There was no motion around him. The unnerving feeling that had swept over Corey when he first saw the blue door came again. He nearly shuddered as he knelt over the pages, feeling waves of unease that were almost physical. Corey didn't know what it was, but something was in this room with him.

"Gramma Marie?" he said. He'd never felt like more of a fool, but he couldn't stop talking. "I hope that's you, because I don't know who else it would be. And if you're here, and if you're talking to me in my dreams . . . does that mean God is up there with you, too?"

Corey had never thought of himself as religious—Dad took him to church maybe once a year, and Mom wasn't much better. They were both supposed to be Christians, but they didn't act like it, just Christmas-and-Easter Christians who didn't say grace over their meals. Corey always said grace to himself when he ate, even if it was a split second, a habit he'd learned on his own because, hell, it seemed like a good thing to do. He didn't take his food for granted, so why not thank God for it?

Corey figured something was out there, but he didn't worry about what it was, since he planned to live a good life so he and God would always be tight. To him, Hell was the conscience trying to be heard, things eating you so you think you have to be punished when you die. He knew a couple of kids who'd already trashed their consciences—one, T.'s brother, had nearly killed a pregnant woman when he ran a red light once. A lawyer had kept him out of jail, but she hadn't helped him sleep at night. Corey didn't like what he saw in people's eyes when their consciences were burning. He saw that look in Dad's eyes sometimes, and he'd probably see it in Mom's eyes too if he looked hard enough. Corey had always planned to treat people right, and if there was a God, he'd figured God would take care of him when the time came.

But now, this was something else. Something concrete. Something to really believe in.

"Is all that white light stuff for real, Gramma Marie?" Corey said. His knees felt like liquid as he crouched, so he sat cross-legged on the floor to keep steady. He realized he was having trouble catching his breath. His body had lost interest in normal procedure, but his mind was afire.

He should run downstairs with the satchel and take it to Mom, he thought. He should share this with her. Mom had known Gramma Marie better than he had, and half the time she was still living in the past, in Gramma Marie's world. This satchel belonged to Mom. If Gramma Marie wanted to reach out for anyone, she was probably reaching to her.

"Yeah, I can see it now," Corey said, imagining the conversation: " 'Hey, Mom, Gramma Marie sent me to find this in my dream. By the way, she says hi. Your mom says hi, too.' "

No, Gramma Marie had called *him* in his dreams, not her. Just like she'd written.

Mom wouldn't appreciate anything about magic. Mom got embarrassed when anybody asked about Gramma Marie's voodoo, like it was something shameful. Mom might appreciate the pages because she loved Gramma Marie, but she wouldn't treat them like something that might be real.

Corey handled the papers carefully, straightening them before he slid them back into the satchel where he'd found them. He'd read this after dinner, he decided. He'd keep it somewhere safe and get to it later, when he would have privacy, after Mom was in bed. If it was selfishness, so be it, Corey thought. Mom was trying to own every piece of him this summer—his time, his thoughts, his moods—but now he had something he owned all to himself.

She didn't know it was there, so how could she miss it?

Corey took the satchel into his bedroom and hid it under his pillow. Then, he stopped by the bathroom to wash up for dinner. He let the water run a long time in the bathroom sink, staring at himself in the mirror with the fancy brass frame that looked like something out of a Chinese palace. His own eyes in the mirror startled him, one of the strangest sensations he'd ever had. His heart was pounding hard enough to make him feel like a hard-core punk.

"That's just guilt you're feeling, *hombre*," Corey told his reflection, like Sean would say.

Gramma Marie's book would be a treasure to Mom, and he was keeping it from her. It wasn't the same as a hurting kind of lie, but it was still a lie. Just like old times, when he'd stolen Gramma Marie's ring from Mom like some kind of crackhead, trying to impress a girl. He'd thought he would feel better about it after all this time, but sometimes he only felt worse.

He planned to show Mom the book when he was finished, but hadn't he said the same thing about the ring? He'd dug it out of her jewelry box, and he'd been surprised when he found it. He'd wanted that ring because he couldn't stop staring at it when she wore it. He'd tried it on for size when he found it, sliding it onto his thumb. *Just for a week*, he told himself. *I'll bring it right back.*

Just like now. But this wasn't the same as stealing. Was it?

As he climbed down the stairs, Corey heard his mother's voice on the kitchen telephone. She was arguing with someone, using her lawyer's voice, not that there was much of a difference most of the time. He lost any idea he'd had about talking to her when he heard her stern tone. Maybe Sean was right. Maybe he was scared of her, in a way.

Corey was hungry, but instead of walking toward the kitchen, he went to the living room instead. He climbed onto the sofa, leaning his elbows against the high, curving back as he stared out of the picture window at the front yard. A couple of fawns usually came around dinnertime, and Corey liked watching them eat the apples Mom left for them in the grass beneath the walnut tree. It was about time for them to show up.

But the yard was empty today except for the rainbow of blooming summer flowers. That was one good thing about Gramma Marie's house; it was damn pretty, like a picture in a magazine.

"Mom, did you leave food outside?" he called, after he heard her hang up the telephone.

"I forgot! Are they there yet?" Her feet scurried on the kitchen tiles.

"Not yet."

When Corey peered out of the window again to see if the fawns were hidden behind the shrubbery, he saw something that convinced him beyond any doubt that Gramma Marie's magic might be as real as its promise: Corey made out the olive-green coloring of a vehicle parked on the road, across the street. His eyes seized on the color, knowing what it was before his thoughts caught up.

Just like that, his father reached the top of the roadside steps with a Raiders knapsack slung across his shoulders, grinning like a fool. Seeing Corey in the window, Dad waved. It was the most remarkable sight of Corey's life. He was afraid to blink, or the mirage would be gone.

"Dad's here," Corey said, before he believed it yet.

Corey felt his mother's hands on his shoulders behind him. He smelled raw onions and chicken fat on her skin, so he knew he could trust his eyes. This was real. She saw him, too.

"Is that Tariq?" Mom said. For once, she didn't sound mad. It was the first time in years Corey had heard his mother say his father's name like it meant something to her.

ᨏ Fourteen ᨏ

"ALL NEGATIVE," the doctor said, fanning Tariq's records in front of him. "No unusual bacteria or cells, nothing showing in your X-rays, no ulcer. And you said you're not having the pain today?"

Tariq sighed, buttoning his shirt after the doctor's quick inspection of his abdomen in the small examination area of his office. Dr. Yamuna was a gastrointestinal specialist, the third Tariq had seen since August. Six different doctors in two years, and all of them with the same bullshit. Tariq had worked hard not to get his hopes up, but he felt something deeper than disappointment, nearly unbearable. "Not right now. It's bad at night and when I first wake up," he said.

"Have you traveled in any tropical regions in the past five years? Somewhere you might have picked up a bug we're not so familiar with here?" The doctor's fingers played with his beard.

"No."

"Did you suffer a fall or some sort of injury? I understand you're with the football team. . . ."

Tariq was so tired of repeating himself after two years of doctoring, he could barely modulate his voice. "I work in the business office, not on the field," he said. "No, man, there's no injury. Just this same damn bellyache, and nobody can tell me shit."

Dr. Yamuna sighed, gazing at him from beneath fuzzy black eyebrows, twin caterpillars. Tariq waited for him to say something more, but

Dr. Yamuna remained silent. Tariq could tell he was preparing to move on, ready to go home for the day. It was after five.

"Don't let me turn around in six months and have somebody tell me it's cancer," Tariq said when the doctor had nothing else to say. *Or I will sue your monkey ass,* he finished to himself. Trouble would rain down on this little brown fool like the skies opening during Noah's flood. Tariq felt his fingers flexing as he imagined what he'd do to this guy if he was fucking around and missed something big like cancer. Something it might be too late to stop soon.

"There is no sign of cancer, Mr. Hill, I'm happy to say."

"Well, it sure the hell is something."

"Have you had any emotional traumas in recent years? Coinciding with the pains?"

This tired old game. Shrinks were nothing but quacks dispensing pills to keep people in a fog. Crack for the bourgeoisie. Maybe Angie had given herself the luxury of losing her damned mind, but he hadn't. As easy as it was to believe otherwise, natural as the temptation might be, he couldn't blame every ache and pain he would feel forever on the death of his son.

This was something else.

The pain in his stomach, at its worst, yanked him out of sleep and made him cry out in the middle of the night. A grown-ass man, yelling into the darkness like a child calling after his mama. He'd broken his arm in two places during a practice his freshman year at U.C.L.A., and then his Achilles tendon had taken him out for good during his senior bowl game. Both times, he'd been in the worst pain of his life. This was another milestone in pain. He'd already racked up more than a month in sick time this year, on the days he couldn't get himself out of bed. A week ago, he'd cried himself to sleep, believing the pain was trying to steal something from him—and was winning at last.

Now here was somebody else trying to tell him it was in his imagination.

"Let me tell you something, Doc," Tariq said, hopping off the examining table. He took two strides toward the doctor, until he stood inches from him. Tariq was a half-foot taller, and he suddenly wanted Dr. Yamuna to remember that. "Don't bullshit a bullshitter, man. I know the difference between imaginary pain and real pain."

"Psychosomatic pains are not precisely *imaginary,*" the doctor said. Whether he realized it or not, he'd shielded his chest with his metal clipboard. "The pain is very real, but sometimes the stimulus is psychological. Especially in the case of a severe trauma."

"I could teach you a couple things about severe trauma, Doc," Tariq said. His face was hot, his whole body was hot, and he knew he would have to get out of here. It didn't take much to set him off lately, like at the club last night, and right now he could feel just fine about knocking everything from that counter to the floor, including Dr. Ranjan Yamuna, M.D., Ph.D. Right now, it was very difficult not to do just that. He wanted to crack this guy's head against the floor with his heel, the Oakland stomp.

Dr. Yamuna shrank away, pushing against the counter full of boxes of cotton swabs, plastic gloves, and disinfectants. Another half-inch and he would knock an empty specimen cup to the floor. "I think we are finished today, Mr. Hill. I'm sorry I could not be of any help to you."

A stone pussy, Tariq thought. All brains and no balls. Tariq eyeballed the doctor, enjoying the way the man's face hardened, bracing. He was scared, and Tariq would love to give him something to be scared about. Maybe that was why his stomach hurt so much—the strain of not being able to act out on the things he really wanted to do. Maybe restraint was bad for his health.

"Yeah, this is a waste of my time," Tariq said, and backed away.

Tariq saw people in the office looking at him funny when he stopped at the billing window to ask if they needed anything else from him. His voice was nice as pie. Nice as a Sunday morning gospel choir. The sister sitting there was what women liked to call "big-boned" but he called just plain fat, looking at him with a stupid expression. He heard a whisper from somewhere behind the partition, Dr. Yamuna's voice, in a hushed tone people used when they wanted to call the police. Over what? Men like that made him sick.

Just to prove Dr. Yamuna a liar for telling stories on him, Tariq tipped an imaginary hat at the big woman behind the window and smiled his best smile. A smile for the kind of woman he thought was fine, the kind of smile that would make her feel good about herself. She smiled back. No mess, no fuss. Just a brother trying to get some decent medical care for a change, against the odds. He turned to go on his way.

He had to shake off his anger. He had to go take his real medicine.

Tariq climbed into his black Toyota Land Cruiser and headed toward Alameda's Bay Farm Island Bridge. If traffic wasn't bad, Martin Luther King, Jr. Way in Oakland was only a thirty-minute trip. Although he loved the size of his newer wheels, he missed the VW. The funny thing was, he dreamed about the van more and more often—he saw himself sitting in the driver's seat, never going anywhere because in his dreams the van always had two flat tires. The flat tires, to him, were a reminder of how the van was falling apart. He'd had it since 1980, and it had been twelve years old when he bought it, so his engine had cut out five times during the drive from Oakland to Sacajawea that summer. But he'd lived in that van for his first semester at U.C.L.A., while he waited for his scholarship money; at night, he'd read from the light above the dashboard, then fallen asleep across the far backseat. He'd first kissed Angie in that van. He'd driven that van to Las Vegas when he and Angie eloped, playing Luther Vandross and Teddy Pendergrass cassettes the entire way, talking about what to name their baby. Marie if it was a girl. Corey or Harry if it was a boy. Both of them scared to death, but happy.

When he'd gone to see her in Sacajawea that last time, he'd known it would be important to arrive in that van. But the van hadn't been enough to do the job. Not enough to make up for the truckload of shit about to hit the fan. Tariq had flown to Los Angeles for Corey's funeral, and he'd never made the time to go back and drive the van home, or to hire someone. It seemed pointless.

He'd tried calling Angie at her office this morning. Her secretary told him she'd gone home for the week, which probably meant she was in Sacajawea. If nothing else, Tariq thought, the van parked in front of Angie's grandmother's house might motivate her to call him back sometime soon, even if it was only in anger. But he was beginning to give up on that notion, too. When Corey died, all of it had died. He couldn't blame her—he'd disappointed her one time too many—but it was probably no accident that he'd left one of the last relics of his past parked at the place where his future had vanished. That place was only a burial ground in his mind now, the empty van a shrine.

Traffic was mild. In twenty minutes, Tariq had reached Marcus Bookstore, which blended into the gray, downtrodden buildings around it, skeletons of better days at the corner of 39th Street on MLK. The essence of Marcus was preserved inside, a new world. Colors and music and knowledge and beauty, everywhere. That was what he loved about the store, the beauty smack in the middle of the street that could use it the most. Tariq walked in and heard Miles Davis on the store's speakers, blowing his horn. Each time Tariq came here, the music was waiting. Miles. Coltrane. Hugh Masekela. Marcus was the medicine a doctor couldn't give him.

Tariq lost himself in books, which crowded every shelf, every space. Books were in stacks behind the desk, on tables, in the window. Tariq had strayed away from histories, the only section that used to draw him after Corey died, when he first started coming regularly. He'd discovered thrillers by black authors, and he was hooked. Then, the mysteries. It had taken him all this time to read Walter Mosley, and he wondered what the hell he'd been waiting for. Now, he'd come to learn there were black folks writing science fiction—and if *that* was true, he wanted to see it with his own eyes. He hadn't known there were any black folks in outer space, not from the movies and books he'd seen when he was a kid. That was news to him.

Tariq had never enjoyed fiction before now. Those kinds of books had seemed frivolous, except for the classics by Richard Wright, James Baldwin, Claude Brown, and John A. Williams, books his brother Harry had passed to him. With so much to learn about the real world, how could he justify wasting hours wandering through realms of make-believe? With so many real problems, he'd never had time to care about imaginary ones. Now, more and more, he found that he *did* have the time. He still read a biography a week, but now he read other books, too, leaving them scattered on his nightstand or in his bathrooms, spread-eagled so he could revisit them at his leisure. There were books all over his house.

Tariq didn't need a shrink to tell him he was replacing his addiction to coke with books, trading one for the other. He could look at his own life and see that. And except for making his eyes ache in dim lighting, Tariq couldn't see a downside to that. He may have lost a hell of a piece of his life after Corey died, but damned if he hadn't found something new. Nothing like the old life, nothing like having his son back. He'd give up all the books he'd read, or a chance to ever read them, if he could have Corey back. But his discoveries at Marcus were feeding him, and there were times he felt almost whole again. Brief, glorious times.

Things were as fine now as they'd ever been since the Fourth of July—except for his damned stomach. That was the only thing that was still very much wrong. He and his stomach fought when he tried to concentrate on reading at night, and each night he read until he dropped to sleep, no matter how much it hurt. He made that decision before he cracked open the first page, and so far it was working. No pain was going to run his life. *Nothing* would run his life.

The store was nearly empty tonight. The only other shopper was a smallish man in a dashiki and a necklace of cowrie shells who called himself Brother Paul. He was a smart man, but although Tariq respected his knowledge of Caribbean politics and history, he wasn't in the mood for talking. He still felt too tight from his doctor's visit. Tariq knew he needed to give himself space, to keep other people out of range for their own good.

Anger management, the shrinks called it. He'd weathered moods like this once a year most of his life, and it had been hell enough then, but now the awful mood came regularly. Three or four times a week, sometimes more. The recurring pain was doing that to him, he was sure of it. It was making him angry. Tariq often wondered if anger might be his natural state now, and his moments of evenness were the exception. Another reason to keep away from coke or booze: He didn't want to hurt someone, and these days he might. He just might.

But there would be no dodging Brother Paul. He was already on his way.

"Evening, Brother Hill," Brother Paul said, cornering him beside the greeting cards, an array of brown faces and African-inspired designs.

"Hey, Brother Paul . . . I'm just meeting someone here. I don't have time to talk." As a truly reformed liar, Tariq had come to understand that truth had its place. This past weekend, his nephew had promised to meet him here tonight, and DuShaun was the only person he felt like talking to. Rather than standing here feeling cornered, he could tell Brother Paul to move on. He let the truth set him free whenever possible, one of the perks of not being concerned about what anyone thought about him, except Harry and his nephew.

Brother Paul gazed at him in a way that made Tariq wonder if he'd heard him. "How's that pain in your stomach? What's the doctor telling you?" Brother Paul said.

Tariq felt himself start, surprised. It was the closest he'd ever come to believing someone was reading his mind, and he didn't like the feeling a damn bit.

"You've mentioned your problem to me, Brother Hill," Brother Paul said when he didn't respond. "I gave you my book on herbs to take home last week. You invited me to sign it for you."

Now that he said so, Tariq had a stray memory of taking home Brother Paul's self-published book on herbal medicines, one with a rainbow on the cover, but he hadn't thought about it since. Brother Paul wrote New Age healing and self-help books, a taste Tariq had yet to cultivate. He suddenly remembered talking to Brother Paul at some length last week about the pain. The brother was pretty far out there, telling him he should look for a new underground drug supposedly made from African blood, or some such pitiful Afrocentric horseshit. Tariq was surprised he'd forgotten a conversation like that, but he'd been doing that a lot lately. Forgetting things, like he had when his face was buried in coke.

"This doctor didn't know anything either," Tariq said.

"Doctors don't know plenty." Brother Paul spoke like a hypnotist, choosing his words carefully, enunciating slowly. "Some afflictions they don't understand."

"Got that right."

"Your pain sounded very bad."

"Damn right about that, too."

"It's time for you to get rid of it, Brother Hill," Brother Paul said. The way he said it, he might have had the answer hidden in his back pocket. "Time to make the pain leave."

Tariq stared again, wondering if Brother Paul was toying with him. More than that, he imagined what he might *do* to someone who tried to toy with him right now, a fantasy that held more appeal than his current conversation with Brother Paul. In his mind, he could see himself grab a handful of Brother Paul's salt-and-pepper dreadlocks, pull his face close to make his point clear—*Didn't I tell you I don't have time for a fucking conversation?*—then throw him backward with all his strength, watching his legs fly into the air as he fell into Blanche's counter in the back. Just enough to give him a real jolt, knock his teeth together. Tariq liked the idea of that very much.

This conversation was over, Tariq decided. Brother Paul was five-foot-six, a moth of a man. Tariq had never hit anyone that much smaller than him in his life, man or woman, and he'd rather not start today. "Brother Paul," Tariq said, sounding as weary as he felt, "it's time you moved on."

Again, Brother Paul seemed not to hear him. He stared at Tariq with eyes that were sincere and brown, sprinkled with green flecks at the pupils' rims. Tariq had never noticed the green before, and it caught his attention long enough to keep his eyes on Brother Paul's. "You've been seeing doctors for the body. Where's your doctor for the spirit, Brother Hill?"

"You got a sequel to that last book you're trying to sell me?"

"I see your smile, but you and me both know there's nothing to smile at. You're stricken. And I'll tell you how I know: I can smell it."

Anger vanished, with numbness washing down in its place. Tariq hadn't mentioned the smell to anyone except doctors, least of all someone he knew only in passing. "You . . . smell . . . ?"

"It's very strong," Brother Paul said.

Tariq knew the smell was strong—there was no arguing that—he just hadn't known anyone else knew, too. Tariq had first noticed the rankness in the days after Corey's death, not very strong at first, but omnipresent. Sometimes it smelled like charred garbage left out in the rain, and often it smelled worse. Like something rotten. Like the dead cat he and his friends had found by the curb outside their building when he was eight. Bloated.

Decomposing under a hot sun, turning black. Wet or dry, the smell came to his skin, seeping from his pores. Sometimes it was weak enough to barely notice, and other times it was so overpowering, it gagged him.

Again, the doctors hadn't been worth shit. When the smell didn't go away—when changing his soap and deodorant and taking chlorophyll tablets didn't work—he'd made his tour of specialists. A dermatologist first, a neurologist next to check for a brain tumor, an internist just to round it out. Not only hadn't those doctors offered any advice on how he could rid himself of the terrible smell, they'd sniffed him up and down and told him they couldn't even *smell* anything. Even on bad days, when Tariq smelled as if he were wearing his intestines outside of his skin.

No one asked him why he smelled that way. No one glanced at him sidelong, or moved away from him, or avoided him outright. Even DuShaun had yet to say a word, or pinch his nose, and they lived in the same house. On bad days, when his own scent made him sick, Tariq sought out crowds to see who would notice. No one did. People brushed against him without looking back. Until now.

Brother Paul lowered his voice, cupping his hand around Tariq's upper arm, his biceps. "Look, Brother Hill . . . forgive my approach this way, but I have to speak. You know me as a man you see in the bookstore, but you do not *know* me. I write books and teach African dance. I'm part scholar, part herbalist, part psychic."

At the word *psychic,* Tariq smiled more widely. He couldn't help it. "Do you see dead people, Brother Paul?" he said, taunting. Corey had loved *The Sixth Sense;* he must have watched that DVD a dozen times in the year before he died, rehearsing for death.

"I don't know much of anything apart from what one of my aunts in Trinidad taught me, a little card-reading, so I don't claim expert status. But I've smelled something on you a long time. I didn't know what to call it, or how to broach it, so I let it be," Brother Paul said. "But it's worse now, Brother Hill. Much, much worse than before. It's . . . *perilous* now. I use that word because I mean it in the strongest sense. It's grave. You know that, too. You must know."

Of course Tariq knew. The thing was, he realized, he'd simply gotten used to the smell, after a time. It was hard to explain, but he wasn't bothered nearly as much by the smell as he was by the pain. It was the *pain* he could no longer tolerate. Brother Paul beckoned him to lower his head closer, and when he did, Tariq noticed that Brother Paul smelled of dried flowers. He wasn't used to standing this close to any man—it made him uncomfortable—

but Tariq liked Brother Paul's clean, untainted scent. It was almost a marvel.

Tariq also noticed how nervous Brother Paul was. He saw a tiny, rapid pulsing in his neck.

"Come let me read you," Brother Paul said, close to his ear. "I live down the street, not far. Or, let me bring the cards to you so we can see what they tell us. There's no time to wait. Let's see what we have to do to stop that pain. Let's stop the fire."

Stop the fire. Brother Paul's voice was music, his words a revelation. Tariq had to stop the fire. He had to stop what was inside him, the thing he couldn't see. Tariq opened his mouth to say yes, he would go with him, but he didn't say what he'd planned. "My nephew's meeting me here. Maybe another time."

Brother Paul's face dimmed as he gazed at Tariq. "Are you sure, Brother Hill? It will only get worse, harder to cleanse. Even if you don't see me, see someone else. You can't wait."

Like most people making life-changing decisions, Tariq made his with barely a thought. "Brother Paul," he said, "you need to leave me alone right now."

There were more undiplomatic words churning in his mind, words he had to struggle not to blurt aloud: *I'm starting to wonder if you're a little on the sissy side, Brother Paul. I don't like the way you're touching me, putting your fucking face close to my ear, and if you don't back off, I may take you into the bathroom and find a plunger to give you what you really want. I can't promise I'll be gentle, though. Like Tina Turner said in "Proud Mary," I hope you like it rough.*

Brother Paul's eyes twinged, but he didn't show real surprise, anger, fear, or anything else Tariq would have expected from someone who could perceive invisible truths so clearly. Brother Paul didn't break his gaze or release Tariq's arm, still holding him gently, like a minister.

"All right, then, Brother Hill. I'm sorry to hear that. I really am sorry," Brother Paul said in that hypnotist's voice again. He couldn't have sounded sorrier if Tariq had just confided to him that his doctor had said he was suffering from an advanced stage of cancer, that he had reached the tail end of the last day of his life.

⎯⎯⎯

The man who was unbecoming Tariq Hill got home and found DuShaun with his feet propped up on the coffee table, watching the wide-screen TV in the dark den, Corey's favorite old spot. "What the hell happened?" Tariq said, slamming open the refrigerator door. Ordinarily, he would reach for a beer in a bad mood, but there was no beer in the house. Instead, Tariq found a bean burrito left over from Taco Bell, and he popped it into the microwave. "Why'd you leave me there waiting at Marcus? I kept trying your cell phone. Did you forget or what?"

DuShaun, like the muted television set, was silent at first. That wasn't like him.

"Boy, what's the matter with you?" Tariq said.

"I was just sittin' here thinking about what you did, Uncle Tariq," DuShaun said, softly. "That wasn't right."

"What *I* did? You hang me up for more than an hour at the bookstore and then you have the nerve to talk about somebody else's shit not being right?" The microwave beeped, telling him the burrito was ready, but Tariq didn't retrieve it.

"I'm talking 'bout last night."

Tariq walked out into the den so he could see DuShaun's face in the glow from the television set. DuShaun was a coal-black Georgia boy, and even the light from a sixty-inch television wasn't enough for Tariq to see a joke in his nephew's face. He was about to ask what the joke was when he saw a woman on the television screen, someone he knew.

What was that girl's name? He liked to keep up with what Angie was doing, and he'd read about this TV movie, how Angie had set this actress up with her new talent agency. The actress was in a pillbox hat, driving a 1960 Buick. This was the movie about Coretta Scott King, he realized, the one that had made her famous. "Naomi Price," Tariq said, answering his own question.

DuShaun's voice cheered some. "Yeah, she's so fine, she makes your eyes hurt."

"Your aunt Angie represents her. I could get a message to her."

DuShaun looked up at him expectantly, and his face reminded Tariq of Corey's. *Did you really say what I think you just said?* Like when he told Corey he would get him a silver PT Cruiser for his sixteenth birthday, before he remembered he'd have to discuss it with Angie first—and *damn,* he realized, she'd probably have said Corey was too young to get a car. She'd have said he should work for it. And maybe she was right, but he'd said he would buy it, so fuck it. That was where secrets came in handy. That was when it felt damn convenient that Angie lived hundreds of miles away.

DuShaun's face went empty, and he switched the channel with the remote, to the game highlights on ESPN. He switched in time for them to see the DuShaun Hill Special from two camera angles, a perfect pass to the five-yard line. DuShaun's eyes didn't light up as he watched. "Naw, man, I'm still pissed," DuShaun said. "Don't try to change the subject. We got to air this out."

"What the fuck are you talking about? I know you're not here moaning because I gave that jackass a shove at the club last night. He'll get over it. Quit being a pussy."

"Why would I care about that drunk fool?" DuShaun said. "I mean *after* that."

The anger had receded before, but Tariq hadn't noticed until now, when it reappeared. That was how it went these days, a few unnoticed moments of calm, and then the anger, an irrepressible, rising tide. He reminded himself that DuShaun might be six-foot-four and two-forty, but he was still a boy wrapped up inside that body. Tariq would have to be patient.

"This time, speak concisely and make your point," Tariq said, as if to a child.

"I didn't appreciate you offering me that stuff, Uncle Tariq."

"Now we're getting somewhere. What stuff?"

DuShaun looked up at him, his face grim. "Oh, so it's like *that?*"

"Boy, quit fucking around and say what you've got to say."

"You know I don't use no cocaine," DuShaun said, so angry he spat. "That pissed me off. You know what I've been through trying to stay clear of that, what Coach said. You give me all your speeches about how you got cleaned up, all the pitfalls, and then you're trying to get high with me? You think I don't wanna be out there with the fellas after the games? I'm praying over this every day, living with you instead of getting my own crib, staying in my damn hotel room after the road games instead of hitting the clubs or whatever, and then *you* come trying to get me high—"

"I haven't touched coke in almost three years, DuShaun," Tariq said. "You're mistaken."

At that, DuShaun looked away, but not before Tariq saw his raging eyes. He admired that. The boy kept himself carefully controlled off the field, but Tariq had seen the way he could spark when it mattered, when he needed to drill somebody in the ribs for an extra yard. DuShaun was fluent in rage. "I don't believe this," DuShaun said.

"I said you're mistaken."

"You need help, man," DuShaun said, shaking his head. "You don't even *remember?* That's plain sad. You're always preaching like it's behind you, and here you are having blackouts. Let me get Reese on the phone. He saw it all play out. Monday night, me and Reese are walking out of the club, we get to your car . . ." DuShaun studied Tariq's blank face. "You're trying to tell me you don't remember none of this?"

"Go on and finish." Tariq was no longer angry, he was interested. Fascinated. He sat on the arm of the sofa, waiting. "You walked out of the club, you got to my car. Then what?"

"That little girl's there with you in the back. And that's another thing—that's sick, man. That girl looked young enough to be my baby sister. What was she, like, thirteen? You've got her on her knees in the backseat, she's taking care of you. And you're like, 'Hey, guys, there's room in this little lady for all three of us. Join on in.' Or some shit. You know Reese ain't down with that since he got married last year. And we don't do no chicken-shoots, little schoolgirls and all that."

"This is a hell of a story, DuShaun," Tariq said. "But it's a lie."

Even in high school, Tariq had never been with a girl that young. He'd played around at U.C.L.A., like everyone, but he'd gotten bored fast with girls who thought a quick roll with a football player would make them matter, would somehow take them the same places they thought *he* was going. He'd met Angie, who had her own dreams in her eyes, her own places to go. Even if he'd gotten high Monday night and didn't remember it—which was impossible—he wouldn't have been in his car with some girl younger than Corey. Anyone would know that.

DuShaun saw his disbelieving face. "I'll call Reese right now, Uncle Tariq. I just got off the phone from talking to him about you. He still can't believe it his own self."

"What happened next?"

"You waved that stuff out the window and tried to give it to me. 'Free of charge for family,' you said. You've got this little Baggie full of coke, and you're waving it in my face. You're telling me to get lit with Reese and then we'll all do the girl. She's saying she has to go, and you're like 'Not so fast,' holding her head down, telling her she's not done. I was like, 'Damn, man, you tryin' to get us all thrown in jail?' "

Lies, lies, lies. Why did everyone tell lies about him? After all of Angie's complaints about his lies—and he had to admit he'd told a few so good he'd believed them himself—she had turned into the biggest liar in the end. She had told the police he'd brought a gun into that house, but he hadn't. He'd been questioned like a thug when he was supposed to be worrying about burying his damn dead son. The worst time of his life, and Angie had turned on him. Fucking crazy-ass bitch.

He had not brought that gun with him to Sacajawea.

He had not brought that gun.

He had not. He hadn't seen that gun in years. He'd had a choice between popping Angie in the mouth to shut her up or getting rid of the gun. He hadn't sold it like he'd told her, but he'd done the next best thing: He'd given it to Luisa and told her to hold it for him. Luisa's was the only place where he had any peace, and he'd explained how his teammate Vince had given him that gun, and how that gun was all Tariq had left of him after Vince got paralyzed and died a year and a half later. Angie hadn't wanted to hear it, but that was all it had been about. Vince had watched over his ass for two years at U.C.L.A., one of the best tacklers Tariq had ever seen, and they'd been like brothers. Angie saw it another way, but that was all that gun had been—a thing to remember his friend by.

He'd taken that gun he loved to Luisa's and told her to keep an eye on it. And long after he told Luisa they had to cool off because Angie was looking at him funny all the time and he'd decided he couldn't keep running around on her, Luisa still kept the gun. She was a good woman, not the kind to hold a grudge. She'd taken the gun with her when she moved to Chicago; that's what she told him when he talked to her on the phone on July fifth, the day after Corey died. She couldn't find it, but she knew she had it somewhere. She swore that gun couldn't have been near Corey.

But it had been there. The gun in the wine cellar had a filed-off serial number like Vince's, the same tape, everything. That had been the thing that bothered Tariq most, not being able to figure out where the gun had come from. And Angela telling lies about him, saying he'd done something he hadn't. Attacking him at his own boy's funeral like that. Telling everyone he was responsible.

But she was wrong. The house was responsible. Staring at the raw disillusionment in his nephew's face, Tariq finally understood the bare, nasty fact of it: That house in Sacajawea, where his van was parked this very instant, had given Corey the gun. The house had wanted Corey to have it.

"You need help, Uncle Tariq."

"You're not the first to say that today," Tariq said, remembering Brother Paul's whisper in his ear. Brother Paul was a truth-teller, and he'd smelled it in him. Tariq wished now he had gone to see Brother Paul, to find out what his cards would have said. Those cards would have scared them both speechless, but it would have been good to know. "None of what you just said happened, DuShaun. You're mistaken."

He'd said it three times now, and suddenly there was nothing Tariq hated more than having to repeat himself. The anger had vanished for a while, but it was back. He could hurt DuShaun before this kid knew what was coming. He could kick his nuts in and choke his ass out. Next time, DuShaun would think twice before he tried to accuse him of things he hadn't done. Tariq hadn't touched coke in almost three years. Books were his only addiction now, and he was proud of that.

"Uncle Tariq, you've got me scared. I don't think I can stay here. I'm for real."

"Get out, then," Tariq said. "You've been here too long as it is."

He'd said it as politely as he could, but DuShaun looked up at him like a wounded dog. "Yeah, I think you're right," his nephew said in that same quiet voice he'd started with. "I thought this was working out good, but things are different than I thought."

"Apparently so. You've got your NFL contract, big man. Go get your own damn place."

DuShaun brought himself to his feet, and Tariq stood, too. DuShaun was slightly taller than Tariq, wider. All the players were bigger and wider than when he'd played. DuShaun could make the Pro Bowl, if he worked on his arm. This boy could be a double threat, something special.

But Tariq's warm thoughts vanished as his nephew stepped toward him. Instead, Tariq imagined what it would feel like to crush DuShaun's trachea with a quick chop to his throat, to make DuShaun's eyes pop open wide as he fought to breathe. *Oops, sorry, you ungrateful sonofabitch.* When DuShaun hugged him, Tariq didn't feel anything. He allowed the hug to last a moment, then pushed DuShaun away. "Go on, man. Get off me."

Those hurt brown eyes, again, and this time the eyes did it: Tariq remembered the last time he'd seen DuShaun giving him these sad-sack eyes.

After the Monday night game. At the club.

There had been a lamp glaring behind DuShaun's head, cutting a dark profile. The music was thumping from inside the club's walls like a muffled war-drum. He'd seen DuShaun and Reese, both of them standing outside his Land Cruiser's window looking down at him. The girl's mouth was clumsy, and Tariq had caught a handful of her hair to hold her still, to keep her damn teeth from nicking him. She had looked up at him, lips shining wet in the lamplight.

He'd rolled the window down and offered DuShaun his palm. "No charge for family," he'd said, showing him the lid of coke he'd just scored from this little tramp's friend outside the club, where they'd both been standing, too young to get in but looking for some of the magic inside. *Are you a football player?* the girl had said to him. That was how it had all started. She had started it.

"Why don't ya'll get happy and climb in here with us?" Tariq had called out to DuShaun and Reese through the car window, waving the powder close to DuShaun's face. "She's got room for three. We can stretch her out if we have to." That was what he had *really* said. DuShaun had it all wrong. If DuShaun was going to tell stories, he ought to get the details right.

"I have to go," the girl had said then. She was scared, that was all. First there was one man, and now there were three, and she'd had second thoughts. He could understand that; she was only thirteen. She'd lied and said she was fifteen, but lately Tariq could see straight through lies. The girl had yanked her head against his grip, and that had made Tariq mad. He'd held her more tightly, locking his fingers into her spiked, sticky hair, close to the roots.

And DuShaun had leaned down closer to the window, out of that light's glare. Close enough for Tariq to see his nephew's eyes. Lost, vacuous eyes, trying to accept what they were seeing.

These same eyes.

Something awful happened at the club, Tariq realized, bewildered. *But that wasn't me.*

The room vanished around him, leaving only that thought to anchor him to himself. His legs lost their feeling as his heart froze, pure ice. He remembered Brother Paul again, the music in his words, and his chest hurt so much he stifled a cry in his throat. It wasn't the same pain that burned his stomach at night, the pain of his long resistance. The pain in his chest was grief, the sheer horror of his loss.

I really did do that, but THAT WAS NOT ME. Jesus Lord help—

"Get out, DuShaun. Please stay away from me," he managed to say, his last words.

Tariq held his nephew's eyes longer than he should have been able to, refusing to blink. But he got tired. He'd been tired to start; his soul had been fighting since the party on the Fourth of July, and that was a long time to fight. Longer than a weaker man could have. At last, Tariq blinked hard.

When he opened his eyes, the pain was gone, all of it. The worry, too. No mess, no fuss.

For the first time in two years, Tariq Hill felt just fine. Truth be told, he had never felt finer. Tariq Hill was a brand-new man, and he was riding the best high of his life.

⚜ Fifteen ⚜

SACAJAWEA

TUESDAY NIGHT

*L*IZA BRUNELL had banned toxic phrases like *I did the stupidest thing today* from her inner monologues a long time ago, but she'd been thinking those words all day. And now that she'd finished chopping apple wood for the backyard smokehouse and helping Glenn with his third-grade science report—(Different Kinds of Leaves!!! screamed the sloppy, leaf-covered mess on the dining-room table)—her mind was free to resume its rant against herself.

She had done the very stupidest damned thing today.

Liza patted Glenn's backside. He was in his typical position, lying flat on the mattress between her and Art, chin resting on his elbows, rump sticking in the air as he watched the television at the foot of the bed. The *Aladdin* video was over, and so was family time.

"Nine o'clock," she said. "Bedtime."

"I'm not sleepy!"

"We don't care if you're sleepy. This is Mommy and Daddy time."

Glenn pretended to be shocked. "You don't *care* if I'm sleepy?" He looked at her, then at his father. Art was on the other side of the bed, his back against the headboard as he sat up with his face buried in paperwork. He was researching the tax bond to improve Sacajawea County schools, thinking he could push that through like he had the new jail, and he was in over his head. Art wanted to help Sacajawea prosper the way he had, through shrewd decisions and no small amount of luck, but Liza wasn't sure he understood the reality of the times. This was a poor county. People didn't have money, and they didn't want new taxes, even for their kids' sake. Not enough people in the county even *had* kids; there were only twelve students in Glenn's third-grade class, and fewer in second grade. At the roots, anyway, she sensed that the area was dying, the schools included. She knew three families who were sending their kids to the private Catholic school in Longview, and the thought had crossed her mind, too. More than once. She had Glenn's future to think about.

"Dad, is that true? Mom said you don't *care* if I'm sleepy or not."

Art didn't look up. "Yep, that about sums it up," he said. "I don't care. You, Liza?"

Liza shrugged. "I'm not giving a big fat darn over here."

"You guys are lame," Glenn said, hopping off the bed. "I don't even get a bedtime story?"

Liza took off her reading glasses and outstretched her arms for a hug. "Come on, sweetie. All kidding aside, Mom and Dad are bushed tonight. If you want to read yourself a story, keep your light on until nine-thirty. But when I look in your room, I'd better see you reading. No G.I. Joe, no Star Wars, no Gameboy. Just reading, or else you go to sleep. You're stalling."

Glenn frowned and grumbled softly, but otherwise didn't argue. Liza gave him a long, tight hug and a kiss on the cheek. A couple more years, she thought, and she'd have to fight for every hug. It could start anytime. "That's my good boy."

"Come on 'round," Art said to him, beckoning. When Glenn bounded over, Liza heard Art stage-whisper to him, pretending they had a secret life without her: "You and me. Four o'clock tomorrow. Our favorite inlet. Those fish better watch out."

"*Yayyyyy!*" Glenn shrieked. He ran out of the room, arms extended, veering like an airplane.

"Teeth!" Liza called after him.

"Yep, I've got 'em all, Mom!" Glenn called back.

"Not for long he won't, that little smart-ass," Liza muttered. "He'd better brush. And since when do you have time to take off to go fishing on a weekday? You're spoiling him, Art."

"Who's spoiling who? Tomorrow's light, and I love taking off to fish. It's good for my image. You know—I'm a regular guy, not some bureaucrat behind a desk."

The way Art behaved sometimes, you'd think he'd won a seat to the U.S. Senate, she thought, rolling her eyes. But Liza had a larger concern, one she hadn't been able to forget all day. She curled her knees against Art, her little-girl pose.

"I did the stupidest thing today," she said.

Art could never resist the little-girl pose, even when he was deep in his work. He stroked her hair, his eyeglasses reflecting her face in the light from her nightstand lamp. "Awwww . . . ," he said in his most coddling voice. "Tell Uncle Art all about it." Uncle Art was his recurring fantasy character in their bedroom; a kind father confessor who was often a molesting pervert in disguise. Tonight, however, Uncle Art was prepared to listen.

So, Liza told him how Angie's face had looked when she heard the story of the mud. "I think Angie went to Longview to get a hotel room tonight," Liza finished. "I can't believe I was so *stupid*. What was I thinking about, to tell her that? And then bringing up her mom, and the Fourth of July. *That* was my crowning moment. The Fourth of July! Christ."

Art grimaced, pained. "Oh, geez. Yeah, I might have tried to find a way to skip the part about the Fourth," he said, forgetting his Uncle Art voice. "That's a bad one. But it's done now, munchkin. Angie knows you didn't mean any harm."

Liza sighed, switching off the television set with the remote. This next part was going to sound crazy to him, but she had to let her thoughts out. She and Art never hid even the small things from each other, if they could help it. Despite a few embarrassing moments, so far that system worked pretty well. "Art, I don't how to say this—but it's as if I *did* mean to do harm. Not on purpose, not exactly . . . but when I started telling that story, I wish you could have heard the way details started pouring out of me. You remember how Grandpa could run a story into the ground, but it's been ten years since he died. I haven't repeated that story to anyone, before today."

"Yeah, not even to me. Thanks a lot."

"Grandpa asked me not to tell, and I've kept my word. He was very specific about it, Art—this whole rigamarole about how it had to be a secret because only he and three other men saw what happened, besides Red John and Mrs. T'saint. They were all convinced they'd seen the devil up close that day, and they took a vow to keep quiet so the devil would keep his distance. You know—you leave us alone, we'll leave you alone. He said the kid in the tub never remembered a thing."

"I bet it was Randall Booth in the tub. That guy was a weirdo."

"Who's Randall Booth?"

"He owned the hotel in the fifties. A *real* weirdo, my dad tells me. He used to—"

"Will you let me finish before you get started on one of your half-cocked gossip tears?"

"Go on. Sorry."

Liza sighed. Art was a better talker than he was a listener, so conversation with him was exhausting sometimes. She'd almost lost her heart to go on, but she did: "When I told Angie that story today, you'd think I'd been reciting it for years. Truly? It felt like I could *see* it happening instead of describing something I hadn't heard in ages. Honest to God, when I heard myself mention the Fourth of July, I wanted to yank out my own tongue. I just couldn't stop."

Art didn't laugh at her, which was a relief. He gazed at her with solemn eyes. "I've got a question for you to consider, Madame Liza."

"What?"

He hesitated. "Let's not pretend we haven't talked about how we'd like to buy that house if Angie puts it on the market. Is it possible you were just . . . twisting the knife?"

Liza gasped. She grabbed her pillow and whipped it at Art, landing a blow squarely on his temple. "Thanks a lot! How can you say that? You must think you're married to the Queen Bitch."

Art wrested the pillow away from her. "I think I'm married to a wonderful woman who happens to love that house," he said in a placating tone. "We both do. It's a ready-made mayor's mansion, staring right over the town from the ridge. Five bedrooms! And picture it . . . one day, when our grandchildren are visiting, we'll be able to tell them, 'Look, kids, this is where Grandma and Grandpa kissed for the very first time.' "

"We never kissed in that house," Liza said.

"It was at The Spot. *Behind* the house. All of it belonged to Mrs. T'saint. I've taken a peek at the property records. She's got fifty, sixty acres back there."

Liza shook her head, laughing. She'd forgotten that The Spot was part of Angie's land, that it wasn't community property. The summer after high school graduation, when she'd discovered that her grades and talent weren't going to garner her any scholarships, she'd wanted to get drunk, so she and Melanie found a late-night party at The Spot. Angie hadn't been there, and Liza remembered the reason: Angie had been depressed over her breakup with Myles. Watching the agony her friend was suffering, Liza had vowed not to get too serious about any boy until she was much older. After college. After she made it to the New York stage.

"There you were, wearing a white blouse, your face shining in the firelight," Art said suddenly, his voice faraway. "I'd had a crush on you since fifth grade, but the way you looked that night . . . I said, 'God, if you let me have Liza Kerr, I will never give you cause to be displeased with me.' That's exactly what I said, a little prayer."

"Are you sure it was God you were talking to?" Her question was only half-joking.

"This was the work of the Big Guy, Liza. No other way to explain it. You'd never given me a glance all through high school, and not fifteen minutes after I said that prayer, we were necking behind a tree. And it's not just us. Melanie and Rob, Doug and Christine . . ."

"Angie and Myles."

"Well, they're the exception. Most every other couple that linked up at The Spot is still together, my folks included. You ask me, that's why the county divorce rate is so low. My folks have never 'fessed up to it, but Dad's hinted that I was conceived there. Can't you just picture it?"

"I'd rather not." The image of Art's pudgy parents rutting in the woods did not appeal to her.

"I've got a stake in that place, and you do, too. And the whole property might go up for sale soon, if Angie decides she wants to dump it. That could be your motive for what happened today, Liza. That's why you told that scary story."

God help her, Art might be right, she thought. How many times since Corey's funeral had Liza nearly called Angie in L.A. to put in an offer? *Oh, everyone's fine here—listen, Angie, we haven't seen you in a while, and we're wondering about your plans for your grandmother's house.* . . . Laurel Everly had shown the house once, and Liza wasn't the only person in Sacajawea incensed that outsiders had gotten the first crack. This week, Liza had planned to give Angie a few days, then pop the question. Telling that story damn well *might* have been deliberate on her part. But . . .

"Okay, that occurred to me, too," Liza said, nestling inside the crook of Art's arm. She rubbed her hand across his pale, ample belly—*More cushion for the pushin',* as he liked to say. "But I don't believe it was some cheap ploy by my unconscious, Art. The way we all felt standing in that kitchen today, I have to tell you—I wouldn't even want the house now. I mean that."

Art looked at her, disbelieving. He took off his glasses. "Oh, come on.

The same person who laughs at me for picking up pennies on the sidewalk and saving my fortunes from Ming's?"

"Yeah, yeah, I know. I still think that's dumb, on both counts. But we felt something there today. All three of us. I don't know the words for it."

"I'll tell you what you felt . . . ," Art said, kissing the tip of her nose. "You felt a stellar performance by a top-notch actress telling a ghost story. You were so good today, you scared your own socks off. Save it for opening night, munchkin."

God bless him, Liza thought. Art always found a way to turn the conversation around to the things he imagined were extraordinary about her. She'd been so superficial as a teenager, it was a wonder Art's earnest, quiet admiration hadn't been lost on her when they really first saw each other at The Spot. He had never stopped seeing something in her she still wasn't sure how to live up to. And maybe he was right. Maybe she'd only been guilty of falling into character earlier today, immersing herself in her actress persona. She hadn't done any real acting in so long, it was no wonder she was getting swept away. That possibility had never occurred to her.

"You're too damned smart sometimes," she said. "You've earned a piece of German chocolate cake. I brought one home from the bake sale at Glenn's school today."

Art rediscovered his papers, frowning. "Maybe tomorrow. No more food for me tonight."

"What's wrong?" Art never turned down food unless he was sick, and he'd never admit to being sick. The last time he got sick, he walked around with pneumonia for days and ended up in the emergency room with enough infection in him to nearly kill him, the stubborn idiot. *Exactly like what happened to Jim Henson*, the doctor in Longview said, telling them how lucky he'd been.

"Just a little something the past couple days. No biggee," Art said. "A tummyache. Stomach flu, maybe, or too much stress. The *News* is running a story about the school bond tomorrow, and I'm as nervous as the new baby-faced kid taking his first shower on Cell Block D. That's all it is."

Liza was not comforted, but she didn't press him. He'd be all right, she told herself.

He always was.

Once the lights were out and the house was quiet, Liza hated to close her eyes. Each time she did, she saw Angela's upstairs bathroom, mud flinging everywhere. Her wide-open eyes began fooling her in the bedroom's darkness; as she stared at the walls and ceiling, she could swear she saw the appearance of stark mud-patterns around her. But they simply weren't there, vanishing when she blinked. They were only shadows, each and every one. She really *had* scared herself telling her grandfather's story today, she realized.

Liza's eyes guarded the doorway of their dark master bathroom, and her ears listened for sounds from the bathtub. The house was carefully quiet, more so than usual. Even Miko, sleeping in his doggie bed in the hall outside, didn't scurry around restlessly, hoping to climb into the bed with them. Beside her, Art breathed heavily in sleep, occasionally snoring softly. And issuing a single angry murmur from his stomach she barely heard.

⚔ Sixteen ⚔

SACAJAWEA
WEDNESDAY

I KNOW—it's a surprise to hear from me," Tariq's voice said, and Angela's heart lurched.

She was checking her office messages from her hotel room while CNN Headline News nattered capsules of world events from the television set. After an hour-long conversation with her assistant about which calls needed her urgent attention, Imani had told her she had a private message on Tuesday's voice mail, that she should listen to it herself. Tariq's deep voice in her ear was a shock.

He sighed on the recording. "It's a beautiful Tuesday morning, and I miss you. That's not what I called to say, but it's the truth, Snook. I'd be lying if I said I didn't. Anyway, DuShaun made the Raiders' cut—you might have heard about that—and now he's one of the star starters. Football's not your thing, and I won't bore you with the details, but he made a hell of a play Monday night. Just thought you'd like to know. He's been living with me, and we both like that. Believe it or not, I'm keeping him out of trouble. He's a great kid."

Angela smiled. Yes, DuShaun was a great kid, Corey's favorite cousin. Good for Harry and Yolanda, she thought. Her in-laws had been the only other family she had, yet Angela hadn't spoken to them since the funeral. Another bridge she'd torn down when she exiled herself from her life.

"Anyway, babe, your secretary mentioned you're away for a few days, and I'm glad to hear it. Hope it's a good trip. I know you're doing great things, and I'm hanging in here, too. A few medical problems, but I'll get that handled. I have a doctor's appointment later today, and maybe that'll shed some light. Send a few good thoughts my way, Snook. Take care of yourself."

Angela picked up her cell phone, dialing from memory. An effervescent recorded voice announced an index of things she didn't care about. Season tickets. Game schedules. Team memorabilia. "Finance. Tariq Hill, please," she said, when an operator rescued her.

The wait on the line, this time, was silent. And short. Tariq had a new secretary, a male one, and he told her Tariq had called in sick. Did she want to leave a message? For the first time, Angela asked herself what the hell she was doing. What was she going to say? *Hey, sorry I went off on you like that at the funeral after you did your part to help kill our son. Hope you feel better.*

"Tell him Angie returned his call."

Hanging up, Angela felt liberated. Her anger at Tariq was a weight, and she was tired of carrying it. She might not ever be able to forgive him, but she could talk to him, at least. She could be civil. He'd been thoughtful to call, considering she'd never said a kind word to him in more than two years. And she felt sad, she realized. The feeling puzzled her, but she recognized the sting. She'd felt a keen sadness last night, realizing what she'd lost with Myles—and now she might be losing something else because of one missed telephone call.

What had she lost? Her chance to hear Tariq finally tell the truth?

Angela steeled herself, then she dialed another number, the number she used to call when she wanted to talk to Corey. The number was still fresh in her mind, a living thing. She expected to hear Corey's voice next, and she almost did, because the voice that answered was youthful, cavalier: "Whassup? This is the Hill residence. Press one to speak to Tariq Hill. Press two for DuShaun Hill. May God's love find you each and every day. Peace." It was DuShaun's voice on the machine, practically unchanged since the last time she'd seen him, when he was about seventeen. This time, Angela hung up without leaving a message. She felt like an intruder.

Angela dialed a new number, moving onward. She had a lot to cover in Sacajawea before she could go back to L.A., and this was going to be a long week. She knew the next number she dialed by heart, too, unfortunately. She couldn't forget it if she tried.

Her high school classmate was at his desk, and he picked up on the first ring. No voice mail, no recordings, no secretary. An honest-to-God human voice. "I figured I'd be hearing from you soon," Sheriff Rob Graybold said, after the initial pleasantries and his condolences on her fallen tree.

"Why's that?"

"I saw Myles at the courthouse this morning, and he said you have a couple concerns about Sean Leahy. Want to come by and talk?"

Sacajawea's grapevine amazed her, yet again. "I'd rather just meet you at Sean's."

"Let's not put the cart before the horse, Angie. Let me hear what's on your mind. That boy just lost his daddy, and we need to be delicate."

"He knows something about Corey, Rob."

"Then we'll find out what he knows, I promise you." Rob paused. "Since you're on the phone, thanks for moving that bus. I was going to bring it up before you left town. It's been an eyesore sitting out there. The kids getting into it, all that. Kind of a hazard."

"What bus?"

"That old VW that's been parked in front of your house is gone. Or at least that's what Joe Everly said when I saw him at the diner last night. You don't know anything about that?"

Angela had no answer. The van had been there when she'd left the house yesterday. Her fingertips lost their sensation.

Sheriff Rob Graybold sighed. "Well, get on over here, Angie. You might as well fill out a police report while you're here."

There was a dead space where the van had been, a patch of grass so dried out and sunlight-starved it looked scorched. With the van gone, the mound of trash that had surrounded it was more offensive; old food wrappers, beer cans, soiled condoms. It had been an eyesore, no question. How could someone have gotten the van to start after two years, much less driven off with two flat tires? Angela's eyes searched for bent stalks of overgrown grass that would have been left by the heavy tires of a tow truck, and she found none. There were no tracks at all, in fact. While Rob waited at the roadside beside his Sacajawea sheriff's vehicle, Angela ran up the stone steps to check the front door of the house for a note of any kind. Nope.

Angela stared down from Gramma Marie's porch at the spot where the van had been parked, and the emptied space disturbed her. "It's nice that you called, Tariq, but you should've told me you were coming to town," she muttered in the silence of the gray afternoon.

No. That wasn't it, she decided. Tariq would have mentioned that when he called. She would have to file the van's disappearance into the growing category of strange occurrences since her return, a long, depressing list. She'd wished that van would disappear, hadn't she? Maybe one of her wishes had finally come true.

There was a crater where the walnut tree had been, filled with new soil marking the place where something big obviously had stood. Angela gazed up at the round attic window, which was cracked in two places, ruined. A small section of the roof's shingles had been swept away where the tree landed directly, revealing splintered wood underneath. The house was coming apart, in pieces.

Feeling more at ease because the sheriff was outside waiting, Angela quickly let herself into the house. Everything inside looked exactly the way it had when she'd left, a relief. Upstairs, she retrieved the index cards from the window seat in Corey's room, hoping Sean would show the same fear when he saw them again. She glanced into the bathroom on her way back downstairs, and there was still mud in the tub, but no more than yesterday, and it had dried. Good.

"Whatcha think? Need to file a police report?" Rob asked from where he waited against the hood of his sheriff's unit. Angela shook her head. The van wasn't worth it.

"Let's just go talk to Sean, Rob."

Sheriff Rob Graybold was lean, standing six feet, with a carriage that bespoke his tour as a Green Beret and medic during the Gulf War. Pot farmers and crystal meth lab operators who set up shop in Sacajawea County made the mistake of assuming that the sheriff of a small county would be short on brains or skill. But Rob's arrest record was one of the best in southern Washington. He'd also killed a man in Skamokawa in the late nineties, taking a clean shot at a tourist attacking his wife with a machete outside their camper. The story went that Rob had shot the man without blinking, so confident in his aim that he'd taken a shot most cops in movies were afraid to try—but only after he'd spent a half hour trying to talk him into putting the massive blade down. *You won't shoot me,* the man had said, a woeful miscalculation. Rob had shot him through the heart.

Rob was one of her few classmates in Sacajawea who had always been intact, turning out to be almost identical to what he'd always been. Even in high school, he'd been serious and aloof, as if he were preparing for unpleasant tasks. Today, his beige uniform was pressed, his western-style hat was slanted at an angle, and his badge, shoes, and leather holster shined. If Sheriff Rob Graybold couldn't rattle Sean, Angela thought, no one could.

Rob had called first, so Sean was expecting them. He met them outside his front door, guiding them to a picnic table under a cedar tree beside the trailer. His white-blond hair was neatly combed, gelled away from his forehead this time, not falling into his eyes. He answered every question without hesitation, calling Angela "ma'am" and Sheriff Graybold "sir." He brought out a pitcher of iced tea and served them politely. Watching him, it would have been easy to believe Sean had been conducting himself admirably in interrogations half his life.

When Angela spread the index cards on the table, Sean barely registered any emotion.

"Yeah, I've seen those," he said. "Like I told Mrs. Toussaint before, those were Corey's. He thought they could do spells."

"And *you* thought they could do spells, too," Angela corrected.

"Maybe a superstitious thing, like you don't walk on the sidewalk crack or you break your mother's back. I've never seen any real-life magic, just stuff on TV."

He was lying! Angela had expected Sean to be evasive, but she could hardly reconcile the calm boy sitting before her now with the quivering wreck she'd seen just two days ago. "Sean . . . ," she prompted, a warning.

Sheriff Graybold tapped her knee under the varnished wood tabletop, silencing her.

"Sean, why do you think Corey shot himself?" he asked.

Sean shrugged. "I don't know, Sheriff. I've thought about that, but I just can't say. It's crazy. It was a shock and everything." He hung his head, which Angela cynically decided was a move for sympathy before she scolded herself for the thought.

"Of course it was, son," the sheriff said. After a sensitive pause, the sheriff pressed on. "Corey wrote something in his notebook we thought you could help us interpret. He wrote the words *We have fucked up big.* Do you have any idea what he meant by that?"

"Yes, Sean—do you remember what you said about the land being tainted? Something you'd done with Corey to taint the land?" Angela could no longer keep silent.

"No, sir," Sean answered, ignoring Angela. "I don't know anything about that. He never showed that notebook to me. He wrote poems in it, I guess. He was private about it."

"Yeah, I guess a kid would be private about a thing like that," the sheriff said. His green eyes flashed Angela a quick but plain message: *Keep quiet.* She folded her hands in her lap, sighing. In the long silence, they heard agitated whinnying of horses in the stable.

"Still got Sheba back there?" the sheriff said.

"Yessir. My aunt sent the other ones back, the studs we had."

"You think you're gonna sell Sheba, you let me know. Melanie's looking at an Andalusian on the Internet now, but they're a fortune," Rob said, his voice sounding breezy, as if they were ready to leave. He even closed his notebook, and they had just gotten started!

"Andalusians are great horses. But I don't think I'm gonna sell Sheba, sir."

"You find a good horse, you keep her," the sheriff said, and he hardly paused before he went on. "What do you know about a kid named Beaumont Cryer, Sean?"

There. Sean kept his expression carefully in check, but all color seeped from his face. He looked ill, suddenly.

"Who?" he said.

"You don't know who Beaumont Cryer is?"

"Well . . ." Sean hesitated. "Yeah. Of course. Everyone called him Bo."

"What else do you know about him?"

Sean's hand wandered to his forehead, looking for hair to flick from his face, a habit. "Didn't he . . . run away or something?"

"He vanished that same summer you met Corey," Rob said. His notebook was open again, his pen poised to take notes. Sean looked at Angela, as if for assistance, but Angela was lost. She'd never heard of a kid named Beaumont Cryer. Apparently, Sheriff Graybold had his own agenda today. "Didn't Bo spend a lot of time at The Spot? You and Corey hung out there, too. When you ran into Bo there . . . did he ever say anything about leaving town? Anything that could help us out?"

Sean opened his mouth to speak, then hesitated. He was weighing what to say, and not hiding it well. "I'm not sure I remember running into Bo Cryer at The Spot," he said finally. "I don't have any memory of that." To Angela, he sounded like a senator testifying at a Congressional hearing.

"You sure, Sean?" Sheriff Graybold said gently. "No little disagreement?"

"That was at Pizza Jack's," Sean blurted, then slowed down. "I mean, it wasn't a real disagreement or anything. No big deal. Bo said some things Corey didn't like, trying to start something. That's how Bo was. But nothing came of it."

That was all news to Angela, but as much as she'd tried to monitor Corey's whereabouts, the life teenagers shared with other teenagers was known only to them. Corey had mentioned some local boys making snide comments and giving him hostile looks, another of the reasons he hated spending summers in Sacajawea. Remembering that, Angela felt pangs of remorse. She'd been so bent on trying to recreate the experiences of her adolescence for Corey, she'd uprooted him every year and isolated him in a place where he felt like an outsider. Since his death, that seemed unreasonable in a way that horrified her. Tears pricked at Angela's eyes. She should never have brought him here. What would she give to have that one summer back?

"You *sure*, Sean?" Sheriff Graybold said again. "You're sure nothing came of it?"

Sean was looking at Rob Graybold as if he knew it was useless to lie, but it was too late to start telling the truth. "Yeah, nothing came of it. Then we heard he'd vanished."

"And how long after that did Corey shoot himself? Do you remember?"

Sean swallowed hard, his Adam's apple fighting his throat. "A couple days, maybe. I dunno."

Angela could no longer keep quiet. "Rob . . . I don't know what you're getting at here, but you're missing the point. Sean, you need to tell us about what you told me. The spells."

Sean looked at her with sad, exasperated eyes. "I don't know anything about the magic, Mrs. Toussaint," he said. "Swear to God. Corey was into it, that's all."

"But you said the land is tainted," Sheriff Graybold said. "Isn't that right? Didn't you say that to your dad all the time? That's what I hear from folks. You said not to go near it."

Sean blinked. He was close to tears, and Angela suddenly pitied him. She hadn't expected Rob to push this hard. "I said it was bad karma, because Corey died there," Sean said.

"Corey died in the *house*, Sean. I understand that. But there's fifty-odd acres of land back there. Why would you warn your dad and anybody else who'd listen to stay away from the land?"

Sean looked at Angela again, this time with fierce eyes. "Maybe *she* gets it. When something bad happens, you want to stay away from it. Don't you? You don't want to talk about it. You want to forget it ever happened. You understand, don't you, Mrs. Toussaint?"

"Yes, Sean, I do," she said, seizing the opportunity to try to get through to him. "But sometimes we can't stay away. We have to go back. Because if we don't, other people get hurt. I can't think of any good that's ever come out of a secret, even if you made a promise to a friend to keep one. Even if you promised a friend who died."

Tell us, Angela thought, wishing she could control Sean with her mind. *Please*. But Sean's eyes had narrowed as he drew more deeply into himself, escaping to his own contemplations.

The sun was low in the sky. It must be nearly five o'clock, Angela realized. She could hardly remember how she'd spent her day, except making phone calls and this conversation with Sean. Days were too precious to waste, and she wasn't looking forward to the drive back to Longview and the confinement of her hotel room. This close to Gramma Marie's house, she almost felt tempted to stay here at home. Almost.

The squawk from Sheriff Graybold's radio was so loud, Angela jumped beside him. Rob pressed the radio to his mouth. "Graybold," he said.

"Rob? There's a report of a possible homicide over by the pier, near the historical museum. Gunnar Michaelsen's waiting there with his grandson. Tommy made the call." A woman's voice.

"What the hell would Tommy know about a homicide?"

"That's the call, Rob. He sounded frantic. You best go check it out."

"Roger that," Rob said, and Angela noticed his body sag. His eyes had gone cold in a way they might have when he was in Skamokawa that day, right before he squeezed the trigger. "That sounds like a shitstorm. Tommy and some friends playing a prank, I'll bet. But I gotta go."

Sean looked relieved to have lost Rob's attention, but Rob had a stern tone for him. "Don't disappear yourself until we've talked again. You got that?"

"Yes, sir," Sean said, already halfway back to the front door of his trailer.

"Rob, we need to talk," Angela said.

"Then you're gonna have to ride with me, Angie."

It began to drizzle as Rob set off for the pier in his Sacajawea sheriff's vehicle, a silver Ford Bronco with a bright blue stripe painted along its body. He drove without his siren and in no apparent hurry, his windshield wipers whining as they made their slow, dragging passage back and forth across the glass. The sight of Toussaint Lane, and Gramma Marie's house perched above it, disappeared in the rearview mirror.

"What was that all about?" Angela said.

"That Cryer kid disappeared around the time Corey died, and it seemed clear as a bell to me just now that Sean knows something about that. And, I guess . . ." Rob didn't have to finish.

2 Jananarive Due

"Corey never said anything to me," Angela said. Rob shrugged, non-committal, and she felt a surge of anger as she realized her son might be under suspicion for a crime. "You never thought there was any credibility to what I told you, did you?"

"Sorry, Angie, but I follow leads. Spells and curses don't hold water with me—facts do. There are a lot of facts tied together with Sean Leahy. If you follow it your way and I follow it my way, maybe between the two of us, we'll figure this out. Like you, I want to know what happened that summer. That was a bad summer in Sacajawea County. We lost two of our boys." His eyes were suddenly intent on the road before him. "Let's hope we haven't lost someone else."

Angela's left arm tingled so badly, she clutched it close to her chest. *Dammit.* What now? "I don't think this call is a hoax, Rob," she said softly, thinking aloud.

"Know what? You could be right. I'm breaking regs bringing a civilian with me without calling it in, Angie—so when I pull in, stay close to my car."

Laney Keane waved them down in front of the huge maritime bell and mounted antique schooner on display outside of the historical society, which abutted the riverfront. She ran to Rob's window, breathless. Angela hadn't seen Laney since the Fourth of July party.

"Tommy's *hysterical.* Everyone's around back, on the pier."

Rob thanked her and bumped his Bronco up onto the curb to drive across the muddy grass leading to the pier—cops' privilege, and definitely faster than walking. A second sheriff's vehicle was already parked several yards ahead of them. Only now did Rob turn on his flasher, which flamed in red against the historical society's rear wall and the water's edge. When Angela opened her car door, a strong wind from the river whipped across her face, tousling her hair. She smelled rotting sea life. Someone was feeding a flock of seagulls nearby, and the birds' cries bothered her ear. Seagulls always sounded like they were in distress.

Eight people were huddled on the pier in light jackets, waiting. Angela forgot Rob's instructions to stay near his car, following him stride for stride. A young child stood at the center of the crowd, wrapped in a police-issue orange blanket while Gunnar Michaelsen stood over him with both hands planted on the boy's shoulders. The child's face and hair were streaked with sandy mud, a sight that stopped Angela in her tracks. There was no hysteria in the crowd, not the way Laney had described it, but the quiet was more unsettling.

The muddy boy's neck was craned upward, his head pivoting back and forth as the adults spoke over him. A lanky deputy Angela didn't recognize pointed out an inlet with a muddy, rocky shoal to Rob, about forty yards from them. Angela saw someone's blue jacket, a tackle box, and fishing poles on the sandy bank across the way, which was littered with tiny clamshells that seagulls had carried into the air and broken on the rocks below. Next, the deputy pointed out the tied fiberglass rowboat bobbing in the water alongside the pier. There was another fishing pole in the boat, a rod and reel that looked expensive.

Even standing a few feet from Rob, Angela heard only snatches of what was said. ". . . All three of them over there at about four-thirty . . . ," said the deputy, reciting for Rob with precision. ". . . says he held his face under the water and strangled him . . . shook him violently . . . then when he stopped moving, he carried the body to the boat, rowed it back . . . saw him put the body in his car. . . . Tommy had to take the path. . . . He ran screaming to Laney, and she called 911 for him."

The crowd listened like a funeral party. Rob nodded and took notes, gazing out at the boat and then toward the shoal, which was accessible either by the water or a rocky, circuitous path winding along the riverbank. He gazed at the path, probably replaying what the deputy had said in his mind. "Colin," Rob said to the deputy, "get me the mayor's law office on the phone."

"He's not there!" the boy said, screaming, the first words Angela had heard him speak.

"We already tried his office. He did leave early today," the deputy said.

"He's already home by now. That's where he said he was goin'!" the boy screeched, and Gunnar rubbed his shoulders to try to calm him. Gunnar's cheekbones above his beard looked tight enough to crack if he spoke. He looked haunted. It was hard to believe that only yesterday he'd been romping on the rooftop of her house, enjoying his friends.

"Get them at home, then," Rob said. "Let's talk to Liza."

As the rowboat in the water floated closer to the dock, Angela made out the bright red lettering painted lovingly at its pointed helm: HIZZONER, it said. That was Art's boat. Had something happened to Art?

Her heart leaping, Angela made her way closer to the sheriff as he took the cell phone his deputy had already dialed for him. "Liza? Hey, this is Rob. Is Art there?" Angela, like everyone else, listened during the ensuing pause. For an instant, there was silence except for the moaning of seagulls and indistinguishable traces of Liza's chipper voice on the phone.

"No, no need to pull him away from that," Rob said. "How about Glenn? Is he there, too? He all right?" The sheriff nodded, indicating to the onlookers that she had said yes. Thank God, Angela thought. Thank Jesus, Allah, and everyone else. But she noticed that Tommy looked more confused than relieved, and Gunnar's face was no less haunted.

"No, nothing's wrong," Rob said. "I'm just gonna swing by there in a few minutes. There's a little something I want to ask Art about. I'll tell him when I get there." He clicked off. Rob summoned his deputy closer to give him private instructions, then he kneeled down until he was at eye-level with Tommy. "I think maybe there was a misunderstanding, Tommy. Do you feel like taking a ride with me in a real police car?"

Despite his tears, Tommy's face brightened and he nodded. Rob led Tommy and Gunnar back toward his haphazardly parked Bronco and opened the back door for them. Without a word, Angela slid into the passenger seat. Rob would probably like to leave her behind—her car was parked outside his office only two blocks away, easy enough to walk to—but she wanted to go with him to make sure Art and Liza were all right. Rob started his engine without glancing at her.

Spruce Street, where Art and Liza lived, was on the other side of the Four, half a mile from downtown, toward the white-tailed deer preserve between Sacajawea and Skamokawa. It was a short ride, made interminable by the silence in the car. Angela glanced at Gunnar's face in the rearview mirror; he didn't look as brittle as he had before, but he was not at ease. Neither was Tommy, who was sitting with his eyes closed, rocking back and forth, singing a quiet song to himself.

"You like fishing, Tommy?" Angela said, trying to distract the boy.

Tommy didn't open his eyes. "I *used* to," he said mournfully.

Gunnar glared at Angela in the rearview mirror, so she didn't say anything else to the child.

Spruce Street was shared by six houses, three on each side with five-acre land tracts, so it was not usually a busy place. But Angela saw the cars waiting as soon as Rob turned the corner from the Four, three of them parked along the road, in addition to another sheriff's unit. Marlene Odell from the grocery store stood leaning against her car, fumbling with a cigarette while she waited. Logan Prescott and Tom Brock were there, too, arms crossed. A neighbor family stood in the front yard across the street, keeping a polite distance but determined to see what they could. The sight of the waiting crowd made Angela feel queasy with dread.

Angela saw Rob touch his holster before he opened his car door, feeling his gun. What the hell was going on? "I thought Liza said everything was fine, Rob," she whispered.

"That is what she said. Just keep clear, Angie. I mean it this time."

When Rob told Gunnar and Tommy to wait in the car, the boy squirmed. "Can you ask if Glenn can come outside?" Tommy said urgently.

"I'll do that," Rob said, and gave Tommy a small smile before walking away.

A lean, broad-shouldered black dog guarded the house from the backyard, heaving himself against the fence as he barked angrily. Art's two-story house was white with forest-green trim, and a cheerful wooden country mailbox waited on a post at the roadside. BRUNELL, it said above the freshly carved jack-o'-lantern grinning out jaggedly on the ground beneath it. For the first time, Angela remembered that Halloween was in two weeks. She'd forgotten all about it. In Sacajawea, holidays were celebrated early, with painstaking decorations, as if it were the law.

Angela followed Rob as far as she thought she could without a warning. Then, she stopped and stood posted like the others, a dozen steps from the front porch. The porch was draped with orange and black streamers, but what stole Angela's gaze was the mock graveyard beside the porch steps, a small patch of soil planted with three gray headstones in diminishing size; mama bear, papa bear, and baby bear. The joke was lost on her. It didn't seem the least bit funny.

The doorbell chimed inside the house. Another long, silent wait. When Liza flung the door open, Angela's sense of normalcy swiftly returned. "What the *hell*'s into Miko? He's making a racket," Liza said, then she shined a smile at Rob. "Hey, Rob. That was quick."

Liza's smile died, however, when she looked beyond Rob and saw the people watching at a distance. Angela had never seen Liza blanch like that. "What's wrong?"

"Probably nothing, darlin'. I just need to have a quick word with you and Art."

Liza's face relaxed some, but she wasn't satisfied with that answer. She turned her gaze to Angela, pleading. "Angie, what's going on?"

Angela lost her last bit of resolve to stay out of Rob's way. She would hear about this later, she knew, but Liza was scared. "Everything's fine, Liza," Angela said, walking to the porch. "Something happened downtown."

"Liza, I know this looks funny," Rob said. "But there was a little problem at the river earlier today, and I need to talk to Art. He might have seen something."

Liza took Angela's hand, squeezing hard, not letting go. Liza's eyes gazed hard at Rob, questioning, and she looked back out at the gathered onlookers. "That's why two sheriff's rigs and half the town are camped out in front of my house? I believe that."

"We should talk inside, Liza," Rob said quietly.

Liza gave Rob a thinly masked glare, then moved out of the doorway. "Okay, Rob, yeah, both of you can come on in. Art's upstairs watching the news, like I told you on the phone. He just got back from fishing, him and Glenn and Tommy Michaelsen."

"Angie has to stay put, Liza. This is private."

Liza's eyes sparked. "Last I checked, this was still *my* house."

"All right," Rob said, giving in. He knew it was best not to rile Liza; as Angela remembered it, when he and Liza had dated their junior year, he'd riled her a lot. Rob pressed his hand against Angela's back, guiding her into the house. He closed the door behind them. The foyer felt steamy, scented with tomato sauce and garlic from cooking food. "Where's Glenn now?"

"Art said he wanted a nap. He's in his room."

"Have you talked to Glenn since he's been back?"

"Well, no, Rob," Liza said, annoyed. "I've been in the kitchen. They came in about fifteen minutes ago, and Glenn had tired himself out. Did Glenn . . . *do* something?"

Art appeared above them on the stairs to the left of the foyer, tucking a plaid shirt into his blue jeans. "Well, hey, Rob. Angie. What's going on?"

"Rob is here asking about Glenn," Liza told him.

"Glenn?" The joviality left Art's face. "Something we can help you with?"

"I'd just like to talk to him, if that's all right. There was a problem out at the river, and we think he might have some information for us."

"Hell, Rob, I was just out there with him not a half hour ago," Art said. "We were fishing. I'm sure Glenn didn't see anything I didn't see. He couldn't have. What's going on? There's something you're not saying." There was a coarseness to Art's voice. His feelings were hurt.

"Art, I'm sorry, but I have to ask you to take me to see Glenn. Once I've talked to him, I'll explain everything. It's a whopper of a story, and it's worth the wait. I promise."

"Rob Graybold, this is some twisted kind of joke, right?" Liza said.

"No, Liza. It's not a joke, darlin'. Can you take me to Glenn's room?"

Liza and Art gave each other a look of mutual confoundment, then

Liza joined her husband on the carpeted stairs. "Come on then, if you're coming," Liza said curtly, waving them up.

At the foot of the stairs, Rob nudged his index finger gently against Angela's collarbone. His whisper might as well have been a shout, from the look in his eyes. "You stay downstairs. If you don't, you'll go back outside. Say 'Yes, Rob, I understand.'"

"Sorry, Rob," she said quickly, embarrassed.

Rob followed Art and Liza, keeping a careful distance behind them on the stairs. Angela watched their procession, suddenly uncomfortable being in their house. She didn't belong here. Whatever was going on with Art and Liza had nothing to do with her. The best thing would be to quietly go back outside, she thought. But she didn't. She stayed at the foot of the stairs, her palm wrapped tightly around the wooden globe crowning the bannister, waiting. She felt physically rooted in place, the way she had after the tree fell. And the tingling was there, too. The tingling hadn't stopped, this time.

An instant later, she knew why. Angela whiffed an odor so rank from above her that her nostrils stung. Her throat shut itself tight as her hand flew to her face to cover her nose. She stepped back. "Jesus, do you smell that?"

The three of them stopped to look around at her. Art and Liza had vacant faces, but Rob was coiled like a spring. "Smell what?" Rob said.

How could they *not* smell it? It smelled like the slaughterhouses she drove past on Interstate 5 in northern California, a stew of cow feces and endless acres of crowded, doomed meat. The odor was so thick, Angela felt as if she were wading through a cattle pen, up to her ankles in rotting waste. She shook her head, and the smell weakened, but it was still there, drifting from the stairs. From very close to her. "You don't smell anything?" she said.

By the expressions on their faces, the answer was no.

"What do you smell?" Rob said.

"It's . . . something . . ." *Dead,* Angela wanted to say. Rotten. Liza looked exasperated, giving Angela a look that begged her not to complicate the visit. For her friend's sake, Angela faltered. "I don't know. I thought it was something, but . . ."

Rob sighed, giving up. He followed Art and Liza around the corner of the staircase, and all three of them vanished. At the foot of the stairs, Angela sniffed the air again. Her arms tingled painfully, as if they were irritated by the scent; absently, Angela scratched herself, crossing her arms. The smell was more faint now, but still putrid. What in the world could be up there?

And why couldn't the others smell it, too? It was impossible *not* to.

Angela *wanted* to follow Rob's instructions. He was already pissed at her, and she didn't want to end up in real trouble. But despite that, her foot rose instinctively, and she rested her weight on the first step. As her shoe sank into the plush carpeting, the scent was sharper, closer. Angela took another step. Once again, a stronger version of the smell waited for her. Her stomach quivered. Fetid filth. Stinking dead flesh. *Inside* Liza's house?

"Glenn, you've got company!" Angela heard Liza call as she knocked on the door closest to the stairs. As Angela's head rose to the second floor, she saw *Spider-Man* posters decorating the closed door. The bone-colored carpeting upstairs was smudged with mud, from the stairs to the door that belonged to Glenn, and Liza noticed it the same time she did. "Art, look at this! Which one of you tracked all this crap into the house?"

"Aw, geez, I didn't see that. Sorry, munchkin. I'll clean that up."

Angela inched closer, sniffing the air. It was closer now, upon her. When its full strength assailed her, she couldn't mistake the source because it was right in front of her nose: The stench was wafting from Art. He couldn't smell any worse if he'd spent his afternoon rolling in cowshit and decomposing meat. Angela felt her throat throb as she leaned closer to Art and smelled his shoulder. *Ugh.* What in the world would make anyone smell like that? The smell wasn't . . .

"We're coming in, honey," Liza said, opening the door.

Too late, Angela realized that she did not want to be here. She should have waited outside. She should have stayed at the pier. She should have stayed at Sean Leahy's gate. Her tingling arms had tried to warn her all along that this was not somewhere she would want to be. But she *was* here, and the motions of the three people around her took on a surreal quality. As the three of them went into Glenn's room, Angela stood in the doorway feeling as if she were watching their actions through a smoky glass.

The bed had been stripped down to the plastic-covered mattress. A four-foot form was wrapped tightly in sheets atop the mattress, prone. Precisely in the center, vertical. Not moving. That might be Glenn, but he was not taking a nap.

"What the hell are you doing? You can't breathe like that! That is *not funny*, Glenn Brunell!" Liza shouted, both furious and alarmed. She clawed at the sheets wrapped around the figure's head, or where the head should have been. After a few skillful yanks, a pale foot flopped into view, falling to rest on the mattress, limp. Angela's mouth fell open. For a moment, she forgot even the smell.

Liza shrieked, panicked. *"Help me unwrap him!"*

Angela, still feeling as if she were witnessing someone else's bad dream, couldn't make herself move. But Art joined Liza, picking wildly at the sheets' folds, trying to free Glenn. Angela heard Rob say something into his radio, his words in machine-gun bursts, but she couldn't understand him. He was speaking in codes, she realized. He also pulled out his gun, a black Glock. Angela knew a Glock when she saw one.

"Art, go stand by the window. *Get away from the bed,*" Rob said.

Art either didn't hear Rob's instructions or pretended not to, because he gathered the bundled lump from the bed into his arms. "No, no, Liza, let *me* do it," Art said, and while Liza stared in horror, Art tossed the heavy bundle onto the bed, until Glenn nearly fell from the mattress to the floor. As the sheets loosened, Angela saw a glimpse of Glenn's red hair. Her blood turned to lead.

"Art, *stop it!*" Liza wailed. She'd grabbed Art's arm, clinging to him.

Art grabbed the bundle again, his knuckles ivory-white. With a grunt, he pulled Glenn back toward him, then heaved him away, trying to unfurl the sheets. This time, a flap of fabric fell away from the head, and Angela saw Glenn's mud-stained face. The tip of Glenn's tongue lolled from his mouth, fat and purple. The boy's clouded eyes were wide open. His neck hung loosely as Art lifted the bundle into his arms with another grunt. The dead boy's face staring squarely at Angela was upside down, dangling over Art's arm.

"He's up now," Art said, beaming with unabashed good nature. "What did you want to ask him about, Rob? If you've got a question, just come out with it. Liza has dinner waiting, and my appetite's come back, so I'm ready to eat. Glenn and I just got back from fishing."

Angela's eardrum popped in pain when Liza began to scream.

✄ Seventeen ✄

TARIQ WAS AWAKENED from the most wonderful dream by incessant barking.

The dream had been this: He'd been fishing, having some quality time with his son. He wasn't himself in the dream, nor had the boy been his real son. But it had felt good nonetheless, watching the boy and his little friend cast out their lines, pointing out when their bait was too loose on their hooks, urging them not to pull their lines away too quickly from the mouths of the hungry fish.

In the dream's most memorable instant, he had surprised his son by plunging his head into the muddy water at the shoreline. He'd seen air bubbles race to the water's surface as the boy tried to yell. *Didn't he know better? Had no one taught him to HOLD HIS BREATH under the water?* It had been a sweet struggle. A valiant struggle, for such a small person. Writhing, kicking, clawing. Tariq had wondered for an instant if he shouldn't release the boy, let him chalk it up to experience. Let him get a good laugh over it, because it was so silly, really, for someone so weak to struggle against someone so strong. Once he truly grasped that, the boy might have laughed until he choked.

But Tariq had been the one doing the choking in the dream, because he'd understood that the purest pleasure in the experience would be when the struggle stopped, a parental symmetry of sorts. What had the comedian said? *I brought you into this world, and I can take you out.*

Besides, he had to kill the boy. *Had* to, because the boy's death had been decided. The boy's mother had to be punished, because That Bitch had been using her, communicating through her. In the dream, Tariq had explained this to the boy beforehand—it was best to deal with people straight, even the littlest people, and even the people who lived in dreams. He'd said, *I have to kill you now, Glenn.* Yes, he remembered—the boy in the dream was named Glenn. And the best part? When he'd said it, the boy had only grinned at him, ready to take his new circumstance like a man.

When Tariq woke up, he was sad to be cast out of his dream. He was aroused, a delicious feeling of physical longing he would have loved to explore, but he couldn't tend to his erection at the moment because of the barking. That yappy, annoying barking was outside his front door, bringing attention with it. Tariq didn't want any attention brought to his door.

The house was dark, the light dying through his windows. He must have slept through the day, he realized. He sat up and blinked, staring with surprise at the unholy mess before him. He seemed to recall a time not too long ago—perhaps it had only been *yesterday*—when this had been a very nice place to live. There had been some order to it, some organization. Furniture standing upright, magazines and mail stacked, large-screen television uncracked, unbothered.

The next time he needed to beat someone's ass, he decided, he'd do it with more composure. Why destroy an expensive television set by heaving someone into it? Was it more important to make a point by throwing a coffee table or having a bit of order in the room? He'd like to be able to walk in the room without stumbling over broken things. He'd enjoyed having a tidy living space. It gave him peace of mind. He should have asked that sanctimonious prick DuShaun to step outside with him, the way western gunslingers and courteous bar-brawlers did.

Losing his temper had been childish. If he'd been mad because DuShaun walked away from the fight instead of finishing it like a man, he should have gone after him. He should have run him down in his Land Cruiser, grinding him against the wall. Shit, he had a baseball bat in his closet—why hadn't he run after DuShaun and knocked the back of his head into the cheap seats? What point had been served by going from room to room, breaking things as he went?

Tariq felt silly for that. He had to learn to control his temper. He had yet to master the concept of taking a deep breath and counting to ten. Wasn't that what Angie had always said?

More barking, this time with whining and frantic scratching at his door.

"I'm coming!" Tariq shouted, and the barking stopped.

Tariq turned on his porch light and opened the door. The dog had been eager to get inside before, but he cowered when he saw Tariq, folding his tail beneath him, trying to disappear into the cement stoop. Pussy furball.

"Well, it's about time, runt," Tariq said.

A fucking black poodle. Not even a standard poodle, which would have been a noble animal, a hunter's companion. Instead, this was one of the miniatures. A fucking toy poodle with flowing, hairy ears, more like a doll than an animal. Tariq leaned over to grab the dog's collar so he could see the name tag, and he felt the dog's limbs trembling.

ONYX, the tag said. At least it was the right dog. That part was the way it should be.

But what about the rest? Tariq stepped outside. He saw his Land Cruiser parked in the driveway, where it had been since he'd driven it home from Marcus Bookstore last night. That was not what he had expected, not at all. Mother*fuck*.

But wait. . . .

A half-block down the street, perfectly illuminated by the wash of orange light from the streetlamp, he saw the olive-green paint of his VW van, parked and waiting. The chrome looked shinier than it had in a long time. Tariq felt his pocket, pulling out a single key dangling from a VW key-ring. He grinned. He liked it when things went smoothly. When things fell into place.

The dog, feeling more courageous, began sniffing Tariq's shoes, ready to retreat at the slightest incentive.

"So? Like your new daddy?" Tariq said.

After more careful sniffing, the dog's tail wagged. He barked, jumping up, his nails scratching Tariq's calves. The scratching annoyed Tariq, but he kept his head. He and the dog had to get along, at least for a while. He and the dog had work to do.

Tariq had thrown the entire contents of his refrigerator onto the floor during his tantrum last night, so he took the dog into the kitchen to let him start lapping away at the linoleum. That would fill him up. He moved the bucket of stale KFC before the dog could get to it, though. Chicken bones weren't good for dogs. He couldn't let Onyx choke, not before he was returned to his rightful owner.

That was how it worked. The *baka* took away, and the *baka* gave back.

"*Bon appétit,*" Tariq said. "Enjoy the cuisine. I've got packing to do."

He wouldn't need much, but there were a few things he wanted to take with him now that his van was here, his rebirth complete. He needed fresh clothes, his electric razor, his dumbbell set. His baseball bat, a few sharp knives from the kitchen drawers, some rope from the garage.

The necessities.

And he didn't have much time. As much as Tariq hated to be rushed, he was in a hurry. It all went back to that sniveling, loudmouthed mama's boy, DuShaun. There were a hundred different ways Tariq might have shut him up for good last night, but he had not. He *had not*, for reasons that would forever mystify him. And because of that one oversight, he had to leave now—because DuShaun was at Oakland International picking up Harry this very instant, waiting outside the security gate. Granted, it was hard to believe Harry would make a special trip from Atlanta over a little old-fashioned ass whupping. Ass whupping wasn't new to Harry; their father had delved out plenty to them and their sisters, worse than what DuShaun had gotten. But irrational or not, his brother was arriving on a United flight this very minute. DuShaun was planning to bring Harry over to his house, and then the two of them were going to surprise him here, or so they thought. Even Reese might show up. DuShaun had called him, too.

Was that some shit?

Well, they would have to have their little Twelve Step party without him. As tempting as it might be to hang around and hear what they had to say, there was a considerable principle in the matter: You don't kill people just because they are annoying you. That was senseless, bad form. Whenever possible, you only kill the people you are supposed to kill. The people who *need* killing.

Take his lovely dream about fishing. Tariq appreciated the dream's symbolism: He and the boy had been *fishing*. Fishing, that is, for answers. Fishing for solutions. For lessons.

He must teach That Bitch a lesson. Her gall was staggering, even now. She hadn't learned her lessons yet, after all this time. Had she thought for a moment that just because her flesh had died, her lessons were over? Had she really expected to hide her remaining line? Her insipid spirit had dogged him for more than two years, scrabbling to confuse him, to undo his future. Tariq knew she was watching still, and that knowledge kept him moored to his undertaking. On task, as he used to say.

Neither DuShaun nor Harry and Reese were a part of his undertaking. And that meddling queer Brother Paul wasn't either, as much as Tariq would like to pay him a special visit. *So close, Brother Paul, so close. You would have died in the process because you underestimated what you were playing with, but That Bitch was trying to work through you. She's a strong one, That Bitch.*

Maybe he'd see about Brother Paul another time, another night. Let her watch that, too. Let her see more innocents suffer.

"Keep watching, *manbo*. Where are your friends Shangó and Oyá now, you pompous bitch? What good is your stolen word now?" Tariq said. He flung clothes into his leather duffel bag so he and Onyx could make their exit without interference or lectures.

Marie Toussaint would have plenty to watch now.

The Tariq Hill Show was about to hit the road.

✂ Eighteen ✂

SACAJAWEA
WEDNESDAY NIGHT

*T*HERE WAS NO OFFICIAL MEETING scheduled in the Sacajawea Town Council chambers at the rear of the courthouse, but by eight o'clock the room was thronging with more than a hundred and fifty people, their faces washed of pigment by the fluorescent lights overhead. The seats had filled long ago, but more people would have come if there had been more notice. A deputy posted at the door made certain no one under eighteen got inside, not even with a parent. "Grown people's business," the deputy told the teenagers, who were circling like hawks. It was an angry-looking crowd, Angela noticed. Faces wore skeptical scowls, and many of the people gathered were twitching, ready for a confrontation.

Angela blinked, and tears escaped from both eyes. She turned to look for Myles. She'd staked out a spot at the rear center pillar not far from the door, hoping he would arrive in time. As much as she'd hated to tip off anyone at the *Lower Columbia News*, Myles belonged here. But where was he? She'd called him forty-five minutes ago.

Rob and Melanie made their way to the front of the room, and people parted to let them pass. They were holding hands, not looking at anyone as they walked. Rob was wearing his uniform, but his hat was in his hand. He and Melanie walked until they stood between the American flag and the painted Sacajawea emblem on the wall; a collage of an eagle, a Lewis and Clark trail map, and the long-haired profile of the city's namesake, Sacajawea. The meeting was about to start.

Angela looked for Myles again. This time, she saw an electric blue shirtsleeve winding its way into the doorway, a shade borrowed from the streets of Rome, and she knew it was him. No other man in Sacajawea owned a dress shirt that color. Myles was trying to ease one shoulder past the crowd in the doorway, a thin reporter's notebook clutched between his fingers.

The deputy tapped Myles's shoulder. "Sorry, sir. No press."

"Colin, give me a break. I didn't bring a photographer. I live here, too."

The deputy hesitated, then waved him in despite grumbles around him. Myles hurried to Angela's side. He leaned over, kissing her cheek. "You all right?" he whispered.

She nodded. "Yes," she said. The more precise answer was a long story—but the gist of it was yes, she was as well as she could be, given what she'd seen today. All she'd noticed in the past hour was a headache and occasional spasms in her legs, when she thought they would buckle beneath her. But even those were subsiding. She was doing better than she'd thought she would.

On the small elevated stage in front, a tech handed Rob a microphone attached to a small amplifier, and Rob rested his hat on the podium where Art usually lorded over town council meetings. When Rob raised the microphone to his mouth, the amplifier squealed loudly, making a few people near the front cry out in surprise. Rob put the microphone down. "Listen, uh . . . I'm not gonna use that thing. Can everybody hear me all right?"

The group murmured yes. Drifting conversations in the rear died, and the next time Rob spoke, the room was so hushed he didn't have to raise his voice. Rob's eyes shone like red marbles.

"Thanks to everybody for coming," he said, and he had to clear his throat twice before going on. "These are unusual circumstances, and I appreciate you coming out to hear what I have to say. I couldn't think of what else to do but call a town meeting, since the phones at my office have been ringing off the hook. Instead of telling ya'll one at a time, I figured I'd better tell you all at once. That way, everybody hears it and there aren't any misunderstandings. But please bear with me. This has been the hardest day of my life, worse than any day I had in the Gulf."

His audience had turned to stone, waiting.

Rob took a breath while Melanie rubbed his forearm. "Art Brunell has been arrested, and he is in custody at the new jail. I'm sad to say that Glenn Brunell died earlier today. Art took him fishing . . . and held his head under the water until he drowned. Those are the facts as they have been presented to me. Art drowned Glenn today. An eyewitness is claiming Art did it on purpose, with the intent to kill him."

Angela heard Myles draw in a pained breath. She'd told him what she knew on the telephone, but Rob's report was still shocking, stripped to its ugly facts.

Rob tried to go on, but the audience had erupted, drowning out his words. "That's *bullshit!*" a tall, lavishly bearded man called hoarsely from the far side of the room. He must have captured the room's sentiment, because their protests grew louder. Rob had to wait a long time for a lull. He stood patiently, allowing them to vent until the room went quiet again.

"Some of you know part of the story—and you know the age of the witness involved, so I understand why you have your doubts. But there have been other developments, people. Others have come forward." The room quieted, waiting. Angela hadn't heard about other developments. She'd spent the past two hours trying to help Liza's mother keep Liza from screaming.

"There are two more witnesses. One is saying Art told her at the market this morning he was going to kill his son today. At the time, the witness thought it was a joke, but now she doesn't. Another has told me Art took out a fifty-thousand-dollar life insurance policy on Glenn in Longview yesterday. Liza knew nothing about it—that's what she says, and I believe her. But we've been presented with a copy of the policy."

"That doesn't mean *shit!*" the same bearded man shouted, his voice more hoarse than before.

"Rourke, I hate this more than you do," Rob said. "I was at the house today. I saw Glenn's body. I had to put handcuffs on Art. I know how you feel. But let me tell you, without disclosing too many details, Art was behaving very, very erratically. And I know there hasn't been a trial yet—"

"*Damn right* there hasn't been!" a woman yelled behind Angela, anger rasping her voice. Angela turned to look at her, and she recognized the stout woman as one of Art's relatives, a cousin.

"I hear you, Sarah. I do. But I have to tell you straight, this thing looks real bad. Art is looking at the serious possibility of a prison sentence for this, even if it gets ruled an accidental drowning. And we can't keep it out of the press. I see Myles here. . . ."

Angela felt an ache of guilt as the audience turned to look at Myles, following Rob's gaze. Now, the anger simmering in the room was directed toward them, the heat of more than a hundred pairs of eyes. Angela felt more like a stranger than she had in years.

"But we can't blame Myles," Rob said. "A TV station in Portland almost sent someone here tonight, except I stonewalled 'em so long. We all want to do what we can for Art and Liza, but there's no such thing as keeping this quiet—it's out. By this time tomorrow, the TV cameras will be here. And maybe not just from Portland. Right, Myles?"

"Could be," Myles said, his voice raw. "He's the mayor, and unfortunately, there's a child involved. I wouldn't be surprised to see a network pick it up. It's possible."

There were new murmurs of anger and surprise. From the stage, Melanie mouthed the word *What?* at Myles. She looked heartbroken that strangers would know their business.

"Well, Art always wanted the limelight, and he's about to be in it," Rob said, a grim joke, and a few people even laughed. "No matter how it all comes out in the end, we have friends who need prayer from us. Liza is . . . well, she's not good. She's at her parents' place. If you're a friend, don't be afraid to go see her, but wait a day or two." He paused, stuck momentarily on his thoughts of Liza. His pause forced Angela to freeze her own thoughts, because she could not allow herself to dwell on Liza. She knew something of how Liza felt tonight, and she'd never wish it on an enemy, never mind a friend. Liza hadn't spoken a coherent word since her visit to Glenn's room.

Rob was exhausted, obviously on the verge of tears himself. "We may never know what happened here, or why. My brain's not making sense of it, and neither will yours, once you hear the whole story. Believe me when I say that. But all of us in this room—in our hearts—know Art Brunell did not want to kill that little boy. Art loved Glenn, and he'd sooner go to Hell itself than hurt his child. We know that about Art Brunell, because that's the Art Brunell *we* know."

The audience murmured loudly, an amen corner. Angela and Myles murmured with them.

"I'm no minister like my dad and granddad, but let's bow our heads a minute," Rob said.

That minute lasted longer than five. No one in the room so much as coughed.

———

Angela wasn't asleep when she heard the soft tapping on her hotel room door at two A.M., but she stared at the door a long time without moving, wondering if she was able to dream at last. "Angie?" a man's voice whispered from beyond the door.

Angela jumped out of bed, startled. She checked herself in the mirror to see if she was decently clothed, and she was. She'd put on pajamas after her long bath instead of throwing on a T-shirt like she usually did, searching for a semblance of comfort. The silk soothed her skin. Candlelight in the room soothed her psyche and spirit. After the meeting, feeling unsettled and miserable, she'd bought two large white candles at the Triangle Mall; one burned on her nightstand, the other on the dresser, coloring the room in a flickering yellowish light. Gramma Marie had always burned candles at important times, when there were prayers to be made, or when her weakest parts needed to be made stronger. Her room now smelled of vanilla, another comfort.

Anything to help her forget that other smell, or at least to try.

When Angela opened the door, she found Myles there, leaning against the door frame. He'd loosened his shirt, and his tie wound across his shoulders. His eyes looked awful.

"You're in luck," she said. "I have a coffeemaker."

"Bless you, lady," he said. "But no caffeine. I need to sleep sometime tonight."

"Herbal tea?"

"Perfect."

Angela's two cups of herbal tea before bed hadn't been any help, and Myles probably wouldn't fare much better, but she didn't want to dash his hopes. Maybe sleep would come more easily to someone who hadn't seen Glenn's body dangling in Art's arms.

Myles walked far across the room and collapsed into the armchair beside the striped curtains, drawn against the night sky. He stared straight ahead, not speaking, and his silence didn't bother her. Angela was glad to have something to rescue her mind, even if it was just filling the coffeemaker's carafe with water, plugging it in, turning it on. Watching her, Myles took a deep breath and sighed as if he were trying to cleanse his lungs. "I just got off the phone with Art's mom," he said.

"You called her this late?"

His sad eyes met hers. "No. I was at my office, and she called me. She wanted me to hold off printing the story about Art's arrest. I had to tell her I couldn't do that."

"I know," Angela said, although she wished to God he had. She'd hoped he would.

"She thinks I'm angling for a big story. She called me a 'slick, opportunistic asshole.' "

"Mrs. Brunell said that?"

"Right before she hung up. Her exact words. Art and I did a school newspaper project together senior year, and she invited me to dinner a few times. His mom was the first person who told me not to be afraid to go to New York for college. She said it would change my life, and she was right. Now I'm a slick, opportunistic asshole."

Angela sat cross-legged on the floor, at Myles's feet. "Don't take it personally, Myles. Mothers are fierce when it comes to protecting their young. I know—I used to be one."

Myles winced. "The things you say sometimes . . . ," he said, shaking his head. He rested his palm on top of her head, firm and heavy. "I hate that you had to go through this. And now Liza and Art—*damn*. It sounds like he cracked, Angie."

Angela's voice grew soft. "I saw him. He did crack." She paused, deciding that wasn't quite right; it was accurate, but it wasn't enough. "Something made him crack."

Gently, Myles's fingers massaged her scalp. "I'm sorry you had to see that. I really am."

"Well, the good part is, I was there for Liza. I keep remembering how Liza tried to put a sweater on me that day we found Corey. In July! I thought, *Why does she keep doing that?* Then she told me I was shaking, and I was. Head to foot." Until today, watching Liza's shaking, she'd forgotten about that, another misplaced memory from that day.

"Liza was lucky to have you there. We're all lucky."

Amazingly, Angela realized that the light dance of Myles's fingertips on her scalp was setting off a burning sensation across her head. Shit. Even now, her hormones couldn't keep quiet.

"I'll check your water," she said.

"No, leave it for now," Myles said, closing his eyes.

If she weren't so tired, if she had spent her day another way, Angela would have lost hope of respecting another woman's dominion tonight. And even with things as they were, she couldn't be sure of herself. She was having a hard time thinking of reasons to stay inside her clothes. She'd learned how to drown her sorrows in sex a long time ago, as a child. Except that sins were punished, weren't they? Sins were punished, and sometimes punishment came without sins. Sometimes punishment just came.

"Can you see it yet, Myles?" Angela said. Speaking the words gave her goose bumps.

He opened his eyes, gazing at her to try to understand her meaning. Then, his head fell back against the headrest. "Yeah. I'm seeing something. Corey first. June McEwan tries to strangle her brother. Rick Leahy walks into a logging truck, grinning all the while. Now, Art drowns his son. A series of violent, irrational acts, like a slow mass hysteria. But what does it mean? What's causing it? That's what I don't know." Myles rubbed his temples, sighing.

No, he didn't see it yet, Angela realized, disappointed. She would have to walk him through slowly. "It's a curse, Myles," she said. "It started with a possession gone wrong in 1929."

Myles patted her head. "Listen to yourself, doll-baby. I can't print that in a newspaper."

"Does everything you believe have to be something you can print in a newspaper?"

"People are scared, Angie. They want to know what's going on."

"I'm just talking to Myles Fisher. What do *you* believe is going on?"

Myles sat up straight, folding his hands between his knees. He looked reluctant to speak. "Angie, I wasn't going to tell you this . . ."

Before he could finish, Angela felt herself withering. She thought of the song from *The Wiz*, "Don't Nobody Bring Me No Bad News." She was bearing up all right under the scope of her terrible knowledge so far, but she was full up.

"That story Liza told you, the one about the bathtub, isn't true," Myles said.

"How do you know that?" she said.

"In 1929, only one of Hal Booth's six children was still living at home. The rest were all grown men, long gone. The youngest was his daughter, Maddie, who would have been sixteen."

"Maddie . . . ," Angela said, on the verge of recognizing the name.

"That's Ma. Her maiden name was Maddie Booth. Hal Booth was her father, and she would have been the one in the story. But she never said a word about it to me, not in thirty years, and Ma told me a lot of family history, especially once she started getting sick. She wanted me to know everything, the good and the bad. I don't believe that bathtub incident happened, Angie—not to her, and not to her brothers. It's apocryphal, some kind of town legend. And I'm worried that if you spend too much time chasing after old ghost stories, you'll miss your chance to find the truth."

Myles's adoptive mother had been the one in the bathtub! It had never occurred to Angela that the child would still be living, but Ma Fisher was at least ninety. "She might not remember," Angela said. "After the demon was cast out."

Myles's look was doleful, and she understood. He thought she was cracking up, too. If his mass hysteria theory was true, Angela was the perfect candidate as the next one to take a kid fishing, or to try waltzing with a truck. She didn't expect it to be easy to bring anyone with her where she was going, but she hoped Myles would be the one. "You don't consider it strange timing that this happened the *day after* Liza told me that story?" Angela said, slowly.

"Of course it's strange timing. It's all strange. But that doesn't make the story true."

"Would you believe me if I told you I smelled it today?" Angela said.

"You smelled what?"

"Whatever it is, the thing that made Art do that. I smelled it on him, Myles. We were on the stairs, and no one else could smell it. But I'm telling you, it was a smell that could not be missed. It was all over Art. Before Rob opened that bedroom door, I knew Art had done something. I smelled it on him. I *knew*." Angela saw concern creep into Myles's eyes, which grew more alert. She must sound like a mental patient. And she *was* a mental patient, wasn't she?

"Adrenaline?" Myles suggested. "Art was nervous. He was probably secreting . . ."

Angela shook her head back and forth a long time. "No, Myles. This smell was something not human. Not living. Something from another place."

He stroked her face with sad eyes. "I can't follow you down that road, Angie. There's almost always another answer. You just can't process how monstrous this has all been."

"But what if it's real, and it's right in front of us?"

"If I thought it was real, I'd find out how to fight it. I'd come up with a plan."

"I have. I need to see Ma Fisher."

"I knew you would say that. You can try talking to her, but you won't get far. She's lucid once in a blue moon, and I treasure those moments. But she hardly speaks. It's gibberish."

"I should visit her anyway."

"Fine. Come by after I get off work tomorrow or the next day, if I have any brain cells left. It'll be a good diversion. I'll make dinner. I don't think I've ever cooked for you. I'm not bad in the kitchen. Cuban dishes mostly." His sentences were hurried, mumbling. Myles was exhausted, a sleeping man holding a conversation. Angela wondered if he'd had a drink on the way to her room.

"I'm sure you're good at anything you put your mind to," she said.

At that, Myles smiled. In the candlelight, Myles's face looked like polished ebony, his teeth the white keys of a new piano. He was probably glad to be done with the crazy portion of the conversation, the part that made him wonder if she was all right.

Their gaze suddenly felt too long for comfort. Dangerous.

"Your water's ready by now," she said, getting up. She felt his eyes watching her walk across the room, and she wondered if the candles gave enough light for him to appreciate the curves of her buttocks through the silk pants. She wasn't wearing anything underneath, which he could probably see full well. She thought about slipping out of her pants while she walked, but when she tried to fantasize about straddling Myles on the chair, all she could see was Glenn Brunell's purple, swollen tongue. Then the memory of that smell came back.

Angela sought Myles's face behind her in the mirror as she stood over the sink, hoping to drive away Glenn's face and the knowledge of how evil smelled up close. "I'm glad you came," she said. "I needed company. I just hope you won't feel guilty tomorrow, Myles."

"If I had a reason to feel guilty," he said, "I wouldn't have come."

Touché. Angela poked his tea bag with the stirrer in the mug, irritated. Had he trained himself not to look at her that way at all anymore, purely out of loyalty to someone he had dated for six months?

"Luisah's not too happy with me right now," Myles said, his voice thin.

Angela turned around, facing him. Myles was wrapping his necktie around one of his hands, agitated. "What do you mean?"

"Last night, she asked me the same question you did. If I'm in love with her."

"And?"

Myles rubbed the corner of one eye with his index finger, quickly flicking his finger away. "I guess 'I don't know' wasn't the answer she was looking for. She said she'd like to get married. She's been expecting me to ask. She asked me if I loved her, and I told the truth."

Angela cringed for the woman, and for him. "What happened?"

"I think we're taking a break from each other right now."

Angela managed to feel sad for Myles, and a shiver of recollection came to her: Yesterday, watching her tree taken apart, she had told Art how much she hated to lose anything, and he had tried to comfort her. Sweet Jesus Christ.

Art was in jail. Art had drowned Glenn. New numbness spread across her chest.

"I screwed up," Myles said. "I wasn't aware enough, I got lazy, and I hurt her. And I hurt Art's mom, too. I had the power to cause her a little less pain, to give her a few more hours to adjust before we went with that story, and I couldn't do it. Because it's news. So, some people right in Sacajawea who've known Art their whole lives are going to hear about it first when they open their newspaper in the morning, and that's going to make it hurt worse. What Art's mom called me was exactly right, word for word. I am a slick, opportunistic asshole."

"Don't believe that for a minute," Angela said. "You're not really all that slick."

Myles smiled at her joke, but it was a tired smile. He wouldn't have come here tonight if he'd had anywhere else to go, Angela realized. He was as opportunistic as she was, but that was all right. They were a matched pair. Quietly, she brought Myles his mug of tea, which he sipped from once before resting it on the seat cushion between his thighs. The coffeemaker heated the water barely beyond lukewarm, so he wouldn't have to worry about scalding any tender parts of his body. Angela sat at the edge of the bed, studying Myles's face, his electric blue shirt's radiance against his richly colored skin, and the mug between his legs.

"When I wake up tomorrow," he said, "I want this week to have been a bad dream."

"Amen," she said. "Except for right now."

"Yes. We'll keep this part. But only this part."

They stared at each other a long time, and this time the gaze didn't make her nervous. She didn't feel a need to fill it, hide it, or question it. It just was, and she enjoyed it. After a time—a long time—Myles closed his eyes. Then, his head drooped. Almost immediately, she heard his breathing draw out as he fell asleep. She'd forgotten people could fall asleep that fast.

Angela took in the sight of him for a while, studying his nuances in the candlelight. She could smell his cologne, weak after a long day, still clinging to him. His shoes were as shiny as Rob's had been. He wore a silver wristwatch that looked sharp but not ostentatious. His skin was the color of dark, fertile soil. All in all, he was a marvelous sight, sleeping in her chair.

Still facing Myles, Angela curled up at the foot of the bed and closed her eyes. She had a new plan for getting to sleep: Whenever the ugly pictures came to her head and tried to drag her back to Glenn's room—and then to the wine cellar and its bloody floor—she would open her eyes and see Myles there. She'd waited a long time for so simple a privilege. Angela would be able to open her eyes at any hour during the night and find a man she loved close enough to touch.

✥ Nineteen ✥

$\mathcal{M}$YLES FISHER awakened bleary-eyed in the chair in Angie's hotel room at six-thirty with a bear of a cramp along the right side of his body. When he opened his eyes, he felt a creeping sense of unreality. He was in a strange room. He was wearing last night's clothes. He must have slept for more than four hours, but he felt more tired now than he had when he'd come.

And he should not be here. That was the worst of it.

He saw Angie sleeping at the foot of the bed in gold pajamas, finally at peace. A line of sunlight from a crack in the curtains spilled across her face below her eyelids, making her cheekbones jump out at him, and he felt blood throb to his groin. Her face looked as soft as a child's. Her shirt was loose at the top, and her bosom was visible where her breasts parted, an intimate view. Myles looked longer than he wanted to, then turned his eyes elsewhere.

It would take everything in him to stand up and kiss Angie's cheek good-morning and walk outside to his car, rather than climb onto the bed and spoon himself behind her until she woke up and realized he was there. Maybe the bed had been his secret motive when he'd gotten here, but in the daylight, he felt a sobering dose of reality: Angie was going through a hellish time, and she was unstable. When Angie was unstable, she ripped his life to shreds. He should not be alone in a hotel room with her. Myles talked to himself that way for ten minutes, staring at Angie while she slept, trying not to look at the swell of her peeking bosom.

She'd committed herself. She hadn't said so yet, but Myles was almost sure of it. When Liza mentioned the rumor that Angie had gone to a mental hospital more than a year ago, he had written diligently, trying to let her know she could confide in him if she wanted to. But she never had. He hoped she'd been able to get herself together after Corey's death, even if she wasn't willing to accept help from friends, but she was still troubled, as far as he could see. The timing was wrong, yet again.

Myles walked to the edge of the bed and kissed Angie's cheek. He could smell her hair, a coconut fragrance in the oil she used. When his lips touched her, Angie stirred, opened her eyes. She smiled, seeing him. Her sleepy smile was unguarded. "What time is it?" she said.

"After six. It's time for me to go, Angie."

She looked disappointed, but he felt a surge of resolve. He'd been playing big brother to Angie since they were fifteen, even when he wasn't feeling brotherly. He was beginning to understand that a brother was all he was supposed to be to her. Maybe that wasn't so bad.

"Have breakfast with me," she said. "Stay."

"No, doll-baby. I shouldn't have stayed this long. I need to get home to change."

Angela's smile grew coy. "I knew you'd feel guilty, Myles. You're so predictable."

"Just a little," he said.

"Why?"

Instead of answering, Myles touched her forehead and smoothed her hair against her scalp, then tugged her ear gently. Touching her was fascinating, even the tiny hole in her earlobe where the needle had pierced her. "As much as I'd like to join you in bed this morning, Angela Marie, I'm afraid we're not cut out to be buddies who sleep together."

She looked surprised. "Who said that's all we'd be?"

"Anything else wouldn't be smart."

"I don't believe in always doing the smart thing," she said.

There wasn't enough time in a single morning to respond to that. She'd missed the past twenty-two years, so she hadn't seen the wreckage: His trips to the therapist at Columbia because he hadn't been able to sleep for two full years after her withdrawal. How he'd married Marta after college, enticed by her aspects that reminded him of Angie—the worst, stormiest parts. Angie didn't know how close he'd come to loathing them both. Marta had made herself at home in Angie's shadow, and now it was a shadow with no name. It followed him. He'd just lost Luisah somewhere in that shadow, he was certain.

"Doing the smart thing is my new policy, Angie. Blame it on age."

"You think I'm a psycho, don't you?" she said. Her eyes were earnest.

He smiled. "No." *Psycho* wasn't the right word. *Broken* was better; and Angie's kind of broken was communicable, practically in the air.

"You promise?"

He kissed her lips, a peck. "I promise. I have to go. Call me if you need me."

Outside of the hotel, Myles managed a dull, exasperated laugh. Last week, he'd congratulated himself on the tidy state of his life: friends, a girlfriend, a job he enjoyed more than he'd expected, his reunion with nature in the Pacific Northwest. It was hard to be with Ma Fisher, harder than he'd thought it would be, but experience made it easier all the time. Lying in bed with Luisah after lovemaking two nights ago, he'd told her how *right* his life felt. Now, Myles chided himself for his blindness. He'd been offering to share his life with her, without ever saying so.

A dying mother tends to cloud your judgment, he thought.

Outside of the hotel lobby, the morning's newspaper was already waiting in the news box, sandwiched between the Portland *Oregonian* box and a stand for the *Nickel* classified paper. He fished a quarter out of his pocket, but he could see the headline through the blue news box's plastic shield: SACAJAWEA MAYOR HELD IN DEATH OF SON, 8.

Art, Liza, and Glenn smiled in a family portrait against a woodland backdrop, Art's campaign photo. The headline didn't have the large print of the Mount St. Helens eruption in 1980, but it was eye-catching. Chilling, to put it better. Surreal. Myles could only imagine how it looked to people in Sacajawea County sitting down casually to read their morning paper over ham and eggs. People who had seen Art and his family at church on Sunday.

The sky was drizzling. Myles was tempted to call Luisah and ask her if he could come by, since she got up by six-thirty each morning to do yoga. He had a change of clothes at her place, and she was only ten minutes away. But what was he going to tell her? That the day after they decided they should cool off for a while, he'd spent the night in a hotel room with another woman? He hadn't lied to Luisah in all this time, and there was no reason to hurt her more with the truth.

He had to go home.

The rainy sky was still pink in the cloud-breaks over the expanse of the river as Myles's Saturn rounded a curve on State Route Four, driving west toward Sacajawea. He kneaded the cramp in his neck with one hand while steering with the other, and his car crept slightly toward the oncoming lane.

The huge grill of an eastbound logging truck appeared around the bend, and the truck shook his car when it passed, too close. The suddenness of the truck's appearance, and the shower of dust and gravel against his windshield, snapped Myles to full alertness.

Myles hated the Four. When he first started driving at sixteen, he'd navigated his car around the narrow curves at speeds that made his blood sing, but his reckless days were over. Since he'd been back, he'd hit a dog during his daily commute to Longview. And then, not once but twice, he'd had to replace his windshield because of falling rocks. *One chance in a million,* said the guy who'd replaced the windshield both times, but Myles didn't think so. Everyone had a story about the Four involving a deer or a cascade of rocks. The roadside was dotted with makeshift crosses built by the loved ones of accident victims, often tourists whose day on the sand at Long Beach had gone badly awry. There were fences swathing the rocky ridges and warning signs at the curves, but when people remarked on how much he must be enjoying the stress-free life in Sacajawea after living in big, bad Washington, D.C., Myles thought about State Route Four.

Everything was relative, he always said.

ENTERING SACAJAWEA COUNTY, the yellow highway sign announced. Myles felt a flood of nerves. He glanced at the passenger seat and saw the newspaper again, Art's jolly face in full color. "I hate this," he said to the empty car.

He knew how Art's family felt. That was the hardest part of it.

When he was eight, Myles had seen a news report of his father's death on TV. *Ain't that Buddy?* his cousin Twyla said, pointing, and Myles had seen his father's angry-looking photograph, an old mug shot, he would learn later. The newscaster's all-knowing voice said he'd been *killed in an early-morning robbery.* Vernon Richardson, *dead* after trying to stop a robbery attempt at the Gulf station on Fourteenth between Pike and Pine. *Dead* on arrival at the hospital. If Twyla had told him not to pay the TV any mind because it was all made up, he would have believed her. But instead, Twyla was on the phone telling someone, *Buddy dead. He dead. Yeah, the news say Buddy dead.* That was how Myles had learned he was an orphan.

Of course, the police never meant to surprise him like that, he knew now. Police tried to inform family members before releasing the names of the dead. But since Myles's mother had died of a heroin overdose two years before, and since his father's parents were dead, the police had thought there was no one to tell. Nobody knew Vernon Richardson had a niece who called him Buddy, his family nickname, and they damn sure didn't know a thing about his eight-year-old son, Myles Richardson, who was living with her temporarily even though she could barely afford to feed him. He didn't exist. So there it had been on the news, his father's face in a bad photograph from an old arrest, before he'd gotten the job at the gas station, wearing a uniform he washed every day. That had been the first and last time almost anyone in Seattle had heard Vernon Richardson's name.

Myles hadn't talked to his cousin Twyla since he was fifteen, and he wasn't sure where she was, or how she was doing. He could still retrieve a kaleidoscope of old images, but most of the time, the images seemed hardly related to him, someone else's memories: His parents' wild days, when they sold drugs out of their apartment in the Hope Circle Projects, and how he'd raced into the bathroom with his mother once, watching her flush packets of powder down the toilet after the police came knocking, her hands shaking like God himself was at the door. Two white police officers had wrestled his father to the floor and chained his hands behind his back like Kunta Kinte on *Roots*. But the really awful thing had been his father's picture on the news, hearing a stranger say he was dead. *Buddy dead*.

Myles's cell phone rang. He glanced at the phone in the cradle above the gearshift, but he couldn't make out the lighted Caller I.D. display and keep his eyes on the road. He couldn't reach for the speakerphone button either. Myles had a rule against answering his cell phone on the Four. There were too many twists on the road, too many surprises.

The phone rang four times and stopped.

Who would be calling him at ten to seven unless it was an emergency? Candace, the weekday nurse, might have news about Ma, who'd been waking up in the middle of the night lately to demand water or cereal, behaving more like an infant all the time. Or it might have been Roger, the reporter assigned to Art's story. Roger had won a Pulitzer after Mount St. Helens and was as obsessive about his stories as any of the ambitious workhorses Myles had known at the *Post*, so he wouldn't be surprised if Roger was on the job this early.

But most likely, it was Angie, wanting answers. He wished he had a few to give her, but he didn't know why he'd been in her room. It was the story of his life: A sweet, stable woman wants to marry him, and he can't love her. Instead, he's hovering around a woman he hasn't known since high school, who's fresh from a nervous breakdown—and who genuinely believes that a demon possessed not just her mother, but his too. He was older but no wiser, he thought.

When the phone rang again, Myles's curiosity gnawed at him. He took a last glance at the road and saw that he was alone in a passing lane now, with a decent stretch before it would narrow again at the curve. He hit the speakerphone button. "This is Myles."

The caller was on a mobile, too, judging by the static. The call sounded far away, but he heard strains from an old Teddy Pendergrass song, "Close the Door." No one spoke on the other end, but Myles heard a small dog barking. All those tiny dogs sound alike, he thought.

"Speak up, please," Myles said.

"Did you get what you wanted?" said the caller, a man.

"Who is this?"

"You know who it is."

"If I knew that, I wouldn't have asked," Myles said. The caller was play-ing games. He had a deep, FM disc jockey voice, and he sounded as if he might be black, or else he was pretending he was. Probably a crank caller. Someone mad about the article in the paper.

UNKNOWN CALLER, the phone display said when he checked.

"Man, lemme tell you, she's still a hot fuck. A stone freak," the voice said, losing its clipped quality, turning conversational. "Her band teacher got her when she was thirteen, plucked her early. That's how freaks are born. She can swallow a cucumber whole. But I don't have to tell you that, do I? You remember, Myles. Out in the woods? That thing she did—she squeezed you from the *inside?* You gasped like you'd seen your mama's ghost. Your *real* mama, I mean."

Myles's sore neck locked. He would have braked and pulled over if he could have, because he was so angry his vision blurred slightly before refo-cusing, something that had never happened to him. "Who the hell is this?" Myles said.

The caller laughed. "Oh, I'm sorry. Was that too personal?"

"You want to get personal, you vulgar ass? Come talk to me in person."

"Count on it, Myles. Try not to die before I get there."

The voice and static vanished just as the passing lane merged back into a single narrow lane and the road bent, following the river's whim. Myles regained his concentration in time to whip his car around the curve with-out veering into the oncoming lane, where any unseen vehicle would have clipped him. His car was the only one beyond the curve on the Four.

The road was empty except for the deer.

Under different circumstances, Myles would have admired the animal: It was a mature blacktail buck with a plush, dark coat and antlers the color of fine mahogany. He must have been more than two hundred pounds, a giant prize Pa Fisher would have been willing to give up a chunk of his life savings for if he'd had the chance to take him down with his bow. Myles had seen a blacktail buck this size up-close only once before, when Gunnar Michaelsen bagged one on the slopes of the Cascades the weekend Gunnar and Pa Fisher took him hunting after high school graduation. This could be its twin.

None of that awe, however, was in Myles's mind when he saw the deer on State Route Four at the moment he was rounding a curve at fifty miles per hour. His head emptied of everything except the sight of the animal directly in his path, as still as a wildlife monument. The deer's glossy brown eyes stared at him, strangely untroubled. Myles didn't have time to reach for his horn, or to do anything except plant his foot on his brake, hard.

That was the thing about the Four: There was nowhere to go. On the driver's side, a flimsy barrier provided slim solace against the prospect of tumbling down the ravine into the Columbia River; and the other side was mostly steep rock-faces, promising a hard impact if he drove too far over in the opposite direction. He was boxed in. His best choice would have been to hit the deer and take the damage, but he'd braked instead because of its imposing size. And he'd braked too hard.

Myles realized his mistake only when he felt the weight of the car drifting, pulling at his steering wheel. The wet road or loose gravel, or both, had thrown him into a skid. He tried to steer and right himself, but there was already too much momentum. Myles lost control of his car.

"Oh, Jesus," he said, as true a prayer as he'd ever uttered. Death felt certain in a way that flushed his body with iced pinpricks, made his face hard as iron.

Myles shouted a dead man's shout, pumping the brake and counter-steering, fighting to break the skid. But the car didn't respond. His tires whined as the road and the deer vanished from his windshield, and instead the rock-face sprang into full view. That passed in a blur, and then he was staring at the road behind him, at the curve he had just passed. His car had turned completely around, still spinning, and the river was coming next. "Jesus . . . Jesus . . . Jesus . . . Jesus . . ."

The car rocked to a stop, jerking Myles's neck back. The quiet was so complete, Myles wondered for a moment if he was dead. His eyes seemed to have shut down. There was no darkness, no light. Utter stillness held him paralyzed in its spell.

I'm alive, he thought finally, hardly daring to hope.

He must be. He was damp with perspiration, his face hot. His heart was a drill in his chest. His hands were hugging the steering wheel as if he would fall to his death if he let go. All he could see through his windshield was the river, but the car had come to a stop before falling over the ravine. The nose of his car had dented the low barrier, giving it little more than a tap.

When he'd oriented himself, Myles turned over his shoulder to look at the deer. The buck was still planted where he'd been, only now he was six yards from the rear bumper. He hadn't moved, except to turn his head in Myles's direction. With the deer's eyes still watching him, pinpricks washed Myles again. *That stupid animal almost just killed me,* he thought. Payback.

Myles sat in his car a moment, facing the calm of the river while his trunk jutted into the oncoming traffic lane. If he'd hit that barrier any harder, he could have tumbled in. He would be under the water this instant, clawing to get out of his car, if he had survived the impact. *Thank you, thank you, thank you, Jesus.* Myles knew he needed to move his car, but he wasn't ready to begin driving again. He wanted some air. His breath was tight in his lungs.

Myles saw a red light flash in his driver's side mirror. A sheriff's unit pulled up behind him, emergency lights on, appearing like an apparition.

"You all right?" Rob Graybold said at his window.

Myles nodded, his breathing heavy. "Yeah. I almost hit that buck."

"Well, get this car moved quick," Rob said. "Drive up to that fishing stop up on the left. I need to shoo that buck before someone gets killed. I didn't even see that giant sonofabitch until you came around the corner. You sure you're all right?"

Myles waved yes, nodding. The disorientation was passing. Jesus had shown him mercy this time. Miracles didn't get any more real than the one he'd just lived through, he thought. His heartbeat slowing, Myles put his car into reverse, away from the water, to turn around. In the distance, he could see an eastbound logging truck in his lane, far enough back but coming at him fast.

"From now on, I'm taking the ferry," Myles said, straightening himself in the road.

Myles drove to the shoulder about sixty yards from where he'd nearly crashed, a strip of gravel large enough for a few drivers to park and fish over the barrier. Turning off his engine set him at ease. Myles had fished here a few times, standing patiently in the shade of the flowering dogwood tree, getting hardly a bite for most of the day and then pulling up a twenty-pound chinook salmon just when he was ready to pack up and go home. One afternoon on his way from work, stopping on a whim right here, he'd caught a salmon as fat as a weasel. That memory calmed Myles, wiping away the maw in his gut.

Rob's police lights were still flashing when he came to Myles's window a few minutes later. "Your day is off to a shitty start," Rob said.

"Man, I don't know where that buck came from."

"A crack in the fence, near as I can tell. He ran right for it when I shooed him. I've never seen a deer down this far. You're lucky to be alive."

"Thank you, Jesus almighty."

Rob stared out at the water. The morning was windy, so the dark waves crested in dancing white formations across the surface. Already, the pinkish tinge was leaving the sky as it grew brighter beyond the clustered rainclouds. "Seems to me you must have come around that corner pretty fast, to skid like that. What were you doing? About fifty?"

Here it comes, Myles thought. Myles was sorry he'd interrupted the sheriff's morning reflection, because Rob wasn't likely to be in a good mood. "Yeah. I got a crank call, I was distracted. I shouldn't have answered my phone."

"They need to outlaw those damned phones on the road," Rob said, still not looking at him. "Someone threatening you, Myles?"

Try not to die before I get there, the caller had said. Had that been a threat? "It's nothing. It's personal." He was sure it must have been Tariq Hill. Tariq's baritone voice was memorable, and Myles had talked to Tariq at Corey's funeral, shaking his hand while trying not to peer too closely into the private well of grief in the man's eyes. Tariq was the only person likely to know so much about Angie, or the details of Myles's sexual experience with her at The Spot. Now, on top of everything else, he had to contend with the rambling of Angie's ex, a former football player. The havoc had started already.

"Folks are pissed at you. Let me know if anything gets out of hand," Rob said.

"I'll take care of it." Tariq must be a pathetic, troubled man, to make that call. The idea of it made Myles sad. "I guess we're the two least favorite people in town today, Rob."

Rob chuckled sourly. "No offense, but I don't see us in the same category."

Myles should have known that was coming. For whatever reason, Rob had never liked him. Sacajawea County High's basketball team hadn't been good, but he and Rob had played themselves to exhaustion trying to show each other up. That competition had never turned into friendship as it sometimes did, although Myles wished it had. Something had killed that possibility a long time ago. Maybe it was Melanie, Myles thought. She'd had a crush on him for a while in high school, or so it was rumored. Myles still saw glimmers of something quick and bright in Melanie's eyes when he ran into her in town, and it was possible Rob's wife mentioned his name a little too often at home.

"I'm sorry you feel that way, Rob," Myles said. "But when my reporter calls today, I sure wish you'd work with him."

"He'll have to take a place in line. I heard from a gal at CNN this morning."

"Already?" And Art's mother had been mortified her son's unexplained breakdown would be known in several *counties*. Myles hadn't expected so quick a response from the national media.

"Yeah, there's a front-page story in the *Lower Columbia News*, and I guess that kind of thing gets around," Rob said sarcastically, eyeing the newspaper on Myles's seat. "Think you could've made that story any bigger? That family photo's a nice touch. Congratulations—you got the word out. The Portland station's on the way to the courthouse now. I figgered I'd better get some peace out here this morning, because there sure won't be none for a long time to come."

That hurt, Myles realized. "Do you really think I was enjoying my job last night?"

Rob didn't answer. Instead, he began writing out a speeding ticket.

Rob yanked the ticket out of his book and dangled it in Myles's window, leaning closer. His breath smelled like coffee grounds. "I'm glad you're all right, Myles. I mean that. And I know you have a job to do, just like I do. But I'm gonna give you two pieces of advice: For starters, pay attention while you're driving, so I won't have to spray you off your seat with a hose. The next thing is, you tell that prick reporter, Roger, to stop calling Liza's mom's house. He called four times last night, and that's plain indecent. I'm surprised at you." His voice shook on the last words, angry.

Dammit. Roger should know better, Myles thought. "I didn't know he was harassing them, and I'll tell him to stop. I apologize, truly. But can I ask a favor?"

"I'm listening."

"I know how tight you are with the M.E. If you get the autopsy report first, will you call us before you call the big news stations?"

"What do you want with it?" Rob said.

"I hear there might have been bruises. On the neck."

Despite his irritation, Rob's sleep-starved eyes burned with awful knowledge he needed to share, like a convert to a lurid religion. "Yeah, there were bruises. That rumor's true. Art choked the hell out of him. I don't know which killed him, the choking or the drowning, to tell the truth. When I have a report, you'll know more. It's public record. But I'm calling you, not Roger."

"Thanks. That's good enough, man. I appreciate it."

Myles remembered they were talking about little Glenn Brunell, and he felt a stupor wash over him. He'd seen that kid only last week, when Glenn's eyes had been glued to his Game Boy while he sat cross-legged outside the town council chambers, oblivious to the mundane world of the adults around him. *Bored?* Myles had asked him, and Glenn had only nodded, not looking up, as if he'd already heard the question fifty times. His neck had not been bruised that night.

Myles could have believed an accidental drowning, horseplay gone awry—but how could Art have accidentally choked Glenn hard enough to bruise him? That was murder, no excuses. He didn't know what to make of a man like that. That funny, lively family had been a lie, and it was gone in a single day. And Myles had grown to like Liza since his move back to town, ever since Corey's funeral. They'd flown to Los Angeles together, and Liza had spent much of the trip trying to convince him not to give up on Angie. *Give her time. It can all work out in the end,* she'd said, forever positive. *Just look at me and Art.*

He needed to mail Liza a card, or send her a fruit basket. He wanted to do something for Angie, too. He wished he knew what else to do for either one of them.

"I hope this is the end of it," Myles said.

"It sure as shit better be."

Rob didn't ask what it was. He'd been clearing away corpses in Sacajawea since Angie's Fourth of July party, Myles remembered. More than most, Rob already knew.

"You're kidding," Angela said.

"Girl, I couldn't make this story up if I tried. We're delayed at least four days."

Angela had answered her cell phone only because she thought it might be Myles, until she remembered he didn't have her mobile number. Still, she was glad to hear Naomi's voice, an anchor to the simpler life she'd had even a few days ago. Not easy, but simpler.

Angela's stride slowed as she rounded Lake Sacajawea in Longview.

She'd been pushing herself so her mind would go empty, helping her forget everything for a whole minute at a time. A whipping wind and cold rain droplets had chased away any other morning joggers, so Angela had the gravel path to herself as she ran beneath the canopy of branches from neatly ordered trees. The rainwater washed her face, and she hoped it was washing her spirit, too. She needed to be as cleansed as possible before she drove back to Sacajawea today.

"We're just about to start shooting, then that crybaby Jake twists his ankle at the gym and says he can't put any weight on it," Naomi said. "Almost all my scenes are with him, of course. So I'm stuck. And after the way I rushed out here, leaving my poor dog in the middle of nowhere. I knew I shouldn't have left, Angela. I'm flying back there tonight."

Angela nearly tripped over her feet. "No, don't do that."

"I can't sit up here while Onyx is out who-knows-where. He's been gone since Sunday! I know you're doing your best to find him, but I'd be looking a different kind of way because he's my baby. Did you set up a reward yet like I told you?"

Angela didn't answer because she barely heard the question. Knowing Naomi was far away was the one nugget of relief Angela had felt after Myles left that morning, when she'd had to fight to pull herself out of the bed in a way that reminded her of those days before she went to The Harbor, when she lived in her bed. Recognizing herself less and less in those days, she'd picked her eyelashes and eyebrows clean off and had to paint on her face when she went out, which had been rarely. She never wanted to revisit that ruined, debilitating part of her mind again.

But that would be hard. The world was in pieces again. She needed to keep Naomi away. The source of whatever she'd smelled on Art could be in the house, in the soil, in the air. Naomi could not come here.

"Sweetie . . . ," Angela began. "I want you to sit down." She'd planned to do this in person, but the time and place were no longer her choice.

Naomi caught her breath. "What? *Shit*, Angela." It was like a plea, asking her not to go on.

"I didn't know how to tell you this, and I'm very sorry. . . ."

Naomi didn't interrupt her, but Angela could almost see Naomi's tears in her pointed silence. This was hard, but not as hard as it would have been if Art had not drowned Glenn yesterday. "Onyx is dead. Myles and I found him in the woods behind the house."

"Maybe it's another dog. Are you sure it's him?" Her voice was stubborn, matter-of-fact.

"I'm sure. He had on his collar." That was a lie, but a forgivable one, Angela thought. "Sweetie, I'm so, so sorry. We both are."

Utter, stark silence again.

Angela stopped at a picnic table and sat against the rough, damp table-top, feeling the rainwater seep into the seat of her jogging pants. From where she sat, the expanse of the rain-spattered lake stretched out on one side while the oldest and most regal homes in town sat tranquilly on the other. This was a peaceful place, she realized. That was why she had come, because she would need to hoard all the peace she could find.

"What happened?" Naomi said finally.

Angela paused, wondering if Naomi really wanted to know her dog had been found in pieces. She chose mercy. "We're not sure," she said. "A snakebite, maybe."

Naomi sobbed, a squeal. Naomi finally believed her, and Angela was sorry both for the lies and the truth. She cursed herself for not knowing better in the beginning. She never should have brought Naomi to Sacajawea.

"I was so scared something would happen to him in those woods. Wasn't I, Angela? That first day, when he was gone, I was so scared he was in the woods all by himself. Before I left, I knew something had happened to him. I *knew* it. I—" Her next sob stole her speech.

Angela let her friend cry. She'd needed that at one time, when she called her friends to cry, until she was sick of hearing her own misery. She waited, gazing at a brown duck paddling between stalks of grass in the water with her line of four ducklings, a sight that nearly mesmerized her. "Here's what you should do, Naomi," Angela said after a time, and Naomi quieted, eager to be told. "Don't stay at that hotel. There's no reason for you to be there. But don't come here."

"What about . . ."

"I've already taken care of Onyx for you. He's buried in the woods." That lie elicited another sob, but this time Angela didn't wait for the spell to pass. "I'll have Suzanne book you a room at the nicest spa she can find up there. Go somewhere pretty, like a hot springs. Pamper yourself. The works. Blow your diet. Eat ice cream. Do you hear me?"

Naomi made a vaguely affirmative sound.

"I think that's the best thing for you now. You're hurting. Take care of yourself for a few days, then go back to work. It's my treat."

"I can't let you do that, Angela," Naomi said. Her voice was tear-racked.

"You don't have a choice. I am doing it. I want to."

"Only if you come with me," Naomi said.

"I can't, sweetie."

"Why not? You took the week off." She was nearly whimpering.

"I'm stuck here for a while. Something's going on."

"Something like what?"

Angela paused. There was no way to explain it, but she decided to try. "Like when Corey shot himself. And when my neighbor walked into a truck. And when you went sleepwalking into the cellar. And when Onyx died. That kind of something."

"Angela, you're scaring me. Just *leave* that place."

"I can't. Whatever's happening here started with my family."

"So?"

"It's mine," Angela said, because she could think of no other way to put it. "I own it."

"You're talking crazy."

"I know," she said, smiling to herself. "Don't worry. I'm sleeping in a hotel, and I won't stay in town long. Will you go to a spa?"

"I'll think about it," Naomi whispered.

"Just do it. Please." She paused. "Naomi . . . have you been sick at all?"

"What do you mean?"

"Have you had a stomachache since you left here? Anything strange?"

"I just got a headache, but my stomach's all right. Why?"

Angela had called Liza's house that morning and posed a single question to her exhausted father, who was the only one in the house who could compose himself enough to come to the line. After apologizing for the intrusion, Angela asked him a single question: *Did Art say he wasn't feeling well before yesterday?* As a matter of fact, Mr. Kerr told her, Liza had said Art had a bellyache the night before Glenn died.

Angela had felt better while she was running, but now the foreboding that had begun in earnest last night was gathering strength. Didn't she feel a slight heat in her arms, the tingling again? She was almost sure of it, and her heart quickened. "There's something going around town. That's another reason you need to stay up there. I want to make sure you're okay, because I love you, Naomi. And I'm so sorry about Onyx."

She heard Naomi's sniffling nostrils as she cried to herself. "If I promise to go to a spa, do you promise to leave that house as soon as you can? Before something else happens?"

"I promise," Angela said, although she doubted it was a promise she could keep.

LES MYSTÈRES

"People ask, 'Why has this Evil come?'

Why does the rain come?

It has its time."

— MARIE TOUSSAINT
Le Livre des Mystères
1929

✠ Twenty ✠

I WAS THE FIFTH OF FIVE CHILDREN, *the youngest; and, some would
say, the most spoiled. My siblings Charles, Gil, Henrietta, and Nadine preferred each other's company, as I was born much later, so I spent my time either
playing alone or at Grandmère's knee. She liked to tell me she had been waiting
for me, asking, "Why did it take you so long to get here, cher?" She chided me as if
I'd had a choice in the matter. "I got here fast as I could, Grandmère," I told her,
laughing as her dry fingertips tickled my soft belly.*

*Grandmère was a manbo, her talents widely sought after. Throughout my
childhood, Madame Fleurette, as she called herself, was visited by all the walks of
life inhabiting New Orleans; colored and white, rich and poor, unschooled and well-
schooled. A white man with a handlebar moustache came to her once because he
wanted to go to the state senate, and he sent our family boxes of sweets and cookies
for six Christmases after he won that gilded seat. He later became a United States
Congressman, but by then his Christmas packages had stopped arriving. Grandmère said he should have been thanking Ogou la Flambo and Shangó, because you
would never want to go to battle without them at your side. People always forget
those who have helped them. I learned this young, but knowing this did not save me
from my fate, from my own forgetting.*

*From the start, I loved vodou and the lwas more than my brothers and sisters,
and more, it seemed, than my own mother, who was a manbo in her youth, favored
with visits from spirits in her dreams. I knew we owed our home, our clothes, and
our luck to the lwas, and to the blessings of Jesus Christ, whose crucifix hung above
my bed at night. Grandmère trained me from the time I was young. I was only*

seven years old when my sweet Papa Legba came to me the first time, when Grand-mère made her ritual call, "Papa Legba! Ouvri bàryè," so he would open the doorway to the lwas, and suddenly I felt as if I was floating into the sky. I remembered none of what happened next, but I was told Papa Legba bent my spine as if it belonged to a twisted old man, and I hobbled about, speaking with Papa Lebga's tongue, a tongue of an elder. I was a marvel, because it is rare for a lwa to mount a child; the danger to young ones is too great because they are not yet strong enough to carry such a burden. Yet, I was that strong as a child. As a child, I am convinced, I was the strongest I have ever been. Papa Legba has always favored me, and my love for him was sown early in my years.

One day, when she feared she was near death, Grandmère bade me to wear her ring. I was but twelve, so the ring was too large for my ring finger, but she fitted it to my thumb. "So I will always be able to find you," she said. I did not know the meaning of her words at the time, but I was happy to take possession of such a lovely ring, especially since she had not offered it to my brothers or sisters. I studied the ring's ritual artwork, and I did not recognize the vèvè as those I had seen her draw on the ground, cornmeal slipping delicately between her fingers as she called the lwas. I asked Grandmère to explain the ring's drawings to me, and she said they were from an ancestor's dream, that the ring had been mined in West Africa. The drawings were clues to a secret language known only to our bloodline, telling our story, preserving our power. "Through this ring," Grandmère told me, "I will tell you the language of the lwas, so you may speak to them as an equal."

Such talk was not unusual for my grandmère, who had often been accused of pomposity, even heresy, thinking so much of herself. I had assumed her critics were only jealous, since no other manbo in New Orleans, in Louisiana, or perhaps in the whole of the South, could claim her power. Hundreds of people came from miles about for her rain ceremonies, and her successes with healing rituals were legend. Grandmère often made the claim that she was kin to the great priestess Marie Laveau, a lie—but there was enough truth ground up in her lies to serve the lwas and the people well. Even people who did not like her arrogance came to her when they needed help.

Grandmère taught me young that I was not bound by the rules that governed others. Our wealth and standing gave us privileges, she said. As a consequence, when I was in town, I dared to go places designated only for whites, much to my parents' mortification. Grandmère gave me courage. In Africa, she told me, our direct ancestors could take wing and fly. It was our birthright, she said, to create miracles. With my ring, she said, I would grow up to make a great miracle take place, something no other manbo or bòkò could claim. I would become the head family spirit.

I have waited all of my life for the miracle Grandmère promised. There are times I have come close to destroying these papers because I became convinced she lied to me, another of her elaborate stories meant to serve as a metaphor, not literal truth. There are times I have wanted to destroy these papers whether her words were lies or not, so great is the power of what lies within these pages. Twice, I have thrown the ring she gave me away, and twice I have retrieved it; once, I had to search an open field for a month before I found it glimmering in the sun. It is a terrible dilemma: I blame the ring, and I blame the word, and yet only the ring and the word can restore what has been ruined. I loathe the ring and the word, and still I must cherish them.

There has been a curse upon me. Perhaps "bad eyes," the plague of too much jealousy, led to my change of luck after Grandmère died. I was blind to the curse until it was too late.

I did not speak for a full year after Grandmère died when I was eighteen, so much did my heart ache. I expected her to come to me right away, in dreams and visions, but she did not. In her homeland of Haiti, the not-speaking disease, pa-pale, is said to usually come after childbirth, but in my case it was after a death. I hardly washed or ate. My family could do nothing with me.

It was Philippe Toussaint, the Creole young man who served as my father's attorney, who drew me from my prison of mourning, with his gentle smile, wit, and constant attentions. For two years, he courted me, and I would not have him. I did not want to be a wife right away, as so many others of my sex did. I went to the Mary McLeod Hospital and Training School for Nurses, to learn nursing to complement my vodou practice, and when I returned, Philippe was still waiting for me. Again, as I said, I was spoiled. Why should I settle for one thing or the other— my education or my suitor—when I could have both?

At last, we wed. He built me a lovely house very near my parents. We had a daughter, Dominique. I was no longer angry at life for the loss of Grandmère, nor for the absence of her spirit.

Then, as if to prove its mean core, life became a horror.

That night is too painful to me to describe in full, but suffice it to say that one can hardly comprehend that human beings would be capable of such monstrosity. It began when Philippe grew interested in politics, encouraging other colored people to register to vote despite the stranglehold of Jim Crow. With my blessings, he could have amassed more power than any colored man in the history of the state, and there were many others who knew it. We were naive not to expect reprisals.

I had no warnings, no dreams. I had prayed for Philippe's safety, but it was not enough.

They came for him with their rifles at night, when we were sleeping. They pulled him from my bed, from my desperate embrace. My baby was too young to comprehend the violence, but Philippe was killed before our eyes. "Remember the sight of this, nigger," one of his torturers spat at me, as if I could forget a sight that could not have been more abhorrent if it had been a rendering from Hell itself.

Those men were all soon dead for their crime—the lwas helped me punish them—but that was small comfort to me. Papa Legba tried to console me by offering himself as my spirit-husband, a ceremony consecrated by a prétsavann from Haiti, a bush priest, with the signatures of witnesses dutifully collected on our marriage papers, and I swore to Papa Legba that no man of flesh should ever touch me on Saturday, my spirit-husband's sacred day. But even as the new bride of so powerful and generous a lwa as dear Papa Legba, I could not shake myself from my mourning.

My heart died with Philippe. I barely had heart enough left for the child of mine, who now knew only one parent, but I did not give the baby to my sisters, as they begged me to. If only I had! Instead, I took my precious Dominique away from New Orleans, away from the South, as far from the place of her father's murder as I could go.

It was then that Grandmère began to find my dreams and visions, offering me the miracle she had promised me as a girl.

It was then that my journey to damnation began.

✒ Twenty-One ✒

THURSDAY

$\mathcal{U}$NDER A RAINY SKY the color of dirty snow, the creature that had once been Tariq Hill drove a 1968 bay-window Volkswagen microbus northbound on Interstate Five in southern Washington, nearly an hour past Portland. Onyx was curled on the passenger-side floorboard, either sleeping or pretending to. Onyx hadn't always been this quiet, but he'd wised up since Tariq caught him with a quick kick in the ribs two hours back. The dog had nearly ruined his telephone chat with that prissy Myles Fisher, with all the racket he'd been making. Tariq had wanted to kick Onyx two or three more times, but he'd stopped himself, counting to ten. He was getting better at that. Anger management.

Tariq opened the glove compartment and pulled out a handful of sun-faded cassette cases, spreading them across the passenger seat. Teddy Pendergrass, Marvin Gaye, Al Green. Coincidentally, all his favorites. When he popped a cassette in the player, "I'm So Tired of Being Alone" mewled from the van's old speakers, distorting Al's voice with a hiss on the high notes. Still, the sound of the music was celestial. He remembered that much about who he had been. Music, so far, was his favorite souvenir of himself.

Tariq drove at seventy miles per hour, the precise speed limit, neither more nor less. He was in a hurry, but he would not be pulled over for speeding. He had no faith that he would be cordial if someone in a police uniform tried to delay him. He had never liked police uniforms much, the fault of a few bad apples. He remembered that too.

That Bitch Marie was a bad apple. She had spoiled everything close to her, everyone she touched. Marie had been lost from her precious grand-daughter for a time, but she would never be lost from the *baka* who deviled her.

It was too bad he had won his knowledge so late, Tariq thought, or he'd have known from the start that Angie's line was spoiled, that she would be impossible, and that the boy would be as greedy as his great-grandmother. Tariq knew the entire shameful story, because the *baka* With No Name had whispered it while it awakened within him, gleefully telling him about the downfall of the silly flesh creatures who tried to be gods.

Eshu had been too good to Marie and her forebears, the *baka* said, favoring them blatantly with his attentions. That was Eshu's way, blinded by his love for his children. Over the ages, when Marie's line had called him from Yorubaland, or Cuba, or Haiti, or the Americas, praying for Eshu-Elegba, Eleggua, or Papa Legba—by any of the names by which he was known to them—Eshu came speedily. He had been generous, his eternal flaw. Foolishness!

One's children, the *baka* said, can only be motivated by fear.

Yet, Eshu had bid his fellow spirits Yemoja and Oyá to hold famines, earthquakes, and hurricanes at bay to save Marie's line a dozen times over. Most of her line had been spared slavery across the sea, but for those he had lost, Eshu had given voice to their prayers in the bellies of the great ships, and they had stayed strong. He had rescued Marie's *grandmère* Fleurette from a shack in the swamp, brought children to Fleurette's barren womb, married her daughter Sonia well to that *passé blanc* she loved so much, showered them in property and riches. And they had grown so vain!

When Marie's husband was killed, Eshu had hastened her grieving pleas to Ogun and Oyá to wreak the penalties against those who had taken the unlucky man's life. Those murderers awakened with boils across their bodies, fire in their genitals, dying at the rate of one a year, and always at the anniversary of Marie's husband's death. Then, Eshu led Marie to the sacred grounds in the far west to begin her life afresh, far from the place her beloved died. He had given her free run of the land to use as she pleased.

And how had Eshu been repaid? Eshu, the great Trickster god, had himself been tricked.

"But you've learned better now, haven't you, Marie?" Tariq said. "You were only a silly flesh witch playing games. You were a child, Marie. You're still a child."

Eshu had led her to the land willingly, to the Crossroads Forest, but when Marie found it, she had become insufferable. She could have offered libations and sacrifices and collected sacred soil in a pouch to wear around her neck, across her breast. That soil would have suited her well enough, and the *baka* there might have slept forever, undisturbed. She could have gone anywhere with the soil and ensured health and happiness for her children, grandchildren, and great-grandchildren.

Instead, That Bitch had been proud enough to steal the land.

Even that, though, was not the worst offense; the land had been stolen by others, and it recognized no owner. The land belonged to spirit, not to flesh. The red men had understood this about the land, and Marie should have known, too.

But even Eshu could not forgive the way she befouled the land.

Oh forgive me, Papa Legba, but I did not know, she claimed in so many prayers to him afterward, when she pretended to be shocked at the potency of her wishes. She, who had been tutored by Fleurette, a priestess who would have been burned as a witch in earlier times because she was so brazen with her gifts, governing crops, rain, and births. She, who had been taught the history of the line from which she was descended. She, whose dreams had revealed forgotten prayers, prayers from long before the Journey of her people across the sea. She, who wore the ring mined from gold blessed by the most powerful circle of priests in her people's original land. It was all the more impudent for her to claim she did not know her power!

And Marie was a clever one. She had kept her progeny in ignorance, stripping them of her knowledge, as if Eshu might be placated with so small a penance, and as if the *baka* could so easily be banished from their trail. But it was too late for penance. And the *baka* could not be so easily deceived. The *baka* had taken Marie's daughter easily. Marie's efforts were feeble. The *baka* would not be banished.

Especially now that it had taken the boy.

Tariq had once loved the boy, as a flesh creature. But silly was silly, whether or not the boy was his son. The boy had been too easy to fool. All flesh was easy to fool. So, the *baka* would take the last of Marie's line, to make Marie an example. The *baka* had nearly fulfilled its lesson. Eshu, in his anger, would not intervene.

Angela Marie—daughter to Dominique, grandchild to Marie, great-great-grandchild to Fleurette—was the last of the line. Angie was the last.

Tariq could feel her nearby. He could see her face in the evergreens his bus drove past on the freeway, painted in the gaps between the trees. Her chiseled brown face was all around him now, bringing its own memories. But the *baka* had warned Tariq: There would be trickery. There would be messengers. All of it was evidence of That Bitch's pride, her effort to preserve her progeny. Marie and her line had held Tariq in sway for two years, through pure strength, or else he would have completed his calling much sooner. He couldn't discount her power, the power of her line.

But Marie's line was not the stronger of them. Tariq would teach her that, at last.

As a revelation came to him, Tariq opened his van's glove compartment and smiled at what he found: The gun lay there waiting atop the old registration papers, maps, and receipts that had migrated their way into the space over the years. Its butt was still wrapped in old tape, but its black barrel shined as it never had. The gun had been taken when the boy died, impounded.

Tariq had lost this gun before. The *baka*, once again, had given it back.

There would be ironic beauty in taking Angie with this gun, Tariq realized. She had always been afraid of it; knowing, yet never understanding what she knew.

The sight of the gun brought back another ghost of memory: In his pure flesh life, Tariq and his brother Harry had heard gunshots through the wall of the bedroom they shared as children, the first time Tariq had heard the terrifying sound so close. Tariq couldn't remember the woman's name, but he remembered the thrill and shock of knowing their neighbor had committed a murder. She'd been a nice woman, that was the thing. A waving and smiling kind of woman whose home was one of the few places he, Harry, and their sisters were allowed to trick-or-treat. When he'd asked his father to make sense of how such a nice woman could turn around one day and shoot her husband to death, his father had told him, *Sometimes you get mad. When you're mad enough, you can do anything.* That was a lesson Leland Hill had taught his children many times before.

And Angie had seen it when he first brought home this gun. She'd seen how the bruises at his father's hand had left him eager to settle arguments with his fists, or with a weapon. He had never touched her that way, but he had wanted to. He may not have aimed that gun at her breast in life, but she knew he had many times in his imagination. She'd seen it in him, just like Brother Paul.

Angie, a true child of Marie's line, had known her future.

LONGVIEW—STATE ROUTE FOUR, the familiar green roadway sign said, announcing an exit that veered into the countryside fifty yards ahead. Even without the sign, Tariq knew he had nearly reached the road to Sacajawea. He was close to the place. He was nearly home.

Tariq had wanted her that summer. He had driven a long way to reclaim her that summer, just as he was driving a long way now. He had tasted her skin and tongue, and he vowed to enjoy Angie's flesh once more the same way he enjoyed his old music: with exquisite, grateful pleasure. He had a memory of the folds of her womanhood, the pink and brown rises and valleys, that made him moan softly as he drove. That memory was better than the music by far.

There would be time for play. The *baka* had promised him that.

But then, Tariq must finish it.

Still, Tariq sped past the Longview exit without looking back, not veering from the Interstate to the road that led to Longview and Sacajawea. In his mirror, he watched the exit retreat behind him. "Good-bye for now, Angie," he said. "I'll see you soon, Snook."

He had never been good at patience, but he would master that trait today.

He had one more trip to make. Five hours north of here on Interstate Five, across the malleable Canadian border, another detail needed sorting. One more special task lay at Tariq's feet before he could go home to his wife.

Tariq had to see a woman about a dog.

⚑ Twenty-Two ⚑

Vancouver, British Columbia
That same day

Y OU'RE POSITIVE YOU CAN'T GO TODAY, Naomi? I could get you
to Victoria by dinnertime."

Her assistant was trying so hard to please her, Naomi felt sorry for the
girl. Naomi shook her head, and marbles cracked inside her skull. She
hadn't had a headache this bad in her life; not the day of the Emmys for
Coretta, not even after Mama June died and then Daddy followed six
months later, the worst year of her life. Naomi lay across the couch in the
living room of her two-room suite at the Sutton Place Hotel, barefoot,
wearing the hotel's white terry cloth robe over the workout clothes she'd
put on before talking to Angela had ruined her day's plans.

Suzanne's mudcloth head wrap and large gold hoop earrings made her
look like a high-toned African shaman, Naomi thought. She felt slight pressure across her eyes as Suzanne gently swathed a cold, damp towel on her
face, above the bridge of her nose. Suzanne had been tending her for an
hour, doing her best, but Naomi longed for the massage Angela had given
her backstage at the Emmys, with perfect strokes at her temples that made
her headache vanish as if by magic.

"How about if I pack you a weekend bag?" Suzanne said, her voice a
gentle murmur. "Then we'll go straight to the spa when your headache dies
down. I booked myself that early flight to L.A. tomorrow, so if I don't take
you today . . ."

"Go on about your business, girl. I can get there. It's only a couple
hours from here."

Let Suzanne go on home, she thought. Hell, maybe she'd fly home to-morrow, too. Or go to Sacajawea and say good-bye to her dog properly, no matter what Angela said. Or maybe she'd lie where she was for four days straight. That sounded tempting, too. All Naomi gave a fuck about right now was having some quiet, so her head would leave her be.

"Naomi, Angela is going to be all over me if you don't go to this spa," Suzanne said, as if Naomi had voiced her doubts aloud. Suzanne sounded nervous and gloomy, more like the twenty-one-year-old she was, not the quick-thinking dynamo she'd been the past couple days. Suzanne was working her heart out.

"Don't let Angela scare you," Naomi said. She almost smiled, until she realized what she'd been about to say: *Angela's all bark and no bite.* New tears, new ripples of pain. Fuck. Anytime Naomi's mind tried to stray from Onyx, her headache punished her. A nasty thought rolled with her tears. "Angela saw Onyx dead in the woods before I left and didn't tell me," she whispered.

"Why would she do that?" Suzanne said.

"Why else? She wanted me to come to work."

It was so obvious now, Naomi felt stupid. Angela was looking out for her ten percent. Bennett had told her to remember that. There's business and there's friendship, her older brother always said, reminding her she was too quick to let people into her heart. Naomi felt her insides churn-ing, spurring her headache. She was on the verge of the wailing kind of crying best done in private. Soul-tears, Mama June used to call it. No amount of Tylenol, massage, or cold towels would ease the pain of losing Onyx.

"I'm okay," Naomi told Suzanne. "You can go now."

Suzanne squeezed Naomi's shoulders, kneading hard. Her grip said she knew why she was being sent out of the room. "I'm always nearby. Just call." She kissed Naomi's forehead.

Alone in her suite, Naomi lay still, trying to will away the pain. Thank God for Suzanne, she thought. When Suzanne finished her U.C.L.A. film degree in January, maybe she would come work for her full-time, stay on a year or two until she made her own industry contacts. Naomi had prom-ised herself a full-time assistant when she got her first million-dollar pay-day; and in January, that would come to pass. What the hell else did she have to spend her money on? Her husband? Her children? Not in this life, honey. Not yet. She didn't have time for vacations, and she was living in the same house she'd bought with her soap-opera money.

She didn't have Onyx to spend her money on either. She was taking this ride by herself now.

And just when things were going so right! She'd finally done it. Everyone said so. She was about to erupt like a newborn sun. The future she'd been striving for since she was Dorothy in *The Wizard of Oz* under Cornelia Dozier at the Eighth Street Children's Theater was happening while she witnessed it, prophecy in the making. This was supposed to be the happiest time of her life.

So why was it so awful? More awful all the time?

She'd accepted how Mama June and Daddy hadn't lived to see it. Their absence lanced each triumph, but she could live with that. And she'd accepted the way her old friends and new men shunned her, as if they couldn't quite find her in all the light shining on her. Angela's friend Myles Fisher was the first new man she'd met in a year who'd treated her like she could be his friend, his sister, or his partner. He hadn't been afraid of her, mad at her, or awed by her. Hallelujah.

That was rare. More than rare. But with Onyx, her growing isolation had been all right.

Now, the all rightness was gone. Onyx had been her daily witness and companion, her baby, her comfort. Onyx had loved her with a fervor, thinking she was his mama since Mama June gave him to her as a puppy on her college graduation day. Onyx had been there from the start, forcing her to think about someone besides herself. Now, with each new blessing, she seemed to lose one more thing to make room.

We ain't meant to know the ways of God, Mama June had always tried to comfort her when no other words fit. The Lord giveth, but with a catch. She accepted that, too, but it hurt.

The doorbell outside her suite rang gently. Naomi didn't move, her eyes still hidden behind the towel. Fuck. Maybe she should go to the spa today so no one could find her.

"Naomi?" a voice said, all exuberance. It sounded like Vince.

With a sigh, bringing herself to her feet, Naomi walked to the door and had almost touched the knob when she stopped before her fingers reached it. She had to be careful about opening her door now. Bennett reminded her there were crazies everywhere. She'd just read a story in one of the tabloids about an actress whose crazy fan regularly masturbated in her rosebushes.

"Who is it?" Naomi said, to be sure. Through the peephole, she saw a man's earlobe. He was looking away from the door.

"It's Vinny, sweetheart. Sorry to bug you, but I have a surprise."

That voice was Vince's, all right, with his Brooklyn accent and cigarette-toughened larynx. Naomi had always thought it was silly for a man as big as Vincent D'Angelo to use a child's nickname. She opened the door, although the tightness she'd felt in her temples was spreading to her neck. It was just a feeling, but it was more than that. It was intuition. The bad kind.

Vince grinned, an ocean of teeth. "How's the most beautiful woman in Vancouver?"

Naomi glanced down at her robe and shorts. She'd forgotten she was barely dressed. "When I see her, I'll ask. What is it, Vince? I'm not feeling well."

Vince's face went deadpan. "I know, and I'm sorry about the whole thing, beginning to end. Your agent called me before, I know you had a problem, and I disappointed you. After this thing with Jake, you're probably ready to tear me a new one. Am I right?"

Naomi didn't say anything, because she didn't have the energy for polite lies today. Onyx might still be alive if Vince had given her the time to search for him. Maybe it wouldn't have made a difference, but she would never know. This gig felt more trifling all the time, a string of bad luck.

While Naomi glared at him, Vince's grin glowed back on. "I'm so psyched to be able to do this, Naomi. Please remember this a year from now, when I'm begging you to work with me again and you're not only still mad at me, you're *way* out of my budget. Deal?"

"What, Vince? I'm really not . . ."

"Your brother's here," Vince said, beaming. "He brought you something you'll want."

"Bennett's here?" Naomi said. Without realizing it, she'd grabbed Vince's arms, ready to kiss his stubbled cheek if he said yes. Bennett hadn't told her he was coming to Vancouver! Bennett never had time to come visit her shoots anymore, and she had almost stopped missing him.

A shadow moved beside Vince, someone outside of her vision around the corner. Then, a tall black man came into view. Vince was six-one, and this guy was taller, rising over both of them. He was not Bennett. Nothing about him was remotely like Bennett.

"That's not my brother," she told Vince, and her director's carefully tanned face went pale.

"You're kidding," Vince said. "I thought—"

That was when Onyx barked.

It didn't matter that Angela had told her only a few hours ago that Onyx was dead. Or that she couldn't see the shadowed animal inside the blue carrier the tall man was carrying at his side, topped with a red bow. Naomi had raised her dog from a puppy, and she knew his call.

"*Onyx!*" Naomi shrieked, and the man laughed. He knelt to the carpet and unhinged the carrier's door. Onyx came bounding out, leaping toward her, his tail going berserk as he barked.

"Naomi . . . you're saying this isn't your brother?" Vince said, troubled.

"No, it's okay. It's Onyx!" Naomi said, whooping in waves of laughter and tears as her dog lathered her face. "Oh my God, *this is really my dog!* He brought me my dog."

Naomi's mind felt foggy, but she recalled that she knew this man: He was Tariq Hill, Angela's ex-husband. She'd seen him last at Corey's funeral, and once ages ago at a party at their house in the Hills. She wondered how she hadn't recognized him before. He was wearing a black nylon shirt and black slacks, the same way he'd been dressed at his son's funeral.

"So all is forgiven?" Vince said. "Everything's okay here?"

"I love you, Vince," Naomi said, and he smiled, relief filling his eyes. Vince gave Tariq a hearty handshake, thanking him. Then, Vince walked away, jaunty and at ease, not once considering the possibility that he might be the last human being to see Naomi Price alive.

Onyx's eyes were bright, and he looked well fed, even pudgy. His coat smelled bathed. Someone might have even clipped his nails, Naomi noticed. Onyx looked good, and he was beside himself with energy, scrambling over her as she sat on her hotel room floor. He'd missed her, too.

Every time she touched Onyx, Naomi felt as if she were slipping into a world of wishes.

"I'm sorry about that mix-up with your brother," Tariq apologized, sitting on the couch. "I lied to the concierge because he was hassling me about the dog, and I figured that was the only way he'd call up to your room. That Vinny guy overheard me and went nuts. He wanted to escort me so he could see the look on your face, and I didn't want to ruin his fun."

"A-Angela told me this morning—"

"Yeah, that's on us, Naomi. We'd already decided to surprise you, and she knew I'd be here in a couple hours. We hoped you'd forgive us once you got Onyx back."

It was the most awful prank Naomi could think of. The idea of it staggered her.

"I'm going to kill that woman. She just doesn't *know*," Naomi said, although she couldn't hold on to her anger with Onyx in her arms. She pressed her cheek against his downy fur, delighting in his fresh smell. After two full minutes of hugging and stroking her dog, Naomi began to gather herself again, and her mind overflowed with questions. She offered Tariq a Heineken from her minibar, so excited and confused that her hands were shaking.

"Who had him?" she said. In her joy, she'd forgotten to ask.

"A kid in Sacajawea found him and hid the collar and tag from his parents, until his father saw a poster in town. I happened to be there when they called Angie, and it's a quick drive."

It sounded absurdly simple, and it was the biggest bunch of horseshit Naomi had ever heard. Why would Angela invite her ex-husband to take part in a playful prank? What could have happened in three days that would put them on such good terms?

Tariq offered nothing else, sitting on the couch with his long legs crossed before him, sipping his beer. Gazing at him, Naomi suddenly didn't want to be in the same room with him. *There is nothing worse on this earth than a liar*, Angela had said when they'd driven into Sacajawea and seen Tariq's van, sounding like someone who'd taken the scenic tour of Hell.

Naomi held Onyx tightly to keep him from squirming away as she rose to her feet from the floor. She could feel the restless thump of his heart beside her breast, meeting hers. "I'm going to the other room to change," Naomi said, hoping Tariq would excuse himself.

"Take your time. I'll wait here, see what's on TV."

Damn him, she thought, but it was her own fault. How could she ask him to leave when she'd just offered him a beer? She was being too nice again. She could hear Bennett in her ear.

The suite's living room was separated from the bedroom by French doors with semi-sheer white curtains, so Naomi closed the doors behind her, turning the lock. Her mind was in a spin.

This had not been solely a *strange* day. She'd had many strange days lately.

Take the time Prince sent her a note in the ladies' room telling her he was a big fan, asking for a quick autograph on a paper towel because he was running late to someplace fabulous. And the day a man gaping at her on Sunset ran a red light and plowed into a Dumpster across the street; and when she ran to his window to see if he was all right, he'd only asked to take her picture, ignoring the blood streaming from a gash in his forehead.

And being invited to the White House Correspondents' Dinner *and* the Oscars on the arm of *the* Robert Mitchell, their meetings arranged by his publicist purely for show, the year he was up for Best Actor, so observers wouldn't know he was gay. Strange days all.

Today had been more than strange. None of its pieces had met at the seams.

Naomi sat at the side of her bed and picked up her hotel phone, still clinging to Onyx. She dialed Angela's cell phone number, hoping the signal would work. Her fingers were unsteady, and she dialed wrong the first time because her eyes were on the French doors, watching for movement. She heard the living room's television set go on loudly, then Tariq flipped through the channels.

Silence on the line. Naomi waited, praying Angela would pick up. Only a busy signal came. *"Fuck,"* she said, her headache rioting. Maybe she'd dialed wrong again.

Onyx suddenly yelped and gnashed his teeth, as if to bite her arm. Gasping, Naomi jerked her arm away, loosening her grip around him, and immediately Onyx went back to normal, wagging his tail, licking her face. Adrenaline drenched Naomi, brought by an awful trickle of a thought.

"What's wrong with you, baby?" Naomi said. She ran her fingers across Onyx's coat while she dialed, and he winced away from her touch when she reached his rib cage. He was tender there, she realized. "Onyx, are you hurt? Did somebody hurt you?"

The busy signal came again, louder and more stubborn than before. This time, Naomi hung up and dialed 502 for Suzanne's room, on the other side of the hall, and the busy signal came without a pause. Her assistant's cell phone number was scribbled on the pad next to her bed, so she tried that next. Naomi's heart fluttered as she dialed. "Please pick up, Suzanne . . . ," she whispered.

The phone, once again, was busy. No combination of numbers worked. This was wrong, too.

"Local TV's not much to speak of, is it?" Tariq called from the other room. He landed on a French-speaking channel before flipping again.

Naomi didn't answer him, forcing herself to sit completely still, fighting the well of panic that had risen from nowhere. The only thing to do now was to ask him to leave.

". . . has shocked friends, family, and supporters in the idyllic river town of Sacajawea, named for the Native American guide who accompanied Lewis and Clark on their historic expedition. . . ." The television's volume in the living room resounded suddenly, startling her. The brassy voice of a female newscaster vibrated the walls.

Naomi stood up, still holding Onyx. The newscaster's voice cut through all her thoughts.

". . . in a town where residents would rather be talking about the latest spaghetti feed or how the steelhead are biting, today only one question is on everyone's minds: Why would their popular mayor, forty-one-year-old Art Brunell, take out a life insurance policy on his eight-year-old son and then allegedly drown him . . . right here?"

Naomi mistrusted her hearing. She had just met a man named Art Brunell at Angie's, the mayor of the town. Had the woman on the news said *Sacajawea?*

Naomi snatched up her bedroom remote. She opened the television cabinet facing her bed and found her TV. She flipped anxiously, and three tries took her to the matching voice on CNN, where she saw an inlet before the image changed to a female broadcaster standing in front of the courthouse she and Angela had jogged past with Onyx a few days ago. Next, Naomi saw an eerily recent photograph of the man who had come to tell her how sorry he was about her missing dog, telling her Angela's grandmother's house was so beloved that everyone called it the Good House. A dry wind seemed to gust through Naomi's mouth and throat.

They were saying this man killed his *son?*

There's trouble and then there's *trouble*, Bennett liked to say, reminding her not to make too much of some things. Keep life in perspective. Don't sweat the small stuff, and all that jazz. Cool as a cucumber, baby. That was Bennett. There's trouble and there's *trouble*.

Staring at her television set, Naomi knew she was in the second kind of trouble. A day this strange was strange for a reason. A day this strange was toying with her. This was the big kind of trouble, even by Bennett's definition.

"Phone trouble?" Tariq's bottomless voice said beside her.

Naomi hollered, a strangled sound. The French doors were propped wide open, and Tariq was four feet behind her. Seeing him, she nearly fell against the bed. He looked like he had strolled into the room without effort. Onyx barked angrily at Tariq, wriggling in Naomi's arms, but she held him with all her might.

"Don't hurt him," she said. Naomi had no doubt now why Onyx's ribs were sore.

Tariq whipped a black handgun from behind his back, holding it at hip level in a stance that looked casual even in its threat. The muzzle staring at her chest looked like a black pinhole in the thick barrel. When she was able to look away from the pinhole, back at Tariq's face, she was surprised by his cheery expression.

"What do you want?" Naomi said. She'd managed to sound indignant.

"I owe you an explanation," Tariq said gently. "Promise me you'll keep quiet?"

He was being nice about this, whatever it was. Naomi nodded, her teeth clicking together. Maybe he only wanted to unburden his heart. He'd tell her how Angela had always misunderstood him, how much it had hurt him when his son died, how awful he felt at the funeral when Angela cussed him out in front of God. She would promise not to tell anyone about the gun and send him away. Sometimes deranged people just wanted someone to listen. She could listen.

"It's not your fault. You didn't know," Tariq said. "Everyone's been telling you your luck's changed because of hard work and your pretty face, and I won't take that away from you. But you've had help—help from Angie, help from her grandmother. They've been pushing things along, wheedling. People in power dream about you and see your face everywhere for two days solid. Did you know that? Ask Vincent. Ask Stan Loweson at FilmQuest. That's what happened to them. That's what people mean when the say the fates are smiling on you. It's all good, right?"

Naomi's head nodded fervently, as if she understood, although she was barely listening, getting madder at herself. This man was the kind of psychopath she'd read about in tabloids. Why hadn't she prepared for this? She'd laughed at Bennett when he'd ask her if she was getting a bodyguard. *Just don't let him get mad,* she thought. *Just let him keep talking, Jesus, and help me find a way out of this.* In her peripheral vision, she looked for places to hide, a towel or a bedsheet she could throw on Tariq to give her a minute to . . .

"But you've been used, Naomi. Marie used you to send Angie back to Sacajawea, back to the place. Marie dragged you in, and now you're involved. But you didn't know Marie was talking to you, did you? You couldn't hear her voice. Well, she was talking to you, baby. You did exactly what she wanted you to do—a little puppet, Naomi. Marie said jump, you said, 'I'm jumping!' "

Tariq sounded like he was getting agitated, and Naomi stared at the glaring pinhole again. If Tariq's finger slipped on the trigger, if he twitched, he was going to kill her. He was *pointing* that gun at her. Sweet Lord, what was wrong with this man?

Suddenly, Naomi felt obligated to listen again. She wanted to cry, but she was afraid to.

"The flesh realm can be a lonely place if you don't know how to reach the ones who've gone, and you never learned that, did you? Don't you miss your father, Naomi? And Mama June? Well, they're right here. They're right here watching."

The names of her father and grandmother froze Naomi still. She gaped at Tariq with a sob that sounded like a hiccup. Her moorings to reality had loosened long ago, from the moment she had seen Onyx again, but now her mind snapped free. She was babbling. She'd never done that before.

"Shhhh. Don't make a sound," Tariq said. "I promise, I won't hurt you. I treat beautiful women with respect. Eshu's happy with your line—Mama June always had pipe tobacco and a walking stick waiting for him at her door. I'm not here to cause you pain. I'm here to punish Marie. You should have been more careful about choosing your friends, Naomi. And you'll have to stop that whimpering, or I'll get mad. I'm not a saint, and I'm having problems with my temper."

Naomi's hand flew over her mouth. She'd thought the whimpers were coming from Onyx, but they were hers. She closed her eyes. In the sanctity of darkness, her terror retreated enough that she could breathe without feeling smothered.

Tariq's broad, cold palm rested against her cheek. "You would have been timeless," he said.

Would have been. The words clawed at Naomi. She decided to scream, at the same instant she realized that the living room television was so loud that no one would hear her. Tariq tightened his grip against her jaw, behind her ear, pushing her head to one side. Gasping, Naomi opened her eyes, a reflex. She had to see what was about to happen to her.

She was an observer now. This couldn't really be happening. It *couldn't.*

And then, as soon as she'd decided it wasn't happening, it really wasn't.

The gun's muzzle was gone. Tariq held the gun up in the air, flipping it in his hand until he gripped it by the barrel. The tape-covered butt was facing her, safe. Harmless.

"See? I won't hurt you," Tariq said again, his eyes studying hers with great curiosity. He pulled her toward him, until he was close enough to embrace her, gently squeezing Onyx between them. But Tariq kept a distance, not pushing himself against her as she'd been afraid he would, a prelude to rape. Out of the corner of one eye, Naomi saw Tariq raise his right arm high, the gun's butt facing the ceiling. Far, far from her.

Naomi's feeling of overwhelming thankfulness lasted until Tariq's gun hand swooped down in a chopping motion, and she screamed, trying to pull away, convinced he was going to hurt Onyx.

"You'll be beautiful for posterity," Tariq said, but she didn't hear him.

She thought she saw an eruption of red light. But true to his word, Tariq did not hurt her.

Naomi Price was dead before she felt any pain.

✄ Twenty-Three ✄

SACAJAWEA
That same day

ANGELA MISSED the old Main Street.

The massive windows of Downtown Foods were darkened, mourning. At the old brick hotel next door, the yellowed marquee advertising Liza's play, *The Last Good Time*, was a savage joke. Orange sawhorses up and down the south side of Main Street blocked residential intersections leading toward the river. Two news vans were parked outside the courthouse, one with a large satellite dish atop its roof, posing a spectacle here in a way news vans did not in Los Angeles. It was lunchtime, and dozens of people had come to congregate around the vans. Older children played on bicycles and skateboards, basking in their town's newfound importance. Angela wondered if school had been canceled, or if parents had decided on their own to keep their children home today, close to them.

Thank God it hadn't been like this after Corey died, she thought. *How did Liza survive it?*

As Angela drove at a crawl, she saw Myles in a crowd of four or five reporters comparing notes outside the courthouse doors, but he didn't see her. In that instant, unseen, Angela felt alone in a way that terrified her, until she deadened herself to the feeling.

Moun fèt pou mouri, Gramma Marie used to say. People are born to die.

Angela braked, and the car behind her honked before driving past her in an impatient roar. Creole! She hadn't been able to remember more than a word or two of Creole in thirty years. When she was young, Gramma Marie had taught her songs in Creole, and she'd recognized many sentences as a toddler, she'd been told, but she'd forgotten the language after a time, living in L.A. with Mama. Mama hadn't known Creole and hadn't wanted to. But Gramma Marie's phrase had just leaped into her mind as if it belonged there.

"Keep talking to me, Gramma Marie," Angela said. "I hear you."

Gramma Marie's whispers came in so many ways now; the tingling, a subtle foreknowledge that made her feel slightly out of sync with the world around her, words and ideas popping into her head. Was Gramma Marie getting stronger? She hoped so. If not, Angela would have nothing but funerals to look forward to, and anyone left would have to attend hers. That was a *fact*, not a fear.

She needed an answer, and now. She was running out of time.

As her feeling of desperation grew, Angela noticed that she was ten yards shy of the driveway to the restored fisherman's cottage that was now the Sacajawea Historical Society, beyond the antique schooner, near the pier where Rob had driven her yesterday. She should stop here, she decided. She swallowed back a bad taste in her mouth when she saw the empty pier, imagining Art carrying his muddy, drowned child from his boat to the car he might have parked exactly where she was parking now. As she left her car, she again noticed the sour, fishy smell of the riverbank. Misty rain caressed her face.

Maybe Gramma Marie wanted her to come here.

A tiny bell chimed when Angela walked inside the historical society building, which was musty despite the air-conditioning that kept the room too cold to be comfortable. The large front room was crowded with tables and shelves of town memorabilia: old oil lamps, uniforms from World War I and World War II, medals, display cases full of letters, historical photographs.

Laney Keane appeared from the back, startled to see Angela. Laney's skin was stretched tightly against her face, too bony to look healthy. Her short hair was limp, barely combed. "I don't believe this," Laney said, frozen in place. "I was about to call you."

Good. There *had* been a reason to come here.

"What about?" Angela said.

"Because . . ." Laney blinked, embarrassed. "Well, how can I put it? I remembered something, and . . . I wanted to tell you . . ." Laney straightened up the tourist brochures on the front table, separating the stacks for the marina, the deer refuge, the Lewis and Clark trail.

Angela watched her work, as patiently as she could. "Go on, Laney."

Laney gazed at her with hollow eyes that looked nearly bruised. "I saw all three of them going out yesterday in the boat, and I waved. They were just grinning, all three of them. I can see where they were fishing from the window right here. If I'd only looked up, I keep thinking. If only I'd seen something. He must have walked right past my window, after. I just didn't see. . . ." Laney gazed out toward the pier and the winding path that led to the inlet. Angela saw yellow police tape strung up across the shoal.

"Is that what you wanted to tell me?"

Laney shook her head no with a sigh, her thin lips tight. She swallowed. "I've been thinking a lot about your party, Angie. About what happened. Is it all right if I talk about that?"

It always came back to the Fourth of July.

"Please," Angela said, although the idea of it made her feel queasy already.

"I've always wanted to tell you about your piano. In your living room."

"What about the piano?"

"I was studying it that day. My grandparents had one just like it, with the piano rolls, and I love those old pianos. I was looking at your piano, and I'd opened the case to see what condition it was in. And it started playing right before . . . right before . . ."

The piano had been playing right before the gunshot. "I remember," Angela said.

"But I didn't do it, Angie." Laney's face was pleading, as if she'd been accused of a crime. "I didn't move your rolls. I would never do that without asking you first. And the bar was empty. It wasn't even moving. I know, because my nose wasn't six inches from it. And then . . . I looked down at the keys, and they were playing. Just . . . *playing*. The keys were moving of their own accord, I *swear* they were. And I looked around for you to tell you what was happening, and I heard you laughing, but then . . ." Her wan face looked like old china, mapped with age lines.

"Anyway, it's always stayed with me. Followed me. And who was standing right beside me when the piano started playing? June McEwan. We both commented on how curious it was, the way it began playing that way. We laughed at the time, we were so startled, but then we looked at each other, and I saw the same question in her eyes: *Well, how is it playing, then?* Then the gunshot right after. We jumped like jackrabbits. I'll never forget it. Later, when June tried to hurt Randy, that was so curious, too . . . and I remembered that damned piano." Laney's bottom lip twitched. "I woke up first thing this morning and wanted to tell you that, Angie. I've been working up my nerve."

Angela squeezed her arm, which felt as frail as an old woman's even though Laney couldn't be older than fifty. The wild look in Laney's eyes reminded her of one of the patients she'd known at The Harbor, Mrs. Shaw, an eighty-year-old widow who had been sweet and smart and utterly gutted by life, haunted by anxiety attacks after decades of beatings by her husband. "Take the day off, Laney," Angela said. "Why are you open? No one's coming today. Close up and go home."

Laney's face deflated, disappointed. "You don't believe me?"

"Of course I do. I know something terrible is happening. Something in the house."

Laney smiled a sickly smile. "Yes. That's it, exactly. It's something terrible, Angie."

"Before you go home, you have to do me a favor, though. I need your help right away. Did Gramma Marie ever give you anything for your archives? Any papers? Or trinkets?"

Laney thought about it hard, her eyebrows furrowing. Then, she shook her head. "I asked her to many times. I asked her about the piano, too. But she never wanted to—" She stopped, and the sun seemed to shine on her troubled face. "But there was an interview once. I'm almost sure I still have it! I started a heritage series when I first came here, interviewing town pioneers. . . ."

Angela's heart leaped. She held Laney's face between her palms. "I need to see it," she said.

"It's a cassette tape. I'll find it for you. Come with me to the back."

The back was the historical society's small library, a carpeted room with two tables for reading, with a few thinly populated bookshelves. While Laney rummaged through a file cabinet near the window, Angela glanced over the book titles: *Beach of Heaven, South of Seattle, The Northwest Guide to Medicinal Herbs and Plants.* Local titles. Nothing she needed right now.

"Here it is!" Laney said proudly, producing a single cassette case. "I don't think she was feeling well, so it's not the full hour. Just the first side, if I remember. . . ."

The typed label on the cassette said MARIE F. TOUSSAINT, 11-23-90.

Gramma Marie had done this interview a month before she died.

Angela's chest locked with guilt. She should have interviewed Gramma Marie a dozen times over and captured this history herself. She should not have left that job to a stranger. Gramma Marie had never liked talking about herself, but she should have forced her to. It was Angela's story, too. "Where can I listen to this?"

"I'll bring out the player and headphones. You can sit right here and do it."

The oversized cassette player Laney brought was labeled SACAJAWEA HIGH, probably an old donation. But it looked like it worked, so Angela put on the large, cushioned headphones and waited for the hum to pass after she pushed Play. Laney slipped out of the room to give her privacy. She closed the door behind her.

"—sure it's on?" Gramma Marie's voice came suddenly, draining Angela's breath. She'd sounded a little raspy as she'd gotten older, but her grandmother's voice and careful speaking pattern were unmistakable, immediate. Angela closed her eyes, wishing she could climb into the recording and wrap her arms around her. How could Gramma Marie's voice be here if she was truly gone?

"Yes, ma'am," Laney's voice came, much more sprightly than it was today. "We're rolling."

"Well, let's roll on along then, young lady."

"You're one of the remaining pioneers in this town, Mrs. Toussaint," Laney said.

Gramma Marie hated being called a pioneer, Angela remembered. A beat later, the tape affirmed her recollection: "Oh, I can't tolerate that word! *Pioneer.* You make it sound as if I should be sitting here wearing a raccoon-skin cap," Gramma Marie said.

"Well, this town is called Sacajawea, and the Native Americans like to honor their elders. . . ."

"I hope the Indians aren't the only ones, or the world's in trouble," Gramma Marie said. "Well, this must be what happens when you reach a certain age. When your hair gets gray and your memory gets long, suddenly you're a pioneer and an elder. Don't waste your lofty words on me, *cher.* I haven't earned them. Not everyone with gray hair is worthy of honor."

"You're being modest. You've made such a wonderful contribution here. Your tutoring—"

Gramma Marie sighed violently, cutting Laney off, and Angela couldn't make out the first words she muttered. She replayed the tape three times, but the sound was too muffled. "—as honest as I can bring myself to be. There's too much resting on my soul, too much done and too much undone. I've spent my adult life trying to mend the mistakes I made when I was young, which is what we all do, I suppose—but my mistakes were so large and my life was so short. There's too, too much on me."

Suddenly, Gramma Marie made a strange sound, and after a few seconds, Angela realized she had sobbed. Angela had never seen Gramma Marie cry. She felt a stab of envy. Why had she opened up to Laney more than she ever opened up to her?

"Should we stop the interview?" Laney said.

"No, go on. It's good to say it. Words are powerful. You know that, don't you?"

"Oh, yes, ma'am. That's why I do what I do. I love to preserve words."

"Not all of them are worth preserving. I'll say that much. Words are treacherous, too. They outlive you. They follow you. You don't know what I'm talking about when I say this, but words can move the earth. Just a mouthful of *words*."

"Yes! That's so profound, and that's exactly the way—"

Gramma Marie cut her off. "You don't understand me, *cher*, but that's all right. It's best you don't. I wouldn't want you or anyone else to live with what I know. My life was sour longer than it was sweet. I lost Dominique, God rest her poor, sweet soul. But I saved Angela from it, didn't I? I sure did."

At the sound of her name, Angela's heart quickened. Saved her from *what? Please let there be something on this tape I can use*, she prayed. *Please, Gramma Marie.*

"Your granddaughter?" Laney said.

"Oh, yes. My grandbaby. She'll be here any day for Thanksgiving. She comes four times a year, her and her husband and her little boy. And if that baby isn't the *spitting* image of my first husband, Philippe. I tell you—those eyes, that jaw. Angela looked like her grandaddy too, but not like the baby does. One of the blessings of God, having Philippe back. Angela gave him the middle name Toussaint in Philippe's honor. As for that first name, I never understood that, but she said it was after a boy on a television series about a nurse in the 1960s. Said it was the first time she'd seen a little black boy on TV. Can you imagine naming the child Corey after a child on TV? Silliest thing I ever heard. But at least Philippe is in the name, too."

Angela rolled her eyes, nearly laughing despite her sorrow. She and Gramma Marie had argued back and forth over Corey's name, and now it was all coming back, an argument in progress. On this tape, at least, time had not moved an inch.

Gramma Marie went on: "God's miracles, God's miracles. You see? I lost Philippe, Eli, and John, so I had three husbands—they were all husbands to me, at least—and I lost them all in a short time. I didn't have more than three years with any of them. But Angie, she's got herself a husband to keep. Smart as a whip, that one, and so good with the boy. He and Angie have their disagreements, but all married folk go through that. Angie's the first one of us to keep a husband since my mother. I don't know if we women are harder to live with or the men are harder to hold."

Gramma Marie had been many things, Angela thought wryly, but she'd been no psychic. True, Angela's early years with Tariq had been good ones, but they had lost their way in their arguments in the years following her grandmother's death. Almost from the time she died, really.

"So despite the hardships in your life . . . it's easier for you because you know you've left your grandchild and great-grandchild behind?" Laney said.

"Well, of course, *chérie!* They're my joy. If not for them, it would be better if I'd never passed this way." Tears came to Angela's eyes. Thank goodness Gramma Marie hadn't lived to see Corey's death.

"What has been the hardest thing, Mrs. Toussaint?" Laney said.

"The worrying," Gramma Marie said. "I thought the worrying would drive me to my death, but the devil must want to keep me here to worry me some more."

"What has worried you most in your life?"

There was a long pause, and the hum on the tape returned for a moment before she spoke again. "That others would suffer for my pride," Gramma Marie said. "I couldn't bear it. That's why I've stayed here all this time, to tend after my mistake. I say prayers every morning. Two hours every morning. Prayers are the water I need to put out the fire."

"I don't understand."

"Well, just think of a forest floor after a wildfire's put out. The flames are gone, the ones you can see, but the ground's still hot because it's smoldering underneath, buried. A poke could set it off to roaring again. *Cher,* worrying about that poke will follow me to my grave! God willing, my grandbaby will be stronger than I was. I hate leaving such a burden for her—I wish I could carry it myself—but I don't think I'll live long enough to see a hundred and three. That's how long I'd have to live to put it out for good. That's how far my words carried, all the way to a new century. But I'll be living in this ring, you can best believe. I'll be with her when it's time, I pray to Jesus almighty." Gramma Marie sighed. "I think I'm tired. Would you mind coming back another day?"

"No!" Angela cried, sitting upright in the wooden seat. Listening to her grandmother's last words, she'd hunched over the tape player so closely that her chin nearly rested against it. But the tape didn't heed her. Almost immediately, the voices clicked away, and the hum filled her ears. Her fingers fumbling, Angela pushed the button to fast-forward the tape, but it was silent to the end. The second side was silent, too. Gramma Marie was gone.

Shit. Angela wanted to throw the bulky cassette player across the room, and overturn the table for good measure. *"Why didn't you tell me?!"* she shouted. She hadn't felt so angry at any dead person since the day she found her mother at the kitchen table. Dominique had left her alone, with no way to fend for herself, and so had Gramma Marie. "Why didn't you give me a *chance?"*

She'd never heard a word of it. Nothing about daily prayers. Nothing about a fire. Nothing about how Gramma Marie expected her to be the one to finally set everything right. Angela listened to the recording twice more, trying to see her way through the fog of her grandmother's words.

I don't think I'll live long enough to see a hundred and three, she said.

Gramma Marie had been ninety-two when she died in 1990. If she'd lived to be a hundred and three, she would have died in 2001. The year Corey died. What was supposed to have happened?

Angela had just slipped the cassette tape into her purse when Laney knocked on the door and peeked inside. Her unkempt hair fell into her face. "Is something wrong?" Laney said.

"Yes," Angela said, on her feet. "But it's my problem, not yours. I have to borrow this tape. Go home today, Laney. Close up and get some rest. You need it."

Laney didn't move right away. Her eyes fixed on Angela's. "My brother in Salem's been dying for me to visit. This would be a good time for a trip, wouldn't it?" she said.

Gently, Angela brushed Laney's chin with her palm. "Yes, a very good time. Laney?"

"Yes?" The woman looked hopeful, as if Angela had a golden answer. She didn't, but she had something to share. Not the whole of it, not yet. But pieces.

"Call me if you get a stomachache," Angela told Laney. "Call me right away."

Laney Keane, who had heard the piano start playing itself at the Fourth of July party just before Corey died, didn't need any further explanation. She nodded fervently. "I'll call you from Salem," she said. "By the time I go to sleep tonight, that's where I'll be."

The Leahy family was packing up a minivan backed up to the trailer doorway. Angela idled on the road in front of their property, watching the purposeful procession of children hauling open boxes, household items, and toys out of the house at a clip that wasn't frantic, but wasn't slow either. Someone had made the last-minute decision to leave right away.

Sean's aunt saw her first, and turned over her shoulder to say something to Sean, who was wearing a tan baseball cap turned backward. After glancing toward Angela's vehicle, Sean wiped his hands on his jeans and began making the long walk down his dirt driveway, until he stood at her car window. Once there, he stared back at his family, his hands hooked into his pockets.

"Taking a trip?" Angela said.

"Few days, maybe," Sean said. By the look of the packing, that couldn't be true. A liar to the end, she thought. Sean was the only piece of Corey still here, and he was leaving. Angela was relieved for his family's sake, but she felt abandoned. She hadn't realized how much she'd been relying on the hope that he would tell her something. Anything.

"I need you, Sean," she said.

"Yeah, probably. But Andres and Tonya need me more."

"I think I know a way to protect you."

For the first time, Sean met her gaze. His eyes were scathing. "You *think?*"

Angela couldn't answer him. Instead, she peered back at his property, toward the corral and stables, which looked empty. "Where are the horses, honey?"

"Boarded." Sean blinked, his eyes glassy. "I might have to sell Sheba. I'm not sure." He reached into his back pocket, finding a crumpled piece of paper, which he gave to her. Angela's heart danced, until she saw he'd only written a telephone number. "Can you give that to the sheriff if you see him? Tell him I'm sorry I had to take off. I was trying to stick it out, swear to God. I wanted Andres and Tonya to have a real home for once, one place they could remember. That was my dad's whole dream, but that's all turned to shit. Anyway, we'll be in Boston. For now."

Something had scared the life out of this boy, Angela thought. Something had scared him from uttering a word of what he knew.

"I'm glad you were Corey's friend, sweetheart," Angela said, touching his face. "I don't know what happened to you two, but he had more happiness in his last few weeks because of you and your family. That means a lot to me. I'll never forget you for that."

Sean nodded, gazing stubbornly at the clay road beneath his feet. Sean kept his voice steady. "I'm real, real sorry about . . ." His face changed, coloring. "You know."

"I know," Angela said. "Be safe. Take care of your family."

"Yeah, same to you. Be careful. Stay strong, Mrs. Toussaint."

Suddenly, Sean leaned into her window and kissed her cheek. The affectionate gesture caught her so off-guard, Angela nearly jumped. She'd forgotten how potent her emotions were, bound up inside her in so many intractable knots. She would have to leave a great deal of herself knotted away if she was going back into Gramma Marie's house today. She'd been carrying her knots a lot longer than the past few days, or even since Corey's death. Sometimes knots felt like all she was.

"Corey could be a pain sometimes, but he really loved you, Mrs. Toussaint," Sean said. "He was just pissed about you and his dad being so far apart. It might not look like it, but I know he didn't want to die. Things aren't always what they look like, understand?"

She nodded. It might be a clue, or just a platitude. "I know. And thank you for saying so."

Sean patted her driver's door, his good-bye. Unspoken words twisted his face for a moment, then he waved solemnly and turned to run back toward his house, where his brother and sister were waiting. Angela watched Sean jog up beside them, playfully slapping the side of his brother's head. The boy leaped toward Sean's legs, trying to tackle him, before Sean shook him off, pulling free. The girl let out a laugh, a peal of pure glee that nonetheless sounded almost desperate. Maybe that was her first laugh since her father's death, Angela thought. She prayed it wouldn't be the girl's last.

"Safe journey," she whispered, for herself as much as for them.

Angela pulled up twenty yards and parked her rented Explorer in front of the stone steps that had awed her since she was young, the steps that led up to her grandmother's castle. She gathered the supplies she'd bought in Longview that morning: a digital camera, blocks of clay, Magic Markers, a small stack of orange posterboard, hammer and nails. She'd walked into the Fred Meyer store, allowing herself to be carried aimlessly through the aisles, stopping when she sensed she should. Only part of her had been thinking at all. The rest, she hoped, had been the hand of someone trying to help her. Gramma Marie? God? Maybe even Corey. She liked that idea.

She would take all the help she could get.

Angela stared up at Gramma Marie's house, unguarded by the fallen walnut tree, and she had to remind herself that she had once loved this place. The house looked plain and grim, all of its imperfections flagrant: the broken attic window, the mangled lawn where the tree had been, the fading paint. She couldn't understand why that man had wanted to buy this house in the first place, luring her back to Sacajawea. Everything she'd believed she'd loved about the house felt like the worst kind of lie. She wished she'd bought some cans of kerosene, too. Gasoline.

"You just give me one more good reason," Angela said to the house from the road, "and when I am finished with you, I will burn you to the fucking ground. Don't think I won't."

With the warm hood of her car serving as a tabletop, Angela began writing a message on the posterboard with the thick tip of a black Magic Marker. Writing slowly, she revealed everything she knew, everything she could think to share:

DO NOT ENTER THIS PROPERTY!!!

COREY HILL DIED HERE 7-4-01.
ART BRUNELL WAS HERE 2 DAYS BEFORE GLENN DIED.
RICK LEAHY HERE 1 WEEK BEFORE HE DIED.
ALL HAD STOMACHACHES.
DOES YOUR STOMACH HURT? CALL 555-2969.

The warning sign was a flimsy gesture, and the constant drizzle would make the ink run, but it was a beginning. She'd already told the Everlys to stay away from her house, so she would tell everyone else. Angela posted one sign on the stone wall at the foot of the steps from the road, one to the cedar tree beside the path leading to The Spot, one to the roadside corner post of the Leahy fence, and the last to the front door her grandfather had built. The orange posters radiated, impossible to miss.

People couldn't say they hadn't been warned:

Long after the sound of her hammering had stopped, Angela's heart had stolen the hammer's rhythm, pumping in a frenzy. She stood on the front porch with her bag of supplies, trying to find the courage to go inside. She might get sick. She must be crazy to think she wouldn't. Whatever soul-stealing illness was infesting Sacajawea, she could hardly get closer to it than in Gramma Marie's house. It had been living here for at least two years, enjoying its privacy. Angela clasped her hand, feeling the ring in place on her finger. Corey had found the ring right on time, or she would have been lost, too. She would be dead by now. Angela knew that like she knew her own name.

Vin pale ou, cher. Come talk to me.

The front door was locked, which relieved Angela. If it had been unlocked, she might not have been able to make herself go inside, primed for a violation before her first step.

The door open, Angela reached for the foyer light, turning on the bright chandelier.

And her foot halted in mid-step.

Dried brown leaves were strewn across the foyer in a thick layer. The Oriental rug and floor beneath them showed only in a random patchwork through the mass of dead leaves. Leaves stretched back to the wine cellar, covered the steps leading to the second floor. Leaves had buried the living room, settling like camouflage across the piano keys. As Angela stared at the mess, a single leaf floated from upstairs, landing on the telephone table in the foyer like paper, in front of Gramma Marie's photograph. Angela's heart scuttled in her chest, an animal looking for escape. Her heartbeat nearly cut off her breath.

"Sonofa*bitch*," Angela said. "*Who are you?!*"

No more leaves fell in front of her, as if by silent agreement to wait until she was gone. Angela dreaded the sound of something scurrying beneath the leaves, but it never happened. So far, the house was quiet, waiting her out. Breathing raggedly, Angela shuffled through the crackling leaves to the library windows. In here, too, leaves had invaded the room, blanketing the books on the shelves, making a new pillow in the seat of her reading chair. Each of the three long, white-trimmed windows along the library's south wall were locked tight, Angela saw after pulling up the shades. She crossed the foyer to go to the living room, a catastrophe she wouldn't allow herself to look at fully. She flung herself through the French doors to check the dining room's coved windows, which were also closed.

The leaves hadn't flown in from outside. She hadn't thought so, but she wanted to be sure.

There were leaves inside the china cabinet, overflowing from teacups and glass candy dishes. More leaves hid the dining room table, the black and white kitchen tiles, the tabletop in the breakfast nook, the shelves of the butler's pantry. The house looked like a ruin, as if there had been no roof to obstruct the leaves in years.

Suddenly, Angela realized why she'd bought a camera.

Methodically, she took pictures, keeping her eye behind her camera's viewfinder as leaves crunched beneath her running shoes, marking her every step. The sight wasn't as frightening when she observed the house through her camera, she realized. Everything she saw was confined in a tiny, boxed image, erasing her presence. Angela walked with her eye pressed behind the camera even when she wasn't taking pictures.

Upstairs was more of the same, as dense as a forest floor. There were leaves in the hallway, leaves in her bedroom, and, of course, leaves in the bathroom. Angela couldn't see any remaining mud as she surveyed the bathtub with her camera, but there were wet black leaves clinging to the bathtub, as if pasted in place. Angela snapped pictures, scene by scene.

Only then did she realize she'd been talking to herself for some time. Or not to herself.

"Is this supposed to scare me?" Angela said as her flashbulb lit up the bathroom, flaring in the bathroom mirror. "You're gonna have to do a hell of a lot better than this. It doesn't get worse than the Fourth of July. Hear me? This isn't *shit.*" She almost believed her own bravado. Holding the camera tightly, she kept her hands from shaking. Rage overwhelmed her fear.

"My mama was sitting dead in the kitchen when I came home from school, where she'd been sitting since seven in the morning on a hot May day—and I mean *hot*, like ninety-five degrees hot—and you think this shit is gonna scare me? You think *this* shit is gonna run me off like that li'l scared boy next door? You messed up *bad* this time. 'Cause I'm gonna get you. You hear me? I'm gonna make you sorry you ever found out where I live. You're gonna be sorry you ever heard my gramma Marie's name. And you're *damn well* gonna be sorry you ever touched my son."

Angela's face shook, silent tears tracing her cheeks as she gazed at Corey's bed, shrouded in dead leaves. "I'm gonna send you straight back to whatever part of Hell you crawled out from," Angela whispered, and snapped another photograph.

Back downstairs, Angela was trembling so much that there were intervals where she had to try to stand completely still, to let the attacks pass. It was hard to remember her reasons for coming back here, and she panicked each time she forgot. She *needed* something from this house. Maybe

Gramma Marie could find her best when she was here. The camera helped her feel better, because she had a job to do. Had she photographed every part of the house? The man at Fred Meyer had told her the camera's computer could take photographs from now until doomsday.

Angela remembered the wine cellar.

She was mad at herself for the coil of fear that tightened her muscles, making her pause for a full minute before she could make herself touch the doorknob. Of course, this was how it wanted her to feel, she thought. It enjoyed her fear. Well, fuck it hard.

To prove she could, Angela turned the doorknob and pulled the cellar door open.

The darkness gaping down the stairs was sudden and disconcerting, a repository of imaginary images. Angela yanked on the light. Her arm had weighed a full ton if it weighed an ounce, but she had done it. The light came on, and the darkness obeyed, vanishing.

Angela put her face behind the camera again.

There was a perfect pool of crimson-black blood on the cellar floor, its edges rounded like a cloud's. Blood ran into the cracks in the concrete, snaking toward the empty wine racks in a thin, jagged line. The smell of blood was so thick, Angela coughed, gagging.

"You *motherfucker*," Angela said. On cottony legs, she tottered down two steps to focus her camera, leaning over to snap her picture. No matter how tightly she held the camera, her hands shook so much they were nearly useless. But she clicked the camera three times, doing her best to capture the blood on the floor, then she lurched back up the steps, slamming the door behind her.

Angela's stomach heaved. She ran blindly through the leaves in the library to the bathroom, a closet of a room that was also overrun. Angela vomited into the toilet, drowning the single leaf that floated in the bowl. Her abdomen tightened, expelling everything in her stomach. Perspiration ran into Angela's eyes. She sobbed as she vomited.

"All right," she gasped, between her stomach's pulsing, sinking to her knees because her legs felt like sand. Her kneecaps banged against the tile floor with currents of pain that forced tears to her eyes. "All right, Gramma Marie . . . you better be right here, and you better start showing me what to do. You better tell me *right now* what happened to Corey, and how to stop some more of these people from getting killed. 'Cause you know what? I can walk away. I didn't start this shit. I will *take my ass home.*"

In the boxlike bathroom, Angela's voice echoed around her. Rain spattered against the bathroom window, and she jumped at the sudden wet *thump* of a fat droplet.

Was that her message? Was it in the hiss of the heater? The hollow noises in the drain? Angela listened with all her being for sounds beneath her words, for a response, for anything that might carry significance.

"You were saying prayers for two hours every morning and you didn't teach me even *one?*" she said. "You taught me all these writers and you didn't leave me anything from *you? What the fuck was wrong with you?!* You thought what I didn't know wouldn't hurt me? This shit is *still here,* Gramma Marie, and it took my son! You hear me?"

Angela collapsed to the floor, her chest heaving.

Shit, shit, shit. Gramma Marie wasn't here. Or if she was, her modes of communication were so esoteric that Angela was exhausted from the effort of hearing her. Angela was sick of symbols and clues and premonitions; she'd *never* wanted to heed the part of her that wasn't her brain. No, she wanted to open her eyes and find a neatly typed note waiting for her, a goddamn stack of papers, written especially for her by Gramma Marie. A *book* on how to kick the ass of whatever was kicking her ass. That was what she wanted, and damn Gramma Marie for not leaving it for her.

"Gramma Marie, I can't do this alone," Angela said. "I can't do this."

For an hour, Angela lay amidst the leaves on the cold bathroom floor and waited for a sign that never came, fixing a hundred interpretations on everything around her. She tried to see order in the leaves on the floor, hear Morse code in the pattering rain, hear muffled whispers in the pauses between her breaths. She tried every way she knew and some she didn't, searching for *anything.*

The answer, instead of arriving as an outside voice from somewhere unseen, glided into Angela's mind as a keen, vivid thought.

Gramma Marie *had* left instructions in the house. Corey had gotten to them first.

☆ Twenty-Four ☆

JUNE 28, 2001

"I FOUND SOMETHING," Corey said.

It was now or never. He'd put it off as long as he could, trying to decide if he wanted to speak up. He and Sean had nearly finished their two large slices of Meet the Meat pizza at Pizza Jack's, crusts sagging with pepperoni, sausage, and ground beef, and they were working on the melting ice of their two Super Large root beers. There hadn't been any customers outside with them at the white plastic picnic tables when they first arrived, but now a monster pickup had just pulled up, full of high school kids sitting beside muddy dirt bikes strapped to the bed, so the place was about to get crowded. Sean probably wouldn't want to stick around if a lot of people were here. Sheba and Chestnut, who were tied to a telephone pole ten yards behind Pizza Jack's, didn't like strangers.

Sean slurped the last traces of his soda, his eyes glued to Corey's. "Did you find money?"

"No, some papers. My great-grandmother wrote them."

"Too bad it's not money. What'd she write?"

"Magic spells." Corey said the words as coolly as he could, as if magic spells were a part of their everyday conversation, but he felt his ears burning. This was embarrassing as hell, and it would only get worse.

"Magic spells," Sean repeated, neither a question nor a statement. He left the words hanging.

"Yeah, she knew voodoo. Well, the actual word is pronounced *vo-DOU* or *vo-DUN*. She was a priestess, what they call a *manbo*. She wrote some spells." There was more to Gramma Marie's papers than spells; it was part personal history, part religious document, part cautionary tale. Some of its pages were so dense, with her talk of gods, demons, and curses, that Corey didn't have the patience to read it all. But the spells were the jackpot. The mother lode.

"What kind?" Sean said.

"All kinds. Good luck. Love spells. Hexes. Bringing back things you lost."

Sean stuffed the last of his crust into his mouth. "No way. Do they work?"

"I don't know yet. I'm trying one tonight, at The Spot. At midnight."

"Are you kidding?"

"No."

Sean's eyes grew to three times their normal size. "You have *got* to let me come watch."

Corey grinned. That was what he'd hoped Sean would say. "Hell, yeah," Corey said, and he and Sean slapped palms and shook hands across the table. Corey hadn't enjoyed the idea of walking to The Spot by himself in the middle of the night, but Gramma Marie's spells were specific about time and place, and he wanted to do it right. Within reason, anyway.

"Is it cool if I spend the night at your place tonight? Otherwise, I'll have to sneak out. You know how that goes," Corey said. He had an eleven P.M. curfew, one more of Mom's dictates.

"No problem. My dad won't care, as long as I'm not out past one," Sean said. "This is gonna *rock!* What kind of spell are you doing? Nothing with negative energy, right?"

The way Sean said that, it was as if he already had respect for it, which was good. Corey had skimmed through parts of Gramma Marie's manuscript, but he'd read enough to know that she didn't think magic was a game. She thought magic had gotten her in trouble, and if she were here, she wouldn't want him to try even the most harmless spell until he'd taken a hundred precautions. But he'd already decided not to do anything dangerous. Corey was glad Sean felt the same way about it, so they wouldn't have to argue later.

"One of the easiest ones is called The Lost," Corey said. "It's a spell to bring back something you lost."

"Like what?"

"I'm not sure. Probably nothing too big. Pick something small."

"I get to pick something, too?"

"Yeah, we'll both pick something. That way, we're in this together."

"I got goose bumps when you said that," Sean said, his face suddenly serious, contemplative. Then, his smile came back. "This is *awesome*. The lost spells of a voodoo priestess!"

Corey waved his hand, warning Sean to lower his voice. Three girls from the pickup had already gone inside to the counter to order, but three boys were standing outside the door, probably talking about the girls who had come with them. The bigger one looked familiar to Corey, and he and his two friends were staring toward their table already.

Corey spoke softly. "Pick something you know *for sure* you lost, so if it turns up later, you'll know it was magic. Something you haven't seen in years."

"What are you going to pick?" Sean said.

Corey hesitated. How many of his family secrets did he want to tell?

"There's a ring of my mom's I lost when I was in fifth grade. I want to get that back for her." That was true, but Corey wasn't ready to tell Sean the rest yet. Gramma Marie had written in her papers that the ring's symbols would help him do the *real* magic, much more than the spells she'd described. If he'd known in fifth grade what he knew now, he damn sure wouldn't have given that ring to Sherita. There were generations of tradition attached to that ring.

"How does this work? You don't have to sacrifice a goat or anything, do you?" Sean said.

"Hey, man, don't laugh, but yeah, you're supposed to use a chicken. I'm using some chicken blood from the supermarket. It's a compromise."

"Will that work?"

"I don't know, but I'm not ready to start cutting off chicken heads. She has a *lot* in there about blood—the meaning of the sacrifice, how blood is the life force of the world. It's deep. I can see the point, for real, but I'd rather not go that route. I might want to be a vet, you know? How am I supposed to go around killing animals?"

Sean went silent. He shook the ice at the bottom of his cup, then took off the lid and flung the ice down his throat. He chewed for a while, crunching, then spat most of it out. "You know what? I think I'm chickening out, *hombre*."

Shit. Suddenly, that sounded like common sense.

Corey had waited this long because he wanted to be careful. No doubt, if Dad hadn't shown up, Corey would have tried a spell right away. But Dad's arrival made everything else less important, and he had barely given the papers a thought for those first couple of days. The three of them were acting like a family, doing things together, falling back into rhythms he'd nearly forgotten. Mom was laughing again. For a while, that had been magic enough for him.

But his curiosity was back. He had changed his mind about experimenting with the spells three dozen times. He wanted to see magic so badly he could barely stand it, but Gramma Marie's papers sounded like a legal document, with every other sentence a caution. *Complete all cleansing rituals before trying to implement any lesser formulas,* she wrote, or *beware of grave danger to the untrained hand.* What was he supposed to do, listen to the parts he liked and ignore the parts he didn't? He read most books that way, but this felt different, like he should slow down and take his time. Gramma Marie said she'd already messed up the magic herself. And she was an expert.

But, shit. Just one little spell. Nothing to hurt anyone or make somebody love you out of the blue, or to try to take anything from anybody. This was a spell to make something come back. A spell to get Mom's ring, which was God-knows-where by now. A spell to undo one mistake.

He would do the cleansing ceremonies later, he told himself. He didn't have time now. Gramma Marie's cleansing rituals were repetitive, and the lists of necessary ingredients endless. When was he going to have time to collect cedar, sage, rosemary, and lavender? How the hell could he find a parchment, holy water, and goats' horns? He didn't want to be a *vodou* priest, he just wanted to see magic. One little thing.

"No problem if you don't come," Corey told Sean. "I'll just hang with you tonight, then I'll go make a major fool of myself, chasing after bullshit in the woods."

"You really think it's bull?" Sean sounded surprised.

Corey shook his head, flicking his finger at an escaped piece of sausage on his paper plate. As usual, Sean could see straight through him. "Nah," he said. "Ritual magic is practiced all over the world. Why not, right?"

"Yeah, that's my point. Just be careful fooling with it."

Corey heard laughter, and he saw the three girls from the pickup walking back outside from the counter through the glass door, cracking up over their pizza box. One, a fresh-faced girl with ringlets of curly blond hair, was laughing so hard her face was bright red. Corey couldn't look away, engrossed by the sight of her. All the girls Sean knew were out of town for the summer or had just graduated from high school, moving on to bigger places, he'd said, so girls were scarce this summer. These girls were older, probably seniors, and they were definitely cute.

As soon as Corey heard the voice, he realized he must have forgotten where the hell he was.

"Who the *fuck* are you staring at, nigger?"

What was he thinking? Here he was in Hicktown, and he hadn't thought about the girls being white, or his being black. He wasn't used to keeping that in his head all the time.

Corey didn't have to look around to see who had spoken, his voice killing the laughter. The boy wasn't big enough to be fat, but he wasn't more than a few bacon cheeseburgers off. This was the boy who'd been staring at him on Main Street the day he'd met Sean, the one in the rebel flag T-shirt. Closer to him, Corey noticed a deep cleft in his chin and a weird gray streak in his black hair, a faint checkmark over his temple. Corey recognized his broad-legged stance; he was a football player, or wanted to be one. He was six feet tall. And he had friends with him.

This could turn into an ass-kicking fast.

"Hey, Bo, you don't have the right to talk to him like that," Sean said, before Corey could step on Sean's foot under the table and tell him to keep quiet.

"Shut up, faggot. Afraid I'm gonna hurt your black boyfriend's feelings?"

The two other boys, who weren't nearly as large but were large enough, chuckled. One of the girls smiled vacantly, too, but the other two were crowding near Bo, as if to restrain him. This wasn't the first time they'd seen him acting like a fool, Corey guessed. He wished he'd invited his father to lunch today. Nobody would start any shit with Tariq Hill nearby.

"Oh, Bo, drop it. Nobody did anything to us. Leave them alone," one girl said.

"Bo, let's just grab the pizza and go," the other girl said, the blonde Corey had been staring at. She didn't look so pretty now, the way the side of her mouth was turned down, her eyes so tired. Corey hoped one of the boys would try to talk the big-mouth down too, but neither did.

Fuck saving face, Corey decided. Dad had told him he'd be surprised how often he could keep out of a fight with a little respect, even if he didn't mean it. "Hey, man, if I insulted you or your friends in any way, I'm sorry," Corey said to the boy, looking him in the eye. "There's no need to call names. I didn't mean you or your friends any disrespect."

Corey was proud of his bullshit, but he must have said the wrong thing. Or said it the wrong way.

The gray-streaked boy took two lumbering steps to their table, fast. Corey rose to his feet, sure he was about to get jumped. Sean sat holding his empty plate, not moving. Sean wasn't going to be any help if anything really went down. Corey could tell that already.

"Are you trying to be a smart-ass? You supposed to be better'n me?" Bo said, so close that Corey could smell his Old Spice. And beer. Bo's eyes were pile drivers, and Corey couldn't look him in the face. If he did, he knew he would either get pissed or start laughing.

"I don't know what you're talking about, man," Corey said. His first week in Oakland, he'd almost gotten thumped outside a movie theater with this exact same conversation. People accused him of being a snob before he'd hardly said a word. Mom told him he should always use proper English, but it sure as hell didn't do him much good.

"You trying to act like you ain't a nigger? You sound white, but a skinny nigger's all I see."

Corey backed up a step, fuming. He had just read about this same shit in Gramma Marie's papers, about his great-grandfather being pulled from his bed in Louisiana in the middle of the night, killed by white men calling him *nigger*. His attackers might have castrated him and burned him and who knew what else kind of madness; Gramma Marie hadn't been able to make herself write it all down. This racist kid needed to learn what year it was, and Corey wished he could be the one to teach him. Mother*fucker*. But there was a big difference between wishes and reality. He knew that.

"Let's go, Sean," Corey said, still keeping his eyes low. He prayed Sean could take a hint.

Sean didn't need to hear it twice. As soon as Corey spoke, Sean was on his feet, headed to untie the horses. There was nothing but woods a few yards behind the telephone pole, and Corey didn't like to think about the kind of hurting three guys could put on him if they were out of sight.

"Where you think you're going?" Bo said. "Did I say you could go anywhere?"

Ass-kissing wasn't going to work this time. This kid was a bully who didn't like black skin, plain and simple. Corey brought his gaze up to meet Bo's, remembering Dad's second lesson: Give 'em something to think twice about. Corey squared his shoulders, raising his chin up to the taller boy. He pushed away the plastic chair that separated him, like he was ready to throw down.

"I ain't scared of you," Corey said. "I don't sound *black* enough for your ignorant redneck ass? How about this? *Fuck* you."

That time, he'd nailed it. He might not have impressed Sean that day they met, but this time Corey had sounded hard-core, his limbs loose, arms flinging, voice dropping. Suddenly, he'd sounded like the kind of thug who had a Nine hidden down the back of his pants, who could drop somebody without hardly thinking about it. He'd transformed himself into Super-Nigger, the only kind of black person a kid from Sacajawea knew, the ones from rap videos, movies, and TV. *You better watch who you fucking with, or I'ma put a cap in yo' ass.*

And he'd nailed it. He could see that by the way Bo blinked, the surprise that shifted over his face before he remembered his mask. When the other boys snickered this time, Corey was sure they were laughing at Bo. *Look what you got yourself into now, man,* the boys were thinking.

"Like you could do something," Bo said, but he didn't sound sure.

"Keep your boys out of it, chickenshit, and I'll *show* you what I'm gonna do," Corey said, sounding so good he believed it himself.

Shit, he'd had three years of tae kwon do, and he'd placed third in a tournament once since he'd gotten his green belt. He wouldn't have picked an opponent Bo's size, but that didn't mean he couldn't take him. He could kick him hard in the gut and follow up with a spin-kick to the head. Corey could see it in his mind.

Chestnut whinnied behind him, popping Corey from his fantasy. With one hand grasping Sheba's freed reins, Sean was already mounting Chestnut, keeping his nervous eyes on Bo and his friends. Last chance for a first strike to shut this guy up, Corey thought.

But he didn't. Instead, he made a dash for Sheba, grabbing the saddletree, his left foot finding the stirrup in time to leverage him up high onto the saddle with one leap, his most successful mount so far. His nuts hurt like hell when he sat, but he didn't care about that. It was time to say *adiós* to Pizza Jack's.

"Where you going? I thought you were gonna show me something," Bo said.

"Kiss my ass, dickhead," Corey said, and he shot a gloating bird at Beaumont Cryer, leaning over in his saddle with his middle finger raised high. That one was for Philippe Toussaint, he thought, for the night his great-grandfather couldn't say it himself.

"You're crazy," Sean said beside him. "Let's *move.*"

"That's a plan," Corey said, and he was tempted to finish with "Hi-ho, Silver, away" as he took the reins from Sean. That was how good he felt, like leaving a gunfight at a western saloon.

Except that he wasn't leaving.

Sheba moved, but she didn't follow Sean and Chestnut, who had pulled ahead to the dusty path beside the Four. Instead, Sheba swung her long neck from one side to the other, snorting. When she did start walking, she walked back toward the pole behind Pizza Jack's. She was circling.

Suddenly, the fun was gone again.

"*Go*, Sheba," Corey said, digging his heels into her sides. The horse lurched, but backward, not forward. Then, she circled again. Sean whistled for her from the road—the high-pitched whistle that usually got her running—but she ignored it.

Sheba was nervous. She knew trouble when she smelled it.

Corey heard laughter from the other kids, and he prayed a good laugh would cool Bo off.

"Kiss your ass? Yeah, that's a good idea," Bo said. "You want me to kiss your ass?"

Corey heard the door to the truck open, and he didn't like that sound. Getting beaten up was one thing, but people kept guns in their cars.

He tried to whip his head around to see what Bo was doing. When all three girls started their frantic chorus of *No, Bo, come on*, Corey felt his heart thunder. He saw the blond girl squeezed next to Bo on the truck's driver's side, trying to take something out of his hands, but he couldn't see what it was. The horse's turn pulled his eyes away. The other boys weren't laughing anymore.

"Hey, Bo, *don't do that!*" Sean yelled. No nonsense, no fooling. Scared shitless.

Snakes of light flew from Bo's hand, toward Corey. He saw pink and yellow flames, delicate weaves sparking in the air, a sight that thoroughly confused him. But when he heard the popping and a deafening whistle beneath him, he realized what Bo had done: That sonofabitch had thrown some kind of fireworks under his horse.

The girls screamed, half-laughing as they ran back toward the building to get out of the spinning rocket's way. At first, Sheba's circling only became more frenzied, but when Corey felt a flare of heat near his right leg, Sheba began bucking.

The jarring motion startled Corey, yanking him so hard he was sure he would bite his tongue off as his teeth slammed together. He was able to hold on, clinging to the reins, but the back of Sheba's neck hit him in the face, crunching his nose and draping him in her mane. "*Shit—*" he said.

Sheba crashed back down to all fours, and Corey shifted out of place in his saddle. He was slipping to the left side, so he struggled to lock his right leg in place, to stay astride. He had almost pulled himself upright again when Sheba bucked for the second time, jerking up her massive haunches, knocking him so far off-balance he couldn't remember what balance was.

This time, Corey flew. He felt himself soar, freed.

Corey's flight ended in a dark patch of soil behind the last picnic table, and Sheba's huge front hoof landed with a haze of dust two inches from his nose. Corey's mind was a dull roar, but his instincts kicked in soon enough for him to pitch himself into a roll when he fell, his right shoulder hitting the ground hard. The roll wasn't smooth or pretty, but it helped him avoid hitting his elbow or knee, the kind of injury he wouldn't walk away from. The worst came at the end of the roll, on the concrete. He scraped his right arm badly, and his shoulder knocked over one of the plastic chairs.

A half-dozen faces stared while Corey lay still, waiting for the pain to kick in.

"Are you okay?" Sean said, standing over him.

He must have flown nearly a mile, Corey realized. Or two or three yards, anyway. He almost smiled, his adrenaline pulsing.

"Yeah, I'm okay," he said, and sat up to show it. His left arm was afire from the bloody scrape from his wrist to his elbow, and his nose was sore, too, but it didn't feel broken. Sheba's hoof would have split his head wide open if she'd stepped on him. And if he'd fallen onto the concrete instead of the softer soil, he'd have broken bones. But all he'd gotten was bumps and jolts. This would be a good story back home, even though he'd fallen. He'd fallen *well*.

"*You asshole!*" Sean screamed at Bo. "You don't traumatize a horse like that when somebody's riding! People get killed like that. You better hope she's not burned!"

"What are you gonna do, sissy?" Bo said, giving Sean a sharp shove that made Sean fall to the ground in a heap, practically on top of Corey. "Send your retarded little sister after me? Or your nigger brother with the fucked-up hair?"

The pizzeria manager and two men who had been eating inside heard the rocket's whistling and came out, staring curiously from the doorway. The manager didn't look happy, walking toward them in an apron while he pulled off his clear plastic gloves. Corey was glad to see adults. That meant this wouldn't get any more out of hand, most likely.

"*Hey,*" the manager boomed. "This ends right now, or the sheriff's here in a minute flat."

That threat was enough to make Bo's friends head back to the truck, but Corey had to lock his arms around Sean to keep him from lunging at Bo. Sean was so mad, he almost scrambled hard enough to free himself. His eyes were wild in a way Corey had never seen.

"Man, just chill," Corey said, laughing. "It's over."

He couldn't believe it. Corey had figured Sean would be one of those sheltered people who would go through his whole life never knowing what it would feel like to really want to hurt somebody. Corey remembered when he'd been one of those people, too.

They didn't talk about it, except to decide on their story: Sheba heard a car backfire, she reared up, Corey fell off and scraped his arm. No Beaumont Cryer. No racial slurs. No fireworks.

They both agreed lying would be easiest. Sean said his dad was cool about most things, but he would *not* be cool about someone setting off a rocket under his $8,000 purebred gray Andalusian show horse. His father would want to call the police (and so would Corey's mother, he knew, and she'd probably call the NAACP to boot), and then they'd be in the middle of some modern-day Earps and Clantons shit. The police might arrest Bo on some kind of lame criminal mischief charge, but he had brothers, Sean said. And cousins. There were Cryers all over Sacajawea County.

So, they didn't tell.

Corey went home and showed his parents his scrape, telling the lie he and Sean had agreed on. His mother got overexcited, talking about taking him to a doctor, but Dad rubbed antiseptic on the raw scrape and said, *He'll be all right. Let him spend the night at his friend's house,* probably because he was dying to have the house alone with Mom. And Mom gave in pretty fast, Corey noticed. Dad knew how to soften her. Maybe he was the only one who could.

Tonight was going to work out for everyone, Corey thought.

After Sheba had been bathed, combed, and fed, she seemed willing to put the scare behind her. Corey helped Sean groom her, gently pulling the rigid teeth of the horse brush through her mane after her bath. She cheerfully ate apples from his palm, rubbing him with her cold snout and rubbery wet lips. If this horse had taken a step the wrong way today, Corey realized, he would be dead now. This was definitely an animal you had to respect. "You did good today, girl," Corey said, rubbing his hands across the horse's sturdy, hulking shoulders.

But he and Sean didn't talk about it. For a lot of the night, they watched TV with Sean's brother and sister while Mr. Leahy repaired a weak wall on the horse-stall outside. When the kids and Mr. Leahy went to bed, Sean put on a video, *The Matrix*. Although it was one of Corey's three favorite movies, his eyes hardly moved from the blue-green glow of the clock on the VCR.

He was waiting for the clock to show 11 P.M. Finally, it did.

"I'm going," Corey said. In the video, bad-ass Morpheus was pulling himself free of his mind-control drugs and chains, running toward Neo's waiting helicopter in a hurricane of bullets.

Sean put down the *Vibe* magazine he'd been flipping through at the other end of the sofa. "I'll get my jacket," he said. For some reason, he'd changed his mind about going too.

The walk to The Spot wouldn't be easy in the dark, Corey realized. He'd taken his parents out here a few days ago, but at night it was a different story, a blanket of darkness shrouding everything he recognized. He and Sean brought flashlights, but a tunnel of ghostly tree trunks hovered in their beams, penning them in, hiding the trail. With a duffel bag slung over his shoulder, Corey leaned on the wooden staff he'd brought from the junk room for his ceremony, digging hard into the soil with each step. They walked slowly, taking their time.

Around them, the woods were having a party. There were so many insects hissing, rustling, chirping, and humming, Corey wondered how the noise outside his window didn't keep him awake at night. There was nothing quiet about the country. His street in the suburbs was a lot quieter than this at night. But even now, when talking might have put him and Sean at ease, they didn't make a sound as they walked.

Finally, the tree trunks vanished, and the sky opened up. Crisp white stars and a half-moon shone above them like rescue lights. They were at The Spot, the clearing. There was a little more light here, but not much. From where they were standing, Corey couldn't see the trail, and he couldn't tell if it picked up again on the other side. He swept his flashlight beam over the ground, trying to get his bearings. He found a circle of stones covered by a grill. Good. He knew exactly where they were. He and his parents had grilled hot dogs out here, another family outing that had seemed more like a fantasy than real life. *Please* let them work it out, Corey thought again. "We need to start a fire," he said.

"Great minds think alike. Bet you're glad I carry a lighter now, *hombre*."

It took fifteen minutes to get a good fire going because the wood they found at the edges of The Spot was damp, but persistence paid off. After only smoking for the first few minutes, their fire finally burst to life within the tower of twigs and branches. It cast so much light in its glowing circle, it reminded Corey of twilight, orange-yellow and beautiful. Moths circled the fire-pit, and the wood popped and spat embers at them.

Once the fire was going, Corey admitted to himself that he'd been getting spooked in the dark. He didn't want to be jumping at shadows all night. He needed the firelight.

Corey breathed deeply, enjoying the air. This air wasn't the same as daytime air, and it wasn't the same air from downtown Sacajawea. It was so sweet and heavy, he had to close his eyes and appreciate it for a while. He could see why people would like sleeping outdoors, breathing this air all night. This was air for a gourmet, someone who took breathing seriously.

"What time is it?" Corey said, not ready to open his eyes to check his watch yet.

"Eight 'til," Sean said.

"Let's do this." Corey's supplies were ready, waiting on the ground beside the fire in the duffel bag he'd brought. He'd rehearsed this ceremony in his room for three nights, recreating the different stages, and he could do it in five minutes flat. Less than that. Gramma Marie said he had to *conclude* the ceremony at midnight. It was almost time.

"You in?" Corey said, rubbing his hands above the fire although his fingers weren't cold. Summer nights were cool here, but not cold. Still, the raw heat felt good against his skin.

Sean nodded. From where he stood at the other side of the fire, he could be a pale phantom.

"Tell me what you want to bring back," Corey said. Without realizing it, he'd dropped his voice to a whisper. It was almost midnight, and it seemed right.

Sean whispered back. "Before she vanished for good, my mom sent me a letter when I was little. But I got pissed and threw it away when she stopped calling. There was a picture, too, wallet-sized. It's the only one I had. I want them back."

"I said *one* thing."

"They came in the same letter. Technically, it's one thing."

Corey was surprised to realize his hands were shaking slightly, the way they had when he'd found the satchel in the closet. Standing close to the fire so he could see, Corey took the readied page from the satchel. In the firelight, the paper looked golden. He had to start now.

Before any ceremony begins, you must ask permission of Papa Legba to speak to the other lwas. As I have written earlier, Papa Legba is the doorkeeper between men and spirits, and you must take great pains not to offend him. Our history has been a stormy one, as you have read. When you speak to Papa Legba, speak from your heart with all the reverence that is due to him. Speak to him with love, as it is only love he craves.

Gramma Marie had written many pages about Papa Legba in her book, and suddenly Corey wished he had read more about why her history with Papa Legba was so stormy. He couldn't remember exactly—it was something about his feelings getting hurt, his toes being stepped on—but he hoped ancient history wouldn't hurt his spell tonight. Corey didn't want to butcher the Creole words Gramma Marie had written, so he read the prayer's translation: "Papa Legba, open the gate for me Ago-e . . . Atibon Legba, open the gate for me. Open the gate for me, Papa, so that I may enter the temple. . . ."

The fire flared brighter with a loud crackle, then ebbed back down. Corey sensed something hidden outside their firelight, and he didn't think it was his imagination. Was Papa Legba here? Suddenly, he felt exposed. It was a struggle to make himself go on. "Please accept my offerings, Papa Legba," Corey said, his voice wavering.

Corey laid out his gifts to Papa Legba in the dry soil beside the fire, as Gramma Marie had written: the wooden walking stick he and Sean had found in the upstairs closet, three shiny pennies, the last drops of rum from a tiny airplane-sized bottle he'd found in the back of the butler's pantry at his house, a pinch of tobacco from one of Sean's cigarettes, and two drumstick chicken bones, which he crossed in an X.

Still kneeling, Corey pulled a bottle of Evian and a bowl out of his duffel bag, carefully filling the bowl with water. Then, he dug inside a pocket and brought out a handful of leaves and twigs he'd gathered earlier. These were for the spirit of the Great Woods, Gran Bwa. He brought out a second bowl and also filled it with water; his hand was so unsteady now, some of the water spilled, but he had enough left to fill the bowl halfway. The second bowl was for Madame Lalinn, the moon spirit. He found a pocket mirror he'd bought at Downtown Foods and dropped it to the bottom of her bowl, peering down to see his image. His face was dark in the firelight, but he saw his grave expression. He looked older than he had expected to.

For an instant, seeing himself, Corey hesitated. Was this a good idea?

But he'd gone too far now to stop. Corey pulled a rusted medal out of his front pocket. This had been the hardest item to find, and he'd nearly given up on it until he'd visited an antique shop on Main Street. It was a St. Anthony medal, one that had belonged to a woman whose husband never came back from World War II, the shopkeeper had told him. He hoped he would have better luck with it.

Corey laid the medal between the two bowls. He cleared his throat to speak. "Gran Bwa, Madame Lalinn . . . St. Anthony . . . please hear me tonight and return what we have lost. Please give me my mother's ring, and please give Sean his mother's letter."

"And the picture," Sean whispered, and Corey was too rapt in the ceremony and the fire's frolicking flames to be annoyed at Sean's intrusion.

The last item in his duffel bag was a sealed plastic container of chicken hearts he'd bought at Downtown Foods, still cold from Sean's refrigerator. He lifted the lid slightly and poured bloody water into the soil beside the two bowls and the St. Anthony medal. It splattered in red droplets into the earth, into a pattern that reminded him of a pinwheel. "Please accept this blood sacrifice," Corey said. "Sorry it's not a real chicken."

Sean's watch beeped. Midnight. The fire dimmed, or seemed to.

"Is that it?" Sean said, after a time.

Corey blinked. Aside from the earlier sensation that someone might be watching them, he hadn't felt a thing. "I think so," he said. "I'm not sure. Let's look around."

They turned their flashlights on, searching the ground. Nothing had changed or moved. Each item was where he had placed it.

"Do we get the stuff back right away?" Sean said.

Corey scanned Gramma Marie's page, looking for her instructions for The Lost beyond the drops of chicken blood. She didn't mention anything about how long it would take. He sighed, frustrated. "I don't know. Maybe something's messed up."

He shouldn't have done the spells out of order, that was it. He should have done the cleansing spells first, to try to banish the evil spirit Gramma Marie had written about, if there was any such thing. Why was everything so complicated? Why couldn't he just make a simple trick work? Corey suddenly felt silly, irritable, and tired. What had he expected? If there was real magic in the world, he would have seen evidence of it by now. It would be on CNN.

He poured out the water in the bowls, dousing half of the fire. Darkness fell over them as they lost some of their light, but the fire struggled to live.

"Man, let's roll," Corey said to Sean. "I don't think it worked."

"Shouldn't we wait to see?"

"We'll come back in the morning. We can't stay here all night."

Sean started to argue, but they both went tomb silent when they heard the sound from the woods, high-pitched and maniacal. If Corey had felt any sensation in his legs or anywhere else, he would have run. Both bowls fell from his hands, one shattering on a large stone near the fire-pit. Sean crouched, pointing his flashlight toward the woods, as wild-eyed as he'd looked when he wanted to lunge at Bo Cryer.

"*Who's there?*"

Corey was impressed by the command in Sean's voice, until he realized the voice had been his. He was also surprised to realize he'd picked up the stone nearest to him, ready to throw it at the first thing that moved. He grabbed the walking stick, too, gripping it hard, another weapon.

The sound was laughter, he realized. The laughter was closer to them, bizarre and childish, but so loud it seemed barely human. Corey heard leaves crunch in the woods under footfall, someone running toward them. The fear Corey had felt with Bo at Pizza Jack's a few hours ago had gotten his heart pumping, but the fear he felt now sat in his stomach like a block of ice. He was no longer Corey Toussaint Hill, high school sophomore, about to turn sixteen in the fall; he was one faceless creature being hunted by another.

Sean yelled out, and Corey spun to look at him. He saw a crystal-clear image in his mind of some *thing* dragging Sean into the fire. "*Holy sh—*"

What Corey really saw, though, was a girl. A tall teenage white girl had dashed out of the woods toward them, her long pale dress flying behind her, and the sudden sight of her had so shocked Sean that he'd lost his balance and fallen too close to the fire-pit. Sean backed away from the heat, rubbing his singed palms on his chest while he gaped at the girl.

She was barefoot, about sixteen. Her hair was in two neat blond pigtails, one flapping on each side of her head, and for a moment Corey thought it was the same girl he'd seen at Pizza Jack's, the one Bo had lost his mind over. But no, she was taller than that girl, and her frame was smaller. She was wearing a light blue dress with puffy short sleeves that struck him as old-fashioned, and although it was a neat dress, he noticed it was frayed at the hem, almost worn to rags. It was late June, but tonight's temperature was only about sixty degrees. Wasn't she cold?

"You should see the look on your faces!" the girl said, doubling over as she laughed.

Corey lowered his rock, but he didn't drop it. "Who are you?" he said.

She didn't answer, still consumed in her laughter. She plopped down onto the ground cross-legged beside what was left of the fire. She didn't pull her dress down over her knees to be modest, so Corey found himself staring at the yawning shadow between her unshaven pale legs.

"Papa Legba, hear my prayer!" the girl cried, mocking, and she fell to her side, laughing.

Corey and Sean looked at each other. Now that he realized his worst nightmare hadn't just come screaming to life, Sean was smiling a little. Seeing Sean smile, Corey smiled, too. He stared down at the items at his feet—the broken bowl, the St. Anthony medal, the crossed chicken bones. He had to laugh, too. A little.

"Yeah, okay, so it sounds funny," Corey said to the girl. "You shouldn't sneak up like that, though. I was about to nail you with this rock."

"You couldn't hit the broad side of an elephant with that rock," the girl said, grinning.

The smile did it. For the first time, Corey noticed how pretty she was. Her teeth were as white as the teeth of the actors who sometimes came to Mom's parties in L.A., polished and scrubbed. Her cheekbones, in the firelight, looked like a wood carving. She wasn't as cute as Vonetta at home, mostly because she didn't have Vonetta's lips, but she wasn't bad.

"What are you doing out here alone in the middle of the night?" Sean said.

The girl gathered up the folds of her dress and squatted by the fire, balancing on the balls of her bare feet. "Watching my entertainment," she said. "Watching you two act like fools."

Corey replaced the page in Gramma Marie's satchel. He didn't want this nutty girl to see his spells, no matter how pretty she was. "First of all, it's none of your business," Corey said.

Intrigued, the girl shot up to her feet. She walked closer to Corey, until she was standing in front of him and he could see her eyes, almost luminescent in the firelight. Were they gray or blue? There was a quarter-moon birthmark high on her right cheek, and she was at least two inches taller than him. "Did he answer?" the girl said.

"Who?"

"Papa Legba. When you called him, did he answer?" Her deep gaze unnerved him.

"I don't know," he said.

She smiled a teasing smile, then shook her head slowly back and forth.

"Sor-ry . . . ," she said in a singsong voice, her eyes knowing things she shouldn't. "Papa Legba isn't here. I'm the only one here tonight." She bumped herself against him, and her loose breasts sank into his chest. They felt like soft, warm pillows against him, welcoming.

Corey backed up, startled. The girl laughed again, and he felt blood rush to his face.

The heat from her body drew him, nearly held him in place, and Corey felt his groin growing heavy, twitching with arousal. There were girls like this at his school, who came on to any guy who passed their way. And this girl might be homeless, the way she was dressed, not wearing any shoes. She could use a bath, too. She didn't smell clean.

"Where do you live?" Corey said.

"Around," the girl said.

"What's your name?"

"Becka," she said.

"My name's Sean," Sean said quickly, probably feeling left out.

Becka gave Sean a quick glance over her shoulder and shrugged at him. "You're not the one I want to talk to," she said to Sean.

Ouch. That was cold, Corey thought.

"You don't live here in the woods, do you?" Corey said.

Becka shrugged again. Her eyes were back on his, that infinite gaze. "Why don't you send your friend home and stay with me tonight?" she said. "I'll show you where I live."

Sean sighed, obviously expecting Corey to leave him. But Corey shook his head. Despite a growing boner that felt like a foot-long iron club as Becka inched closer to him, the situation struck him as wrong. He touched her hair, feathery and light. He could honest-to-God get laid tonight, he realized. But he didn't want to, not like this. She smelled wrong.

"Nah," he said, before he could talk himself out of his decision.

"Why not?" she said.

"Don't you even want to know my name?" Corey said.

"I know your name."

"What?"

"Toussaint," she whispered, saying the name like it was treasure. His neck thrilled.

"I go by my first name," he said. "Corey."

"Stay with me tonight, Corey. I'll teach you real magic."

"Corey?" Sean said, sounding nervous. "We better head back."

Becka's index finger poked Corey in the chest, and she let it trail downward, toward his navel. Corey's stomach fluttered violently, and he grabbed her hand. Once her hand got below his belt, his brain would shut down and he'd stay out here tonight whether he wanted to or not. Already, anticipating her touch, his dick was swelling in a way he couldn't remember, on a mission. His jeans felt confining, painful.

"My friend's right," Corey said, too embarrassed to adjust himself in front of the girl. "Listen, you're really pretty, but we have to go. Maybe I could see you some other time?"

The smile never left the girl's face. "Why not?" she said. She backed up one step, two, then she waved and turned on her heel. She was running back toward the woods, into the dark.

"How can I get back in touch with you?" Corey called after her.

"Say my name," she said.

"Are you sure you're okay out here?" Corey called again. But the girl didn't answer. Corey watched her retreat until she was out of the firelight, and then she was gone, with only the sound of her feet in the leaves and twigs in the darkness, running.

"What the hell was *that* about?" Sean said quietly, at Corey's side. They both watched the woods to see if she would come back, but she didn't. Her brief appearance felt dreamy to him. If Sean weren't here, Corey might have believed he'd imagined her.

"I don't know," Corey said. His heart was thrashing. He shifted himself so his jeans wouldn't pinch. Then, he slapped his rigid biceps when he felt a mosquito bite his arm.

"That's the weirdest girl I've ever seen."

"You're just jealous," Corey joked, then he patted Sean's shoulder. "No, man, I know what you mean. She looks homeless to me. I don't think anybody lives back there. I thought that was just woods."

"We should report her."

"I guess we could, but she won't get found unless she wants to be."

"You're not going to sleep with her, are you?" Sean's question was a judgment.

"Nah," Corey said, although he wasn't sure. If she *wasn't* homeless, that was different. She might be a little weird, but she was cute as hell. There were worse ways to lose his virginity.

"I wouldn't if I were you," Sean said. "Remember Glenn Close in *Fatal Attraction*. When girls you don't know are that eager, watch out. There's a catch. What's up with the way she showed up as soon as you finished that spell? I don't like it. I say we get back home."

Now that Sean had put it that way, Corey realized he was right. It *was* weird, all around.

But he was sorry he'd sent Becka away.

Corey's dream about Becka began the same way she had appeared at midnight, crouching by the fire in her dress, her legs teased open, daring.

But in the dream, Sean wasn't there. Corey was alone with her.

Her eyes heavy-lidded with promises, Becka took Corey's hand and pulled him out of the firelight, into the woods. She walked quickly, knowing her way, pulling him past his blind spots as they ventured deeper into the parts of his mother's property he didn't know. He saw a log cabin covered in moss with a dim light glowing from the open door, blending so well into the woods around it that he'd never have seen the low-roofed structure without the light.

'Good, he thought. She *isn't* homeless. "Who lives here with you?" Corey asked her.

"No one else lives here," she said. "Just me."

There was no furniture inside the cabin, and no windows, like a cave, but the entire floor was covered by an enormous bearskin rug. Vaguely, Corey wondered where the hazy yellow light inside the cabin was coming from, because he couldn't see a lamp or a burning candle. The cabin also had a sour smell, the same smell he'd noticed when he'd met her, but he forgot to be bothered by it when Becka closed the cabin door and pulled her dress over her head. Her raised nipples were bright pink, her areolas staring at him like wide eyes. Corey gawked, riveted. He had never been this close to a naked girl. Without a word, she began pulling off his shirt. Then, she yanked on his pants and slowly slipped them down, too. When he was naked, she pulled him until they were lying together on the rug's rough fur. She clung to him, a garment of soft, warm skin.

Becka sat astride him, her bare breasts bobbing as she squatted. When Corey sank inside her, the shock of the pleasure made him spasm, curling at the waist. He hadn't expected her insides to be so fevered, or her grasp to be so tight. His mouth opened wide without a word, his eyes closed.

Shit, he thought. His loins wanted to burst, but he couldn't yet. He didn't want her to know he'd never had sex before.

In the dream, Corey opened his eyes and realized his raised head was directly beside the dead bear's, those sharp, yellowed teeth as close to his nose as Sheba's hoof had been. Big teeth. So big, in fact, that Corey realized this rug wasn't from a bear. Its head was bigger and narrower than a bear's, its teeth longer, thinner, and curving more sharply. Like Bigfoot, he thought, if there was any such thing. Bigger than that. The creature's carpet of fur covered the cabin's floor, with extra pelt climbing up the walls. No animal could be that big! While he lay naked with his back against the thick fur, Corey felt something wriggle beneath the dead beast, jostling against his shoulder blades.

Waking.

With a gasp, Corey woke up.

He was in a sleeping bag on the floor in Sean's overcrowded room. His heartbeat alone might have ended his dream, because it was raucous in his chest. There was a faint glow through the window, although the sky was almost dark. It was five A.M., Sean's clock radio said on his desk. He could smell Sean's shoes somewhere near his nose. The sour smell in his dream, he realized.

Corey was so hard, his testicles felt swollen, sore. Damn. A second ago, he'd been having the most realistic dream sex of his life, and now it was gone. Why did that damn bear-thing have to show up and ruin it? Already, Corey had forgotten the image of the creature's face, but he knew how it had made him *feel*, especially when it moved. It had scared him awake.

That scare might have been part of his dream, but Corey's blue balls were real. Corey squirmed in the sleeping bag. *Blue balls* was the wrong term for it, he decided; they should call it *red balls*, because he was burning up. This was worse than when he'd necked with T.'s eighteen-year-old cousin from Detroit last Christmas, who'd shocked him when she let her hand rest on his crotch, squeezing. Her boyfriend had been in the next room playing hoops on PlayStation 2 with T., so the touch had been a game to her—but to Corey it had been a revelation, one of the most memorable things that had ever happened to him. Later, T. told him his cousin was always coming on to him, too, even though they were blood kin. That girl in the woods might be a freak, too, but she had wanted him for real. All he'd had to say was yes.

What if he went back to The Spot right now? Would he find her there?

Corey glanced up at the bed, where Sean was snoring, his arms crossed over his eyes. As wakefulness sharpened Corey's memory, he recalled the way the girl's hair had felt, and the primal, unbathed smell of her skin. The thought of her loose breasts pressing against him nearly made Corey moan. He could probably sneak out to The Spot and come back before Sean woke up. Sean was too uptight, and he wouldn't have to know.

"Man, you can't do that," Corey whispered to himself, sitting up. "Forget that girl."

No matter how horny he felt, he wasn't desperate enough to have sex with a homeless stranger in the woods who didn't smell right. He would get up, go to Sean's bathroom, and take care of his blue balls himself. Hell, he was used to that by now. He could write a damn book on it, just like Gramma Marie.

Corey climbed stiffly out of the sleeping bag and walked down the hall to the bathroom in his underwear, covering his crotch with his hands in case anyone saw him. It would be just his luck to run into Sean's dad, or his little sister, giving them an unintentional salute. *Ten-HUT!!!*

The bathroom was a mess, mildewy and crowded with bath toys. Corey closed the door and locked it, checking it to be sure no one could walk in. *Damn,* that dream had been real. Corey could still feel the way Becka had enveloped him, grasping. He turned on the hot water in the sink. With damp hands and a little soap, he would close his eyes and recreate the dream as well as he could. He cupped warm water in his hands beneath the faucet.

Corey noticed a yellow glimmer in the sink, something shining through the tiny space between his fingers. A bath toy was about to get sucked down the drain, he thought. But it wasn't a toy, he saw when he looked more closely.

A gold ring with a thick band was nestled against the drain stopper, in danger of falling into the pipe. The girl in the woods vanished from Corey's mind. The water he'd cupped in his hands spilled over his bare thighs as he drew back, shocked. "What—"

He grabbed the wet ring, careful not to let it slip past the stopper. He brought it to his face, staring at it with a shaky hand. There were symbols on the ring's sides. Drawings.

Oh, God. Oh, God. Oh, God.

This was his mother's ring. This was Gramma Marie's ring.

"Holy *shit,*" Corey said.

He said it a dozen more times before he could remember his own name.

ᔓ Twenty-Five ᔓ

THE FISHER HOUSE was on the southwest side of Sacajawea, closer to the marina, a three-bedroom bungalow with its own dock on the river. The house was nearly cloaked behind bigleaf maples with bright yellow leaves, their trunks wrapped in twisting ferns and vines. The leaves were falling, so the yard was buried much the way Gramma Marie's house had been, until Angela had spent hours sweeping up the mess, bagging as many of the leaves downstairs as she could. These yellow leaves were more colorful, and still looked more alive than dead, so she didn't mind them. As Angela walked up the curving walkway, she passed Myles's Saturn instead of Pa Fisher's old red Chevy pickup, and the missing truck jarred her. So much was the same, yet nothing was.

When Myles opened the door, he looked surprised. He was still wearing a dress shirt, although he'd taken off his tie and unbuttoned the shirt midway. He hadn't been expecting company.

"We said I'd come over for dinner tonight," she said. "Remember?"

"I thought that was just tentative. Where have you been? You never returned my calls."

"I didn't get a message," she said. "My phone's not working today."

Angela hadn't been able to make any calls from Gramma Marie's house, and her cell phone's signal, which usually worked in Sacajawea, had died. She suspected her telephone problems were part of it, too, another tiny piece. There were no more coincidences from now on.

Myles looked like he felt awkward. She would too, in other circumstances.

"It's okay if you don't have enough food," she said. "I'm not hungry."

Finally, he smiled, almost shyly. "I just wanted to do it up special for you, Cuban chicken and black beans and rice, the whole number. All we have is frozen stir-fry."

"Don't worry. I'm not here to eat."

"You're relentless," Myles said, squeezing her waist with a gentle teasing, and she smiled somehow. It felt that good to be standing near him. A few hours ago, she'd thought she would never have time for smiling again. "Come on in, Angie. I know why you're here. She's in the dining room, and it's a good night."

The living room looked unchanged to Angela, old family photographs and uninspired furniture encased in plastic, but the dining room was so bright and full of new life that it startled her. The paint was a tropical peach color, and the walls were decorated with masks, most of them carved from painted coconut shells. Here, the furniture was festively white, nothing like the plain but courtly dining room at the Fisher house years ago. Angela didn't recognize it.

But she recognized the woman sitting at the head of the table while her nurse spooned food into her mouth. Ma Fisher looked every single day of her ninety years, her skin riven with wrinkles, her hands as thin and delicate as a bird's feet. Much of her hair was gone, and what remained looked like tufts of stringy cotton clinging to her head. Some essence of her face was preserved in her eyes, though, and between her deep wrinkles. Angela smiled when she saw Ma Fisher's birthmark, the quarter-moon beneath her right eye. Even her posture was the same, rigid and proud, as she leaned forward in her seat, waiting to be fed.

Seeing Ma Fisher again, Angela almost forgot why she had come.

"Ma Fisher? Do you remember me? I'm Angela Toussaint, Myles's friend."

Ma Fisher's gray eyes came to hers, and Angela saw them snap to lucidity. She smiled at her, chewing the last of her food. "I remember," she said. "Hello, Angela."

Disappointment jabbed Angela. Ma Fisher was pretending she knew her. She wouldn't have repeated her name as Angela, only Angie.

"How are you doing?" Angela asked her, although she already knew.

"Watching my entertainment," Ma Fisher said. "Watching you two act like fools." Her earnest eyes locked with Angela's, an eerie sensation. Maybe Ma Fisher *did* know who she was.

Myles shrugged apologetically. "Sorry, Angie. Could be something she saw on TV. "

"Or something she heard somebody say on the phone," the nurse said, and Angela looked at the woman squarely for the first time. She was a young, ruddy-faced woman, about thirty, and she gazed at Angela with an unabashed intensity that made Angela remember how much gay women loved her short hair. Her gay friends assured her she would have been a queen in the all-girls' circuit.

"Anyway, this is Candace. Candace, this is Angie Toussaint," Myles said.

Candace smiled knowingly as she shook Angela's hand. "*The* Angie Toussaint. Well, well."

Myles cleared his throat. "That's enough from you. Angie, want me to fix you a plate?"

"Sure," Angela said, although she didn't have any appetite. She only craved the warmth of this room, the ease of smiling and forgetting in here. That must be why Myles had painted the room this way, she thought. He'd needed brightness in the house, something to dull the pain of watching his mother slowly disappear. "Is it okay if I eat with you tonight, Ma Fisher?"

"You couldn't hit the broad side of an elephant with that rock," Ma Fisher told her insistently, and Myles and Candace laughed, startled.

"It's always a mystery," Candace said, shaking her head.

"Wow. She hadn't been using full sentences tonight," Myles said. He sounded thrilled.

Angela stood over Ma Fisher, behind her chair, and rested her hands on the woman's bony shoulders. Then she leaned over and slowly buried her face in Ma Fisher's hair, smelling her as deeply as she could. Perspiration, maybe shampoo. She didn't smell anything she shouldn't.

"I love you, Ma Fisher," Angela whispered, nearly tearful. This woman had spent hours telling her about her youth in Sacajawea, her work with the Red Cross during World War II, and how much she loved her son. She had rarely, if ever, used the word *adopted*. In some ways, Angela had been privy to more details of Ma Fisher's life than Gramma Marie's. But the one secret Ma Fisher and Gramma Marie had shared, apparently, they had kept to themselves.

"Why don't you send your friend home and stay with me tonight?" Ma Fisher said to her.

"My friend?" Angela said. "Who's my friend?"

Ma Fisher lowered her voice to a whisper. "I know your name," she said.

"What is it?" Angela said. She kissed the top of Ma Fisher's head, a patch of downy hair.

"Toussaint," Ma Fisher said, bending her neck backward so she could meet Angela's eyes.

"Very good," Angela said, although something in Ma Fisher's backward gaze unsettled her.

Myles and Candace applauded, pleased by their exchange.

The food was bland, as warned, but Angela didn't mind. She enjoyed watching Myles and Candace dote over Ma Fisher at the table, the verbal games they played trying to keep her mind occupied so she wouldn't get restless and bolt from her seat. She was so much like a young child! Every once in a while, Ma Fisher sought Angela's eyes again, gazing intently.

From her seat beside Ma Fisher at the table, Angela squeezed the woman's hand, which felt cold to the touch. "Ma Fisher, do you remember what happened on July 4, 1929?"

Myles's lighthearted expression faded across the table, and Candace looked puzzled.

Ma Fisher nodded eagerly, squeezing Angela's fingers. "Stay with me tonight, Corey," she said, enunciating so clearly that there was no mistaking her words. "I'll teach you real magic."

———

Myles had moved into his parents' master bedroom, which had a glass door leading to a deck overlooking the river. This room, too, was decorated with a bright color, mustard yellow, and the walls were covered in intricate masks accentuated by track lighting. Unlike those in the dining room, the bedroom masks were carved from rich wood and looked more African than Caribbean, and Angela knew from her clients who collected African art that they probably had been expensive. The room was overcrowded for its size, since Myles had been forced to cram so much of his life into a house that was already furnished.

There was hardly room to walk around the king-sized bed, and Myles's massive computer desk and its bookshelves took up nearly an entire wall. Beside it, picture frames and awards hung on the wall. One was a photograph of a young boy who looked Latino, grinning a gap-toothed smile on a beachfront. Another was a master's degree from the Columbia School of Journalism, beside a column-writing award from the National Association of Black Journalists. The last was an award for Volunteer of the Year from Big Brothers/Big Sisters in Washington, D.C.

The only item in the room she guessed might have been here all along was Pa Fisher's traditional wooden bow, which leaned against the wall in a corner by the glass sliding door. Angela smiled when she saw the bow. She'd criticized Myles for hunting when she was younger, but he'd told her plainly that he did it because he'd dreamed about spending time with someone like Pa Fisher when he was in foster care; Pa Fisher reminded him of his uncle Guy, who had lived in the country and died when he was seven. Usually, he'd admitted, he was happy when Pa Fisher's arrows veered off-course in the wind and his game scurried to safety. Angela doubted Myles was still hunting now.

Then again, maybe he was. She didn't know this man, she remembered sadly.

Angela stared through the glass door at the deck, which was lighted by the orange fire of the dusk sun. The slivers of the river she could see beyond the backyard trees looked like sheets of flames. Myles had strung up a hammock on the deck, and when she noticed a sudden movement from the corner of her eye, her gaze found an odd, tubular-shaped feeder hanging beside the hammock. Two redheaded hummingbirds with impossibly long, thin beaks were flitting around the feeder, sipping from the clear liquid that had nearly been drained inside. Their wings beat so fast they were invisible, making the four-inch, delicate creatures look like they were floating instead of flying.

"What do you feed the hummingbirds?" Angela asked, intrigued by them.

Myles didn't answer at first. He was sitting at his desk in silence, as he had been for several minutes, gazing at the photographs stored in her digital camera. He squinted at the camera's lighted display, tilting it back and forth for the clearest image.

"Myles? What do you feed the hummingbirds?"

"Sugar water," he said, distracted. "They're small, but they're greedy. I've already filled that twice today. Have you reported this to Rob?"

"Reported what to Rob?"

"This vandalism, Angie. Is this *blood* on the floor in your wine cellar?"

"It smelled like blood. Yes, I'd say so."

"We need to call Rob right now. Why did you wait this long?"

His voice had the let's-do-something-about-this quality she'd always loved about Myles. He was a fixer, just like Pa Fisher had been. Every time she'd visited this house, Pa Fisher had either been under his car or in his shed, fixing things, and usually he'd shown his son his skills. In high school, Myles had known how to change oil, chop wood, build a radio, and shoot a bow, capacities that made him unlike any other high school boy she had met in L.A.

Myles stood and walked to her, peering into her eyes. "Angie, are you listening to me? We have to call and report this to the police."

"There's nothing for the police to do," she said. She wished he could understand that, because then they could move on to the conversations that would mean something.

"This morning, I got a crank phone call from someone who might have been your ex-husband. I don't know how he got my cell number, but he said something that sounded like a threat. So, in light of that, someone vandalizing your house and leaving blood in your wine cellar is not something I'm ready to dismiss. Do you get where I'm coming from?"

"Tariq called you?" This was new, and unexpected. But she should have known Tariq would have something to do with it, she realized. The way his van had vanished like that.

"I said if he had a problem with me, he should see me in person. He said he was planning on it, but I should try not to die before he gets here. That's another reason I called you today, so you'd keep an eye out for Tariq. I left you messages both at your hotel and at Gramma Marie's house this morning. I tried calling you both places again two hours ago. I was planning to swing over to Gramma Marie's after dinner because I was getting worried."

"I didn't hear anything at Gramma Marie's. It must not be letting my phone ring."

"It?" Myles said. His eyes, concerned before, were downright alarmed now. He sighed, patting her shoulder. "Angie, sit on my bed. We have to talk."

Photographs would not be enough for Myles, Angela realized. He would have to see something for himself. But that was all right, because he would. She had no doubt of that.

"I want you to wear this," she said, and she pulled out the round clay necklace she'd made for him that day, imitating the shapes and order of the symbols on Gramma Marie's ring the best she could. She'd strung a leather cord through the clay pendant after allowing several pendants to bake and harden in her oven, and she hung it around Myles's neck. It was long, hanging midway down his chest. With his shirt open, she saw the gold chain of a large cross he wore. The cross would be good for him too, she thought. She wished she had a cross herself. She and Jesus hadn't been on speaking terms in too long.

"What's this?" Myles said, examining the crude pendant. He sounded impatient.

"Something to keep you safe. I hope, at least," she said. "It would be better if you packed up Ma Fisher and went away, but I know you won't do that. So, I made a charm for you. Promise me you won't take it off."

He didn't argue. "Yes, I promise. Thank you," he said politely. "Now, sit. Let's talk."

Once she sat on the neatly made-up bed, Angela realized how tired she was. She'd had a long day at Gramma Marie's house, with so much to think about. She lay down and curled on her side, enjoying the cool bedspread against her cheek. The bed smelled like Myles. He'd told her he always made his bed as a kid because his group home in Seattle insisted on it, and he'd apparently never broken the habit. She felt the mattress sag slightly as Myles sat beside her. He massaged her upper arm, squeezing rhythmically.

"I'm worried about you, Angie," he said. His voice cracked.

"I know."

Through the closed door, Angela heard Candace trying to coax Ma Fisher into bed. After dinner, for some reason, Ma Fisher had felt an obsessive need to empty out her bureau drawers, endlessly rearranging her belongings. Another aspect of her illness, Myles had told her.

"I know it's none of my business," Myles said, "but I heard about your hospitalization."

Angela chuckled. From his viewpoint, *crazy* was the easy answer, all right.

"What's funny?" he said.

"That was day, Myles, and this is night. I spent three months at a hospital, but that was only because I didn't want to uphold family tradition and hurt myself. I shut down my heart and let some other folks take care of me for a while. That has nothing to do with this. You heard what Ma Fisher said at dinner. She called me Corey. She was channeling something that talked to my son about magic once upon a time, and you still can't see it. You don't want to."

Myles didn't respond right away. Through the wall, Angela heard Ma Fisher demanding to know where all of her socks were. She sounded furious.

"Listen to her," Myles said. "Doll-baby, I'll admit my heart went pitter-pat when Ma Fisher said that about Corey. I won't pretend I have an explanation for it. But my mother is suffering from dementia. Unfortunately for all of us, there hasn't been a day in a long time when she hasn't said something that doesn't make sense. That's who she is now. But *you* have a serious problem. Somebody came into your house and—"

"Or some*thing*."

"Rob needs to be informed," Myles said. "I should have mentioned my call from Tariq when I saw him today. I had an accident this morning, by the way. I went into a spin on the Four. So, yeah, I'm feeling jumpy and cautious, Angie. I lost control of my car right after Tariq called me."

Angela closed her eyes, shuddering. "Shit," she whispered. She had known it would try to take Myles, too. She felt despair try to slip over her, a burial cloth. "Does your stomach hurt?" Angela asked, afraid to hear the answer.

"No. Why?"

"I think Tariq's stomach might be hurting. He said he was going to see a doctor."

"You talked to him? When?" Myles leaned closer to her on the bed, reclining.

"Tuesday morning. He left a message at my office. He sounded good, but he said he'd been sick. Art was sick, too. Did you know that? Liza said his stomach hurt the night before he killed Glenn. And Rick's stomach hurt. You can ask Sean yourself. Corey's did, too."

"What are you getting at, Angie?"

"Your mother was brought to my grandmother's doorstep when she was sick in 1929, and people are still getting sick today. I'm talking about an outbreak of some kind. Open your eyes."

Finally, Myles looked intrigued. "I'm listening. What kind of outbreak?"

"Possession," she said, and Myles sighed again. He would stop listening now, she knew. Still, she went on. "I don't think it's still inside Ma Fisher, but she has some kind of connection to it. I think that's why she said that about Corey at dinner, and why she called me Mrs. T'saint the other day on the phone, talking about San Francisco. I think when Ma Fisher talks to me, she's remembering old interactions with this thing, whatever it is. The memory of it is stamped on her. It echoes inside of her, maybe." As she spoke, Angela felt her level of understanding deepening, and that gave her fleeting hope. True understanding was the only weapon she would have.

"God, you sound sure of yourself," Myles said, more amazed than skeptical.

"I'm not always. But sometimes, I know things. More all the time, Myles."

Myles was no longer massaging her arm. Instead, he'd begun stroking her, his fingertips grazing the side of her face. The giddy arousal she'd felt last night was gone, but something more staid and calm came in its wake, a glow that made her limbs melt into the mattress.

"As of right now, we start trusting each other," Myles said. "I'll grant that you might know things, but respect my hunch, too. Please, Angie. I consider Tariq to be dangerous."

Angela nodded. Tariq hadn't sounded dangerous on his telephone message to her, but she didn't know what had happened to him since then. "Agreed," she said.

"And I'll say it again: Rob needs to know about that blood."

"Come to the house tomorrow," Angela said. "If you still think it's vandalism, we'll call Rob right away. Cross my heart, Myles. Is that a good compromise?"

"All right," Myles said, looking relieved. "But don't go back there now."

"I don't plan to. I have a room in Longview, remember?"

"Yes. I remember." Myles exhaled, and his breath was as familiar as a favorite blanket. He slipped his palm beneath her sweatshirt and let it lie on her belly, pressing as if to keep her fixed in place. Tariq's palms had always been callused from the weight room, but Myles's palm was as smooth as a boy's. Beneath his touch, she felt her nervous system awaken after hours of retreat. Her stomach jumped. "You could stay here," he said, as if she'd willed the words from his mouth.

"I thought you said that wasn't a good idea."

Myles's eyes searched hers, new pennies shining at her. "Angie, sometimes I look at you and see a woman who's a complete wreck, and that scares the hell out of me. That's the truth as well as I can speak it. But sometimes I see . . ." He shook his head.

Myles must have made up his mind. He hoisted himself closer to her, wrapping one arm around her lower back to pull her against him. His lips glided over hers lightly, then sank hard, his tongue washing hers. Angela had kissed Myles many times before, but never as a forty-year-old man. His hungry kiss was foreign to her, as if he meant to prove to her that the timid boy she'd known was gone. Angela cupped Myles's face between her palms as she kissed him, afraid she might hurt him from clinging too hard. Their bodies sought each other, cleaving together. His erection dug hard against her stomach through his slacks. He was as wide as the Nile, she remembered.

Angela wrenched her mouth away. Kissing Myles had absorbed her so much that she hadn't been taking in enough breath. "I miss you," she said, stroking his bare scalp, feeling the fuzz of his shorn hair trying to return.

"No need to miss me," he said. "I'm here."

"Tell me everything about who you are, Myles."

His hand beneath her shirt scurried upward, resting on her breast. His thumb found the firmness of her waiting nipple, and he rubbed a circle atop her nylon bra that made her thighs press together, hoarding the pleasant tingling trapped between them. "What can I tell you?" Myles said.

"Who's the boy in that picture on your wall?"

"That's a very old picture of Diego, my stepson. He's seventeen now."

"You were married?" Of course he must have been, but she hated the idea.

"For three tumultuous years after grad school. I thought Marta was you. I was wrong." Myles lifted her sweatshirt, and she watched the earnestness in his face as he stared at her bare skin, at her bra. He looked almost saddened, anxious, as his eyes traveled over her. Slowly, he lowered his head, kissing her navel. The quick, wet warmth of his mouth made her start.

"I went running this morning. I haven't had a shower," Angela said, suddenly self-conscious.

"I've always loved your sweet, salty funk, Angela Marie," Myles said. He licked her stomach with his broad tongue, bathing his way upward. He freed her breasts, and his tongue found them, too. Angela's whole frame shuddered as he swallowed her.

Myles slid one hand past the elastic of her jogging pants, furrowing inside her panties. His fingers waded through her pubic hair, lighting gently atop her clitoris, and Angela stiffened. She was sensitive, and often Tariq's fingers had been too rough, uncomfortable even when he tried to be gentle. Instinctively, Myles kept his touch light, so fleeting that she yearned for him to press *harder*. Her hips rose, begging.

Myles's index finger rubbed and teased until it was inside of her, sure and deep, and she felt her body kissing him, moist. His tongue flicked one nipple while his free hand gently squeezed the other. When Myles hooked his index finger inside her as if he were beckoning, massaging her in the precise place so few men knew, Angela clamped her mouth shut and screamed in her throat, where only Myles could hear. Her pleasure astonished her so much that tears came to her eyes.

It couldn't touch them here, she realized, arching against Myles.

It couldn't touch them tonight.

Angie was half-asleep beneath his rocking, so Myles was careful not to wake her. Even dozing, she'd naturally slipped her hand to grasp him tightly as she always did, as if she planned to keep his organ for herself. Then, her hand helped guide him inside her.

He'd found three lambskin condoms in the drawer of his nightstand, thankfully, but this was the only one that had survived their night together. He'd planned to save it until daylight, but when he'd awakened and felt Angie's hot skin against him in the dark, he'd wanted her again. He hadn't felt this kind of urgency since he was a teenager, and he was trembling as her warm dampness absorbed him. The condom seemed to disappear. He felt her skin against his, a fusion.

Angie mumbled, and her internal muscles clenched like a fist, momentarily holding him in the place of her choosing. Her mastery always startled him. Myles locked his elbows, feeling himself swell in her intimate embrace. His teeth ground together as waves of longing coursed through him, tightening in his testicles, an irrepressible tide. *You gasped like you'd seen your mama's ghost,* Tariq had said, and he nearly gasped again now. Only the unsettling memory of the taunting words saved Myles from expelling himself too soon.

Myles wanted this to last. His head was quiet, the deepest kind of quiet, the kind he'd felt his first time inside Angie, when all the loose strands of the world had knitted themselves into something that made sense. At home inside Angie, he understood everything he wanted to know.

Angie's grip relaxed. Maybe, he thought, she had drifted to full sleep.

Myles slowly began his strokes again, moving in quarter-inch probes, nudging inside, withdrawing at a snail's pace, then nudging inside again until their pelvises were joined. With his chest high above her, the charm Angie had made for him dangled from his chest, swinging between them. He didn't wear jewelry except for his gold cross, which never left his neck, so he'd nearly whipped off the leather chain a half-dozen times because it felt out of place. But he had promised Angie he would wear it, and although he'd had to bite his tongue not to tell her he had all the protection he needed from the good Lord above, he would honor that promise to her. She had made it for him. While Myles rocked inside of her, Angie's clay charm swung on.

Angela shifted slightly beneath him, her face still pliant in sleep, her worry gone. She made a small sound, a murmur. "I love you, Angie," Myles said, and he thought he saw her smile. "Don't you run from me, lady. Don't do that again."

Myles didn't know what made him turn around when he did, but two years at home with Ma had given him razor-sharp hearing. He turned over his shoulder to stare at the his door, and he was surprised to see it was open halfway. A slight figure stood in the darkness, barely visible except for a nightgown. Candace had gone home tonight, and she would never open his door without knocking.

Myles could have sworn he'd locked that door.

"Ma? You know you're supposed to be in bed," he whispered. He rolled away from Angie, tugging off the condom and covering himself. Miraculously, Angie didn't stir. The poor girl was beat to her socks, as Pa Fisher used to say. Myles climbed into his pants, which he'd left on the floor in the past few hours' frenzy. He was glad the room was so dark. Even if he'd had to wash and wipe Ma Fisher more times than he could count, he still didn't want to stand naked before his mama.

Ma Fisher stood stock-still in his doorway, one hand leaning against the frame. It wasn't like her to be so still, or so quiet, and Myles felt a charge. As much as he fought against the wild forays of Angie's imagination, he'd thought about it himself, and he'd heard others say the words when he visited the support group at the hospital in Longview on the days he needed fellowship: *It's like they've become possessed.*

"Ma, are you thirsty?" he said. He left his bedroom, closing the door behind him so they wouldn't disturb Angie. There wasn't enough light in the hallway to read Ma's expression. She might be thirsty, or hungry, or afraid of the dark, or convinced there were imaginary intruders outside her window. Ma wasn't the same wreck she'd been when every lost memory terrified her, or sent her into a rage, but she was rarely at peace. If Myles could give her one thing, it would be only that. Peace. He brushed her forehead. She was sweating. Maybe her room was too hot.

"If you keep getting up like this, we'll have to restrain you at night. Or send you away. I know you won't like that. I want you to be happy as long as possible. So you have to stay in bed. Got it, Ma?"

To her, he was only the man who lived in the house, and although she was happy to see him when he came home, she called him every name except Myles. Most often, she called him Jake, thinking he was Pa Fisher. Still, he couldn't stare at Ma in the face and not keep talking to her the way he had since the day she'd first appeared at his group home and told him he was just the little boy she'd been looking for. Myles reached for his mother's hand, but she snatched it away. She often did that, too. Sudden movements made her nervous.

"Come on, Ma," he said patiently. "Back to bed."

She relented, slipping her palm into his. "I'll see you soon, Snook," Ma said softly.

Ma had never called him Snook, but the affectionate nickname sounded uncannily as if she were talking to *him*, the way she used to. Sometimes, honest to God, he was sure of it.

"Yes, Ma," he told her. "You'll see me soon."

—

Myles was in deep sleep, entwined nude around Angie, when the phone on his nightstand rang, a tranquil trilling. He bolted upright, feeling as if he had been on alert all night, waiting. The rain outside pelted his rooftop, spilling noisily into the downspouts. Angie stirred but didn't open her eyes, frowning in the cloudy morning light creeping in through his glass door. He'd forgotten to close the blinds. He'd forgotten a lot of things last night, frankly, most of which he would probably regret in a very short time.

Sighing, Myles slid his hand across Angela's bare waist where it dipped above her hip, sunken and lovely, and he wondered how many more times he was likely to be able to touch her before the price was too high for any sane man to let himself be bargained up to. Angie's exits had always been grand, and this one would be no less so. Fate had been against them from the beginning, and it was still putting up a hell of a fight.

Myles cut off the phone's second ring. Chaos was an early riser, he thought.

"You told me to call you before the I call the big guys," Rob Graybold's voice said.

"What's up?" Myles croaked, glancing at his wall clock. It was only seven. This guy must never sleep, he thought.

"Art's ready to talk. He's asking for Angie. He said you'd know where to find her."

◄ Twenty-Six ►

*E*VEN IN JAIL, being the mayor must have its perks, Angela thought, as Rob handed her a carton of Marlboros for Art in the hallway of the new Sacajawea County jail. Ironically, according to Myles, Art had helped raise the money to build this addition in the rear of the sheriff's office, a fourteen-bed jail with no kitchen that had been open two months and still smelled like plaster and paint.

Art was one of his own first customers.

Angela's hands were shaky, so she slid the carton under her arm to keep from dropping it. She hadn't held a carton of Marlboros in years, since she used to buy Tariq's from the Safeway in Hollywood Hills. More convenient by the carton, he said when she complained.

Then, she realized the peculiarity of it. "I've never seen Art smoke," she said.

"Neither had Liza," Rob said. "But he sure smokes now."

They stood outside a blue-gray door marked CONFERENCE, beside the empty holding cell where Art had been kept since his arrest. Two jail guards nearby crossed their arms and huddled close in conversation, deliberately not noticing whatever regulations Rob was flaunting by bringing Myles and Angela here instead of to the glass booths where everyone else was sent. There was barely room for all of them to stand in the narrow corridor.

In the rush to leave his house that morning, Myles had put on a pair of glasses that looked exactly like his gold wire-rims from high school. Whenever Angela looked at him, she felt time vanish. "How long do we have with him?" Myles asked Rob.

"Not long," Rob said. "He seems all right now, but let's play it safe. Go in for a hot minute, say your hellos, and come on back out."

Angela's heart plunged, then raced. Who was the woman she'd been yesterday, methodically photographing the leaves and blood in Gramma Marie's house? That clearheaded resolve had left her now. She could hardly make herself move, uncomforted by the guards. She wished she were back in Myles's bed, savoring their first waking morning together. And if she couldn't have a moment's happiness with Myles, she'd rather be at Gramma Marie's house than here, somehow.

"Are you coming with us?" Angela asked Rob, noticing that he was the only one with a gun.

"For Art's sake, I'd better not. Legally speaking, it's best if I don't hear too much. Think of this as old friends jawing, nothing official. You all right, Angie?"

"How is he?" Angela asked Rob, ignoring the question she'd be lying to answer yes to.

Her terror must have shown on her face, because Rob leaned toward her, touching her elbow, and Rob wasn't prone to physical gestures. Right after Corey died, there had been many times she'd wished he was, because the news he gave had always been blunt and hard.

Rob shrugged, his eyes misting. "Some ways, good. Some ways, bad. You'll see."

"You don't have to go in there, Angie," Myles said. He wrapped an arm around Angela's waist, hugging her against him, and she clung to him, grateful.

"Yes, I do, baby," she said. She reached into her pocketbook and retrieved one of her remaining quarter-sized charms, holding it out to Rob. "I need to give this to Art."

Rob took it, held it up to the fluorescent light above them to examine it. His face soured. "Sorry. It's a choking hazard, or he could break it to make a sharp point. I can't let you do that."

Angela had expected Rob to say that, but disappointment made her fear more keen. "Will you keep it, then?" she said. "Those are Gramma Marie's symbols. For luck."

Rob looked puzzled, then he noticed the similar charm around Myles's neck. She saw condescension in his eyes when he looked at Myles, and she wondered if Myles's eyes had warned him, *Just humor her, man, 'cause you know how it is, her being nuts and all. Runs in the family.*

Rob slipped the pendant into his breast pocket, looking at Angela with amused warmth. "Tell you what," he said. "I'll give it to Melanie. She'll be glad to wear anything from Mrs. T'saint."

The conference room was as small as a crypt, one table and four chairs crammed in a too-small space, and Art sat at the table at the far wall, his hands cuffed in front of him in a pose that looked like a prayer. He was wearing his glasses, his head resting at an angle on his knuckles, staring toward the door, waiting. The pine-green inmate's uniform he wore made him look like a surgeon.

Art sat up straight when she walked in. He was so happy, his face broke into something that was supposed to be a smile, but twisted his mouth into a terrible grimace instead. His skin looked loose on his face. She tried not to look at his eyes, but she couldn't help it. His eyelids fluttered when he spoke, evidence of the effort it took him. "Angie . . . thanks for coming. Thanks s-so much."

Those eyes seared her. They were Art Brunell's eyes, unaltered. Nearly insane with pain.

"Yes, Angie. Thank you," Liza breathed behind her.

Liza's nose and upper lip were bright red, her eyes glassy and anxiously wide. She was standing against the wall opposite Art, her arms wrapped around herself. Her baggy clothes were mismatched, an afterthought, and her hair looked as if she'd just finished a long hike in the rain.

"Oh, sweetie. I didn't expect to find you here today," Angela whispered, hugging Liza. Her friend leaned hard, shuddering. Angela heard her sob softly, immobile in her arms.

"I can't help it," Liza said, a whimper. "I love this sonofabitch, Angie."

Angela hugged her more tightly, swaying with her, feeling the pain flowing from Liza's fevered skin. Liza had given her this same hug after Corey, she realized. The uncanniness of the mirrored moment made Angela screw her eyes shut from the memory, fighting off the temptation to sag to the floor. Liza needed her today. This was Liza's time to sag.

But maybe Liza was stronger than she'd been. When it had been her turn, Angela had not been here for Tariq. She'd lost her mind when she'd seen that gun. She could have survived Corey's death without The Harbor, finding shelter in Tariq's shared grief, but the gun had been there when it had no business being there, and she had blamed Tariq because he'd been the closest one to blame. She hadn't wanted to ask herself the uglier questions Liza must be asking herself now.

Like Myles, she hadn't allowed herself to see it.

"W-we don't have long, Angie," Art said, with an almost inaudible stammer in a voice that was otherwise measured, nearly unchanged except that it sounded so weary. "I've got to talk while I still can. We're on the clock." He sounded so much like himself, she forgot everything for a moment. Like Rob had said, it felt like old friends jawing. But as soon as she saw his eyes again, she remembered why she would never want to be the person living behind that abyss.

Holding Liza's hand, Angela walked to the white plastic chair in front of Art's table. All of the chairs looked like picnic chairs, probably so they couldn't be used as weapons. This room was claustrophobic, with no windows, not even a window in the door so the others could see inside. Their only link to Rob was an intercom on the wall beside the door, where Liza had been standing when they'd walked in. Angela sat, and Myles stood behind her, his hands gripping her shoulders. Liza sat in the empty chair beside Art, covering his folded hands with hers. When her nose began to run in a thin stream, she wiped her nose on her shirtsleeve, not letting go of him.

"Angie, b-break out one of those cigarettes?" Art said, sounding like he hated to trouble her.

"Sure." Angela had forgotten about the carton. She opened it and dug out a pack. "I don't know if he sent matches. . . ."

"I brought a lighter," Liza said, searching in her pocket.

"I've been jonesing since last night. First thing I asked for was a cigarette," Art said, and Angela noticed how much Art's hands were shaking, his fingers hugging each other for support. "Hell of a thing, I'll tell you, because I don't smoke. Only that one time . . . Liza, remember that?"

"Yeah, in Tacoma. We smoked a pack at the Pink Floyd concert." Liza smiled faintly, wrapped in the recollection. "We were what, Art? Nineteen? Smoking cigarettes because we couldn't find any grass. We coughed 'til we had tears in our eyes."

Art didn't seem to have heard her; he was focused solely on Angela's fingers as she tore the plastic from one of the packs. "The guard gave me a couple smokes last night, but they weren't Marlboros. They *have* to be Marlboros," Art said, shaking his head to emphasize the point, as if he couldn't understand how anyone could think otherwise. "Rob's a godsend. If not for him, I don't know w-what I'd . . ." Art paused, thinking better of whatever he'd wanted to say. Angela saw a shadow emerge in his face, something that wanted to steal him back to his pain. While Art clamped a trembling cigarette between his lips, Liza lit it for him, and Art held it with both of his hands, drawing in the smoke. He closed his eyes, and Angela waited for him to exhale. It was a long wait.

Too long.

As casually as she could, Angela pulled against Myles's protective grip so she could learn forward, closer to Art. To try to smell him. Finally, a cloud of smoke billowed from Art's mouth, the last in the shape of a perfect O. But he smelled fine. The rankness was gone.

"Look at that—I can blow smoke-rings now. Did you see that, Liza?" Art said.

"I saw it." With the wide-eyed look of a child seeing a falling star, Liza stared up at the dissipating smoke as it elongated and fractured. Art watched it with her, equally transfixed.

"This is just one more thing, Angie, the cigarettes," Art said, once the smoke ring was gone. "I feel like I'm dying without them, but that's just a teeny thing, really. I wish I knew what to do about my *stomach*." He blinked painfully, and took another long drag on his cigarette. "Jesus God, it hurts."

"I know," Angela said. *My stomach's not right today, man.* The memory of Corey's voice locked Angela's elbows against her chair's armrests. Her precious baby had been in trouble, showing all the signs, and she hadn't known. She hadn't seen them. She hadn't been able to help.

Art went on. "Well, what the fuck? If I stop trying to remember, I think the pain goes away. If I talk, I feel like I've got a spike stuck through my gut. Some choice, huh? Eenie meenie miney moe." An unspoiled part of Art was trying to make a joke and failing, the way Art so often did.

Liza squeezed his knuckles, sniffling again. "Tell her what you told me, Art."

"I want this cocksucker dead," Art said, his mirth gone in an impossible instant. His voice rustled in his throat like dry brush. "You follow, Angie? I want this devil cunt sent back to Hell. This is the only way I can hurt it back." His voice shot up an octave on the last three words, but he swallowed several times, composing himself. "I saw it. I had to *watch*. It *wanted* to make me watch. So this is my fight, and it's all I've got, Angie. Hating this thing is all that's left of Art Brunell."

Art seemed spent, momentarily. He hung his head, wiping strands of his thinning hair across his scalp. Most of his hair was pushed to one side, uneven. She saw perspiration gleaming on his crown. Miraculously, though, although his jowls trembled, he did not sob. Liza, beside him, had closed her eyes, her face so stricken it looked as if it were sinking from her bones.

"This was a very bad idea," Myles said gently, in Angela's ear. "We should go."

It was tempting to see this visit through Myles's eyes, casting Art as a psychopath in the full throes of a mental collapse. That was how she wished she could see it, too. Angela had hoped something would shatter her fledgling belief in curses and invisible predators, because she liked the world better without them. Myles's conviction that Tariq or some vandal had thrown leaves in Gramma Marie's house and poured blood on her cellar floor was comforting, one she'd hoped might redeem itself one day. But she couldn't see Art's face and hold on to her illusions.

He was ready to give her a report on where he'd been. What had taken him.

"What does it want, Art?" she said.

Art's eyes looked saddened, if it were possible. "You, Angie."

To Angela, it almost seemed that she heard Art's words before he spoke, an effect exactly like hearing him say it twice. Her limbs shivered, so much that Myles must have felt her tremor where his hands held on to her. "Then why did it do that to you? Why did—"

"To hurt you. For sport. To punish anyone who tries to help you see it's there. All of the above. It's not real picky about the reasons."

Myles sighed impatiently, shifting behind Angela's chair. Silence fell on the room while Art took in more smoke. He was midway through his first cigarette already, gobbling it with his long draws he held in his lungs too long, but never coughing. His cheeks hollowed as he inhaled.

"Your friend Naomi," Art said finally, hoarse.

"What about Naomi?" Angela hadn't been prepared to hear Naomi's name from Art's lips. It sounded like a desecration.

"We got her," Art said, nodding to make sure she knew he had spoken the word deliberately. He breathed out again, fanning smoke across the table. "*We.* He. It. It's all the same, or it was. I dreamed the whole thing yesterday, before it let me go. In the dream, *I* was the one it sent to her. *I* was the one who stuffed her in the trunk of a junk car on a farm in south Vancouver, and let me tell you, she's as dead as they come. Her brain hemorrhaged when she got hit with the gun, and a dry-cleaning bag stopped her breathing. A bag from the hotel. I used to know exactly where she is, I think, but I don't anymore. I tried to hang on to it, but it's gone now. I'm sorry, munchkin."

Oddly, he didn't sound sorry. There was a shading of playfulness to Art's words that chilled Angela, beyond the horrible information he conveyed. Almost as if part of him enjoyed telling her.

"Angie, don't listen to this," Myles said, alarmed and angry. He slipped his hand beneath her armpit, trying to lift her to her feet.

"Myles, *hush*," Angela snapped, pulling herself free. If she didn't press on now, she might lose herself to the grief she'd aborted when she heard Art say the words *She's as dead as they come.* "What else? Who's next?"

"Tariq," Art said.

"What about Tariq?"

"It ate Tariq. Ate him slow. It was harder for it to get Tariq, him being so far away, but it's strong, like I said. It used the bus he left—the bus was on its grounds—and it got to him that way. Objects we've had a long time, they carry parts of us. . . ." He shook his head, exasperated. "All the whys aren't important. Tariq is gone now. That's what you need to know. He killed Naomi."

"Is Tariq coming here?" she said.

"He's already here."

Angela's legs tensed, cramping. "Where?" she said.

"It wouldn't let me see that. But you'll find him. He'll come to you." Art's eyelids were fluttering again, harder now, as if they were trying to fly from his face.

"What happened to Corey?" Angela said.

"Corey woke it up," Art said, sighing. The fluttering stopped.

"How?"

Art's face wrenched in pain, and he paused, shifting in his seat. "Marie put it to sleep, but Corey found something he wasn't supposed to. A little knowledge is a dangerous thing, as they say. Corey learned enough to get in trouble. Marie expected you to bury the cocksucker for good, but something happened and she couldn't find you. Something about the ring. It was out of place."

Angela blinked as tears flooded her eyes. She couldn't speak.

Art went on. "You didn't have the ring, and something was blocking your dreams. End of story. When she tried to talk to you, the dreams strayed. They went to Corey. He was more open. Closer to his spirit self."

Angela nodded, nearly blind in her tears. She fought to speak. "How do I fight it?"

Art half-chuckled. "Fight it? Good luck. The ring protects you, but it isn't everything. The ring only makes it work harder. It won't keep you alive, I'm sorry to say." He still sounded too indifferent. Maybe from where Art had been, it was all the same one way or the other. One death here, one death there. His son was gone, so nothing else mattered quite as much.

"What do I have to do?" she said.

Art pulled on the cigarette again, wretched eyes honing on her. "When it comes for you, kill it. You'll know it by the smell. You didn't always, but Marie's helping you with that. She's helping you when she can. You'll probably have to kill the body, and once you've done that, you have to kill the *thing*. It's not of flesh. It's stronger now than it's ever been. And it hides. I don't think it wants me anymore. Too much trouble. But it can walk without a body to carry it. And you can't run from it, not once it's got a bug up its ass for you. Like Naomi couldn't run. The safest place for you is on your property. Just like Marie. You wait, and you kill it."

"Art, *how?*" Angela said, rising to her feet. "How do I kill it?"

"The body'll die like any body does. That's the easy part. The rest, Marie will show you. *As long as you keep the ring.* But she's not as strong as she wanted to be, or this little situation we have here wouldn't have gone so far bad. This wasn't supposed to happen like this. But *c'est la vie.*"

The ring again. Yes, Angela had always known she was supposed to keep Gramma Marie's ring. When she had discovered Gramma Marie's ring was gone—when she'd walked into her bedroom and seen the broken glass and the mess on the floor, *knowing* it would be gone because it was the only thing worth taking—Angela had stopped believing she could have anything in the world. In that light, everything afterward had made sense. Tariq going to Oakland. Corey running after him. Corey dying. She wasn't supposed to have a goddamned thing.

"You may not win, Angie," Art said.

"But I might?"

"Might."

It was a small word, not the least comforting. But it was all she had.

"Art . . . what is it?" she said, because she had to know.

Art's breathing seized, and he doubled over, clutching his stomach. Liza let out a cry, leaning over him while she rubbed his back with soothing strokes. Art raised his eyes to Angela's, his upper torso shaking as if he were carrying a refrigerator on his back. Already, his eyes were beginning to look like a stranger's again, like the man who'd told her the day before yesterday that he'd worked up a mighty appetite taking Glenn fishing.

"A spirit," Art said. "In your woods. Some of them . . . are *wonderful*"— he blinked as if he saw celestial lights, his eyes alone illuminated in a sunken face that was suddenly pale, sickly—"but they live alongside . . . the other ones. This one was too wild, banished. The Chinook buried it because it liked . . . death. It brought disease. They wouldn't speak its name. But Marie . . . Marie . . ."

Art nearly spat Gramma Marie's name, as if it left a bad taste in his mouth, then he shook his head. He couldn't finish. He slumped in his chair, trying to catch his breath. "I don't remember. I d-don't remember, Angie. It doesn't want me to. *Shit*, it hurts. I'm sorry. I'm so sorry. Liza . . . Jesus, honey, I'm so sorry."

As Art spoke, smoke drifted from his lips in an unfailing stream. This time, it didn't smell like cigarette smoke to Angela; it smelled like charred flesh. Art's chin fell to his chest and he closed his eyes. Even when she could hardly tell if he was breathing, the smoke still appeared from his mouth, clouding his face, showing no sign of abating.

The smoke kept coming long after what little was left of Art's cigarette fell to the floor.

"What's the tag number on that van?" Rob said, scratching notes on his blank report.

"It's a vanity plate. T-A-R-I-Q-1."

Rob nodded, taking that down. "Gotcha. I remember noticing that once."

Rob was very curious about Tariq, suddenly. And Angela had heard him make a call to have Art transferred to a high-security mental health ward in Cowlitz County. Art's case had just changed.

The photograph on Rob's desk had been there the summer of 2001, Rob and Melanie in rain gear from a long-ago camping trip, probably when they'd been in their mid-twenties. As she always did, Angela wondered again why Rob and Melanie had never had children. Angela had never seen Rob smile the way he was smiling in that picture, which was the only personal item on his desk. Rob's military training had followed him here, because his books and papers were in neat stacks, and a cup of freshly sharpened pencils at arm's reach.

The two deputies and the dispatcher were the only other people in the sheriff's office, and they stood listening beside a nearby file cabinet, somber. Myles sat at one of the empty desks behind them, on his cell phone. Myles had finally reached Naomi's assistant, and Angela tried to overhear what he was saying to her, but his voice was too low. Myles had asked Angela for Naomi's numbers so he could settle the question of her friend's whereabouts and put her at ease, but Angela knew he was only confirming Naomi's disappearance. No one was answering Naomi's cell phone.

Still, her grief hadn't broken free. She wasn't still fighting for hope, not anymore, but some kind of shock had set in, she decided. Something that needed to happen to her now.

"Has Tariq shown hostile behavior since your divorce?" Rob said.

"No. I've barely spoken to him, Rob. It's not Tariq."

Rob gave her a look that was part pity, part aggravation, a trick of his eyebrows.

"Naomi's assistant is back in L.A.," Myles said, snapping his folding cell phone shut. "She's calling Naomi at the spa in Victoria, then she'll get right back to us."

"Naomi isn't at the spa," Angela said. "Art's already told us that."

Rob tapped his pencil eraser against his desktop in an impatient staccato, glancing at Myles. The voices had been too low for Angela to hear the exchange between Myles and Rob after they left the jail, but she'd seen Myles giving the sheriff the kind of earful a man like Rob Graybold rarely stood still for. Rob's face had turned bright red, whether from anger or embarrassment. Angela guessed Rob was recalling the same moment now, kicking himself for putting two crazy people in a conference room together.

"Sorry again about this morning, Angie," Rob told her. "Liza talked me into it, against my better judgment. She's got a way of doing that. Always has. Art's been all but catatonic since he was arrested, then last night he came out of it sounding so . . . *normal,* or so I thought. Liza said he wanted to see you. I must have been out of my mind to call you like that."

"Don't apologize, Rob. I was supposed to go there."

He wanted to believe her, but his eyes told her he didn't. No matter. He would soon.

The room was silent for a long time, longer than six adults usually managed to keep silent without creating reasons to talk. There was chatter on the police scanner, but the deputies ignored it. Angela heard the hum of the vending machine where Myles had bought her a muffin for breakfast, although she hadn't touched it. She wasn't hungry. The idea of taking even a bite had made her feel sick to her stomach, and feeling sick to her stomach had scared the shit out of her until ten minutes later, when she was sure the feeling was gone.

Angela forgot what they were waiting for, until Myles's phone rang.

Myles picked up, anxious. When his expression flagged, Angela knew. Suzanne Ross, somewhere down in Los Angeles, was freaking out. Myles thanked Suzanne, apologized, and assured her everything was fine, in a voice that sounded unsure himself. Slowly, he hung up.

"Well?" Rob prompted.

Myles didn't speak at first, his expression lost. The impossibilities were running through his mind, looking for a plausible place to rest. He was two steps behind her, but he was catching up.

"She never checked into the spa," Angela said, since Myles wouldn't say the words.

"No. She didn't," Myles said. "After Suzanne called the spa, she talked to the film director, a Vincent somebody?" Myles shook his head, still perplexed. "A very tall black man returned her *dog* yesterday, that dog she lost here. He lied about being her brother, and nobody's seen her since. She left a note saying she'd gone to the spa."

If Angela had been capable of grief today, she would have grieved for Tariq, too.

"Holy fuckin' baloney," the younger deputy muttered. His face was chalky. *"Art knew."*

"Darlene . . . ," Rob began, turning toward the curly-haired dispatcher.

"On it, Rob." The dispatcher pirouetted toward her desk. "I'll get Vancouver P.D."

Through the window across the office, which overlooked two drab barges, Angela saw rain spearing the river. Her watch told her it was nine in the morning, but under the thick cloud cover, the muddy sky held barely enough light for dawn. Distantly, just within her hearing, she heard a low grouse of thunder. It was only the third or fourth time Angela had heard thunder in Sacajawea, and she wondered if anyone else had noticed it.

The thunder might be something they would all remark on when they talked about this day later, Angela thought. If any of them survived to tell.

RECLAMATION

And I'm standing at the crossroad,

Believe I'm sinkin' down.

— "CROSS ROAD BLUES"
ROBERT JOHNSON

We paused before a House that seemed

A swelling of the Ground—

The Roof was scarcely visible—

The Cornice—in the Ground—

— EMILY DICKINSON

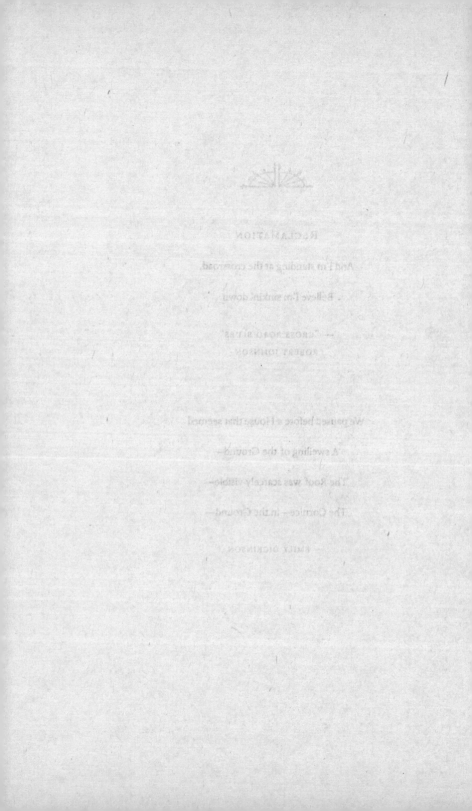

☒ Twenty-Seven ☒

*W*HEN YOU HAVE REACHED *a place of spirits, your bones know it.*
You feel their company in the gentle call of the wind, in the laughter of
the creek, in the silent conversations between the trees. I have been to many such
places. Grandmère took me to a bayou a few miles from our home as a child that
was thick with spirits, harboring one in each water moccasin, in each dragonfly,
in the fissured trunks of the saltbrush trees, in each lick of the marshy water, even
in the whining mosquitoes. There, she introduced me to my forebears, calling them
by name, one by one, and although I could never see them, I knew they were em-
bracing me.

Such was my feeling upon reaching Sacajawea, upon finding the Place. How
did I find it? The route was a long one! My plump little Dominique and I spent a
year in San Francisco after I dreamed of that countryside rife with visual marvels.
The beauty of that part of the country alone convinced me that this must be the
spiritual home I had yearned for, the place that would heal my soul after Philippe's
death. Yet, after only one short year, during which time I felt both very close to and
quite remote from my destination, Papa Legba came to me in my dream and showed
me a walnut tree. I also saw a house built on a ridge, but it was the tree I remem-
bered most. It was the tree I was determined to find.

I was happy to leave San Francisco by then. I had encountered a Chinaman
being ridden by a baka, like the corruptions whispered about by Roman Catholic
priests dispatched from the Vatican to carry out the dangerous feat of banishing the
Evil One. Bakas are perceived in many forms by human eyes, most often as mis-
shapen beasts—so it is rare for one to invade a man in such a way. But any manbo

knows there is danger of mischievous spirits riding the head in place of the lwas if a curse has been cast, although I do not know why this Chinaman was cursed. Perhaps the spirit followed him from Peking. Perhaps there has been a marriage of demon spirits in this part of the New World. Of this I can only speculate. The baka I met when he was brought to me was no more Satan himself than I was the Virgin Mary, but it proved a worthy adversary. It was almost the end of me.

With Papa Legba's blessing, and those of Ougu la Flambo and Simbi, I was able to send the Chinaman's baka away from him. Perhaps it flew to one of the forests of majestic redwood trees I visited so often as tears streamed down my face in witness to their beauty. Certainly spirits live among the redwoods, and bakas claim their rightful place among the spirits. One could not wish for a world without bakas because they are willing to carry out the work shunned by the more gentle spirits. But no sound-minded person would invite a baka into her head, nor her home.

These are words I should have remembered.

The encounter with the baka in San Francisco taught me much I had not known about my own facilities, but it wearied me as no other exercise before it. I was bedridden for thirty days, my body covered with a rash that itched almost to the end of my tolerance. I took daily cleansing baths with anise, mustard seed, lavender, and rosemary, to no avail at first. In fact, I feared I had reached the end of my usefulness as a manbo, just as all people are reduced to a fearful state from time to time. Fear is inevitable, as is fear's parent, death. Moun fèt pou mouri.

Papa Legba stayed at my side during this trying time, reminding me of my own strength when I chose to see it, when I was not swallowed in my misery. I think Papa Legba was disgusted with me and my tears, or else I might have healed sooner. He conveyed my messages to the lwas in his own time; often my prayers met silence because Papa Legba stood in my way. This made me angry, but it taught me patience, a trait I wish I had learned better. Impatience has been my undoing.

During this time of rash and fever, as I thrashed in my bed, I had vivid dreams about the walnut tree and the lovely house on the ridge. When my illness left me, I knew I must find them.

Sacajawea is not as close to San Francisco as it might seem by studying a map. I did not know the name of the town where my tree grew, an obstacle few would hope to conquer. With Dominique on my back, I wandered from town to town, not unlike a madwoman, traversing the northern coast of California, then to Oregon, where I spent three long months; and then, finally, I came to Washington, in our nation's uppermost western corner. I always stayed near the water, because I knew water was not far from the place I sought.

I have no memory of why I came to Sacajawea, except that it was not my destination the morning I set out. I came upon it accidentally, as one must happen across all places of great importance in life. I do remember, however, that as I arrived on Main Street in the back of a kind traveler's wagon, one of the first people I laid eyes upon was the tall, sturdy Chinook whom townspeople had come to call Red John, reducing him to the color of his skin. He saw me right away, given that there were no other people of my skin color in the little town. I think my brashness amused him, because he had a grin waiting for me. I could not have known then that John would soon be my husband, but I knew I was near the Place.

"Do you know a house on a ridge with a great walnut tree?" I asked John as I gathered my traveling bag on my arm and my child on my back, much like an Indian squaw; perhaps like brave Sacajawea toting little Jean-Baptiste on her trek with the white explorers, arriving before me.

"Sounds like the Goode house," John said, and he pointed the way. "He has a few black walnut trees. Do you have business with Mr. Goode?" he asked me.

"No," I replied. "I have business with his land."

That answer satisfied him, so he nodded and wished me well. I would discover later that John knew of the land's power, because he had sojourned there to say prayers since he was a boy with his grandparents, who remembered the place when it was a burial site in their own grandparents' day. When the plague came, John would tell me later, his people's dead outnumbered the living, and there were barely enough men with the strength to hang the burial canoes from the trees. Once, he told me, there had been a forest of canoes in Sacajawea, until the white men removed them.

I saw the tree immediately, precisely as my dream had promised; a large tree with a broad trunk and a large canopy across its crown, although I could tell the tree still had growing to do yet. The tree was young. Like me, the tree was a transplant, brought out of its natural environment to make a new home in the West. The house also appeared as promised, and my dream's vision was fulfilled.

And imagine my surprise! Grandmère was waiting for me in the tree!

You have done well to find me, chérie, she called from its branches. This will be our new home.

Dominique and I slept in the forest that night, and I felt the rumbling beneath the soil of all the souls that had passed this way. There was so much life, and so much death, that I had to shut my ears so I would not go insane. Sometimes a very spiritual place will overwhelm you, and I had never visited a place as restless as this. When I thanked Papa Legba and the lwas for leading me to such a vibrant place, my whispers went directly to their ears with the force of a thunderclap, and theirs to mine. I smelled roses and lavender where there were none. I cried from joy until I slept.

But while I am a woman of spirit, I am also a woman of practical matters, and I knew I could not hope to live in that wonderful forest undisturbed, not so long as a deed proclaimed it belonged to another. The next morning, I went to the service entrance of the house on the ridge and introduced myself to the man who lived there, a pharmacist named Elijah Goode.

He was an older man, white-haired and portly, and he walked with an elegant wooden cane. He was very polite, as if he had been waiting for me. "You've come in reply to my advertisement?" he said.

I knew of no such thing, but I nodded my head. Coincidences are commonplace in the life of a manbo, so I took it as a sign.

He admitted he had reservations about hiring a colored cook and housekeeper to live in his home—that there were no colored people in Sacajawea, and that his neighbors would not understand—but after he'd voiced his concern, he laughed and shook his head. I think he was taken with Dominique, who kept reaching for his cane, calling Leg-ba, because she recognized the symbol of her spirit-father. "Blast them all!" Elijah Goode said. "I'll give them something to talk about."

Well, talk they did. I had been in Eli's employ for only a month when he complained that he had seen a decline in business. Many of his neighbors assumed I was too young and beautiful to live in a house alone with Eli—which, in the end, perhaps was prophecy on their part. They were quick to attribute lustful motives to him, and more so to me, although our lives were very separate. Dominique and I did not have a room in the main house; instead, we were consigned to a small, windowless room in the attic, where the rising summer heat was nearly unbearable, as if Eli meant to prove to any visitors that his colored domestic understood her "place."

Eli was very concerned about his business, which is understandable. He'd been born into some money in New England, which enabled him to build the house and buy the land, but he was not wealthy enough to discount townspeople's gossip. The solution, to my mind, was simple.

"Mr. Goode," I said to him, for that was what I called him then, "if I may say so, you haven't used your land's endowments to their greatest potential. I could make you a rich man."

I then introduced Eli to my teas from the herbs I grew in my garden, and he was much impressed. He had suffered from arthritis since he was in his fifties, and he noticed a marked improvement once he had tasted my blend. I cured his sleeplessness next; and the last blend, though I did not tell him its intent, restored his carnal drives. From that time on, Elijah Goode no longer saw me as his colored maid, but as a healer in my own right. We became friends, reading our favorite books in his library in the evenings while Dominique played on a quilt on the floor.

And we discussed business strategies. He agreed with me that a mail-order company would give him financial security for years to come, if I would be willing to give my assistance.

"But there is something I must ask in return," I said.

"Name your price, Marie," he said, reclining in his great Turkish parlor chair as if he were President Coolidge himself.

"You have no wife and no heirs," I said. "All I ask is that you leave this property to me in your will."

The way he stormed! It was blackmail, he said. Preposterous! He had to consider his nieces and nephews in Boston, his brother's children. Not to mention the scandal it was cause in the town, he insisted. Eli was always preoccupied with the specter of scandal.

"It's no one's concern but ours," I said. "Once you're dead and gone, no scandal will touch you. That's my price, and nothing less."

He was very angry for weeks, only grunting at mealtime, shifting his eyes away from me when I entered the room. He tried to cultivate herbs himself, but he had already seen the difference my prayers made, so he knew he could not hope to carry out his dream without my help. Eli also probably feared me by then; I believe he realized I could simply take what I wanted from him, and that asking his permission was a formality on my part. I also believe he blamed me because he had grown so alarmingly fond of me, which I knew long before he confessed it; although I will swear with my dying breath that I had no hand in swaying his heart. I had given him tea to improve his manhood, but I had not expected him to fix his attentions on me.

He came to me one day in the kitchen, standing unusually close behind me. "Marie," he said in a gentle voice, "I don't cotton to blackmail. But I've come to see this question another way: In a different time and place, without the curse of your dark skin between us, I might have taken you as a wife to comfort me in my twilight years. We both know your mind and soul are as white as mine." He meant this in a complimentary way, so I struggled to hear the words as he meant them despite the way they rankled me.

"As my wife," he went on, "you would have been entitled to this house and my land after my passing, so you and your daughter wouldn't have needed anything from anyone. Custom may govern me while I live, but I won't deny you and Dominique what my heart says is yours. I'll change my will, by God, just as you asked."

That night, for the first time, Eli and I shared his bed as we would for our next three years together. Did I love him? Not the way I loved Philippe, certainly. And not the way I would love John. But I loved Eli as well as I could. He was kind to my daughter, and he had welcomed me into his home, giving me access to his land, so I could ask him no more than that. I honored Papa Legba, thanking him for bringing me to his Forest of the Crossroads, where it seemed my life had finally turned for the better. Eli was one of my blessings there.

I made Eli a wealthy man. We shared the profits from his mail-order business, which performed well once customers realized his products lived up to their promises. Our teas could improve eyesight, cure impotence, promote alertness, and bring peace of mind. Within two years, we had more money than two people could spend, so he secured trust accounts for his nieces and nephews, and I did the same for mine in Louisiana. I took care of my family's every need, exactly as I'd hoped I could, fulfilling my duties as the head family spirit.

Our secret remained. Townspeople suspected what we were all along, though they did not suspect our enterprise. Eli and I chuckled over their ignorance, since he continued to prosper although his pharmacy in Sacajawea languished. They never knew what kind of miraculous venture was operating right in their midst!

Then, in the fall of 1926, Eli left for two months to visit his brother in Boston. He never returned. His brother found him dead in his bed, most certainly from heart failure. He died at the age of sixty-eight, far too soon.

I grieved alone, since I alone knew what Eli had been to me.

Within a week of the news of Eli's death, I received the first telephone inquiry from his brother. Did we have any needs? How long would it take me to move my daughter out of the house? I mailed him a copy of Eli's will, assuring him that all of our needs had been taken care of. The scandal Eli had feared arrived with hurricane force.

Eli's brother hired a battalion of lawyers, and I hired my own in matching numbers. In the end, after many prayers, I won the battle for what was rightfully mine at last.

John moved in with me six months after Eli's death. He had been a constant visitor while Eli lived, a handyman and groomsman, and he had also been my only friend during the terrible period after Eli's death. It was natural that we should have developed feelings for each other, and we did. His sterling soul reminded me of Philippe's.

John hesitated to share the house with me, fearful of the neighbors. He had lived so long as the town's favorite pet Indian that he dared not be a man. "What can they say? The house is mine," I said.

Finally, he agreed, and John, Dominique, and I became a family.

I had been subjected to profanity and terrible glares since Eli's death, but my neighbors' rancor intensified when I took John as my common-law husband. When legal strategies and exorbitant tax bills failed to drive us away, the attacks began.

Perhaps they saw me as a terrible force "corrupting" their good red man, and feared John's remaining people would become equally bold, following his example. Perhaps they feared a mass migration of colored and red people, soiling their town. I cannot speak to the motives of such hateful hearts.

But I will confess this: The longer I was hated, the more I learned to hate in return. I hated my daughter's tears as gunshots awakened her in the dead of the night. I hated the memories those gunshots unburied in my own mind, forcing me to relive again and again the horrible fate brought upon Philippe. Often, John tells me, I woke up with Philippe's name on my tongue, sobbing pitifully. I feared that I would once again be forced to stand and watch harm come to those I loved. I hated my fear most of all.

There are many remedies I might have sought if I had not been blinded by so much anger and hate. I could have prayed to Ezili to foster love in my neighbors' hearts, to quell their senseless fears. I could have relied upon Papa Legba's protection, realizing that he would never allow harm to come to us in so enchanted a place.

But one June night, the night of a rare summer storm, the attack was more horrible than usual. Perhaps our enemies felt emboldened by the shroud of heavy rains, but from the time the sun set, gunshots boomed before our house for hours, shattering windows. I opened my front door to face the cowards, with John at my side with his gun to protect us, and I saw how our door had been savaged by buckshot and lead. Our attackers had left by then, but the damaged door sent me into a rage. I had vengeance in my heart as I made my way through the Crossroads Forest in the driving rain.

That night, instead of praying for peace, I prayed for war.

Papa Legba ignored me. I brought him offerings, and begged him to open the gates so I might evoke the lwas and bakas who would give me the power to harm others as they had harmed me, to send plagues upon them as plagues had beset the Chinook and other tribes who had preceded them here. But Papa Legba laughed at my agitated state. I heard his deep laughter in the thunder above the treetops: Stop this silliness, Marie. You are better than this, my spirit-wife. Pray to me again when you have regained your senses.

I might have heeded dear Papa Legba's wishes. He is the highest lwa, the lwa who holds the secret of the language of the gods, and is worthy of the highest respect. Papa Legba brought us the gift of communion with the lwas and the highest God, opening the gate between us.

But in my half-crazed state, I remembered Grandmère's messages to me in my dreams, which had been stronger all the time since I had found the tree where her spirit dwelled. I remembered how she wove the symbols of my ring into language, creating a single word—one word only—that she claimed our ancestors had stolen from Papa Legba in the time before time. I had never uttered the word, nor considered uttering it.

But on that stormy night, I did.

"——," I said, raising my arms high, beseeching the gods against Papa Legba's wishes, barren of his blessing. I committed the offense at midnight, Papa Legba's sacred hour, and on Saturday, his sacred day. With the utterance of a single word, I sinned three times and scarred my life beyond recognition.

But I did not know the scale of the calamity on that night.

The ground trembled beneath my feet, and I reveled in my power. "Come to me, spirits," I called to the weeping sky. "Vinn jwenn mouin."

Before my startled eyes, the ground became a sea of mud.

⚔ Twenty-Eight

JULY 2, 2001

TWO DAYS BEFORE HE WOULD DIE, Corey Hill nodded to sleep at
the edge of The Spot. His back leaned against the deeply grooved
bark of an enormous fallen trunk, a Douglas fir that had lived for four hundred years, although Corey didn't know the age of the tree, nor how close
he sat to death himself. Corey had to sleep in naps now, because he had forgotten the habit of sleeping at night.

An animal made a snuffling sound high above him. Corey woke up
with a cry of surprise, spilling the bag of food he'd been balancing in his
lap, and three apples rolled at his feet. He saw a massive gray animal's
breast and legs. Then, hooves. And a snout, above an iron bit.

Sean was sitting astride Sheba, practically on top of him. Corey was so
startled, he felt dizzy.

"You scared the *fuck* out of me," Corey said, tugging his baseball cap
down to cut the sun's glare as he stared up at Sean.

"Sorry." Sean flipped his hair out of his face. Sheba's long neck arched
down so she could rip a clump of flowering weeds from the ground beside
Corey, chewing a huge mouthful. The weeds stuck out of the sides of her
mouth, vanishing as she chewed. "Where you been?"

"Around," Corey said. He quickly collected the spilled apples and
stuffed them back inside the Downtown Foods bag before Sheba could get
to them. He'd also brought cans of Chef Boyardee ravioli, a loaf of bread,
a jar of peanut butter, a can opener, and some plastic forks and knives.

"We're going to pretend like nothing happened?" Sean said.

"I didn't say that."

"What's the deal, then? I've been trying to find you for three days."

Sean sounded like a love-crossed girl after she'd given it up to a player who'd ditched her, Corey thought. He wanted to laugh at how hurt Sean sounded, but he couldn't.

"Hey, I'm sorry, a'ight? I'm just trying to get my head on straight." From habit, he slid his hand across his knuckles to feel the ring there, safe. He always wore it now, except in the presence of his parents. He had a feeling he was supposed to.

Sean leaped from Sheba's back and pulled her to the trunk of a thin fir tree beside Corey to tie her. He gazed curiously at Corey's shopping bag. "What's that for?"

"Just some food."

"For her?"

"Why are you in my face? That's none of your business."

"I'm just asking. Drop the attitude," Sean said, and Corey lowered his eyes. Sean was right, he was being a jerk. But he hadn't been able to sleep for three nights straight, and he felt like shit. He didn't usually get nervous when he came to The Spot looking for Becka, but seeing Sean again made his heart trip out. If Gramma Marie's papers were right, Sean had been here the night he might regret the rest of his life.

"Sorry, man. I'm just . . . I don't know. I'm freaked out."

"Well, so am I. Why have you been trying to avoid me? I'm going out of my mind. You told me not to say anything, but come *on*, Corey. This amazing thing happened—this *miracle*—and we can't even talk about it?"

Sean pulled an envelope from his back pocket and held it up for Corey to see. Corey glanced at it and saw that the ivory envelope was addressed to Sean in a handwriting that looked feminine, postmarked from 1992. After seeing the date, perspiration sprang to Corey's palms, the way it did often since the last time he and Sean had been here. Corey didn't want to touch the letter. He had hoped it wouldn't come back, too. Miracle hell.

"Where was it?" Corey said.

"In the mailbox. I found it after you left the other day."

"The picture, too?"

"Just like when it came to me the first time." Sean opened the envelope and pulled out a wallet-sized photograph of a woman with a slightly up-turned nose who almost looked like a teenager herself. "That's my mom. I haven't seen her since I was six. She mailed this when I was seven. But like I told you, I got pissed that she never called me, so I threw it away. I *burned* it with the cigarette lighter in my dad's car." Sean's eyes pranced, maniacal. "Every time I think I dreamed it all, here it is in my hand. My head is coming unscrewed, Corey."

Corey sighed hard, hiking up his knees so he could rest his elbows. He held his head between his palms, feeling his teeth grinding. He couldn't keep this to himself. It wasn't fair. It was different with Mom and Dad, because they weren't involved, and he wanted to keep it that way. But Sean had come with him the night of the spell, so he was probably in this just as deep. The magic had touched Sean, so the rest of it might have, too.

"I thought you'd be *psyched* about this," Sean said. "You don't look like a guy who could conjure himself up fifty million dollars if he wanted to. I thought we'd be figuring what to do next. You know—world peace? A free cure for AIDS? What's wrong with you?"

"Sit down, man," Corey said. His voice hurt his throat, and he was terrified that he was about to cry. He couldn't look at Sean's face. "I didn't tell you everything before."

"What does that mean?"

"Just sit down, and I'll tell you."

"No, you tell me first, and *then* I'll decide if I want to sit down."

It was too late to stop it. A tear smarted in Corey's eye and escaped before he could wipe it away. He'd floated through his day when the ring came back, full of a kind of joy he'd never known he could feel. He'd felt staggered by the idea that there was *nothing he couldn't do*. Then, that night, he'd read every page of Gramma Marie's papers, every word, straight until dawn.

His joy had disintegrated.

"Hey," Sean whispered, seeing Corey's tear. He sank down in front of Corey like the Scarecrow from *The Wizard of Oz*, boneless. "What's going on?"

"We have fucked up *big*," Corey said.

"How?"

"The spell I did—I don't think it worked right."

"What are you talking about, Corey? It worked *exactly* right."

Now, Corey looked at Sean. He had to work to keep his breathing steady, because the thought of admitting the things he'd been keeping imprisoned in his head was bringing him close to panic. "In a *vodou* ceremony, you try to pray to gods, right? There's a whole bunch of them. Whole families of them. There are different gods for different things. They all have different roles."

"Yeah, so?" Sean's eyebrows dipped, scowling.

"When I found Gramma Marie's papers, I skimmed around. It's practically her life story, and I was trying to skip ahead to the good part. But I should have read *all* of what she wrote, because if I had, I would have known better. She was under a curse. It was a bad one, a curse that could live for generations, she said. One of the most powerful gods, Papa Legba, was mad at her for something she'd done, so he left her on her own. This is the first year the curse could have been broken for good, seventy-two years later. It has to do with stars' alignments, things like that. But since I didn't undo the curse *first*, like her papers said I should . . . I don't think the gods heard us."

Sean half-grinned, but his face looked nervous. "I don't get it. Then how'd you get your ring and my letter back?"

"That's what I've been trying to figure out. I think something else brought them back."

"Something else like what?"

"She calls it a *baka*. It's a kind of evil spirit. *Bakas* have powers, too. I think that's what happened that night. What we did was like . . . praying to a demon. And when I prayed and fed it that chicken blood, I might have . . ." *Woken it up*. Those were the words in his mind, the words from Gramma Marie's papers, the words that kept him from sleeping. But he couldn't make himself say those words to Sean, as if there were a physical barrier in his throat.

Sean's face was pasty, nearly the shade of Sheba's coat. "That's why you have this food? To try to get rid of the curse?" He sounded hopeful.

At that, Corey sighed again. Sean would never understand why he brought Becka food, nor would he understand why he'd walked half a mile to the gas station on the Four to buy a box of condoms. Maybe Bo had been right about Sean—maybe Sean wasn't into girls—so he wouldn't appreciate how sometimes a girl could shake you up, how she could get inside your thoughts and make herself at home. Corey's memories of Becka's touch by the fire and their lovemaking in his dreams were more vivid now than before. He *needed* to think about her, or else he started shaking. When he wrote poems about Becka, his heart rested.

He had come here looking for her every day since the spell, waiting, calling for her. Sometimes he could feel Becka watching him, but she didn't come out. But each day, when he came back to look for the food he'd left, the bag was gone. Why would she take it unless she was hungry?

"I don't want to talk about that," Corey said.

"Why are you so hung up on this girl?"

"I said I don't want to talk about that."

"Corey, don't you remember how she showed up here laughing like a freak? She has serious damage. What's wrong with you?"

Sean might as well have been talking about his girlfriend—hell, his *sister*—because rage welled up in Corey, volcanic. "I *said* to shut the fuck up about her. Stop acting like such a little faggot," Corey said. He never used that F-word because he knew gay kids at school and he thought all prejudice was the same bullshit, but it had slipped out before he could stop himself. In fact, he'd wanted to reach over and pop Sean in the mouth, just like the day he'd met him.

Sean's face colored. He pursed his lips, not saying anything.

"Forget it, man. I'm sorry," Corey said. "I don't know where that came from."

"Call me whatever you want, but you've been *way* too strung out on that girl from the minute she showed up here. It's not gay to think something feels wrong about her," Sean said, sounding calmer than he looked. That said, Sean looked away from him, staring back toward the fire-pit.

Corey was shocked to realize he was on the verge of shedding another tear. What *was* wrong with him? He'd said only three or four sentences to that girl, and his emotions were barely within his control. Maybe Sean was right—it was some kind of obsession. Maybe that was why he kept dreaming about her, and why the dreams were so *real*.

"I need to do something about this while I still can," Corey said. His knees were shaking, so he sat cross-legged, hugging the bag of food. "Before something happens to me."

"Let me help you," Sean said, looking back at him, clear-eyed again.

"It's not safe for you to get involved."

Sean waved his mother's letter in front of Corey. "This is a letter from my *mom*. I don't care how I got it, and I'm not giving it up," he said. "That makes me pretty involved."

Corey stared at the glistening gold of the ring on his finger. "Yeah. Same here. I'm keeping it," Corey said, studying the designs that were identical to the ones drawn in Gramma Marie's papers. Those ritualistic symbols were a key, she had written, a coded word of pure magic. Sacred. "If there is an evil spirit, he already made his first mistake—this ring makes me stronger, so we're already ahead of the game. Maybe he didn't have any choice when I asked for it. This ring can help me with the cleansing ceremony. So I can banish it."

"When are you doing it?"

Corey took a deep breath. "Tonight, I think. If I can make myself get ready. Shit, I said the same thing yesterday, but I punked out."

"Then let's do it tonight," Sean said. He held out his palm, ready for a shake.

Corey smiled, hooking Sean's palm, sliding away soul-style. "I'm really sorry, man. I was acting ignorant before. And I'm sorry I brought you out here the other night."

"I'm not sorry," Sean said. "We saw *magic*, Corey. How many other people can say that? My life's going to be different now, even if nothing else like it happens again. It's like, I don't know—it's like seeing *God*. It's the best thing that's ever happened to me."

Seeing Sean's earnest eyes, Corey remembered his day of joy, sparked by the sight of Gramma Marie's ring in the sink, in a place and time it didn't belong. His body shivered and he blinked, nodding. It really had been like staring God dead in the eye and seeing Him smile. He only wished he could forget the dread chewing away at his insides.

"You're right," Corey said. "We just have to fix the curse. After that . . ."

Corey's mind couldn't peek around the corner to *after that*, but he knew something large and important was waiting for him, something that would make retrieving a single ring look like a small feat. Gramma Marie had said he came from a powerful line. Once upon a time, she'd said, his people could fly. That meant he could banish the demon. He *could* do it.

"Come on," Corey said, invigorated, feeling more energy than he'd felt since he'd read Gramma Marie's warnings. "We need to find some raven feathers. And some other obscure stuff it's probably impossible to find in Sacajawea."

"Nothing's impossible," Sean said.

"That's the truth."

While Sean untied Sheba, Corey wrapped up the bag of food and left it beside the fallen tree trunk. He thought about bringing the bag with him for a second, but he decided to leave the food behind—there was no harm in *feeding* Becka. Even Sean didn't ask about the bag, preoccupied with quizzing Corey about what they needed to conduct the banishing ceremony.

Corey's offering to the *baka* sat against the ancient tree, waiting to be found.

Dinnertime was torture. His parents were playing the *Cosby Show* riff, everyone sitting together like a family in the dining room, trying to think of happy things to say. The jambalaya tasted like wood chips in Corey's mouth; his appetite was long gone. But he had to sit and fix a pleasant expression on his face, trying not to fidget, trying to keep his eyes away from the clock on top of the china cabinet, trying to remember to make responses when he was spoken to. His mood pissed off both his parents, but he couldn't help it. His mind was holding him prisoner.

By nine o'clock, as Will Smith's *Willennium* blasted from his bedroom CD player and the sky outside was finally turning dim, Corey wondered how he would find the stamina to pull himself off of his bed and walk to Sean's house. He'd gotten permission to spend the night there, although his mother had asked him why he never invited Sean to spend the night at *their* house. They both knew the answer to that, although he didn't say it: Corey had more freedom at Sean's. He would need it.

Corey left his CD player on all the time now, hoping his parents would assume the music meant everything was fine. No curses, no magic, no problems. But he'd lost his way to the music; it was only the background noise to the thoughts that rang in his head and made his skin feel hot to the touch. Maybe he'd come back to Will and OutKast and Nelly one day, but for now the processed sound was meaningless, like the living room's old piano rolls sitting forgotten in the corner. These songs had nothing to do with him. His music only reminded him that he could be in Oakland thinking about less pressing things, like whose house he would hang out in for the weekend, what movies he'd have to see on opening night, and what clothes he'd buy for school. And oh yeah, that PT Cruiser Dad had promised him in the fall. Those were another person's concerns now. Sometimes, though, the music shut off his brain some and helped him sleep, no matter how loud it was. The louder the better, in fact. Corey welcomed sleep whenever it found him. Ten minutes, maybe twenty minutes, that was the best he could do, but it was better than nothing.

Corey thought he was dreaming again when he heard something scrape against his window, so he ignored the noise. When the scrape became a knock, he opened his eyes.

In the window, Becka was waving at him, bending her fingertips up and down without moving her palm, bobbing gently in the air. Her shadow lurched across his wall, back and forth, in the dusk light from outside. Corey had been staring at her for almost ten seconds before he realized he was wide awake. He sat up with a gasp. *Becka was floating outside his second-story window.*

But she wasn't, of course. Once he dared get to his feet to take a closer look; he realized she was sitting on a tree branch. Granted, it wasn't a branch he would want to sit on—she was high up, probably thirty feet from the ground, and the walnut tree was not a climbing tree. The walnut tree's branches were a long way from its trunk, and those branches were a jumble up there. The branch where she was sitting couldn't be all that sturdy, not growing this close to his window. The gardener sheared the big branches that grew too close to the house, leaving only the thinner ones behind. Yet, Becka was sitting there like an aerialist in a high-wire act. Like it was nothing.

"How'd you get up there?" Corey said, pulling on his windows, which opened into his room like cabinet doors.

Becka smiled, and he noticed again how beautiful her teeth were. "I couldn't always get in this tree, but you should see me climb it now. I climb like a monkey."

Corey didn't like the way the branch was swinging under her weight. It looked like it could snap if she turned her neck to sneeze. "Becka, you better come inside. Just keep quiet so my parents won't hear." Corey peered down at the ground and felt his stomach roll when he saw how high she was. "And hurry, before you fall."

Becka leaned over, resting her elbows on the windowsill. Corey heard something fall when she moved, maybe some walnuts she'd shaken loose. "Thank you for bringing me the food, Corey. That's the nicest thing anyone's ever done for me," she said, ignoring his invitation. Her eyes stared at him with a private message. He hadn't been able to tell if her eyes were gray or blue before, but they were definitely gray. It was possible he'd never seen gray eyes, and he'd certainly never seen any like Becka's. All she had to do was look at him, and Corey's jeans squirmed. He was hard.

On *Willennium*, Will was rapping about the Wild, Wild West, and Corey turned his music down so he could hear if anyone came near his door. Luckily, the wooden floors in the hall were noisy. That was how he knew Dad traded bedrooms sometimes after Corey was in bed.

"I thought you were probably hungry," Corey said. "Where do you live?"

"Out there," she said. "Not far."

"But do you live in a *house*? Do you have a family?"

The sides of her lips curled downward, bored. "Corey . . ."

"Yeah?"

"I came here so you would kiss me. What are you waiting for?"

Corey squatted to meet her at eye-level, leaning close to her in the window, where he could smell her breath. He wasn't quite sure he liked the way she smelled—the pungence bothered him some, although not as much as the first night. Maybe she just needed to brush her teeth. "I wrote you poems," he said.

Sweet honey cream. That was Becka. Wild woman of his dream. That was Becka.

"I wouldn't expect anything less of you," Becka said. "That's why I picked you."

Their lips came together. Becka's wet mouth made love to his, and he followed her lead, until he was sucking on her tongue. They washed each other, tasted each other. She took his hand and led it to her chest, inside her dress, allowing him to feel the pliable mounds of her bare breasts. Her nipples felt like pearls to his fingertips. He had never touched a bare nipple. Corey's face was under a sheen of sweat by the time the kiss ended, and he pulled away, his crotch making his jeans feel as if they were full of rocks. No, not rocks. Hot coals. An eager agony.

"Come with me," Becka said. "Sneak out the back door and meet me outside. I'll show you where I live. Don't you want to see?" Becka's hand dropped to his knee, and she rubbed a circle with her index finger. His knee trembled so badly, he had to lean against the wall to keep his balance.

"Right now?" he said.

"Yeah, right now. Meet me outside, out back."

He could do that, he realized. He could tell his parents he was leaving for Sean's and meet Becka instead. He could go into the woods with her. *He could do it.*

"What's in your pocket?" she said suddenly, and he was sure she must be talking about his boner, but his erection was shifting left and Becka was pointing right. He stared down. He was carrying the ring in his right pocket, where it had been since dinner. It was so small, it looked like nothing more than a crease.

"You can see that?" he said.

"What is it? Show me."

Corey reached into his pocket for the ring, but he felt a jolt of uneasiness. As weird as his first meeting with Becka had been, this one was weirder. Weird squared. The girl had risked her life to climb a tree, and now she was fishing after Gramma Marie's ring right off. Corey imagined how a drunk must feel when he first starts feeling sober, wishing he could feel drunk again.

Corey slid the ring onto his ring finger, securing it, then he held it up for Becka. Wearing it, he felt better. Becka leaned further through the window to stare at the ring with wide, eager eyes. Again, Corey heard something from the tree fall, thumping softly to the grass far below.

"The *boy* puts the ring on the *girl's* finger," Becka said.

"Stop being crazy, girl. Come in out of the tree."

"Can't I hold your ring?" She was gripping his hand tightly. So tightly, really, that he wondered how she could exert so much strength without it showing in her face. She ran her thumb across the ring, and each time she touched it, he felt more jumpy.

Sherita, all over again. That was how it had started in fifth grade. "I don't think . . ."

Becka's gray eyes talked to him, pleading. "Corey, don't you like me like this?"

She sounded hurt, and suddenly he felt awful for hurting her. "Of course I like you, Becka. I told you, I wrote poems for you."

"Don't you like my face?"

Maybe it was the light, something about the purples and oranges in the space between dusk and night, but in that instant Becka looked like a dancer on an MTV video, fresh and impossible to own. "Becka, you have a beautiful face," he said. "Everything about you is beautiful."

"Let me hold your ring," she said. "Pretty please?"

Corey's heart thundered. What was wrong with him? The girl just wanted to hold the ring. She was outside *in the tree,* for God's sake. He didn't have to be such a dick about it.

There were two knocks on his door. "Corey?" his mother's voice called.

Corey shot up to his feet as she tried the doorknob, but the door was locked. His door was always locked now, because there was too much his parents might see if they walked into his room unannounced. Things he would have to explain, but wouldn't know how to.

"This door isn't supposed to be locked," Mom said, knocking again.

"Just a second!" Corey called. Becka was smiling at him, already pulling away from the window, her branch bobbing more violently beneath her. "Are you okay out there?" he whispered.

She nodded, still smiling. Somehow, he believed her despite the way she was rocking. Her face was so cocksure that Corey could believe she *lived* in a tree. "Sorry I have to do this. Stay there a minute," he whispered, then he closed the windows, hiding them behind his heavy curtains.

His room went dark.

Another knock, louder. This time, Corey heard his father's voice instead. "Corey, your mama said open the door." Dad rode him harder when he was around Mom, trying to score points with her.

"Dag, I'm just taking a nap!" Corey said. The irritation in his voice wasn't a lie. He quickly closed his desk drawer first, then his closet door. Especially his closet.

"I thought you were spending the night at Sean's," Mom said.

"Yeah, I am. Guess I dozed off." Corey fumbled to unlock the door.

His parents were together in his doorway, a united front. They didn't usually stand this close together, as if they were afraid to brush each other's skin, but in his doorway they looked like old times. Better than old times. Shorty and the Giant, he used to call them, because Mom made Dad look like Shaquille O'Neal, and Dad made Mom look so little, like a doll.

"If you're so tired, why in the world are you going over to Sean's?" Mom said, flipping on his light. "Stay here and get some sleep."

"I'm okay," Corey mumbled. He heard the tree branch bump against the windowsill, and his eyes went back toward the curtains to make sure his parents couldn't see Becka swinging outside. There was a small crack in the curtains, but he couldn't see anything, so he felt himself relax. A little. "I'll leave in a minute."

Mom wasn't the kind of person to wait for an invitation to come into his room, so she walked past him to get a look around. Corey could see her head working: His door had been locked, so she figured he was doing something he didn't want them to see. She glanced toward the window first. Mom didn't miss a trick. She was like Miss Cleo, that psychic on TV.

Please let her stay away from the window, he thought.

He also hoped she wouldn't look under his bed, where she would see the bowl of water he had left there because it might help Gramma Marie find him in his dreams. Or the closet, where he'd hidden the items he and Sean had collected during their wild run to Portland in a car Sean borrowed from a friend. Corey had seen a listing for a Portland *botanica* in the Yellow Pages, and he was thrilled at how much he'd found in the large store, labeled as plainly as supermarket shelves: John the Conqueror root, virgin parchment for petitioning the gods, goats' horns, coconuts, cowrie shells, scented candles, and incense. He had enough to do a simple cleansing ceremony tonight. The ring's symbols were more important than the ritualistic items, she said; but the more complete his offerings, the better his chance of putting the *baka* to sleep for good.

Sean's brother Andres had even killed a raven for them with his BB gun, like he'd promised he could, and Corey and Sean had stripped the dead bird of its feathers. Those, too, were in the duffel bag in his closet. Andres didn't know or care why Sean wanted the raven feathers; he just liked shooting birds. For once, Sean said he was glad his brother was so trigger-happy. The raven feathers would make Corey's blessings stronger. Maybe the raven could substitute for a dove.

First, Corey had to get past Mom and Dad tonight. Especially Mom, who was gazing at him with questions in her eyes. Corey didn't have the energy to come up with lies that would make her questions go away. He was too tired for lies tonight. He could sleep for a month solid.

"Next time," Mom said slowly, "Sean should spend the night here. All right?"

Corey nodded. She didn't like it when he didn't answer verbally, so he said, "Yeah, okay."

"And could you remind Sean and his father about the party Thursday? I need to know how many people to plan for."

"I don't think they'll come," Corey said. He had no intention of telling Sean's family about his mother's Fourth of July party. He wished he could skip it himself.

"Well, just ask him, please."

"Yeah, okay."

"We're thinking about hitting a movie in Longview tomorrow," Dad said. "The three of us."

"Great," Corey said, trying to smile.

The branch hit the window harder this time. Corey forced himself not to look again, or he'd be busted. He wondered if Becka was playing with him, making noises on purpose.

"Don't you want a vote on which one?" Dad said. "*Dr. Dolittle 2* or *Pearl Harbor?*"

"Whatever's good," Corey said. "Doesn't matter, as long as we all go."

Corey congratulated himself on that last line, because it had an immediate effect on their faces, wiping away most of the suspicion in Mom's eyes. Mom smiled, satisfied, and Dad winked at him, even curling his arm around Mom's waist, something Corey hadn't seen him do since he'd been here. Something he hadn't seen Dad do in *forever*. Even while they still lived together, Mom and Dad hadn't kissed each other hello or good-bye or shown any signs of liking each other for at least a year before Dad left, maybe longer. Corey had been wishing for this for four years—for *this* exactly—and his heart was giving him a big *So what?* It didn't feel fair.

Maybe this will all hit me later, he thought. He hoped so. He felt sad, almost tearing up.

But Corey couldn't feel sad long. Suddenly, he realized he was still wearing Gramma Marie's *ring.* He'd forgotten about it. He'd been too worried about hiding Becka, too worried his parents would see the hard-on that refused to die in his jeans. Cursing himself, Corey shoved his hand into his pocket, hiding the ring.

He had to finish this soon, before he cracked up. He wasn't a good liar, not like Dad, who thought Corey was too stupid to notice he liked to get high sometimes, leaving traces of white powder on his nose-hairs. Even before, in L.A., Corey had heard Dad on the telephone talking to some woman all the time; he could tell it was a woman just by the way Dad's voice changed, loosening up and laughing for somebody who wasn't Mom.

Corey couldn't live like that. He couldn't live like *this.* He wished he'd never found those papers in the closet, that Gramma Marie had stayed dead and gone.

Bag this shit. He could get *laid* tonight. Why was he fucking around with spells?

As usual, Mom saw through him. She'd always been able to. *Always.* As soon as Corey thought about Becka again, Mom's eyes went straight for his curtains. Becka hadn't made a noise this time, but something was pulling Mom's attention there. Knowing Mom, she could probably smell her.

Mom walked toward the curtains slowly, taking her time like it was a stroll, glancing around the rest of his room. "Corey, you know we want you to have a good time"—as she passed his desk, her eyes swept over that, too, and he was glad his notebook was closed, his poems for Becka out of sight—"but your dad and I are worried about the way you've been acting the past couple days. Is there something you need to tell us?"

"No." His voice wasn't convincing. "Like what?"

Dad slapped Corey's biceps, his version of a hug. "We're still tight?" he said, sounding phony. Dad didn't like hard conversations, just easy ones. He must want to get laid tonight, too.

"Sure, Dad," Corey said, but his eyes were on Mom as she made her way across the room. He tried to think of a reason to tell her to stay away from the window, or a way to warn Becka she was coming, but his mind was a blank. And his back was soaked with sweat.

She knows. Corey's brain couldn't move past that thought. And sure enough, as if Mom were purposely trying to surprise someone, she flung his curtains open and stared out of his window. Fuck this, Corey thought. Fuck it. He would have to tell. He'd tell everything.

When his mother turned around to look at him, Corey couldn't believe his eyes: She was smiling. "Did I ever tell you this used to be my room when I was your age?" she said.

"Yeah." Corey's lips had almost stuck together when he tried to speak.

"I knew a boy who climbed this tree to ask me to my senior prom."

"For real?" Corey was so relieved, he managed to sound genuinely interested, although Mom told him that same story each summer.

"You keep on reminiscing, and I'll cut that tree down," Dad said, pretending to sound jealous.

"Over my dead body, fool."

Corey stood beside her, gazing out of the window over her shoulder. The branch where Becka had been sitting was empty, but it was still swinging, as if she'd hopped to the ground. Seeing the branch more closely, noticing how thin it was, Corey wondered how it hadn't snapped under her weight. That girl was crazier than he'd thought. She was Rick James's Super Freak, come to life.

Dad came to stand near them, draping one arm over him and one arm over Mom. Shorty and the Giant both wanted to be near him, and near each other. This was really something, Corey realized. This was a miracle as big as bringing back Gramma Marie's ring.

"Snook, go on and keep hold of your memories," Dad said. "I'd never touch that tree. That tree's got tales to tell. Besides, you know I wouldn't hurt something you love."

"I know that, baby," Mom said. For a long time, she didn't say anything else. When she did, her voice sounded soft like Becka's. "But I sure love the way it sounds when you say the words."

They had both said the word *love*, one after the other.

This was going to be his last summer in Sacajawea. That night, standing near his parents, Corey just knew.

☙ *Twenty-Nine* ☙

FRIDAY AFTERNOON

$\mathfrak{M}$OST OF THE SACAJAWEA COUNTY Sheriff's Department was on Gramma Marie's property by noon, with Rob Graybold taking blood samples from the wine cellar while four deputies searched the woods for signs of Tariq. Neither Tariq nor his van had been spotted in Sacajawea, but at the jailhouse Art had said Tariq was here. Art's word counted for a hell of a lot suddenly.

Instead of making her feel safe, the police presence felt foolish to Angela. And temporal. The police would not be here long, she knew, because they would be needed elsewhere. The future was no longer a mystery to her, at least not the pieces she was closest to. Her foreknowledge had shown up ugly so far, but she didn't have to hold her breath or cross her fingers or make a wish. She knew.

When Tariq finally came for her, she was going to be alone.

In the end, she remembered, you are always alone.

While she waited for Tariq, Angela saw Gramma Marie's living room with new eyes. Gramma Marie had collected porcelain figurines, their stunted shapes crowding the mantle, the windowsills, the top of the piano. Most of them had smiling faces, idyllic representations of how little boys love puppies or how little girls love pigtails, and how grand a man and woman look on their wedding day. Other porcelain pieces depicted fat, luscious strawberries on the vine or watermelon slices so ripe they were the color of strawberries themselves. Even the stout black mammies in their red handkerchiefs were smiling, offering wishes for a happy day.

But there were other figures scattered among them, and Angela was noticing them for the first time, not just in passing. Really *seeing* them.

Angela had never liked these rude clay dolls. They weren't smiling like the other figurines. Most of them lacked clearly defined features, but even those with cowrie shells for eyes and noses had no mouths for smiling. These figurines were at work, not at play.

They were Gramma Marie's gods, hidden in plain sight.

Each time Angela found one of the mud-colored clay figures, she took it to the table in the dining room, where she had amassed a large collection of them, nearly thirty. A white votive candle burned in the center of the table, one she'd found easily by opening the china cabinet's lower drawer. She knew where things were more and more, if only she paid attention, her knowledge coming with the feeling of a sudden, sharpened memory, as if she'd placed everything there herself. She'd never emptied that drawer since Gramma Marie's death, one of the few spaces left unchanged.

Angela felt sorrow as she remembered how carelessly she'd dismantled Gramma Marie's altar in her bedroom after she died, boxing up her crucifix, her candles, her shells, her cigar boxes, her bottles, and her beads, setting the crammed box out in front of the house to be taken with the next trash pickup. Destroying that altar was the first thing she remembered doing as the new owner of the house. She'd almost felt *hostile* toward it, as if that altar stood as a reminder that no matter how much she loved and respected Gramma Marie, the woman had been primitive at heart, victim to the silly superstitions that thrived in places where people felt helpless to control the world around them. Africans who needed rain. Slaves who needed to feel their souls were free. Sharecroppers and poor farmers desperate to believe they could feed their families.

She'd wanted to bury that part of Gramma Marie as soon as she could. Looking back on it now, Angela realized she'd been afraid of it. She'd been trying to run away.

Luckily, or due to circumstances where luck wasn't even invited, more of Gramma Marie and her *loas* remained in the house than Angela had remembered. The figurines, for one. For another, a beaded rattle made from a dusty gourd that had been on top of the refrigerator for so many years it was embarrassing. But instead of throwing it away, Angela had always asked Mrs. Everly to keep the rattle in place. Now, the rattle had a place on the dining room table, beside the candle. Between the figurines. Under the gaze of the photograph of Gramma Marie and Red John she'd placed here, too. Her ancestor altar.

The sepia-colored picture was staged: Gramma Marie wore a puffy-sleeved white dress very unlike her usual manner of dressing. At home, she'd preferred housedresses spun from light, colorful fabrics; and if there was company, she'd been rigid about her navy blue skirts and plain white blouses, something that had reminded Angela of Mary Poppins when she was young. Although Angela had never met John, she guessed he'd felt as awkward as he looked in the formal woolen suit he'd buttoned to his neck, pinching his face. The blurrily painted background, a farm scene of a wheelbarrow filled with hay, was also wrong. That hadn't been Gramma Marie either.

But their faces were in sharp, clear focus. Gramma Marie was a young woman, her skin rolling smoothly across every rise and hollow of her face. Angela had never favored her grandmother, but she felt as if she were staring at herself, transplanted. The photograph looked so vivid now, she expected to see Gramma Marie blink her eyes.

Finally, Angela thought. Gramma Marie was here.

Angela had put away the white linen tablecloth that had been on the dining room table since her arrival in Sacajawea. In its place, she'd gone upstairs and found an African-patterned scarf Naomi had left behind in her bureau drawer. She had to dig beneath the dead leaves still hiding in the drawer to find it, but the scarf greeted her eyes with its pink and purple patterns. Angela had seen Naomi wear this scarf many times, and she smelled Giorgio when she pressed it to her face. Angela's insides blistered at the unexpected reminder of her friend's essence. The smell went deep, past her walled-in thoughts, bringing Naomi's voice to her head—*To Angela Toussaint, the strongest, smartest woman I know*—and an image of Naomi's smiling teeth that nearly knocked her from her feet. Smell could do that. Smell just took you where it wanted you to go.

But the moment passed. Angela had sucked in a tearless sob, closed each door upstairs as if she were quarantining the house after the police search of every room, then brought Naomi's scarf downstairs with her. There was important business at the table. Naomi's spirit belonged there, too.

The official word had come an hour ago: Naomi Price's body was in the trunk of a rusted Plymouth Gran Fury at a farmhouse a few miles south of downtown Vancouver, half an hour from the Sutton Place Hotel. She had been dead at least twenty-four hours. Blunt head trauma and asphyxiation, or so the police thought. Six different people had seen a man who looked like Tariq loading a large, overstuffed suitcase into the sliding door of his green VW van outside of the hotel. With a black poodle on his heels.

Art was right about the dry-cleaning bag, too. Naomi's face had still been wrapped inside it.

"Angie?" Rob spoke quietly from the kitchen doorway, hat in his hand as if the dining room were a cathedral. She didn't know how long he'd been in the room with her. A stern-faced young man stood behind him shaking rain from his hat, a deputy she remembered from Art's house. Both of them were fitted with navy blue bullet-proof jackets. Angela noticed that Rob was also wearing the pendant she'd given him at the jail that morning, listing off-center across his vest.

"I've got some samples of that blood, darlin', and we'll send some more analysts out here later," Rob said, and Angela didn't dispute him, although she knew no one would ever come to study the blood in her cellar. That part of the day had already been decided. "Have you met my under-sheriff, Colin McBride?"

The young man reached for her hand, and Angela accepted his firm grasp. "Pleasure, ma'am," he said, and Angela couldn't answer his lie back.

"There's been a pileup on the Four, near the county line," Rob said. "I called Colin and Maritza in from their sweep of the woods. I have to shift some manpower."

"A rockslide," Angela said, knowing an instant before she spoke.

Rob's eyes lingered on hers a moment, but he didn't ask how she knew. "Yeah, it's a bad one. A logging rig and a bunch of cars tangled, and both lanes are closed. Probably at least one fatality, Darlene says. That means I've got to go, and I'm taking two of my men with me. But Colin and Maritza will be here as long as I can spare them."

Angela glanced at the young man again, who nodded assuredly at her, lowering his chin. He looked like a boy. She'd given pendants to all of the officers on her property, but as far as she could see, Colin wasn't wearing his.

"Can I speak to you alone, Rob?" she said.

Rob shifted his weight impatiently from one leg to the other, but he gestured for the man to give them privacy. Angela waited until she heard the back door open and close before she went on.

"Don't leave those kids here," Angela said. "There's nothing they can do for me, except die."

"Those are my two best officers, Angie. Top-flight. Colin is—"

"That's not what I mean and you know it."

Rob frowned, staring out of the dining room window toward the deck, where Colin waited restlessly, glancing at his watch. Maybe it was only swagger, but the young man looked eager to find something most people wouldn't dare go seeking. "Don't give me problems, Angie," Rob said. "That car wreck is my responsibility because we've got a dead person, and that trumps *maybe* or *might*. I also have to make sure you're not here alone when we all have a damn good idea Tariq is coming after you today. I still don't see why the hell you won't just—"

"Leaving this house isn't the answer. Did it help Naomi?"

"I'm sick of arguing. But if you're here, my officers are here. Period."

"Any officers on this property have to wear the pendants."

"Fine by me," Rob said. "Can't hurt."

Angela hoped no one had died on her behalf in the rockslide, and that no similar mishap would find Rob or his officers. Would the ferry from Westport develop sudden mechanical problems, too? Maybe cutting off the town from the south and the east was part of whatever was coming for her. Maybe it didn't want anyone else leaving, anyone else coming. No interference for its work.

"Where's Myles? Is he gonna stay with you awhile?" Rob said.

"He said he'll be back soon." Myles was taking Ma Fisher to a nursing home in Skamokawa, where he thought she might be safer. Angela was glad Myles hadn't decided to take Ma Fisher to Longview, or he'd have been cut off by the rockslide. Maybe the charm was working for Myles, she thought. *Please, God, let it work.*

"Angie, do you have a gun in the house?"

"No. We've never had a gun in this house." It was a relief to say it, vindication.

Rob bent over, reaching inside his right pant-leg. With a gleam of metallic light, he pulled out a handgun that looked like a toy. "Take my .38," he said. "Do you know how to fire a gun?"

She shook her head, smiling sadly. "A gun won't help me, Rob," she said.

"That's right, and a piece of shit-colored clay around our necks won't help me or my deputies. Take the damn gun," he said, and Angela relented. When she held the heavy gun in her palm, Rob stood beside her with a calm instructor's voice. "Safety's here. See? There's the trigger. Just takes a squeeze. Aim for the chest or the back, where there's the most body mass. Never fire blind. See what you're shooting. You have five shots."

Angela tried to thank him, but her mouth wouldn't open. She felt wearied by the realization that Rob was teaching her how to kill someone. And he was good at it.

Rob surveyed the altar, then his eyes came back to hers. "My family had ministers to spare, so I know about praying. Praying is fine, so you go on and pray, as long as you don't forget Jesus while you're at it. I'm praying, too. But God helps those who help themselves. If you have to fire that thing, Angie, *do it.*"

"Thanks, Rob," she whispered.

Tariq's soul was already dead. She could shoot a dead man if she had to.

Rob hugged her, a solid embrace that nearly cut off her breath, so quick it was over as soon as it began. "I'm sorry about your friend. We'll catch that sonofabitch," he said.

But as he made the vow, Rob's eyes were dim with doubt.

Myles had left his house only thirty minutes ago.

Thirty minutes ago, he and Candace had coaxed Ma into the car and driven to the Riverview nursing home in Skamokawa, and the move had been as smooth as satin. Ma had no complaints, no questions, no concerns. Ma thought it was a beautiful day despite the rain, chatting about how pretty everything was as she stared out of her car window. Her smile had faded when they parked in front of Riverview—which wasn't a bad-looking place, more like a little retreat than a hospital—but when he asked her to give him her hand so he could help her out of the car, she'd agreed more readily than usual. He'd been surprised when he looked at his watch and saw the move had taken only twenty minutes. Candace had stayed with Ma, and Myles thought he was free.

But he had misplaced his phone. His mobile wasn't in the car cradle, it wasn't on the seat, and it wasn't in his pocket. Now that he thought about it, he could *see* where he'd left it, on his kitchen counter in the Mexican clay bowl Diego had sent him for a birthday a couple of years back, one he'd gotten on a cruise to Cozumel with his mother. The bowl was home to Myles's keys, his wallet, and his cell phone, the first place he looked.

On the day of an emergency, he thought, you don't walk out of your house without your phone. It was bad enough he hadn't had time to put on his contacts this morning, but he couldn't do without his mobile. He had to go back home.

Besides, he needed a weapon today.

Myles had cut off the news station in his car because Ma preferred music, but he found his favorite AM station with one jab of a button as he drove east on the Four, back toward Sacajawea. ". . . back to this bizarre story about the death of Naomi Price, who was found stuffed in a trunk in Canada. Caller, you're saying she was in the Portland area a few days ago?"

A teenage girl sounded like she was hysterical. "Oh, my god, *yes*. She signed an autograph for me at the airport last week, and she was *sooooooooo* beautiful. I'm in line at the gift shop at PDX and I'm, like, 'Isn't that Naomi Price?' And she sees me looking over and she *smiles*, all friendly. . . ."

The story had already leaked to the press? There couldn't have been time to notify Naomi's family properly, Myles thought. He'd been at the sheriff's office when Rob Graybold got the news, exactly an hour ago. Somebody up in Vancouver must be whispering, *Hey, you'll never guess who we found stuffed in a trunk today*. Maybe the farmers who owned the Gran Fury were hawking tickets to their neighbors. Naomi's family must have learned the hard way.

Back when Myles was still writing newspaper obituaries because he hadn't yet moved up to stories about the living, a college professor had died, and the college's public relations department efficiently faxed him a list of friends of the deceased. Calling from the list to get the reactions of people who cared about the dead professor—because Myles had taken pride in writing good obituaries, getting the facts right, resurrecting souls for at least a day—he had identified himself and his business to one of the professor's listed friends. "Could you tell me what kind of man he was?"

The stranger's voice had crumbled. "He's dead?"

Buddy dead.

"Naomi Price, you've got strangers crying on the radio, sweetheart," Myles said as his car pitched gently into his driveway, rolling over roots that felt like speed bumps. "Bless your heart."

Myles looked over both of his shoulders for Tariq's van, surveying the road to the house, the yard near the shed. Clear. He thought he'd seen that van on the way to Riverview, but it had turned out to be an SUV painted the same color, driving toward Longview. Did he really think Tariq would leave himself in sight? Have the van waiting in his driveway?

Myles turned the radio off and got out of his car. He didn't have the stomachache Angie was so terrified of, but his head hurt like hell. Myles had studied Rob's face as Rob took detailed notes during his call from police in Vancouver—when they both realized Art knew things Art had no business knowing—and Rob knew a war when he saw one.

Somehow, Art Brunell and Tariq Hill were buddies, twisted soul mates. Maybe Art had managed to get a call to Tariq from jail, or the details of

Naomi's murder had been planned far in advance. Maybe Art and Tariq had run into each other in the River Saloon one day years back and struck up a conversation. *I'm fine, how 'bout yourself? Kids are a royal pain in the ass, aren't they? How 'bout I kill my kid, and you kill that actress—you know the one?* Art had plotted to kill Glenn when the time was right. Then, together, they'd orchestrated the death of Naomi Price, with Art spilling his guts just in time for the sensational discovery of the body.

Their plan, whatever it had actually been, was brilliant in its senseless sickness. Myles had spent years documenting human sickness, the price of his job as a police reporter back at the New York *Daily News*, the Miami *Sun-Sentinel*, and then *The Washington Post*, when he'd decided he wanted to sit behind an editor's desk instead of reporting from the field. Myles was glad he'd left D.C. before the Twin Towers fell or the sniper rampage in his old backyard, because he'd had his fill of human monstrosity long ago. David Wolde, the black serial killer in Miami, had ruined Myles's appetite for news-gathering. The man's wife, Jessica, had worked with Myles on the Miami newspaper staff. Myles had met David Wolde and the little daughter he killed, his last victim. He'd known that child since she was a baby, and he'd had to write the 1A story about her murder at her father's hands.

No need to blame demons, Myles knew. There were plenty of humans to spread the misery.

Angie didn't understand that. She was shaping every new discovery to fit her conviction that human behavior alone could not explain Art and Tariq. She and Liza had sat under Art's spell, eager to believe his psychopathic fantasies. Myles's brow hardened with anger as he remembered being roused from sleep, summoned to that lunatic's jail cell. Since when could an inmate demand a guest? And why the hell would Rob subject Angie to something so awful? Rob *knew* better.

The world had gone insane overnight.

Myles stood in his driveway, nervous about walking into his own house in full daylight. He studied the house again, taking visual inventory. Curtains drawn in the living room. Lights off. No sounds that he could hear, except squabbling seagulls on the water out back.

Still, a deep unease tickled Myles, and he suddenly realized why: It was an *empty* house. He hadn't thought about it in the commotion; in the haste of packing Ma's things, trying to get her to Riverview before registration closed at noon, and, incidentally, trying to dodge a murderer who might be coming after him personally.

But here he was. He had sent Ma away, and she was gone. Maybe he could bring her back when this problem with Tariq passed, but he probably would not. He was losing her. *This* was the true state of his life, not the bubble of denial he'd been living in the past few months, telling Luisah how good he had it. He didn't have it good. A wonderful actress, a friend of Angie's, had been murdered, and after Angie already had lost so much. He had an ex-wife so unhinged that she still couldn't speak a civil sentence, and she'd only allowed Myles to see his stepson ten times in fourteen years because he had no legal power and she was so jealous of the boy's time. He had one mother dead, another dying. And he'd been doomed to cross paths with men like David Wolde, Art Brunell, and Tariq Hill, who were a mystery to him, who appalled his soul.

On days like today, it was hard to see God's hand at work in the world.

Are you seeing it yet, Myles? Angie had asked. More and more, Myles couldn't blame her. He had learned the scripture from the Book of Matthew in Sunday school, one he'd memorized to recite for Ma and Pa Fisher: *Put on the whole armor of God, that ye may be able to stand against the wiles of the devil.*

"For we wrestle *not* against flesh and blood, but against principalities, against powers, against the rulers of the darkness of the world . . . against spiritual wickedness in high places," Myles murmured as he walked the S-shaped path to the front door of his first real home, the home God had brought into his life in answer to his prayers as a boy. This home had been his *evidence* of God. Ma had always expected him to be a preacher, and he might have gone to a seminary if he hadn't loved writing about the world so much. God still might call him one day.

Maybe God was calling him today.

Myles climbed the two concrete steps to the narrow porch of his parents' bungalow. "Wherefore take up the whole armor of God, that ye may be able to withstand in the evil day, and having done all, to *stand.*" Myles's voice cracked as he remembered Naomi Price's painfully lovely face, how he'd held her hands and helped her pray. Hot tears moistened his eyes. Myles whispered the rest. "*Stand* therefore, having your loins girt about with truth."

The front door came open with barely a touch, unlocked. Hardly closed.

Inside, wreckage awaited him.

The living room's furniture was upside down. The sofa and chairs were on their backs, the coffee table's legs in the air. The photographs on the mantel were facing the wall, lined up meticulously. Vandalism was one thing, but this felt planned to the minute. Myles's skin went cold.

The dining room—which Myles had painted and decorated himself, struggling not to lose touch with his life—was a contrast, the picture of rage. The table and chairs had been sliced and splintered to pieces, thrown around the room like cracked chicken bones. His masks were broken. Left-over food from the refrigerator was spattered over the dining room walls and the kitchen floor; streaks of red sauce, grains of cooked rice, curried chicken from Ming's, sour-smelling milk.

The kitchen's black tiles were covered in powdery white flour tracks made by a small dog, by the look of it. Onyx. How they'd orchestrated *that* part, Myles didn't know, but the thought that Art might have helped Tariq steal the woman's dog before killing her was another peak in sickness.

They were monsters, both of them. The human kind. And Tariq had been here.

Diego's beautiful Mexican bowl was broken to dust on the tiles, deliberately crushed nearly beyond recognition, but the mobile phone on the floor beside it looked fine. Myles picked it up and dialed 911. The dispatcher picked up on the first ring, but the static was awful. "Emergency," he heard a woman say amidst an ocean's roar.

Myles's head pivoted around the room as he watched for motion, speaking softly. "Darlene? This is Myles Fisher, over at 620 Eagle's Nest. Tariq was here. He's trashed my house."

A sustained *sssssssssssssss* sound made it impossible to hear most of what she said, but her voice came back at the end, clear as a summer sky. ". . . on the Four. The road's blocked, and without units from Cowlitz County, we may not have the personnel to run out there. But I'll tell Rob—"

Myles's line beeped, cutting her off. Myles saw the UNKNOWN CALLER identification, and the back of his neck twitched. He clicked to the incoming line, but he didn't speak. No voice taunted him this time. He only heard music playing, Al Green's "Let's Stay Together." He didn't hear any music playing in the house, so maybe that meant Tariq was gone, Jesus help him.

But gone where?

"What can we do to put a stop to this?" Myles said, his voice even, not betraying the part of him that wanted to curse nor the part of him that wanted to beg. "Tell us what to do."

He heard breathing, or he thought he did, maybe a chuckle huffed into the phone. But whatever the noise, it was the only response before the line died. He lost his connection to Darlene, too. When Myles tried to dial Angie's number at the house, his hands felt as if they'd been immersed in freezing water, rubber weights at the ends of his wrists.

Angie's line was busy. That didn't surprise him. She'd told him the phone wasn't working.

"Rob, you'd better be standing right beside Angie like you promised me," Myles said to himself. He'd have to bring more than this dead-ass phone with him to Angie's.

Myles crept his way quietly through the house, his heart thrashing as he neared each hidden corner. They were clear. He made it to his bedroom, which was worse than the rooms he'd left behind. His computer screen and glass sliding door had been shattered, his books and picture frames were strewn across the floor, and there was a mud-colored mound in the middle of his bed that reeked of human feces. But the worst was the feces on the *wall* above his bed, four crude words smeared in shit:

SEE YOU SOON SNOOK

Ma's words. His last good memory with her, when he'd put her to bed and believed she was talking to him; not to Pa Fisher, not to someone of her own invention, but to *him*, her son. Had Tariq fed those words to Ma? But when? How? In that instant, it seemed as if the devil had used Ma to say what was on its mind, and the devil had made a special visit so Myles wouldn't mistake whom he had been talking to. A final fuck-you from Hell.

"This crazy son of a *bitch*," Myles said. The back of his neck felt numb. He had to get to Angie before Tariq did.

Myles was afraid he wouldn't find Pa Fisher's wooden bow intact in all this destruction, but as he stepped gingerly over the thick glass chunks and shards near the deck, he saw the bow against the wall. It had fallen over behind his nightstand, directly beneath the first S in the stinking message on the wall. "Ugh." Myles covered his nose, stooping to reach for the bow.

It would be too much to ask that the bow's string would be intact. Yet, the string was pulled tight, taut and ready. He hadn't hunted since he was twenty, since Pa Fisher died, but the bow-handle fit his hand just right. Myles had fished this bow out of the back shed soon after he came home, looking for good memories to dull the ache of why he was there. He'd laughed when he found the traditional wooden bow, since Pa Fisher rarely hit anything except tree trunks. Myles had grabbed both the bow and the new box of six aluminum arrows, just in case he might feel nostalgic enough to try hunting again. The arrows were supposed to be under his bed.

"Please, Jesus, let them be there," Myles said, because he didn't think he'd have time to go to the shed and look. He'd used up all his time already.

Pulling up the bedspread to gaze under the bed, Myles forgot what had happened to the rest of his room—and the defilement on the mattress—because it was pristine down here. His hiking boots were on the other side of the bed, standing where he'd left them. Two inches from his nose lay Pa Fisher's camouflage-colored quiver and the box of new arrows, their feathers bright green. Myles didn't even remember bringing the quiver from the shed to his room.

That would have been too much to ask.

"Where's Rob?"

Myles stood in Angela's foyer with a bow readied, its arrow tip sharp. He had a quiver strapped to his leg, and he wore a brown parka, ready to hunt. Seeing him, Angela was pulled out of her lethargy: Myles might be the most welcome sight of her life. She was so relieved, she felt a knot loosen in her chest she hadn't known was binding there.

She'd been almost sure Myles was dead, that he'd died at his house. Maybe he had brushed close to it. "Thank God, baby," she said, pressing her lips to his. "Was Tariq at your house?"

"I just missed him. Where the hell is Rob?" Myles glanced around the house, his eyes unblinking. "I only saw Colin out there."

"There are two deputies here, but Rob had to go. There was a rockslide. He gave me this." Angela showed him the .38 she still held in her hand, keeping her fingers far from the trigger. The gun felt like a living creature, subject to an unexpected, deadly tantrum.

Myles looked more alarmed than impressed. "Rob promised me he'd stay *here.*"

He was still missing the point. Angela pressed a palm to his cheek, trying to slacken Myles's knitted face. "Myles, hush. This isn't police business. You know it isn't."

Myles's eyes softened as he looked at her, pitying. But the memory of their lovemaking came to his eyes, too, and the pity vanished. He kissed her, cupping the back of her head with both hands. He kissed her hard and long, as if he needed her mouth to breathe. His kiss was ardent at the start, but resigned at the end. Like good-bye, she thought, unable to help it.

When his mouth pulled back, Angela missed the taste of Myles instantly. Kissing him, her thoughts had politely let her be. Now, Angela had a bad feeling that someone she knew and liked had been killed in the rockslide, another punishment meant for her. But the strongest feeling had been fifteen minutes ago, when she had been sure Tariq was standing on Myles's bed, pressing the linens to his face, trying to smell her.

"Let's get the hell away from here," Myles said. "This is the first place he'll come."

"No it isn't," she said, reminding him. Art had said she would be strongest on her grandmother's property, and maybe Tariq knew that, too. She packed the gun Rob had given her into her handbag, which fit her like a knapsack across her shoulder. She had Corey's index cards there, too, safe and ready. "But there's something I need before I go."

He gave her a look of naked confoundment.

"Can you come upstairs with me, Myles? I think it's upstairs. It's high in the house."

"What is it?"

"Something I need." She didn't know enough to explain it beyond that.

Myles glanced toward the living room, the wine cellar, and then, more warily, at the staircase. She'd swept up all the downstairs leaves yesterday— as many as she could, an act of defiance—but the leaves on the stairs and upstairs were still in plain view. Since yesterday, there was a new incursion: clusters of dry leaves wrapped around the staircase by stringy brown vines entangling the handrail and bannister. The vines looked as if they had been growing for years. Myles didn't comment on the dead vines. He probably wasn't letting himself notice them, she thought.

"Did Rob search this house before he left?" Myles asked.

"Rob and three others. Tariq's not here."

"Well, if he isn't now, he was before. Tariq made this mess, Angie. He made a mess at my place, too. And you should assume he's coming back."

"That's why I need to find what I'm looking for."

Myles considered that, nodding. "All right, let's do it. But quickly."

On the stairs, the leaves were worse than yesterday, in their second or third layer, thick, damp, and spongy beneath their feet. This time, blackened walnut casings—the fruit that covered the shell—were hidden among the leaves, rotting against the floor. Angela nearly slipped on a walnut when she mashed one with her foot on the second-floor landing. "Careful," she warned Myles.

"Sweet Jesus," Myles said. She heard his breathing grow heavier behind her. He must be realizing by now that it wasn't just the leaves that were wrong; the smell was wrong, too. The upstairs smelled dank, as if it hadn't been visited in generations. The air was thin, like a cave.

Upstairs, all the doors were wide open. The doors were open to the bathroom, Gramma Marie's old room on the left, Corey's on the right, Tariq's room down the hall, Naomi's room beyond it, the junk room. And the door was wide open to the attic at the far end of the hall, the last place Rob and the deputies had searched. Angela had closed them all, but she didn't dwell on that.

What bothered her most was Corey's doorway, the first one facing them from the landing. Corey's doorway was blocked by a mountain of leaves, like a giant pile Mr. Everly might have raked up in the yard for burning, as tall as her shoulders.

This mound had not been here a few minutes ago, when Rob had walked straight through that doorway. Angela froze before the mound. As she gazed at it, a voice flew to her from somewhere beyond hearing: *I came so you could kiss me. What are you waiting for?*

A girl's voice. Not a child, not quite a woman.

The memory of a stench—the smell of Art at his house—came in an instant so quick that Angela almost didn't register it. But it was enough to make her throat gag, and she pressed her hand against her face. This time, the smell was from Corey's room. She hadn't always been able to smell it, but the stench had been here all along, under her nose.

"What, doll-baby?" Myles said.

Angela had forgotten Myles was standing beside her. She could think only of Corey.

"*It was here,*" Angela said. As knowledge flooded her, Angela's lips bobbed together before she could go on. "It was *in this room*. My baby was . . . my baby was *talking* to it and didn't know."

Myles lowered his bow, hugging her with one arm. "Shhhh," he said, his face pained. "Angela Marie, hon, let's go back downstairs. We need to get you out of this house."

A sound came again; something she could *hear*, but from beyond her ears. Angela heard a girlish laugh from Corey's doorway. The sound was coming from the leaves.

Angela's thoughts scattered like billiard balls, hiding in any pockets they could find. Suddenly, she understood: Like Sean had told her, things weren't always what they appeared to be. These leaves were not leaves, not the way she knew them to be. The leaves were another mask over something that didn't want to show its face. Or couldn't.

"You bitch!" Angela spat suddenly at the four-foot mound, at someone her eyes couldn't see. She almost lurched at it, except that Myles held her with such a firm hand.

"Don't, Angela. What are you doing?"

Angela panted, not taking her eyes away from the pile of leaves. She didn't blink.

"Are you back here with me?" Myles said.

There was movement from atop the pile; not much, but enough for her to notice. A curled, dried flake *jumped* a half-inch and then fell still. Although her heart dove, Angela felt victorious. Whatever this was, it wanted to hide, but she was seeing it better all the time. She *wasn't* crazy.

"I'm okay," Angela said, smiling for Myles to prove it. Her eyes tried to go back to the leaves, but she made herself remain fixed on Myles's worried face. He obviously hadn't noticed anything strange about the leaves. He would never believe her.

"You're not behaving like someone who's well."

"I'm fine."

"Angie." Myles ran his fingers beneath her chin, a brotherly flutter. "You're not fine. Tell me you understand that. Otherwise, I'm going to have to carry you downstairs. Hear me?"

"Will you *open your eyes?"* she said. "It's as if you don't *want* to see it."

"You're not making your case, sweetheart." Myles's tone was resolute. He would carry her out against her will, she realized. Myles could get them both killed.

Angela backed up a step, in case she would need to run from him. She'd do anything to avoid it, but she might have to. "Myles," she began softly, calming her voice. "Did you enjoy yourself last night, sweetness?"

"Of *course,"* Myles said, blinking.

"Was I just a crazy woman to you last night? You thought you'd better hit it quick before I had a meltdown?"

Two full seconds passed before Myles spoke, his expression rigid. "You know me better than that," he said, but his pause told her he'd asked himself the same question.

"I'm no crazier now than I was in your bed."

"Hon, I just think I might have . . ." Myles paused, maybe trying to soften his words, but the word he chose was not soft. "Misjudged."

"So I'm crazy, period, because you can't decide what another answer might be?"

"You sound more lucid now," he conceded.

"Tell me if I was crazy last night, Myles. Tell me if you misjudged."

"I hope not, Angie, because I love you."

Myles was the first boy who'd spoken the words *I love you* to her, when he was sixteen and the revelation had shocked her into laughter, but this time she craved the words' music in a way she hadn't dared before. Angela kissed Myles's lips, a light caress of her mouth. Their breath mingled, and she felt his breath seep down to her toes.

"I love you, too, baby," Angela said. "You didn't misjudge. Now stand aside and let me do what needs to be done. If you try to stop me, we're about to fight." She had Rob's .38 in her bag, and Myles knew it. Angela did not want to fight.

With a sigh, Myles stepped away from her.

The moment he did, the bathroom toilet flushed.

Myles pinned Angela beneath him against the wall, gazing toward the bathroom, hardly six feet from them. He expected Tariq to fly out of the bathroom and swoop down on them, she thought. But Tariq hadn't flushed that toilet. Angela knew that.

From the bathroom, they heard water splashing down the toilet bowl, taking care of its own business. Myles silently held up a single finger to her: *Stay here.* Like hell. Angela shook her head. This wasn't Myles's burden, it was hers. As he readied his bow again, Angela's hand wandered inside her bag, to touch her waiting gun.

Myles took three steps toward the bathroom, ready to let loose an arrow if anything moved, and Angela followed him. Standing behind Myles in the bathroom doorway, Angela saw the toilet's pull-chain swinging back and forth, its porcelain handle brushing against the wall. But there was no one in the room. The bathtub was empty, including the tub, the best place to hide. The shower curtain was wide open.

"Tariq?" Myles said.

No answer. Myles kicked the bathroom door back, and it slammed against the wall inside. There was no one hiding back there either. But Angela heard the floor squeak in the hall behind her, soft enough to be imagination.

It wasn't. She sensed motion in the corner of her eye and looked back toward Corey's room.

The pile of leaves was now a foot beyond the doorway. *It had moved.*

"Myles," she whispered, tugging his sleeve.

Myles looked where she was pointing. When he did, his cheeks hollowed.

The mound of leaves rustled. A dozen leaves suddenly flew from the pile in a looping dance. They flew as high as the ceiling, deformed butterflies, then floated apart, scattering. As one of the leaves drifted near her nose, Angela yanked her face back. The leaf reeked of decay.

"*Fuck,*" she said. Her skin recoiled.

Somewhere inside the remaining pile of leaves, which seemed bigger now, more cohesive, Angela heard a dry, rattling hiss. The mound hiked itself up, then *crawled* forward, snail-like, before falling still. In that moment of stillness, Angela's heart shook her chest. Her mind begged her to run, but she stared, dumbstruck, as the pile of leaves began to sway. Then, it shot itself two feet closer to her with a fluid, sudden motion Angela had never seen from a living thing.

This time, Angela screamed.

She heard a sound near her ear, Myles's bow. An arrow cut the mound of leaves straight through the center, imbedding deep in Corey's doorframe beyond it. Leaves scattered to the floor, individual pieces again, losing all sense of ever having been a single entity.

But they had been. And Myles had seen it. He couldn't deny it now.

Myles's eyes were riveted to the floor and its bed of half-broken, withered brown leaves. He didn't move, hardly breathing. The lack of an answer had frozen him.

"Am I crazy now?" she said.

Myles shook his head, dazed. He stepped gingerly to the leaves and nudged them with his foot before quickly drawing back. "What *was* that? Where'd it go?"

Good question, she thought. Where was the invisible thing that had been in the leaves?

Angela heard gurgling from the bathtub, and then she knew. "The bathroom," she said.

The whole bathroom was clean, the only room upstairs that could make that claim. The tub sparkled, and no leaves or mud remained. If Angela didn't know better, she'd think Mrs. Everly had come to straighten up today. This was the way she had hoped the bathroom would look when she first brought Naomi here. Well-preserved. Attractive.

But the appearance was a lie. Like Sean had said, things aren't always what they seem.

Don't you like my face?

Angela heard the same chilling, disembodied female voice she'd thought she heard in Corey's doorway. This time, the voice seemed to have come from the bathroom mirror. Angela stood in front of the sink to face the beautiful mirror that was this bathroom's prize possession.

The mirror's reflection showed no trace of her.

Instead of her face, the mirror's glass showed the bathroom behind her; the spanking clean tub, the toilet with its lid open, the washboard on the wall. Seeing her removal from the place she knew she was standing, Angela's mind shriveled. She closed her eyes tightly, like a toddler trying to make something ugly go away.

When Angela opened her eyes, a girl with golden pigtails stared back at her from the mirror, her face caked with mud. Grinning in blackface. The girl's gray eyes laughed at her.

Angela screamed, more in rage than terror, although the terror made her hands shake and rendered her thoughts silent. Spittle flying from her lips, Angela spun in the bathroom for the first heavy thing she could find. She jiggled the porcelain toilet seat to loosen it, yanking with all her strength, then wrenched it free. Regaining her balance, she heaved the seat against the glass.

The grinning girl cracked down the center; the middle of her face, and her eyes, fell away. With another shout, Angela hit the mirror with the toilet seat again, breaking her thumbnail with a sharp ripple that made her yell again, this time in pain. The seat clattered to the floor.

"Sweetheart, *stop,*" Myles said from behind her. He grabbed her hand, leading her out of the bathroom as broken glass cracked beneath her feet. "What the hell are you doing?"

"*I saw her,*" Angela said. "*In the mirror.*"

"Who? Who did you see?"

Angela realized who, and she couldn't bring herself to tell him. Maddie. Ma Fisher. Her face as a girl. She'd recognized Ma Fisher's eyes, gray as the sky outside. Angela clasped their fingers together, and she felt Myles's pulse clambering. Poor guy, she thought. It was selfish to keep him here. But would he leave if she asked him to?

"What did you see in the bathroom?" Myles said.

Angela shivered despite her newfound calm. "The girl who took Corey from me."

"What do you mean? *How?*" He sounded desperate to understand.

Angela shook her head. The girl in the mirror was the ghost of a woman who had yet to die. An echo. She hadn't been like Tariq, not exactly. She'd been something else.

Angela didn't have time to try to explain.

A metallic clang tolled from the bathroom, shaking the walls like the night the tree fell. Myles readied his bow again, and they backed away from the bathroom doorway, farther down the hall. The clang came again, followed by a loud groaning—wood or metal, she couldn't tell—and this time the floor trembled, too. The hallway lights flickered once, then died.

"What *now?*" Myles said, exasperated, not asking her. Asking God, maybe.

The third clang was thunderous, and mud sprayed from the bathroom doorway, as if from a hose. The foul-smelling mud spat across the hall, drenching the floor and walls near Gramma Marie's open doorway. Mud ran down the wall like a soupy human stool. Another spout of mud arced out of the bathroom door—from the *bathtub?* —and this time, the sickly splatter reached as far as the staircase and Corey's room. Watching mud land within an inch of her foot, Angela cried out. She leaped backward, bumping against Myles.

Staring down at the mud, Angela noticed a clump of something drenched inside it, and it took her long seconds to recognize what it was: bird feathers. A lot of them. Chicken feathers.

Rejected offerings, she thought, not sure where the thought came from, or how she was able to think at all. The smell in the hall was overwhelming, dizzying. Angela wanted to vomit, but her throat was paralyzed. All of her was paralyzed.

Almost as if to wash her, water came next.

Grimy water sheeted down the walls of the hallway. Water dripped in droplets from the ceiling, puddling at her feet. Angela couldn't remember when the water had started—from one breath to the next, the water was just *there*. Another clang sounded, and water poured from the ceiling, nearly too heavy to see through. Myles yelled out, trying to shield the top of his head from the dingy, muddy water, as if he expected it to burn him. "We have to *go!*"

Those simple words were a revelation.

The attic, Angela thought, another displaced whim that didn't feel as if it were from her own mind. *We have to go to the attic.* Angela took Myles's hand to lead him, semi-blind in the sudden onslaught. Myles followed, cursing words she'd never heard him say aloud. The leaves beneath their feet were slippery from mud and water, and both of them skidded trying to run toward the attic at the end of the hall. Myles's bow caught in the doorway, nearly knocking him off-balance, but they pulled the bow inside and slammed the door closed behind them.

It wasn't raining on the attic stairs. Here in the narrow attic stairwell, there was peace.

Their breathing mingled, shallow and panicked, in too much darkness. Not enough light from the attic window was reaching them at their odd angle on the stairs. "Light," Angela whispered, a prayer. If she didn't see light soon, she would faint from pure fear. Images of dancing leaves and flying mud glutted her mind.

A circle of light switched on. Myles had brought a flashlight, she realized vaguely, grateful. The grooves between the planks of the wall came into sight, and everything behind the closed attic door suddenly seemed very distant. She could still hear the water falling in the hall, but it wasn't in here. It *couldn't* come in here, she realized.

This was the place. This was where Gramma Marie wanted her to go.

Behind her, Myles's breathing was a labored wheeze; she hadn't known until now that fear made it so hard to breathe. She climbed the stairs, toward the hazy light above them, clinging hard to the wooden pole that served as a bannister.

"When Gramma Marie first came to work here, she and my mama had to sleep up here in the attic. The man who owned this house thought people would gossip if she lived in the main house. She was young then. And *pretty*." Angela knew she was rambling, but rambling gave her solace.

"It's not leaking up here," Myles observed, ignoring her. He had gravel in his voice. He needed to understand why it was raining in the house. He didn't know yet that he never could.

"In summertime, it was hard to sleep up here at night," Angela went on, feeling her fear unclogging. "All the heat collected until you couldn't do anything but swim in it. The baby didn't mind, but Gramma Marie would lie awake all night and wait for morning. She was just so grateful to be on the land, on *this* land, she never complained. Not once. She would read by an oil lamp. And sew clothes for Mama. And cry over her husband who died. You know how I know, Myles?"

Myles didn't answer her. For now, he was lost from her, trapped inside his questions.

"She never told me, but I remember it now. I *remember*," Angela whispered.

By the time they reached the attic and the dim sunlight, Angela was blinking away tears of relief and hope. She had walked here before. Through Gramma Marie, the soles of her feet had touched these stairs before she'd been born.

The ceiling was so low that Angela could barely stand at her full height, and Myles hunched over as he walked behind her. Dust teemed in Myles's flashlight beam as they surveyed the space, which spanned the entire second story of the house. Boxes were piled neatly against the walls, leaving the unfinished floor almost clear. Spiderwebs swathed the corners like party decorations. Angela lifted a tarp and found a stack of wooden planks, old building materials. On the floor, there were cans of blue paint, the color of the house, the color of the closet door in the junk room.

Gramma Marie had painted that closet door downstairs herself, Angela realized. To make it easier to find. And one small part of the wall was painted blue up here, near the attic window.

"It's completely *dry* up here," Myles said, crouching, feeling the dusty wooden floor. "Could that water be coming from pipes below us? Is there a way Tariq could be doing that?"

Angela didn't answer. Let Myles surrender his logic in his own time, she thought.

She needed to find the room where Gramma Marie slept. In her imagination, the room was no larger than a walk-in closet, with barely space enough for a bed and a chair. Angela couldn't see a sign of any room like that now. She saw no doorways and no door the entire length of the attic.

Instinct drew her toward the attic window, the highest point in the room. The window was in a cove, with high walls on either side. The round window stared out at Toussaint Lane below, and Angela could see the steady rain outside. The window was still cracked in at least three places, and a triangular shard of glass had fallen out, maybe during that awful clanging, that shaking of the walls.

Angela studied the cove's walls. She knocked on the right side. She wasn't sure what she was listening for, but the wall felt dense against her knuckles. Next, she knocked on the left side. That knock was very different. "It's hollow," Myles said, noticing at the same time she did.

"There's a way to get in there."

With Myles's beam to assist her, Angela ran her fingers along the sloping wall, looking for some kind of entrance around the left corner, outside of the cove. That brought her to the narrow section of the wall that was painted blue. A rusted, old-fashioned heating stove that looked like it weighed a hundred pounds sat in front of the wall, its steel panel inscribed

Oakdale Sunshine. Beside the stove, there was a three-legged gadget, some kind of butter churn. At the frailest time of her life, soon before she died, Gramma Marie had dragged these items here to protect something.

Downstairs, the angry clang came again, and the floor trembled. Angela's knees nearly folded beneath her. That sound was a horror.

Only the sound of glass clinking behind the blue wall, from the hollow, helped her smother the impulse to run out of the house before it was too late. There *was* something hidden here. "L-let's move the stove," Angela said.

"What are you looking for?" Myles said.

"I don't know. Just help me, please."

Myles helped her drag the stove away from the wall, knocking over the flimsy churn. A thick, knotted rope came into sight where the stove had been. Angela had to stare at the rope a moment to realize it was a door latch. She couldn't see the door, but she saw indentations in the paint that betrayed a door that had been painted over. Angela pulled on the rope, but the door stuck.

"Hold up," Myles said. He took the rope, turned, and tugged. His first tug yielded nothing, but he shifted his body to put more of his weight into the pull, and his second one loosened the door. By his third try with a hard grunt, the door flung open with the strong fragrance of incense.

This little room had a sharply sloping ceiling, and it was dark, too. "Light, Myles," she said.

The beam flew inside. In that instant of light, Angela saw a shock of bright colors—green pervading, but also flaming red and orange, white and gold. Colorful banners hung from the ceiling, mirroring the rainbow on the walls. An altar, she realized. Angela had thought Gramma Marie's bedroom altar was intricate, but she could see now how reserved it had been, almost entirely lacking in color, and taking up so little space in her bedroom, on a corner table of white wicker. Gramma Marie's true altar was almost too crowded to take in at once, its colors marvelous.

But Angela's eyes were drawn to a wide, six-foot wooden cross, painted red, bound with thick, heavy rope. The cross had half a human skull planted on top, with only the twining rope where the lower jaw should be. Ropes lashed the cross with upside-down bottles and a small white chair, all of it bound tight. Dusty bottles hung upside down from the cross. Rag dolls without faces swung on ropes from the ceiling, six of them dangling near the cross. The dolls were upside down, too. They looked like a nightmare come to life.

Sweeping his flashlight over the cross, finding the skull, Myles made a sound Angela couldn't distinguish. Disgust. Or terror. He took a step back. "*Holy* God. What—"

Angela felt her heart bounding, too. Whose skull had this been? How had Gramma Marie gotten it, and what did it mean? Why was the skull on top of the cross? And what were the dolls for? One by one, the images repelled Angela. No wonder Gramma Marie had never let her see this altar, she thought. Gramma Marie's religion was a foreign language to her, its symbols alien.

But Gramma Marie was in this space, waiting. Angela knew that much.

She took a step inside the room, and the potency of the incense doubled, a cloud of scents over her. Deep scents. Earthy, musky, tart, sweet scents. Sage, lavender, rosemary, cedar. The smell was so luxurious, she forgot to feel afraid. This room smelled like God.

"Give me the flashlight, Myles," she said.

"Be careful," he said, but handed it to her, raising his hand to his nose as if the skull's owner had died in here. She couldn't blame him, but she wished he would come beside her and smell what the room really was. It was a celebration.

Angela could see celebration in the bright chalk drawing on the floor, a symbol far more complex than any of those on her ring: crossed lines, four dots, bulbous ends to the vertical line, feathery flourishes at the ends of the horizontal line, a symbol that meant more than she could understand. She saw celebration in the faces painted on the wall by an amateur hand, the lines uneven and faces too big for the bodies, but nonetheless rendered with love. Brown faces against green clothing in gilded paint, with haloes and light behind their heads. Her eyes lingered a long time on the rendering of an old man with a white beard, bent over, leaning on a walking stick.

A drum stood in the corner, Red John's drum, another celebration. The sight of it made Angela long to hear it played. She mourned suddenly that she had never seen her grandmother dance to the drum. What a sight she'd probably been. Gramma Marie had *danced*.

Directly beneath her, Angela heard the clang again, and the floor jumped. Swinging bottles in front of her clanked together dully, and two small green ones on the floor tinkled, falling over. "Angie, I don't like this," Myles said behind her. "Nothing should be shaking the house that hard. That feels like it's from the *ground*, at the foundation."

Whatever kind of intuition Myles had, it was working for him, too. He was right. They would have to leave the house soon.

"Give me a minute. Let me feel her," Angela said.

Angela's flashlight beam went back to the bottles at the foot of the cross. There, between two bottles at the base, she noticed a small covered pot that looked like it was made of clay. The pot was too small to be promising as a weapon, but this was what Gramma Marie wanted her to have. Angela grabbed the earthen pot and cupped both hands around it, holding tightly.

A *govi*, she realized. She had no idea what the word meant, but a *govi* was what she held.

"Done," she said, and Myles gave her space to back out of the worship room.

Tears crept down Angela's face as she thought about the things she would never know about that room, about that altar. But she had rescued a piece of Gramma Marie.

Maybe, she thought, she had rescued her grandmother's soul.

If a house could feel pain, Angie's grandmother's house was in agony. As nonsensical as the thought was, Myles couldn't discard it as he and Angie raced down the muddy stairs from the second floor and found the chaos waiting downstairs.

In the foyer, where dead leaves were a foot high on the floor, the grandfather clock chimed maniacally. In the living room, the player piano's sour keys wandered up and down, playing a song with no real melody, an affront to the ear. And above them, the terrible clanging sound came every fifteen seconds now, shaking the house each time.

But there was an explanation. There always was. He wouldn't give in to fear, Myles vowed.

He didn't see Angie dart away from him. By the time he noticed that the swishing sound of her feet through the leaves was going in the wrong direction—*away* from the front door, toward the living room—only the swinging French doors remained to tell him where she'd gone. She was in the dining room. "Angie, we have to *get out of here!*" he shouted, going after her.

Angela stood over the dining table and its neat white tablecloth that looked freshly pressed for a dinner party, and her face seemed yellow, pallid. Her hands were raised to her mouth.

The floor was littered with the remains of a host of broken clay figurines; detached torsos, heads, and limbs. In the mess, Myles saw a picture frame he recognized—that wonderful old photo of Gramma Marie and her husband—and although the frame was cracked, Myles rescued it from the mess. Angie kneeled down, clutching a colorful scarf from the floor while she pressed the clay dish from the attic to her breast. She sobbed, an awful, keening sound, as if a horrible blow had been struck against her. He heard defeat in her cry.

"Angie, come *on*. It's an earthquake," Myles said, the first outright lie he had told in many years. He knew, in fact, that this was *not* an earthquake, that earthquakes came in abrupt shudders with aftershocks. What was happening in this house felt more like dynamite blasts from somewhere deep underground. On a timer of some kind. Methodical.

But even dynamite would not explain the water running from the walls and ceiling upstairs. Nor would it explain why there were so many leaves in the foyer where none had been when he and Angie went upstairs. Nor, in fact, would it explain the *crawling* pile of leaves, nor the mud he'd seen shoot out of the bathroom. But the word *earthquake* fit Myles's tongue; it was something he understood, and it called for the same plan of action as whatever was really happening here, events he couldn't quite grasp. The house might topple, he realized. The ground beneath it seemed to be shifting.

And Angie was oblivious, mourning over trash on the dining room floor.

"That's *enough*," Myles said, and he hauled Angie onto his shoulder, a fireman's carry. Maybe it was the adrenaline cascading into his system, but Angie was so light, he nearly lost his balance because he'd expected her to be heavier. She didn't struggle the way he'd feared, and Myles thanked God for small blessings. Angie lay still while he carried her from her grandmother's house.

Outside, on the porch, Myles looked in the yard for that deputy, Colin, who'd been posted at the front door when he arrived. He wasn't in sight.

"*Shit*," he said. He'd known it wouldn't be the same without Rob here.

"Put me down, Myles," Angie whispered, so he did. He was glad he didn't hear the terrible keening sound in her voice anymore. He took her hand, and together they ran from the porch into the yard. The picture frame fell from where Myles had nestled it tightly against his armpit, but neither of them turned to retrieve it. At the top of the stone steps, Myles looked down at Toussaint Lane and saw the deputy's rig still parked where he'd seen it last, near the mouth of the woods. Empty.

"Colin!" he called, cupping his hands. No movement. No answer.

Only now, outside of the house, did Myles allow himself to sink into the terror he'd felt from the time he'd seen those leaves upstairs twirl a minuet and that pile launch across the floor. There *was* a way to explain it—every extraordinary, impossible moment of it—but Myles didn't know the explanation, couldn't even *begin* to know right now, and not knowing had immobilized him. Fear bound him in place, digging his heels into the grassy soil at the edge of the ridge.

"Look," Angie said, pointing toward the ground.

On the highest of the stone steps leading to Gramma Marie's house from the road, there was a single muddy paw print in the center, identical to the ones that had crisscrossed his kitchen floor.

"He's here," Angie said, voice hushed and fearful. "We have to go to The Spot."

The only plan Myles wanted to hear was one that involved getting into his car and driving like hell as far from here as they could go. But although Angela's plan didn't appeal to him, he was impressed that she had the presence of mind to come up with one. Myles, for the time being, had run out of plans. He stood motionless at the top of the ridge while he watched Angie flying, flying, running down the stone steps, running past the empty deputy's rig.

Running into the woods.

✍ Thirty ✍

IT WAS ALMOST IMPOSSIBLE to follow the barking. Maritza Lopez had been sure the dog was dead ahead, but now he sounded north of her. Maritza hadn't planned to stray so far from her post on the backyard deck, but she'd gone so deep now that she'd lost sight of the Toussaint house on the ridge behind her. All because of the barking.

She'd been standing on the deck when she first saw the wet footprints on the wood, and the barking began as soon as she saw them. It was a no-brainer. Rob said Tariq Hill had a small black poodle with him. The dog barking out there behind the house could be a poodle, a shih tzu, or a Chihuahua, any one of the small breeds, but it seemed damned likely it was the right dog.

It was also likely to be a trap. She and Colin knew that. And when they'd radioed Rob to tell him about the barking, his orders had been clear: Stay at your posts. Wait for backup.

She wasn't supposed to be out here wading through the Toussaint woods with her Glock drawn for the first time in her career. With three older brothers and her father to please, Maritza Lopez had been taking orders since she was five, so she understood the consequences of ignoring them. Especially from Rob. The homegrown deputy she'd replaced two years ago had been fired for breaking Rob's rules, and far lesser rules than *My deputies follow orders.* She didn't understand why she was out here chasing this dog.

If she'd had time to think about it, if she'd been meditating instead of relying solely on her eyes and ears, she'd have recalled that this dog's bark sounded uncannily like a Chihuahua, Bebe, who'd lived with her family when she was a toddler. When Bebe died, she'd learned what death was. She waited at the door for him to come back every night for a week. She'd never stopped looking for him, never stopped waiting for him, and this dog sounded like Bebe. Even if she didn't know it.

"Come on out, you little *comémierda*," she muttered, her favorite curse in Spanish, *shit-eater,* a Cuban word she'd picked up from an old boyfriend, and one of the few words she knew in her parents' native language. She'd learned the full glossary of dirty words from her cousins, so she was content with her Spanglish even if her grandparents in Guadalajara couldn't understand what she said.

Colin's voice came into her radio earpiece. "Status," he said, annoyed.

Colin had lit into her when she radioed him and told him she'd climbed down the embankment behind the deck to look for the dog. But since she was back there, he'd decided he had to back her up. Now she'd involved him in her silliness, and she felt truly bad about that. She pressed on her tiny microphone, which hung across her shoulder for easy access. "He's moving. I'm due east now."

Colin groaned. "Rob's gonna fry both our asses," he said. "Help me find you."

Maritza studied her compass, watching the needle tremble. She was no Eagle Scout—or whatever the equivalent was for girls—but she knew how to use a compass, and this one was intent on pointing north, even when she faced the opposite way.

"*Comémierda,*" she said. "You're not going to believe this."

"What?"

"My compass is acting screwy. This damn thing's no good."

"Forget it, then," Colin said. He sounded out of breath from following her. "I thought you said you were *right* behind the house. I don't see you. Darlene said this suspect was last sighted on Eagles' Nest, and that's . . . what? Six minutes from here? We should go back to the house."

Colin was right. Tariq Hill could be ambling into the Toussaint house this very moment, although the house had been quiet as a graveyard. Not a peep. Not a whimper. Colin had made a joke about it just before she heard the first bark: *You should see this guy with his bow and arrow, like he thinks he's Tarzan. Now that her man is here, I guess it won't be so quiet in there now.*

The high-pitched bark came again, to Maritza's left. Twenty yards at most. Ten yards, even. If not for the ferns wrapped in spiderwebs, she would be able to see the damn dog now. "I've got him," she said. "Give me one second."

Maritza surveyed the overgrown thicket before her, noticing a cedar tree with a huge crevice shaped like a heart, and a creek not too far down the way. She could hear the gentle water.

"Be careful, Maritza," Colin said. "Come back in."

"I'm east. Just keep straight," she said, and she waded into the ferns.

Spiders had never bothered her, so she calmly snatched away any webs that brushed her face, unmindful. She hoped this stunt wouldn't stain the application she had sitting over at Portland P.D. She couldn't stand another year in Sacajawea. Searching for dogs in the bushes wasn't her idea of police work.

"Negative," Colin said. "We go back to the house. We stay there until Rob sends over another unit. Stop fucking around back there."

Maritza saw black fur scurry away from the creek that gurgled a few feet to her left; a fluffy ball at the end of the dog's tail vanished behind a shrub. Maritza whistled and made kissing noises, crouching. "I need thirty seconds. I just *saw* him. What's this dog's name?"

"I forget. Ebony or something. Don't let him bite you."

"I will *step* on that little dog before I let him bite me," Maritza said.

"You still due east?"

"Yes. Northeast."

"Make up your mind."

"East, mostly," she said. "I see a clearing now. There are three fence-posts."

Maritza was grateful for the landmark of the three old fence-posts, which had come into her sight after she rounded the last tangle of hedges. This was the only good landmark so far, and she'd needed something more concrete to give Colin. She was about to call for the dog again, but her voice trailed off in surprise. The neatly trimmed black poodle sat directly in front of her, beside one of the fence-posts. With his bright purple collar, she couldn't believe she hadn't seen him immediately. Had he been there the whole time? She'd overlooked him on first glance.

"Which way after this creek?" Colin's voice tickled her inner ear.

"I got him," she whispered. *"Shhhhhhh."*

Maritza surveyed her surroundings to make sure Tariq Hill wasn't in sight. It would be a hell of a trick for him to have trained the dog to lure her out here, but nothing was impossible. He might have a camp here they'd missed during the sweep.

There were too many stands of fir trees, towering wild shrubs, and high stalks of grass surrounding her to put Maritza at ease. This area would be a nightmare to cover. But she didn't see anyone, and that was good news for now. Kissing and cooing, trying to sound nonthreatening, Maritza crouched, duckwalking closer to the dog. His gaze was questioning, inasmuch as a dog's face could be.

"Come to Mama, little pooch," Maritza said. "That's right, Ebony. I won't hurt you."

This was the dog. It *had* to be the one. How many black poodles were roaming around Sacajawea? If she helped capture Tariq Hill, she thought, her application in Portland would shoot straight through the bureaucracy. In fact, screw Portland. She'd apply to the FBI and go back home to Fort Worth, where she could get a tan, good barbecue, and real tacos again.

"Tell me which way after the creek," Colin's voice said.

"Left. North. But only slightly. Hence, *northeast,*" she whispered. She kept a big smile on her face for the dog, who had stood up on all fours, as if to run from her. She hoped dogs weren't like porpoises, where grinning teeth were considered a threat. What was the rule for dogs, anyway? No prolonged eye contact. Maritza purposely shifted her eyes away from him, toward a clump of some kind of flowering bushes to her right.

"*Díos mío,*" she said, falling to one knee.

She thought she'd seen him. Would have *sworn* to it. She was looking for a six-foot-three black man, and he'd seemed to be standing ten yards to the side of her. Her finger was so tight against her warm trigger, she almost thought she'd pulled it.

Yet, it wasn't Tariq Hill. Instead, Maritza stared into the face of a wispily built teenage girl in a beautiful white dress, much like the traditional dresses her mother made her wear on the Day of the Dead as a child. The girl was pretty, as blond and sweet-faced as the girls she'd known in high school whose hips didn't bulge and who always had boyfriends hypnotized by their flaxen hair.

"Miss, you have to leave this property," Maritza told the girl. She stood up, embarrassed to be pointing a gun at her. Maritza dropped her hand, slipping the gun back into its holster.

"Who's there?" Colin's voice crackled in her ear, excited.

"A kid," Maritza told him, then turned her attention back to the girl. "There's a manhunt under way, miss, and this is private property."

The girl's face was blank, expectant. Standing closer to her, Maritza marveled at her gray eyes, round and almost fawnlike. She was pretty enough to be a model, except healthier, fuller. Maritza couldn't remember seeing anyone prettier, except in a magazine.

"Did you hear me, miss?"

"I'm sorry," the girl said. A single tear streamed down her face.

"Where are you, Maritza?" Colin's voice said, frustrated. But Maritza barely heard him, because the girl's melancholy had moved her. The girl's apology carried the weight of sins too great for someone so young.

"What's wrong?" Maritza asked her.

"I'm sorry," the girl said again in that world-weary voice, and her jaw began quivering, making her look ten years younger. The sight of this girl was making her heart ache in places she didn't know it had. "What, *linda?*" Maritza said, in her own mother's voice. "What happened?"

The girl's eyes brightened, her jaw went still, and her lips lost their sorrow. The transformation happened so quickly, Maritza doubted her eyes.

"This happened," the girl said. She pointed lazily over Maritza's shoulder. Behind her.

After turning halfway around, Martiza saw the motion of someone *big* about to come into her vision, and her hand flew back to her gun.

But not quickly enough. Maritza felt a shove and sharp pressure against her side, at her waistline. The push was hard, because she was no longer on her feet. She saw blood spouting above her holster, bloodying her hand. Maritza had never seen herself bleed this way before, in a fountain. The sight of her blood made her lose the idea she'd had about reaching for her gun, which didn't matter because a stronger hand was already tugging her department-issue Glock away from her.

Examining herself, Maritza saw something that needed her undivided attention: The black, grooved handle of some kind of tool the size of a large ice pick or a screwdriver was affixed to her waist, protruding from *underneath* her bullet-proof vest. When she touched the handle, her body contorted in pain, as if she'd shocked herself. This was the source of the blood, she realized. Something was buried to the hilt inside her. It had punctured her kidney for sure.

People died like this.

Maritza grabbed the handle to try to pull it free, but somewhere in her haze of panic, she stopped herself. No, she realized. If she pulled it out, she might bleed to death more quickly. *Maybe it's the only thing keeping me alive.* She saw how awkwardly her legs had splayed beneath her, devoid of feeling. Movement was out of the question, and shock would be here soon.

Tariq Hill stood above her, impassive. She'd forgotten all about him, just as she'd forgotten about the girl in the white dress, who was nowhere in her sight. When Tariq stood above her, Maritza's brain chronicled everything she could about her killer: black male, age thirty-five to forty-five. Six-three or six-four. Short-cropped hair. Black shirt and black slacks. If she had a chance to speak to anyone again, those would be her last words.

Tariq leaned over, his palm reaching toward her. Maritza turned her face away from him, thinking he might hit her. But he didn't. He wrapped his hand around the charm hanging from her neck and yanked, hard. She felt the leather string cut into her neck before it broke away.

"You won't be needing this," Tariq said. His voice seemed to shake the ground.

Tariq tossed the charm over his shoulder, then scooped the whimpering dog under his arm. With neither pity nor boasting in his eyes, Tariq turned and made long strides toward a stand of fir trees. Maritza watched him retreat, gulping at the air. Her lungs couldn't have been penetrated—she was certain of that—but she had to labor to breathe anyway. Her system was shutting down.

But he hadn't killed her yet. Any chance at all was a big chance.

The pain roiled, making everything in Maritza's sight seem to turn a bright shade of red. Even as her nerves awakened, screaming, she felt more determined to survive. She fumbled to press her radio's microphone. Colin's voice had been in her ear for some time, yelling her name.

"Officer down," Maritza said, hoping she was yelling, too, although she suspected her voice was a squeak by now. "Colin, I'm down. Tariq Hill is here. I'm down."

"Come again?" Colin's voice responded, panicked. "Maritza, come again?"

Maritza's mouth moved in response, but her throat only bubbled beneath a moaning sound she hadn't noticed until she could no longer speak. She hoped the bubbling in her throat wasn't blood. Her mouth tasted terrible—like panic, like death—and if any blood came up, she'd know for certain she was about to die here. Until that happened, she had a chance. A small one.

Maritza thought God was talking to her personally, but it was Colin in her ear. "Hang on, hang on. I'm almost there! I see a post."

The red sky twirled above her. Maritza closed her eyes.

She thought she had died, until she heard the gunshot. Her first sight was Colin running toward her in a full sprint, his gun aimed. Her mind celebrated. Colin nailed that *puta*, she thought.

But Colin's stride turned ungainly, and his midsection twisted as if the top half of his body had decided to run in another direction. While

Maritza watched, Colin's legs buckled beneath him and he fell in a tangle of his own limbs, not five yards from her. She saw a large bloodstain soaking his crotch. Colin was wearing his vest to protect his chest, back, and side—Rob had insisted on it—but Colin had been shot in the groin. Almost like an afterthought, Colin began screaming.

Maritza saw Tariq stand over her friend, aim, and fire once at his head. The dog under Tariq's arm barked, frightened at the sound. Tariq turned to Maritza next, his expression determined but washed of malice. He aimed his weapon like a man with a job to do. A man on his task.

Maritza felt sorrowed. She and Colin *both* down on the same day, she thought.

She didn't dwell on it long.

—

There is no place like home, Tariq thought as he appraised the uniformed man and woman dead at his feet, not unlike lovers at arm's length from each other. His gun's last report rang around him, a powerful sound. Birds were taking wing from the treetops, afraid his bullets might be meant for them. But soon, silence. At least to the untrained ear.

But Tariq could hear things and feel things others could not. Tariq felt the earth vibrating beneath his feet, the stirring of the house. The reclamation.

All of this land, now, belonged to the *baka*, and the *baka*'s plans had not included these two police officers, unfortunately for them. The *baka* had made their ears deaf to the sounds of its reclamation inside the house. If they had heard, perhaps they would have realized they had more pressing problems than a barking dog. They would have heard Death coming for them.

Flesh was so easy to fool. At times, the match didn't seem fair.

Tariq rolled the dead man over with his foot and knelt beside him to pull the talisman from his neck. He scanned the herbs and overgrown grass in the clearing for the one he'd taken from the woman. Finding it, he stepped on them both, delighting in the muted cracking sound beneath his sole.

He had to admit, That Bitch had her moments.

The *baka* would have enjoyed using the police officers to kill Myles Fisher. As a boy, Myles Fisher had seen police officers wrestle his father to the floor, convinced he was watching his father's murder. If the *baka* had hidden inside the officer's skins, Myles would have given it more fear to feed from before he died. And how much more terrifying for Angie would it have been to watch Myles Fisher slain by the hand of their protectors?

The sheriff would have been best, naturally. But That Bitch had protected them all, using Angie and her rudimentary clay, preventing the *baka* from riding them. The *baka* could inconvenience them and fool their ears, but it could not liberate them as it had liberated him.

That Bitch could never be underestimated, Tariq remembered. But in his own way, Tariq was glad Myles Fisher was still living. At the man's house today, smelling Angie on Myles Fisher's bed, Tariq had felt a rage that made all his previous rage feel puny. This man's hands had touched his wife. His fingers had violated her. His mouth had violated her. His *manhood* had violated her.

And Angie had gladly allowed him to.

Tariq knew he was still capable of mercy. Hadn't he shown mercy to the actress? The uniformed woman had suffered, but not long. And the uniformed man had died quickly enough. Frankly, that was more mercy than the *baka* would prefer.

But there would be no more mercy.

"No more mercy!" Tariq shouted, hoping his voice would carry to the place where Angie and Myles Fisher were fleeing on the other side of the property, mere acres from where he stood. They were fleeing toward the place they would be easiest to find, where the *baka* wanted them to go.

He would make Angie watch him kill the man she had betrayed him with. He would have her, his own reclamation. Then, she would die. Depending on his mood, her dying might take time.

This land belonged to him now, and to the *baka*.

The *baka* was feeding here now, on the new blood that ran into the soil.

The *baka* was always strongest after a feast.

✤ *Thirty-One* ✤

*M*IDNIGHT WAS COMING, but The Spot looked like midday, crisp and bright. The moon was nearly full above the bonfire, and a shower of orange sparks flew toward the sky.

The mosquitoes must have been expecting them, Corey thought, because an army swarmed in welcome. But Corey felt good tonight, in control. A few mosquitoes wouldn't ruin that.

Corey arranged twenty stones he and Sean had found in the woods into a large square shape next to the fire-pit, the beginning of his ancestor altar that would help bring Gramma Marie's spirit close to him. "There's a lot of ritual magic practiced in the world," Corey said quietly to Sean as he worked, thinking aloud. "But you never hear about it on the news, somebody doing what we did. I think people who can really do magic keep it quiet. Like Gramma Marie."

"Why?" Sean said. His cigarette tip glowed between his fingertips.

The square of stones was finished, its four lines straight. That done, Corey laid a white bowl inside the square, filling it with holy water from a bottle he'd bought at the *botanica*. Sean had helped him scavenge the area for loose twigs and leaves, so Corey spread those inside the square, too.

"Well, think about it: Here she was, this powerful priestess, right? But she messed up." He suddenly felt as if Gramma Marie were sitting in front of the fire's radiance, watching, so he spoke as if she could hear him. "No disrespect, Gramma Marie, but things didn't go right. Now it's all these years later, and it's *still* messed up. Think about what happens when there's an oil spill. Or an accident at a nuclear plant."

"It's hard to clean up," Sean said.

"Right. It's *powerful*. And the more power you get, the bigger the stakes. Gramma Marie wasn't the only one with power. There are probably other people who could do all kinds of magic if they wanted to, but they stick to what they need, the basics. So the price isn't so high."

"Fine by me," Sean said. "I told you already, I've *seen* it now. You made something that was gone come back, and that's all I need, Corey. I was kidding about that other stuff we should do. Everywhere I look, I see miracles."

Sean was right. They knew something other people didn't: Death *wasn't* the end, because a dead woman was communicating with him. Gramma Marie was watching him, standing alongside relatives he'd never met, people born hundreds of years ago. It was all different now.

But Corey couldn't forget the rest: What did you call a miracle in reverse?

They stood in silence a moment, listening to the licking of the flames and buzzing mosquitoes. It would be time to begin soon. To *really* begin. Gramma Marie would help him open the door, but when you open a door to a place you've never been, you never know what can come popping out from the other side. He'd read enough horror books to know *that*.

"Let's say this works," Corey said quietly. "We break the curse and we decide it's safe to have one more wish. It doesn't have to be the same spell— it can be *anything*. We just shouldn't be greedy, because if you disrespect magic, it disrespects you back. What would you want?"

Sean thought, but not for long. "I'd make sure nothing happens to bust up my family. Miguelito's paperwork isn't final, and I keep having dreams about this guy who comes to take him from us. That's my nightmare. My dad couldn't deal with it. I couldn't either. That's my little bro."

Corey nodded. Sean's dad was a good guy. Everything was about his kids, from what Corey could see. He'd set up his life so he wouldn't have to do anything except raise his kids, except maybe boarding horses and occasional house-painting. Mom and Dad weren't that way at all. Both of them would feel lost if they were shut away from the world like Mr. Leahy. Mom and Dad both seemed to believe they were better people at work than they were at home.

"How about you?" Sean asked him.

The taste of Becka's tongue and teeth flooded Corey's mouth. He saw himself in his bedroom again, squatting by the window, kissing her lips, touching her breasts. The fantasy drew him away from The Spot and Sean and his altar to Gramma Marie. Corey sighed, trying to shake away the thoughts before he got excited.

"I want my parents to stay cool and work it out. That's my biggest wish right now, no doubt. But I almost feel like that's handled already, like they've decided on their own something has to change. So if I could pick another wish . . ."

Becka's tongue, massaging the roof of his mouth.

"Man, to be honest, I want to get past the mystery. I want to be with a girl and not have to wonder how far she'll let me go, or if she's power-tripping. And not a skank who would lie down with anybody, but I mean a girl I *like*. I want to know that feeling when she wants you as badly as you want her, and she says yes. And then you get to see what she feels like on the *inside*. I want to *know* it. All of it." As he spoke, Corey felt fevered.

"You don't have to waste a wish on that," Sean said. "That'll happen."

"Not soon enough," Corey said, realizing he'd almost called Sean T., because T. was the friend he could talk to about his true thoughts, not just movies and music and ball. "This girl Becka's got me ready to bust. I never thought I could fall for somebody I hardly know, but I'm *sprung*. I want to see her every day as soon as I wake up. I want to take her away and send her to school, whatever she wants. I dream about her. I'm writing *poems* for her. It's never happened like this for me. See what I'm saying?"

Sean sighed, and he turned to look at the fire, avoiding Corey's face. He'd kept his silence when Corey told him about Becka's visit to his window. "Just be careful," Sean said quietly.

"*Mos'* def. Definitely," Corey said, and checked his watch. Eleven forty-six.

"Feast time," he said.

Gramma Marie's instructions said to bring a feast that could be shared by Gramma Marie and his other ancestors, among them his great-grandfather Philippe Toussaint and his great-great-great-grandmother, Fleurette. He'd brought leftover jambalaya Mom cooked that day from one of Gramma Marie's recipe cards, and since Mom was part of the bloodline, Corey hoped it was all right he hadn't cooked the food himself. He also had hard candy and canned corn for Papa Legba, since Gramma Marie said he loved those foods, and he was her spiritual mate.

With the food in place in a bowl beside the holy water, the night felt more like a party than the awful reason he was really here. He kept hoping

Gramma Marie was wrong—that the demon had disappeared long ago or let go of its grudge, or that there was no such thing as demons to begin with—but the possibility that she was *right* had been hard to live with these past few days. Corey stared at the photograph of him and Gramma Marie he'd found in Mom's albums in the library; an old woman he'd never had a chance to know with the little kid he didn't remember being.

Corey poured the last of his bottled holy water into the soil, a libation. "Gramma Marie, please accept these offerings and help give me strength," he said.

Instantly, Corey felt his stomach cramp, a fist. His dinner whirled inside him.

"What?" Sean said.

Corey didn't answer. Trying not to panic, he picked up the satchel and thumbed through Gramma Marie's papers, looking for a page he'd marked with a red paper clip. He'd organized her papers: yellow paper clips for personal history, green paper clips for spells, and red paper clips signifying pages with warnings. Most of the pages with spells also had warnings, but there was one section marked with pages only in red. He found the one he wanted.

The closer you come to harming the *baka*, the more it will try to interfere with your spiritual center, which will often manifest as pains in your stomach. Cleansing baths may help ease your stomach pains, but do not stray from your objective. After banishment, the *baka* will be unable to harm you, but until then, wear the ring to prevent the *baka* from riding your head in the form of a *lwa*. Make certain that no *baka* or *bókó* who wishes you ill touches your ring. If the ring is violated, it must be passed to another in your line. In a very rare case, you might become a puppet to the *baka*. I have seen such cases.

All possession is loss of control, whether one is ridden by an ancestor spirit, a *lwa*, or a *baka*. But while ancestors and *lwas* visit us to give us guidance, a *baka* breathes only contempt for its host.

The first time Corey had read the papers line by line, he'd imagined he felt a little nausea during that passage about the *baka* and stomachaches. But he'd decided it was fright and nerves, exactly what had happened when he'd read *The Stand* by Stephen King and felt every symptom of Captain Trips. But this was different. Although the cramp had eased now, he hadn't imagined it. It had been sharp and specific.

Corey closed his left hand tight, caressing the indentations on the ring with his fingertips. What had he done wrong? He'd been wearing the ring since he'd left the house, no longer afraid his mother would see it. Had he left it off too long after dinner? Had he been infected by the *baka* so soon?

Corey was scared now. More than scared. His brain felt shorted out.

"What, man?" Sean said.

"We have to hurry," Corey said. "I think it's messing with me."

"Messing with you how?" Sean whispered, alarmed.

Corey shook his head, unable to answer. The night's festive, philosophical mood was gone. Midnight was coming—the best hour to reach Papa Legba—and he'd been wasting time. He and Sean had been here talking like this was summer camp, and he was supposed to be working. With unsteady hands, Corey flipped to the next pages on banishment, all of them dual-marked with red and green paper clips.

"We have to be quiet," he said, and Sean nodded, taking a step back, squatting beside the fire.

Corey methodically pulled out the other items he'd brought: the goat's horn, copper pennies, a few drops of the dead raven's blood he'd collected in a black film canister. He had the raven's feathers in a paper bag, he'd filled another paper bag with chicken bones (a quick stop at KFC had taken care of that on the way home from Portland), and the final bag was full of soil from The Spot, which Gramma Marie said was some of the most powerful soil in existence.

The guy at the *botanica* had explained that the parchment was so expensive because it was made from the vagina of a virgin lamb, which had made both him and Sean chuckle because it sounded so funny. But it wasn't funny anymore. Corey was glad he'd decided to pay the seventeen bucks for a single sheet, and he suddenly appreciated the lamb that had been sacrificed to make it. "Thank you," he whispered, touching the parchment.

Gramma Marie's papers had encouraged him to use dove's blood ink, but the *botanica* didn't have any. Corey hoped one of Gramma Marie's old fountain pens would be good enough, because he'd found one that worked on the desk in her library. Holding the pen, Corey could imagine it in his grandmother's grasp, between her dark, lined fingers. He'd brought everything except something flat to write *on*, he realized. His tried to glide his pen gently across the paper on the ground, straining to see in the firelight. Luckily, the paper was sturdy and didn't break beneath his pen's point as he copied Gramma Marie's words onto the parchment.

> *Dearest Papa Legba—A treasure has been stolen from you, and*
> *I wish to return it. Please forgive Marie Toussaint for her abuse of*
> *what was yours. I ask that you will please accept the return of your*
> *sacred word and restore my ancestors and progeny to your favor. I*
> *also ask that you will open the gates to the lwas and allow them to*
> *hear my prayers as we must banish this unwelcome baka from your*
> *Crossroads Forest. Please, Papa, help me tonight. Do not forsake me*
> *for the mistakes of my ancestors.*

As soon as Corey stopped writing, his stomach cramped again. This time, he clutched himself with both arms. He knew the pain could be worse, but his suspicions about the pain's source made it excruciating. With his heart racing, he felt light-headed. Was he about to die out here?

Almost finished, he told himself. Go on.

In her pages, Gramma Marie had drawn the symbols from the ring with dark ink, taking her time, detailing them. She had also drawn the *vèvè* symbolizing the individual gods, but the symbols from the ring were less flowery and complex, more like shapes from geometry. Corey had copied each symbol onto individual index cards, numbering each one. Careful to preserve the proper numerical order, he laid each card down on the soil until the twelve of them encircled his parchment petition. Perspiration dripped from his nose to the ground, making a dark spot between two of the index cards. He hadn't realized how badly he was sweating, but his body felt soaked through. He was also cold, suddenly.

The stolen word was preserved in the symbols on the ring. It had been all along.

On a single page, by itself, Gramma Marie had drawn a large wheel without spokes, only symbols and letters. The symbols on the ring were outside of the wheel, matching letters of the Latin alphabet inside. With her key, he could write the word—*speak* the word, which was more important—and offer it back to Papa Legba, its true owner. Afterward, Gramma Marie had written, Papa Legba's silence might be broken. He should help banish the *baka*.

> The word should never be spoken, except in the Returning ceremony. Your eyes must not see the word in alphabet form before it is time for your offering. You must not think of it, and you must forget it once the offering is complete. You must write it only once. The ring is ours to keep, but the key inlaid within the symbols cannot be preserved. You will

write the word only once and speak it only once; afterward, these papers must be destroyed by fire. This will show Papa Legba that the word is his alone, that he may reclaim it. Only then can you make prayers to have the *baka* destroyed.

"Papa Legba, please accept your stolen word. Please open the gate for me."

Corey's hurting stomach told him two things: how close he was, and how treacherous a place he was approaching. His stomach was burning now, as if he'd swallowed battery acid. But he pushed on. Referring to the wheel key in Gramma Marie's papers—and checking it once, twice, three times—Corey slowly wrote down the first letter of Papa Legba's word, the word his great-grandmother had uttered in a rage in 1929: *M*.

Writing the single letter on the parchment wore him out. Corey hurriedly wiped his brow, afraid his sweat would ruin his precious petition. His heart was lunging into his throat. Why was writing one letter so much like taking his first step on a tightrope ten stories high? He felt dizzy.

"Take it easy," Sean whispered, and Corey nodded, grateful to remember Sean was there.

Corey couldn't focus his eyes in the firelight, so he had trouble matching the second symbol to its alphabet twin in Gramma Marie's key. This was the double-wave, and his eyes fooled him, drawing him to a symbol that looked similar, but had a dot in the center. *Shit.* Forcing himself to be still and take a deep breath, he tried again.

This time, it seemed to jump from the page: The second symbol was above the letter *U*. As Corey worked, he forgot both his stomach and his thoughts, matching one symbol to the next, copying them onto his petition. The word emerging wasn't familiar: *MUFR*, it said so far, with eight symbols remaining for translation. He tried to keep his eyes away from the letters as he wrote them, afraid he would accidentally commit the word to memory.

He heard a noise. Something moved in the woods near the trail, out of sight. Whatever it was, it made a sound like a whimper before thrashing as if it were shuffling from side to side, then forward. Until now, Corey hadn't remembered the beast he'd seen in his dream the first night he performed the ceremony of The Lost, but its image sprang back into his mind—it was huge and hairy, with sharp yellow teeth that curved like claws. That beast wasn't a dream, he thought. It was something real, about to charge out at him from the woods.

"*Shit,*" Corey said in mid-stroke, his eyes torn to two clearly lighted tree trunks standing like guards before a bank of darkness.

"Finish it. Hurry," Sean said urgently.

The thrashing came again, and Corey felt his bladder slacken.

But the figure that came into view from the woods wasn't a monster—it was Becka. Her movements had sounded erratic because of the way she was walking, as if she were weighted on one side, lurching. She stumbled, and Corey heard her sob softly, almost a wail. When she was close to the fire, Corey saw dark marks on Becka's face that might be bruises or mud. Something was wrong.

"Becka, what's wrong?" he said, standing up to take her arm. Becka's eyes were red, glazed with tears. Her tears shocked him, making him feel a swoon, as if he'd lost his strength. She was trying to hide her face from him, but he needed to see her. Was one of her eyes *swollen?*

A thin spot of blood peeked from her bottom lip. The blood made Corey numb with rage. Even his stomachache was suddenly gone. "What happened? Becka, tell me what happened."

Becka wrapped herself around him, burying her face against his shoulder. She was taller and older than he was, but she pushed herself against him like a child. Her full breasts pressed to his chest again, but this time he wasn't captivated by her body. He needed to know what was wrong.

"They're coming," Becka whispered in his ear, her breath hot. And sour.

"Who's coming? What happened?"

"They're coming here. They're on their way."

For the first time, as Corey stroked Becka, he noticed that the collar of her dress was ripped nearly to her mid-chest. He could see now that she wasn't wearing a bra, and too much of her bosom was showing, the pale flesh quavering when she moved. Corey knew, then. Knowing felt as if someone had jabbed an ice pick into his spine.

"Who hurt you? Becka, who did this to you?"

Her only answer was a sob. She clung harder, her weight nearly pulling him from his feet.

"Let's get her to my house, Corey," Sean said. "We should call the sheriff."

Hearing those words, Becka pulled herself from Corey's arms, red-faced. "*No!*" she screamed. "That's a *stupid* thing to say!" She was hysterical.

Seeing her face more clearly, Corey noticed that her jaw looked swollen. There *were* bruises on her face. Someone had beat the hell out of Becka. And she was shaking. She looked like someone had just pulled her out of freezing water.

"Oh, shit, Becka," Corey said, holding her shoulders. His ignorance was making him miserable, as if he might cry. "Who did this? What did they do?"

"Corey, seriously, we should take her and go until we know what's going on," Sean said.

Sean's words made sense. Corey heard them, and he felt himself wanting to say, *Yeah, you're right, let's get her to a doctor. We'll let the police take care of it.* His parents would know what to do. Sean's father would know what to do.

But he couldn't make himself say that.

The wondering was too much as he stared into Becka's eyes. The wondering was worse than a fever, more like the bonfire lighting everything in his sight. He had to *know* what had happened. He had to *know* who had put his hands on her. There was something about the way she was clutching her dress to herself, bunching it up near her thighs. A word came to his mind, and he felt tears in his eyes even to *think* the word, but he had to ask.

"Becka . . . did somebody rape you?"

Becka shook her head, but the shake didn't seem to mean no. It meant something else: *Stop asking me.* Corey felt bad about how tightly he was gripping Becka's shoulders, but his hands were thinking on their own now. His hands had become the part of him that *had* to know. "You tell me what happened," Corey said, locking their eyes. "Tell me *exactly* what happened."

Becka turned her face away. She was blushing bright, ashamed. "They saw me and jumped on me. They knocked me down, and I fought them, but they kept hitting me. They wouldn't stop."

A rocket burst in Corey's skull. "*Who* the fuck jumped on you?"

"They'll hurt you if they find you here."

There was more to it. Corey knew that by the way Becka's eyes looked away from his.

"*Who*, Becka? Who is it?"

Becka whispered. "I think he's called Bo. I don't know the other ones."

The mention of Bo's name made Corey remember the flash of fire near his leg while he was riding Sheba, the way she had been so terrified, bucking. *Who the fuck are you looking at, nigger?*

"Bo Cryer?" Sean said, standing closer, until they were both huddling around her.

Becka nodded, raising her hand to her face, trying to hide herself.

Sean's voice was hushed. "A girl at school said he did that to her last year. Becka's right—we have to take her and get moving. If there's a lot of them, this is bad news. *Really* bad news."

Suddenly, Corey could *see* Bo's hand ripping at Becka's dress, burrowing between her breasts, groping and pulling at her soft flesh. He saw Bo sitting atop Becka while he lashed her face with his open palm, and then his fist. He saw Bo thrust his hand between Becka's legs, then hoist her leg around him while he thrust himself inside her, invading her. As the images swallowed him one after the other, Corey heard a voice from the woods, from the direction where Becka had come: *"You guys are so fucking dead!"*

Bo's voice, full of careless laughter. The voice was far off, but coming closer.

Corey felt his face smolder. "Get back," he said, pulling Becka toward the huge fallen tree where he'd left food for her, a tree with a trunk five feet tall on its side. It was hollow enough for Becka to hide inside if it came to that, but for now he thought she would be safe enough behind it, out of the firelight. He gently pushed her until she was crouching, and he gently kissed her lips, trying not to hurt her where she was sore. Her lips belonged to him. All of her belonged to him.

Becka squeezed his hand. "I'm sorry," she whispered.

"Sorry about what? You've got nothing to be sorry about. I've got this, Becka."

"Corey . . ." Sean sounded nervous, always afraid of a fight.

"Shut up, man. This isn't on you. Go run home if you want."

"I'm sorry this happened to Becka, but do you know what you're *doing?* There's just two of us! This is crazy. I mean it, Corey."

As Corey walked back to Sean, he accidentally stepped inside the ancestor altar, spilling some of the holy water from the bowl into the soil. He felt wrong about it, that he should tend to it somehow, but he couldn't take his mind away from Becka hiding behind the dead tree, violated, shaking, and scared. He stood an inch from Sean, staring him down. "What if somebody did that shit to your sister one day?" Corey said. "What would you do?"

Sean didn't blink. "I'd go call the cops. Same as now."

"That's why you're a punk," Corey said. He had to restrain himself from shoving his palms against Sean's chest, because he felt sickened by him. "You take care of your *own*. That's why Bo does this shit, 'cause of people like you. You watch this."

Corey wished he had T. with him; T. and his brother and maybe Levon, a black belt in his tae kwon do class who moved like a cat. Levon could kick you before you saw him lift his foot. But it didn't matter. No matter what— if Corey had to pick up those stones to knock somebody out or throw somebody into the fire, whatever it took—anybody who had touched

Becka was going to pay for it. *Anyone*. Two, three, or four, it didn't matter to him.

Only one person emerged on the trail.

Bo was running in a near-silent sprint, but he stopped when he came to The Spot, seeing them. Corey wouldn't have recognized him except for the white streak in his hair, because his face was covered with soot or grease and he was wearing plastic goggles. Bo was dressed in camouflage pants, almost like a soldier except for his orange vest with yellow strips that glowed in the dark, an appearance so unexpected that Corey wondered if he could be dreaming. Bo had a long, black gun in his hand that looked almost like a machine gun. Becka hadn't said anything about a gun.

"What are you doing here?" Bo said. He whipped off the goggles, and Corey could see his eyes, two pale rings. "We've got a game going. Get moving."

"You guys are playing paintball at midnight? How can you see anything?" Sean said to Bo, making conversation as if Bo hadn't raped Becka, as if they were just catching up on things. Except that his voice was so shaky.

Corey was glad Bo didn't have a real gun. Corey had never seen anyone play paintball, but he'd heard about guys who went out into the woods and played war, trying to shoot each other with paint. Well, Bo wouldn't have to play at war. He had found a real war now.

"I said to get the fuck out of here, asswipe," Bo said, ignoring Sean's question.

"This is my family's property. *Asswipe,*" Corey said. He took three steps toward Bo, his fists tight. "Why'd you put your hands on my girlfriend?" Corey said, sounding as if he were the one with the gun instead of Bo. His rage had taken control of his mouth.

Beside him, Sean made a sound like a groan. So softly that Corey barely heard.

Bo let out a laugh. "What?"

"You heard me. Why'd you put your hands on my girlfriend?"

"I wouldn't put my hands on any slut who'd let *you* touch her, monkey."

"She says you did. You and your friends. You must like forcing yourself on girls. Maybe you learned it watching your daddy fuck your mama."

Bo's face hardened, and his eyes suddenly reminded Corey of how his own eyes must look, boiling with rage. "You crazy motherfucker," Bo said. "I never forced *nobody.*"

Corey heard a shriek behind him; again, he thought of the monster from his dreams. Becka was lunging toward them, pinwheeling her arms. She stopped beside Corey, just short of Bo. "You *liar!*" Becka screamed. "You're a *liar! You know what you did!*"

In retrospect—in the two days Corey would have to think about this night, recalling it detail by detail whether he tried to or not—Bo looked shocked at the sight of Becka, with her torn dress, swollen eye, and bleeding lip. She was bleeding more now than when Corey had last seen her, a line of blood spilling across her chin. Bo's face lost its anger, becoming empty as he stared at her. Corey didn't recognize it at the time, but there was something else in Bo's face: fear. Cold and deep.

"Who the fuck is this?" Bo asked Corey.

Becka shrieked at him. "You and your friends Trey and Scott and Griffin saw me walking on the trail and you jumped me, and you tore my clothes, and you beat me, and you put your hands all over me, and you stuck your thing in me. You were laughing and you said, 'Let's do her like I did that bitch Ariel,' until I ran away. *You know you did it, so don't lie and say you didn't. I'll swear it in court. I'll swear it on a stack of Bibles.*"

"You goddamned liar," Bo said. "Did Ariel put you up to this? Ariel *admitted* it was all a lie. She was mad I broke off with her." He was making his case to Corey and Sean, trying to reason with them, man to man. His voice sounded as scared as Sean's had been.

"You just wait until I tell Sheriff Graybold. He's gonna lock you up!" Becka screamed. "You're gonna go to the state pen like your grandfather and your daddy and your uncle. And you *know* what happens at the state pen, because even though your daddy won't tell you, *something happened to him in there*. You know he's not a man anymore, not a *real* man. And it's gonna happen to you, too, because that's what you did to me! *Then you'll be just like him!*"

Bo couldn't have looked more startled if Becka had thrown a rattlesnake at him. His eyes went wide, and the gun in his hands popped suddenly. Even Bo jumped at the sound.

The paintball hit Becka. Her white dress was suddenly showered with red paint across her chest, like bright blood. She hissed low through her teeth, although she didn't move, as if she hadn't felt any sting. Paint covered her exposed bosom and her neck, as high as her chin. Her eyes leveled at Bo as if she could make him drop dead from a stare.

Corey felt his mind recede, and he heard himself give a yell. He spun, his right leg flying to kick Bo squarely in the gut. The kick was a thing of beauty, faster and more accurate than any kick he'd ever produced at the dojo or a tournament. Bo was too surprised to try to block, and the kick landed with all the force of Corey's training. It was the best kick he had in him. Corey's heart swelled with triumph.

For a time.

Underneath that blubber in Bo's belly, there was a shelf of muscle. Corey felt the unexpected impact against his foot, unyielding. Bo grunted, knocked off-balance by the kick for a single backward step. But he didn't fall. He didn't even double over. He just looked madder than before.

Shit. This couldn't be happening. He'd given Bo *his best kick.*

Suddenly, Corey remembered that Bo was six inches taller than him, and twice as wide. He snatched the gun from Bo's hands to try to club him, but Bo was quick for someone so big and solid. Bo sidestepped Corey's chopping blow and lunged, bear-hugging him. The gun flew from Corey's fingers. Bo pinned Corey's arms to his side and pitched him off his feet, landing with his full weight on top of Corey.

Corey couldn't catch his breath. His ribs felt crushed. He wished he'd been taking wrestling instead of tae kwon do, because Bo had him pinned.

"Don't you listen to that lying bitch," Bo breathed into his ear, tightening his arms until Corey groaned. "Me and my friends never touched nobody. We're playing paintball, and I've never seen that crazy bitch in my life. Say it and I'll let you go."

"Fuck you!" Corey said. He knocked the side of his head against Bo's, hoping it hurt Bo as much as it hurt him.

"Say it!" Bo roared, and hoisted himself high before burying his knee in Corey's groin.

This pain was so raw that Corey screamed, sure his crotch must be gushing blood. Corey had been kicked in the balls accidentally before, and it hurt even with a cup, but he'd never been hit by anyone Bo's size, or with Bo's driving strength. It was like a *claw*, he thought. Bo had clawed out his midsection, leaving his guts dangling. He couldn't move, because all his strength had vanished. Corey understood how Becka must have felt beneath Bo's weight, helpless.

"Say she's lying or I'll do it again!" Bo said.

Corey saw Sean reach under Bo's armpits to try to pull him away, and he tried to open his mouth to cheer Sean on, but his mouth wouldn't move. When Bo's fist ground into Sean's nose, Sean fell back with both hands pressed to his face, bloodied.

When Bo leaned over Corey again, Corey elbowed him in the jaw, hitting him squarely, which felt like a miracle. Bo stumbled backward, standing up, but the blow didn't buy Corey enough time. When Corey got on all fours to try to stand, Bo's foot flew into his stomach with a *whump.*

Corey wheezed. He'd felt like he couldn't catch his breath when Bo first jumped on him, but this was worse. Now, all the air felt like it was gone. His body was stone.

He could die tonight, Corey realized. This guy might be beating him to death.

"If anybody raped that trashy whore, it was *you,*" Bo said. He kicked Corey's stomach again, grunting with the effort, and this time Corey felt something give inside him, folding on itself. He fell into the fetal position, sparks of red light flying before his eyes. Somewhere behind him, Corey heard Becka crying, the only thing he was aware of except how much he hurt.

And how much he wished he could breathe.

"*Say* it wasn't me!" Bo said.

oh jesus please don't let him kick me again please don't let me pass out

"Wasn't . . . you," Corey panted. Tears spilled from his eyes.

No kick came. Bo grinned a bitter grin at him.

"Fuckin' right it wasn't, and I better not ever hear you say different. You got it? You will be *dead,*" Bo said. He scooped up his gun, which had landed a couple of feet in front of the fire. "If this thing's scratched, I'm gonna break your head open, crybaby. I thought niggers could fight."

Suddenly, Corey's throat opened, and he could taste the air again. His lungs sucked at it, desperate. One breath, two. He was breathing.

He saw Becka sitting cross-legged close to him, sobbing into her paint-stained hands. When her eyes found his, Corey felt hot shame far worse than any physical blow. He'd been taking tae kwon do for three years, competing in bullshit tournaments, and he couldn't *fight?* He couldn't step up for his own girl? Thank God his father wasn't here to see what had happened, or Tariq Hill wouldn't believe Corey was his son.

With one arm braced against the ground, Corey sat up. His stomach flared, constricting. The air thinned out again, his lungs hitching in protest.

"What the hell is all *this?* You say your girlfriend was raped, and you're having a little picnic?" Bo said, walking to the other side of the fire. He kicked at something Corey couldn't see, and Corey heard the breaking sound. One of the bowls.

With all his effort, still hunched over, Corey pitched to his feet. Between the agony in his balls and his cramped abdomen, he could barely take a step, but he tried. His own weight burdened him. "Leave that stuff alone," Corey wheezed.

"Or what?"

Corey didn't dare provoke Bo again. He had only one plan: Once he retrieved the petition and Gramma Marie's papers, he'd get Becka the hell away from here. Sean was right. They should have called the police right away. What had been *wrong* with him?

Corey limped, making one painful step, then another, toward what was left of his altar. Bo had stepped on the parchment, leaving an ugly scuff down the middle. One of the bowls was broken, and jambalaya had spilled all over the ground. The satchel with Gramma Marie's papers was safely off to the side, but the parchment and index cards were in plain sight. Under Bo's nose.

Bo gave Corey a shove, and Corey had no idea how he didn't fall.

"If you're still here when me and my buddies get back, we'll show you what happens to liars. It's not gonna be pretty," Bo said, kicking soil and index cards at him. "Got it?"

"Yeah," Corey said. He crouched to pick up the parchment, but Bo snatched it from his fingertips. It was too sturdy to tear, but it was gone.

Bo only scanned the paper before grinning and dangling it above the fire.

"*Don't!*" Corey yelled, leaping toward him, but Bo's fingers released it, and the unfinished petition to Papa Legba fell onto the tower of flames, immediately burning black.

"Oops," Bo said.

The fire, the woods, and Bo seemed to spin, tilting at a strange axis. Corey was beyond dizzy; he felt as if he were literally floating now, separate from himself. He gazed once more at Becka, rumpled and crying in a paint-spattered heap. He remembered the most important thing again: *You take care of your own.* All sound vanished from Corey's ears.

"Have you ever seen magic, Bo?" he said. Corey felt himself smiling.

Bo glared at him, but there was fear in his glare. Bo turned his back on him, walking away. "Fuck off, psycho," Bo said. "Just remember what I said."

"You didn't know this land is magic? It goes back to Indian times. They used to string up their canoes here in the trees, burying their dead. There's spirits here. Want to see one? Want to see a real magic demonstration for free?"

Sean tugged his shirt. "Cut it out, man. Let him *leave*," he said, his nose plugged with blood.

"*Do it!*" Becka screamed, leaning forward from where she sat. "Get him *good*, Corey!"

Corey fell to his knees, breathing hard. He was shaking as badly as Becka had been, but air poured into his lungs, breathing strength into him.

Please let me punish him. Please show me a way.

Corey's fingers knew what to do while his mind was whirling. He fumbled through his paper bag of chicken bones and brought out two drumsticks, crossing them the way he had the night of the first spell. He saw the film canister with the raven's blood in it—the blood he'd brought for the cleansing—and he opened it. Corey poured a stream of raven's blood across the bones.

Bo had rounded the fire and nearly reached the trail.

"Hey!" Corey called after Bo, hoarse.

Bo stopped walking and looked around at him, his head at an angle.

Corey grinned at him. "Watch *this*," he said. He didn't know what "this" would be. He only knew he had a simple prayer in his heart, not caring whose ears it reached: *Help me punish him.*

The earth tremors began right away.

That was how mundane it seemed at first. Corey felt the earth vibrate beneath his feet. Sean and Bo must have felt it, too, because they both stared at the ground. Corey didn't know whether or not Becka felt the vibrations, because Becka was gone. She'd been sitting on the ground a few yards from him, but now there was no one where she had been, an empty space.

If Corey thought about it, she seemed to have vanished while he watched.

Bo suddenly screamed in a way Corey had never heard anyone scream. Bo's body twisted back and forth, writhing. From where Corey stood on the other side of the fire, it looked as if Bo were doing a crazed dance, his arms thrown above his head. Corey took a few steps closer even though he didn't *want* to see, because he thought something might be *eating* Bo, chewing at his legs. But it wasn't that. Not exactly.

There had been an accident.

Bo was sinking into a manhole-sized pool of mud, a perfect ring around him. Somehow, he and Sean had never seen the tarlike quicksand only a few feet from the trail. Any of them could have stepped in it, Corey's mind told him. Maybe it had been hidden beneath some leaves.

Bo was already up to his knees in the mud, screaming as he tried to pull himself free. "*Fuckfuckfuckfuckfuck . . . ,*" Bo was saying, yanking at his legs. His face was bright red. The mud had already climbed to Bo's thighs. Bo screamed and cursed.

"G-grab him!" Corey shouted at Sean, who was behind him making whining noises. They both raced to reach Bo, grabbing his meaty arms. Something yanked hard at Bo's weight from underneath the gaping sludge, and Bo's thick, rigid arm slipped an inch between Corey's hands.

Bo wasn't sinking. He was being *sucked* into the ground.

Corey couldn't see through his tears. The stink of Bo's fright assaulted him, a smell that was both primal and unearthly. He felt shudders as Bo's body jerked downward, and Corey was pulled over into a stoop as he struggled to keep his grip. Bo's arms thrashed, scratching Corey's face, grabbing a handful of his hair. *How could this be happening?*

"I got you! I got you!" Sean was saying, and Corey prayed it was true, but it was a lie.

Sean didn't have Bo. Only the mud had Bo.

"*G-get me out!*" Bo said, losing his breath. He had sunk to his chest. He tried to use his arms to leverage himself up, his muscles straining to pull onto solid soil, but everything Bo touched turned to mud. Corey felt his foot sucked downward into warm mud, and he pulled it free with a panicked shout. His shoe came halfway off his foot. The mud smelled like a waterlogged graveyard, worse than mere rot. Worse than death.

Bo's gasping became horrible. The mud reached Bo's neck, but his hands were above his head, grabbing at whatever he could. Feeling Bo's frantic hands clenching his jersey, Corey realized he and Sean were about to get sucked down, too. They couldn't rescue Bo. They could only die trying. Sobbing on phlegm and spittle, Corey tried to pry Bo's fingers away.

To leave him to die.

"*Help!*" Sean cried from the other side of Bo. In his panic, Bo had flung an arm around Sean's neck in a headlock, and Sean was on his knees, bending over, his face precariously close to the mud. The mud was climbing above Bo's nose, silencing him at last except for a frantic bubbling sound, but Bo was hanging on to Sean with all his strength.

Corey slid out of his shirt, freeing himself from Bo. He went to Sean, pounding his fists against Bo's rigid arm, trying to straighten it enough for Sean to slip away. For endless, terrible seconds, he thought he would have to watch both of them get sucked down. Bo's head was buried, vanished from sight in the pool of sludge, but his arm wasn't loosening, as if in a death-grip.

Then, at last, Bo's arm snapped open before it was yanked into the muck. Bo had either passed out, given up, or set Sean free.

The black Raiders jersey was visible for a moment, half-buried in the mud, and Corey reached for it, hoping it could be a lifeline to Bo if he and Sean pulled together.

An inch from his fingers, the fabric dove from Corey's sight, under the mud. Gone.

Corey and Sean screamed together.

They patted the ground, searching for the place where Bo and the shirt had sunk. Their digging fingers met dry soil and nothing else. The ground was unchanged, as if Bo had never been. Corey and Sean flung themselves away from the hexed spot, sobbing so hard their bodies heaved even as their shuddering cries were silent, their clothes soaked by what was left of the phantom mud.

———

It was nearly dawn. Light was coming.

All Corey remembered was digging. And more digging. He had a shovel in his hands, and his palms were so raw that cracks in his skin bled. His shoulders and back screamed with each new pitch of the earth. There were holes all over this side of The Spot, most of them several feet deep, as if land mines had ripped the ground to pieces, bringing Bo's war games to life.

When possible and impossible had first switched places, Corey had thought if they got shovels and found Bo right away, they might be able to save him. Now, that logic felt dumb. In a full-out run, stumbling in the dark, it had taken him and Sean more than ten minutes to make it to Sean's house, and ten minutes back. Bo would have suffocated by the time they were halfway there. Before then. Bo had suffocated before they stopped clawing at the ground with their fingers, trying in vain to find him somewhere in the soil.

But what else should they have done? Called the police? To do *what*?

Maybe he could try another spell, Corey thought. A spell to bring Bo back.

He'd thought of that right away, of course. He thought of that before he thought of running back for a shovel. But the first time it had occurred to him to try to resurrect a corpse, the thought had made him vomit, and he'd never been far from vomiting since. *You don't bring back dead people,* he told himself. Even if he hadn't read *Pet Sematary* three times, he knew better than to try something like that. It was wrong. More wrong than killing someone. The dead belonged to God.

And he *had* killed someone. He had killed Bo as surely as if he'd shot him with a gun.

Corey quivered in the predawn breeze, new tears spilling. His face itched from layers of tears and mucus. His eyes and nose were sore, and he was nearly crippled by the pulsing ache shooting between his abdomen and crotch. His body was almost as miserable as his memories. Almost.

Sean looked as bad as Corey felt. Sean's face was grimy, his hair caked with dirt and mud, his eyes as dead as a living person's eyes could be. He and Sean had not spoken a word in hours, working silently to earn their membership into the macabre club they had joined overnight. They made their holes at The Spot, looking for a body Corey was now sure they would never find.

They were all dead now, Corey thought. They were as dead as the charred wood and glowing gray ashes of last night's fire. T. had told Corey his brother died when he had his accident, when he'd hit that pregnant lady, killing her unborn child. T.'s brother hadn't died in the flesh, but he'd died in his head, T. had said. *Like my dad says he did in 'Nam,* T. had told him.

With daylight approaching, erasing the night, Corey felt remade, too. He'd been sucked down into the earth with Bo and his Raiders jersey, and his new mind was finally waking.

There were things to think about. Things to do.

"You were never here," Corey said to Sean. He no longer recognized his own voice. Now he knew how Mom had felt when puberty made his voice change, when she looked at him with such wonder, saying it was as if he'd turned into someone else overnight.

"I'll say I was the only one," Corey said.

"D-Doesn't matter." Sean plunged his shovel deep into a mound of soil, leaning against it with both arms, exhausted. "I can't keep digging. I'm d-done."

"Yeah." Corey dropped his shovel. Despite his aching muscles, giving up hurt more than digging. Corey felt burning behind his eyes, but no more tears would come.

Sean was trembling like an old man. He crossed his arms over himself. "I j-just thought . . . m-maybe if there was a body . . . his parents c-could, you know . . . *Fuck.* What happened, Corey? What happened?" A crazed quality shook his voice, halfway between laughter and tears.

Corey shook his head. He didn't know. He'd thrown those bones together and tossed some blood over them, making it up as he went. It had been bullshit. It hadn't been a real spell, just something from his head, trying to scare Bo. As if it had happened by itself.

"Maybe nothing really happened," Corey said, hopeful. "Maybe he's okay somewhere."

He had a cloudy memory of the three other boys coming to The Spot after Bo disappeared, all of them dressed for paintball. Maybe it had been too dark for the boys to see their faces—maybe they hadn't heard Bo screaming, although how *couldn't* they have heard?—but they'd only asked, *Hey, you seen Bo around?* And he and Sean must have answered some kind of way, because the boys had left them alone, cursing about Bo leaving them hanging. The boys had not come back. Maybe they had called Bo's house and found him safe in bed.

"He's *not* okay," Sean said forcefully. "He's d-dead."

Guilt smothered Corey, dogging his breaths, embers in his lungs. "Yeah. He's dead."

Sean's eyes gleamed with weary satisfaction, as if everything else would grow from that admission. "It's n-not your fault," Sean said. "The Old Testament t-talks about lying. B-bearing false witness. B-because it's evil. It's evil, Corey. You got t-tricked by something evil. Me, too."

Even her name, Becka, sounded like the *baka*. She'd been playing with him the whole time. Corey bowed his head, sobbing a rough sob. "You warned me," Corey whispered.

"Yeah, but I thought she was just a freak. I d-didn't know she was . . ." Sean's voice died.

Corey's eyes rose to gaze at the woods where Becka had come bounding out in her torn dress. He probably would faint in terror if he saw her, but what he felt wasn't only fear; it was fascination, even now. A bruising kind of longing. If he'd been able to, he would have killed Bo with his bare hands because she said Bo had touched her. Becka had taken control of him, like it was no work at all. And he had let her touch Gramma Marie's ring. Corey's skin went cold.

He had to go home and take a cleansing bath. But how could he go home now?

"Finish it," Sean said. "Tonight. We have to."

The thought of another spell made Corey's limbs shake. He sat beside one of the holes he and Sean had dug and felt nauseated again, beyond tired. He leaned over and spat into the hole, clear saliva. His stomach, like the rest of him, was empty.

"He burned it," Corey said. "It has to be on that paper."

"We'll get more paper. Let's do it tonight."

Corey shook his head firmly. Once he left this place today, he could not come back so soon. He might not be able to come back at all. "I can't."

"You *have* to!" Sean said, a roar. *"Somebody else might die."*

"Well, *fuck you!* I said *I can't!*" Spittle sprayed from Corey's mouth. A horde of wings flapped from the treetops behind them, birds disturbed by the noise.

Corey was more grateful for the dawn light than he could say, but he had to leave here. If he sat here another minute, he might lose his mind. Even with the light making last night feel more dreamlike, he could *see* Bo flailing in the ground, his face beet-red. Mud up to his neck, then up to his nose. He could hear Bo's screams, the hysteria and disbelief and terror all mingled, useless.

He could not come back here tonight. He could not.

"We can try tomorrow night," Corey said. "The Fourth of July."

Sean nodded, satisfied. "Let's fill up these holes and p-pack up our stuff. It's almost six. If we get b-back before seven, maybe we can sneak in before my d-dad gets up. . . ." Mr. Leahy went to bed early most nights, but he might already know he and Sean had not come home last night. *Last night?* Last night was a lifetime away. What could they say to him?

For the next half hour, Corey and Sean filled the holes the best they could, scraping dirt into the hollowed ground. Whatever he had done here, Corey knew The Spot had been changed by it. He could tell by the way it looked, wasted and perverted.

He had given the *baka* a human sacrifice.

And it would not want him to come back. It would try to stop him.

Corey kicked the crossed chicken bones into the fire-pit. Then he shoved his other ritual items into the duffel bag, taking care only with Gramma Marie's satchel and the papers inside. At least Bo hadn't burned those, too. He collected the index cards and wrapped a rubber band around them, then shoved them into his back pocket. His photograph with Gramma Marie went into his other pocket. Then, one by one, he picked up the three paper bags; the raven feathers, the soil, and the remaining chicken bones. He'd take those bags home with him later today, but he'd leave everything else at Sean's.

"I'm gonna keep most of this at your place," Corey said. "Gramma Marie's papers, too."

"Why?"

Because he didn't trust himself, Corey realized. Because if he couldn't make himself come back to The Spot, he might give up and try to destroy all of it. Gramma Marie said she'd thrown her ring away, and now he understood why. Corey thrust the satchel into Sean's waiting hands. "If something happens to me," Corey said, meeting Sean's eyes, "you have to burn those papers. Understand?"

"*Burn* them? But . . ."

"It's not about your family, it's about mine. I'm the last one. Burn them."

"What about your mom?"

Thinking of his mother, Corey pursed his lips to quiet a moan in his throat. He had tried to convince himself he didn't need Mom while he'd been living with Dad, but he did. She brought out some of the best parts of him, and soothed him in a way no one else could. What if he went straight home, fell on the floor at her feet, and told her everything? What if he could tell her the truth?

She would know her son was a murderer, he thought.

"Gramma Marie kept this a secret from her for a reason," Corey said, deciding. "She kept the *baka* away from Mom somehow. Mom says she hardly ever dreams, and I think that's why. I don't think it knows how to find her. Gramma Marie wrote about how some people are more open to forces, good and bad. I'm one of those people who's open, maybe. Mom's closed to it, and that's better for her. I'll give her the ring back. Maybe it'll protect her, and she'll never have to know." It was the most Corey had spoken in hours, and the effort of speaking parched his mouth and throat.

"Nothing's gonna happen," Sean said. "You'll banish it."

"But promise me, Sean. No matter what. Promise me you'll burn the papers, and you'll never tell what happened. You'll never tell what I did, how I . . ." He couldn't say it, and he didn't want to think about it too long. Bo's screams were bottled in his mind. "*Promise.*"

Sean blinked, his glassy eyes shining in the faint sunlight. "Promise, man."

They hugged a long time. Corey had never held on to anyone except family that tightly, or ever needed to. "Fourth of July," he whispered, barely audibly, in case the *baka* was listening.

And it *was* listening. It lived here.

"Fourth of July," Sean whispered back, a vow.

But no matter what day he chose, the *baka* was not going to allow him to come back. Just as Gramma Marie had described her feelings when she first discovered this place of spirits, Corey knew it in his bones.

⚞ Thirty-Two ⚟

$\mathcal{W}$HEN ANGELA HEARD THE FIRST GUNSHOT, her legs twined as she stumbled over a vine-shrouded root on the trail. The second and third reports helped her place the direction of the noise, and she stopped holding her breath. The shots were southeast of her, from somewhere on the other side of the house. Nowhere near Myles, probably.

But near the deputies.

Angela didn't have long to mourn, because she heard swishing brush behind her on the trail. With a shudder, she remembered the way the pile of leaves had crawled out of Corey's doorway and shot across the floor. But this sounded like someone with two legs, a creature she understood. Someone was running not far behind her.

Angela felt a gulf growing inside of her, something that was *not* her, speaking an undiscovered language in her mind; and that part of her was asking her to let Myles go. The aware creature buried in her psyche did not think Myles could follow her where she was going. Angela prayed it was Gramma Marie's voice steering her, but even if she could have known it for *certain,* she didn't think she could want Myles any less.

Without Myles to want, her heart was dead.

Angela couldn't call out, so she hid behind the nearest brush, the fingers of the damp sword ferns caressing her forehead as she peeked out. She reached inside her handbag and found Rob's .38, which was in a separate compartment so it would not disturb the *govi* she'd carried from Gramma Marie's altar. She could not allow the *govi* to fall or break, not before it was time.

Maybe Tariq was coming behind her. Somehow, that idea scared her less.
"*Angie?*"

Myles was trying to whisper, but he was still loud. Angela waited until
his parka was in sight as he ran from behind the leaning trunk of a fir tree
with his bow at his side. Vision alone no longer gave her real certainty, but
he smelled right, too. "I'm here," she said, standing up, the instant before he
would have passed her by. She would have stayed hidden if she had thought
he would turn back.

Myles's face was set so hard, his jaw looked like it ached. He didn't
smile, but she saw relief in his eyes as he slid to a stop on the mud and fir
needles. "There were gunshots," he said.

"I think it's the deputies." She brushed tiny dead fern leaflets from her
hair, trying to summon knowledge, but nothing more came. Gramma
Marie only showed her what she needed to see.

He eyed the gun in her hand. "Where are you going?"

"I have to face him."

"Please tell me you're kidding. Is this your idea of vengeance for Naomi?"

As soon as Myles said Naomi's name, Angela felt her hand squeeze
the gun more tightly. It might feel like vengeance, but it wasn't. This was
beyond her, Naomi, or Tariq. And it was beyond Myles, she realized. She
had to let him go.

Slowly, without speaking at first, Angela aimed her gun at Myles's chest.

Myles's face went harder still, as fixed as one of the centuries-old trees
surrounding them. Myles's expression triggered a memory in Angela that
was not her own: Red John. No, *John*, his true name. Angela had reached a
similar juncture with this man, or one with a twin soul.

"I won't hurt you," Myles said patiently, believing she was confused.
"This is Myles."

Angela's eyes batted away tears. "I know who you are. Go back, Myles."

"Don't point that at me unless you're prepared to do something about
it," he said, angry. His voice dared her.

"I am."

His eyes cut into her. "Like hell you are."

Maybe it's Dominique, John. Hell it is.

The memories were chattering voices in the rainfall now. Angela felt a
déjà vu so vivid that she could see John hidden in Myles's face. John had
hunted with a bow, too, skills he had learned from his grandfather. John
had hunted in these woods long before he met Gramma Marie, and he was
still somewhere here now. So was Gramma Marie, and she was trying to

come to her. Gramma Marie's memories were overrunning Angela's, melting time, a feeling as unsettling as it was astonishing. Angela didn't like relinquishing control, not for a minute, yet her mind was no longer hers alone. She needed Gramma Marie's memories if she was going to prevail over whatever was driving Tariq.

But Myles was a distraction. Angela hoped Myles couldn't see her hand trembling on the gun. He would only leave if he believed she would shoot him. First, she had to believe it herself.

"I'm about to count to ten, Myles," she said huskily. "Turn and go back. This has nothing to do with you. You'll hold me back. We'll both die like those deputies."

"Then we'll both die," Myles said. He didn't blink, and his face didn't change. His breathing had become very calm. He'd made up his mind, too. He was probably as afraid as he'd ever been, but his serenity was still in place, damn him. "I don't have a choice, Angela Marie. I can't make you come with me, but I'm not leaving you here."

"You stubborn idiot," she said. "Why can't you just trust me to do this?"

"*You* need to trust. Let yourself need somebody for once. I don't think you've trusted a soul since the day you found your mother with that gun in her mouth, sweetheart."

Angela squeezed her mind's eye shut to keep away the image of Mama with the gun. Even today, that memory cut deep. "You're bringing that up *now?*"

"Now is when I have to. I'm trying to save your life," Myles said. "Angie, I *am* here for you. I was always here. Don't run from me."

Angela felt her frightened heart surge, but her mind whirled with confusion. How could she tell the difference between the inklings from Gramma Marie and the deep, frightened parts of her that had always tried to send Myles away? Angela crouched down into the ferns to get out of easy view of the trail, and he crouched beside her. They both breathed a few seconds, not speaking.

"I can't bring you unless you're willing to admit what you're seeing," Angela said finally, hushed. "You freeze when we get in trouble, trying to think it through. We don't have time for that. You have to admit this is magic. This is a curse. If you can't admit that, you're no good to me."

Myles's jaw shook. "Angie, if you want me to admit I'm scared, hell, yes, I'm scared," he said, and his eyes looked plagued enough to prove it. She heard the growing tremor in his voice as he spoke so quickly and softly that she had to strain to hear him.

"That's not good enough. You have to accept what we're facing."

At that, Myles's composure cracked. His face looked ready to shout, but instead a strained whisper emerged from his trembling mouth. *"I don't know what I just saw at your house.* I have no way of knowing that, Angie. The only thing I *do* know is that I'm not leaving you out here alone."

She would never talk him out of it, Angela realized. She wished she did have the nerve to shoot this man in the leg, to save them both. "I do want you to be with me," Angela said, and the words felt like burrs in her throat. "I always have, even when I acted like a fool."

"You've got me," he said, reaching out his hand. "Come back with me, Angie."

Shit. She pulled away from him, deeper into the bush. *"This* is what I'm talking about. You don't understand. That's the quickest way to get us killed."

"No, no, don't go," Myles said, grabbing her arm tightly to pull her close. "I'm sorry. I had to make one last plea." He sighed, glancing over his shoulder, toward the trail behind them. "You say you're relying on your instincts. Okay, I believe you. If I'm out here with you, I don't have a choice. Just tell me why you're out here."

Angela looked away from him. "I have to go to The Spot. I don't know why."

"What about Tariq?"

Angela wished she had an answer, for both their sakes. All she knew was that she had to go to the Crossroads Forest. She imagined herself rubbing her body with soil there, pouring out the contents of the *govi*, burying them in the ground. That image of the burial had been in the wings of her mind since she'd first seen the *govi*, she realized suddenly. But that didn't tell her what to do about Tariq, or exactly how. "I'll know when the time comes," she said.

"That time is *here.* He's minutes away, if that."

"Don't argue with me, Myles. I have to do this."

"Then let's get moving."

Yes, it was time to start running again.

Angela ran in the lead, keeping a steady pace. She darted and ducked past the overhanging limbs and awkwardly placed tree trunks that steered the trail right and left at whim. She heard Myles behind her, matching her pace for pace. The rainfall against the forest's leaves and needles was a blanket of sound around them; steady, unyielding, harder and louder than it had been minutes ago. As more water seeped down to the trail, it would be harder to keep their footing. She could already hear water collecting in furrows around them, turning soil into slick mud. Much of the trail was already muddy, splashing as they ran. Her feet sank with each step, demanding more effort to pull them free, slowing her stride. Mud was appearing from nowhere.

Like the mudslide, she remembered, jolted.

Just keep running, she told herself. If she surrendered to fear, she and Myles would die.

The trail was nearly impossible to follow beneath the gathering mud, so Angela concentrated on landmarks as she ran: the moss-covered dead tree that looked like it was wearing a gown. A stand of dead Douglas firs still standing upright, their stunted limbs sticking out as if the trunks had been pierced by an arsenal of thick arrows.

But new memories were sailing into Angela's head, making her feel as if her mind were literally *expanding*: She recognized the place where Gramma Marie's favorite red huckleberry shrub had grown. And where John had been hiding when he shot a black bear the size of a grizzly. She recognized the place where Art Brunell's father and his friend Lance accidentally started a fire in 1945, which had burned a quarter-acre before dying out; and they'd never told they did it. She saw the unfriendly root that had tripped Dominique and skinned her knee when she was eight, days before the demons started laughing—and then tripped Corey and skinned his knee fifty-five years later, when he was eight, too. The memories made Angela dizzy, gathering strength with the beating rain. These new memories were only the ones closest to the surface, the ones tethered to her and Gramma Marie. These woods were a haven for spirits, and spirits lived on memories.

A question came to Angela that was so unsettling that it nearly made her stop running: *How could she distinguish between the voices of Gramma Marie and whatever forces her grandmother was fighting against?* What if she was becoming like Maddie Fisher in the bathtub?

"The ring will protect you," she whispered, trying to believe. "As long as you wear it."

Angela saw a dark spot on the ground ahead of her, something black, so she slowed, approaching cautiously. Was the clump real or an illusion created by another unfamiliar memory?

"What?" Myles said behind her.

Angela crouched, staring. It was a muddy piece of clothing. Her arms tingled decisively. She touched the fabric, lifting up the soggy rag with two fingers. It was mud-soaked except in spots; she saw shiny silver-colored numbering peeping through on each side. Hot blood flooded Angela's veins.

This wasn't Gramma Marie's memory, or anyone else's; this was *hers*.

"This is Corey's," she said. "This is Corey's shirt."

"Are you sure?"

Angela nodded. "Tariq brought it for him when he came that summer. A Raiders jersey."

"What do you think it means?" Myles asked.

Reluctantly, Angela dropped the shirt where she'd found it. She should not carry anything more than she needed today; she had to leave everything behind her. "We're closer to wherever I lost him," she whispered. Whatever happened to Corey had started before the Fourth of July. It had started in these woods. At The Spot.

They were closer to The Spot than Angela realized.

Angela saw Tariq's van parked in the clearing ahead, on the other side of the fire-pit. Its side door yawned open, but the van was dark inside because the windows were curtained. All she could see through the open door was the empty backseat.

Angela stood stock-still as fear coiled through her limbs, and not only because of the sight of the van. Her feet told her that she stood at the heart of a site that was accursed. Corey had experienced a horror here. The demon—the *baka*, its name occurred to her suddenly—had bested Corey here. Her son had watered this spot with tears. Someone had died here.

"*Down,*" Myles whispered, yanking her backward.

Together, they crawled away from the trail, following the long, thin trunk of a fallen fir tree that had been crowded out by taller, stronger trees. They climbed over the trunk, finding refuge in a thick patch of ferns. From the end of the trail, the van had been directly ahead of them, but now it was to their right. They saw the back window, the closed curtains, and the TARIQ1 tag.

"The police didn't see this parked here?" Myles whispered.

"It wasn't here."

"He couldn't have driven it back here. There's no way to pass."

"He didn't have to drive it." Like the gun had just come to the house. Like Onyx and the van had vanished a few days before. Ordinary travel routes were not necessary.

Myles leaned close behind her, his wet parka draped over her, and she could feel his heart pounding beneath his clothing. He whispered directly into her ear, practically soundless. "We have to know if he's there. Are you ready for that?" His lips touched her.

She nodded. Her heart wasn't ready, if its feverish beating was any sign, but she had to be.

Myles sighed, wiping rain from his brow. "Have you ever fired a gun?"

"No." She stared at the van's curtains, watching for movement from inside.

"Well, be ready to use it. I have to keep the bow. We both have to be armed."

"Agreed," she said.

"This is the safety. Keep it *off,*" he said, and he checked the pin on the body of her gun. She nodded, her palm tight and damp against the revolver. Thank God Rob had pressed her to take the gun, she thought. What had she been thinking to try to refuse it?

"I'll try to draw him out, to see if he's in there," Myles said. "If you see him, stay *out of sight.* Don't shoot unless one of us is in danger, and make sure I'm clear. How much ammo do you have?"

"Five shots, Rob said."

"Then conserve them. Don't fire more than twice. Don't pump away on the trigger. *Two* shots. Hopefully that'll be enough to distract him, and maybe I'll get my shot." He was speaking so softly, his words were no more than sweet breath in her face.

"Then I should shoot at him again right after you, or he might get you."

"Use your judgment, Angie. Handguns aren't good distance weapons, not like rifles. You have to worry about what happens to *you* later. This is a dangerous game we're playing. So, I'm asking you one more time: Are you *sure* this is what you want to do, doll-baby?"

Wanting had nothing to do with it. "Yes."

Myles looked disappointed, his face tightening, but he nodded, too. His expression reminded her of the way a condemned man might look at the cook bringing his last meal: He'd eat, but it wouldn't taste good. Myles kissed her, rolling his mouth and tongue across hers. Again, the kiss ended too soon.

"I'm trusting you," Myles said, resting his forehead against hers. "If we get separated, we should both head straight for the police."

Angela's knowledge came again, full-blown: They *would* get separated. She didn't know if it would happen now or later, but it would happen before the day was finished.

"I love you, Myles," Angela said. "I never stopped, not for a minute."

"I knew that, Angela Marie." He grasped her hand tight, kissing it, then closed his eyes. "Lord, please watch over us fools today. Please keep us in the safety of your arms as we struggle to prevail against the cruel forces that have been pitted against us. In Jesus's name we pray, amen."

Cruel forces. Maybe Myles understood, even if he refused to utter the word *demon.*

"Amen," Angela whispered beside him, hoping God's ears would not be deaf to her.

Her whole life, deep down, she'd suspected God never heard her or Mama at all.

———

Myles had first gone hunting with Pa Fisher when he was ten, a month after he moved to Sacajawea, and on that first outing, Pa had taught him to respect the odds.

Hunting was a game of wits. Men might have superior weapons and pure intellect, but big game animals had a primary advantage: the senses. An elk could hear a limb snap a half-mile away. Or smell a human presence up to a mile away if the wind was right, and pick up the scent of the spot a human had passed through a day after you were gone. With eyes protruding on the sides of their heads, deer and elk had better than three-hundred-degree vision. Their eyes took in nearly *everything.* Even with camouflage, decoys, and mating calls, Pa told him, the hunted had the advantage. The more he appreciated that, the better his odds would be.

Today, Myles was both hunter and hunted. Angie thought Tariq was no mere man, but when Myles's thoughts plunged in that direction, he felt himself seize up with childlike fear. A man with a gun in the woods was dangerous enough, but a beast with a gun in the woods could be invulnerable.

Myles's lungs seemed to have climbed into his throat as he crept in the brush outlying The Spot, trying to find the best approach to Tariq's van. Despite the cold rain, the air felt hot. The old lessons came back to Myles: patience and silence. A single misstep could betray him, so he couldn't hurry. He'd seen part of the interior of the van at first glance, and that had been clear. If Tariq was inside, he was lying across the front or hidden in back.

Myles blinked away rain and stinging perspiration trickling into his eyes. His glasses were so spotted with rainwater, he cursed his decision not to take the time to put in his contacts today. Eyeglasses had no place in the rain, the beads of moisture blurring his vision. He wished he could forget the glasses and take his chances with the twenty-eighty vision God had given him, but in a jumble of forest tones, he couldn't afford to miss a single shadow, jostle, or nuance. This hunt would be over if Tariq saw him first.

Myles made his way closer to the far side of the van from ten yards behind it; he was approaching the gigantic trunk of a fallen Douglas fir between him and the van. That tree could give him some cover, if it came to that. But first, he had to make sure Tariq hadn't thought of it first, that he wasn't stooped somewhere behind it. Myles's arrow was already pulled tight, ready to fly. He nestled the nock against his cheek, staring past the arrowhead to the spot it would hit if he fired. "Steady . . . steady . . . ," Myles whispered with each step.

The beating rainfall worked to his advantage, helping soften the sound of the dead leaves, but Myles still took care not to let his feet land heavily enough to crack the twigs on the forest floor. He'd been unsettled by the thick mud covering the trail earlier, but he missed its silence now. His hiking boots were bulky. He and Pa had worn padded fleece boots on their hunting trips, and Myles would give a finger for a pair today. He crept as quietly as he could, four feet from the tree trunk. Two more steps, and he could see if anyone was hidden on the other side of it.

POP

The only gunshot Myles heard was in his imagination. There was nothing behind the massive trunk except weeds and crabgrass. Myles swallowed hard, so relieved he had to blink to send his attention back to the VW. He wouldn't approach the VW from the open side because it would be easy for Tariq to come storming through the open door with his gun blasting, or to ambush him from the woods. The front seat windows were the only ones that weren't hidden behind curtains. The front windows were closed tight, so the bow would be useless even if Tariq was even three inches from his face. But at least he would know where Tariq was.

Driver's window first. Then, he'd step around to look through the windshield.

And then Tariq Hill is going to turn your face into a gaping hole.

Myles had known a guy in grad school with one of these old VW hippiemobiles, a red one with curtains partitioning off the front from the back of the bus. If Tariq's van had the same curtain, he'd be exposing himself at the windshield and see virtually *nothing* inside.

"But you knew this was insane in the beginning," Myles breathed to himself.

Today was the definition of insane, from the moment Rob Graybold had called his house and asked him to bring Angie to Art's jail cell. The insanity had only multiplied.

Myles ventured toward the clearing. Just like stalking a buck, he told himself.

"Myles?"

He had only taken his first step when he heard a woman's voice behind him. He whipped around, uncertain, still ready to fire. It had damn near sounded . . .

"Myles? Don't leave me here. I'm *scared*, Myles. I promise I'll leave my socks alone."

Myles's testicles seized up. It was Ma's voice, faint but unmistakable. The voice had come from the woods, where the cedar stand grew thick behind him.

The plaintive voice flew to him again. "Myles, take me back *home*. I want my fish. You *didn't* bring my goldfish. You left them in my room."

As he stared back at the woods, Myles's lips parted, dry. Through the beads of water on his glasses, he could see someone ahead, perched on the low-hanging branch of a leafless maple tree. Ma's hair was tied back, and she was dressed in the bright yellow sweater she'd been wearing when he took her to Riverview. Her legs were swinging gently back and forth, like a child's. She must be ten yards high, he calculated, stunned. *How could Ma have climbed* . . .

Myles's heart curdled, and he swallowed back a sickly taste in his mouth. However she was up there, he had to get to her. If she fell, she'd break a hip, or worse. He could climb over that Douglas fir trunk and claw his way through the tight thicket of devil's club that grew in his path, protected by yellow, spiny bristles.

But he didn't move. He was rooted in place by a discrepancy his mind couldn't dismiss: *His mother could not be in that tree.* His mother was in Skamokawa with Candace, where he'd left her.

"Let me go home, Myles. My memory is fit as a fiddle. We'll talk over old times. Remember the day we brought you home and you saw the room we'd fixed for you? I remember, Myles."

The skin on Myles's back itched up and down his spine. Whatever he was up against had the power to create illusions in his mind. A woman *did* seem to be sitting in that tree, and that woman looked like Ma, there was no denying it. But it was a lie, a trick of the senses.

"I can't live this way anymore, Myles. I can't be a burden to you. I'm going to jump."

Myles battled his instinct to run toward her. As he stared at Ma, years seemed to fade from her face, and she became a teenage girl, the way she looked in her old family photographs. Shockingly pretty. He blinked, stunned. She was only Ma again.

"No. That's not Ma," he whispered. "That's *not* Ma."

Don't look at her, Myles told himself. *Look away.*

Fighting tears, Myles forced himself to turn his eyes away from the apparition. His hands were no longer steady on the bow and arrow. He would regain control if he kept his focus on the VW in front of him. Only trouble was behind him.

"*Myles Richardson,* do you hear me? I'll *jump!*" the woman in the tree said.

When he was a child, Ma used to call him by his old name, Richardson, when she was angry. He'd known she was using emphasis the way some parents did with middle names, but it had always sounded like a reminder that he was adopted.

You have to admit this is magic. This is a curse.

Don't look back. Don't look back. Don't look back.

Myles's teeth ground as he took another step toward the VW.

"Two blind men cured . . . the dumb demoniac healed . . . the shekel in the mouth of the fish . . . the deaf and dumb man of Decapolis . . . ," Myles whispered, digging up buried memories. As a boy, when he'd asked Gramma Marie why she believed in miracles, she said she'd witnessed miracles here and there, the way another person would mention seeing a bald eagle. When he asked her to specify *what* miracles, she challenged him to memorize the miracles of Jesus in the back of her St. James Bible. *If you think of them all, one after the other, you'll see your way to believing.*

". . . a blind man of Bethsaida cured . . . Jesus passes unseen through the multitude . . . the great catch of fish . . . the widow's son is raised from the dead . . . a woman is freed from her infirmity . . ." Comforted by his miracles, Myles kept his eyes on the VW six yards from him. If that driver's side door opened suddenly, he was ready to shoot.

"See you soon, Snook!" the woman in the tree said. Myles did not look around.

Instead, he darted to peek quickly into the driver's side window.

Two seats, the gearshift, a Wendy's bag, and cassette tapes all over the passenger seat. Empty. And there were no curtains blocking the back. Good.

Breathing hard, Myles ducked down. Keeping out of sight, he crawled to the front of the vehicle, eye-level with the spare tire on the car's nose. He took two breaths and popped his head up to peer through the windshield, his eyes trained toward the back. The first backseat was empty. The second backseat was out of his view. Even a man Tariq's size could be hiding there.

Myles ducked again. This time, he didn't hesitate. One, two, *three*, he thought.

He ran around to the still-open side door. Angling his readied bow, Myles climbed into the VW and surveyed it: The interior smelled awful, like rotting food and old condoms, and the floor was covered in garbage. Clumps of dead leaves sat atop food wrappers and cigarette packs.

But there was no one inside.

Myles ran back into the woods to hide. He ventured a look toward the tree where Ma had been sitting—or whatever had wanted him to *believe* it was Ma—and the branch was empty. Decoys don't always work, Myles thought. Any hunter knew that.

Angie was where he'd left her, waiting. Embraced by the salal leaves, she looked like a girl again.

Approaching her, he thought of the two times she'd tolerated him during the summer when they were young kids, playing hide-and-seek on the endless expanse of her grandmother's property. Her Gramma Marie had *made* her play with him, Angie never failed to inform him. With Angie's intelligent eyes, bold attitude, and jet-black hair she wore in two pigtails, he had decided he was going to marry this girl the first time he'd seen her. But even then, life made it plain that he would never have Angela Marie Toussaint. *Never.*

But he had her today. Angie gave him a full, soft kiss.

"Tariq's not there," Myles said. He wanted to tell her about the woman in the tree, but didn't. He felt weak, manipulated. Maybe he was losing his grip. Even now, he wanted to go back to make sure Ma wasn't back there in a tree.

"I was worried when I didn't see you for so long," she said.

"I had to take my time. What do you need here, Angie?"

"I need to do a ceremony," she said. Her eyes were earnest, unself-conscious. Angie believed everything she said, a lunacy that would either save them or doom them.

"What does that mean?"

"I need you to watch over me, Myles. While I sit."

"Sit where?"

Her chin gestured toward The Spot, behind him. "Out there."

It was bad enough to be hiding this close to Tariq's van, inviting a chance meeting. But to sit out in the open? "Angie, that's foolhardy."

She nodded, agreeing, her cheeks drawn sadly. Despite the nonsense of her words, her eyes spoke perfect sense. He'd had the same reaction to her eyes inside Gramma Marie's house, when she challenged him upstairs.

There was a fever in her eyes, as if she were in the throes of a mild ecstatic state. But there *was* sense, too, undeniable. God might be talking to her.

"You're bent on getting me killed today, Angela Marie," Myles said. He'd meant it as a joke, but it sounded more like simple-told truth.

Angie shook her head, her face distraught. He knew that the tear gliding down her face was for him. "*No*, Myles," she said, pressing her palm to his cheek. "That's why I asked you not to come. I'm still not sure you understand."

"I . . ." Myles sighed, surrendering. "I saw someone in a tree who looked like Ma."

"It wasn't her," Angela said, her eyes fervent. "You see? It was trying to trap you."

Myles nodded. That felt more true than blaming his imagination. He shivered to his soul.

"I don't know what happens next, Myles. I *don't*," Angie said. "But this thing won't want me to do this. It's going to fight us as soon as I get close to finishing what I need to do."

"So you need me," Myles said. "Admit it."

Angie gave him a full smile, a sight that made his heart gladden despite the terrible new weight it carried. "Yes," she whispered, her face soft in a way it hadn't been all day. "I need you."

She pressed her hand against his parka, at mid-chest—to be sure he was wearing his pendant underneath, he realized. When Angie felt the hard clay pendant she'd given him safely in place, her smile relaxed. He thanked God he was wearing it, too. He thanked God for his cross of gold. Jesus help poor Art Brunell. Jesus help them all.

"I'm still me," he said, touching her cheek.

"Me, too," she said.

They kissed as if it were their last chance.

———

There are moments when time seems to slow, and others when it gains speed. Good times race past, memories before they're properly under way; and bad times linger, interminable. To Angela, from the moment she walked to the center of The Spot, time became a fog. Seconds and minutes were indistinguishable to her.

Only one moment mattered: *Now.* Her future depended on it. Much more than that depended on it.

The Spot wasn't muddied like the trail, Angela noticed. That didn't surprise her.

Myles was out of sight. He had chosen a strategic spot to watch her and the surrounding areas, hidden. He'd used what sounded like military terms: The van was at twelve o'clock; the trail, Tariq's likeliest entry point, was at six o'clock. Myles was hiding in the bed of salal at four o'clock, at a slight angle from the trail, which gave him a view of the trail, the entire clearing, and some distance beyond the van, except for one blind spot behind it. Myles had spoken his last word to her earnestly, holding her cheeks tightly between his palms: *Hurry.*

Everything rested, it seemed, on time.

Angela sat cross-legged as close to the fire-pit as she could, trying to anchor herself to the center of The Spot. Her gun remained in her hand, as Myles had instructed, the safety off. The *govi* was at her feet. She was as prepared as she could be.

Immediately, stillness enveloped Angela, a sensation so immediate that it startled her. Her heart had been racing when she left the sanctuary of the woods, but now it was so calm it was nearly silent. Angela was afraid to close her eyes. When she did, she felt as if she were releasing a part of herself, allowing one part of her to sleep so another could awaken. Her arms tingled violently, and then all sensation left them. Her feet tingled next, vanishing from her.

Frightened, Angela gazed toward Myles again, although his parka made him nearly invisible in the thicket. But she could see the brown spot that she knew was his chest, and she imagined where his face might be; where his eyes were gazing out from hiding, watching over her. She almost smiled at the place where she thought Myles's eyes were, until she remembered not to give his position away. Tariq might be watching. He most certainly was.

During the most dangerous time of her life, how could she feel so safe?

Angela gazed upward, toward the soaring treetops. As she stared at the trees, Angela realized she could already see something she had never noticed before: All of the trees bordering The Spot leaned *inward*, toward the place where she sat. They did not lean precariously, so it hadn't been obvious in all these years, but Angela saw the slight bend in their angles now, as if the trees themselves were bowing in worship.

It's happening now. I'm losing myself now, she thought, and she went rigid.

This felt like bedtime all over again, when she slowly surrendered to sleep and jumped to wakefulness as soon as she slipped into new territory, into places that scared her. She ran from the memories. She always ran. But she would not run now. She could not. With a deep sigh, finding strength in the scents of cedar and fir around her, Angela closed her eyes.

And slipped, as if through a hole in her mind. A low hum surrounded her; not a machine's hum, but a hum that sounded like a chorus of human voices in soft unison. She heard the pattering rainfall, which sounded like drumming. She heard repeated rhythms, endless patterns inside the rain. One in particular transfixed her:

Tap-tap-TAP-taptap Tap-tap-TAP-taptap Tap-tap-TAP-taptap

Her body swayed gently to the call, and she slipped again, deeper into herself.

Corey is here. Corey's spirit is strong, and he makes Gramma Marie stronger.

The realization came to Angela so vividly that she nearly snapped back to herself, wanting to reach out to her son somehow, but she willed her mind to remain calm. She allowed her heart and mind to follow only the sound of the rain.

Bad images came, because she could not avoid them.

She saw Mama standing beside her dresser in house shoes and a thin pink nightgown, a pistol stuck in her mouth like a toothbrush. *Don't worry, Sugar. It's not loaded.* She saw Mama's cornrowed scalp on the kitchen table beside a glass of orange juice. She saw Mama as a girl with bows in her hair, clapping her hands over her ears and screaming the day the demon came.

Have you ever seen magic, Bo?

Involuntarily, Angela stiffened when she saw the next image: Corey and Sean yelling and crying as they witnessed a horror, trying to pull someone out of the mud. Then, she saw Corey climbing down the stairs to the wine cellar, grinning back at her. *I'm gonna take care of you good, Mom.* And Corey's blood on the floor, snaking toward the wall.

I can't do this, she thought. *I can't do this.*

Yes, cher. Yes, you can.

The images faded. Instead, she felt herself floating, flying.

"Come to me, Gramma Marie," she whispered. "I surrender to you. Come."

Then, Angela felt herself digging her fingers into the damp ground, pulling out clumps of soil. When she had two hands full of soil, she raised them to her face and smeared the soil on her skin, rubbing it into her hair. She felt her entire body tingle the way her arms had been, coming to life.

Vinn jwenn mouin, Angela Come to me

With her hands that no longer felt sensation, Angela reached for the *govi*. More than ten years ago, three days before her dying breath, Gramma Marie had blessed this *govi*, leaving strands of her hair and clipped nails inside to preserve her *gros-bon-ange*, her life-spirit, which would become her *esprit* when she crossed to the plane of death. She had labored to paint the wall blue so she could send Angela or Corey to find her when the time was right. She had screamed from the effort of pushing the stove in front of her altar, so it would be hidden. She almost hadn't bothered with so much effort, but she'd had a terrible dream the night before that the *baka* was perched in her walnut tree, reminding her that *something could go wrong* with the papers she'd left in the closet.

The *govi* was her secondary plan. If the papers failed to bring someone to rid this place of the *baka*, she would have to find the strength to come back through her *govi*. With Corey's spirit beside her, she had that strength at last. She herself would set it right.

Angela poured the hair and nails from the *govi* into a hole in the soil, then she buried them, patting the soil down. She was nearly finished. She had only to remember the word now, speak it.

But the smell was here already, rancid, as if it were rising from a mass grave directly beneath her. The *baka* was still strong. The *baka* would fight. This was its last chance to live.

Angela's index finger burrowed into the soil, drawing the characters from her ring in a circle around her, to spell the stolen word Papa Legba craved to have returned to him.

But hurrying was useless. The fight had begun.

A terrible shout came. Angela leaped to her feet dizzily, popping back into her own head. Her limbs felt awkward to her, difficult to control. She swayed and blinked, confused by the trees bowing around her. Why was she outside? *Where was she?*

Then, she saw Myles.

Myles stood outside his hiding place, his face in a grimace, his arrow pulled back to his cheek. He was going to shoot her. His face looked as if he had waited all his life for this opportunity to shoot an arrow through her chest. Angela felt more disappointed than frightened when she saw the alarm and hatred in Myles's face. The *baka* had circumvented his charm, and now poor Myles was suffering just like Art Brunell. The demon was probably making him watch.

Nearly too late, Angela thought to raise her gun. But her gun was no longer in her hand.

"*Down!*" Myles shouted at her.

Angela didn't pause to think. She dropped flat to her back like a rag doll. She immediately heard a *shwwwwwuNNk* sound, and she watched Myles's arrow fly only three feet above her eyes, gone in a blink. Behind her, someone howled.

Angela turned toward the cry. Tariq came limping out of the brush with his Glock, his mouth wrenched with pain. Myles's arrow was buried in the meat of Tariq's upper left thigh. He must have been hiding on the other side of her, ready to shoot, but Myles had seen him first.

Tariq's gun was aimed directly at her.

The last time Angela had seen Tariq was in divorce court, when he was all composure and his pain-reddened eyes turned from hers after she'd ignored his attempts at a greeting. He had not seemed so big then. She would have felt sorry for him, if her anger had allowed it. Seeing him now, Angela remembered how much she used to cringe when the anger in Tariq's voice passed the danger point, when she knew he was ready to hit her. Or, if he could have his wish, to get his gun and kill her. All these years later, he was ready to use his Glock to shut her up.

Another arrow flew, this one lodging in Tariq's left shoulder, inches from his heart. With another howl of pain, Tariq stumbled, turning off-center as he absorbed the impact of the arrow, but he did not fall, and he did not drop his gun.

This time, he didn't aim at Angela. He aimed beyond her, toward Myles.

Angela saw Myles reaching for his quiver. For an arrow.

Her hands grabbed her .38, her last gift from the man whose grandfather had run a mile to tell Gramma Marie that her daughter wouldn't stop screaming, a kindness Gramma Marie never forgot. Angela had a firm grasp, and she aimed the gun toward Tariq.

Five bullets. Shoot twice. Her mind knew what to do.

She squeezed the trigger.

The trigger held firm, not moving. Still, a gunshot exploded in the quiet woods, crumbling Angela's thoughts and chasing away the birds that had been nesting silently around them. Angela tried to pull the trigger again, but there was silence this time. She checked the safety, and it was still in the *off* position Myles had shown her. How had she fired if the trigger hadn't moved?

A moan made her look back at Myles. His bow had fallen, and he was doubled over, making a terrible noise she had not allowed herself to hear before she looked at him.

Tariq staggered behind Angie, within five feet of her, so close she could smell the stink of the *baka* on him. The terrible reeking almost drove her to vomit. "I'm disappointed in you, Angie," Tariq said, his voice surging low from his throat. "He's the best you could do?" Tariq was festooned with the two arrows, wincing in pain, but he grinned at her.

With a scream of frustration, Angela aimed directly up at his broad, smiling face, tugging on the trigger again. Again, it stuck in place. The *baka* hadn't been able to still Myles's arrows, but it had frozen her gun. Her body felt full of sand, heavy and useless.

"Angie, *run!*" Myles groaned, and she turned in time to see him fall to his side, curled in a ball.

"No, Angie, please stay," Tariq said gently. "I planned this especially for you, Snook."

"*Leave him alone!*" Angela cried. As Tariq strode toward Myles's prone form, Angela hurled large stones from the fire-pit at him. As a stone sailed over Tariq's head, she heard Myles's bow crack beneath Tariq's foot. The next stone hit Tariq squarely in the back with a *thunk,* but he only turned and wagged a finger at her. Then, he aimed his Glock at Myles's head.

Angela begged, blubbered, bawled. She felt as detached from herself as she'd been as she poured the contents of the *govi* into the soil, present and yet not present. Her mind was breaking.

"Run—" Myles implored again, through gritted teeth.

Tariq fired.

With a scream, Angela wrenched her eyes away. But not before she saw the spray of blood.

Angela's legs rediscovered their strength, and she pitched herself toward Tariq's van, pushing off the rear bumper to help her run faster into the woods. When she heard the third gunshot, Angela's legs felt so drained of strength that she had to cling to a tree trunk to keep her balance. Her scream became a sob. The tree was friendly, covered with soft moss that caressed her face as she fell against it. She swung by her arms, steadying herself. The tree helped her run on.

Angela was crying and blind from tears of grief and fright, but she ran; leaping over fallen trunks, squeezing between standing trees, fighting her way into vine maple and salmonberry.

She ran as if she were flying.

✥ *Thirty-Three* ✥

JULY 4, 2001

S O, WHAT DO YOU THINK you'd like to do with your life after college, Corey?"

The woman had to ask him twice, because although Corey heard the
question, he didn't remember to answer. He kept looking toward the foyer,
watching new people come into the house, hoping to see Sean. Corey had
been stuck at a movie with his parents yesterday, and he hadn't had the will
to leave the house since. He wanted to be near his parents, even if he was
only sleeping in his room with his blinds pulled down and his curtains
closed tight.

But tonight was *the* night. Within twenty minutes, he and Sean needed
to start driving to Portland, or they would never make it to the *botanica* before it closed at eight; they were lucky it was open on a holiday. Sean was supposed to come pick him up in his friend's car, but Sean was baby-sitting until
his father came home, trying to win enough points to be in his good graces.

Corey didn't know what had happened between Sean and his father,
but Mr. Leahy had knocked on Sean's door at eight yesterday morning and
told Corey he had to go home. He sounded mad as hell, and Corey wondered what Sean had told him. Even without knowing Corey had been out
all night, Mom had been riding him from the moment he came home.
*Where did you leave your jersey? You look like you didn't get a wink of sleep. Why
are you so quiet?*

Corey felt himself pulling away from his surroundings, his mind floating, which had been happening a lot since yesterday. He gave himself a

reality check: He was in the living room talking to a doctor at his parents' party, a woman in her thirties he'd never met. Her hair reminded him of Becka's, so he kept his eyes away from her hair.

"I write lyrics. I think maybe I'd like to work with horses, too, be a vet or something," Corey said, answering her question at last. He was thinking about Sheba.

"My sister is a vet," the woman said. "Let me know if you have any questions about schools."

"Yeah, a'ight," Corey said, but he drifted away from her and her hair, staring toward the door.

He wanted to go back to bed. He didn't remember *ever* feeling as sick as he felt today. Like *death warmed over,* as the saying went. Every part of him felt wrong, wrecked. Whether it was because of his beating or reasons he didn't want to know, his entire body felt as stiff as a slab of concrete, his stomach worst of all. His mind felt sick. His heart felt sick. He wanted to crawl into his closet and sit in the dark, if he weren't so afraid of what he might see in the shadows, the way he felt afraid whenever the walnut tree bumped against his window.

He wanted to close his eyes and feel *nothing.*

What he really wanted, maybe, was to be dead. Maybe Mom's mother had known what she was doing when she took all those sleeping pills. No pain. No worries. No guilt. Freedom.

Bad, bad thoughts.

Corey didn't like having such bad thoughts, but he'd given up on having what he wanted. He *wanted* to be able to go back to The Spot and change what had happened. He *wanted* to take back his wish against Bo. He wanted to stay safe in his house tonight instead of having to walk back into the house of whatever spirits had been toying with him at The Spot. He didn't have a damn thing he wanted. All he had was bad thoughts.

And a stomachache.

Corey couldn't be sure, but the bad thoughts seemed to be hatching in his stomach. The stomachache he'd first noticed at The Spot had never left, and it only felt worse after three cleansing baths, even when he followed Gramma Marie's instructions *to the word.* Nothing soothed the grinding ache in his stomach. Some of it was a souvenir from Bo, but there was something else hiding inside the pain. Maybe it was the *baka,* Corey thought. Maybe this was what it felt like when the *baka* crawled inside you.

Fuck that, he thought. He'd rather be dead.

Mom gave him a look from the other side of the room, checking on him. She was talking to a family wearing identical T-shirts in the foyer. Corey smiled, trying to pretend he was having a good time, but he knew it must be one sorry smile. He tried to duck out of Mom's sight on the far side of the living room, where there weren't as many people. The jazz saxophone from the speakers squealed in his ear. Coltrane. "A Love Supreme." Mom played that all the time.

A woman's voice near him broke through the music. He heard her say *Elijah Goode.*

The woman who was speaking was standing near the piano, with a thin face that could use some sun. "He chose this place because he said the land felt 'blessed beyond all description,' or in any case that's what he wrote to his brother. Marie Toussaint worked for him for a time, and he left her this house in his will."

Gramma Marie worked for him, all right, Corey thought.

"Are you kidding me?" said the man who'd been talking to Mom, the T-shirt man. He lifted his red-haired son to his back the way Corey's father used to give him rides when he was little. Watching, Corey wished he were young enough for his father to carry him again. "I never heard that. I figured it was something to do with Mrs. T'saint and her teas."

"Oh, no. It's much more than that," the woman went on. "In 1929, three years after Marie Toussaint took ownership of this house, a mudslide destroyed the other homes on this side of town. . . ."

The word *mudslide* made Bo's sinking head pop into Corey's mind, and his stomach squirmed, this time with nausea. Why had she brought *that* up? It had to be a bad omen to hear someone talk about the mudslide, today of all days. The *baka* was proud of the mudslide.

Corey didn't want to hear the rest. He slipped past the French doors into the dining room, hoping he could find some quiet. He was in luck. Although the people in the kitchen were louder than he wanted them to be, the dining room was empty, a sanctuary.

Corey walked to the rear picture window, where he could see Dad standing over the grill on the corner of the deck, basting ribs while he talked to three or four guys. Corey wondered if the other men were standing close enough to get a good whiff of his father in the breeze; even though Dad loved soaking in the bathtub, he smelled like shit today.

Corey watched his father a long time, pressing his palm to the window. He felt like a prisoner in his new life, locked away from Mom and Dad both. Corey had never known he hated lying so much.

You just have to go to The Spot one more time. Tonight, it's all over.

For once, good thoughts came. Uplifting thoughts. He could do this.

But first things first. He had to give Mom's ring back. The *baka* had ruined it for him.

". . . He said it was voodoo for sure," the man's voice floated in from the living room behind him, and people laughed as if he were telling jokes. *Art Brunell, that's his name. But he won't think that's funny before too very long. He'll learn some respect.* The thought appeared, sure of itself, although Corey didn't know the man's name and didn't care.

Not all of his thoughts were his own anymore.

As he shivered, feeling disoriented, Corey *smelled* the mud that had killed Bo, and the smell reminded him of Becka. As soon as he thought of her, dead leaves blew across the dining room floor, fanning near his feet. He heard something fall over inside the china cabinet, glass toppling. Leaves were in the china cabinet, too, bunched against the glass.

When Corey gasped, the leaves were gone.

But it was here. It didn't look like Becka anymore—that was only *one* way it could look—but Corey felt something slide past him like a jellyfish, cold and soggy. The smell alone made him take two steps back, covering his nose. One of the dining room chairs skittered to the side, rocking back and forth on its legs before settling again. Corey swallowed, trying to dislodge what felt like a rock in his throat. His heart was pummeling him. Gramma Marie's blessings should have prevented the *baka* from walking inside the house, but it was here. Had *he* allowed it to come inside?

The French doors shuddered. The thing was moving into the living room.

Corey burst through the French doors, trying to follow its invisible trail. But there were too many people in here, and how could he track something he couldn't *see*?

He saw Gramma Marie's statues on the piano, the mantel, and the shelves, and suddenly he knew them on sight: They were Papa Legba and Shangó and Labalèn and Oyá and Oshún and Oggún and Simbi la Flambo and Gran Ibo and Ezili la Flambo. Gramma Marie had written about them all. They should be protecting the house. As Corey stared at them, the silent statues seemed to weep.

WE HAVE FUCKED UP BIG.

Mom wasn't in the living room, even if everyone else in town was. Corey thought there must be at least fifty or sixty people crowded in the room, even though Mom had invited thirty *exactly*. It wasn't a costume party, but the flock of people standing near the picture window on the other side of the room wore black top hats and tuxedos, their faces covered with masks that looked like grinning skulls. The masked figures fanned themselves with thick, leafy twigs, screeching at each other like ravens. Mom had not invited them. Corey knew that.

Maybe he was dreaming now. Maybe that was it.

"Where'd my mom go?" Corey asked the man in the matching T-shirt, Art Brunell. This man wasn't wearing a mask, but he was laughing as if his head would burst. While Corey stared at the man's laughing jowls, he saw streams of smoke escape from his nostrils although he wasn't smoking.

The man leaned close to him, cupping his ear. "How's that?"

Corey forgot his question, staring up at Art Brunell's son, who was on his back. The boy's lips were purple, his eyes vacant and white as he grinned at him. His neck was ringed with bruises.

Welcome to death, kid, Corey thought, and suddenly the boy looked normal again.

"You seen my mom?" Corey mumbled, remembering his question.

Art Brunell pointed toward the foyer, winking. "Thataway, kiddo," he said.

Mom wasn't in the foyer, but she'd probably gone through the butler's pantry to the kitchen, her favorite route. Corey paused before walking inside the butler's pantry. He gazed at the door to the wine cellar beyond him, at the end of the hall. He heard a clanging noise beyond the cellar door. Where Corey was standing, the floor shook as if a train were racing past.

Hellbound Express, he thought.

He must be going crazy like his grandmother, Dominique. But there was one thing about his grandmother Dominique worth admiring, Corey thought: When it came to demons, she'd had the last laugh, hadn't she?

Curiosity almost made Corey open the cellar door, but he had to find his mother first. He had something important to do. Something to give her.

There were no strange smells or sights waiting for Corey in the kitchen, and he breathed with relief. Gramma Marie was strong in this room. This room had not yet been overtaken, and people seemed to know it, because the room was bright, crowded, and full of laughing. Corey saw his mother standing over the sink with a wineglass, digging into the sink for ice. She yanked her hand out of the sink, cursing. Gramma Marie was trying to talk to her, to warn her.

"Mom? Can I talk to you? I have to give you something."

Mom's eyes studied him. Even with Gramma Marie so close, Mom didn't know how to listen. But she would, one day. Gramma Marie would teach her.

"Baby, how's your stomach?" Mom said.

"Whatever, it's a'ight," he said, his first of many lies. As soon as he'd walked into this room, his stomach had begun screaming. He had to go back to the foyer, near the wine cellar. He had to shut up his stomach. He led Mom where he wanted to go, away from the people, away from the pain.

"Mom, I did something, and I have to make it right. It's been heavy on my mind."

The sound of his own voice, so controlled and rational, surprised him. He'd been trying to think of what to say—trying to remember *why* he wanted to talk to his mother—but luckily, his mind knew how to speak for itself. The ring was in his hand, ready. He opened his palm so his mother could see it, and the joy in her eyes helped him fight the feeling that he was melting away like the ice in the sink. Melting like the Wicked Witch of the West.

"At first, I was gonna play like I'd seen it at a yard sale or something, and say, 'Hey, Mom, look what I found, it's just like Gramma Marie's.' But it's the same one." Corey was proud of how lucid he sounded. He must not be as crazy as he felt. Besides, so far, he was telling the truth, and the truth felt good. "*I* threw the brick and broke your window, Mom. It sounds dumb, but there was this girl I liked, right?" Before he knew it, he was telling her all of it, how Sherita had refused to give the ring back, how he'd panicked. His stomach still complained, but Corey's heart loosened, freed.

TAKE the ring, Mom. TAKE it, he thought, because he was fighting the urge to pull it away from her, not to let her touch it. Whatever had invaded the house did not want Mom to have the ring because it might serve as a weapon for her later. Whatever had invaded the house was creeping into his thoughts again, making him wonder why he was so eager to banish the *baka* when the *baka* had always done as it was bidden. *Why not throw the ring down the bathtub drain where it belongs?*

"How'd you get this ring back?" Mom whispered, taking the ring at last.

He almost told her, because he enjoyed the freedom from his lies. The new lies he'd invented refused to leave his mouth, so he glanced away from her. But then he imagined Mom sinking into a pool of mud, screaming and flailing her arms, and he told Mom what he'd rehearsed: He had written to Sherita, and she'd sent the ring back to him. Voilà.

He visited his old life for a minute or two with her mother, actually *talking* to her the way she always complained he wouldn't; even joking with her *(Like they say on TV, I cared enough to give the very best)*. When he saw in her face how much he'd hurt her by stealing her ring, he suddenly didn't care about anything else. He was sorry. He would rake leaves, pick up trash, and pull weeds all summer without complaining, just to make things right.

"I know you're mad at me, huh? Well, I've been thinkin' about a punishment—"

"Corey . . ." Mom cut him off, touching his chin. There was something about being able to rest his chin in her warm palm that made Corey feel more like himself than he had since before Dad moved away. "I don't know if you remember, but not long after you took this ring, everything fell apart for us. Your daddy and I lived in separate houses, in separate cities, and we forced you to choose between us. I think maybe that's punishment enough. What do you think?"

I'm sorry, I'm sorry, I'm sorry. The longer Mom touched him, the more he was sure he would lose himself to sobs. He could curl up in her warm palm and sleep, safe and free.

"Come here, baby . . . ," Mom said, and she hugged him.

Corey clamped himself tight, stiffening. He could barely let himself listen as Mom told him how he'd grown into a young man, how proud she was, how much she loved him. If he couldn't keep his emotions under control now, he never would. Not in time to go to The Spot.

Corey didn't think he could pull himself away from her hug. She would do *anything* for him. Maybe she could help him tonight, somehow. Maybe she knew more than she'd let on. Maybe she already knew about the curse. Corey imagined going to The Spot with his mother to finish the banishment, and his heart soared. They were stronger together than they were apart, he realized. With their spirits combined, it would be harder for the *baka* to bother them.

How hadn't he seen it before?

"Mom, did Gramma Marie tell you stuff about the ring? Like, those symbols. Did she tell you what they mean?"

Nothing showed in her face. "It's West African, she told me. She got it from her grandmother, and I forget how far it goes back before that. At least another generation. I guess she thought it was a good-luck charm."

He had to make her understand what he was asking. Corey paused, taking a breath. "But what about the symbols? She never told you anything about them? Like . . ." *Like Bo Cryer being sucked shrieking into the mud.* ". . . if they're supposed to have powers or something like that?"

Mom's face was all ignorance. "Powers?"

"You know," he said. "If they could . . . make things happen?"

"What kind of things, Corey? I don't understand."

Corey felt his heart breaking. She didn't know. Gramma Marie hadn't told her anything, so it was all on him. No one else could carry this weight tonight. Even if he tried to tell her now, there wasn't time to make her believe him. He had run out of time.

"Nothin'. Forget it," he said, whispering.

Mom seemed to feel bad then, as if she'd failed him. He hadn't meant to make her feel bad, so he tried to throw her a bone or two, teasing her about how Dad was sneaking to her room at night. When he said that, her face nearly flushed, and he realized how pretty she must have been when she was sixteen. No wonder somebody had climbed the tree to ask her to the prom.

Then, Corey felt his stomach lock, as if someone had a wrench and had tightened his insides. The pain dazzled him, making him forget what he'd been saying, something about trying to fix mistakes. But some of them couldn't be fixed. He knew that now.

"Corey, you look awful," Mom said. "Are you sure you're all right? You don't have to help with the fireworks if you want to lie down. I'll explain it to your dad."

With the arrival of the pain, his mother's voice tortured his ear. He wanted *quiet*. He had to get himself together. His thoughts were rolling around him, hard to capture. He was sinking in his own mind, like Bo had sunk into the ground.

"I'm *fine*, dag," he heard himself say.

"Then do me a favor and go to the cellar and bring some sodas up, okay? They're stacked in the corner. Bring up a couple cases. And you might as well bring up the fireworks, too."

Why was this fucking bitch always telling him what to do? Why couldn't he stand still and have one fucking moment of PEACE AND QUIET?

"I have to go to Sean's," Corey said. He had his own plans tonight, and that was that.

His mother's mouth began nattering again, making excuses, saying I-told-you-so, giving him orders. *She never listens—she only talks. If she doesn't shut up, I'LL LOSE MY MIND.*

Maybe losing his mind wasn't such a horrible thing, Corey thought. His problem was, he *needed* to lose his mind. His mind was holding him back. He should have celebrated when that fat-ass redneck got sucked into the mud, because even if Becka had lied, that didn't mean Bo wasn't a waste of air. He and Sean had acted like punks after it happened. What was all the drama about? *He'd WANTED it to happen, so why had he been crying?*

Again, the mind-twister came to Corey: Since the *baka* had been so good to him, why did he want to banish it? Exactly *what* was the point of that?

The logic was fucked up. No matter how much Corey turned the question over in his mind, he could not think of an answer that made sense. The *baka* could give him anything he wanted. That was the *point* of having a word stolen from the gods.

It was so obvious, Corey couldn't fathom how Gramma Marie had missed it.

Mom was looking at him with her puppy-dog eyes, so desperate to know if Corey loved her even if she didn't give a damn about him. If she did, she wouldn't have let him move out. She fought for everything else, but this time she'd shed a few tears and let him go. Well, fuck her for not trying. Fuck her for deciding not to be his mother.

Corey gave his mother the smile he knew she wanted from him, all sweetness and sunshine.

"I'm gonna take care of you good, Mom," he said, winking. "You wait."

——

Becka was waiting for him in the wine cellar.

As he climbed down the stairs, he saw her sitting naked on the floor, her shiny blond hair hanging gently across her shoulders. Her bright areolas gaped like bloodstains against her pale skin. Corey knew he was mad at Becka, although he couldn't quite remember why. He didn't let himself feel glad to see her, even if he wanted to be.

The walls in the cellar were thickly overgrown with vines. The bearskin rug—or whatever kind of skin it was—lay across the entire floor, just like in his dream.

Becka stood up, her lithe body unfolding. His eyes traveled from her breasts to the ridges of her ribcage, then to her pelvic bone inviting his gaze to the thatch of blond hair between her legs. Becka smiled as he looked at her. She walked along the wall where the wine shelves were hidden from sight by vines and moss. Corey's eyes followed the slope of her buttocks, the deep dimple in her ass cheek that appeared when she flexed her leg.

"Stay here with me, Corey," she said.

"I can't," he said. "I have to bring up the sodas. And the fireworks."
That was it. *That* was why had come down here.

Becka bared her teeth. "Why?" she said. "Because *she* told you to?"

Corey didn't have an answer for that. It *did* sound ridiculous when Becka put it that way. Humiliating, really. Becka posed seductively against the wall, one arm raised high. She looked like a centerfold from the stack of *Playboys* his father kept under his bed.

"You lied to me," Corey said, remembering that, too.

"Sorry, Corey, but you needed help. You were too slow. You were going to let him *get away* with it. You could have died when that horse threw you."

"True," Corey muttered.

"The Beaumont Cryers of this world make other people miserable their whole lives."

"True."

"So I just helped you take care of your business, Corey. What's wrong with that?"

"Nothing's wrong with that."

There—he'd admitted it. Bo got what he deserved.

"It's survival of the fittest. And you're the fittest, Corey, because you have *me*."

But that was only a trick, wasn't it? How could he have someone who wasn't *real*?

"I heard your wish when you were at The Spot," Becka said. "You wished for me. I'll be anyone you want me to be, Corey. I can be Vonetta. Would you like that?"

Before he could answer, Becka had vanished and Vonetta had taken her place; skin the color of caramel, full lips, wide hips, a fuller ass. Vonetta's areolas were the color of chocolate syrup. Corey's eyes savored her, amazed. He took a step toward her, not realizing he'd moved.

"There's no reason you should die a virgin, Corey," Becka said through Vonetta's mouth.

"Who said anything about me dying a virgin?" Corey said, surprised. Who had said anything about him *dying*?

"It could happen. It would be a tragic turn, don't you think?"

Corey couldn't think of anything more tragic. The idea of it almost brought tears to his eyes.

Vonetta knelt, reaching under the edge of the carpet of fur. She pulled out a gun—Dad's old gun with tape wrapped around it. It was the gun Mom had forced Dad to give away, bossing him around, as usual.

"I don't want that," Corey said.

"Yes, you do. You've wanted it a hundred times, to *shut her up*."

That was an exaggeration. He might have thought about it once or twice, in the same fantasy part of his head that liked running over old ladies with his car when he played Grand Theft Auto 3 on PlayStation2. But T.'s brother had run over someone in real life, and there was no fun in that.

It was *Dad* who'd wanted his gun back. It was *Dad* who sometimes wanted to kill her.

Now, Becka was Becka again. Presto change-o.

"You'll need to be a man and do this, Corey," Becka said. "She's a ball-breaker."

She showed him a vision in his head of how easy it would be: He would take the gun, climb the stairs, and see Mom talking to a black man with a shaved head who'd just come through the door. The man was an old boyfriend, and Mom was flirting with him like a skank, with her husband right outside. Corey would shoot the man first, and then he would shoot Mom. *Pop. Pop.* Quick and dirty, to the head.

Then, *he* would be the only one left in the line. He could have his ring back. He would have Becka all to himself.

Becka smiled. "That's good, Corey. The more you want to do it, the more you'll like it here. It doesn't have to hurt."

She was right. Already, Corey's stomach felt good again. The twisting pain was gone.

"Do you want me, Corey?" Becka said.

Corey nodded. "Yes," he said. He couldn't deny it.

She held out the gun to him, dangling it. Corey took it and wrapped his palm around it. He'd always wanted to shoot this gun. *Pop. Pop.* Quick and dirty.

"Bossy people are slave drivers, and they deserve what they get," Becka said, and Corey couldn't argue. Mom had been driving him like Kunta Kinte all summer. "Go on, Corey. I'll play music for you on the piano, to give you a grand entrance."

The piano introduction would be a nice touch. Becka thought of everything.

"The music's playing, Corey."

And it was. It was muffled and off-key, but Corey heard music floating from the foyer, one of the old jazz ballads. "Getting to Know You." He imagined himself dancing to the music with Becka like Fred Astaire and Ginger Rogers in one of those old-school musicals, gliding across the floor.

"I'll be here when you come back," Becka said.

Corey felt his foot climb up the first step to go back to the foyer. He had already forgotten where he was going, or why, but he hoped he would remember when he got there. *Pop. Pop.*

You be careful on those steps, Li'l Angel.

On the stairs, a dark-haired black woman stood above him in his path. Although he could not see her face, her hair was in cornrows, and she wore a long dress showered in colors, with bangles and bracelets of cowrie shells draped across her wrists. She was an amazing sight.

Becka shrieked. *"You can't come in here, YOU BITCH!"*

Sure enough, the woman was gone, as if he'd imagined her. Had he brought Gramma Marie in here? Was he strong enough to do that? Tears came to Corey's eyes as he thought of his great-grandmother. *She'd been here.* Realizing that, he couldn't pretend he didn't see the horror of what Becka wanted him to do. Becka was trying to make him into someone else, like she tried to do that night with Bo at The Spot.

But he could still fight. He would *believe* he could fight even if it wasn't true.

Corey stepped down, away from the stairs. He faced the *baka.*

Corey's stomach knotted immediately, and he doubled over in pain. This wasn't the pain from Bo's kicks. This pain went deeper, to his soul. The *baka* was taking him by force.

Already, Corey felt a curtain falling inside him, everything going gray. Corey felt words come from his throat, the last remnants of himself he could find. "I love my mom, and I won't shoot her for you. I won't do *anything* for you."

Becka's grin turned hard, cocky. "Oh, I see it differently, Corey. You're going to shoot the man and then you're going to shoot your mother. *Count* on that. I get what I want."

Corey's body seized, shaking. He was aware of a feeling of struggle, even if his mind was so stripped that he couldn't recognize what the concept of struggle was, or whom he was fighting. Still, he held on, clinging to his fight as the pain swallowed him.

Corey felt the gun's muzzle brush against the side of his head, his temple. His heart flew.

Fuck you, he thought, remembering himself once more. *Mom will come for you.*

With all his strength, Corey Toussaint Hill won his last fight.

✤ Thirty-Four ✤

FRIDAY

*A*NGELA SHOULD HAVE FALLEN fifty times by now. She was running so hard that her head leaned forward as if she were burrowing her way into the woods. She kept her eyes down as much as she could, but her feet were on their own; stepping around knots, roots, holes, stones, and myriad other hazards in her way with each step. Each time she took a misstep, an overhanging branch or stable tree trunk was there to catch her before she fell too far, before she had to slow.

POW

Another explosion cracked in the woods behind her, a gunshot. Angela didn't hear the bullet near her this time, but the last time Tariq fired, his shot had ripped into a tree within inches of her, flicking bark into her eyes. Maybe he was falling behind.

"I've got an idea, Snook," Tariq's voice boomed from the growth behind her. "I'll count to ten, and you go hide. Isn't that how you used to do, Angie? You'd hide so Myles couldn't find you? I can't say I blame you. I don't know about you, but Myles seems kinda stiff to me. Especially now, if you know what I mean. The brother doesn't have much personality."

Angela sobbed once, and the half-second loss of concentration made her trip, nearly twisting her ankle on a vine maple root. Her legs tried to buckle as she climbed across the slippery bark, but she stumbled on, venturing a look behind her.

She saw only thickets of huckleberry, ferns, and evergreen stands behind her, a sea of green and brown. No visible movement. And she didn't hear Onyx's incessant barking anymore, a relief.

Maybe she had lost Tariq, or else he was tiring out, succumbing to his injuries. Before, never more than a second or two had passed before his head emerged from behind a shrub or a tree trunk, pursuing her in his wild, pivoting gait. Myles had hit Tariq solid in the thigh with his bow, but the injury hadn't prevented Tariq from running within ten yards of her, sometimes less.

Shit. *There he was.*

Tariq appeared behind her, and he was *moving.* He pivoted off his injured leg as if it were made of wood, galloping. He'd pulled the arrow out of his shoulder, but the arrow in his leg was cracked in half, the arrowhead still embedded in his skin. The *baka* was helping Tariq run, Angela knew. Here, the *baka* could give Tariq monstrous gifts. If Myles hadn't shot Tariq, he could have caught her three times over by now.

He aimed at her again, and Angela ran on, ducking.

At least her legs were strong. They *had* to be strong.

POW

The sound of the next gunshot made her cry out, anticipating a hit. But he missed again.

Each new gunshot made it harder for Angela to control her legs, made the signals from her brain misfire. *Fast* meant *slow. Right* meant *left.* Her legs had to teach themselves how to run from scratch, but they always did it, driving hard. It was a killing effort, and now she understood why so many heroines in horror movies gave up, falling flat on their asses just when the monster got close. Their fear made them fall.

Be still, cher. *Pas desplase.*

Let me come to you.

Gramma Marie's voice was potent, calling to her from the cascading rainfall, singing from the water as it passed from needle to needle, from needle to soil. Grunting to heave herself over another trunk blocking her path, Angela couldn't free up the energy to answer Gramma Marie. Minutes had been winnowed down, each moment taking forever, full of dangers. Thorny bushes that might take out her eyes. Rotted wood that would break under her weight. Hidden nests and holes that could trip her, breaking her neck. And Tariq behind her, a madman propelled by a demon.

Slow down? Angela wished she could do more than that: She wanted to lie down and give up. She had given all she could. She had given her son, her husband, and her love. She had given her friends and her friend's child. There was nothing else, no one else. Angela was empty. Her legs seemed to know what to do, but the rest of her was dead weight.

Yes, you're hurting, cher. *Pas desplase.*

Angela tried to slow down. She told her legs to slow, but they would not.

As she ran, Angela heard a deep cracking sound ahead of her, a sound she remembered from her house a few days ago: A tree was falling. A massive Douglas fir trunk about three yards ahead of her was bending downward, toppling sideways, bringing an avalanche of limbs and needles down with it. But Angela still couldn't make herself stop running.

I'll outrun it, she thought, an instant before she realized she *couldn't*. It was falling too fast. But it was too late to stop running now.

Angela let out a hoarse yell, surging ahead.

The tree crashed behind her, shaking the ground. Angela couldn't hear herself in the tumult, which sounded like an explosion, jarring her legs. Debris from the fallen tree flew into her neck and back, scratching her. But she had outrun its fall. She wasn't dead yet.

Maybe it had been a friendly tree, she thought, and she almost felt glad. Angela's last true moment of gladness had come two hours ago, when she'd seen Myles's arrow soar above her. She thought about Myles's sure arrow as she ran. Without that arrow in her thoughts, Angela knew she might have died by now. She wished her memory ended with the flying arrow.

That fallen tree had slowed Tariq down. For now, at least, Tariq's voice was farther away.

"Angie, I've got it all planned out for us," Tariq called, muffled by the trees between them. He didn't seem to be breathing hard; his voice was too vigorous. She heard twigs crack as he pushed through dense growth. "We'll have a romantic night in the woods, just you and me, babe. I thought we'd pick up where we left off. We've got some talking to do, Snook. *Real* talking."

Angela didn't answer, crawling beneath a bed of ferns, praying he was still tangled behind the fallen tree, that she would have long enough to lose him this time.

"I was hoping you could show me what you and Myles Fisher did out here on prom night. Or, hell, you can show me what you did *last* night. I'm good either way. I'm sorry about that little execution at The Spot, Angie, but the man was working my nerves. Myles isn't here to fuck you, so you'll just have to close your eyes and use your imagination."

Angie had to suppress the scream of rage that tried to rise in her throat. She suddenly wanted to wait for Tariq and lunge at him, clawing at his face with her bare hands if she had to. Maybe that was what she would do. She knew the *baka* was speaking through him, but it sounded like plain old Tariq to her, the part he'd always kept hidden under his skin. He sounded like the same Tariq who'd secretly wanted to hurt her, the Tariq who'd always been jealous of the memory of Myles in her.

"Where'd you go, girl? Don't be shy. It'll come back to you, Snook. You know what I like."

Breathing heavily, Angela scurried like a crab to skirt around the upright trunk that had appeared in front of her after she emerged from the ferns. Maybe she'd bought herself a yard or two. She would start in a new direction, back toward The Spot. She would confuse him.

Somewhere behind her, Angela heard a shrill whistle.

"Onyx!" Tariq called. "Here, boy! Tell me which way Mommy went, then we'll both go say hello. *Come on*, boy." He clapped his hands.

Angela heard the barking again, sounding closer than she'd like. *Shit.* Spurred by the noise, Angela ran faster. Her legs quavered at first, but then they obliged her, giving her more speed. Her ancestors had run from dogs in the woods, she realized; this flight was embedded in her psychic memory. If she had allowed her heart to fall still a moment, she might have learned their names.

"Oh, that was *good*, Angie. Nice try, Snook. But he's on your scent now. Don't be fooled by the fucked-up haircut. This little mutt's got a nose. And he can *run!* He's got you, babe."

Despite herself, Angela turned to look back. She didn't see Tariq. She saw thick, dense woods behind her, knots of trees and brush growing wild, untended. And too much darkness for so early in the day. It was late afternoon, but the sky was on the way to night.

The woods were getting dark.

Slow down, cher. *Let me come to you.*

Be still. Pas desplase.

After a leap over a thin fallen tree that nearly pitched her off her feet, Angela had no choice but to listen to Gramma Marie. Her legs didn't want to work. Her instinct to flee flared, then died. Angela stopped, leaning against a hemlock tree for support while she caught her breath. She was no longer hearing messages from the trees and land out here; no one in her family had ventured this far before now. She was in new territory.

Angela raised her gun again. She'd never dropped the .38, even though she'd almost cast it aside many times, believing it was slowing her down. Her hand ached from holding the gun so tightly. If only she could greet Tariq with a surprise gunshot!

Was the gun still jammed? If she tried to test the trigger again now, she would give herself away if it fired. But it might be worth it. Angela decided she wanted to know.

Aiming for a tree trunk, Angela tugged on the trigger. It didn't budge.

"*Shit,*" she whispered, her terror renewed.

"Oh yeah, Snook, somebody should have told you about that gun sooner," Tariq called, his voice closer, although he also seemed to have slowed, walking. Taking his time. "My friend has me covered on that gun. If your Gramma Marie had any kind of juice, it would have fired last time around. But it didn't. Not working now either, is it? It's like I told your girl Naomi—you need to be more careful when you're picking your friends."

Finish what you began, cher. *Let me come to you.*

Pas desplase.

She had to pretend Tariq wasn't there. She had to shut Tariq out of her mind.

Angela sat on the wet ground, crushing damp fir cones beneath her weight. She reached inside her bag for the index cards Corey had kept in his bedroom. Weeds waved in her face, at eye-level, but she ignored the tickling. She also ignored the barking, which was closer.

She ignored everything except her heartbeat.

At The Spot, Angela hadn't had to think about writing the symbols in the soil with her finger, but whatever connection she'd had with Gramma Marie at The Spot had been broken, or else weakened. She was on her own. Angela lay the cards in a circle around herself, preserving their order by checking the numbers Corey had written on each one. Her sweet, smart boy had prepared these cards for her. Corey had brought her this far. The rest was up to Gramma Marie.

"Gramma Marie, help me," Angela said, closing her eyes. She rubbed her hands across her scalp, where some of the muddy soil from The Spot still clung to her hair. She rubbed the sacred earth from her fingers across her lips. "Help me."

The sensation didn't come to her as sharply as it had at The Spot, but Angela experienced a shift inside of her. Slowly, the beating of the rain around her sounded more acute, and her mind could once again discern the rhythmic patterns that had been lost to her while she was running from Tariq.

Tap-tap-TAP-taptap Tap-tap-TAP-taptap

She leaned from side to side, allowing the rhythm to gently lift her shoulders. She invited the rhythm inside her, and it invaded. Suddenly, she felt as if she were teetering at the edge of a rooftop high-rise, ready to fall. Angela tensed, squirming and dizzy. For a moment, the expansive feeling inside her vanished. Once again, she was an exhausted, helpless woman sitting in the rain.

Onyx's barking was so close, he could be here already.

Don't fight, she told herself. *You have to do this. Don't fight it.*

This time, Angela sat still. She met the edge of the rooftop again, and she felt herself *jump.*

Angela flew. She did not fight, even when she felt her body rise to its feet, when her body began shuffling rhythmically within the circle of her cards. Her heartbeat blended into the drumming.

Drum, John. Drum for me. Drum for me, Myles. Drum for me.

Tap-tap-TAP-taptap Tap-tap-TAP-taptap

Angela's hips swayed, lifting high. She whirled, but she didn't feel dizzy. She felt *light,* the drumming serving as her wings. Angela barely heard Onyx when he came springing out of the brush with a wagging tail.

As the skies bathed her, Angela fluttered her arms, her hips bucking. She saw the first letter of Papa Legba's word in her mind, an *M.*

She's coming, she thought. *Gramma Marie is coming.*

Angela Marie Toussaint danced.

And spoke a single word.

Tariq was losing his patience.

The *baka* had promised him he would be shielded from harm, and yet *two* of Myles Fisher's arrows had pierced him, one only a twitch from his heart! The *baka* had promised him he could take Angie with ease because his legs would be faster than any man's, and yet he was chasing her in the woods like a starving bear or wolf. In the Crossroads Forest, he was supposed to be a *greater* creature. He should have had her at The Spot.

He had seen it beforehand, perfect visual prophecy: killing Myles Fisher first, then dragging Angie to the exact place where she had lain with Myles as a girl, forcing her to stare at what was left of her lover's face while he took her.

It would have been exquisite.

She was not supposed to have escaped him. That Bitch Marie was to blame. Instead of running for safety, Angie was summoning That Bitch this very minute. Tariq could feel Marie stirring, gathering strength as she sailed in the treetops, seeking a flesh form below, very near to him. That Bitch was especially emboldened now that Angela had buried her *esprit* in the sacred grounds.

But it was too late.

The little mutt had found Angie for him. Tariq could hear the change in Onyx's bark.

Tariq grinned, leaping through a bed of ferns, but his grin disappeared when he landed on his injured leg and felt a spike of pain. The pain shocked him so much, he almost fell from his feet. The *baka* had dulled his nerves, making that leg as numb as stone, but what he'd felt that time reminded him of the moment the arrow had first torn into his flesh. That *sonofabitch*. If Tariq could bring Myles Fisher back to life, he would do it just so he could kill him again—and this time, he would shoot him in the balls before he shot him in the head, just to repay him for the pain.

But Tariq was happy to forget Myles Fisher.

Angie was in front of him, whirling and dancing before a cedar tree. Seeing her, Tariq's anger gave way to relief. The *baka* should never be doubted. The *baka* had promised this day.

Tariq kicked the dog, who was jumping against Angie's legs as if he expected her to pet him. Stupid creature! The dog yelped and ran to hide.

"Are you here, *manbo?*" he said to her.

The whirling stopped, and Angie looked at him with her head lolling slightly to one side. Her face was all Angie, but her gentle, bright eyes were not hers.

"I'll cast the *baka* from your head," Marie said with Angie's mouth. "Take my hand."

"Awww, you'd do that for *me?*" Tariq said sarcastically. "Did you check with your granddaughter on that one, *manbo?* I think she'd rather see me dead about now."

"Angela knows you aren't who you seem to be."

Tariq nodded, unbuckling his belt with one hand while he leveled his Glock at her with the other. "Is that right?"

"You fought a good fight, Tariq. *Two years*, you fought. You're a very strong man."

"Marie, if you're going to lick my balls, I prefer the real thing." He whipped his shirt over his head, wincing when the fabric pulled at the bloody wound on his left shoulder. His shoulder throbbed, but the cool rainwater soothed the raw, torn gap where he'd yanked the arrow out.

"Don't be foolish, Tariq," Marie said.

Tariq strode up to Angela Marie, pinning her against the trunk. She didn't struggle, standing soft and still beneath his weight. That was good. That would feel more like old times. Now if only he could convince her to stop *talking*, too.

He nestled the muzzle of his gun against her temple. Holding her against the tree with his lower torso, Tariq ran his hands across Angela's breasts, squeezing them hard enough for her to understand that this body now belonged to him, not to her. Now that he was with her, so close to her face, he did not want to hurt her despite all her transgressions. She was too beautiful. Angie had been taking care of herself. He suddenly felt reasonable.

"We can do this a couple of ways," Tariq said, breathing heavily. "Either you take those clothes off, or I'll have the pleasure of removing them myself."

"The *baka* has made a home in your anger, Tariq," she said. "But you can release it."

Tariq took her hand and pulled it into his pants, forcing her to touch his ready nakedness. He felt himself jump at her touch, his senses thrilling. Even her lifeless, reluctant fingertips sent currents of pleasure through him. "I'll decide what I want to release," he said.

Her hand remained where he held it, unmoving. "Where is your powerful *baka*, Tariq? Why would he let any pain touch you?"

"Pain makes the man," Tariq said, tugging on the wet sweatshirt that hid Angie's flesh from him. "That's what good ol' Leland Hill used to say." With two more rough tugs, he'd pulled the sweatshirt over her head and thrown it over his shoulder. Angie's brown skin gleamed with perspiration. He buried his face in the soft cleavage captured in her bra. Her scent was intoxicating.

He felt her shift beneath him, trying to move away from his touch while she pulled her hand out of his pants. "I'm sorry you got lost, Tariq," Marie said, stealing Angie's voice. Or, maybe that *had* been Angie, fighting her way through her grandmother's spirit.

"You'll be much sorrier before too long, Snook, I'm afraid to report."

"No," she said, her tone certain. Tariq felt something cold at the nape of his neck.

That .38, he remembered. The one Sheriff Rob Graybold had given her.

Tariq laughed, shaking his head. "Bad judgment has always been your problem, Marie. You know that gun is a piece of junk." The *baka* had been very unhappy with the way the boy circumvented its will in the wine cellar, firing the gun to kill himself rather than doing as he had been told. The *baka* would not let another gun fire in its presence unless it was its will.

"Take the gun from me then," Marie dared him, her voice as sure as the rainfall.

Tariq hesitated, unsettled. Could Marie have wrested control from the *baka*? The *baka* had promised him he could have Angie easily! Again, Tariq felt doubt.

"Don't make me kill her so soon, Marie," he said. "I wanted to fuck her first, *then* kill her. The sequence is important."

"You'll do neither," Marie whispered huskily. "This was not to be, Tariq. None of it. And it ends here. It ends today. I've returned Papa Legba's word to him. I spoke it while I danced."

"He won't be so easily placated as that! You've always underestimated him, Marie. His ruined love for you can't compare to the *baka*'s love for me."

Her calm eyes didn't blink. "What do you see in your future, Tariq?"

For the first time since his transformation, Tariq saw nothing at all of his future before him. The *baka* seemed to have retreated from him, taking its knowledge. The pierced muscles in his thigh pulsed with a new jolt of pain. What was happening to him?

This woman must die now, he realized. She was dangerous to the *baka*.

Tariq pumped the trigger of the gun his son had used to kill himself in the wine cellar. This time, his gun did not buck in his palm. His trigger did not yield.

Yet, he heard a gunshot. The deafening sound came from behind his ear.

Freed from the *baka* at last, like his son before him, Tariq felt a bittersweet joy.

Angela woke up shivering and soaking wet, curled in a hollow at the base of an old cedar tree.

She was naked from the waist up except for her sports bra. She was cold, but that wasn't why she was shivering. *Gramma Marie was here*, she realized, and her body trembled. Gramma Marie had come inside of her, had become a living part of her, speaking through her mouth. Gramma Marie had . . . had what? The memory had been there, but as soon as she turned her attention toward it, it faded. She remembered dancing, though. She remembered Onyx coming. She remembered seeing Tariq. But she couldn't remember anything else.

Cramped, Angela crawled out of the hollow, wiping wet needles from her skin. Her sweatshirt lay on the ground near her. Angela picked it up, wrung it out, and tied it around her waist. She didn't need to wear it anyway. Her skin felt burning hot.

Tariq should be here, she realized, confused. But he was gone.

She needed to get home. Right away. But she had no idea where she was, except that she was somewhere in the heart of her woods. It was bad enough she didn't have a compass, but fog was descending over the trees. It would take her forever to find her way out of here, she thought.

There was an incline ahead of her, a small ridge, so Angela walked toward it, hoping she could get her bearings with a wider view. Maybe she would see as far as the Four, or she'd see Gramma Marie's house; either one would help her decide which way to walk. Her feet slid on the drying mud, slowing her progress, but she climbed to the top, clinging to a branch.

There, below her, she saw something large dangling from a nearby tree branch, facing the west. It was wooden, probably cedar, hanging vertically, slowly twirling. Finally, it faced her and she recognized it: a dangling canoe. The hollowed wood was crammed with wrapped bundles strung in place with coarse rope. One of the bundles, she saw, was the size and shape of a full-grown man.

There were others. Wooden canoes were strung from all the trees as far as she could see in one direction. Like great ornaments, hundreds of them decorated the woods. All of the canoes were filled with the dead and their belongings.

The fog was thickest where the canoes were strung, shrouding many of them from her view, but she couldn't understand why she had never noticed them before. Her grandfather John's people had been buried here, she realized. This was a burial ground. The canoes were the last remnants of a people, and their spirits had been here all along, whispering stories as they hung. Angela's skin shivered.

She turned back the way she had come. After passing the tree where she'd been sleeping, she saw a thin path, maybe a deer trail. She followed it. As she walked, squirrels, moles, and wild rabbits conducted their pursuits around her, unconcerned by her presence. A cow elk wandered in front of her, stopping in her path to tug at a dripping huckleberry bush. Angela only realized later, when she'd walked a good way past the elk, that wild animals usually had more fear of her. This was a new experience, she realized. She had come to a new place.

Gramma Marie had brought her here.

That was when Angela heard drumming. This wasn't the hidden drumming she'd heard in the rain earlier; this was the sound of human hands on real drums, at least three of them, one of the instruments pitched deeply, the others higher, more teasing. The drumbeats raced and chased each other, their rhythms clashing and then blending. Angela heard applause and human cries, calls of appreciation for the drummers. Although it was growing dark, she saw firelight glowing ahead, not too far. The Spot. Were some kids having a party, making a mess? She was almost home now.

The pain and sadness she felt was barely a prick. Angela knew what was waiting for her at The Spot—what had happened there today—but she refused to bring the memory out for air.

As Angela got closer, she heard more and more voices, as if she were at an outdoor concert instead of in her family's woods. This was not a typical teenage party, she realized. The light from the fire was brilliant, offsetting the arriving evening darkness. Walking grew easier, without so much tangled brush. Soon, she was on a clear trail she didn't remember seeing before, not from this direction. She was grateful for it, because it seemed to lead her straight where she wanted to go.

The van was gone. None of her heartaches awaited her here.

Instead, Angela smelled cooking meat. A large animal was roasting on a spit where the van had been. Angela stared a long time at the giant, charred rack of meat, trying to recall where she'd seen such a beast, which must have been the length of three horses. She couldn't remember, exactly, although she couldn't quite forget.

Whatever it was, it couldn't hurt her now.

The Spot was teeming with people gathered around a bonfire, two hundred or more people standing shoulder-to-shoulder. They swayed together, clapping and laughing. Their eyes were trained toward the fire, where Angela saw men and women leaping high into the air, their heads soaring above the crowd. They leaped higher than Angela thought should be possible. All the revelers were colorfully dressed, their clothes clashing and blending like the drummers' rhythms.

It was like stepping into Africa, she thought.

No, not Africa—Haiti.

There were a few whites swaying and clapping with everyone else, but most of the people here were black. And Native American. A tall Native American man with black hair that draped down his back walked past her wearing a loincloth. Passing her, he smiled, and she smiled back at him, mesmerized by his face. She *knew* him. He wasn't her grandfather John, but he was close to him. John's *grandfather.*

"*Kouzen!*" a woman's voice called to her, and Angela strained to see who had spoken. She saw a woman's frantically waving hand, but then the woman was gone, woven into the crowd.

Another young woman shimmied away from the back of the crowd, her head wrapped in a purple scarf, topping off a dress as colorful as Christmas lights. The woman hiked up her skirt as she danced toward Angela with a euphoric expression on her face, shaking a rattle. The woman was young, about thirty, her dark skin drenched in perspiration. Her hips rolled as if they were barely attached to her body.

"What you think? Nice party?" the woman said. Her voice had an island lilt.

Angela nodded. "What's the occasion?"

The woman peered at Angela incredulously, stepping closer to her. "What kind of fool question is *that?* You know the occasion, *cher.* Today, we are free."

That time, Angela heard the husky quality in the voice she had known her whole life, and she gazed at the woman with disbelieving eyes. She stared at the broad nose and eyes, seeing them for the first time. This was how her grandmother had looked before Angela was born.

"Gramma Marie?" she whispered.

"Yes, yes," Gramma Marie said, sounding impatient. Then, she grinned, outstretching her arms. Angela fell against her grandmother, hugging her. Gramma Marie held her, laughing from her bosom before she let out an excited cry, squeezing more tightly. "Yes, Li'l Angel. You did a very good thing today. A very, very good thing. But that's no excuse for you to come here and not know your own *grandmère,* not to know her face!"

If she had hugged the woman right away, she would have known it was Gramma Marie by her scent. The smell of her skin was unchanged, talcum and a hint of peanuts. She also smelled as if she had been standing in a cloud of the incense from her altar.

"You've changed," Angela said, assessing her. Her grandmother's face was much more playful than Angela ever remembered, her eyes brighter. And the way her body moved, so unrestrained! From the way Gramma Marie's chest jiggled, she couldn't be wearing a bra. This was not the same Gramma Marie who had sat primly in her library while she tutored in Sacajawea, wearing the same navy blue skirts and white blouses day after day.

"We don't wear only one face," Gramma Marie said, shrugging. "I let you see one or two of mine, the ones you needed to see. The rest belong to me."

"You should have told me, Gramma Marie," Angela said, with more sadness than scolding.

Gramma Marie's smile faded. "Yes. I should have," she said, and nodded briskly, as if to say, *Yes, but let's be done with it. It's behind us now.* She patted Angela's rump hard, something else she'd never done. "Next time, I'll know."

Angela scoured the crowd for other familiar faces. Gramma Marie took her arm and steered her away from the bonfire; steering her the way Corey had at the Fourth of July party, when he gave her the ring.

"Fleurette, you know, will be sorry she missed you," Gramma Marie said. "She's always bragging about you so. You would think she was the one who raised you."

"I'll stay and see her."

For the first time, a frown blemished Gramma Marie's face. When Angela saw her grandmother's frown—an old woman's frown on an inexplicably young woman's face—she felt more than a prick of pain. This time, the pain burned. Bad memories were waiting to erupt in her.

Gramma Marie squeezed Angela's arm to pull her from her thoughts, clicking her tongue against her teeth. "Don't look so sad, *cher,*" she said. "I'd love for you to stay, but *je peux recevoir personne.* I'm not allowed any guests. See the dirty looks? They're jealous of you. Your own blood! Don't be fooled, because it isn't nearly so lively here all the time. Today is special. Today, we're celebrating a miracle."

Angela saw a young, dark-skinned girl in pigtails run in front of her before disappearing into the lively crowd. She knew that girl, too. *Mama,* she thought, amazed. Angela tried to follow the girl's dress, but her eyes lost her in the maze of colors. As she gazed at the celebrants, Angela's feet shuffled to the rhythms. She wanted to dance with them!

"Do you know what you did?" Gramma Marie asked her.

She had felt Papa Legba embrace her. She knew that much.

"I think so," Angela said. "Is it gone?"

Gramma Marie raised her hands over her head, swinging her head with delight. She snapped her fingers. "Yes, yes, the One With No Name won't trouble us again. See how we're blessed with the favors of the *lwas?* We are no longer exiled. But that's the start, not the finish. God is smiling on us. This is a miracle day."

"What's the miracle?"

Gramma Marie playfully bumped her nose against Angela's. Angela couldn't get used to this new incarnation of Gramma Marie, so girlish and excited. This woman felt more like a girlfriend than her grandmother. "You choose," Gramma Marie said.

"Me? Why me?"

"You were brave enough to let me ride you, so you banished the *baka.* You preserved the line. You choose your miracle today."

Angela couldn't choose a miracle. She didn't dare hope for one. She wanted too much. The sadness trapped inside of her was working its way free. Angela sighed, shaking her head. "I don't know if I believe in miracles, Gramma Marie."

"What! You're afraid to believe in a *miracle*, but not afraid to believe in the *baka?*" Gramma Marie's girl-face frowned again. "I should have taught you better."

A woman cackled loudly from the crowd near them, and Gramma Marie turned to shout at the woman in Creole, waving her arms in annoyance. Angela had rarely heard Gramma Marie raise her voice, either. She would love to have spent a day with *this* woman, to have known her.

Gramma Marie turned back to her, shaking her head. "Fleurette is laughing. She was always telling me, 'You didn't show that child *who she is.*' Everyone knows best! But you're ready now, Angela. It's time." Her eyes gleamed with pride, as if she were gazing at a newborn. Gramma Marie hugged her again, swinging energetically back and forth. "*Adieu, cher.* You were brave today. I knew you would be."

Adieu? Suddenly, Angela's mind tumbled with unanswered questions. She locked her arms around Gramma Marie's back, resting her chin on her shoulder, refusing to let her go. "Not yet. I miss you," she whispered.

Gramma Marie looked at her face, surprised. "Why? We talk every day."

That was true. A part of her was talking to her grandmother all the time. "Yes, but . . ."

"Come visit us here. Bring food, from time to time," Gramma Marie said.

"And rum!" an old man shouted, waving his cane, and there were waves of laughter.

Angela felt suddenly cold. She wrapped her arms around herself, glancing toward the trail that would take her to her grandmother's house. Despite her unanswered questions, she was eager to go. There were too many faces she had hoped to see here and hadn't, people more dear to her than family she had never met. The ache of that disappointment grew worse the longer she stayed. This celebration was beautiful, but she had not been invited. She didn't belong here.

"I'm going now," she said, kissing Gramma Marie's sweaty neck.

"Yes, you go on home!" Gramma Marie said, dancing her way back into the crowd, closer to the fire. "On your way, think about that miracle. You've earned it. Don't put it to waste."

Trying her best to believe in miracles, Angela set out on the worn trail home.

MIRACLE

And he said, Young man, I say unto thee,

Arise. And he that was dead sat up, and

began to speak. And he delivered him

to his mother.

— LUKE: 7:14–15

Where there is mud, there must be water.

— WEST AFRICAN PROVERB

✒ Thirty-Five ✒

*A*NGELA SAT AT THE TABLE on the backyard deck, waiting for her dizzy spell to pass.

Shit on me, she thought, taking deep, even breaths. What was wrong with her?

The dizziness had overwhelmed her in the house, making her nearly swoon over her pot of jambalaya on the stove, but it seemed to be gone now. Maybe it was nothing, she thought. Whatever it was, it hadn't been any match for the fresh air outside.

Before Angela stood up, she gazed out at the green awning of trees that grew north of her, toward The Spot. She had been able to name most of the trees when she was in high school; cedars and Douglas firs and western yews, all of them pointed out carefully by Gramma Marie, but she rarely thought of them now. She'd spent too much time away from her land. In the time she'd been here this summer, she hadn't taken the first walk by herself, too busy working the phone or cooking or shopping or supervising Corey.

And Tariq, of course. Tariq was her toughest challenge.

"Do you love him, Angie?" she asked herself aloud. "Does he love you? Because if there isn't love here, these bedroom games have to stop. Neither of you is looking for a fuckbuddy."

The longer she sat outside in the fir-heavy air, the more Angela's thoughts sharpened, as if she'd been living in a misty, undefined version of reality until now. She'd been trying so hard to make these past two weeks with Tariq work, she hadn't bothered to ask herself *why*. She and Tariq had been separated for four years, and they were supposed to pretend this was a friendly visit? If this experiment turned ugly, Corey would be caught in the middle again. He'd already seen them break up once. Sitting outside in the late-afternoon air, Angela made that vow to herself: She had to ask herself what she really wanted, what she really felt. What was best.

As she walked through the back door to the kitchen, Tariq was standing in her path, his shoulders almost as wide as the doorway. She jumped, startled by the sudden sight of him.

"Sorry," she said, her heart racing, as always. "You scared me."

"Just checking to see if you need help with dinner."

Tariq was not a cooking man except on the grill, so his offer sounded as conciliatory as he'd meant it. Tariq *was* trying hard, bless him. Maybe he was trying harder than he ever had. But his presence in the doorway made her uncomfortable. As if he were blocking her.

"Thanks, but I just have to pop in the cornbread," she said. "Where's Corey?"

"Still in his room. Want me to bring him down?"

Angela was about to say yes, since she'd rather let Tariq battle Corey's moodiness, one of the perks of having another parent in the house. Corey had been withdrawn the past few days. But as Tariq stepped back and Angela closed the door behind her, she changed her mind.

"Maybe you should put on the cornbread, Tariq. I'm going to talk to him."

"He goes through a teenage funk every once in a while. I just ride it out. If we get out to the city and see a movie tomorrow, he'll be fine."

A teenage funk. That could be it, but Angela didn't think so. Corey had been *glowing* when Tariq first came, but his mood had shifted wildly since the day he'd scraped his arm falling off that horse. There was obviously more to that story, and she was tired of Corey's evasiveness. More than that, though, she was worried about him. Something was wrong. She'd always been able to count on Corey's appetite, but he barely ate at mealtime. This didn't feel like any of the other times her instincts had warned her about Corey. This was very different.

"I just want to be sure," she said.

"Want me to come with you?"

"No. I think I'll try it alone."

Tariq smiled, deciding not to argue. "Your call, Snook." Angela had been glad to hear Tariq use her old pet name in her bed last night; but this time, it grated on her. He had lost the right.

Upstairs, Angela knocked on Corey's door, her old room. She heard him scurry around like a crack dealer trying to flush his stash, she thought. Her instincts roared. "Corey?"

"Coming!" Corey called hoarsely. Will Smith he was blasting on his CD player, but she heard him close a desk drawer, then she heard the squeaky hinge of his closet door. She tried the doorknob, but it wouldn't turn. "This door isn't supposed to be locked," she said.

He was hiding something. Maybe it was only an embarrassing teenage masturbation moment, but it could be anything. *Anything.* Corey might get away with murder at Tariq's house, but he would not get away with it here. "Corey, open this door *now.*"

The door opened.

Corey had gone upstairs only about an hour ago, but she felt her insides melt when she saw her son, a feeling that had nothing to do with worry or anger. Just *look* at this boy, she thought. He was three inches taller than she was. There was a whisper of a fuzzy moustache above his upper lip. His eyes twinned hers. His frown was identical to Tariq's, except gentler at the edges. The sight of her son amazed her. She felt herself thinking a prayer, something she hadn't done in years: *Thank you, God, for giving me this boy. Thank you so much.*

How could she have relinquished the raising of her son for almost four years? No *wonder* Corey was so angry, she thought.

"What, Mom?" Corey whined, a toddler with a man's voice. "I'm taking a nap."

Angela gazed into his room over his shoulder, her eyes drawn to the window, where a shadow played through a tiny gap between the curtains. Was that movement out there? Angela touched her son's warm cheek with her palm, then nudged her way past him into his room. "Honey, I want to visit with you a little while," she said.

He barely gave her space to pass. "*Visit?*" He repeated it as if it were a foreign tongue.

"Yes, visit," she said. "Is that all right with you?"

His stonelike face, staring at her, clearly said no. Often, that look had been enough to turn her away, to silence her, to shut her out. But she was never again going to be afraid to mother her son. She could find ways to be more kind, but she would have to fight back.

"I thought it was time to eat," Corey said, stalling her.

"Soon," Angela said. As she walked into his room, her eyes took in as many details as she could: his closed notebook on his desk, CD cases, a duffel bag half-stuffed into his closet. She thought she saw an old-fashioned walking stick pushed back in the closet, barely within sight in the cracked door. She'd never seen that in here before. She'd have to ask him where he found it.

For now, though, her priority was the window.

The thing was, the closer she got to the window, the worse it smelled. She couldn't pinpoint the scent the way she might if it were old meat or a rotten egg, because it wasn't any kind of scent her nose knew. In a strange way, it almost seemed that she wasn't smelling it with her *nose*, but another one of her senses. Whatever was outside that window didn't smell right.

Angela walked to the curtains and threw them open. The window was closed, but the branch outside was shuddering and bouncing as if a great weight had just sprung from it. The branch thumped against the closed windowpane.

"Corey, was someone out there?"

He looked confused now instead of only irritated. "*What?* Like who?"

Her instincts told her he was telling the truth; if someone had been there, he hadn't known. Not yet, anyway.

It wasn't time for him to see yet, came a faint whisper in her mind, one so quick and slight that she did not question it. *He would have seen after dinner.* Angela locked the window tight, but before she closed the curtains again, she stared out fondly at the walnut tree, whose branches were laden with unshed green walnuts. She remembered like yesterday when Myles Fisher had carried his crazy butt up here, asking her to the prom. Thinking of Myles, Angela felt a keen sadness she forced herself to release. Wherever Myles Fisher was, she wished him well.

Then, Angela turned to her son. She sat on his unmade bed, patting the spot beside her.

"Sit down, honey."

Corey's mouth fell open. He looked both surprised and full of dread. "What?"

"We have to talk."

"About what?"

"About you and the way you've been acting. You're worrying me. Something happened the day you fell off that horse, and you're not telling me. You're a terrible liar, Corey."

He shrugged. "Mom, I don't know—"

"Corey, I'm not *blind*. You're too smart to think you came from stupid, so tell me what's bothering you. Does it having something to do with Tariq? Are you upset he's here?"

His face softened, suddenly earnest. "No, Mom. It's *great* he's here."

Angela nodded, smiling. That was good to hear. If she wasn't trying to make this work with Tariq for Corey's sake, then why else? She just had to figure out a way to do what was best for Corey *and* best for her. Since Corey had never sat beside her, Angela stood up again, walking toward his closet. This time, he grabbed her arm to stop her.

"No, Mom. That's *my* stuff. Don't go in there."

"Corey, you're hiding something from me. Why?"

She saw his face break. She'd seized on an inner conflict, and he was crumbling. He didn't answer, so she went on. "Honey, I know this feels unfair to you, but I *am* going to look in that closet if you don't start talking to me. Do you hear me?"

"That's not right."

"That may be, but that's the way it is."

"Mom, why do you have to act like this? Why are you in my face?"

"Sweetheart, I'm here so you can *talk* to me. Why is that so hard for you?"

That was when she noticed it: Corey was wearing a gold ring. He followed her eyes, and his face crumpled with disgust. "*Damn . . .*" she heard him whisper. He stared at the floor, and she saw him blink as if he were about to cry.

Her eyes must be fooling her, she thought. It looked like Gramma Marie's ring.

"I should have told you about it before," he said, his voice barely audible. Then, slowly, he pulled the ring off his finger, holding it out toward her.

"Oh my God," Angela whispered, staring. The feeling of déjà vu reminded her of her near-swoon in the kitchen, as if she were separating from herself. That was nearly as strong as her joy.

Corey's eyes had suddenly become adult. He held the ring in front of her. "I could tell you a lie, or I can tell you the truth. The lie is easier to understand, but it's not the truth. The truth will scare you. Which one do you want?"

Angela's mouth dropped open, soundless for a moment. "The truth," she said finally. "You know I always want the truth, Corey."

Corey sighed, giving her the ring. Angela examined it, turning it over in her hands. Oh God, this *was* Gramma Marie's ring, she realized, down to every detail of the symbols around its band. She slipped it onto her finger, remembering the day Gramma Marie had given it to her, right before she died. How had he gotten this? The ring had been stolen!

Angela was so transfixed by the ring, she barely heard the squeak as Corey opened his closet door. The next time she looked up, he had a stack of pages in his hands, spotted with yellow, green, and red paperclips. "I should have given this to you when I found it. I was just being a brat," he said, and he gave the papers to her.

Le Livre des Mystères, the title page said. Her French came back to her: *The Book of the Mysteries.* What in the world was this? What did it have to do with her ring?

"I don't . . ."

"There," Corey said, pointing to the bottom of the page.

Marie F. Toussaint, the familiar signature read. Dated 1929.

—

"Mrs. Toussaint, you're the last person I expected to be here tonight," Sean said, grinning widely from the edge of the bonfire. He reached into his back pocket for his cigarettes, but Corey gave him a cutting look.

Mom was being cool so far, but he didn't want to push it.

"Well, Sean, to tell you the truth, I don't like you and Corey sneaking around in the middle of the night. But this ceremony was important to Corey." Mom looked at him and smiled when she said that. She'd been pissed when he first told her about her ring and hiding the papers, but the more he told her, the happier she'd been to find out he was so interested in Gramma Marie. She'd gotten very quiet for a while, then she'd said, *Well, Corey, maybe we can find some common ground.*

Corey smiled back at her, but he felt shy, lowering his eyes. He was glad Mom was here, but it was hard to smile at her. He didn't know how to handle her when she was being nice, he realized, almost as if he was afraid to *like* her. That was messed up. He had to put that in check.

Mom looked like a kid, sitting on the ground with her arms wrapped around her legs, wearing jeans and a Seal T-shirt. Dad had asked if he should come, but Corey had taken him aside and said he thought he and Mom should do it alone.

Corey hadn't had the heart to tell Sean he couldn't come. For a moment, the three of them were silent, listening to the rollicking bonfire and buzzing insects. At least there weren't any mosquitoes, Corey noticed. He didn't have any bug spray, and even if he did, he wouldn't mess up the new

Raiders jersey Dad had just brought him—number 81, Tim Brown. *The* man.

"Sean," Mom said quietly. "I'm sorry to pry, but is it true that you found a letter in your mailbox from your mother? A letter you'd burned?"

Sean glanced at Corey, unsure of how to answer. Sean might be irritated he'd told his mother that part, since he'd made Sean swear not to tell his dad. Corey nodded to let him know he could talk. "Yes, ma'am, the letter came back," Sean said. "It was hard-core magic, something most people don't see in a lifetime. Same thing that happened with the ring."

Corey studied his mother's face, wondering what she was thinking. She'd listened to his story and read the manuscript since dinner, but he knew she didn't want to believe in magic. She'd told him he should consider *other* ways the ring might have come back to him, even though they both knew there was no other way to explain it. But maybe she'd figure it out before long, after tonight.

Corey was just grateful his mother hadn't forbidden him from conducting the cleansing ceremony. If she'd really believed in the curse, she wouldn't have let him come, and she would have stayed far away herself. But she'd been fascinated by the ritual items in his closet, especially the walking stick, and even the raven feathers and blood hadn't bothered her the way he thought they would. When she said she wanted to come with him, he'd been shocked.

Maybe she couldn't resist the idea of having a wish of her own one day. Corey wondered what his mother's wish would be.

With the ancestor altar arranged and his petition to Papa Legba finished except for the ritual symbols from the wheel, Corey could already feel the difference with Mom sitting beside him. The air seemed to be *humming*, a sound he felt tickling his stomach, unless it was his imagination. He felt a bubble of protection around them he hadn't felt before, as if bad things could not touch them. Together, they were too strong. All the fear he'd felt was gone. Maybe there *was* no curse.

Corey took his mother's hand. "I'm going to return Papa Legba's word now," he said.

Mom squeezed his hand, and she felt the heat of her ring against his skin. Still holding his mother's hand, Corey wrote the letters one after the other, using the key in Gramma Marie's papers. About midway through, he heard a sound in the woods that made him look up toward the trail. It was a soft sound, but it was enough to get his attention.

Becka was standing at the edge of the trail. Her expression looked sad, lost, and Corey suddenly realized she *had* to be mentally unstable. Becka wouldn't come any closer with Mom here, he thought, and that was fine with him. He had been thinking about Becka almost nonstop since the night he had met her, when she came shrieking out of the woods—and now he didn't feel anything. He didn't feel love, lust, or excitement; only a little pity. Gazing at Becka, the truth of Sean's warnings resonated: He should keep away from her. He'd known that all along, but his ears hadn't been able to hear it.

If Mom saw Becka standing there, she didn't say anything. The next time Corey looked up at the trail, Becka was gone.

Corey wrote the last letters of Papa Legba's word. He blinked, staring at the word on the parchment, awestruck by its power. As the wood on the fire crackled, Corey took a deep breath and spoke the word as clearly as he could, saying it loudly so he would never have to say it again.

"Papa Legba, please accept your stolen word," he said. "Please help us banish the *baka.*"

His hand tightened against his mother's, and hers clung back. The air around them seemed to vibrate. Something *was* happening, he realized.

They couldn't enjoy the ceremony long. Bo Cryer showed up cursing and laughing, although he stopped cursing when he saw Mom with them. After Mom told him this was private property, Bo reluctantly answered her questions about what paintball was and why he and his friends were playing in the middle of the night. Satisfied that nobody would get hurt, she said they could stay on the land as long as he gave them privacy at The Spot.

Bo looked nervous the whole time, probably thinking Corey would tell his mother what had happened with Sheba at Pizza Jack's, but since Bo was respectful toward her, Corey let it go. He even heard himself wish Bo good night, and Bo gave him a puzzled glance as he walked away, mumbling good night in return. Corey never gave Beaumont Cryer another thought.

He had bigger thoughts to occupy him now.

Before he went to bed that night, Corey Toussaint Hill wrote a poem about what he'd felt when he returned the stolen word to Papa Legba, when he felt the gates open to receive his prayers.

Souls fly, he wrote.
Night woods dance.

✄ Thirty-Six ✄

*A*NGELA TOUSSAINT'S Fourth of July party began well enough, but no one would remember that because of the way it would end. That's what everyone would talk about later. The way it ended.

Tariq Hill was to blame. At eight-thirty, when Rhonda Somebody from Portland, June McEwan, Rick Leahy, and Laney Keane had already made their apologies and headed home, Tariq came downstairs with a bag full of CDs. "I'm sorry to break this to ya'll—but if this is a party, white folks or no white folks, there's about to be some dancing," he announced.

Groans and cheers competed in the living room, along gender lines. The women wanted to dance. The men, with the exception of Art Brunell, did not. When Tariq put on his Kool & the Gang CD and the brassy fanfare of "Celebration" blared out, the question was settled: Dancing had its own volition. As furniture was cleared to make a dance floor in the living room, Rob Graybold pushed himself as far as he could against the wall, despite Melanie tugging on his arm.

"Angela, talk to him," Melanie said. "Make him dance!"

Angela gazed at Rob's face, which had grown ruddy after a few beers. She had never been close to Rob, but she felt a rush of warmth for him, glad to see him relaxed. She didn't have the heart to embarrass a man who gave so much of himself trying to be a guardian for others. "I don't know what to say, sweetie," she told Melanie. "That's up to the sheriff."

"*Thank you*, Angie," Rob said, relieved, giving her a half-bow.

Myles emerged from the French doors behind the Graybolds, and Angela was impressed anew with his stylish shirt, hugging his shoulders and the lines of his chest. There was a time this man would have done anything in the world for her, she remembered. She missed those days.

Myles wasn't looking in her direction, though. Instead, he held out his palm to Melanie. "Dancing sounds good to me. May I?"

Whatever pinch of jealousy Angela felt couldn't compare to the spark in Rob's eyes. "Never you mind that, Twinkletoes. *I'll* dance with my wife," Rob Graybold said. He grabbed Melanie's hand, pulling her toward the crowd at the center of the floor. Melanie mouthed *thank you* at Myles over her shoulder, grinning. She bobbed to the beat while Rob shifted stoically from side to side, his eyes never far from Myles.

"Celebration" was too much party pop and not enough funk for Angela, but she figured it was a good enough warmup before they started laying out the heavier stuff. The next track on this CD was "Jungle Boogie," and she'd show these folks something when *that* came on. Tariq grabbed her and pulled her close, swinging his hips midway between slow dancing and real dancing. He'd surprised her, and she felt awkward. Dancing with Tariq in front of everyone felt like a lie.

Angela ventured a glance in Myles's direction, but he was gone. The French doors swung gently, signaling that he had just left the room. Myles's absence made the music seem less bright.

Tariq was her *husband*. What was wrong with her?

The Brunell family was a spectacle. Liza had excellent command of her hips, and her gyrations provoked enthusiastic catcalls from her classmates. Not to be outdone, Art attempted a pained version of what might have been the Funky Chicken, thrusting out his chest in occasional synchronicity with the beat. The man clearly wasn't afraid to make a fool of himself.

"You better cut that out, Art. You're losing votes!" Rob called.

"You're just jealous, Rob," Art said. "If stiffness was against the law, we would've locked you up back in the eighties."

Angela couldn't help laughing with everyone while Rob's face turned red.

Glenn Brunell grabbed his mother's hands, trying to follow her movements with studious concentration. Mother and son whirled in a slow, private circle of their own. "Hear it, Glenn? One, two, three, *four*. Do it on the beat," Liza said. Glenn was spastic, moving to rhythms no one else could hear, but he improved with his mother's coaching.

Angela noticed Corey and Sean standing in the foyer entryway, both drinking cans of soda they had brought up from the wine cellar. They'd brought up the fireworks, too; in an hour, it would be dark enough for the show.

Staring at her son, Angela remembered the surreal adventure she'd had with him the other night. The power of the memory still arrested her. She felt her finger for her ring again. If she hadn't seen the ring on her finger this morning, she might have thought she'd dreamed that ceremony and the charge she'd felt in the woods the night before last.

Last night, she'd had the first dream she could remember in ages, about the attic. A blue wall.

Angela motioned for the boys to come dance, but they shook their heads.

"Too old-school," Corey said. "Let *me* deejay."

"Oh, hell, no," Tariq said. "This is called *music*, scrubs. You'll read about it in your history classes one day." Corey pursed his lips, and both he and Sean waved Tariq off, feigning disgust.

For an instant, Angela almost felt like she was home.

—

The party guests gathered on the deck for the fireworks, since there was a clearing to give the rockets room to fly. Angela watched, delighted, when the first bloom of purple and white light jettisoned overhead, spraying sparks that lit up the property for acres. *Beautiful*, she thought.

It was impossible to tell the children from the adults as Tariq, white-haired Gunnar Michaelsen, Corey, Glenn Brunell, and three young boys fussed over the bag of fireworks, plotting their next explosion. Sean had left early to help keep his horses calm, he said. Art joined the fireworks committee, echoing his son's argument in favor of noise over plumage. "The Good House is going to give Sacajawea a show tonight," he said.

Angela made her way back to the kitchen to pour herself another glass of Pellegrino to enjoy the show with. She was digging into the nearly melted ice bag in the sink when she felt someone standing behind her. The spicy-sweet cologne scent found her nose before she turned around.

It was Myles. His dark skin looked especially appealing in the kitchen, against her white walls. He seemed to have been behind her for some time, in silence.

"You're not leaving, are you?" she said, disappointed.

"I promised Ma's nurse I'd be home before eleven."

Damn. With all the guests, she and Myles hadn't had time to speak much beyond polite chitchat and family introductions, since Myles had never met Tariq or Corey until tonight. "I'm really sorry Ma Fisher is sick, Myles. I'll have to come see her. What time is good?"

"Anytime. She'll be happy to see you. She asks about you."

"Really?" That was surprising, since Myles had told her his mother had Alzheimer's.

"You're hard to forget, doll-baby."

Angela felt blood rush to her face. Myles was staring at her with yearning; part brotherhood, but mostly openhearted regard. Again, as always, she didn't know how to answer that look on his face. Suddenly, she didn't know what to say either.

"It was good to see you, Angie. I'm glad you're doing well," Myles said in her silence.

Angela opened her mouth to say thank you, but instead she decided to say what she was thinking. "I may not be doing as well as appearances imply."

"I'm sorry," Myles said. "I hope it's nothing serious."

"Tariq and I are separated."

"I . . ." Embarrassed, Myles checked over his shoulder to make sure no one else was in the kitchen. The party was wholly preoccupied outside. Angie heard a chorus of *oooooooohs* as another rocket exploded. "I'd heard that. But I thought . . ."

Angela gazed out of the breakfast nook window at the flaring red brightness as the rockets' sparks fell. She shouldn't be talking this way to Myles, but she suddenly wanted him to *know* her again. Once upon a time, Myles Fisher had been her best friend, and she missed him. "He's been here a couple weeks, and it's been good. I was starting to think . . . maybe." She shook her head. "But, no. I don't think so. There's a reason we're separated. You can't keep walking over the same ground. So, wish me luck. I think we're going to have one of our bad talks tonight."

"Sorry to hear that," Myles said. "My ex-wife and I had those."

"How long were you married?"

"Three years, right out of grad school. I plead youth and stupidity."

"How did you know when it was over?"

He laughed. "When I had to get the restraining order."

"I hope that's a joke."

"Just barely. She wasn't very emotionally balanced."

Angela nodded. "I know what you mean. Tariq is . . ." There, she stopped. Talking about Tariq felt disloyal. She didn't want to make Tariq sound like a monster. He wasn't.

"He's a big man," Myles said perceptively.

"Yes. A big man with some anger problems. He's trying, but that kind of thing . . ."

"Goes deep," Myles said. "I know."

Myles nodded toward the butler's pantry. He was ready to go. She walked with him out of the kitchen into the long, narrow pantry that led to the foyer. The space usually seemed large, but while she and Myles passed through, it felt startlingly intimate. His breath was on her neck.

"Something has to change," Angela said as they emerged in the airy foyer and her self-consciousness passed. "I live in L.A. and Tariq lives in Oakland. Corey lives with his father. I get him on holidays and in the summers, and that isn't working. It isn't fair to Corey."

"No," Myles said. "It isn't."

She glanced up at him, almost irritated. But that was only Myles being Myles, she remembered. He told the truth. The truth was annoying only if you didn't want to hear it.

"Tariq and I have to figure out how to be in the same city, even if we're not living in the same house," she said. "One of us has to move."

"Do you think Tariq would be willing?"

"If he won't, then I'll have to. Besides, I'm not sure it's right to pull Corey out of his school and away from his friends. I could swallow my pride, I guess. Maybe this is a good time for a change. I've been at the same law firm for ten years, and I've been thinking about becoming an agent. The industry needs more good black agents. It's better to be in L.A., of course, but some clients would take their chances on a Bay Area agent. I could commute for my important lunches. It would just be for a couple of years, until Corey goes to college."

Myles's eyes shone. "I see you've got it all figured out."

"Actually, I'm making this up as I go. I made this decision . . . right now."

It seemed clear, inevitable. She would have to be closer to Corey. Angela gazed toward the living room, at the piano and all the reminders of Gramma Marie. If she'd been listening to her grandmother's spirit, she realized, she would have made this decision a long time ago.

"An agent, huh?" Myles said. "So, you want to create greatness."

"Damn right. I have a few greats in mind."

"Like who? Anyone I know?"

"Naomi Price. She's mostly done daytime, and a couple of TV movies. For now."

Myles shrugged. "I know the name, but I'm not seeing a face," he said.

Angela smiled. "You will. She's beautiful."

"And she'll have a beautiful agent. Just like Corey has a beautiful mother."

Angela's ears flamed. "If I can't be a good mother, beautiful is a nice consolation prize."

"Oh, I *know* you're a good mother. And you'll be a better mother when you're closer to your son, sweetheart. Take it from me. If not for e-mail, my stepson and I would be strangers. I finally gave up trying to work around my ex-wife's power plays, so I rationalized my way out of it. I lived with Diego for three short years when he was very young. His mother remarried. He forgot me. It still hurts. Take your chance with Corey while you have it."

"I will. You're right." Because she couldn't make herself stare into Myles's eyes, Angela glanced toward a clay figurine on the fireplace mantel, riveted by its cowrie shell eyes. She looked at the ring on her finger again.

"I remember your Gramma Marie wearing that ring," Myles said.

Angela felt flushed with memories, both recent and distant. Gazing at her hand, she imagined the ring on Gramma Marie's finger. "I had the strangest experience with Corey and this ring the other day," she said. "And the most wonderful experience. I'm still a little spun by it."

"What happened?"

So, she told him. She told him about her conversation with Corey in his bedroom and his sudden confession, returning her ring. She told him about Gramma Marie's papers and the ceremony at The Spot. She told him about the reappearance of Sean Leahy's letter. She hadn't even told Tariq all of the details yet, feeling shy about it, but she didn't feel shy with Myles.

"What do you think of all that?" Myles asked when she finished.

She shook her head. She'd been wondering that since the night it happened. "To be honest, Myles, I don't know what to think of it. I don't believe in this kind of thing. But I have to admit, when Corey performed that ceremony, I *felt* . . ." She realized she didn't have the words to express it. She'd felt a presence. She'd felt Gramma Marie. She'd felt as if she were standing at a crossroads, just like Gramma Marie's papers said; between realms. The experience had resonated with her so deeply that she and Corey had agreed not to perform any more spells from Gramma Marie's papers, not right away. They would learn more about *vodou* first. And her family. She had cousins in Louisiana whose names she didn't know.

"Anyway, I was proud of Corey," Angela went on. "He was so directed, so *focused*. I've never seen him that way about anything, except maybe the music he writes, or his poems. I've been trying to imprint Gramma Marie on him his whole life, and now out of the blue he found this connection to her without me. It's all so surprising. I can hardly take it in."

"It's not out of the blue," Myles said. "Without your work, it wouldn't have happened."

"But there's so much I didn't know. He learned it himself."

"It's a wonderful thing, Angie," Myles said. "Truly. Your son is helping you learn about your grandmother. If that's not God's hand at work, I don't know what is."

They had lingered by the door long enough, so they went out to the front porch. Angela didn't turn on the porch light even though the sky was velvet, dark except for the distant glitter of stars. The pops and whistles behind the house were louder here, but not so loud that they raised their voices. They spoke softly.

"What about the rest, Myles? Do you believe in magic?"

"I can certainly see how some people could."

"That's a very diplomatic evasion."

"Thank you. I'm proud of myself for that one." He laughed, just before his eyes became earnest. "Magic? Well, I can tell you from experience, sometimes life has magical qualities. I can think of one time life felt magical to me."

Angela's heart bounded. She didn't have to ask what time he meant. She knew.

Myles clasped her hands, holding tight. "If I have to, I could get to like Tariq," he said. "So I hope everything turns out the way you want, Angie. When all the dust has settled, call me either way. I'll be back in town awhile, and I'd like to know you again. I'll make you dinner, maybe *arroz con pollo*, something Cuban. Just tell me how many places to set."

"I'll do that," she said. "Is it the same number?"

"Same number," he said, and smiled. "It's good to have you home, Angie."

"It's good to be home."

Angela could feel the deep crevices carved by the lines on Myles's warm palms, the story of his future. Angela already knew hers: Her family was about to have a bad time. But it was also about to become something entirely new, better than it had been.

With a thunderous pop, the sky flooded with artificial daylight. For an instant, Myles's face came into perfect, luminous view, like a snapshot; his shiny shaven head, those coppery eyes, the warm, pensive smile on his lips. When the rockets died, his face went dark, hidden by the night.

But Angela knew it was only for a time.

If she waited, the skies would flare again.

⨯ *Acknowledgments* ⨯

First, thanks to Jackie McArthur, for sharing the details of the tragic loss of your son, Justin. I wish I could turn time back for you.

Thanks, and apologies, to the town of Cathlamet, Washington, in Wahkiakum County, which I erased from the map and fictionalized as Saca-jawea. The virtues described herein are yours, and the flaws are Saca-jawea's. Special thanks to Dennis and Audrian Belcher, owners of the Bradley House of Cathlamet, a charming bed-and-breakfast that bears a striking resemblance to the Good House, but *without* the curse. (See the house at *www.bradleyhousebb.com*.)

Thanks to my literary agent, John Hawkins of John Hawkins Associates, as well as his assistant, Mathew Miele. Thanks to my film agent, Michael Prevett of the Firm. Thanks to Tracy Sherrod, who first acquired this novel for Atria Books, and to my current editor, Malaika Adero, for her insights as she shepherded it. Thanks also to Malaika's assistant, Demond Jarrett.

Thanks to Richard Dobson, for his patience in sharing his knowledge of Native American magic traditions as well as his guidance regarding the premise of this novel.

I intended *The Good House* to be a story about the consequences of abusing magic, and I wanted to base that magical system within black traditions—which is why I chose *vodou*. But this is not a *vodou* book. Anyone who is curious about *vodou* and other African-based religions in their truer form should read works of nonfiction, as I did. The books I found most helpful were *Flash of the Spirit* by Robert Farris Thompson; *Jambalaya* by Luisah Teish; *Mama Lola: A Vodou Priestess in Brooklyn*, by Karen McCarthy Brown; *Vodou Visions* by Sallie Ann Glassman; *The Way of the Orisa:*

Empowering Your Life Through the Ancient Religion of Ifa by Philip John Neimark; *Divine Horsemen: The Living Gods of Haiti* by Maya Deren; and *Voodoo Search for the Spirit* by Laënnec Hurbon. (There are no references to a word being "stolen" from the *loa* Papa Legba in any of these texts; this fictitious premise is the author's invention, as is the manifestation of the *baka*. In *vodou* lore, a *baka* is a demon who usually comes in animal form.)

Sacagawea, a young Shoshone woman, made a critical contribution as an interpreter and guide on the Lewis and Clark expedition. In this text, I use the common misspelling of her name, Sacajawea, with apologies to those who know better. Thanks to James LeMonds, author of *South of Seattle: Notes on Life in the Northwest Woods*, for the poetry of his own writing as well as his observant eyes when reading mine. Other books that were helpful: *Beach of Heaven: A History of Wahkiakum County* by Irene Martin; *Chinook: A History and Dictionary* by Edward Harper Thomas; and *Trees and Shrubs of Washington* by C. P. Lyons. Thanks also to Karen Eisenberg, for our hiking adventure, and to novelist Chris Bunch, for his archery lesson.

Thanks to the Cowlitz County Hall of Justice and Joannie Bjorge, a corrections officer with the Wahkiakum County Sheriff's office. Thanks to Peter Ellis, managing editor of the Longview *Daily News*. Thanks to Lydia Martin and Alexis Mulman-Cajou for assistance with translations.

Thanks to playwright Caroline Wood, Joe Daggy, Roger Werth, Cindy Lopez, and Steve and Kim Plinck for providing faces and spirits for some of these characters. And to Angela and Courtney, power-couple extraordinaire, for the faces and spirits of Angela and Myles.

Thanks to writer Joan LeMieux for hosting those wonderful writers' dinners, which I will miss. Thanks also to Yolanda Everette-Brunelle, Rosalind Bell, Mukulu Mweu-Mijiga and Brian Mijiga, Ronn and Felicha Hanley, Farryl Dolph, and all of my other friends who tolerated my long disappearances and helped me make a home in a new place. Thanks to O. B. Hill, owner of Reflections Bookstore in Portland, for your support and your struggles. Thanks to Olympia Duhart, for your advance reading.

Thanks to Mom, Dad, Johnita, and Lydia, who are always with me even when they aren't. Thanks to Steve and Nicki, for the joy of a new family.

Thanks to my grandmother, Lottie Sears Houston, for her fight.

Thanks to God.

Thanks to the ancestors.

www.tananarivedue.com